Of Lovers and Kings

And

Monstrous Things

By Elizabeth A Murphy

Dedicated to
Robert M Murphy
Husband Extraordinary

With deep appreciation for Rachel Reilly McKenzie who volunteered to edit this work. She was exacting and honest and tireless and particular: everything I needed.

Table of Contents

Prologue

Ranald sat up in bed. He shook the sleep from his head. Why was he awake? Had he indicated the need to be roused at this time? Sleep still would not release its hold on him. His mind would not function. He could not remember having given orders for his waking or why he needed to be awake. He stared at the room. He could not return to sleep. Something was keeping him awake. Some fact, some pressing need had woken him and now kept him awake.

What day was this? What time was it? Then he felt the room shiver. His bed bounced against the floor. The shiver was short. It lasted long enough to wake Ranald completely. That was what has woken him. He stared at the walls of his room as if they had come to life. The shaking lasted a lifetime. He could not gauge how long it lasted. He could only sit in his bed wondering what he should do. Was he bespelled? Was his castle under attack? He could not stay in bed. He dared not call for his servants. If there was an attack he did not want the enemy to know he was awake. Though how they could expect him to sleep through such a shaking he could not explain. Ranald stepped out of his bed just as the shaking stopped. There was a gentle rap on his door.

"Your Majesty, King Ranald, are you safe?"

Ranald sighed in relief to hear the sound of his own servant frantically calling him.

"Good you are here. We need to get dressed. Have we any reports on this event? Are we under attack?"

"Your Majesty, immediately. There are no reports, Your Majesty. I do not know if we are under attack. Battle dress your Highness?"

"For riding. Send for reports. Send for the Council. I need to know what has happened."

Weirhass stared at the fall of rocks. He watched as stray pebbles fell with rattles and puffs of dust. The earth was cracked and scarred. Rubble lay scattered across the landscape. These were small signs. Weirhass knew if he looked at the horizon it would bear little resemblance to the shape of his memory or of his ancestors' memories.

Mountains had fallen. Well not fallen, but surely they had shifted. The fabled edge of the world had proven to be not eternal, not immutable, or maybe not even the edge of the world.

He had volunteered to see if anything was beyond the edge of the world. The rim affixed by the Gods to keep the World from pouring into the Sky was broken. His peers had felt that someone needed to see if their world were truly sliding into the Sky. Most wanted to stampede into Llwegania to take their chances against the Dragon. Better to face the sword of the Dragon than the endlessness of the sky. Weirhass never ran without reason. His faith in the world had been shaken in his youth. He did not believe blindly in anything.

Still as he sat preparing to ride into the crack in the rim, he felt nervous. What if his fellow leaders were right to believe the priests? The priests had been very wrong once before to Weirhass' knowledge. Weirhass could still see his wife's dead face. He could see the dead body of his small, unformed child in the pool of blood at his wife's side.

The priests had promised him she would be fine once she accepted counseling. Once the priests blessed her, she was supposed to put aside her hate of him. Once the priests educated her, she was supposed to accept her place in his household.

Weirhass tried to push away her memories. He tried to forget her bitter words. How she hated bearing him children. How she tried to never conceive. Of all his wives only she had borne him children. When she became pregnant for a third time.....Weirhass shook his head. He would not think of those times. She was gone. The priests had been wrong. If they had been wrong then, they could be wrong now.

Weirhass urged his mount into the opening in the rim. He looked at the ground to watch for footing for his horse. Behind him Weirhass could hear the muttered prayers of his troops. They followed him but not without great trepidation. When he reached the other side Weirhass stopped so abruptly that his followers feared the priests had been right. Then they heard the deep laugh of relief.

"What a land to plunder."

Dragon read the reports for the third time. She did not like the mystery. Her fellow Head of Households answered her inquiries with bland advice. Be happy the Sarn are quiet. Don't look a gift horse in the mouth. Rest, repair, replenish, and be ready for when the Sarn come.

She was taking advantage of the respite. Her armorers were working furiously to build up her weapons stores. Horses were being reshod. Soldiers' uniforms were being repaired. She could not enjoy this lull. The breather had gone on for too long. The Sarn were up to something dangerous. To defend her borders, to fulfill her responsibilities she had to know what the Sarn were doing even when they weren't attacking her. She had no interests outside her military duties.

She would have to send scouts into Sarna. There was no option. There were times when the Sarn were less active but never had this length of time passed without a raid, an incursion. There was no record of a time of quiet in her Household's history. None of her husbands' histories included such a pause.

She was very good at her duties. She successfully contained the Sarn. Her stretch of border was heavily fortified and entrenched. Even with her might, planning, building, she had not completely closed the border to her determined enemy. Her fearsome reputation across the border was not enough to keep the raiders away.

She wished she knew more of the Sarnese culture. They had been fighting for generations but she knew only military facts about her enemy. For scouts deep in enemy territory the small store of information she had would be poor protection. But, she had no choice; she had to know what the Sarn were doing, so she would send them out with what little she had for them. At least they could speak the language. She would send male scouts only.

There was a sound. She turned from the window. Sun streamed around her. It turned the white paper in her hand incandescent against the dark of her clothes. Petron stood before her.

"You have decided."

"Yes. Male scouts, send them with the sunrise. I do not trust this quiet. I must know."

"Being thankful to the Sarn does not sit well with you?"

Dragon looked hard at Petron. She would not give him the satisfaction of an answer.

"You know the old Sarn saying: fool me once shame on you; fool me twice shame on me. We won't let the Sarn bring shame to themselves. We won't let them fool us even once."

There were moments even now he was afraid. He had traveled in Sarna for nearly a harvest. There had been some sticky moments but he had managed to squirm his way out of them. He had his life. He had the information he needed. He could go home but he was almost to the rift itself. He had to see it with his own eyes before he left.

He was a stickler for detail. He planned to cross into the opening if possible. He knew the new passage into the new land of opportunity was well guarded by Weirhass its discoverer. His report would not be complete until he saw the land. He was competent. He has traveled this far on his skill and a bit of luck. His luck could hold a bit longer. The trip home would be easier. He could travel the wastelands. He did not need to expose himself to discovery on the return trip.

The next day he reached the rift. It was a bright day. He watched as a long line of raiders poured through the opening. He brought his mount near the staging area. He regretted his lack of a proper horse. The Sarnese animals were all right for riding but in a dangerous situation, such as treacherous ground or battle, he longed for his Llweganian bred and trained mount. Still, he urged his horse into the opening. At the end, he was not noticed.

Mansa watched in horrified despair as the raiders boiled over the edge of the horizon. She dropped her hoe in the field. Her legs pumped as she ran. She did not look back. She pushed her legs and lungs on towards her village. She did not have breath to scream. She could only race with all her soul to the community that was her home and family. Someone was coming towards her. Didn't they see her pursuers? Then she saw the hands raised to her. She felt the strong grip urging her to an even faster pace away from danger. She could hear nothing beyond the sound of her blood pounding in her ears. She felt the top of her head begin to ache. She did not slow. She was drawn into a doorway. Then she watched the chests of horses as they passed by her.

Above the sound of her panting she heard screams and yells. She closed her eyes as she tried to regulate her breathing. They would not remain closed. They kept popping open. She looked at her rescuer. It was her brother. She had been annoyed that he had been late coming to the fields. She had been thinking evil thoughts of him as she worked her hoe. Each whack into the weeds had been accompanied by a dire threat against him. Now she was simply glad to see him; to know that he had come for her.

They could not stay here. The rest of their family was in danger. She had to get to them. She was able to draw breath now. She couldn't think beyond her need to get to her family. She backed into the house.

No one was home. No one should have been. Those who weren't in the fields were busy with everyday life. No one was home in the middle of the day. All the town's wash was done today at the town well. The younger children and the married women would all be in the center of town. Some of the men would be chopping wood. Some of the older children would be tending the fires.

Mansa watched as her brother grabbed fire irons from the kitchen fireplace. She grabbed a heavy iron pot. Slowly they advanced from their shelter. Mansa noticed a lone figure hanging back from the fray. She looked into the watching eyes. They noted her and her brother. She shot a hand to her brother. He turned to see their audience. The three were frozen for a moment.

Then the rider threw off his cloak. He ripped his tunic from his shoulders. A gleaming black jacket appeared. His mouth opened. A huge sound came out. It pierced the air. He drew air into his lungs again. Again he yelled. Mansa saw the riders pause. They milled for a moment. They turned to the source of the sound. They stared at the lone rider. Mansa noted how different the single man looked from her and from the raiders. She clung to her brother in confusion. There was an answering shout from the raiders. Then there was a short exchange of words in a language she could not understand. Finally the rider pulled his sword free from its scabbard. It sang as it came free. Its blade gleamed in the sun. Then, with his sword raised high he rode straight at the raiders. As one they turned towards him. They raced to meet him.

Mansa was released from her paralysis. She swung her pot wildly at the swirling mass. She saw her brother for isolated moments as he slashed at riders and horses. Her people so beleaguered only moments before mobilized. Burning logs were thrown. Cloth steaming hot and filled with lye soap flew at horse and rider alike. Even buckets of boiling water flew into the air.

The surprise and fury worked. Mansa held her hand against a bruise over one eye as she watched the raiders flee. Many empty horses went with them. Those raiders luckless enough to become unhorsed lay dead on the usually pristine cobblestones of the square. Mansa looked around frantically. Where was their rescuer?

She rushed to where her brother was trying to help the lone stranger from his mount. Mansa saw the flow of blood and closed her eyes.

"Does he live?"

"Barely. Who is he? Where did he come from? Why did he help us?"

"I do not know. I am thankful he came when he did. We must get to the castle. They will protect us. Can he be moved?"

"We will have to use a litter. They will be back. We must leave now."

Strange faces came and went. Gentle hands worked on him. He could not remember any of the faces. He did have a sense of this being right. Sometimes he would become afraid. Mostly he knew he was safe. The sounds were strange; though he knew what some of them meant. He knew water. At least there was a sound he connected with water. He thought one set of sounds was asking him how he was. Only in rare moments did he realize any of this. Most of the time he wandered in and out of a grey world filled with pain and anxiety.

Mansa had been stubborn. She had seen him first. So she had remained adamant about taking care of him. She did not care that she was unmarried and young. All she cared for was that he live.

In her moment of deepest terror he had stood between her and death.

She washed his body to prevent a raging fever. She turned him gently to change his sheets. She spoon fed him water and broth when he seemed awake enough to swallow nourishment. Now she sat looking into his aware gaze. She had to blink to realize that he really was awake. This time he knew that he was living. She knew he did not speak Masfin so she only smiled at him. She could not ask him the myriad of questions that pounded in her head. She settled for a smile and a simple attempt at communication. She put her hand over her heart.

"I am Mansa."

"Mansa."

She smiled. "Mansa." Then he closed his eyes prior to slipping into a deep but finally natural sleep.

Ranald sat in his throne. He knew the story of this man's heroic effort to save a small village. He saw the thinness from the wounds and their aftermath. He understood in his mind the great debt the villagers felt they owed this man and so felt he owed this man. He did not like the feeling.

"We are glad to meet you finally. We hope you are feeling well."

"Thank you, Your Majesty. I am much better." The words were strangely accented but understandable.

"We understand you are a scout from another country beyond our mountains."

"Yes, Your Majesty. I am very far from home. I was studying the Sarnese military movements for my leader when I followed them into Masfin."

"You are ancient enemies of the, as you call them, Sarn people."

"Yes your Majesty. They call their country Sarna."

"Well at least We now have a name for them."

He remained silent. He had been a scout too long to volunteer information. However, he did not wish to antagonize this king. There might be an opportunity here for Dragon. He felt the thin line under his feet.

"So is your leader a king also?"

"No, Your Majesty, my leader is responsible for the estates that border Sarna, their protection, their administration. When the Sarn stopped attempting raids, I was sent to discover what was happening, Your Majesty."

"Who is in charge of your leader?"

"No one Your Majesty, there is a Council to which my leader belongs."

Ranald considered the answers. If there were no king then this Council was the only source of authority with which he had to deal. The members of such a council probably had some standing.

"We will send a communiqué to this Council. Will you deliver it for Us?"

"I would be honored Your Majesty."

Part One: Monstrous Things

Chapter 1

Sablor looked at his mother. Her face was flushed with terror and sleep. Her hands were shaking. Sablor was terrified. His mother was the cornerstone of his life. If she were frightened what was he to do?

"You must marry, my son. That is the only way to ensure our safety."

Sablor closed his eyes in fear. To marry meant giving up his favored position. Not many women set such a store by their children as his mother did. He would have to leave his pampered existence for the great unknown.

"The House already has an heir from your sister. We do not need a First Husband position. Our only consideration will be the strongest alliance." Sablor watched his mother pace through the room. He had not heard her words well enough to absorb their meaning. All he had heard was "marriage".

"What do we have to offer? Soldiers? Currency? A vote in Council? I have been too long from the inner sanctum of the Council."

"What have you dreamed Mother?" Sablor's voice came out weak and thready.

His mother turned to him in irritation. As her face contorted to a stern reprimand, she heard his question as an answer to her query. "Of course, you are exactly right: the dream holds the answer to my needs."

Sablor remained crouched on the floor. He did not dare to move. If his mother returned and he was not where she expected to find him; well, he just chose to remain where he was. He was indulged and pampered but he was not stupid.

The day was greatly advanced when Sablor's mother returned. She was not easier of mood. She did not reprimand Sablor, so he was happy. He was happy until she spoke.

"Get up from there son. Sit down at the desk." Sablor sat tentatively at the ancient wooden structure. He barely touched the seat. His mother came to stand behind him. She placed parchment before him. The parchment was of the purest white. The snowy surface reflected the light from the windows. A quill was placed in his hand. A red quill, the color of passion, the color of war, the color of strength quivered in his clutch. Sablor stared at the ink well. The well was filled with blue ink: marriage proposal ink.

"What character should I inscribe?"

"Death riding a Dragon, boldly but well decorated. She is strength, but we are proposing marriage not declaring war."

The messenger was hot and tired and unhappy. She stood at the top of the stairs. She watched with a jaundiced eye the training in the yard. She had been sent on a foolish mission. Why would the head of such a Household even consider the proposal of a pampered, sheltered, soft heir? Sablor had no battle-training nor raids to his credit. He had never lived the hard life of a soldier.

As the messenger watched the action in the training yard she became convinced of the foolishness of her errand. Male, female, young and old, all the bodies heaved in effort and proficiency. There would be no room for pretty toys in this Household. To be hot, dirty, tired, and hungry for a fool's errand annoyed the messenger greatly.

"Lady, drink?"

She looked at the young servant. The glass offered held mead cut with lemon water. She could see the refreshing liquid swirl in the container. She nodded gratefully as she took the glass mug from the girl. Warm, small rolls were offered as well. She had to force herself to refrain from stuffing the welcome food into her mouth.

"Training lasts another quarter day. Would you like to refresh yourself, and then lie down until my Mistress can see you?"

She smiled her acceptance. There were many things that made this a Great House; not the least of which was its hospitality. Generosity of spirit was an important indicator of greatness. She enjoyed the bath and the massage. The nap was wonderful.

Lying in the soft sheets she could savor her comfort. Soon her sense of well-being would be shattered. She would have to present her presumptuous proposal. She would have to stand firm under the glaring eyes of Devouring Dragon. She turned her head on the pillow. In the dying rays of the sun she saw her clothes, brushed and pressed.

The messenger stood quietly before the head table. Devouring Dragon's ten husbands filled the table. The Dragon's face was bland. The men looked in mild curiosity at the strange female. They were all hardened men: strong of feature and body. Their heights varied as did their coloring but they all had the look of fighters.

The messenger bowed deeply as was fitting from a courier to the Head of a Household. She assessed the occupants of the surrounding space. Warriors all lined the room. No ornaments, all were of the same mold as the ten at the head table. Foolish errand, she was engaged in a most futile endeavor.

"I am come from the house of Westering. My Lady's Heir has sent a proposal. I pray you look on it favorably."

The Dragon's face remained bland. At the lifting of her hand a tall, rangy man came to accept the bundle from the messenger. Devouring Dragon drew out the red quill. She laid it on the table in front of her. She handed the proposal to the same man who had brought the bundle to her. As he read the document Devouring Dragon focused her attention on the messenger.

"Are you assigned to this House?"

"Yes, Lady."

"Tell me of the candidate."

"He is the Heir of the House. He is young. He is learned in language and protocol. He is well versed in music and botany."

"And he has an interest in this House?"

The tone was not condescending. She was puzzled. She appreciated the value of these accomplishments, but hers was a fighting household. A political machine of war and Spartan living did not seem the choice of the Heir of a refined household.

"His lady mother decided on this course. The Heir is a good and obedient son. He was happy to send the proposal."

"My lady wife," a deep voice interrupted the conversation. Devouring Dragon turned her face to her husband. "Their offer is sincere. It seems they are most desirous of the alliance. Soldiers can be trained. If the man has brains he can be useful."

The Dragon looked at the proposal for the first time. They were begging for this marriage. "How old is Sablor?"

"He has seen only summers."

A child still, practically, what was she to do with such a husband?

"Wife, we would consider this."

She stared into the eyes of her Fourth husband. She relied heavily on his advice on dealing with the Council. Oh right, Westering controlled several blocks of votes. She felt the decision slipping from her. She could see the future weighing down on her.

"Thank Heir Sablor for his proposal for me, messenger. Tell him this is a warrior household. If he is truly intent on this course of action, he should come personally to present his proposal."

Sablor was torn. He had not expected his proposal to be accepted. Devouring Dragon had more husbands than tradition dictated. He would have been insulted, if his suit had been turned down. It still could be. So, he remained confused in his wishes and feelings.

Added to his distress was the pressure now placed on him. He had never been answerable for anything, not really. Now his mother made it clear that his coming meeting with the Dragon's Household would decide the fate of his proposal. No one could go with him to support him or to guide him. He had to do this impossible task by himself. A task he was not sure he wished to perform. He did not wish to marry the Dragon; then, again, he did not wish to fail; nor, did he wish to cause his mother any distress.

She sat behind the desk. The wide expanse of polished stone stretched between her and the applicant. His written proposal lay under her right hand. Absently she pushed the parchment in a circle. He was young. He was as young as her oldest child. It had been many years since she had taken a husband. Her oldest child, her first-born daughter had already set up her Household and was pregnant. Why was she even considering him?

Political and military matters were very volatile right now. Taking a young new husband would complicate her life beyond everything. Ah, but the proposal had been elegant. The offer had been generous. Fresh blood could be just what she needed. The alliance would be advantageous for her in the Council. Her husbands recommended the move.

"Why do you want to marry us?"

He gazed at her. She was neither old nor young. Her face, unlined by exposure or indulgence contained experience, power, intelligence, authority, and ruthlessness. Muscle covered her bones. The ability to use that muscle gave her frame grace. A mother seven times, she retained no slender innocence. An earth mother she sat there before him. He wished for something witty or charming to say.

"My mother had a dream. In the dream a snake enters the clearing. It begins to swallow a lion cub. From the sky a hawk swoops down to kill the snake. Our wise woman has interpreted only part of the dream. She says you are the hawk. My mother sends her army to you."

The truth came out before he realized his mouth's intent. He had meant to be eloquent and romantic. He tore his eyes from his sweating hands. Her eyes were steady on him. The parchment still rotated.

"My husbands have urged me to accept you based on the need for your armies. I am fertile but I cannot guarantee you an heir."

"My sister had already borne a child not pledged to any other House."

"Good. I already have ten husbands, all of whom I treasure. They are predisposed to accept you but they must meet you before I decide."

"That is appropriate."

"You would be answerable to the First husband and ranked last."

That rankled. He had always hoped to be First. Coming from his House he had counted on that. Even now he had still hoped for some standing. Yet to be last of Her Household was a far greater honor than to be First anywhere else.

"I understand."

"We keep the old customs here. I hold to the old laws as is my right."

He understood what she said, understood and felt light-headed. As the female Head of a Household she could legally kill him on the spot for any reason, but most likely for infidelity. He could leave, dissolving the union if she failed to provide for him or if he were unsatisfied in the marriage. This was a political marriage: he would not leave unless she killed him.

"At your will, my Lady."

She rose to her full height. She reached his shoulder. She seemed much larger. Her spirit added inches to her size.

"My husbands are in the training room. They wish to judge your abilities in hand-to-hand combat."

She led him from the room. She spoke over her shoulder. "They are very good and…. they cheat."

Sablor swallowed loudly. He frowned in desperation. How could he admit to this particular lack? Even in this modern age everyone studied the martial arts. He should at least be proficient at the use of weapons. He cursed his mother's indulgence for the first time ever. What good was poetry for marrying into this Household?

"Lady, I am a scholar not a soldier." His voice cracked on the sentence. She turned to face him. Respect shone at him from her face.

"Very good, I knew that. Your messenger described you to us fully. It is good that your pride did not stand in the way of good sense. You will still need to face my husbands. They will not test your ignorance or knowledge of the arts of war. If they deem you teachable, we will see."

Jorin lay dozing on one side of her, and Marjas, the other. Petron stood at the window gazing at the night.

"So, Husband, how did the man-child do?"

He turned to her. Twenty years they had been together. In some ways she had changed very little, in others, well that eager girl was hard to reconcile with this woman.

She assessed his silence. "Is he teachable? Can you make a fighter of him? At least, can he be trained to some useful occupation?"

At his continued silence, she sighed.

"It doesn't really matter."

Rising carefully so as to not disturb the sleeping men, she came to stand in the circle of his arms.

"If his presence will disrupt my Household I am not interested."

He chuckled as he rubbed his cheek against her hair.

"You could tire twenty husbands, my heart. So don't worry on that score. True he is young and spoiled but those traits will be matured out of him. What his addition means is that we will be taking on the ability to do more. I worry for you."

She leaned back to gaze at the dear, familiar face.

"Ah, my First, it is more treacherous than even you imagine. To stave off enemies on one side we are going to become allies with their enemies on the other. We need to crush the Sarna between us. The Masfin have indicated an interest in my proposal to help them with military matters concerning the Sarnese. They have begun to feel the bite of Sarnese raids on their borders. They are engaged in an attempt to resolve the issue through negotiation but they are not opposed to discussing some move against Sarna if the talks fail. The Council wavers. The strategy is sound but the Council fears to commit itself to any such radical schemes.

"If I marry this man-child we will have some more votes in the Council, but, more importantly, we will have the armies to act independently. Either way we will be in Masfin before the dust has settled."

"Wife, Wife," Petron rocked them both in his concern.

"We must crush Sarna."

"Then we must marry this suitor. I will train him personally to guard your every move."

"Just my back, Petron, just my back."

"It's such a lovely back."

Petron was strong: muscled into manhood, tall and scarred in her service. His concern for her touched her heart and warmed her blood.

Sablor sat in the Great Hall of the House. His bride stood before him. She had just finished her promises. Her body was turned towards him awaiting his responses. Fear suddenly raised its sensible head. He had spent several days training with her husbands. He knew how much work he would have to do to be as skilled as they were in the necessary knowledge of war. Children trained with them.

Watching those children he had thought that he would never be able to become proficient at the art of war. Years went into the training of a soldier. She had not judged him on that. She had taken his strength and made that his asset. He was to study their new ally so that the Household would not go blind into this next venture. His scholarly hobby at home had become a weapon of sorts here. As he thought of her gift to him, Sablor relaxed. He looked differently into her eyes. She would not treat him as a pampered child. She would require he be an adult. She would demand and expect from him responsible behavior. That was frightening him but it also reassured him.

His voice was strong and true as he spoke his vows. His words echoed confidently in the Hall. The witness from the Council bowed deeply to both of them before leaving to announce the marriage to the surrounding countryside and to the Council.

From his kneeling position Sablor had to look up to see Dragon's smiling face. That friendly expression looked strange atop her unrelieved black shroud figure. Even in this moment she was ferocious. He closed his eyes as terror returned. He had asked for one thing as a gift. He had asked for one week alone with her as a husband. He wanted one week when he did not have to compete with the more experienced marriage partners. He also did not want his ignorance to be exhibited before his new brothers.

He was shaking with his eagerness and his terror. His body seemed to have a mind of its own. His mind filled with the anxiety of this step. It wondered at the roads not taken. His body saw only the woman he had married. His mind noted that the Hall emptied.

"Come, our horses await. It will be a lesson in trail life as well as in marriage." Sablor looked into her face. Her eyes seemed even more atilt in her face. She drew a steady finger down his cheek. He had no idea where he was going but he would follow her there happily.

Sablor shook away memories of the days leading to his marriage with impatience. He no longer had time for the child he had been. In the time since his wedding Sablor had come to rely on his fellow husbands. They were mentors he could only hope to emulate. Their skill and dedication were to be highly admired. He had improved dramatically in his fighting skills but he would never have the ease and grace of one who had spent his entire childhood training. He felt a stab of self-pity for his short-comings. Then he shook his head in denial.

He did not have time or sufficient reason for this line of thought. He returned his attention to his priority. He had become an expert on Masfin and Sarnese cultures and activities. On the table before him were the lineages of several Masfin families. He had difficulty remembering the lines of descent. As lineage was not reckoned in the same manner by Llweganians as the Masfin, Sablor had a hard time learning the various ins and outs of Masfin inheritance.

Devouring Dragon stood at a window in her study. Beyond her window she could see the new troops training. The latest communiqué from the Council lay open on her desk. Next to it was the request from Masfin. The decision was made. At sunrise she would begin her Walk of her Lands. Good thing Wind Rider was not pregnant. She needed her Heir to ride with her.

Wind Rider was approaching the House. She strode with the long gait of youth, impatience and country living. That impatience had better be well-restrained. Dragon watched her daughter walk through the shadows and light. She noticed the light shining on the dark hair. She was a good Heir. She knew how to obey and to reason.

"Daughter," Devouring Dragon greeted her child with open arms. They exchanged a kiss of peace. For a moment Dragon held her child with hard hands by the upper arms.

"The Council has rejected our advice."

"Fools."

"In this case, yes. That means we do this alone. I shall go to Masfin. You will lead the army."

"Yes, Harbinger."

"You will ride with me on my Walk. This will establish your right to use the Rights of Way."

Wind Rider nodded. She glanced at the map of Llwegania. Her mother's House lands and Rights of Way were in green. Her lands which she had the right to use through marriage were in blue as were the Rights of Way. Wind Rider's marriage lands were in red. Looking closely Wind Rider noticed that now the trail of color stretched unimpeded from one border of Llwegania to the opposite along the Sarnese border. Sablor's Rights of Way completed the chain.

"Will we discuss your instructions while we travel?"

"My instructions are simple. In a random pattern conduct maneuvers on all our lands. Use the Rights of Way. Just be sure that the first week after the first full moon of spring you launch an invasion into Sarna. I will attack at the same time from the other side. We will crush our enemy between us."

Wind Rider nodded. Simple direct instructions were her mother's trademark winning style.

"How do you like having a young husband?"

Dragon glanced at her daughter's slyly amused expression.

"I've had several before. They have not changed much in the intervening years. How's your old husband?"

"Much the same as yours I suspect."

"Fresh child."

"The fruit doesn't fall far from the tree."

They were both chuckling when Sablor walked into the room. He watched the pair as they nodded with barely restrained laughter. He wondered what he had done to elicit such mirth. The quiet, watching habits of women unnerved him. When Harbinger was her direct, commanding self he found her slightly intimidating. When she was the flame that consumed their bed she was invigorating. When she was with other females she became mysterious and secretive. She gestured her daughter out of the room. A feral gleam entered her eyes as she looked at Sablor.

He held very still. As he watched her circle the room Sablor wondered what he had done to bring this dangerous animal out in his wife. He dared not breathe for fear she would turn on him. As she moved forward Sablor edged away from Dragon. A sinuous grace moved her body as she stalked him. Her chin came forward leading her body as Dragon approached Sablor.

Sablor stopped his instinctive move away. He was no child. If she meant to kill him Sablor would stand his ground to take his punishment. If only he could recall what he had done to earn her violence. Then she had him. Her hands racked him with restrained strength. She did not mean him harm. His relief made him weak. His hands were tied and his body prone on the floor but he did not care. Her mouth traced every swell of his newly won muscle. Her teeth scraped his ribs. He wanted to thrust. Her strength held him hostage to her will.

Her deft fingers slowly unlaced the opening of his leggings. He wriggled trying to hurry her motions. She slowed even more. Those strong fingers fondled his seed sac until he could not draw a steady breath. She planted a hand in the middle of his chest. Her mouth traced a path that led to his throbbing shaft. That large mouth, an erotic slash in her face closed over him. Her tongue caressed him. His hips thrust up towards her. His body bowed in his pleasure. With a feral gleam in her eyes she left his member to lick the path of his body hair up the center of him. Her fingers made short work of her own laces. In a powerful thrust of her body she enclosed him with her nether mouth. Sablor groaned his pleasure and his relief. On the third downward thrust of her hips he emptied his seed and soul into her body.

"I trust you are ready Husband. We begin my Walk tomorrow. Then you will have the opportunity to use those skills and that knowledge you have been acquiring so conscientiously."

Sablor could only grunt in acknowledgement of her statements. He was still floating in the sensual net she had woven. He drank in the sight of her above him. Light streamed around them. She swung off him in one fluid motion. She pulled her clothes together with steady hands. Sablor envied her composure. He was still trembling in the aftermath of their passion.

Chapter 2

Lord Jeffeaux sat in the King's privy chamber stroking his mustachios and gazing thoughtfully at the newest royal ward. Her pouty mouth and pert breasts attracted his attention. The strength of her protector became a challenge to his ability to circumvent obstacles. To seduce a royal ward was foolish and dangerous and thus impossible to resist as an attraction.

The door to the chamber opened. The King stepped into the room. Jeffeaux sat up straight, surprised by the royal presence. He had expected a servant to summon him. The King gestured to Jeffeaux. Arm-in-arm they walked through the palace. Out, into the pale sunlight, they walked, still not speaking. Once they entered the palace grounds the King continued to walk but now he spoke.

"We have been in closed negotiations with the Llweganians."

"Who? Pardon, Your Majesty."

"The country to the north and east of the Sarna; We have formed an alliance with them. We have held off making plans until We were certain their envoy was safely through Sarnese territories. They have sent one of their military leaders with entourage to coordinate our efforts."

Jeffeaux looked in amazement at the King. He would never have expected this ability to keep a secret and to make plans of the soft spoken man.

"We are telling you this because We know you are not in league with the Sarna."

Jeffeaux nearly snorted. His loyalty was not at issue. His self-interest lay with the Crown for the moment. He was not pleased that politics interfered with his only real interest, ah, that ward was so tempting but Jeffeaux suspected he would not taste that particular dish right now.

"We have offered your fortress at Malso as headquarters for the envoy."

Jeffeaux snapped back to the issue at hand.

"I am honored of course, my Liege, but, why Malso?" Jeffeaux felt the lie fall from his lips. It came easily: Jeffeaux had many years practice at deception. In his mind all he could do was chaff at the idea of entertaining military types in the cold drafty castle.

"Strategically it is well suited to her needs and it has the capacity she needs for her entourage."

"She?"

The King hesitated. He felt as if he were setting the fox to guard the chickens.

"Yes, *she*. Women hold military rank and political positions in Llwegania."

"Interesting."

Jeffeaux lost his interest completely in the royal ward. Foreign, exotic females coming to him, to his household were much more enticing.

"How many in the entourage?"

"Fifty in all: her household guard, servants, messengers, they will all be with her."

Jeffeaux calculated swiftly, he could still move part of his household and invite a few guests. This situation became more and more interesting. Some of his excitement showed on his face.

"Jeffeaux, remember, this is a military endeavor. We have had little contact with the Llweganians. Their choice of envoy highlights a basic difference in our cultures. Be discrete. I do not want to make an enemy here."

The Count looked at the strangely serious King.

"She has requested the presences of several of my military staff."

The size of Jeffeaux's household was shrinking.

"Surely, I must be there as host."

The King pondered the question.

"You, your mother, your sisters, ladies of standing that should be sufficient to do honor to the envoy. They do not have a king in Llwegania. They have a Council which rules. The envoy is a Council Member. She is very important, as is her goodwill. Show her respect at all times."

Jeffeaux hardly heard the advice. He was anticipating the presence of his mother's wards at Malso.

"Go, Jeffeaux. Make ready for Our guest."

Malso was cold and dark. The gloom invaded his spirit. A serving girl scrambled to right herself after their tumble. Even the momentary diversion of the juicy wench had not eased his mood. He could hear the echoes of his household in the background.

His mother and sisters had arrived yestereve. The elegant wards Ilissa and Marma had come as well. The sophisticated Junla had arrived in a snit that she was to be exposed to the coarse manners of the foreigners. Jeffenza had come with starry-eyed dreams of dashing exotic princes and impossible romances. Jeffeaux shook his head at his sisters' attitudes. All he looked for was relief from his everlasting ennui. In the distance the warning sounded; finally a change in the routine.

Jeffeaux donned his best casual finery; then sauntered down to the Great Hall. It was late afternoon. The fading sun drew long shadows on the ground. The beat of the horses sounded long before the visual sighting from the gate. Fifty, he had not thought fifty horses would make so much noise. His mind tickled. Fifty people might have a guard. No, fifty military people would come with two hundred horses. Malso's grazing space made it ideal for this size group.

As Jeffeaux came to this deduction, the group rode into the fortress courtyard. He could not make them out very well. In the lengthening shadows of the afternoon their unrelieved black merged many of them with the dark spots of the courtyard. Black horses, black helmets, black clothing filled the space. His young stable hands rushed towards the horses. They were forestalled.

The outriders quickly dismounted. They left their horses standing obediently still. The ring the outriders formed around the dismounting inner riders became a living barrier. Once all the riders dismounted there was motion from the inner circle. The shifting of horse and people took only a few heartbeats. A young man from the innermost group came to where Jeffeaux's mother stood.

"Greetings, Madam. Thank you for your hospitality." The words were strongly accented but Jeffeaux could understand them.

"We have ridden hard to beat the Darkfall here. Devouring Dragon would like to settle her Household before meeting with her fellow military experts."

"Devouring Dragon?" Jeffeaux breathed the name with contempt. Not quite hearing him, the young man glanced inquiringly at Jeffeaux.

"This fortress is held by my son the Count Jeffeaux. I am Lady Zona of Chantiera. The chambers are ready. Of course you must rest, eat before any serious business is conducted."

There was a hiss, almost as if in fact a dragon were present. The youth glanced back at the innermost circle.

"The chamber for Devouring Dragon should have two adjoining rooms large enough to accommodate twelve people."

Jeffeaux stared. His mother's smile froze in place. Only his suite or hers would fit the request. He was about to refuse reflexively when he noticed the size of his guests, the seriousness of their weapons, and the ease with which they wore their arms. His mother glanced at him: her chambers.

"Of course, give us one moment to ready the chambers."

"Very well, thank you Madam. We need to see to our horses."

The stable boys led the troop. They walked quietly, orderly away.

"Devouring Dragon!?!"

"Did you hear that sound?"

"Could you tell the men from the women?"

"I wonder how he looks."

Jeffeaux listened to the women around him buzz with excitement. He had told them nothing of the guests except that they were soldiers, some of whom would be women. Twelve in one suite, what kind of people were these?

The Llweganians filed silently in taking him by surprise. Helmeted soldiers stood station around the room. Upon close perusal Jeffeaux determined that most of the guard was female. Their helmets shadowed their faces. They stood with their hands resting on their weapons. The center group was male. Their helmets were tucked under their arms. Strong features, varying ages, hair color, eye color they were all tall, muscled and quiet. In the center of the group stood a woman.

The youth, still slight and fuzzy cheeked stood behind her right shoulder. She drew the eye; still of feature, strength not grace in her stance bowled one over. Her hair was cropped close to her head but lay there in tight dark curls. Her helmet was cradled under her arm, held against her hip with negligible effort. Everything about her suggested an ease of doing.

She approached him. The group of men followed her. Their eyes constantly searched the room.

"Count Jeffeaux I am come from Llwegania. I am called Devouring Dragon for everyday use or Harbinger of Death in my military capacities. I appreciate the use of your fortress. I recognize the respect extended me by having your King's own blood greet me." The strangely garbed woman executed a graceful, elegant bow to his mother. "This is Sablor. He is my liaison. Any concerns about my household should be directed to him. This," at a flip of her hand a weathered, scarred man strode to her side, " is the Captain of my Guard: Petron. He deals with all matters of my Household and of my Soldiers."

Harbinger of Death, Devouring Dragon, names or titles, they were comical except she had the air of being able to fill the phrases. She was done with speaking. She waited, at ease, for his mother to lead the way.

"Yes, well, I see the rooms are ready. My mother will show you the way."

"Jorin, see to the troops."

There was a brief nod in reply to the order.

Jeffeaux found himself staring at the impassive face of another seasoned warrior. The Count flexed his shoulders in a resigned shrug. Waving a lace covered hand he indicated the way to the barracks.

Lady Zona led the smaller group of troops and the Devouring Dragon. Some carried gear, while others walked with their hands resting on weapons. Sablor directed the stowing of the gear. Petron searched the rooms. Lady Zona stood to one side to allow her servants with trays of food to enter the room. A slight female detached herself from the group to begin tasting the food.

Lady Zona watched as windows were checked, furniture moved and floor boards stamped on. She stifled a gasp as her expensive silk sheets were stripped from the bed. Calloused hands dropped yards of material unto the floor. Did these barbarians think to sleep on her bare mattresses? No, out came priceless cotton sheets. They had been freshly laundered. The sweet smell of them invaded the room.

Where were her manners?

"The journey was long?"

"Longer than most."

Perhaps this was a sensitive topic. Lady Zona tried again.

"Are you married Devouring Dragon?"

"Yes."

"Do you have any children?"

"Seven."

Obviously this was a woman of few words. Most mothers could be counted on to contribute several paragraphs about their children to any conversation. Lady Zona paused in skepticism. She could hardly envision this hardened warrior as a mother. As Lady Zona had stopped speaking, Dragon had turned to direct the arrangement of her maps and papers in clipped, business-like tones.

"It must be hard to leave young children to come to this far place."

"Yes but they have their older siblings to guard them. Strangely I think I will miss the changing of my grandchild the most."

Lady Zona stood transfixed by the statement. She had ten years on this woman and she still had no grandchildren.

"You became a mother very young."

Dragon understood the implications in the statement.

"Your son has not yet secured his line of succession?"

Lady Zona swallowed. "He has yet to find the lady of his heart."

"I married at fourteen. Before my fifteenth anniversary of my birth I had secured my heir. I knew my duty to my House." Unemotional, cool tones answered. Lady Zona faced the realization that here was a product of a culture beyond her imagination. One of the guards came to speak in low tones to Devouring Dragon.

"These rooms are satisfactory. Thank you. Tomorrow at first light I will be available for consultation with the military leaders. Have some tables placed in the Great Hall."

Armor started to litter the floor as Lady Zona hurried from the room.

"Dismissed like a servant." Becoming color flushed his mother's cheeks. "Sent from my own rooms." Her indignation warred with her love of gossip.

"Would you believe she is a grandmother? You my son are very remiss to have waited so long to secure your line of succession."

Jeffeaux stared at his mother. A surprised laugh erupted from him. "They are different from what we have known or from what I expected."

"What did you expect?"

"I don't know, something softer perhaps. After all she is a woman."

"You think she really is female? Devouring Dragon? Harbinger of Death?" Ilissa spoke disparagingly.

Lady Jeffenza heard nothing. Her jaded imagination had been caught by the liaison officer. His tall good-looks and youth appealed to her. She would like to seduce one of the newcomers. The others held no appeal for her. Sablor's freshness and inexperience called to her. Why she thought of him as inexperienced she could not say. She was to the point of fantasizing him a virgin for her taking.

"He is so tall and handsome. Don't you agree?"

"Who?" Jeffeaux looked at his sister as if she had lost her mind. "Sablor, who else?"

Jeffeaux snorted in disgust. She would be mooning over the youth forever now.

"They are all tall and attractive." Marma spoke matter-of-factly. She moved around the room to stand at the window. Night had completely fallen. The light from the torches in the courtyard danced on her profile. "The boy is most likely a lackey or something."

"More likely a younger son sent for seasoning." Jeffeaux spoke absently.

"Well I would like to season him." Jeffenza stared into the space where their guests were housed. Her face had fallen into a look Jeffeaux recognized from his own soul. The poor boy would never know what had hit him.

"These guests are very important to the welfare of Masfin. Don't do anything to upset them or to embarrass us. We are representing our King here."

"Since when did you care about the King, brother? Your motives are always pure: purely your own best interests. Well, for now, my best interests lie in the direction of that young, juicy, liaison officer."

Jeffeaux looked to his mother for support. The lady Zona glanced from son to daughter. Her eyes strayed into the shadowed interior of the fortress.

"I would think it very unwise to upset the Harbinger of Death on principle alone. I would not like her attention turned my way. She would not have untried me….soldiers in her company. Whatever that boy's appearance, he is seasoned. I would venture a guess that all of her followers have only one loyalty: the Harbinger of Death."

Jeffeaux looked away from his mother's suddenly bleak gaze. She was the descendant of warriors. Her father had died on a battlefield. The Count was his father's son. His refinement and civilized behavior held no strain of belligerence. He felt his mother's disappointment in him strongly for the first time since he had attained adulthood.

"I intend to rest up for the exhausting rounds of talks sure to start tomorrow." Jeffeaux's voice was admirably languid. None of his internal reactions to the day or to his mother showed. He moved slowly, elegantly out of the room. He was sure his mother wondered what he could possibly think to add to the discussions on the next day. He walked past both his mother's wards' rooms. He paused briefly outside Ilissa's. She was the harder of the two to convince. She would represent more of a challenge of the two to his skill. She had yet to succumb to his seduction.

He turned to look back at Marma's door. Marma, he knew her skills. They were inventive and very pleasurable. There would be no challenge of the chase or thrill of victory, but the time would be very satisfying.

As he stood in the hall he could hear the echoes of the castle's life. The breezes, the settlings, the small sounds of the inhabitants all went into his ears. He sorted through them instinctively, identifying each sound. His head cocked to one side. That sound, he knew that sound. He followed the sound through the corridors. When he neared the hall leading to his guests' quarters, he stopped. A guard stared impassively at him. Her stern features reflected a life outside his experience.

She stood in the flickering light contemplating him. Under her leather tunic he could follow the line of her frame. She did not flirt with her eyes nor did she stand with provocation. She was a well-trained sentry at attention. He backed slowly. He knew that sound. Somewhere beyond that imposing shoulder, sex was happening. He would visit Marma. He wanted immediate respite from this world spinning off center. And he needed to be sure he did not sleep. He would have an easier time showing up for a dawn meeting if he never went to sleep.

Harbinger looked at the line of grim faces. She felt the wall of their disbelief. They stared at her as if she were an exhibit at a raree show. Perhaps the Council was not totally wrong: these Masfin would never take advice from a female, never mind allowing her to lead their armies. Her host sat at the far end of the table. He looked as if he had not slept in a while. She grimaced at this further evidence of the vast differences in their cultures. What powerful leader would come to a war council with less than his best faculties at hand?

"We are here to present our capabilities as well as some options. We have an army; there is not in your language a word for its size. The army is one thousand times fifty. It is immense and expensive to maintain. It is on a series of training actions now. It will be at an appointed place at an appointed time. The leader is of my House, loyal to me and obedient. She has the experience of years of fighting the Sarn."

"Another woman." She did not turn her head to find the source of the comment. She knew who had spoken.

"Yes, she is my Heir. She is blood of my blood and bone of my bone. Have you some further comments to make? There are many differences here. I understand that. We are not a people accustomed to luxurious living. We have been at war with the Sarn for many generations. I have spent half my life killing them. I expect to die killing them. I have come to this foreign place with its foreign culture with the best of intentions." She released part of her aggression. Her fist landed on the table with a resounding thud. The wood trembled under the force of her blow. She rose with the action to stand, leaning against her fist.

"I was not elected nor appointed to the Council. I earned my seat in battle. I hold my power with this hand." The gloved fist uncurled to stretch at the end of her sweeping hand. "How many kills can you claim? The Sarn turn to you because you are easier pickings than we are. I do not need to be here except I wish to defeat the Sarn. It pleases me to do so."

She paused. She did not wish to reveal any information to these strangers. These were different people. They had different values and traditions.

"There is an army that will strike. It would be best if an army from here struck at the same time. I will tell you what I have learned from my experience fighting the Sarn. I will even suggest a plan of action, several plans. You may do what you will with them. If this alliance does not work, I will go home.

"We have many differences. I believe that our common goal is a strong enough motivation to put aside the difficulties of trying to deal with our differences."

"I cannot understand female soldiers."

"We can field a larger army when everyone fights. A body is a body when you are filling a hole." Her tone was casual bland. The simple statement reflected a world of experience that the Masfin generals had not considered.

"Your entire society is structured around fighting?"

"Fighting Sarna, yes. We are their creation, you might say. Everything is centered around what we must do to defeat the Sarn. Everything. They are new enemies for you. You have yet to feel the impact of total war. That is how we fight.

"Do you understand the issues that drive the Sarn?"

"We are not blind."

She was not deterred by sarcasm or disrespect. She ignored the tone.

"It is a reproductive issue. The Sarn will be coming for your women. Sarnese men have ten to fifteen wives not because they enjoy variety but because there are few females who are compatible with the Sarnese sperm."

The Masfin generals squirmed in their chairs. Her direct words were strange to male ears from female lips.

"Sarnese men on average produce one child for every ten women they take to wife. They need more and more females to produce more and more children in order to field more and more armies. This is not a land war. They are coming for your wives and daughters, sisters and mothers." She looked at the circle of faces. The morning sun showed every line and the lack of lines.

"You are a civilized people. We are barbarians. Like the Sarnese we eat, sleep, and breathe fighting. It is useful when you are fighting barbarians to have barbarians in your corner. You cannot impose your structures on us but we will not try to force ours on you. We will do this thing, then leave. The Sarn will be a buffer between us. I have a vision of Sarna fighting you, then us, then you, then us, establishing a cycle that will trap generations in war."

Jeffeaux stared at his guest with respect. For one second he believed she understood a subject better than he did. Then he shook his head. She simply saw something that was not there. Like any trained beast she would have her use but she could not understand the intricacies of the situation. What kind of people had women who waged war?

"Gentlemen, we have decided on a defensive war. By defending our borders we will dissuade the Sarn from their course. After a resounding defeat they will learn the error of their ways." The speaker turned to face the Harbinger of Death. "With all due respect to our honored guest, I do not think this situation will last very long. We will be able to negotiate peace with the Sarnese."

Dragon did not allow her thoughts to creep into her face. She was relieved. The Sarn would not negotiate. They would capture, slaughter, or lie to all envoys. She would bide her time. Meanwhile, she would train these generals in the art of war despite themselves.

Jorin wondered at Harbinger's patience. These fools did not realize the danger they could be in by showing such disrespect to Devouring Dragon. Their ignorance was a shield in this instance. How long she would allow that shield was the question.

"How many men did you bring, Lady?"

She did not answer. Her face turned to the impatient speaker. He was a young man. His face held no scars of battle or lines of thought. He had an air of importance that only those elevated by favor owned. She sat abruptly.

Across her steepled hands he studied the maps on the table. Her invitation from the King gave her a great deal of freedom. She would use it.

"A defensive position you say. I will study the maps provided by my host, King Ranald. Defensive." She rose from her seat. She left the hall, her entourage trailing behind her. There was an ugly pause in the room. She was the only one who had any first-hand knowledge of Sarna battle tactics and topography. All those left in the hall had only suffered the random raids and thorough trouncing by the Sarn. With her gone the reason for having a war council was gone.

"Smooth Yandeasu. In her country she is as powerful as our King is here. That aside, when you are wooing a woman you don't treat her as if she has to open her legs for you at your command. You wait for that until you are married. Even then your behavior would have been inadvisable." Renfrew muttered under his breath. As the youngest of the generals present he did not want to draw attention to himself.

In the ensuing silence the hall echoes crept in from the castle training yard. Voices high and low resounded in a strange tongue. Everyone stayed in their spot. Eyes looked right and left. No one was willing to be first. Jeffeaux indulged his curiosity. After all, he had nothing to lose. At his move everyone followed.

From the balcony high above the yard, he saw tens of bodies twisting and heaving in hand-to-hand combat. Male and female bent and threw with lethal looking skill. As they watched Harbinger strode into the yard. Her uniform had been stripped away. She stood on the packed earth in the same loose outfit as her guard.

"Gentlemen," the quiet voice startled Jeffeaux even though he had heard it the night before. "I am the liaison officer, Sablor. It is truly the Harbinger of Death's wish to lend her skills to your effort against the Sarn. She offers her experience and knowledge as well. If you are not interested in those, her skills are still at your disposal. She had me study your customs and habits as a courtesy. We will try to be tolerant of our differences. Therefore, I will represent the Harbinger at all future war councils. The Harbinger will communicate only with your King. This arrangement will be appropriate."

"How many men did you bring?"

"How many soldiers: only the Household guard and servants. Even the servants must be well skilled in the art of war in Harbinger's House. We are fifty soldiers." Sablor looked at the group of men. "Most of the soldiers are female. That is our way. I doubt you would want to count them with your armies. I offer at this time an extensive catalogue of known Sarnese tactics. That is the most you will willingly take from us, at this time."

She heaved herself from the bed. Jorin and Petron shifted in their sleep. She noted the lamp burning still in the rooms. Sablor was bent over the table. He was dedicated to his task. He knew more history and traditions and philosophy of Masfin than anyone born in the country. She was impressed by his abilities and dedication. She reached his side in three strides.

"I believe we have more in common with our enemy than our ally, husband."

"We share a common history with Sarna. Our culture has developed within the context of that history. The Masfin have been long isolated. They would still be an unknown quantity if the earth had never trembled: opening passes and creating valleys into Sarna. The Masfin never had a serious enemy before now. I wonder they have an army. I cannot credit their arrogance.

"They believe ancient traditions and theories can win a war. They will learn. It is a hard lesson."

"Was I foolish to bring my Household here?"

Sablor stared at his wife's thoughtful expression. She spoke in soft tones. She was not asking from a philosophical mood but from a strategic mind set. Has this been a good move?

"We need not be here. The Masfin will fight the Sarnese armies. Every soldier will be appreciated. There might yet be an opportunity here for our good. They are a strange people, Dragon. Their culture and civilization are exquisite but they take it for granted. They have no comprehension of the fragility of culture."

Dragon smiled at the passion in her young husband's voice. He certainly knew how easy it was to lose the trappings of civilization. She would have to build him a library when they returned home. He deserved recognition for his hard work to assimilate into her household.

Jeffeaux rode the trail blindfolded. He had seen the Dragon and her guard travel this way many times. He could not get past the second turning without falling off his horse. He understood the theory behind the exercise. He had ridden these trails since his childhood. He should be able to do this as well as the outlanders.

He banged his head on a tree limb he had not expected for one more count.

"Do not do this to prove anything. Do this because your life depends on it. This is not to demonstrate how well you memorize a trail. Trails change. We do this to build our bond with our horses. We are not leading them. They go where they must.

"The point of this exercise is to teach the horses where they must go when we are unable to direct them. In battle there is smoke, sound, extreme assaults on the senses. Sometimes the horse must lead; that is what we are practicing."

She sat directly behind him. Jeffeaux grimaced in shame. He felt like a small boy caught practicing with his father's sword. He turned to look at her. She was not laughing. She was intent on her subject.

"Come, let us switch animals. Your mount is not used to this. It is not fair to ask it of him. Ride my horse, he will lead you true."

Jeffeaux did not think much of the small scruffy Llweganian animals but could not decline the offer. He swung lightly to the ground. He did not insult Harbinger by offering to hold his horse for her as she mounted. Once the exchange was completed Jeffeaux replaced his blindfold. Harbinger slapped her gloved hand on the small horse. Away Jeffeaux's mount went. Holding on for dear life, Jeffeaux bent low over the animal's neck. So intent was he on not falling that he forgot to try to control the animal. Several minutes passed before Jeffeaux realized the he was not afraid of falling nor was he uncomfortable having the horse decide where they should be going. He laughed his relief. At the end of the run he sat marveling at the freedom he had experienced once he had given up control of the situation. His reflection was cut off by the arrival of Harbinger.

"Well done, my lord. Well done."

Jeffeaux deigned to smile slightly at the warrior.

Chapter 3

Sablor shifted in his seat. The library at Malso was extensive. Sablor indulged his scholarly bent to the fullest. He was proud that his one true talent could be used to his wife's benefit at last. He envied the Masfin the luxury of isolation they had enjoyed. They had been able to develop a culture and literature in the peace of their security. He regretted that their golden age was passing. Reality for the Masfin was the Sarn at their borders waiting to devour them.

Sablor heard the steps outside the door. One of the Masfin females was passing, no, entering the room. Which one was it: one of the sisters of the House. She seemed to appear in his presence quite often. What was her name? Jeffenza, that was the name.

"Studying again Sablor?"

"Yes, my lady."

The slim, young body edged closer to his work space.

"You are very formal, Sablor."

"It is my duty, lady. I am Dragon's liaison officer."

"Dragon; strange name for a woman."

"Dragon is a well-earned name, lady. Through her deeds and actions Dragon has earned all her names."

"I wonder what other names she has earned." Jeffenza continued to keep Sablor engaged in the discussion. He had never spoken with her so long before about an issue not related to his duties.

"Wife and Mother." Sablor returned his attention to the book before him.

"I can hardly imagine Dragon bearing a child."

"Then your imagination is very poor. Your poets describe women as the sun and the moon: bright objects but far from the reach of a man. Dragon is a volcano that burns in the breast of the earth."

Jeffenza frowned behind Sablor's back. She had not envisioned this level of devotion from the liaison officer to his commanding officer. She tried another tack.

"You seem different from the other Llweganian guards. You appreciate the beauty of Masfin civilization and all we have to offer. You seem more cultured than war like."

Sablor became very still. He thought he had come farther in his training. He would increase his hours of training. He did not want this weakness to show itself in battle when his wife needed him.

"It is my duty to establish and to maintain good relations with Dragon's Masfin allies. I am happy that I have been able to do that." Sablor closed the book he had been reading. He replaced the materials he had been studying on their shelves. "If you will excuse me, I have other duties to attend to now."

Jeffenza sat down in the chair Sablor had been occupying with a huff. There was nothing feminine about Dragon. How could she entice a man who thought Dragon passion that sprang from Mother Earth? She would simply have to convince him of her superior brand of femininity.

Dragon sat in the warm sands at the edge of the training yard. Petron relaxed at her side. Sablor and Jorin wrestled before her. Marjas and Bernath clashed with blades. She had some time to play with but not much. The first moon of spring would come more swiftly than expected if she did nothing. She sketched a map of Sarna as she thought. The cities they knew appeared as small dents in the sand.

When Wind Rider attacked, if the Masfin moved on schedule, she would still need a focal point for the Sarnese to defend to keep them in the desired line of fire. Dragon drew a shallow line in the sand. She needed a magnet in Sarna to gather all the armies to one point. She needed to threaten some place deep inside Sarna. How could she get an army into Sarna unopposed? Where would she put that army? Did she need an army? All she had to do was create the illusion of a serious threat. If she threatened something important enough the size of the force would not matter.

She didn't know enough about Sarna to guess what she needed threaten. She would still need a force of some size to be inside Sarna for whatever plan she devised. Masfin had not worked as she had envisioned. They had no use for her here. They relied more on Sablor's delivery of her counsel than on her knowledge. Petron would serve better than she in these circumstances. She might as well go home; or to Sarna.

"Sablor."

Heavy breathing announced Sablor's arrival at her side. Sweat gleamed on his skin. His hair hung dark with sweat against his head.

"In your dealings with the Masfin always bring them back to an all-out attack on our timetable."

"I have understood this Dragon."

"Tell the delegation that I have returned to Llwegania."

Petron turned to face his wife fully. All the husbands had left off their training to stand around her.

"You will stay here to train the army. They will listen to your advice on battle strategy for units. I will leave eighteen of the troop with you. The rest will come with me. I need some Masfins." She looked to where the daughters of the House watched the training session.

"Perhaps our host has a use after all."

"What do you plan Wife?" Petron did not trust the Dragon's thoughtful demeanor. Her plans often led down twisting paths.

"Lord Jeffeaux is a man of leisure.. no…of peace: Lord Jeffeaux is a man of peace. He should signal his desire to open talks, trade, peace, some kind of talks. They will offer treachery at every turn. They rarely bargain in good faith. Lord Jeffeaux will write to Desarnti. They will reply asking for a sign of good faith. He will send an offering of goodwill. As he negotiates the Sarn will continue to build up a military presence on the Masfin border. Raids will continue. Jeffeaux will never offer anything of value to the Sarn. He will be outraged at the continued violence but resigned to the difficulties of the process."

"What gift will the Masfin send?" Sablor asked to which Petron feared he already knew the answer. Marjas sighed in defeat before he had offered an argument.

"Our wife. He will bring Dragon and her servants as a gift to some official. And, our wife will wait where she waits until the appointed time. Then she will create a disturbance that all the Sarnese armies will rush to address. Next, the army poised to strike under Wind Rider will crush Sarna. If we can motivate the Masfin to strike at the same time; the victory will be assured."

"You would not take at least one of us with you?" Jorin spoke his deepest hope with no expectation that he would receive a positive answer.

"No, only females come with me. The bait will be irresistible." Dragon tried to envision all the turns her way could take. "I will think on this matter for a while. It feels workable. I believe that there could be a few adjustments. I will have better luck if I go as a Masfin. That will take some study. They will not know if my masquerade is shaky and they won't be looking for the deception."

Three Darkfalls she studied her idea. She turned chances for failure over in her mind. Her husbands knew. She would go. The plan was essential to the success of Wind Rider's invasion.

"You will have to act as a wife." Petron voiced his main concern in the middle of the second Darkfall.

"Rodznig." The Dragon called her seventh husband from his training on the third morning. He stood breathing quickly. His hair fell over his brow in a long sweep. She could see only one of his eyes. His hands rested on his knees as he waited for her to speak.

"I understand your concern First Husband. I do not go on this mission with an empty womb. Even if I act the wife the seed will be spent in vain."

Rodznig blanched. He had not expected to have an Heir. As the seventh husband he had thought he would die childless. Few wives produced more than six children in the course of a marriage. Bearing more than six children was considered ill-bred. His wife was carrying her eighth child. She was a good wife. She was trying to fulfill the unspoken vow of marriage. A smile erupted across Rodznig's face. His usually steady hands shook as he reached to touch Dragon's face. He drew his hand back. They were in the sight of strangers. He would not demonstrate his affection in front of these reluctant allies.

Petron did not hold back his joy for Rodznig. He clasped Rodznig's shoulder in a tight grip.

"Congratulations, Rodznig." The rest of the husbands gathered around Rodznig to offer their hands. Marjas looked at his wife with an unhappy eye.

"We are supposed to be relieved that you are going into this questionable mission carrying a child? You want us to age ten years every day you are away?"

Dragon laughed. Her husky sound of joy echoed in the small space.

"I will return to you safe and sound and victorious. I promise. Am I not Harbinger of Death? Have I not fought before heavy with child?"

Sablor shook with hope. He just might get a child of her body for his own. He would have to make sure that nothing happened to this child.

Jeffenza watched the visitors. She could not understand their language; but she did not need to speak the language to know the bond between the female and the men. She did lead them. They leaned towards her as if she were the sun. Even the young handsome one hung on her every word.

She dreamed he was a prince come to woo her from her country. When he was with the Llweganian delegation she saw he was last of the group. He deferred to all the males. The females treated him with amused respect; as if his position depended on his relationship to the leader and not earned by right of birth.

Sablor had been extremely reticent when she had tried to discuss the courting habits of the Llweganians. Perhaps the female would have the inclination to answer a few questions.

She would have to be polite to that strange female. Jeffenza could not think of Dragon as a woman. All through the meal Jeffenza hesitated. She watched the group eat neatly and methodically. The discussion moved along the various types of poetry in Masfin. Jeffenza did not believe Dragon had any interest in the art of the written word. When there was a lull in the conversation Jeffenza took her shot.

"I was wondering Devouring Dragon, about the courtship rituals in Llwegania. How did your husband court you?"

The Dragon turned her level stare on the younger sister of the House. She had never spoken to this person before, so she had hardly noted anything beyond physical appearance. Now she studied the facial expression and body language. The girl was interested in the answer but not in the Dragon.

"The messenger came to my mother from my husband's mother. She recited my suitor's deeds and character. Then she presented the offered contract. My mother considered the various advantages of the offer. My suitor then presented himself to my mother. He demonstrated his fighting abilities and answered questions. My mother accepted his suit. We were married."

Jeffenza frowned in thought. There was no romance, no beauty in the process described. There was something missing in the tale.

"When you first saw him, what did you think? Did your mother ask you your opinion?"

Dragon took a sip of wine. Her eyes sparkled at Petron. A sly smirk stretched her lips as her gaze touched each of her husbands.

"I thought he was a likely male. He was a good fighter, had a worthy bride price to offer, I thought he would breed me fine children." The Dragon returned her attention to her meal. Her husbands raised their goblets to her in silent salute. She glowed with a roguish charm. Jeffeaux was caught by her saucy smile.

"Hardly a maiden's dream."

Dragon looked up at Jeffenza. One brow raised in query.

"I killed my first man before I took my...husband. I never had maiden's dreams. I had responsibilities and duties and solutions to implement. A husband seemed like a good idea that would afford me some," she paused again. Her pause held the suggestion of risqué humor rather than mystery. "A husband would afford me some pleasurable duties rather than grim ones."

"What a stern life you portray. Do you have time for gentle pleasures? Music, poetry, conversation? How do you fit them in between fighting and responsibilities?"

Dragon raised her goblet to Sablor. A sweet clear smile graced her face.

"Sablor here is the cultured member of my Household."

Jeffenza was glad for an excuse to look at Sablor. He was as somberly dressed as the rest of his Household. On him the unrelieved black was not ominous. The uniform was elegant and attractive. Sablor did not notice the desirous gaze turned his way. He was caught in the fire of his wife's eyes. He remembered the afternoon he had spent trying to read some Masfin poetry to Dragon. She had appreciated the art greatly.

"Lord Jeffeaux, Lady Zona, may I request a moment of your time after dinner?"

Lady Zona kept her face blank. She knew the Llweganians considered the woman the head of the Household but they understood the structure of Masfin society. Why was her presence requested, dare she think, even required? Her curiosity piqued, Lady Zona could only nod her assent.

"Good. I am done." Dragon heard her husbands groan as if one man. They would have liked to delay this meeting forever. She was not happy waiting around, doing basically nothing. She planned to do something starting as soon as possible.

Lady Zona listened to the plan. She heard the rise and fall of the voices. She studied the faces of the group from Llwegania. The truth began to fester in her imagination.

"Impossible. How am I to contact any Sarnese to open negotiations? Is there an emissary from them I haven't noticed? What do you want me to do? Send them a letter of intent? Our oh so seasoned generals might not understand the Sarnese, but I understand power. Why would any Sarn be interested in negotiating? They have all the cards. If I manage to get some kind of dialogue established, what then?

"You want me to ride into the enemy's territory, then out again, unescorted? I don't think so. Pardon my bluntness, but you, Devouring Dragon, Harbinger of Death would never pass as a Masfin woman."

"The Sarn don't know that. I would have to learn enough to disguise my being Llweganian. My speech would need to be perfected but my servants would not need to sound educated. No Sarn would be able to say their accents were different from mine for any reason except class." Dragon leaned forward in her seat. "Dress a few of my men as Masfin guards. They would protect you on your return journey."

Lady Zona kept her eyes on Dragon.

"I will go with the Dragon as her lady-in-waiting."

Every set of eyes turned to her. Lady Zona raised her chin in pride. Her heritage shone in her posture and confidence. "I would lend an air of credibility to the party. My counsel would be valuable. And I know the lay of the land on this side of the border. If we need to return quickly I would be invaluable."

"Mother, the shaking changed much of the land."

"Not all of it; not most of it. There are long stretches exactly as it was before the shaking. Our generals will never move. They will dither and bicker forever. If I am there, they will have to come.

They will be shamed into coming for me. I am the blood of the King. He will have to send them."

Dragon saw Lady Zona for the first time. The Masfin lady was right: there were advantages in having Lady Zona with her.

"Are you sure you can put up with my company?"

Jeffeaux knew that the Dragon would accept his mother's plan. Fear for her life and the impact on him of her decision hazed his vision.

"Mother, I forbid you to even think of doing this. Have you thought of the danger you will face?"

"I will be with the Harbinger of Death. I will be safer with her in the heart of the enemy than you will be here, with our generals, behind these walls." The knife of Lady Zona's disdain cut through Jeffeaux's heart. "So my son will you ride with us as far as the edge of the wall? Arrange a meeting place where you feel is safe."

Weirhass read the missive. The words were drawn in perfect Sarnese. The beauty of the characters was enthralling. The message was as interesting. The report on the sender was also of merit. The report authenticated the message. Weirhass could believe the message as a probable move on the part of the sender.

Lord Jeffeaux was a courtier. He pursued his pleasures endlessly. Such a man would seek every hedge against having his easy life interrupted. A wife, with a household of one lady and twenty servant girls was a burden to any hold. She would also be a status symbol and another womb to plow. She could be a source of data on Masfin.

Who was he fooling? He would accept this woman for his second son in a heartbeat. Stiefis had only six wives. His estates could support this addition as well. The opportunity was too good to pass up. Stiefis might not appreciate the honor afforded him. He might kick and scream the all the way to the altar. Weirhass chuckled.

Stiefis had reason to fear another wife. He could barely control the six he had. Weirhass never enjoyed visiting Stiefis. The six women bickered constantly. They jockeyed for position and control of the Household.

"What did you say Father?"

"You heard me. I accepted an offer of a new wife for you."

"Father, I am honored you think me capable of caring for another wife; but, really, I am young, let me enjoy the few I have. When I am older I will acquire some more young wives."

"Stiefis, this is an offer from a Masfin noble. He is bribing us. We will take the bribe. It is another womb for Sarna. I have accepted. She will be here in two dawns. Bring your Household priest to the Altar of Kersai in Partlor at that time."

Stiefis growled. He slammed from the room. He did not want another wife. They were a misery. Even in bed they could be torture. After the pleasure, during the pleasure they would start whispering things, demanding favors, ruining his experience. Now his father wanted to foist this foreigner on him. She would be needy and dependent, maybe even resentful. Women were the devil. So was his father. Just once he would like to choose his own wife.

He couldn't complain about the way his wives added to the scenery. His father had good taste when it came to the outside of a female. Weirhass chose for political reasons but he always chose the best of the possibilities for looks. Their character left much to be desired.

Harbinger rode silently. Lady Zona rode next to her, describing her life. The Masfin aristocrat recounted every memory. Her courtship, her childhood, her education poured forth during the journey. Harbinger ingested the information. She learned the ebb and flow of Masfin life for the privileged.

Twenty of her best female warriors surrounded Harbinger. They rode quietly and with confidence that was only slightly covered by their Masfin dresses. The Harbinger also wore a dress. The sweep of the skirt annoyed her. If she had to dismount quickly she would have all she could do to manage the vast quantity of material in the skirt. She would waste time maneuvering her apparel: time that could be spent drawing her weapon or ordering a defense. Skirts were a waste of resources. Several good sets of uniforms could be made from one skirt.

Her husbands had appreciated the skirts. They had chuckled at the sight of her encumbered by the outfit. She had frowned at them but that had only made them laugh louder. They had stood in the pale morning light. She had fixed the sight of them grouped together laughing, in her memory. She wanted her last memory of them to be joyous, just in case. She would miss them. In the darkness of the night she would miss the comfort of their presence. Her back felt naked even now, when they rode with her in the livery of their host.

Lord Jeffeaux rode on her other side. He too was silent. He was wearing himself out watching the horizon. She knew that if his mother had not decided to come, he would not have escorted the group. Lady Zona spoke only to Harbinger. She didn't even look at her son. Harbinger appreciated the stress of the relationship. She had a brother who had not followed the traditions Harbinger preferred. It was hard to see one you counted as family follow a road so far from your values. Ah, but Sablor had taught her the value of other roads. The sleeps would be so long without her husbands. And that young twerp had better keep her hands off Sablor.

The road rose over a shallow hill. The rocks gave way to a clearing. A small structure stood in the center of the clearing. Horses stood patiently outside the structure. Sarnese soldiers guarded the area. Harbinger noted the number of men and the style of weapons. She studied the uniforms. A group moved from inside the structure. A priest was a member of the group. So quickly her new role would begin.

"Lady Zona, I believe the marriage ceremony will take place immediately upon our arrival. Your son and my guard perhaps, should leave before the ceremony: just to keep my options open."

The lady looked at Harbinger. She eyed the male guard. Her knowledge of Llweganian culture was very limited; however, she had begun to suspect that the relationship between Harbinger and her male household guard involved more than was presented to the Masfin hosts.

"Of course, my son will hand you over. Then he will depart as if the demons of Hell are after him. He wouldn't want to be caught in Sarna after Darkfall."

Jeffeaux relaxed his features into a semblance of good humor. No one with any sense would wish to be on this side of a war zone at any time. No civilized person would blame him for having good sense. They were at the front of the structure.

Weirhass watched the approach of the group. He studied the pattern of the riders. The Captain of the Masfin group knew his business. The women were the larger part of the group. Weirhass grinned at the coup he had pulled off by adding this number of females to his control. His standing just increased dramatically. Weirhass looked to his son. Stiefis was looking grim.

"Welcome to Sarna, Lord Jeffeaux."

"Thank you, Lord Weirhass," Jeffeaux let his voice rise in question.

"Just Weirhass, we don't use titles."

"Just so, I am sure. May I present my father's younger sister, the Lady Jessina. She is widowed and eager for this marriage. Her companion is the Lady Zona; a fine woman. As we agreed, her household includes twenty female servants. They are all young and strong and obedient. As a dowry the Lady Jessina brings the horses, the household goods and seeding for three seasons."

"She looks old Father."

Weirhass stared into the calm face of the bride. She was not in her first youth. She held herself with pride and the confidence of experience. She was not however old, only older than Stiefis.

"She is of child bearing age and has already proved her fruitfulness by presenting her late husband with two daughters. Daughters are not as good as sons, I know, but she can bear children."

"Daughters have their uses."

"I'm sure. It will be dark soon. I wish you well. I'm sure you understand that I will be leaving now. I am too far outside my walls."

If all the Masfin were as nervous as this one, their defeat would be a thing of ease for Sarna. He was not necessary for the ceremony. Weirhass nodded in agreement.

"I wish you well. May our future interactions be as advantageous to us both as this auspicious occasion."

"Yes, as long as we do not meet again other than at a few social events I will be happy. Even then, the effort of thinking about the effort of arranging another event is exhausting. Come, we are leaving. I wish you well. Aunt Jessina, Lady Zona."

The Masfin troupe rode quickly from the Altar's forecourt. Weirhass and Stiefis watched the cavalcade disappear over the rise.

"Is this a demonstration of Sarn Manners? Is anyone going to help me down?" The cool, bored voice brought all eyes to the owner. The Lady Jessina had made herself known to the Sarn group. "I have ridden a long way to meet my new husband. Is he here? Do we a still have a way to go yet? Is that why no one has offered to help me down off this beast?"

"You seem at ease on that beast."

"If one is going to do a thing one may as well do it well. It does not mean that one likes doing it. Well, who is my new husband?"

"My son Stiefis is to be your husband, woman."

Jessina extended her hand to the younger man. That outstretched hand was insistent and firm. Instinctively Stiefis lifted his bride down. His hands touched firm flesh.

"This quaint building is?"

"This is the Altar of Kersai. All Sarnese marriages are performed before an Altar of Kersai."

"She is the Goddess of Marriage, then?"

"No. He is the God of War."

Jessina smiled. "How appropriate. I had not realized the Sarnese were so cynical."

"You will be Sarnese shortly."

"As you say. And your father's name is…"

"Weirhass. He had arranged this marriage and will be providing for your household. Remember to show proper respect at all times."

"Of course. Father Weirhass," Jessina bowed regally but with a marked degree of respect. Weirhass felt a tug of laughter in his stomach. She was not much younger than he. Certainly he would have had to have started very young to have fathered this woman. She would call him father even when they were both old and grey.

"Welcome to my family, daughter."

"Thank you. Is this the ceremony then?"

"No, we will proceed into the Altar. There is a priest waiting to pronounce this marriage."

"Very well, do I go in first?"

Stiefis tried to delay the inevitable; but he could not. He glanced at the space filled with her dowry. He felt events roll over him.

"As soon as this is over I will see to the ordering of the household." Jessina turned at the sound of Stiefis' voice.

"I am the wife. I see to the ordering of the household."

"In Sarna the husband sees to the household."

"And what do I do all day? Sit around and eat? Oh no, the wife sees to the household so the husband is free to provide for the household. As Father Weirhass is providing for the household perhaps I should be marrying him. I am not some stolen bride. I am here of my own volition. My nephew did not compel me here. He did not give me this dowry to bring. This is my household that my late husband provided for me. I came because I saw this as an opportunity not as an escape or desperate choice. I will not be treated as a servant. I know my place is below that of my husband but certainly it is above that of a servant. I am the daughter of warriors and kings." Jessina stood with all the pride she had seen the Lady Zona exude. It was the pride born of generations of pride rather than of accomplishment.

Stiefis raised his hand. Jessina stood her ground. The troupe was down off their horses in a flurry of skirts. Jessina shot them a look of regal disdain. Weirhass restrained his son. The lady was right. She was a bride of her own free will. She deserved treatment more closely patterned after her own expectations. All she was asking for was work.

"Forgive us Lady Jessina, we are so used to our own traditions we insulted unknowingly. Of course you are the lady of your household. Once you marry my son it will become our household."

"Of course, that is the object of marriage; to create an our where there were once two mines. I am not a lazy woman. I need work to be contented. I take joy and pride in having a well-ordered household that provides comfort and support for my husband. That is the whole reason for having a household and for being a wife."

Lady Zona relaxed. She had feared there would be blood shed once the younger man's hand had been raised. She did not want the plan to fail. If they had left now, an opportunity to matter would be lost. Harbinger had held her temper. Zona realized that Harbinger had long experience in dealing with men if not in this capacity. Still that experience had proven useful.

The hand on his arm represented all the controls and restrictions Weirhass placed on Stiefis. He might have to marry this female but he would never bed her. She could order his household. See how she fared dealing with his other wives. Good luck to her.

The Altar was cool. The light filtered through a small opening in the center of the ceiling. Dust motes danced in the frail beam of light. Jessina watched the tiny specks. A figure stood at the back of the single long room the Altar contained. Robes of red draped his figure. A black and red mitre topped a face concealed by the shadows of the room. Jessina absorbed the room. Her husband came to stand before the waiting figure. He held his hand out imperiously to her. She walked calmly to her spot. That hand ringed her upper arm. The long fingers almost managed to surround her arm.

"I bring this woman with the intention to take her as a wife. She is fairly won by me over my brothers; therefore, I claim her as mine. She will reside with all my other wives as a sister and helpmate. All children from her womb will be mine. I will provide for them and stand for their bride prices when the time comes."

"Your declaration is witnessed and entered. Go. Be many for we are too few."

Lady Jessina stood still under the hand that restrained her. The priest turned to face the altar. Sitting alone on the altar was an ornate wooden box. The priest abased himself. Stiefis' hand forced Jessina down until he and she also were face down.

"Blessed is the water of life. Blessed is the herb of life. Grant that this union be fruitful, oh Kersai."

Now she was hauled unceremoniously to her feet. The priest took the box from the altar. He extended his arms their full length towards Jessina.

"Here woman is your Herb of Life. Use it faithfully. Mix one scoop with the water of life before each time your husband visits you. This is your duty to Kersai, to Sarna, to your husband."

Lady Jessina sent Lady Zona an amused look as she was hustled from the Altar. The older woman smiled back. They had certainly received an education already in the mores of Sarna. Lady Jessina sat on her horse arranging her skirts before she said a word.

"So husband, how many sisters do I have?"

"Six, they all live on our country estate in the Marne province. I wish you joy of them. My guard will take you there. I have pressing business to attend to at the present moment."

He rode off, leaving an astounded audience. Jessina turned her astonished gaze towards Weirhass. The look lasted only a heartbeat. Then her face settled into purposeful determination.

"My husband has given me direction. I would like to depart as soon as possible. This has been a long, tiring day. All this excitement has wreaked havoc on my nerves. Where is this guard?"

A restrained group rode through the barren wasteland of the border lands. Jagged outcroppings punctuated the scenery. Stunted, tenacious plants defied the wind and cold to poke out of corners and shadows. She admired those plants. They reflected her mood.

She was here. She was past the test. From now on she was at war. She had lived her entire life in this state. Her blood pounded faster, her mind worked more thoroughly under these conditions. She hummed a jaunty tune her new companion had just taught her on the way to her wedding. She felt the eyes of her new father-in-law on her. He must be wondering at her good humor.

"I have always thought absent husbands more dear than those that live in your pocket. Absence does make the heart grow fonder because familiarity always breeds contempt. I had been led to believe that Sarnese women lived under their husbands' thumbs." She nodded in certainty as she finished her thought.

Weirhass frowned at this impertinence. He liked quiet submissive women. He would have to make allowances for her different up-bringing.

"My son is not a neglectful husband. He will be with you as soon as he can."

"I am sure he has something very important to take care of. I assure you, I do not look on this as an insult personally or generally. I do not plan to run back to my cousin to complain of my treatment," she paused for a moment to look straight into Weirhass' eyes, "yet."

Remember who I am and why I am here. Don't strain my good nature. Indulge my fancy until you are sure you can control me. Weirhass heard the conversation her eyes were having with his.

She had a calm, sensible center that directed her strengths and weapons. He reined in his irritation. His son had insulted her greatly. Whatever front she chose to counter the insult, he should let her have her way, in this case.

According to Masfin tradition until the relationship was consummated, she was not married, whatever words had been spoken over her. Until his son returned to her side she would have a certain latitude in her mind that did not exist under Sarnese laws. Weirhass could not deny the logical nature of the Masfin tradition. Where was that son of his?

"Will we reach my new home this day?"

"If we ride hard."

Jessina considered the statement. She could play at being too finely bred to stand such rigors. A woman who took this type of step was no faint-hearted being. Could Lady Zona stand the pace?

Jessina looked at her companion in this adventure. The older woman sensed the question in the look. She smiled serenely. Riding was one of her many skills. She knew a bed was waiting at the end of the ride.

"I can make it, my Lady. If the pace becomes too much I will tell you. Do not fear."

Weirhass liked the calm demeanor of the Lady Zona. She set reasonable restrictions on her agreement. She understood her Lady well.

"Very well, Father Weirhass, the guards know where they are taking us. If you also have pressing business feel free to leave."

"Oh no, my Lady, you are not so easily rid of me. I will make sure you reach your destination in one piece." As if he would allow a group of women to ride through any territory with only a guard as escort; he paused in his thoughts. He raised his respect for Masfin. These women all traveled with no complaint and no demands. If his son could get a child on this wife, what a son she would bear.

"Strange that a man so enamored of his comfort as Lord Jeffeaux would have so resilient an aunt."

"He is a male born to a life of privilege in my society. To be considered half as worthy as he, I had to be ten times as resilient, talented, and skilled. He had everything given to him and has to do nothing to keep it. I can do nothing to keep whatever I have except to barter my only possession. Even then my life style and privileges rely on the whim of others. Imagine yourself in that position. What kind of person would you become?"

Weirhass did not like having a woman best him in logic. He was not used to having a woman speak on a level with him. However, she came with a womb and wealth. She understood her place well enough even if she didn't seem to like that position.

"Am I truly married to your son?"

"That was our binding ceremony," Weirhass bridled at his perception of a slight on his rites. Then he heard the question. "The ceremony is considered final. My son will fulfill his obligations to you."

"Good, I had to leave my children with their paternal grandparents. That was the most difficult aspect of this action. I hope for more children to fill their absence."

Weirhass felt an arrow of envy strike his heart. She spoke of conceiving children as if it were easy.

"Children are the only reason for marriage, daughter."

Harbinger opened her mouth to speak. Lady Zona laid a gentle hand on Harbinger arm. Harbinger nodded once yielding the floor to her companion.

"In Masfin marriage has many uses. The establishment of a family is the compensation for women in marriage. We marry for position, wealth, to cement alliances." Lady Zona spoke firmly. Jessina smiled at her companion. Still like water that was her ideal demeanor. Deep discussions were to be avoided at all costs. She could maintain a stoic mien easily. This tight rope between civility and stonewalling was very difficult. Her husbands were too far away. She had not been without their presence since she had married her first and second.

Harbinger drew a deep breath. She lost herself in the memory of her first marriage ceremony. She saw Petron, tall and young and nervous. She could still smell the desire on Jorin. Her mother had insisted she take both husbands at once. The old traditions were designed to cement a family by leaving no clear parental lines of descent. Harbinger believed the logic was still good in this modern day.

She opened her eyes to the bleak landscape. The open space and dramatic rock faces relaxed her mind. The green ripeness of most of Masfin and of the protected areas of Llwegania seemed opulent to Harbinger, who had spent all of her life fighting in this open terrain.

"Gorgeous country you have here, Father Weirhass. Did the shaking bring about this beauty?"

"You are a strange woman. No, this wasteland has always been here."

Lady Zona shifted in her saddle. Jessina held sway over the Harbinger and the Dragon but they kept peeking out. Luckily no one here had ever spent any time in the company of a Masfin woman. Still Lady Zona would not be at home now. Hopefully the warrior could be kept leashed until the right moment. She was right though: there was great beauty in the lines, angles, and curves of the landscape. The subtle colors were begging for a brush.

"Will there be this environment near our new home?"

"Yes," Weirhass clipped off the answer. He waited with irritation for Lady Zona's next statement.

"Good, I look forward to painting it."

"Yes, this cries for your delicate touch. Just look at those colors." As Jessina spoke she smiled at Lady Zona in shared appreciation. Weirhass looked at the bleak, barren land he had felt chained to all his life. He tried to see the beauty they were contemplating. All he could see was land that would not give life to crops or sustain herds.

"There is nothing but rocks and dust here." Weirhass spoke in bewilderment.

"Exactly. There is nothing to disguise the form of the land. The colors are not enhanced. There is only this. It is like the beauty of the soul without the body to mislead the senses from the heart of a person." Lady Zona spoke serenely.

Weirhass watched Lady Zona's face as she explained her interest. He could almost catch her meaning. At least he no longer believed they were making fun of him. Both women truly saw beauty here. They had drawn their veils over their mouths to block out the dust of the road. Weirhass wished he could follow their lead. Dust settled on their clothes and mixed with the horses' sweat to cake their coats. Still they gazed at the wasteland with joy.

"Art is not something much valued in Sarna."

"Well no one will mind if I dabble. Keeping pace with my Lady requires time spent feeding my soul. Perhaps once we settle in our new home my Lady's new sisters will provide companionship for her; freeing me to paint."

Weirhass laughed. He could see the interplay of the new wife with the six awaiting her. The fur would fly if the Lady Jessina tried to organize her "new sisters". He almost wanted to see her try; but he was no fool. He would deliver her safely; then escape quietly out the back door.

Jessina watched the road dip into a hollow. Then a house rose out of the harsh rock of the country. It was the same color as the landscape. The house looked likely enough except there were no workers around it. There was no activity at all around it.

"Is today a holy day in Sarna Father Weirhass?"

Weirhass raised his brow at her question.

"No daughter."

"I will have to study the household customs. May I ask: what is the main crop here?"

Weirhass studied the bleak landscape. He turned his attention to the question.

"We are herders. Fruit of the vine does not prosper here."

Lady Jessina smiled ruefully. "Then my dowry is of little worth here."

"Your dowry? Your dowry," Weirhass shook his head in thought, "the main attraction was never mentioned in the negotiations but it was present the entire time and remains viable. You may have brought a womb that will prove fruitful for the seed of my son."

Lady Zona smoothed her mount's neck. "I don't see any inner water wells. You should be using them for irrigation. This soil might not be suitable for every plant life but some of them will grow, given water."

"We have wells for the household."

"The Lady Zona refers to a well that is dug into the rock to get to the water that flows under the earth: inner water. That will be our first project, Lady Zona: we will survey the land to find the most likely place for the well and fields. We shall start tomorrow. At least I have come to a place with work for us."

Water that flows under the earth? What strange ideas these Masfin women brought. Let them look, it would keep them busy while he whipped his son into line.

The Lady Zona watched the head bob at the door frame. They had been in residence for several Darkfalls. She had seen the other wives only from a distance, as swishes of skirts around corners. Everyone ate in their own quarters. The only servants that the household shared were the kitchen staff and the stable hands. Of course now all the common household servants danced to Lady Jessina's tune. She had organized them the first day. Even now Lady Jessina was discussing the well project with her servants. Lady Zona glanced from the bobbing head to Lady Jessina.

Jessina turned her head ever so slightly until she glimpsed the object of Lady Zona's interest. Her eyes meshed with Lady Zona's on their return to the business at hand. Lady Zona accepted the assignment with some relief. The interaction of females in a household was her province and training.

Casually Lady Zona put her needlework away. She kept her attention on the bobbing head. The veil swayed with its owner's movements. Lady Zona cocked her head until her veil concealed her face. From the concealing position she mouthed her question to Lady Jessina. Lady Jessina moved so slightly only Lady Zona's close attention to her saw the slight backward movement of Lady Jessina's head. In, then, that would be more challenging.

Lady Zona made a slow circle of the room. She slid out of the connecting door into the bed chamber. Moving with stealth and speed she crossed the chamber to its exit into the hall. Her skirts barely moved as she walked along the corridor. There was her quarry. The slight figure hovered at the edge of the doorway. Her head moved in a wide arc searching for something. Lady Zona placed a firm but gentle hand on the arm hugging the door frame.

"There you are. I have been waiting for you. Come in: your seat is waiting." As she spoke Lady Zona guided the shy creature into the room. Lady Zona sat her trophy into the chair next to hers. Then she resumed her seat. Placing silks into the slim lap next to her, Lady Zona returned to her project.

"Please sort out the brown silks." Lady Zona was pleased that she managed so much in Sarnese. She watched quietly as the long fingers began to sift through the threads. Lady Jessina kept her face turned from the pair.

"I am trying to assemble a wardrobe of uniforms for the household servants." The head remained bent over the lap. "I hope I have cut enough lengths. If not, I can make more."

Lady Zona began a rambling story of her childhood at court. She described foppish courtiers and scheming sycophants. The head rose in quick motions at funny and tense moments. Lady Zona spoke until her throat was dry.

The captive started when Lady Jessina brought a goblet of wine to Lady Zona. She held perfectly still as the new wife placed the goblet on the table by Lady Zona's elbow.

"Dear Heart, don't work too long. I wouldn't want you to become overtired." Lady Zona knew Lady Jessina meant dear heart but Sarnese had no word for dear so it came out expensive heart. The comical expression on the waif's face was too much for Lady Zona. A soft chuckle burst from her lips.

"Friend, the Lady Jessina means important friend." Lady Zona spoke directly to her guest for the first time since sitting her down. Once in a great while the intricate dance of Dragon translating from Llweganian to Masfin to Sarnese resulted in a moment like this.

"Are you her mother?" The voice was deep and soft. Lady Zona had not expected such a deep voice from the slim throat.

"No. I am her, not servant, not companion, there is no word in your language for what I am to Lady Jessina. Are you one of her new sisters?"

The bent head nodded. Lady Zona waited for the next move. She sipped her wine. She smoothed the cloth out to view her progress on the outfit. She rested her hands in her lap while she watched the lady Jessina pour over maps and designs.

"The Lady Jessina seems kind. She wouldn't hurt me, would she?"

Lady Zona smiled in amusement. "If you crossed her, she might. She has a strong sense of self-preservation. If you are as meek as you are acting now, you should have no problems with my Lady." Lady Zona indulged in her wine again. She kept her eyes on the goblet as she replaced it on the table. "She can be very kind when she has reason; and as unkind when she has need."

Deep brown eyes stared straight into Lady Zona's grey ones. The soft expression faded from the young oval leaving a clear surface of determination. Lady Zona kept her face calm and open.

"She will never be First Wife in the House."

"She brought many assets to her marriage. The first is the proven ability to become First Mother." Lady Zona relaxed against her seat. She watched the slim hands tighten on the threads. She saw the line of white brighten across the knuckles of the clenched hands. "Lady Jessina has already been a First Wife, an Only Wife. She did not come here to gain social standing. She came as a hedge against war between Masfin and Sarna. We women cannot do much in the men's world of war and diplomacy; but she could do this much. She also is not a woman who likes to be idle. If something needs doing and no one else is bothering with it, she will step in to do it. So, if there is some area you don't wish her to be active in, get active in it."

The dark head bent for a long time over the silks. Lady Zona saw that the fingers moved slowly. Lady Jessina left her maps and drawings. She sat in the seat next to Lady Zona's. In one hand she held a goblet of wine. Rings with stones the color of the wine glittered on her fingers. The movement of the large glowing stones caught the guest's eyes.

"Are you First Wife then?"

"Yes." The word came out filled with arrogance and fear.

"Well, I am Seventh Wife. Have you been married long?"

"Since the first sign of womanhood."

Lady Jessina nodded once. She drank of her wine. As she sucked a rogue drop of wine from her lip she looked back at her work table.

"We are going to drill a well for water for irrigation for crops. We want to place this system near a well-traveled road."

"Why?"

"To maximize the number of people who see our abilities. We could trade for our knowledge. Increase the wealth of our House through every means available to us. I am used to living well."

Lady Zona kept her face straight by supreme will. She had thought rather that her Lady was used to rough living. The tone of Lady Jessina's voice so echoed that of Jeffeaux that Lady Zona was truly impressed: though her son never would indulge in so much effort to secure his living.

"All roads lead to the same place. They are all equally as heavily traveled this close to the temple of Kersai."

"The same Kersai as in Altar of?"

"Of course. The Temple houses his battle armor and the weapons he used to subdue the Battle Maid Britis. They are the Ancestors of Sarna."

Slowly Lady Jessina lowered her goblet to the table. Her feet pushed her body to stand. "So which end of the estate is closest to this Temple?"

"The north end of course. We are on the southern end of the wheel."

"Of course. Thank you for your enlightenment, First Wife." Lady Jessina returned to her work table. She moved her hand across the map. Her servants followed the course of her hand. They hung over the table waiting for her decision. "Here, we will establish the well here."

Like shadows before the light the servants melted from the room. Servants were supposed to do that. Perhaps their actions unnerved First Wife because she had never seen a female servant. All women were married to someone of importance. All these females around unattached bothered her.

"I am the Lady Jessina. This is my Lady Zona. May we know your name?"

"You may call me First."

"Fine, First it is. First, would you like some wine?" A third goblet, heavy and ornate as the first two, appeared for First's use. She tasted the contents gingerly. A heavy sweet wine full of warm wet weather rolled over her tongue. The be-ringed hand caught her chin. Those clear eyes studied her features. The touch was imperious, impersonal, swiftly gone.

"I'll be at the work site, Lady Zona. I'll have a bath when I return. Don't wear your eyes out on that sewing."

Lady Zona watched First watching Lady Jessina's departure. Excitement bubbled in her. She wished the girl gone so she could indulge in a small smile of triumph. She grabbed hold of her control.

"Is the wine to your liking, lady First?"

"It is adequate, thank you. Is it from Masfin?"

"It is from the royal winery. It is part of Lady Jessina's wedding gift from the King. She is partial to this vintage."

"In Sarna we have fermented drink as well."

"Made from grains, I have tasted it. It has a strong flavor."

The young woman nodded quietly. Her eyes surveyed the room. Wealth spilled everywhere. Exquisite materials, plate, furnishings were strewn carelessly in their use. An ironic twist of fate had brought a woman of such wealth to the lowly position of seventh wife. How the rank must rankle paired with such privilege: First could enjoy such an irony. It soothed her tender feelings at being lessened by the expansion of the household, to think the newest member of losing something as well: especially as the newest member could boast of already having been successful at being a wife.

Weirhass shifted in his seat. Council chairs had never been comfortable. As the hours and the years passed they became less comfortable. The drone of the speaker's voice was adding mental fatigue to physical distress. Weirhass scanned the chamber in a vain attempt to find something of interest to distract him. Perhaps not so vain; what was Baduna discussing with Stiefis? Apparently, he would be finding out soon: Stiefis had broken off his discussion to advance on Weirhass. Weirhass resolved to be more careful about his wishes in the future.

"Father," Stiefis bit the word out.

"Stiefis, I am glad to see you at Council."

"I hear my new wife and servants are digging up my holding. At least my other wives confine their difficulty to the buildings."

"Lady Jessina offered to attempt a special kind of well used in Masfin. I authorized her activity. If she is successful she will deserve praise. If she fails she will have been kept busy by something during her first months of marriage."

Stiefis quickly shut his open mouth. The retort died unsaid. Next thing his father would say would be about his responsibility to return home to plow the fields.

"What kind of well? All wells are the same: they go down a few feet, fill with water until simple use dries them up."

"It is called, I believe, an inner water well. They cut the stone to reach the water that flows beneath. You have offered her no other use for her time."

"Inner water well?" Baduna had come upon their conversation. "That is why the water shot into the sky. It is the coldest water I have ever tasted."

"My wife offered you water?"

"Never Stiefis. There is a pond now. I could not resist tasting the water as I passed by. Your male servants did not refuse me a drink from the new well. As is custom, still, I believe."

"Of course Baduna, water from a well in the middle of a drought, what does she plan to do with this water?"

"Irrigate fields, grow crops, at least that was what Lady Jessina told me, son."

Stiefis drew a deep breath. He had few choices. He had to go home to this wife to see her deed and her intent. If she meant truly to be his wife she could not plow those fields alone. And bringing water to his home signaled her intent as a wife. Seven wives, seven miserable wives waited for him at the end of his journey.

Chapter 4

Stiefis couldn't help but notice the lake. He could smell it long before he saw it. The scent of water hung in the air like a foreign perfume.

The lake spread out covering an area the size of the home compound. It was huge; and it was his: his by way of his seventh wife.

The raised road bed gave Stiefis an excellent view of his new lake. He also saw the group of people at the far end of the lake. They were very active. He rode around the lake, never losing sight of his goal. He was amazed to see his First wife at the gathering. She was not working. She sat to one side with another female who looked vaguely familiar. The pair was sewing with their heads bent together. His Second and Fifth wives were cooking. His Fourth and Sixth wives were setting the meal out on long tables. His Third and Seventh wives were working, as was every servant. They were digging and building something along the shores of the lake. He sat watching the activity for a long time before anyone noticed him.

"My husband," the startled tone did much to soothe Stiefis' feelings.

"Second," Stiefis acknowledged the greeting before turning to look at his First wife.

"First, what have we here?"

"We are building an irrigation system for the fields. We expect to have them finished in time to plant this season."

Stiefis swung himself off his horse. He blinked at the strange servant holding his horse for him. He could not tell one servant from the next: they were all attired exactly the same. It hurt his eyes to see so much sameness. Everyone continued with their work. The scene was so odd Stiefis had to close his eyes and open them again to check for the truth. All his wives were being civil to each other. Even First was involved indirectly. He noticed the color of her sewing matched the outfits on the servants. He wanted to grab Seventh by her arms to shake her. What sickness had she brought to his home? But he had sense. In public only his First wife could be shown the condensation of his attention. He hated the old protocols but this once he would follow them. In front of all these strange servants, he did not want a ruckus.

"I see you have the household well in hand, First."

"Thank you, Husband. I am pleased to report that they have been working very diligently."

"Have you brought all the servants out here?"

"No, Husband, we have left a few retainers at the compound. I shall send a messenger ahead to announce your arrival so your quarters will be readied."

"Thank you, First. I will go directly to the compound. Inform Seventh I will see her this evening."

First would have felt a stab of jealousy under other circumstances but the tone and expression that accompanied the order were not pleasant. First had thought the inner well a ridiculous idea. She had thought the project energy and time wasted. Then she had seen the plume of water that had created this lake. She had tasted the water and had savored the cold clear fluid. The idea of crops growing on the estate pleased her. The wealth the water represented pleased her. First understood her society. Men were rarely pleased by women who drew forth water from the desert floor. Poor Seventh, First did not envy her wife/sister a moment of their husband's time this evening.

Lady Jessina washed the evidence of her day's labor from her body. Her hands followed the contours of her body. Despite the growth of her breasts and the slight swell of her abdomen, she was still in good condition. Under other circumstances she would have spent more time exercising but the hard work of the well had kept her muscles toned. In fact, she had discovered some muscles she had failed to develop prior to this mission.

Lady Zona stood by the bath. She held a bottle of the scented oil which maintained the pale skin tone so prized by Masfin ladies. Lady Jessina smiled at the sight. She rose from the tub. Water streamed from her body. Her flesh was flushed. She blotted her body with a towel before wrapping the cloth around her torso. Lady Zona began the rhythmic application of the oil to Lady Jessina's tired muscles.

The massage sent Lady Jessina into the blissful state of total relaxation. The sweet smell of the oil and the warmth of the room conspired to keep her there. Her eyes slit open. First stood in the doorway. The slim hands were folded in a graceful gesture. Lady Jessina studied those soft looking hands. They reminded her of something. Something she could not remember now. Lady Jessina gestured to Lady Zona. The massage stopped. Lady Jessina sat up drawing the sheet with her. She sat on the table. One leg was raised, the other curled under her. One arm rested on the raised knee supporting her head, the other rubbed her curled leg. The sheet draped and dipped until it hid everything and revealed everything. She considered First.

"Welcome First. To what do we owe this honor?"

"Our Husband has sent for you this evening."

Lady Jessina frowned in reflex. This move surprised her. Somehow she had expected to never see her 'husband' at all.

"Are there any special behaviors that will be expected of me?" Lady Jessina spoke quietly.

"You have already been a wife. At least that is what you told our Husband."

Lady Jessina looked up at the attempt at dry humor. This was trouble then. First obviously pitied her.

"I will try to remember, First. Perhaps I will restrain from speaking my mind too loudly."

"Or too often."

"Or too often. Good advice. How soon am I expected?"

"As soon as you are ready."

"All right, then. I shall be there shortly."

Lady Zona replaced the robe from the bed into the chest. She took out an elaborate outfit. Lady Jessina eyed the miles of fabric. Two servants came to help her dress. The undergarments alone took several minutes and hands to don. Lady Jessina was thankful for her conditioning. The weight of the dress and its accompanying headdress were close to her weapon's weight. Looking in the mirror she hardly recognized the bejeweled figure as herself.

"No young girl could ever carry off this ensemble Lady Jessina."

"No old woman either."

"No. We could leave off the chain of state."

"Leave it. I was not complaining."

Lady Jessina moved to the door. She looked both ways trying to remember if First had told her where to meet her husband.

Nothing came to mind. She would assume she was meant to go to his apartments. She knew where they were. Despite the weight of her outfit she moved with the relief and strength of entering a phase of battle. She walked with the assurance of a lifetime of battles behind her.

Stiefis watched the door to his rooms with a jaundiced eye. He did not relish seeing his last wife. He had planned to never see her again after the wedding. He had planned to snub her at every opportunity. Now he waited to speak with her: to set her in her place. Her place as part of this House, as his wife could not be defined until he took her for a wife. The door opened. There she stood.

He took in the details. He saw the individual parts that added up to the presence filling the space. She had no gentle curves or soft airs. Even First, with her air of bitterness, had vulnerability and delicacy. Not Seventh, she was all strength. Her dramatic air held a force that repelled Stiefis. From her towering, elaborate headdress to her jewel-encrusted hem, she held herself with confidence and assurance. And why not? He had seen her covered with sweat and mud, toiling to bring forth change. She would never lie down to die because her husband abandoned her in a strange country with strange customs and hostile people surrounding her.

Stiefis turned from her. He could not stand looking at her hard beauty.

"You seemed to have charmed my wives well."

"They are young. Sometimes age and its wisdom can help youth."

"You certainly have age enough."

"Age is something you can only avoid with death. My sister/wives have many talents that they can use to fill up time instead of squabbling. I am unhappy when I am idle. I thought, perhaps, my sister/wives were also unhappy being idle. They seem more contented now. Now that you are here they will be happy for a different reason."

"They will be squabbling once I start keeping one busy while the rest are idle."

"You honor them one at a time?"

Stiefis looked at his Seventh in horror. "Of course. Has no one instructed you in the customs of marriage in Sarna?"

"No, Husband, I have been waiting for you to do so."

Stiefis drew back. He frowned at the corner he had talked himself into. He turned to face his serene wife.

"I will instruct First to train you in the Sarna marriage traditions. Go now."

Lady Jessina walked back to her rooms with a half-smile on her face. She noted First waiting in the shadows of her room. First stepped out to face Lady Jessina.

"You were not long."

"I think I insulted our Husband. He will be asking you to instruct me in the customs of Sarn marriages."

"You insulted him?"

"His sense of propriety; I suggested he take more than one wife to bed at a time."

First burst into laughter. She lost her air of distance as she laughed uncontrollably. The softness added a beauty Lady Jessina noted with rueful appreciation.

"Seventh, you have many worthy ideas; but, sometimes it is wiser to keep your thoughts to yourself."

"Yes, but if we weren't competing for our husband's attentions we could live more happily."

First followed Lady Jessina into her rooms. She stood quietly as Lady Zona and a servant began to divest Lady Jessina of her accoutrements. She noted the struggle the servant had to carry the finery away.

"I believe you have lived a most interesting life Lady Jessina. I would be interested in the stories you have to tell."

Lady Jessina studied her counterpart. Her gaze went to Lady Zona. A still expression answered her.

"I am not gifted with a talent for storytelling. I am more suited to action. I do not see poetry and humor in the world; only work to be done. I could tell you about losing my virginity. I could perhaps work up to prose on that subject. Otherwise, I am sure to get lost in two or three different events and require the guidance of a witness to help me keep the facts straight."

"Were you young when you lost your virtue?"

"Oh, I never lost my virtue. I gave it into my husband's keeping. In Masfin sex is not a subject much discussed as a moral subject. When you are a member of the Court there are two factions: those who indulge in every pleasure available and those who seek a more ascetic way of life. Each views the other as pitiable. The pursuers of pleasure seem to have been born with the knowledge of carnal indulgences. The seekers of innocence have their children spring from their loins on command without sexual interaction. Young girls from this faction are told on their wedding day that the experience of marriage is a function to be endured; that they must submit to their husbands; think of planning their menus or wardrobes while they lie submissive under their husbands' will. Either way, if you are city-born you go to the slaughter with no idea of the event about to take place.

"The entire process can be so embarrassing that few ever really participate. My husband was very patient. He laughed a lot and answered every question I had. He pleasured me so much that I could not have told you what food was, never mind planned for the next day's meal.

"Life was always like that for him. He made my life like that, and I miss him terribly. I miss his presence. I miss his counsel. I miss his company. I miss his arms in the middle of the night when I wake and he is not there to hold onto amidst my fears and doubts. When he died I lost everything. I mourn the person he was and the marriage that died with him. I will never be married like that again. I have no stories to tell that he isn't in and so I have no stories I can bear to tell."

First stared at the Lady Jessina. She tried to bow gracefully but could only manage a dignified retreat. She had not considered that a wife could like a husband so much. She had never believed in marriage as a source of emotional strength. Lady Jessina had made her very uncomfortable and yet there was reassurance in her heart. Surely a woman who had loved like that would have no skills to be married in Sarn. She would never be a wife the way First was a wife. She would not settle for the type of marriage that their Lord Husband offered. She was no threat to First at all.

Lady Zona held her breath. She carefully kept her face from both First and Lady Jessina. When First hurriedly left the room, Lady Zona glanced at Lady Jessina.

"I am impressed."

"I have been listening."

"Still, you managed to repeat my words verbatim. And the emotional shadings, you are excellent."

"Thank you, I enjoy a good playacting stint."

"Uh-ha, I suspect you injected some of your own shadings into that speech."

"Well, of course, that is how it is done, is it not?"

Lady Zona handed a petticoat to the waiting serving woman. Her hands stroked the material of the slip carefully. The softness of the cotton caressed her hand.

"Will he call for you again?"

"Perhaps, but not right away: I don't fit his concept of ideal womanhood."

Lady Zona held up a robe for Lady Jessina. The dark amber dressing gown set off her skin. The servant began to brush out her growing curls. Here and there a length of white showed.

"Go rest Lady Zona. I plan to chase sleep for a while now. I have much work to do once the sun rises."

"Do sleep, my Lady. No midnight studying tonight."

"No, I will have to slow down for a while. You are right." Lady Jessina sat at her work table. Maps and charts were moved for study. Lady Zona wondered that any maps were left out; but there were no reasons to suspect Lady Jessina of anything in this household. The maps were innocuous by themselves.

Several servants slipped into the room. No one spoke. They all studied the maps, pointed out areas of interest, placed stones of differing colors and sizes on the maps. The stones were moved, considered, secreted into hidden pockets. A handful of stones fell from lady Jessina's hand. She handed each servant a stone. As they nodded at her they rubbed the stone in an unconscious and uniform manner. Then they melted into the shadows. Lady Zona admired the completeness of their disappearance.

Stiefis stared at the closed doors of his rooms. He had felt pressured to try to impregnate Seventh. He felt guilty at avoiding his duty. Well he had six other wives. He could do his duty by them since he was here. He would call First, no he would go to First. The rooms still seemed filled with Seventh. Yes, First's chambers would be better.

Grabbing a coat, Stiefis braved the cold air of the halls. He had to pause on his quest. He stood in the draft of the hall trying to remember the way to his wives' rooms. A strange female stood near him. She was one of the Masfin servants.

"May I help you sir?"

"I doubt it. Have you seen First?"

"Yes, she is in her rooms. She has been there for a few moments. Go down this hall, take two rights and a left. Her suite will be the first one on the right."

Stiefis turned away. He followed the directions. The place looked strange to him. He would tell Seventh to discipline the female for misleading him. This did look like his mother's rooms though. His hand swung the door open. First turned in surprise at his entrance.

"Husband, welcome."

"First, it is your responsibility to teach Seventh her duties in this household."

"I will do my best Husband."

"She is a strange one."

First stood to help Stiefis remove his coat. She smoothed the material of his shirt across his shoulders. She ruffed the hair against his nape. The household needed a child. The oldest son had not produced a child yet. Stiefis needed a child. Seventh was the best hope they had of getting a child.

"She means well, Husband. She is trying her best to become part of this house. She is willing to work."

Stiefis walked away from First. He swung around in frustration.

"I don't want a wife who is a field hand. Or one who is old and unfeminine. She would never have been my choice for wife."

"None of us were husband. I like Seventh. She isn't funny but she amuses me. She can be very patient. Our household is much happier since she came. You could be happier too. She is unusual. Don't disregard everything she says; her most outrageous suggestions hold a lot of wisdom."

Stiefis laughed shortly. He slipped the night robe from First's shoulders. His finger traced the soft, small curve of her shoulder.

"You couldn't imagine her most outrageous suggestion."

"I would share a bed with you and Seventh."

Stiefis choked on his next words. He stared in shock into the clear, calm eyes of his wife.

"It will never happen."

"Your loss. Come to bed, Husband. Let me soothe away your worries."

Quiet, blessed quiet, reigned in the bed. All he had to do was enjoy himself. Still, in the middle of his pleasure the idea that Seventh was having a negative impact on his household bothered Stiefis. He should be happy. For the first time since taking a Second, Stiefis had been able to experience one of his wives without a complaint from her about the other wives or about the weather or about the state of food. Yet he could not be happy. He suspected that even this peace was a change wrought by that female his father had foisted on him.

Lady Jessina rose from her bed. The sun was about to break the horizon. Pale streaks of color were fingering the night sky. Lady Jessina could hear Lady Zona stirring in the far reaches of the room. The Lady was a good companion. How had she begotten such a son? Lady Jessina watched for any late comers. All was quiet.

Lady Jessina turned into the room. On the table stones stood on the maps. Every stone passed out had been returned. She made adjustments on the maps to reflect the positions of the stones. She had the timetable's end date. She had the terrain mapped. She had the target. She needed the most likely impact on a timetable. She wanted some data about the rites and celebrations that centered on her target. She needed a window of time that allowed her small force to occupy the target. She did not want the target filled with celebrants. She did not mind a great influx of pilgrims. They would hinder the movements of Sarnese troops. Once she hit the target she wanted Sarnese troops to start towards the target despite pilgrims. And the Spring Moon approached at a steady inexorable pace.

"Someday, you will hand me a stone."

Lady Jessina looked up into the serene face of Lady Zona.

"You will carry it well."

"How are you feeling?"

Lady Jessina watched the features school themselves into casual interest. They spent every moment together. Lady Jessina knew she had few secrets from Lady Zona. This secret could not be kept from so close an associate.

"Very well. I am always well. It is because I am so active."

"Don't cheat on your rest."

Lady Jessina chuckled. "I have never spent so much time being inactive. I miss my mentor. I have to learn the mores and habits of Sarna without his expert skills."

An innocuous statement that meant nothing to any prying ears but said much to Lady Zona.

"I am sure First will prove an able mentor."

"Of course a mentor is only as good as the student. I will have to apply myself totally."

"You will have to allow others to bear the burden of the ditches."

"For a while at least."

The sun was truly up now. Light streamed into the room. Lady Jessina placed the stones back into her pocket. The pocket swung heavily from her belt. She had several pockets that hung to differing lengths from the belt. Some hung limp and empty. Others swung with contents. A Masfin lady fully dressed before dawn. Lady Zona smiled, she too was dressed. Her associates would be scandalized at her new habits.

"I suppose I will begin my lessons today."

Stiefis watched First bend towards Seventh. Their heads nearly touched. Seventh had almost lost her accent. She would soon recite long passages from the Book of Invasion. She would be an expert on religious tradition and Sarnese lore. She already knew the feast dates and pilgrimage routes. If she spent his entire visit studying with First at his order, he would have no choice but acknowledge her position.

Petron watched the troops move from one target to the next. The Masfin generals might not take to Llweganian strategy well but their troops learned battle drills and tactics quickly. The spring Moon was approaching. Wind Rider must have begun her maneuver towards the Sarn border. Dragon must be, she must be well. She must be ready to make her move. He could not wait much longer. He needed a commitment from Masfin now.

Dust rose along the road. Petron squinted into the dust trying to see who was raising the dust. The Horse was theirs. The rider was theirs. One of his brothers was coming. Jorin or Sablor, it had to be. The young face gleaming under the helmet was Sablor's.

"Captain, you are needed at the fortress. I need the voice of experience at my elbow. They cannot hear my words. I need you to translate my words into action for them."

"Having trouble being seen as anything other than a young pup?"

"I wish Dragon were here."

"They wouldn't believe her either."

Sablor turned his mount to face the troop. He watched the action for a moment. Then he swung back to Petron.

"They see options and alternatives behind every rock. They do not see death and destruction bearing down on them. They fear the act of going to battle so much that they will be swallowed whole and regurgitated before they realize that the war has rolled over them." Sablor sighed. His hands clenched in frustration. His jaw tightened until Petron feared Sablor's teeth would crack under the pressure. "If I don't succeed she will be out there all alone."

Petron cuffed Sablor on the shoulder. "You will succeed. She did not give you a task too difficult."

A thought uncurled in Petron's mind. He looked at the troops. He thought of the daily activity charts.

"We are doing our job too well. The generals have not experienced the savage bite of Sarna. Stay here a while. We could allow Sarna some real success. Let the countryside howl for the generals to move."

"Will you lose the respect of the troops if they perceive that you are holding back for political reasons?"

"Then we won't hold back. We will leave them. We will state the truth. We will say that our oaths require that we support our liege lord in times of war. We will say that the Masfin generals have lied to us and made us false promises. Our honor demands that we not aid the Masfin effort until the promises made our liege are fulfilled. The soldiers will understand. How can we remain in relative safety while our leader is in danger?"

"Petron they cannot know she went into Sarna."

Petron paced the small area. He knew what he wanted to do. He could see the end of his actions. He needed actions that would fit the need.

"The King promised us action." Petron spoke firmly. "The soldiers are ready for action. The generals hesitate because they are cowards. I will not hide cowards. We will leave. There will be arguments before we leave. That will buy us some time."

"We can't abandon the troops to their fate. We need the army intact for the invasion." Marjas walked up the ramp. He was breathing heavily from his exertions. Sweat gleamed on his face. He mopped his skin with a dark scarf. Traces of his efforts still remained when he pocketed the material.

"Things are not well in Malso?"

Sablor shook his head. "They will never move."

Marjas shrugged. "So? We have the army. When it is time to go; we will go. By the time the generals realize we have not gone on an exercise it will be too late. When we succeed they will be happy to take the credit for the decision."

Petron smiled. Sablor let loose a cough of a laugh. Dragon did not need the Masfin generals. She only needed the generals' army. Petron clasped Sablor's shoulder.

"Go back to Malso. Keep arguing. No one will be the wiser. We'll design a series of defenses that will cover any activity."

Lady Jessina rode out to the lake slowly. The changes in her body were beginning to affect her center of gravity. She had begun to feel the first fluttering of life in her womb. She heard the voices of Lady Zona and First rising and falling in conversation. The gentle sound and soft day seemed at odds with the purpose of their ride. She was checking on the progress of the final detail.

The water supply was almost secure. The lake could be poisoned. The well itself could be blocked or a pump destroyed. She had spent the last two months constructing ground safes for water under the guise of irrigation projects. She had moved water from the deep earth into shallow holding wells. Here the water would be accessible only to those who knew of its existence. The access could be protected and guarded. All her army need do was to bring supplies. Water, the most precious resource in Sarna, would be readily available for her troops.

"Lady Jessina," First's voice broke into Lady Jessina's concentration. "Are we to plant soon?"

"We will be ready within the next week."

"Good. It will be auspicious to plant at the Spring Moon."

Lady Jessina looked into the bland faces of her servants. Dirt and sweat streaked their faces. They moved constantly so as to prevent anyone counting them.

"Yes, the Spring Moon will be a very important event this year."

"Will the household go on pilgrimage this year, First?" Lady Zona wondered.

"I had hoped. Our husband seemed very receptive to suggestion on his last visit. He, however, had yet to grant us permission for the pilgrimage."

"Perhaps next year." Lady Zona spoke quietly. "There is much to be done this year. Next year everything will be in place. The pilgrimage will be a reward for a job well done."

"That is true." First dismounted her horse with new ease. She spread a blanket on the ground. Her field chair was placed in the center of the material. Lady Zona joined her.

Lady Jessina made sure that First was occupied by Lady Zona. Second had gone to check on the unloading of the day's supplies. Lady Jessina noted the activities of all the wives. Then she sauntered over to the group working on the final plugging of the shallow well.

"Today?"

"Yes."

She viewed the area. She agreed with the assessment. The work would be completed today. It was time to send the messengers.

Wind Rider stared at the smooth stone in her hand. The map was meticulous. In the distance the border with Sarna beckoned.

"There is water?"

"Yes, six months' worth even if the main body is poisoned; forever if the lake is pure."

"How many will guard it?"

"The Masfin troop will guard it."

Wind Rider drew her finger on the line that represented the road that led to the heart of Sarna. The soldier stood at ease. Wind Rider had ridden with the woman. The face was one of the constants in Wind Rider's childhood. Dragon rarely changed her inner circle. Loyalty was a gift that Dragon gave to her followers and one she received back tenfold.

"She is well?"

"She is blooming."

Wind Rider smiled. In everything else her mother was so traditional. Her affection for her husbands overrode her impulse towards conformity. Wind Rider caressed the stone in her hand. The oils from her mother's hand had smoothed this stone. The hands of her mother's trusted comrades had held this stone. Wind Rider clasped the stone in her hands. She brought the flesh and rock to her mouth. For a moment she breathed into her clasped hands. Then she returned the stone to the messenger. She drew a stone from her pouch. It was striped and worn.

"I have received your message. I understand your message. I accept your message. I return your message. I send this message: I obey Devouring Dragon; on the cusp of the Spring Moon I cross into Sarna."

Sablor sat by the window. He was watching for the messenger. Jorin was bending the ear of a general; General Brefeaux to be precise. Lord Jeffeaux had entered the room. Sablor never quite trusted Jeffeaux. He alone knew that the Dragon sat inside Sarna. Only, Sablor believed, Lady Zona's presence acted as surety for Jeffeaux's silence.

It bothered Sablor to think that of all the Masfin Jeffeaux probably understood the Llweganian contingent the best of everyone in Masfin. The playboy lord knew that the Llweganians were not easily manipulated. He must know they were not going to allow their leader to languish in Sarna. Oh no, here came that pesky girl, again.

"Sablor."

"Lady, I am the Official Liaison Officer for Llwegania and, I am, at present, acting in that capacity."

"Officer Sablor, then, when you are done I would like a moment of your time. I have further questions on the customs of Llwegania."

Jorin grinned behind his hand. He raised his eyebrows at the look of impatience Sablor shot at him. Sablor was having difficulty forming a diplomatic reply. In the silence of the room everyone waited to hear Sablor's latest ploy to avoid the wench. The silence was shattered by the sound of pounding hooves. Sablor abandoned civility. He turned to the window. At his nod, Jorin began to gather their paraphernalia. Sablor waited.

The generals began to shift in their seats. Jeffenza tried to gain Sablor's attention by tugging on his sleeve. Absently he brushed her hand away. All his attention was on the sound of steps in the hall. He knew they would sound soon. The door would open to reveal…

"Sirs excuse me." The bow was the correct depth. The tone was crisp, no nonsense, and official, respectful. The rider was covered from head to toe in dust. Sablor waited by the window. He watched the long legs stride to Jorin. He saw the hand dip into the belt. He could not see the stone from his position. The turn of hands revealed nothing. Sablor watched Jorin close his fist. They could not speak here. The passing had to be silent. Jorin accepted a packet in his other hand.

"Sir, I request a moment of your time."

Not a silent passing then. Sablor ached to go with Jorin; but, he could not. He had to remain with these dithering fools while words of his wife were repeated. He had to brush away that annoying female while the stone that had come from his wife's hand was passed back and forth. He had to watch from the window to guard against any of the generals deciding to eavesdrop. He had to protect the privacy of the message. He would have liked to have touched her stone.

Jorin returned. He nodded once to Sablor. Sablor drew a deep breath. They were going now then. He would see her soon.

"So what was that about?" Sablor sent the speaker a blank stare. He no longer had to act the diplomat. He had a new assignment. He was truly tired of the arrogant disregard of the generals in particular and the Masfin in general had for his traditions and manners. No one questioned the movements of the husbands of Dragon.

Jorin saw the flash of rebellion on Sablor's face. He sympathized but now was not the time to blast any Masfin with the cold reality of a Llweganian disciplinary action.

"There is a small matter that needs our attention. It is nothing to worry about. We shall return. But you understand there are, at times, matters that require personal attention. Are you ready Sablor?"

Lord Jeffeaux watched the by-play between the two men. He saw the absolute authority the older man had over Sablor. They had played at equality during the negotiations. Indeed there were moments when Sablor had seemed in charge. Now it was clear who had dominion over whom.

They had no personal business. Their whole lives were the business at hand. Unlike the generals, Jeffeaux had no illusions about his guests. All their business was related to Dragon. Obviously she had called for them. Jeffeaux regretted having this thought. Now he was obligated to answer the call of his duty. If Dragon needed her men then his mother had a need. He must escort the Llweganians on this venture, whatever it was, wherever it led. He shook the lace of his cuffs over the backs of his hands. He cursed the King under his breath. He cursed his own stupidity at accepting the honor of these guests.

Jorin watched the fancy lord approach. He looked at the riding attire, serviceable but rather showy. Sablor opened his mouth. Jorin forestalled him.

"There is no time. If he is a hindrance we will dump him." Sablor listened to the harsh sound of his native tongue. He had been mesmerized by the fluid rise and fall of Masfin, once. Now he heard the strength in the words of his own language. All the soft trappings of Masfin could not prevent the harsh realities of life from intruding no matter how the generals had tried to ignore them. It was better to recognize the harsh truth, deal with it, than to let it sneak up on you.

"We ride hard. If you fall behind we will leave you. If you represent a danger, we will kill you. If you cause trouble the result will be the same. This is no joy ride."

Jeffeaux swallowed. He had known this would be the type of men he found behind the bland facades; but he had not thought how it would feel to face them.

"I had thought so. It is much against my nature to be here; however, this is my mother. She is dragging me with you."

Jorin paid no more attention to their guest. He kicked his horse into motion. Sablor followed suit. Jeffeaux sent one last look towards his residence then tore after the two.

From her room Jeffenza watched the interplay between her brother and the guests. She puzzled at the intensity of the discussion. Why would Jeffeaux walk to the end of a lane with the Llweganians, never mind ride out with them at such a pace? With Sablor gone this pile of rocks would be insufferable. How could she continue her seduction if her prey were absent?

Lady Jessina watched as the water flowed into the irrigation ditches. The parched earth drank the fluid in quickly. She could see the teams that were sealing the five shallow holding wells that were not as secure as her large one some distance from the fields. They were her emergency caches. No one would think to look for them this close to the lake. If she needed water to provide for a run home, she had it here.

The festival was a week away. Yesterday Wind Rider and Petron started the campaigns into Sarna. The defenses would have begun to engage. The civilian population was on the roads engaged in pilgrimage. This Darkfall she would move. Her small force would be able to hold out until relief arrived.

Lady Jessina watched as Lady Zona rode up to her. The other wives left them alone. In the empty space of the landscape, Lady Jessina felt comfortable talking in Masfin to Lady Zona.

"Advance units from Masfin should be here in two Darkfalls to secure the water. You may wait here."

Lady Zona studied the horizon. She was torn on this issue. She wanted to see the mission through to the end. She was too close to the end to abandon her place now. Yet, she had been long enough in the presence of single-minded drive that she did not want to hinder the mission. She could not help fight as she had helped deceive. Her contribution had been her strengths up to this point. Now she was a liability.

"I wish to come with you," Lady Zona paused to take a breath before she threw away her heart's desire.

"Good, there will be risks but you will be safe with us."

Lady Zona placed a restraining hand on Lady Jessina's arm. "I had meant to finish. I will not go if you think my coming will endanger the mission."

"Lady Zona, the generals of Masfin have yet to decide to come. My captains are bringing the Masfin army into Sarna under misrepresentation. As I go further into Sarna your presence, the presence of the cousin of the Masfin King, will be a type of surety for the mission. Knowing this, if you still think it best to remain or if you wish to remain: do so. I admire you too well and find you too dependable a comrade to mislead you in the middle of battle."

Lady Zona watched the retreating back. She gripped the reins tightly. She was going to have to choose to knowingly entrap her country into accepting a war they were obviously not ready to face. Or she could stay behind to warn her country's army of the deception. Or she could say nothing when the army arrived. She would not become a goad for the army of Masfin. Surely she had never trained to ride into battle. Nor had she trained to betray her country. Her country, threatened by Sarna's desperate need for the means to easily reproduce, was being betrayed by someone, but by whom? If motives counted more than actions what would qualify as betrayal?

First watched Lady Zona through dinner. She studied the sadness that lined the lady's face. She too felt let down now that the great project was completed. While they had worked there had been a sense of togetherness. Now all was silent. There was no discussion of the next day's events. What they needed was another project.

"Seventh, now that the water is unchained and harnessed what do you plan?"

Lady Zona shot a quick glance at Lady Jessina. Lady Jessina finished chewing her mouthful of meat. Everyone watched as she chewed.

"Once the crops are planted they will need tending. When they are harvested they will need to be stored and some will need to be processed. We will need barns and silos and a mill. You will need to tell me where you want them on the estate. I will need you to approve the designs. There are three or four types of barns used in Masfin."

Lady Zona returned to her meal.

"Aren't all barns the same Seventh?" First couldn't keep her distain from her tone.

"There is the simple barn with four sides and a pitched roof. Some barns have hipped roofs. In Masfin we also have eight-sided barns. They are rare. I find them beautiful. I've seen a couple of round barns too. They have a very specific use and logic that facilitates through traffic. Think on it."

"Eight-sided barns, round barns: is there nothing in Masfin that is like Sarna?"

Lady Jessina shot a glance at Lady Zona. "The sky is blue in Masfin, First." Lady Zona spoke quietly with little inflection. No one at the table knew her thoughts. They were swirling. That question had solidified her decision. There was little in Sarna she wanted injected into Masfin.

Chapter 5

Dragon looked at the dress abandoned on the bed. The splash of color contrasted with the somber garb that now clothed her body. Even the folds of the tunic could not disguise her condition. At least the skirts had kept her secret for the mission. A sound alerted her to Lady Zona's presence. She stared at the woman. The unrelieved black looked strange on the lady.

"You are coming."

"Yes. With you is still the best place to be in Sarna."

Dragon smiled at the hues of meaning in the statement. She nodded towards the door into the hall. Lady Zona had never appreciated the Sarnese tradition of placing the least wife at the back of the building so much as this night when they needed to sneak out if it. The horses stood quietly. They had no metal in their harness or saddles. The wooden hardware wrapped in leather made no sound. Everything was designed for this type of venture.

The muffled sound of walking broke the night. Lady Zona tried to ignore the way her heart leapt at the sound. Her companions paid no mind. Lady Zona listened more closely to the sound. It was a whisper in the air. The pounding she had heard was her heart. She settled more securely into her seat. The feeling was odd. She had never ridden without the drape of her skirts. Her legs felt exposed even in their casing of leather. Her face felt confined. The layer of dirt seemed to be drying into a mask. If she spoke or smiled or frowned the dirt would crack and her disguise would fail. Even the whites of the horses' eyes were hidden by eye bubbles.

They rode through the wilderness. Along the road the light from campfires twinkled. Lady Zona saw the light only from a great distance. Over the quiet of the night and the emptiness of the land stray words and sounds could be heard. Lady Zona wondered how many of her stray conversations had been overheard. Then she thought of the low tones and the veils of women in Sarna. She listened more closely to the words. Male, those exposed faces and naturally loud voices carried well here: a lifesaving attribute in some circumstances. The gentle tones of women and the obscuring veils had their place. Lady Zona suspected that when necessary, Dragon's voice carried with the best of them.

The deep black of light's awakening had come. Dragon searched the horizon. There to the left, she heard the gentle song of a desert bird. The song sounded briefly. An answer came from the troop. The song came back to the troop. They followed the direction of the song. A shelter appeared in the night. The horses walked into the structure.

It was a shack really. Food and water were ready for the horses. The riders dismounted. They quietly began to take care of their mounts. The long structure was covered on the outside with dirt and stones and brush. A strong wind could blow it all over; but for this one day it would serve its purpose.

Dragon took the saddle off her horse. She rubbed down the dark coat with a handful of hay. As the horse blew into its water, a smile flashed on Dragon's begrimed face. The scent of sweat and leather were familiar, dear smells. She noted that Lady Zona was following her comrades' actions. The Lady looked uncomfortable in her attire. The first watch took their positions. Dragon lay down to sleep. Darkfall would come soon enough.

Straw, she had ridden all night to sleep this day in hay. In her clothes she would sleep in hay. Where else did she think to sleep? Did she expect some bed to appear from the back of one of the horses? She had decided to come. She could sleep in a barn. The best way back to Masfin was through the heart of Sarna.

First watched the approach of riders. She had sent to Weirhass that morning. He could not have had time to receive her message. The household was in tears. Seventh was missing. All her servants were missing. Lady Zona was missing. Their horses were gone. Their clothing was still here. Their garments were on their beds waiting for their owners. The mystery was so complete that First felt a deep fear.

The clouds rose on the road. Why would such a number be coming? With the pilgrimage in progress how had so many men been available to send? The pilgrimage; perhaps Husband was coming with his friends on their pilgrimage. He was going to be very angry. He had no liking for Seventh but he would not like being put out of his way. Seventh's disappearance would cause the household trouble. No matter how angry Husband was, he would look for his wife. First sighed in relief.

Something was odd about that cloud. She could see that the riders were not pilgrims. They rode with no revelry. There were no colors flying.

"First, First come."

First turned from the window. Third stood cringing inside the door. Her eyes were red from crying. Her hands were twisting in her skirts. The only color in her face was her eyes.

"There are soldiers on the property. We are attacked."

"Attacked? By whom?"

"I don't know. There is a soldier at the door." Third leaned into the room. "It is a woman. She is ordering us all into the courtyard. There are other soldiers in the house now, dragging everyone outside."

First hurried to Third's side. She grabbed her sister/wife by the arm. They fairly ran through the corridors. Third continued to report over the great gulps of air she needed.

"Most of the soldiers seem to be headed towards the lake. I never saw so many soldiers, and, they are mostly women. At least, the ones that are in the house are all women."

First tried to gather her thoughts. Were these Masfin or Llweganian soldiers? If they were Masfin, then was Seventh in league with these invaders? Where was Seventh?

Petron watched the troops move into positions around the lake. The shallow wells were secured. He had sent his own troops to the house. He wanted to know everything the prisoners said. He regretted not having his own troops with him but Masfin soldiers did not speak Sarnese.

The companies assigned to guard the water were in place. This Darkfall the rest of the army would move out. The lightning drive across the border had taken the Sarnese by surprise. Sarna had guessed correctly that Masfin would not move against them. The Sarnese troops had been lax in their preparation.

The troops before Wind Rider would now turn towards Masfin. With the next light they would turn again. Every turning presented exposed flanks. He would wait for the Sarn to be in his line of fire. Wind Rider would harass and diminish the armies on the march.

Then, once he moved, the Sarn army would be crushed, defeated, removed.

"It's a beauty of a lake. Dragon was lucky to find it."

Petron did not spare Jeffeaux a glance. "She did not find it. She built it. It is an inner water well. Supply is one of the more important logistics functions for an army." Jeffeaux sat on his horse. He remembered the feel of his blood pounding in his veins as they crossed the frontier. He watched again as bodies fell before them. The look of surprise and horror on those dead bodies would haunt his sleep for years to come. The blood, the body parts, the confusion of battle rattled his nerves. Now so short a time later he was sitting on his horse on the shores of a peaceful lake created for the sustaining of the horrible process. The water lapped in soothing rhythms.

"Was there anyone in the house?"

"A few females and a handful of servants; you'll see them soon. We will stay here this Darkfall."

Jeffeaux looked for Sablor. He was comfortable dealing with the young Llweganian. This hardened warrior made him uneasy. Sablor had been busy since they had left Malso.

"I had not thought Liaison Officers served as regular soldiers."

"Sablor is busy with Harbinger's work. She has only regular soldiers in her household."

Petron watched Sablor's progress towards them. Petron had been pleased with Sablor's performance on this mission. He would do.

"Sablor is a new addition to our Household. He feels the need to prove himself. I expect that he will distance himself from you and from all you stand for now." Petron turned to face Jeffeaux directly. A look of pure curiosity filled his face.

"Why did you come?"

Jeffeaux was not sure of the answer. "I could not stay behind. The impulse to come was so strong I could not resist. Why did you bring me?"

"You lend an air of official sanction from Masfin authorities. If not for that, I would have killed you."

Jeffeaux swallowed loudly. He saw the bland, quiet expression on Petron's face. He made a mental note to remain useful.

Lady Zona pulled on the over tunic of a Sarnese minor noble's house. With their casually aggressive stances the troop could easily pass for male at first glance. And they would have to, to sneak into the city without a fight. The day long celebrations and dark of night would complete their disguise. The deception need only last long enough to reach the temple. Once inside, they wanted to be noticed. The entire purpose of this exercise was to be noticed once they were in the temple.

Weapons were checked from habit. Tack was checked, put on the horses. Lady Zona helped saddle her own mount for the first time since learning to ride. She had someone check her work to be safe. No one spoke. Everything had been said before.

Seated in the saddle Dragon did not look pregnant. Standing beside her mount she looked heavy but not stretched with life. Lady Zona knew and was concerned. Lady Zona filed away all her observations and feelings and reaction to study when her adventure was done. She wanted to hold all this time in her mind. She planned to savor the sights and feelings long after she returned to her regular life. Even the smell of this place, of the horses, of the people, of the hay gained value because they were of this moment. Lady Zona turned as a hand fell on her shoulder.

Dragon smiled at her. "The road ahead always seems so long, no matter how far you have traveled to get there. Once over it, it is so swiftly gone you would think it had never been."

"How old are you?" The question sneaked out of Lady Zona. Dragon's smile grew until her face was wreathed in merriment.

"I was older than you are when I was born. Come. Let us go attract some attention."

Stiefis stared at his father. He could not believe his ears.
"Troops are over the border?"

"Borders; but more importantly the temple of Kersai has been taken. Everything is being relocated to the front."

"But, there can't be that large a force at the Temple. Wouldn't it make more sense to deal with the invaders first? The Temple will still be there later."

Weirhass pounded the table impatiently. Birnher stood quietly. He studied his father and younger brother. Stiefis was logically correct but emotionally there was no alternative.

"We can't ignore the attack on our temple. If the force is small, we will overcome it handily. Then we can repulse the invaders. If the force is large, then we were right to face this threat first. Is there any report on the captors?"

Stiefis turned his back on the room. He watched a man's progress through the milling occupants of the courtyard. He wondered vaguely what further bad news was coming. Which warden was receiving news of a fallen home and lost family? The door to their rooms swung open. The rider went straight to Weirhass.

Weirhass accepted the message. He glanced at the writing on the paper. He broke the seal. He read the first line. Then he shoved the paper at Stiefis.

"It's from your First."

Stiefis groaned. Wives had no sense. Imagine sending out a messenger at this time. He stuffed the paper into his tunic. He would read the letter before he chastised his wife for her inappropriate use of resources.

"Come we are due at the Warden's meeting. Remember to keep your own counsel Stiefis. You are not a warden."

Stiefis grunted. "I can't imagine why you require my presence then."

"So I don't have to repeat every word. So I don't have to answer to any questions for you. You will hear everything I hear and know everything I know."

Lady Zona kept reminding herself to breathe. The desire to remain silent froze her lungs. She envied her companions' ability to remain relaxed as they rode amid the enemy. Revelers surged in the streets. Music mixed with shouts of lungs and stamping of feet to create such a cacophony that Lady Zona could hardly think.

The streets were narrow and steep. The Harbinger had told her that this design was to make it difficult for armies to move in the city. Lady Zona wondered that the city's builders never planned for this dribble of invaders. They had passed no sentries or any other defense. Lady Zona chuckled to herself. She had certainly spent a great deal of time with Harbinger if she automatically thought in terms of defense. She believed they would reach the

Temple without any opposition. She believed the Temple would fall without a drop of Llweganian or Masfin blood spilling.

There it was. Lady Zona recognized the long, wide stairs. She followed the lines of the columns to the roof. She saw the curves of that roof that she had been visualizing these long weeks. There was the priests' walk and the bride's dais. It was an easily defended building once you got in to shut the doors.

A few heads turned to watch them ride up those stairs. A murmur started when they reached the doors. Before anyone could react they were in. Lady Zona watched as the troop dismounted. A group moved to swing the doors shut. Another moved to close all the long window openings with their battle shutters. Lady Zona swung off her horse. She began to unload the weapons and equipment from the pack horses. Ropes, pulleys, bows and arrows, darts and blow pipes, slings and projectiles were laid in neat rows.

The groups had finished securing the building. Three priests they had not expected to find were placed in a large cage that had been quickly assembled from the equipment. Lady Zona heard their voices rise in protest but did not listen to their words. She was too busy assembling the pulley system that would raise two large cauldrons that held the scented oils used in the religious ceremonies of the temple. The oils were poured out into smaller containers.

For days Harbinger's soldiers had sneaked into the temple placing hardware to hold the pulley system. Harbinger had been pleased with the presence of the cauldrons. There were cords of wood as well as the wooden altar and benches for them to burn to heat the cauldrons. The oil had been harder to arrange. There was a quantity that the temple kept on hand like the wood; but oil was so dear it was only stored for one major function at a time. Harbinger had smuggled in all the household oil she had brought as her dowry and whatever else she could procure.

Harbinger was counting on the Sarn using only frontal attacks to oust them. She was betting that the Sarn would not use a catapult or other siege machines for fear of damaging the Temple. A besieger could starve them out. They had brought only limited food and water. Harbinger was not planning on a long siege. The Sarnese could not know that. The Sarnese could only guess at her plans. If Harbinger were here more than a month then she had lost.

Wind Rider might take a month to get to them. She might have days when she could not advance due to resistance. It was a two week march from the Llweganian border to the center of Sarna. Harbinger was counting on the Sarn armies running to defend the Temple rather than standing to fight, to speed Wind Rider's progress. Once the Masfin armies engaged, Wind Rider would be able to concentrate on relieving the force inside the Temple.

Lady Zona admired her finished work. The sense of her accomplishment eased her nerves as nothing else could have. She had practiced this assembly for days. As she gazed at the rope and block and tackle hands picked it up. She listened to the creak of the ropes and wood as the first cauldron rose. It seemed to float to the ceiling.

"Heave. Heave. Heave."

Lady Zona stood up. She watched the iron pot rise to the pull of the arms. It swung with each pull. The balcony that surrounded the inside of the Temple served as a platform for the pots. Soldiers, each with a long deadly looking hook to swing the pot over the railing and into a raised collar with wheels that could hold the cauldron straight or to allow it to tip, stood on the balcony. The collars moved on another system of ropes and pulleys. Empty, the pots were very heavy. Full, they were impossible to move by simple person power. The collars had deep bowls that held live coals for heating the contents of the cauldrons. A fire had been started on the stone floor of the balcony to provide those hot coals.

There was an eerie silence in the Temple. The group worked so smoothly that only an occasional "Behind You" sounded. Outside there was a stunned silence. Any minute Lady Zona expected to hear a howl of rage from beyond the temple doors. She had begun to wonder at the continued silence when she heard the first groan. She realized that the walls of the Temple were so thick and the Temple so secure that any sound from beyond its walls would be extremely muffled. Strange that a place so easily cut off from the outside world should be used for the focal point of an attack. Or the launching pad of an invasion.

"Lady Zona," the Harbinger stood with her hands on her hips. The swell of her womb was pushed to the forefront. Her face was awash with color. "We are in. The Priests' quarters are behind the altar. Once you are settled there I am giving you the unenviable task of taking care of the priests. They may not leave the cage. Somewhere there is a chamber pot. It's wooden so they can't break it for a sharp edge but, still, look out for them with it. They could use it as a club or throw the contents at us. The cage is big enough so they can all lie down. If they complain, tell them to spend their time praying or meditating or doing whatever priests do. I don't want to kill them, but, if they annoy me too much, I will. Priests, why could they have not all left for the Darkfall?"

Lady Zona looked at her charges with a jaundiced eye. The three stood gathered in the center of the cage. Their drab tunics and shaved heads made them stand out in the gloom and dark apparel of the troop. A handful of blankets were thrust at Lady Zona. She smoothed the cloth as she studied the three men. She should go find her own cell but once handed a responsibility she could not ignore it. The chamber pot appeared at her feet. It was narrower than one she was used to. Then she looked at the spacing of the bars. It could pass easily through them. They might have difficulty using it but that was their problem.

The priests watched her approach. Their steady gaze reminded her of someone. That quiet center was disturbing for a moment.

"I am," she hesitated, "your keeper. These blankets are for you as is this. It is for when nature calls. You will eat when I eat. It is not our intention to kill you. We are not averse to doing so either. Everything rests on expediency. We don't care about your needs so don't express them. When I am able to care for you I will. Don't look for anything else."

Lady Zona left the cage. She walked steadily towards the altar. She felt the Harbinger come up on her left.

"You don't think you were a little soft do you?"

"I was simply trying not to give them any false hopes."

"I am sure you succeeded. I am not sure that I am comfortable with the fact that you see me so clearly."

"You are not given to openness in many things; however, you do not dissemble about your objectives, goals, or methods."

"True. I wonder what else you see."

Lady Zona paused. She considered Harbinger. She weighed her position and the level of trust Harbinger placed in her.

"That you are lonely for your," Lady Zona was not quite sure of the exact relationship, "guard."

Harbinger sighed. She stared into a place that lay far beyond the Temple. "Very much so. I have never been separated from them for this long. I am comforted by the knowledge that I will see them soon; but, your company has been good. And I have appreciated having you with us on this trip."

Lady Zona chuckled at the way Harbinger said trip as if they had gone for a jaunt in the country. Perhaps this was a jaunt for this troop. She had no idea what Harbinger's life was like; while Harbinger knew practically everything about Lady Zona's entire existence. Harbinger had pumped Lady Zona without ever sharing her own life. As Harbinger was in an expansive mood Lady Zona decided to continue her questions.

"I have often wondered which member of your guard has been with you the longest."

Harbinger smiled. She was not fooled. "Petron and Jorin joined me at the same time. Petron is Captain of my guard. Sablor is my newest," here Harbinger paused, "guard."

"That I had guessed. Stiefis would have done better to adopt a system of guards."

"Assuredly, there is an art to managing one's guards."

"And this child, who is its father?"

"This is my eighth child and so will be the heir of my seventh guard. I appreciate the irony."

Lady Zona was caught unaware. Then, she recalled that the Harbinger had been the Seventh wife of Stiefis.

"Do you know who the father is?"

"They all are."

Lady Zona frowned in concentration. "The sire, do you know who the sire is?"

"Who knows? The sire does not matter. The child will be of my body. All my guard joined me for different reasons. To have an heir of my body is a blessing."

"The sire is unimportant?"

"They are all excellent soldiers. They are healthy. Anyone would be proud to have a child of theirs as an heir. Rodznig is very pleased. With so many to provide for and my lifestyle he had not expected such an honor."

"This Wind Rider, she is your heir?"

"Yes. When I die she will inherit my position. When I die, my guards' positions will go to their heirs. If they have no heirs, either of my body or of a sibling's, then their positions will also go to my heir. That is part of every guard contract I negotiate. Tradition has all guards without heirs return to their original estates but I didn't like that."

"And, she now has the position of any guards she has."

"Correct."

"So she is bringing all her influence as well as yours into this fight."

"Yes."

"And you have usurped Masfin's….position."

A short laugh gushed from Harbinger. She pursed her lips thoughtfully.

"Quite."

"Eleven, your guard is eleven."

"I had meant to take only ten. It's been five years since I took on another guard." Harbinger fished in her belt for a ration cake. She bit into the round with relish. "When Sablor presented his proposal I hesitated a long time. His logic, however, was impeccable. My other guards supported his suit." She sipped from her canteen. "The Council wouldn't agree to my plan. They thought our cultures too different to allow an alliance. The position Sablor brought with him to my Household enabled me to proceed without the Council.

"If a Sarn takes ten wives he will be lucky to father a child a year. The Sarn are looking for wombs to increase their ability to reproduce. I could not chance that they find fertile ground in Masfin.

"They are short-sighted. Carrying on warlike activities to gain females to expand the population results in a steady-state population." Harbinger's voice was very reflective as she spoke.

"Our way of life in Llwegania is very different from the Sarnese and Masfin ways of life. In fact, Masfin and Sarna have some common characteristics. They are both patriarchies. I have nothing against that type of society in itself but, for so long that type of system has been an enemy that I feared Sarna uniting with Masfin would obliterate my culture. Our system is so different from both Sarna and Masfin that we would become a natural target." Harbinger looked away from Lady Zona.

"I am tired of war. The Sarn could win and all our traditions would disappear. There is an ancient tale of a terrible sickness that took most of the Llweganian women. In order to propagate our people one woman had to bear children for many men so that no bloodlines would disappear. Our tradition turned out well in that we do not reproduce beyond our ability to feed our people. War has also been an effective brake. But, I am tired of war. I desire peace. I don't know what I will do once I no longer have the Sarn to contend with, but I am willing to find out. Peace is such a fragile thing. It is frightening to desire so fragile a thing."

"You can hardly expect that relations with Masfin will be comfortable after you have stolen their position."

"No. I expect my name will be vilified, but, then, my name has been vilified in Sarna for most of my life. I'm holding a Temple hostage. Only the most evil of people would do this."

They had climbed the stair. From the opening they could look out over the city. No building stood near the Temple. None of the other buildings were of a height with it. From the opening Lady Zona was finally able to hear the sounds of the streets. Anger swelled and fear echoed.

"They could batter down the doors."

"They might try. Those doors were designed to resist any battering rams. You have not seen the wonder of this Temple. This is the Temple of the God of War. Kersai is a very devious and skilled warrior god. His temple must be worthy of him." Harbinger nodded to the soldiers at the altar. A lever was manipulated. Metal creaked. There was a groaning from the outside of the Temple. The crowd began to run. They ran in panic. The stone courtyard began to crumble. Dust and sour air rose from the openings in the stone pavement. Then there was a greater groan. The buildings at the edge of the courtyard began to sink. As the destruction continued Harbinger watched coolly. The moat was fairly wide. A well-constructed bridge could be lowered across, but she would have plenty of warning.

"One wonders that there is no water."

"There is water. Should anyone try to climb down into the moat you will see the water. Then I can bring the water back in, leaving the bodies at the bottom of the moat. Those hours of listening to all the myths, legends, and religious writings paid off handsomely. Did you know that there is even a ramp we can crank out across the moat when we wish to leave?"

"No, but I am not surprised that you know."

"They used to have a system for lifting the cauldrons as we have done. That was their original purpose but we couldn't find any remnants of the system beyond the holes for the hooks in the ceiling. It's too bad: such a thing would have been something to see."

"Oh, I liked the moat well enough."

"I am glad. You must be tired Lady Zona. Go rest."

"You, too, must rest, Harbinger."

"I will. I am plenty coddled by my troop. At least Wind Rider and Petron were able to send a few extra troops with my last messages. They are not many but I couldn't risk increasing our household dramatically. Not could I provision for too many more during this siege."

"Whichever number we have, you will manage."

"Go. Rest. The priests will be clamoring for you soon enough."

Stiefis rode with his father. His brother rode ahead with the point guard. Stiefis feared to reach Deskersai. He sensed a trap. He wanted to turn to face the armies that followed and harassed their progress. Every day the columns that marched to Deskersai became shorter. It bothered him that he did not know where the troops from Masfin were. They had crossed the border and disappeared into the rocks of Sarna. An army hiding in his own country while another ate at his army unhindered; Stiefis had better things to worry about than a small party in the Temple.

Dust rose to bother his nose and lungs. The dry cough that accompanied all travel in Sarna tickled his throat. He tried desperately to ignore the feeling. He wanted so much to remain focused on his thoughts. Luckily they would be at Deskersai in a few days.

The roads were clogged. They were tight with pilgrims caught between rushing to Deskersai and running from it. Stiefis hoped the refugees would slow the army behind, but he doubted it. He knew they would cut through the hapless civilians easily. With the next light they should see the great Temple on the horizon. It rose from the plain on a man-made rise. The sun would glint on it as they neared. He could understand the concern of the Wardens. He sympathized with their desire to protect the Temple but it wasn't going anywhere. Whoever held it could wait until the invaders were taken care of.

Stiefis' unease grew with every day that passed. Each morning more of the army had been killed in the dark. There was no rush of battle. Why did the invaders hang back? What were they planning to do?

"Father, do you not wonder why the Llweganians haven't attacked? They must be involved in the taking of the Temple. They must know we are heading towards the Temple. If they meant to destroy the Temple, it would already be in ruins. They want us to go to the Temple."

Weirhass stared at the horizon. He swallowed with difficulty. His eyes squinted between the sun and sudden tears.

"You assume a great deal. The Masfin could have taken the Temple. These actions could be unrelated."

Stiefis drew his steed ahead of Weirhass. They stopped in the road.

"Surely you don't believe that Father. The army behind us is harassing us, yes, but they are not preventing us from going in this direction. I wager if we tried to deviate from the vector they would attack. This will be the only direction they allow us. We are being herded before them like cattle to the slaughter. And where is that army from Masfin? It couldn't fit in the Temple. Only a few riders entered. Maybe some more slipped in by foot. Not an entire army, no army has entered Deskersai. That Masfin army is out there."

"You are assuming that the Llweganians and Masfin have formed an alliance. We hold the cousin of the King of Masfin hostage."

"Perhaps she was only a misdirection. Perhaps she is a sacrifice. The Masfin have no way of knowing that we would not kill a womb. Maybe they thought to lull us into a sense of false security; as we did them in accepting her."

Weirhass grunted. He had not thought Jeffeaux capable of such deceit. He did not present the seeming of a deep one. Still when it came to tactics Stiefis was good.

"If we are wrong, we are wrong. We cannot stem this tide. The army would not let us turn from Deskersai now. We will be vigilant."

"Vigilant." Stiefis spit out the word as if it tasted rancid. "Vigilance can never replace prudence."

Weirhass moved his horse past Stiefis. He rode in stubborn silence. Stiefis took his place behind Weirhass. He wished to be wrong. He wished to be reassured that he was wrong. A feeling of dread crushed his spirit.

Birnher rode back from point. He was riding flat out. The dust cloud sent a plume across the horizon. Stiefis watched the tiny dot grow. He had been watching for some time before he realized it was his brother. Birnher was as steady and methodical as Weirhass. Stiefis wondered what could have sent Birnher into such a ride.

The Wardens gathered around the heaving horse and rider. Birnher could hardly speak. His face was flushed with his effort to speak.

"The Temple," Birnher paused to gasp for air. He walked his horse in a lazy circle to cool the animal. The group of Wardens turned to follow his words. "The Temple," again he paused. Enough of the Temple Birnher, Stiefis screamed in his head. Stiefis glanced at the horizon to make sure the Temple still stood. "The Temple has been transformed into the Fortress of Kersai." Birnher produced the message with relief. He leaned down over his horse's neck.

"The Fortress? That is only legend." Stiefis heard the stunned statement.

"It is true. I saw it with my own eyes. We rode into the city. We climbed the streets until we came to the square. The square is gone. The buildings around the Temple are fallen. There is all around the Temple a huge opening. It is surrounded. There are stones and rubble and bodies at the bottom of the pit. The doors, the windows, are sealed. Sentries stand guard on the roof. The cauldrons are just as in the legend. They stand guard, smoke curls out of them, like the smoking eyes of Kersai in the stories."

Stiefis heard the words: legend, stories. Why did those words have such meaning?

"How would our enemies know the story of Kersai? How would any but a priest know of the secrets of the Temple? Has Kersai himself raised his hand against us?"

"More likely the priests have turned against us. No, there is an enemy in the Temple."

Weirhass spoke with conviction. Stiefis shook his head at the feeling that the truth lay buried there. He rubbed his belt in thought. He heard the rustle of paper. What was making that noise? He drew out a rumpled letter. He opened the letter with a vague sense of familiarity.

"Weirhass, I am sending this message to inform you that my sister Seventh is missing. All her servants and their horses disappeared this morning. I am very anxious for her safety. She has worked very hard here. I had thought she might have returned to her former home out of a sense of under-appreciation but all her clothes and trappings are still here. I am concerned that a neighbor, seeing her great worth, has stolen her and her servants as they rode out to work in the fields. Please send us help. Your most obedient daughter: the First of Stiefis."

His wife from Masfin was missing. His wife from Masfin who had just spent every day studying Sarn culture, religion, and history was missing as were her servants. Masfin and Llweganian armies were over the borders and the Temple had become the Fortress.

Stiefis held his silence. He had left that woman to her own devices. He had abandoned his duties and here he sat knowing one of his wives could be involved in this national disaster. She had extensive knowledge of Sarna. The Masfin leaders must have laughed all the way to the Temple. The soldiers sitting in the Temple probably knew more about the myths and legends of Kersai than any soldier in the Sarnese army. His Seventh had become an exemplary student of theology at his command.

Stiefis shifted impatiently in his saddle. He wished his Father away from the meeting. He wanted to throw the results of this meddling in his father's face. With each passing moment Stiefis became more certain of Seventh's involvement in this catastrophe. Alarms sounded from the right.

Stiefis swung his horse towards the sounds of drums and horns. Yells rose in surprise and anger. Stiefis called to his father.

"We don't have time." The sounds of battle drifted to them. From behind Stiefis heard more alarms. He knew who was behind them. To the right was that lost army: it had to be, it had to be the Masfin forces on the right.

Petron surveyed the building. Outside the army was digging into the ground. Holes in the ground would serve as shelter and camouflage while they waited for the moment to strike. The building would serve as stables. The cavalry that went with this army would overflow even this building but the remaining horses would not be noticeable in the household herd. The handful of servants and women of the house had been closed in the cellars. The Masfin was annoying him about those women.

Petron knew they would not suffer in the cellars. They would not be down there long enough to suffer anything more than inconvenience. Jeffeaux was too soft-hearted for his own good and for Petron's patience.

"They could catch a draft in that hole."

"Lord Jeffeaux, they have blankets. They have food. I see no reason to expose our mission to any chance interference by allowing them freedom."

"Let me make sure they are all right."

Petron eyed Jeffeaux. He knew the Masfin noble well. Had there been only the old male servants in the cellar this conversation would not be happening. The thought of six young females stimulated more than concern in Jeffeaux.

"You may not go down there. If you wish, have one brought up for questioning. She will have to return to the cellar once you are through with her."

Jeffeaux did not wonder at the tone Petron used. The way the Llweganians used the word 'through' bothered Jeffeaux.

"What do you think I plan to do?"

"I don't care, just be quick whatever it is."

"You think I am moved by base motives."

Sablor passed by them. He paused as Jeffeaux spoke. He leaned near them.

"My Lord Jeffeaux, I would not allow you within ten paces of any female in my family. You have only one use for them, one plan, one interest. And it is not their well-being. I wouldn't say you are malicious but you certainly aren't kind, more predatory."

"I am shocked at your opinion of me. I am a gentleman."

"As you say. Petron, everyone is in place. The lookouts are ready. The lake is still clean so we are using it for our water. The Sarn armies are still several Darkfalls out. Wind Rider is pursuing them."

"Very well. Place one of the guards at Lord Jeffeaux's disposal. He wishes to be sure the prisoners are well."

"What harm can have befallen them? They are safer than a …," Sablor stopped speaking. He saw the look on Petron's face. What had he been thinking to question Petron?

"Immediately. Please come with me Lord Jeffeaux."

First watched light appear at the head of the stairs. The soldier climbed only a short pace down the steps.

"Who is in charge here?"

First stepped to the bottom of the stairs.

"Follow me." Years of training pushed First up the stairs. The automatic obedience annoyed her. She wanted to resist the urge but she was halfway up the stairs before she realized she had moved. Seventh would have asked why or where.

Soldiers moved everywhere. Horses filled every room. The smell and sounds confused her. Her home seemed like a foreign place. She tried to notice every detail as she walked. Male and female soldiers worked together in a manner that frightened her. A door swung open, she shook her head. She should know where she was. This was Third's suite. A strangely dressed man stood in the room. His clothes, though dark as the soldier's, were of a fine material. He wore them with an air that was odd to her.

He spoke strange words that were familiar because she had heard Seventh and Lady Zona speak them. She did not understand them. She watched the interplay between the man and the woman. The woman was not his subordinate. She held a lower rank somehow because she spoke with a slight degree of respect. The respect, however, was begrudged, as if some outside force required the woman show the man a politeness she did not feel.

The man was very respectful of the woman. The soldier had some power he feared. She had her influence from a different source than he did. First had spent her life studying power, influence, and manipulation. She could influence the male because she was female. The soldier would be immovable by her regardless of sex. The female was clearly a soldier, the man clearly was not.

"Jeffeaux, who has some standing in his society, wishes to be assured of your and your companions' physical well-being. This is not a question of comfort. Has anyone any injuries?"

The tone spoke volumes. First had no wish to give this soldier any reason to harm her or her household.

"We are fine. One of our number is missing with her servants. We are concerned for her safety."

"We have killed no Sarn females," came the answer. The man looked blankly between First and the soldier.

"She is Masfin, as are her servants."

"The only Masfin that have died, have died at Sarn hands."

First felt an arrow of fear quiver through her flesh. Surely Seventh would have kept her servants safe. Lady Zona would have come to no harm.

"It is a large group of women. Did you see any signs of such a group when you," First hesitated. She did not know how to describe the invasion without upsetting the soldier. The man looked at the pair with troubled eyes. He did not like being out of the communication loop.

"Have you seen such a group?"

Jeffeaux chose that moment to jump into the conversation. First frowned ferociously at him.

"What is she saying?"

"She is concerned for the well-being of your mother and of Harbinger. She is very worried about their disappearance."

Jeffeaux blinked. He looked at the woman with considering eyes. What had happened here? The implacable, hardened Harbinger did not seem the type to engender such concern. He could not reconcile his memory of the warrior with the distress of this finely built creature.

"But otherwise the group is well?"

"Other than this missing party, you are all well?"

"Yes, yes. It is dank and dark in that infernal hole but we are fed and have suffered no physical damage."

"We have not yet encountered such a group dead or alive. If we do I will convey your concerns to them."

"Are we to be prisoners long?"

"As long as is necessary. Give some sign of respect to this man. His culture requires it."

His culture not ours; he was separate from the soldier. Very separate from her, from the soldier, the female soldier, how slow she had been. The female was Llweganian. The male was from Masfin.

"Tell this man that they are Masfin women. Tell him, Llweganian. One of the women is cousin to the King of Masfin."

The soldier hesitated. She looked at the hand tugging on her arm. If the Masfin lord had not stood at her elbow the Sarn female would be across the room on the receiving end of a back-handed hit. With great restraint she removed First's hand.

"I will tell him." The soldier replied condescendingly.

"What is she going on about?" Jeffeaux spoke in arrogant tones of his own.

"She is still trying to get us to search for her missing household members. She reminds me that one of the women is related to your King." The soldier answered already bored with the exchange.

"I hope Harbinger remembers that."

"Harbinger would never forget. Have you seen enough?"

Jeffeaux did not know what further he wished to know. He did not feel comfortable with the cold way the Llweganians were treating the prisoners. He chewed the inside of his lip. If he pushed much more the chance the Llweganians would dispose of the prisoners seemed likely. He could hear Petron declare that all Jeffeaux's concerns were solved as they stood over the dead bodies.

"Yes. Thank you for your time. Return her to the cellars."

First wanted to fight for her answers. She wanted to force the hostile female and cowed male to help her; but she couldn't. She had a duty to stay alive. Her only true duty was to retain life until she could not possibly produce a child. She would not risk her life, even for Seventh and Lady Zona.

Lady Zona stared at the puddle next to the cage. She was rapidly losing her sympathy for the three priests. At every opportunity they made her life difficult. The Llweganians seemed to take the trouble in stride. They almost respected the three men for not caving in to their lot. Lady Zona eyed the impassive faces behind the bars with disfavor. A low chuckle alerted Lady Zona to her audience.

"You must admire their obstinacy. Either they are very stupid or very brave; which as far as I am concerned is the same thing. Anyway, let them remain fouled. We will not be here long enough for it to do them any harm."

"I take my duties very seriously Dragon, or is it Harbinger now?"

"Call me what you like. I carry every name on the same person. My troops will be calling me Harbinger. We are at war now." Harbinger looked at the wet spot on the floor. Her eyes went to the three priests.

"Here is your responsibility: offer them care. If they refuse that care, it is their responsibility. I believe in free will."

"Then give me some more duties. This sitting is trying."

"Join the troop in their exercises. That will pass the time. Go easy at first."

Lady Zona had not envisioned herself learning to tumble and to throw an opponent, but here she was. It did serve to pass the time. Once she stopped paying attention to her charges they began to behave with more restraint. She could still feel the burn of the hate in their eyes but they were careful not to antagonize her. She replaced their fouled clothing and blankets. In her spare time she improved her Sarnese. She used the books she found in the Temple. The grammar was a little different from the Sarnese spoken in the Household but not so different she couldn't figure it out. Most of the books didn't test her understanding of grammar. They held family genealogies. She was intrigued by some strange thing that she couldn't pinpoint until she found the book containing the family listings with Weirhass and Stiefis.

There was a second set of books that at first glance looked like genealogies but weren't.

They divided families into groups based on criteria decided on by the priests of the Temple. She came to this conclusion because she couldn't immediately see the criteria from reading the lists or the accompanying texts.

It was the final set of books that gave lady Zona her hint. She found these hard to decipher because of their formal language. She had been pouring over them for two days when she thought she knew what was going on. She gathered a book from each of her first discoveries. Then she brought out the set of three tomes.

Harbinger looked at the pile of books on the dinner table. She looked at Lady Zona over the rim of her goblet.

"You have decided to continue my education in the habits of our hosts."

"I have been reading some literature that is lying around. Your box of herbs..."

"Box of herbs?"

"That the priest gave you. Do you remember it?"

"I don't have it with me."

"If I showed you a picture would you recognize it?"

"Probably."

Lady Zona opened one of the heavy books. Harbinger rose from her seat to look over Lady Zona's shoulder. She studied the two pictures.

"This one."

"Are you sure?"

"Yes. I only looked at it once, but, yes, this is the one."

Lady Zona nodded thoughtfully. Her mouth compressed in thought. She sat back in her seat. She laid a hand on one book.

"These are lists of all the biological connections of the people of Sarna going back at least twenty generations. There are special notations for the captive brides. You're in there.

"The next book is from a set that divides all those people into different groups. Your answer to my question leads me to believe that this book categorizes people into groups that the priests want to reproduce, those they will allow to reproduce, and those who will never get to reproduce.

"These books describe the physical attributes the priests deem necessary for the survival of Sarna. They give strict guidelines for who should have children and who should not. They tell exactly how many people Sarna can support at any given time. You can see how much rain fell in any year of those generations listed; how much land was under grazing or the plow in those generations; and how to mix the herb of life. The box you got contained a mixture with an herb I recognize from its picture. It prevents pregnancies. In sufficient quantities it produces miscarriages."

Harbinger looked at the wide-eyed priests.

"It's a good thing I never used it. This continual war with Llwegania would also keep the population in check. I see the logic."

"But."

"Quite right: but."

"You cannot think to defeat the Sarn armies, woman."

Lady Zona turned her head to look at the source of the words. The youngest of the priests had spoken. They were all young. The lowest orders had been left behind while the main body went out to prepare the route for the processional. On the final day of the festival the triumphant march was recreated. The relics were marched through the streets then replaced on the altar.

"For every moment we are in control of the Temple we are triumphant."

"It seems that Masfin women are no different from Llweganian females."

Lady Zona laughed to herself. Any Sarnese soldier would have figured it out by now. You could not mistake the stance of a Llweganian soldier. Watching the Harbinger, now Lady Zona would be able to discern the figure anywhere. Even in repose the stance was alert and wary.

"No, we are all three very different cultures and people."

"Your leader is mistaken if she thinks to hold this Temple. She will be starved out eventually."

"You are correct there."

"Stupid, blind, we will defeat you."

"Isn't today the day the relics return to the altar?" Lady Zona turned her back to the cage. She gave a feigned start. "Oh look there they are." She turned back to the cage. The priests were uncomfortable. She knew it irked them that she knew so many of their traditions and customs. "That's right, they never made the procession. Why didn't the most holy of processions happen? Could it be because we control the most holy of holies of Sarna? How many days have passed and we still retain control? I am not fond of camping. I prefer the comfort of my home. I have traveled many miles and slept in many places since I began this mission. If you don't have anything of importance to say to me: be quiet."

Harbinger chewed her food carefully. She trained her steady gaze on the cage.

"Don't let these boys upset you, Lady."

"How can you risk yourself? Think of the children you might have."

Lady Zona laughed. "I am well past bearing children. And, I have always been more than that capacity. I have many talents and skills that are of worth besides an endowment of nature."

"Come. It is of no use. We already tried talking with the Sarn. They have no use for logic."

Her meal half-eaten, Lady Zona rose from the table. She tried to match the loping stride and confident set of shoulder of the Llweganian soldiers. She began her final exercises of the day. Her muscles would ache at the end of the day. She had not asked them to work this hard since she had pushed children out into the world.

"You need not train as an expert, Lady Zona. Simple exercises will do."

"Harbinger, I know I will never achieve the skill of a lifetime soldier but I can achieve satisfaction for a drill well done." Lady Zona looked at the cage where her charges sat watching her.

"Are all the Sarn males so obstinate and dull?"

"No, their military leaders have more finesse. These three are hardly more than children. Look at them. It is a week and still they hardly have shadows on their cheeks. They are frightened and embarrassed to be our prisoners and of being frightened. Show them some mercy."

Lady Zona sighed. It was easier to be compassionate when the object of your compassion did not belong to a sex that had always held some form of power over you.

"You do not hate the Sarn, Harbinger?"

"No. They are a danger. They will not listen," she paused to find exactly her meaning, "they cannot hear words of wisdom from the mouth of a woman nor can they respect a society that has so different a set of values as mine does. Your culture, they could deal with because Masfin culture is closer to Sarnese in basic ways. Not the monogamy you practice, but the relative position of women in society is the same. In Masfin the women's position is more subtly subservient.

"I was right to usurp Masfin as an ally. You would have come to terms eventually. Some of Masfin's culture would have seeped into Sarna's traditions. Masfin would have looked at Llweganian society as a horrific aberration. I remain convinced Masfin would have eventually joined Sarna in war against Llwegania."

"I don't know. It is easier for the women of Masfin to hate Sarna with its practices. We might have influenced our men to some degree."

"True. That influence might still be needed." A sad smile curved the Harbinger's mouth. "We might win this battle but I could still lose the war in this victory."

Wind Rider saw the towers of her goal on the horizon. She saw the hurrying armies before her. Somewhere beyond her sight lay her mother's husbands and their allies. Victory was a hope now. She would not consider it secure until she saw her mother striding over the field filled with the dead Sarnese. The flat land made the horizon seem a possible day's ride but she knew better.

Her way would be swift because the army did not turn to fight. It fled with every day towards her goal. She wondered that no one in power had decided to face her. Her army was strong but the Sarn could not know that. The Sarnese had not even sent scouts to assess her strength or skirmishers to test her strength. She had no liking for the Sarnese. She had spent her entire life fighting them. She respected their abilities on the battle field. They were a formidable enemy. This flight was foolish. Were she the commander of the Sarnese, she would be expecting ambush every step of the way.

A rider came up on her left: the appropriate side for a messenger. A stone appeared. Wind Rider rubbed the surface of the stone. Not one of her mother's the stone had striping across the surface. The color indicated the source was a member of her mother's Household. The stripes indicated Petron. He was in place. She had her maps brought out. The lines and curves held her mother's touch. The Masfin troops were entrenched here. The Sarn armies were moving at a steady pace. She had the South and West armies before her. Petron had crushed the East army when he crossed the border. The only army still out of line was the North army. The South and West armies would be crushed in a few days' time. Then the combined armies she led and Petron controlled would turn to face the North army. True, while they subdued the armies the North could over run the city. That was of no importance. Harbinger would reduce the city to rubble, burying the North army in its own stones.

Wind Rider wanted very badly to crush these armies before they joined up with the North army. She would with Petron's forces. No use dwelling on a future that might not be.

Lady Zona groaned as she lifted a length of wood. The wood was very heavy. The concave curve was lined with iron. A set of hands grasped the opposite end. Lady Zona sent her helper a smile of thanks. Together they manhandled the length into the rope cradle.

"All hands away!"

Lady Zona backed up carefully. The cradle swung free. Up it went until hooks snagged it. Then hands had hold of the ropes. Feet scuffled on the scaffolding.

"Whose idea was this?" Lady Zona wondered under her breath.

"Yours, Lady: you are the one who remembered the tale. We only went looking where you suggested."

The matching segment was secured. A long spout was forming. As it rose the spout became narrower but still it was large enough for her to stand in. Deep under the temple was a wellhead. The end of this spout attached to that wellhead. In the story, once the wellhead was opened a stream of liquid would erupt. That liquid could be ignited. The flaming would spew over the moat unto any attackers. Lady Zona wondered how the flaming would be controlled. Harbinger smiled serenely.

"Lady Zona, you worry too much."

"What if the fire goes down into the source of the liquid?"

"In the history this worked."

"In the **story**, the legend, the myth it worked. There is no written history in Sarna only myth."

"Ah, Lady Zona, in a culture that has no written history, the oral tradition is fairly accurate. Every other *legend* about this temple had proved true."

"This could be the one exaggeration."

"I don't think so. What say you priests?" The Harbinger reached out to bang a fist on the bars of the cage. The sleeping young men scrambled to their feet. They blinked in distress. "I asked you a question priest. Is it true that the Temple of Kersai shall belch fire at the enemies of Sarna?"

"That is the tradition." The reply was whispered. In the time of their captivity the three had learned to fear the strange women. The colorless faces looked younger to Lady Zona everyday she tended them. Soon she would pity them.

"This will be the first time a priest has seen it happen in living memory. You probably don't even know how to work it. Lucky for me this fine lady paid attention to your traditions. I didn't fancy riding out into battle across a bridge in the full glare of my enemies. Now I will rain fire down on their heads. Thanks to the ingenuity of ancient Sarnese priests. There is an elegant irony to this situation. Sablor will have to compose a song on this campaign for me."

"Our armies will subdue you as Kersai subdued Britis." The whisper reached the Lady Zona's ear. She smiled in the direction of the cage.

"Perhaps Britis did not mind being subdued. The courting dance can seem like battle. Certainly there is an element of acceptance in her actions. After all, once the passion had passed she could easily have killed Kersai. A pillow over the face is always effective." Lady Zona spoke absently. Her gaze followed the Harbinger's. The final sections were being secured.

Harbinger ran her hand along the polished wood. The finished cylinder fitted into the groove around the top of the ceiling. The base rested on a ball joint. This joint fitted over the pipe that ran to the wellhead. Lady Zona sighed. This was constructed to work. This was no decoration or half thought out contraption.

Harbinger continued to rub her hand along the wood. A devilish smile lit her eyes. The long pipe meant to direct the flow of burning fluid brought a gleam to those dark eyes. Lady Zona tried to pretend she could not read the expression. She bit her lip to restrain the answering smile. The troop did not. They caught the expression on their leader's face. A jolly laugh rang through the temple. The three priests looked on in confusion.

Lady Zona would not enlighten them. She might enjoy the joke but she could not recognize it publicly. Harbinger had no such compunction.

"Don't fret. We are just admiring your," a silent laugh," cannon."

For another moment the priests puzzled the joke. Their eyes went from Harbinger to the wood where her hand rested. Lady Zona knew the moment they caught the joke. She watched their eyes widen in shocked comprehension. As they watched Harbinger turned her head towards them until her mouth almost touched the wood under her hand. Her mouth opened. Her tongue appeared to flick her top lip. Almost, her tongue touched the wood. Then she smiled.

Lady Zona heard the priests release the air from their lungs. Lady Zona had never imagined such blatant sexuality could sit so easily on the warrior. Nor had she thought a woman could look so beautiful indulging her sexuality. Harbinger looked so playful and happy that Lady Zona could not find fault in her actions. Somehow the Llweganian made priest baiting seem like harmless fun: although it was neither. Harbinger did nothing without a reason.

Something distracted Harbinger. Her hand rose to her stomach. A look of joy colored her face.

"The child is very active. That is good. I spent most of my third pregnancy riding. That child slept most of her time. Once she was born she refused to sleep. The poor nurses were driven wild with her activity."

Petron saw the dust in the dawn's light. He watched the cloud grow dark against the rising sun. It was time.

"Marjas, wake the troops. We march."

There was a feeling of energy through the camp. Everyone moved with practiced ease but their body language betrayed their mood. This was no drill, no mock battle. The event, the action they had trained for stood before them. Petron breathed deep the morning air. He tried to fix this moment in his memory. Jorin came to stand by his shoulder.

"Sablor wants to know if you want Jeffeaux roused."

"No, but we will anyway. We can't leave him. He might run back to Masfin or into a Sarnese patrol. Don't let him know we expected to see battle today. Just get him on a horse."

"Should Sablor guard him?"

"No, Rodznig should watch him. Sablor will have enough to do guarding himself. Get 'em up. Move 'em out."

First heard the thunder of the house emptying. She held Second's and Third's hands. She waited until all was quiet. Then she waited some more. Finally she climbed the stairs to the door. She moved quietly and gingerly. Every silent fall of her foot caused her to cringe. Each breath she exhaled echoed in her mind. Finally she reached the door. She laid her hand against the wood. She drew a deep breath. It swung free.

She slid from the door. The house smelled of horse and sweat and emptiness. The silence roared at her. She walked slowly. Each step she took confirmed her belief that the invaders had left. She went to the front doors. They hung open. She stood watching the horizon. Towards Deskersai a dust storm was gathering; only, there was no wind and the sky was not the color for a storm. First walked through the house until she reached a window that faced Masfin. She knew what she would find: nothing. Nothing lined the way back to Masfin. She closed the shutters tight against the empty skyline.

She needed help to close the front doors. Hopefully there was food left in the kitchens. Water, at least they had plenty of water in the casks in the cellars.

Jeffeaux tried to reach Sablor. The young pup was out of earshot. The soldier on his right always cut him off from Sablor. Jeffeaux did not like being alone in the midst of this army. The infantry had become more Llweganian than Masfin. Jeffeaux was dismayed by this occurrence. He had not expected that anything could influence behavior as deeply as this common effort. In moments of instinct Jeffeaux found himself responding to the focus, and, yes, the comfort of the Llweganian military structure.

"Do you have a need Lord Jeffeaux?"

"Yes. I need to speak to Sablor. He is the Liaison Officer."

"He is busy now. I will stay by your side. I have more experience in dangerous situations. As we are riding through the heart of enemy territory, you have more need of a guard than of a liaison officer."

Jeffeaux halted his next words. The logic was correct. He would rather have a well-trained soldier right now. Of course, he would also like to have a stream of information about this situation that necessitated a guard. And, his original desire to have a fellow non-soldier around remained. Watching Sablor now, Jeffeaux paused in his thoughts. The young man was not a non-soldier. He had the same determined, set expression as every soldier in the army. He, Jeffeaux, was the sole useless cog in this machine: a hindrance since a soldier had to be spared to protect him.

Petron never carried useless baggage. Jeffeaux set his mind on the exercise. Anything to keep his thoughts from the terror that he suspected waited at the end of this ride.

As the sun rose, the ride ended. The Sarnese army was rising from sleep. The pickets fell like saplings under the rush of the spring floods.

Wind Rider heard the crash as the battle began. She issued the order her lungs had been aching to give for weeks. There were no heights to gain. Her archers and darters had little use. This would be a slugfest. She urged her horse away from its position. Her sword swung free of its scabbard. The sweet song of the metal coming free brought a smile to her stern face.

Harbinger stood just inside the door on the ramparts. She watched the army from Masfin slam into the Sarn positions. She fancied she could pick out Wind Rider as the Llweganian army joined the battle. Her eyes swung to the north and east. She could not see anything from her vantage point. If she were leading the Sarnese North Army that is the direction she would take.

The commanders of the North Army had to know by now that the East Army was destroyed. The Masfin armies would assume no danger rested at their rear. The exposed right flank and rear would be the softest spot to hit. A cautious North commander might try to swing through the west to join up with the West Army. Coming through the city had its points as well. The city offered the only cover on this battle field. By holding the city the North Army could supply covering fire for the South and West Armies to retreat into its protection. The North Army had the disadvantage of not knowing where the Masfin and Llweganian were until this battle. The North commander would come through the city. The Temple was besieged. He could affect a rescue while the invaders were busy with the other Sarnese armies.

Harbinger walked the length of the balcony. She nodded to her troops as she went. Below, she could see Lady Zona attempt a close combat throw. The peace of the Temple contrasted strangely with the battle at their feet. She reached the opening at the far end of the Temple. There, from the northeast, she saw the column of Sarn troops marching.

"Should we ignite the city to draw their attention?"

"He will turn. Petron will have considered this possibility. He will not leave an exposed position. This is a feint. They will turn. Don't move the spout yet. We do not want to give him an excuse not to turn. When they are well into the city, then we will turn the spout to burn them out into the battlefield."

Lady Zona landed with a definite thud. She lay on the ground regaining air in her lungs. The priests sat in silence as they watched her performance. For some reason their attention drove her harder to achieve competence.

"Lady Zona, may I interrupt your display of martial skills?"

A chuckle issued from Lady Zona's mouth. "Any time Harbinger, you may interrupt me anytime at all."

"The battle has begun."

Lady Zona paused in the act of rising. She had known this day would come, but she had never realized it would. She had always thought that like tomorrow it existed but never arrived. She rubbed a cloth over her face and neck. The damp, clean material hid her momentary loss of composure.

"Should we fill the moat?"

"Not yet. When we start burning the city, then will we fill the moat."

"The people have not tried to storm the Temple?"

"No, they are streaming out of the city towards the northeast. The refugees are clogging the roads. It means our quarry will take a little longer to get to us."

"I better feed the priests now, then. I will be too busy later."

Lady Zona lifted three wooden plates. They held the same stew the Temple invaders would eat. A wedge of field bread rested in the edge of the broth. Lady Zona found field bread edible only with stew or soup. Without moisture the bread was very chewy, though it tasted fine. Lady Zona passed the wooden rectangles through the bars of the cage.

The tall slim priest watched her. His eyes held none of his previous disdain or mockery. He studied the group of soldiers with resignation. No help had come. This foolish prank had become a dangerous, successful move.

"You will be leaving soon."

"I don't see anyone forcing us." Lady Zona answered reflexively. She didn't even muster a stern tone or thinking expression.

"You will go of your own will."

Lady Zona paused in her readied answer. She had been bandying words so often with the three young men; she rarely listened to their tone anymore. Something in the voice held interest for her.

"We have the situation under control."

"Are you planning to kill us when you leave?"

Lady Zona stood very still. She turned to find Harbinger. The commander came to stand by Lady Zona.

"It would be the kindest thing."

The three priests leaned towards Lady Zona. They did not disagree with the bland statement. They nodded in unison. Lady Zona frowned in thought. When she left this temple Sarna would be defeated, in ruins. These three men could not live among their own people. Someday, someone would blame them for their helpless role in this campaign. They would be blamed for failing to protect the Temple. They would be suspected of aiding the enemy. How else had Harbinger known all the secrets of the Temple? For the very first time she saw them as boys and not work, annoying work.

"Take them back with you."

"Bring them home with me? I already have eleven men dependent on me. I don't need or want three more." Harbinger heard her words. She looked at the concerned face of Lady Zona.

"If you care so much, you keep them: you don't have any..guard."

Lady Zona reared her head. She was speechless. Guard? Take them back with her to Masfin as her Guard? Lady Zona had no illusion about the Harbinger's use of the word guard.

"Women don't have a guard such as this in Masfin."

"Start a new trend. It's a practice I highly recommend."

Lady Zona imagined her son's face if she were to return with the three. She blinked at the three faces pressed to the bars.

"They would be more trouble than they are worth."

"I am sure you could handle them."

"What are you suggesting?" The slimmest of the three spoke with hushed tones.

"Lady Zona feels pity for you. She has found some redeeming quality in you, despite your constant poor manners. She might be willing to take you with her as her guard; her personal guard."

"Why would we willingly go with her?"

"Being her guard is a better situation than being freed into the city as we leave; in my poor woman's opinion, that is."

The three faces paled in fear. They would be stoned in the streets. They would be trampled and crushed. They had taken an oath to the Temple but their religious fervor wavered in the face of the fate that Harbinger offered. They turned their faces as one towards Lady Zona.

"Why don't you kill us?"

Harbinger compressed her mouth. She glared at the three boys.

"I will not be known as a priest killer. You are not warriors or soldiers. You are scholars. There is no honor in killing those who cannot defend themselves."

"When did you ever have scruples?"

"I am responsible for dispensing justice in my Estates. Your only crime has been to be in the wrong place at the wrong time. If I kill you it will have ramifications which I am unwilling to create. Now I am a feared and hated enemy. If I kill you: I am a monster. That would give the Sarnese defenders too much power."

Lady Zona listened to the brusque words. She understood the meaning and implication of the situation. There was little choice.

"I can't believe I let you talk me into this."

"It will be all right. You'll see. You will enjoy yourself greatly."

Harbinger returned to her place on the balcony. She watched the battle rage until Darkfall. She could see the valiant effort the Sarn armies were making. She expected with the next day to see an end to the fighting. As Darkfall came a voice called her to the north side of the Temple. The army had turned. They did not stop with the dark.

"It will be quite a sight."

"Yes Harbinger."

"When half the army is in the city: begin the turn. When all the army has entered the
city: fire it. Start with short arcs."

Chapter 6

Stiefis felt tired in his heart. His bones ached. His teeth hurt. Dirt had worked its way into every pore of his skin. Sweat had soaked his clothes. Now, the chill of the evening was creeping into his damp clothes and tired bones. Around him his troop lay dead and unburied. He could see his father in the distance trying to call his troop into some order. Dark was falling. Stiefis wanted to slip away in the night but knew that he had to be here for the next day's fighting.

Tomorrow had some hope. The North army should arrive before dawn. Sarna would have fresh troops to field while the invaders would have only tired soldiers. But, this enemy fought so well. They had come so far into Sarna that they could already be said to have won a great victory. Even if the Sarnese forces managed to turn back these invaders, Sarna's forces were ravaged. All these dead, Sarna's plans and cause had been set back generations.

The hand Stiefis raised to his face shook with fatigue and reaction. He wiped the sweat and dirt out of his eyes. The silence of the battlefield unnerved him. The occasional groan or scream split the night with eerie echoes. The complete darkness was broken by no fires. Neither army wished to reveal its position.

Barely able to lift his hand to the task, Stiefis sheathed his sword. He moved towards his father. A field aide went by dragging a dead body. Stiefis stopped his motion. He followed the field aide's progress with his eyes until the darkness swallowed the figure. Stiefis let out a great sigh. He bent to the body next to him: dead. He waited until another field aide went by him. Then he followed, dragging his own burden.

He spent hours dragging bodies. There was no end to the Sarn who had fallen. He imagined the enemy in the same activity. He felt the weight of his sword as an added burden. That weight grew with each passing hour. Almost, he thought to take the sword off; but, the comfort out-weighed the burden. Stubbornly he suffered the drag of the metal.

He bent to gather up one more body. He stopped. A huge groan filled the air. Stiefis looked towards where he imagined the enemy to be. The groan swelled to a bitter cry. Stiefis dropped his burden. He whirled, desperate to find the cause of the sound.

A glow filled the night: a glow that came from the city.

"All clear." The sound of running feet resounded in the Temple. The cage was pushed far to one side. The three priests hung on in fear as they were shoved out of the way. There was a whir. Then the long spout began its motion. It slid along the groove with majestic beauty. The polished barrel gleamed in the torch lights. Harbinger stood with her hands on her hips. The curve of her child pushed forward. Her chin was raised as she watched the spout's progress.

"Everyone: clear the balcony." Harbinger did not quite trust the Temple's designers. She was not going to risk any troops on the balcony once the fire began to spew. If it worked then she would send a lookout back to the balcony and only if it worked.

"Only the baggage train remains outside the city, Harbinger."

"Begin."

There was a creak as the wellhead was opened. Two of the troop stood on the roof of the Temple. Lady Zona tried to imagine the figures crouched below the wall on the roof line above the opening for the spout. In her mind's eye she saw one woman readying the flint and the other notching her arrow. Then with the rush of liquid sounding in the spout Lady Zona saw the flint strike and the arrow fly. Lady Zona held her breath. Even now she half expected the Temple to succumb to fire. She though she heard a rush of air. She felt the floor of the Temple tremble. A young trooper came running from the back of the Temple.

"It works. We are raining fire on the city."

At the base of the spout the troop began a gentle arcing motion with the spout. The barrel seemed to move only inches but the reports from the lookout described an ever widening swathe of destruction.

"Have there been any attempts on the moat?"

"Not yet, Harbinger."

"We are ready on the water Harbinger."

This was desert country. Harbinger doubted that swimming was a wide spread skill. Still it was better to wait. Troops trying to climb in the moat would be hampered by gear and weapons. Once they were well caught in the moat the water would act as an offensive weapon as well as a defensive tactic.

"Hold on the water. Wait for my order."

Harbinger turned to Lady Zona. She stood calm and cool as she spoke. "Patience is the best weapon in battle. Good reaction times are important but patience is essential."

"I should think experience would be needed as well."

"Without a doubt. Experience is the spark that lights patience into action. Come, let us see how we are doing."

Lady Zona climbed with some trepidation behind Harbinger.

"If we are burning the city; how do you plan to get out of here?"

Harbinger ignored the question from the priest. She reached a hand to help Lady Zona the last few steps to the top. They stood under the lip of the groove. The spout would pass over them. Lady Zona preferred not to stand under the spout, despite its seeming safety. She didn't quite dare to flinch next to Harbinger's nonchalance. Luckily, they were not walking towards the spout.

"Already everyone is running from the city. The shells of most of the buildings are stone. The roofs and insides will burn but the fire will spread slowly. Still, no one can guess when I will stop, so everyone should run."

"The question was worthy."

"I have enough water to fill the moat twice over. When I am ready, we will flood the city."

Lady Zona looked out over the city. She could see the shadows of the great armies moving through the city. She wandered along the balcony until she could see the leading lip of the fire. It burned sullenly, leaping from rooftop to a shed. The arc from the spout gleamed with a deadly beauty.

"You will burn it all."

"I earned my names."

"You will use boiling oil on all comers in the moat."

"If there are any. It will not help our escape. I hope to avoid it. As the water spills from the moat the oil would go first. The fire would ignite the oil. It would be very hot and slippery to ride through the city under those conditions."

"Even twice the moat's capacity is not a tidal wave."

"No, but the moat is filled with the debris from the surrounding square. The water was calculated on an empty moat. The dead bodies take up space. There is some risk. This is after all a battle."

There was a cry from the city. No, it was from the battlefield. Harbinger signaled the controller. The spout swung in a wider arc. Lady Zona eyed Harbinger warily.

"I should see about securing my guard."

Harbinger laughed. "We could use a variation on their ceremony or use one of yours."

"I think a Llweganian rite would be more appropriate." Lady Zona turned back from her descent. "And I don't believe you take chances on the small things like a burning city. You'll gamble on big things; but in battle you will find water in a desert or a safe passage through fire."

"You can't be married to plans in battle, Lady Zona. You train your soldiers. You provide them with the best supplies and weapons you can. You secure any geographical advantage you find. It helps to have more soldiers than you think you will need. You give clear goals and objectives.

"If you have a much larger army and your enemy is very determined, you don't need to win every battle to win the war. Don't focus on controlling the battlefield at the end of the day. Every battle you make the enemy fight, you win. A smaller enemy cannot afford to lose as many soldiers as a larger army. If my army has a hundred soldiers and yours has fifty when we have a battle where the kill ratio is one to one: a loss of twenty five soldiers on each side reduces my force by 25% and yours by 50%. So even if you control the battlefield I have won the military victory. If in the next battle the ratio remains the same, you are down to twelve soldiers to my fifty.

"Ratios and numbers don't win wars by themselves. You must have goals and objectives. The enemy has some behavior you are trying to alter. You want to be sure they stop raiding your borders. You have tried to work out a political or diplomatic solution. These means have failed. You are going to war to force the enemy into such a position that they stop raiding. You punish them so terribly that they would not think of crossing you in several generations. You effect a change in the political structure that raiding is no longer a sanctioned activity. You destroy them so they are unable to raid. You force them into your political structure. You force them to accept a political structure you designed. You find a solution to the need they had that started the raiding behavior and force that solution on them. Some combination of the above actions is the answer.

"Every plan you make for your army is based on your goal. Your commanders have to be clear on this goal and the means you wish to use to achieve this goal. You can't be mealy-mouthed or unclear about these issues. You are sending soldiers to their deaths. Good information is a powerful weapon. Your soldiers should have and use every weapon they need."

"Are you trying to tell me you don't gamble ever? I won't believe you."

"The Llweganian marriage rite is very complicated. You have no Household to witness for you." Harbinger ignored Lady Zona's statement.

"I accept you as a legitimate witness."

The three young men looked very different in their somber clothes. Their wan faces stood out above the soft rolls of their collars. Soft down had begun to grow on their heads. Lady Zona stopped to consider them. Was she really going to do this? They could simply be her guard. She didn't have to act on the rite. They were priests. Where was that lady who had ridden into Malso to play hostess to a foreign dignitary?

She looked at the watching eyes. They had gathered their courage to take this leap. They could have begged for release into the burning city. They had asked for death but had not been willing to take their own lives. Maybe they would betray her.

"Do you think they will kill me in our marriage bed?"

"If they do I will give them a slow and agonizing death. But I don't believe they will break their promise. Will you priests? Will you go back on your marriage vows?"

"Marriage vows? We are to be this lady's guard."

"In Llweganian law the only male guards a woman may have are her husbands. She has male soldiers but her personal guard consists of husbands. If you leave here with us you leave as Lady Zona's guard. You will swear to her on the Altar of Kersai. You will be bound by blood and fire. If you betray her your souls will become dust. This is the choice I am offering."

"We are Sarnese. We are not bound by Llweganian rites."

"Any Llweganian or Masfin females your males steal you expect to abide by Sarn marriage laws. This is the bargain I offer. You may not remain in the Temple. You must be seen leaving this building alive and in good health. You come with us, severing all ties with Sarna or I cut you loose outside the Temple."

Lady Zona waited until she had walked several steps from the cage. The three young men sat talking quietly. She listened to the soft sound of the spout swinging on its support. The loud whoosh of the fire pushing out of the earth echoed not with sound but with vibration under her feet.

Harbinger stared at the growing sea of fire. The yellow, red, and orange moved with an intense beauty. She felt like the fire. She had been startled when Petron had moved without the Masfin generals. She had wondered how she would pacify the Masfin authorities. Then she had thrown the word pacify out of her thoughts. She would become the tide that was pushing the situation. She had no choices now, only decisions. The Council had been right: the Masfin culture was too different for a working alliance. If they would not be allies, they would become enemies. First she would use their army to destroy her old enemy.

Wind Rider watched the fire. She saw the pattern of growth. In the glow she could see the black shapes running from the city.

"There is the North Army."

"The army is rested. They can be ready. She will be coming out soon."

"How can you know that?"

Petron and Wind Rider turned to find the source of the interruption. A dog-eared Jeffeaux blinked at them.

"She has no more reason to stay. We need to be ready to meet her. She will fight her way to us."

"Through the Sarnese army with her small troop and my mother?"

"Yes dressed in the robes of night."

Marjas edged his horse closer to Jeffeaux. He grabbed the horse's cheek strap. Steadily he urged the horses away from Wind Rider and Petron. Jeffeaux cringed at the action. He didn't, however, try to resist the Llweganian's direction.

"Come, my lord. We need to change horses and to eat before we do anything else."

Around them the army shifts gears. Like a sleeping dog it raised itself. It shook off fatigue and pain. Weapons were being checked then discarded or readied for use. Jeffeaux did not need light to visualize the rows of dead that littered the land Wind Rider and Petron were planning to reenter. Some bodies had been cleared away but not all, not nearly all. And they were planning to go back in this deepest darkness of the night; except, it no longer was dark. That glow called both sides back.

"Have you decided, priests?" The hard sound of her voice startled the three. She was older than their mothers. She had neither the lines of care nor the stoop of a hard life but she had the air of having seen much. She stood in the company of a hardened warrior. If she swore to them she would fulfill her duty. They were different men. They had some things in common. The most important thing was they were too young to die.

"If you promise to Lady Zona I will expect you to honor your word. This is a choice we are giving you. You could choose to die by your own hand. You could kill each other. You could take your chances in the city. Lady Zona does not wish you to die. We will take you with us or leave you in the city streets. If you come with us it will be as Lady Zona's sworn guard. This oath will be given on the Altar of Kersai."

"I understand; we all understand. We choose Lady Zona."

"Fine, let them out."

A knife and a bowl filled with burning incense sat on the altar. Harbinger raised the knife. She cut open the flesh on her forearm. She dripped her blood into the bowl.

"I, Harbinger of Death, Devouring Dragon recognize the Lady Zona as of my House and swear on my blood to defend her and hers to the last drop of blood in my body." She passed the knife to Lady Zona.

"I, Zona, recognize Harbinger of Death, Devouring Dragon as the Head of my House. I swear on my blood to defend her and hers to the last drop of blood in my body."

The knife passed to each of the kneeling men. Their blood mingled into the bowl with incense. Harbinger watched the smoke curl from the bowl.

"I, Zona, take you Wintraub, Stea, and Brir as my husbands, as my Household, as my Guard. I will provide for all your needs according to the rules of the covenant of the ancestors. If I fail to keep the covenant: you are free of this binding. If you fail: I will kill you."

"You reply: my life is yours, your life is my only duty, honor, respite, joy."

The echoes sounded odd to Lady Zona. She remembered her marriage to her first husband. This ceremony was so short and unadorned. There would be no wedding feast to follow, only a terrifying ride into battle. The words were so abrupt and harsh. The sting on her arm accentuated the difference of the moments. Harbinger gently clasped her arm. Cool ointment eased the pain in Lady Zona's arm. The small pot of cream was pressed into Lady Zona's hand. She ministered to her three new guards. She returned the ornate pot to Harbinger.

Harbinger was down the steps of the altar in a bound. Her feet hardly echoed in the vaulted space.

"Cap the wellhead." The order sounded through the ranks. There was a groan as the mechanism moved back into place. Running feet sounded. Everyone moved to the next duty. Lady Zona signaled to her guard. They finished saddling the horses. Ten days rations were all they packed. Then they led the entire troop of horses down into the lower regions of the Temple until they reached a door at the base facing the burning city.

"Release the water."

Everyone had spent days oiling the cranks and hinges. There were no groans or hesitations. The gates lifted easily and swiftly. The only sound was the gurgle of water. Then the rush of water swelled to a dull roar. The moat filled quickly. Debris rose and swirled. The edge of the moat away from the Temple was the lower side. The water spilled out onto the city. There was a great hiss as the water met fire.

"Let out the ramps."

In the rush of water and the dark of night Lady Zona could hardly discern the bridges that went out from the base of the Temple. The downward swing of the ramps used gravity to speed the action. Still the ramps did not show above the rush of the water.

Lady Zona mounted her horse. Her guard swung up onto the empty pack horses. Bodies came from every place in the Temple to claim a mount. Finally Harbinger arrived. She swung easily into her saddle. Lady Zona had a moment's fear: she had never ridden a horse across so deep a body of water. Then she gritted her teeth. These were not the pleasure mounts she was used to riding. These horses had seen battle and hard use. She could trust to their training if not to her skill. Then she had no time for thought. They were down into the wild rush of water.

The sound of the water was deafening. The roar of the fire and the hiss of the water meeting the fire added up to so great a noise that Lady Zona felt isolated. Even the sound of her breathing was covered up. Lady Zona clenched her teeth. She fastened her eyes on the rider ahead.

Water reached high on her thighs. She gripped her knees tightly to her horse. She bent low on the neck trying to reduce her mount's work. His head was bravely stretched to stay in the air. It seemed forever until she felt the water recede from her legs. She felt her horse strain up out of the moat.

The route had been carefully selected. Harbinger hoped that she could maintain some speed once they cleared the fired area. She wanted to race around the Temple now but she dared not risk the horses' footing on the wet stones. She wanted to be out of this forsaken place. She wanted to be with her army. The smoke was bothering her eyes. Her lungs weren't too happy either. She drew her veil more tightly across her nose and mouth. Her sight though couldn't suffer. This darkness was handicap enough without all the tears blinding her. There, the first turning was coming up on the right.

She counted slowly. At thirty she squinted into the smoky darkness. The next turning loomed. The sounds of the fire and flood were fading. The fretful hiss was becoming dominant. After the next run she heard the faint echo of battle. Her eyes still stung. Her lungs felt a little better. Bodies were running through the night. No one even looked at the cavalcade. Everyone was intent on fleeing the city. She hoped they had planned well enough to avoid any refugee congestion. They turned back towards the fire.

If they came out close enough to the leading edge of the fire, they should have a clear field for running. The sting was back in her lungs.

"Why did they fire the city? How did they do that?"

Stiefis paid no attention to his older brother. He reached wide with his sword. The enemy ducked. Stiefis backed away from his opponent. Who knew what caused disasters in the middle of battle? All Stiefis could think was how to stay alive for one more minute.

He could hardly see whom he was fighting. The smoke from the city was blinding him. The stars and the moon had disappeared. He marveled that the enemy continued to press the attack. Surely they were suffering from the same hindrance. He heard the sound of a blade slicing into flesh.

The Sarnese army was trying to defend the entire front of the city. It was spread like a wall around the part of the city not yet on fire. Stiefis wanted to reach one of his father's peers. They should start to slide north of the city away from this position. Under the cover of darkness the army should retreat in order to regroup. Deskersai was lost. The army had to survive. He had to get to his father.

Movement caught his attention. He swung his head quickly. He watched a group of horsemen emerge from the smoke of the city. The whites of their eyes glittered in the night. Their teeth were bared as they tried to breathe. Was this a sign that the North Army had escaped the fire's destruction? Was relief on its way? Stiefis felt the breath of death on his left. He spun around. He raised his arm to take the force of the downward stroke. Stiefis buried his dagger into the exposed stomach. He turned back to the mounted group. He tried to catch a glimpse of the riders' faces.

The lead rider glanced his way. His eyes locked with hers. He blinked. Then she melted into the enemy lines. Pain radiated from his chest. His head ached. Seventh, he had not been immediately able to recognize the grim, determined face, but it had been his last wife who led the group; his wife that emerged from that burning city. She had passed through his lines dressed as a Sarn; just as she had come to him dressed as a Masfin. He would follow that thought later.

Now he had to get to his father. If she had come from the city then the North Army would not. She had not come running from anything. She had moved carefully, quietly, in an orderly, planned manner. He pushed away from his newest opponent. He swung to his right. He dodged through spears and swords. As he moved the pressure of the enemy eased. His brother followed him. They moved without speaking.

A body hurdled against his shoulder. Stiefis shoved back. He brought his fist hilt first down on a head. His foot slipped in a puddle of blood. He threw himself in the opposite direction. Tears began to run down his cheeks from the smoke.

"Have you seen Weirhass?" Stiefis pushed his face into a drooping soldier's line of vision. He repeated the question until it was almost dawn. Then he saw his father standing with the other leaders.

"They will finish us today. We must leave. Slip north. They will come again soon. You know they will come again."

Stiefis did not bother with pleasantries or explanations. He hung onto his Father's shoulder for support.

"We cannot abandon Deskersai."

Stiefis did not even look at the speaker. He focused on his father's face only.

"Deskersai is lost to us now. It is half burned and half drowned. We must save Sarna. We have to leave. Now."

"The North Army is not yet here."

"It will never come. It would be here already. If you want to find the North Army: look in the burned half of Deskersai." Still Stiefis looked only at his father as he spoke. "Let us take what is left of our army to regroup: then wait for another day."

"There won't be another day. They have taken Sarna."

Stiefis looked out over the battlefield. Beyond them he saw the solid lines of the enemy.

"They have fought as much as we have. There is still a chance if we leave now. If we stay there will never be another day; then they will take all of Sarna."

Jeffeaux dozed in his saddle. He was not allowed near the fighting. He was happy to be away from the violence but not out of the loop. He chaffed at being shunted to one side when he could remember to think. Fighting at night was idiotic. Battle was confusing enough in daylight but in the dark it was a hopeless mess. Yet these soldiers seemed to be sure of their actions. They moved confidently into the fray.

Marjas had returned. He motioned Jeffeaux to move back. They rode for some distance. The army was heaving itself back with them. Skirmishes were abandoned. As suddenly as the assault had begun it was over. Jeffeaux stared around in confusion.

"What's happening?"

"We are finished for the moment. Wait here. I'll return shortly."

Jeffeaux had lost track of the time. In the dark he could not gauge the passage of time. The smoke from the fires obscured the sky so he had no clue from there. It felt as if ten dawns passed before anyone made their way towards him. It was Marjas. The Llweganian led Jeffeaux towards the encampment.

"Is that it?"

"For now. Come, there is someone to see you."

Who would be here? Oh, the King had sent help. Jeffeaux sighed in relief. Then he frowned. The King would not be pleased with anything that had happened. If there was a messenger from the King it was for someone's head and that someone's head the King wanted could very well be Jeffeaux's. Jeffeaux swallowed. The Llweganians would protect him. They still needed him. He added an air of legitimacy to the endeavor for the Masfin troops.

Metal clinked everywhere. Weapons, gear jangled in the encampment. People were too tired to speak. They moved slowly, conserving energy, trying to stay awake until their duties were completed. Jeffeaux watched helmets swing free from heads. He saw faces grimed by the night resolved into grey as the sun rose. In that moment there seemed to be no color in all the world.

At one tent people milled about with some energy. They came and went with purpose. Faces, ashen with exertion had a glow Jeffeaux could not understand. Heads turned towards him. Jeffeaux turned to his companion for enlightenment. Marjas had the same air of suppressed excitement. Jorin himself held their horses as they dismounted.

"All is well."

Marjas smiled. Jeffeaux realized that he had never seen any of the guard smile until this moment.

"What is happening?"

"Come." Jeffeaux resolved to express his displeasure at the cavalier treatment he received from the Llweganians. In fact, since everyone seemed to have left the battle, he would express himself now.

"I would appreciate answers to my questions. It is not too much to expect common courtesy. I am after all of some standing. You need me."

Jeffeaux followed Marjas and Jorin into the tent. His eyes adjusted to the change of lighting. The flare of lamps was very abrupt.

"You are right Lord Jeffeaux: I believe I will be needing you."

The Dragon stood before him. She was obviously pregnant. Blood and dirt streaked her face. Her expression was enigmatic. Jeffeaux studied the faces of her court.

"Where is my mother?" Jeffeaux did not bother to disguise his anxiety. He could not find her in the tent. Perhaps she had gone to another tent to rest.

"I am here son." Jeffeaux studied the owner of the voice. The voice was his mother's but the seeming of the speaker was not. A woman of the right age stood there. She was dressed in an outfit similar to the Dragon's. She stood with the same assurance and ease as the Dragon. Jeffeaux moved close to her.

"Mother?"

"Yes, it is I, Jeffeaux." Lady Zona rubbed her hand over Jeffeaux's unshaven chin. "It is good to see you. I had not expected to find you here, now."

"Well, you are not in the condition I expected to find you."

"Where are the generals?"

"Probably trying to figure how to punish us."

Dragon grunted. "Too right. I am sure we have made an enemy of the Masfin King. Hopefully Sarna won't figure out the opportunity this means for them for an ally."

Petron and Sablor stood quietly. They did not try to explain the chain of events that had led to this moment. Jeffeaux almost said something in their defense.

"The generals were no loss. As long as we fight the Sarn, the Masfin troops should be manageable. Once Masfin decides what to do, then we could have trouble." Harbinger walked around the room. She rested her hand on the swell of her stomach. Jeffeaux watched her move. He watched her close on him. Her route brought her to stand before him.

"You are the King's cousin. Lady Zona what are the lines of your descent?"

"Hold on." Jeffeaux took a breath to stop whatever insanity was coming. He lost his chance.

"The King's grandfather and mine were brothers."

"Who was older?"

"My grandfather was the older. He begot daughters."

"Daughters; but you have a son: a son who has ridden into battle with this army; while the King and his advisors did nothing."

"I will not pretend to the throne. I do not wish to be King."

"Excellent. Very good. You aren't pretending to the throne. You are protecting Masfin's interests as you see them. You perceived a danger, you saw the inaction, you sought a solution."

"It could work." Lady Zona stood next to Harbinger. She studied her son through neutral eyes.

"I do not want to be King."

"He is perfect. Keep saying that."

"You cannot force me to help you."

"Son, be quiet. You're already here and implicated in this entire action. Just keep your head low. Let us worry about getting you out alive."

Jeffeaux noticed three shadows that followed his mother. He did not recognize the youthful faces. He thought they belonged to the Harbinger, but they stayed close to his mother.

"Who are these boys?" Jeffeaux tried to avoid any commitment. He sought any distraction.

"They are my guard."

"These? Where did you acquire a guard? Or the need for a guard?"

"They are my guard. That is all you need to know. What was it you use to tell your sisters? Get them young, train them right?"

Jeffeaux drew back. He drew his breath in with a hiss. The implications behind that statement appalled him. The implications for his mother, the implications for Harbinger were so incredible he was not happy with this line of discussion either.

"Just do whatever you want. I will be in my tent."

One of the trio moved to stand before him. The young face held an expression of such grimness that Jeffeaux hesitated.

"You will show respect for your mother at all times. Do you understand?"

Jeffeaux raised his right hand to his heart.

"Pardon me. Mother please, excuse me. I have had a very tiring few days. Call off your guard, do."

"Darling boy, go lie down. Get used to my guards."

Harbinger sat down with little grace. She was tired. Finally she was where she could expect a good night's sleep. She didn't have time to sleep. Wind Rider was coming.

"Mother, the Sarnese army is moving off to the west."

"North, they'll turn north. When the light comes, you take half the army to pursue them. I will lead the rest of the army east and then north."

"You will lead the Masfin troops?"

"No, mix them up. If I am going to take this army I will take it. Let them become bonded with us. Call up the commanders. Let us begin. Oh, and get Jeffeaux back here."

First was frightened. She did not let her sisters see her fear. They ate and slept as always. They did the chores they had begun with Seventh. Only at night, when she lay alone in her bed, did First feel her fear.

No one had answered her message. The invaders had occupied the house. Once they left, she had sent another message. There had been no response to that message either. Even though she had been alone for most of her marriage, First had always felt protected. Somewhere there was someone else responsible for her well-being. Now she felt herself alone and responsible for others.

The work helped. In the burning sun, with her muscles aching from effort, she could forget her fears. Bringing food from the earth assured First that she could provide somewhat for her responsibilities. Working with her, her household gained confidence not in themselves but in her. The fear paralyzed First when she saw the riders on the horizon. She could not provide for her household in this instance.

"Come. Gather up your tools. We can get to the storage cellars in good order."

"Is it our husband?"

"We cannot think that way. Most likely it is the invaders returning. Be wary." She was proud that her voice did not waiver. She watched her steady hands gather her hoe. The length of wood felt comforting in her hand. It had a long reach and sturdy handle, with a sharp blade at the end. No one spoke again. Everyone worked with tight faces and determined expressions. She willed her belief into them.

The stream of horses turned straight for the lake. The dust from the earth clouded the sky. First saw smaller, darker clouds following the horses. Foot soldiers too headed for the water. The entire landscape seemed to fill with foreign bodies of some shape. First increased her pace towards the cluster of buildings. She did not look at the road or anywhere except her goal. She did not see the group of riders that approached the same buildings.

Feeling a vibration she turned her head. Several riders were going to reach those buildings before her. In her heart she knew. The invaders had returned, in greater numbers. She did not try to reach the storage cellars.

First and her group entered the courtyard. The guard bowed in respect. First nodded coldly. She wondered that the horses were stabled in the stable this time. She tightened her grip on her hoe then forced her fingers to relax. Turning to the servant just behind her, First handed the hoe to him.

"Put everything away. Then come up to the house to wait for me in the kitchens. I'll be down by and by."

Her sister/wives flocked behind her. She raised her chin a notch. So did her sister/wives. She shook out her skirts; so did they. She turned to Second to rest her hand on the younger woman's forearm.

Many of the faces were different but the uniforms were the same as the Llweganian dress she knew. No one directed her but her steps were directed by restriction. They were allowed only one route through the house. She had never been to this part of the house. She walked steadily towards her father-in-law's wing. A heavy door bound in iron swung open at the urging of a soldier's hand.

"Seventh!?!" First went to rush towards her lost sister. Swords scraped in scabbards but First paid no attention. She nearly tripped in her haste to touch Seventh. Then she stopped short. Seventh was dressed as a Llweganian soldier. First noted that absently. What she could not believe was the incredible swell of Seventh's stomach. The curve that distorted Seventh's shape and posture was so beautiful that tears came to First's eyes. Hesitantly her hand went out. Her fingers that had not trembled in fear of her life did now. She felt the hard contour of Seventh. She measured the width of the swell and its length. Under her questing fingers she felt movement and then to her delight a solid thump. Startled her eyes flew to Seventh's face. First's mouth let loose a delighted laugh. Seventh smiled serenely back at her.

"You are safe Seventh."

"Decidedly so. I have a name you may use. I am Harbinger of Death, although I suspect my co-council members would say I am in fact Devouring Dragon at this moment."

First looked at the other occupants of the room. She looked at the place of honor Seventh held in the group. Her suddenly knowledgeable eyes saw Lady Zona dressed in the same manner as Seventh.

"Lady Zona, how good to see you." First's haughtiness was ruined by her hand still resting on Harbinger's womb. First suddenly remembered where her hand was. She snatched her hand back. Harbinger laughed.

"You remember Lord Jeffeaux? He is Lady Zona's son. This is my," Harbinger paused. She considered First solemnly. "This is my **First** Guard of my Household: Petron." First heard the emphasis. She looked at the group of men around Seventh. She blushed as she caught the meaning. She looked with knowing eyes at the three youths hovering around Lady Zona.

"How long will you be with us?"

"I couldn't say. I am sorry that the last time my Household were your guests you had to stay in the cellars. That won't be necessary this time. However, you will understand if your movements are somewhat restricted."

"Perfectly."

"I was informed that Lord Jeffeaux looked out for your welfare the last time he was here. I am sure he will do as fine a job this time."

"I am sure."

"Good. I have had a long journey here. I really need to rest now."

First began to leave the room. Her thoughts raged in her head. She tried to guess what had happened. She wanted to leave an impression of some sophistication, intelligence, something."

"How did you find Deskersai?"

"The question is: how did I leave it."

Harbinger lowered her body onto the bed as she heard the last echoes of First's leaving. Lord Jeffeaux rushed from the room. Lady Zona smiled at her son's departing back. Then she too left taking her guard with her. Harbinger felt Petron begin to ease the clothing from her body. She was so tired. She had anticipated savoring the comforts of her return to her husbands but all she could do was to close her eyes.

Lady Zona approached her own set of rooms with some trepidation. She knew she would complete the binding of her guard to her this Darkfall. They knew it as well and they followed behind her like the anxious bridegrooms they were. Since her husband's death five planting seasons before, Lady Zona had not been with a man. She had never thought to take another man to bed after her husband's death. Now she had three.

One thing about having a guard: she no longer opened doors. There always seemed to be a hand there to perform this service for her. She watched that hand on the knob pushing the door open for her. What had Harbinger's advice been? Everyone together from the beginning. She could give each one his own week but after that always together to build the married unit. Well she had no desire to go through this first night three times in one moon.

She was in her suite. Her husbands stood uneasy before her. She could see the flush rising on each face. A heaviness formed in her chest. These three were hers to do with as she pleased. She felt an intense tenderness for them.

Before she fell asleep Lady Zona had one thought: Harbinger must never sleep.

Lord Jeffeaux bowed out of the quarters where the Sarnese women were being held. They seemed to be indulging in amusement at his expense. As well they should be; his mother, at her age, taking a set of lovers: much younger lovers. The idea repelled him. His father, he wouldn't have minded if his father had acquired some comfort in his old age; but, his mother?

Two days he hadn't seen her. Food and drink had been delivered to her rooms but only empty dishes had come out. Two days he had endured the sly, knowing glances of the rest of the Household. He would not put up with this type of behavior. He stood before the door to his mother's suite. He raised his hand to knock. The rap sounded loudly in the hallway. A trooper walked by, her eyebrows raised in query. Jeffeaux ignored her. He knocked again. Still there was no answer. His hand lay flat against the wood.

"If you are looking for Lady Zona, she and her guard are training this morning. There is a meeting soon. She will be present there." Jeffeaux watched the retreating figure with disfavor. His hand slid to the handle. He turned it, then he pushed the door open. The smell was strong and familiar. A servant was stripping the bed of sheets. The huge bed that would have looked inviting once now looked obscene. Jeffeaux backed away from the scene and scent. He would be damned if he let this continue.

First appeared at his elbow. Her cool elegant features held a look of affection as she surveyed the rooms. Her eyes became dreamy.

"They have markings on their faces."

"What?"

"They are priests. Your mother has seduced three priests from the Temple." First spoke with respect in her voice.

"This is intolerable."

First looked directly into his eyes. She studied his expression and soul.

"You are not happy with this situation?"

"In Masfin respectable widowed women do not, no that's not true. This is not the usual state of affairs," Jeffeaux cringed at his words.

"I was not sure, Harbinger is not Llweganian?"

"Harbinger is Llweganian, my mother is Masfin. This is all Harbinger's doing."

"Seventh is a remarkable woman. However, I think this is all your mother's talents." First nodded at the rooms. "In Masfin do people truly marry one spouse at a time?"

"Yes."

"Do you miss your wife?"

"I am not married."

"At your age? Why ever not?"

Jeffeaux drew himself up to his full height. "I have yet to find the one woman that will please me for the rest of my life."

"Well there is the problem with your system. If you have more than one wife, you are bound to be pleased with one of them at all times."

"I couldn't possibly support more than one wife."

"Then I guess the Llweganian system has the advantage there: everyone provides for themselves to a large extent. Simply marry rich wives, widows, there you go. Lady Zona has a widow's portion; and she has been granted an income by Harbinger so she will be well able to support her," First hesitated. Of all the residents of the estate only Jeffeaux seemed to be in true ignorance of the exact nature of the Llweganian marriage customs. He clearly did not realize he had three stepfathers. For some perverse reason First did not wish to enlighten him. "Lady Zona is well able to support a husband, should she wish."

"I can't marry her, she's my mother."

"I am sure there are other women in her same position. Marry a few of them."

"Madame, if you will excuse me, I have a meeting to attend." Jeffeaux stopped at the door. He turned his head to one side. "What do you know of the Llweganian system? What husband no matter what system he is from would welcome the child of another man?"

"Seventh's child is not my husband's. He never went to her bed. What I know of the Llweganian system is very limited."

Harbinger had been pregnant when she entered Sarna. She had planned to expose herself to violence knowing she carried a child. She was capable of anything.

The room was filled with people. Jeffeaux moved towards Marjas and Sablor. He refused to look at his mother and her guards. He did not want to see the flush on her face; or the smiles on her guards. Everyone else seemed very serious.

Harbinger sat on a low chair. Her legs were stretched before her. A low table in front of her, held maps. Petron stood by her shoulder as did Rodznig. Jeffeaux wondered which man in this group was her husband. One of them had to be. No matter what the system no man would not be with his wife at this time. They all seemed equally close or distant from her emotionally.

"We will be leaving at first light. The Sarn army has moved north towards the new mountains. There is a fairly defensible position in their line of advance. I have already sent out scouts to reconnoiter the location. We'll have a way in when we want. We're marching. Those are my orders."

Everyone there knew Wind Rider was following the same path as the Sarnese army but from the opposite direction. The meeting was almost unnecessary except the word had to be given and Harbinger liked giving the word personally. Jeffeaux wondered at his presence.

Then he knew. His being here represented Masfin and gave him standing he did not have in truth or want in reality. He could not backpedal. He had been here and now the word would go out. The Masfin commanders would see him leave with the Llweganian guard and assume things that weren't. She was so devious. He could believe that she had ordered the kidnapping of the Masfin army if he hadn't been there when the decision had been made.

Harbinger was happy that her time would be soon. She was tired of being pregnant. The last months were the hardest. She had little choice. She could not bear to give up her husbands. She reached a hand out. Strong arms bent to aid her.

The King of Masfin was furious. He blamed his generals. He blamed himself. He blamed Harbinger. Oddly to his advisors he blamed the woman least.

"But sire, she is a woman."

"Fools. She was your peer. She had fought more years than some of your soldiers have been alive. She took one look at our army and saw that they were vulnerable to attack. We are lucky she only stole it and did not destroy it."

"Are we going to do nothing, Your Majesty?"

The King bent his head. He squeezed his eyes shut. "No: We have the reserves. We shall call on each province to provide additional recruits."

"Do we have any reports from Sarna?"

"Our army has joined the Llweganian army in victory. The Sarn capital has been razed. Most of the Sarnese army is moving towards a region near our northwest border."

"Then we will have a defeated army to worry about close to our border."

"If they threaten Masfin I know our troops will desert their present army to defend us."

"We can't be sure."

The King listened to the debate rage around him. "If the Sarnese attack Us: the Llweganian will chase the attack. Our troops will see themselves as coming to our rescue. We believe the Llweganian army will be coming to conquer Us."

Renfrew drew his finger along the edge of the table. He tried to keep his mouth shut. He was least of the generals. He had seen the present trouble developing but had said nothing. He dreaded speaking but felt saying nothing again would be close to treason. "Lord Jeffeaux is with them."

The words echoed strangely in the noisy room. They were so different from the rest of the conversations that they stood out in stark loudness. Then someone chuckled.

"Lord Jeffeaux is cousin to the King. He is related to the throne through the female side of his house. He is riding with the Masfin army that is defeating the Sarnese. He will be riding with those same soldiers when they return home."

"Lord Jeffeaux never was so deep or ambitious."

"No, but she is. She might not have arranged this but she will see its uses. He might not even be interested in being put out like this but she will sweep him along. She made the army that is defeating Sarna. We gave her the men; she trained up the army. We gave her Jeffeaux."

The thought distressed the King. He wanted to push it away. He wanted to run from it. But, it stared back at him relentlessly.

"If We denounce him that gives him status and perhaps legitimacy for some. If We say nothing, that gives him control."

"Renfrew could be wrong."

"Can We risk that he is right? Jeffeaux, lazy self-centered Jeffeaux, is the best kind of tool. Go back to Malso. Bring Us his sisters."

Renfrew stayed quiet. He had said enough, but he was willing to bet the sisters had already left. Since he believed they had already left he saw no reason not to volunteer.

"I will go." He didn't want to remain where he was. He wanted away from court. He was a soldier. He would find nothing he needed to fight at court. He needed to return to Malso to look for clues. He needed to remember everything he had observed of the enemy. And he needed time to reflect. His brother was in that army over the border. How well did he know his brother? Would his brother defend the King if the situation looked murky enough to offer another solution? If a charismatic leader convinced the army Masfin was best served by Sarna's destruction wouldn't that army follow its leader even to overthrow the King? To defy the generals who had hesitated before danger? Would Masfin fight against Masfin? That thought was anathema to the Masfin generals. They would never believe until they saw it happen.

Renfrew feared that thought. Once an avalanche started it was impossible to turn it aside. Renfrew clenched his teeth. Those sisters weren't at Malso and only he knew it.

Chapter 7

Jeffenza sat impatiently on her horse. Junla rose behind her.
Ilissa and Marma followed. Around them were Llweganian
troopers: female Llweganian troopers that had no respect for rank.
Jeffenza was tied to her horse. She had tried to dismount to force a
slower pace. Her present position had only been allowed when she
stopped complaining about being tied upside down. These
unnatural women cared nothing for pain or fatigue.

They had been riding all night. Since they had stopped to allow
Jeffenza up there had been no stops. Junla and Ilissa spoke rarely.
They asked for water occasionally. Marma said nothing. She
hung on grimly. Darkfall was leaving. The thin strip of light that
spread on the horizon comforted Jeffenza. Once they were visible
someone would report them then help would arrive shortly.
Something was odd about this countryside. It didn't look right.
Jeffenza noted the landscape in the midst of her plans for the slow
and terrible deaths for the troopers.

The world was the pink of a new day before she understood what
was so odd. She wasn't in Masfin anymore. This was the new
desert she had only glimpsed from the battlements of Malso.
Masfin was miles away by now. They had been riding at neck-
breaking speed for the entire night.

"Where are you taking us? I demand an answer. Do you know
who we are? My sister and I are the King's own cousins. He will
come for us." Jeffenza injected all her inherited arrogance into her
voice. The cold tones had no effect. The pace was slowed only
when the day began to warm. They stopped in the noon day heat.

Jeffenza wondered what the leader was doing. The horses were
going fairly slowly. They had been following no visible road with
alarming speed, but now they were on a path at a snail's pace.
Then they stopped for nooning. A rock was rolled by three of the
troopers.

Jeffenza watched the strange sight of three women placing their
shoulders to the rock to heave. The muscles bunched and sweat
poured but the sight was odd. Everything was off-center this day.
Jeffenza smelled water. She had not thought water had a smell. If
anyone had ever told her she would be able to smell water she

would have laughed. The scent was immediately exciting to the horses. They quivered as they waited for permission to move. Before any person had water the horses drank.

Junla, Ilissa and Marma stood quietly. They drank next. The troopers produced clever collapsing cups for them to use. Jeffenza had sat on her horse while it drank. She had gripped the pommel of her saddle in sudden fear that she would slide into the water then drown. Now she glared at the troopers. They purposely had left her on her horse so she could not drink.

Rough hands hauled her from her mount. A cup was pushed into her hands. Dried meat was presented. She had to fill her mouth with water to soften the food before swallowing. The horses were walked around gently. Damp rags were smoothed over their sides. Sweat and grime disappeared from them. Saddles and tack were checked. Jeffenza watched the scene over the rim of her cup.

"Rest. Now." Junla sat wearily. Ilissa and Marma sat with her. They leaned together creating a support of sorts out of the dirt.

"Untie my hands."

"Be quiet."

Jeffenza looked at her bound wrists. She studied the out-stretched arms attached to those wrists. An unhappy thought crossed her mind: maybe she had no influence in this situation.

It was almost Darkfall when she woke. Her muscles were stiff and sore from her hard bed. The horses were saddled. She was given a few minutes to relieve herself with an ever-present guard. Then she was back on the mount riding in the dark. She lost count of the days. The landscape never changed. Once she saw a house on the edge of her line of sight but when she turned her head to look full at it, they had gone by it. Her voice grew hoarse from her complaining; so she had to save her complaints for really big ones at the end of the day.

Her outfit was beginning to smell. She did not like to think of her clothing. She was exposing the shape of her legs in the Llweganian leather pants. The dark leather was very hot in the sun. She didn't like to admit that she sweated but in the leather attire in the hot sun she sweated so she smelled. She smelled of her sweat and of her horse's sweat. She smelled of the dirt in which she slept and of the water she spilled because of her bound hands. She smelled of the oil in her hair and of the oil on her saddle. Someone was going to pay at the end of this ride: if she survived it.

Junla and Ilissa and Marma were traitors. They had become indistinguishable from their captors. They sat like the troopers. They spoke only the simple words they had picked up from the Llweganians. They could say water and horse and food and I have to relieve myself. Right now, as Jeffenza was contemplating her miserable state, Marma was learning how to repair her own tack. Her clumsy fingers were trying to manipulate the thin strips of leather.

Jeffenza felt a hand push her head to the ground. A cloth was pushed into her mouth then secured by another strip of material. Her feet were quickly bound together then to her hands. She was unceremoniously dumped in the far corner of the camp. Marma, Ilissa, and Junla gathered around her. They sunk down into the dirt. Against the gray rock their grayed outfits blended until with their faces covered with dirt, from a distance they looked part of the rock.

The troopers melted away. Here was their chance to escape. Jeffenza tried to struggle as she tried to speak around the gag. Marma pushed her ruthlessly into the rock's surface. Junla pinned her to the ground. Ilissa joined her weight to theirs. Jeffenza was outraged. She tried to renew her struggles. Marma looked for something. She brought a rock close to Jeffenza's head. She drew back as if to strike. Jeffenza looked into the stark eyes. In her shock Jeffenza stayed still. Junla eased the rock from Marma's hand. Junla placed the rock near them but out of immediate range. They waited.

In the silence Jeffenza listened to her own breathing. She could not hear anyone else's. Then there was an earsplitting howl. The clash of arms followed. Yelling filled the air. Male yelling, loud and aggressive, Jeffenza tried to hear words but could not. Then the yelling stopped. It was cut off abruptly. The sound that followed was the thud of bodies and an occasional grunt. They all jumped when a body fell from the top of the rock. It landed with its sightless eyes facing them. Blood, black with dirt decorated half the head. Its hands gripped a deadly looking blade. Jeffenza closed her eyes in fear. This was no game. Marma had been right. They were dressed as Llweganians in the land of a Llweganian enemy. Away from troopers they were dead. They would be dead of thirst or hunger or predators or soldiers.

The shadows grew. Jeffenza remained still. She waited for the troopers to return. She hoped they did. She hoped they had won and were coming back. Another body dropped but this one was alive and it was one of the troopers. It turned to look at the four huddled women. A smile cracked its face. The face was covered with blood and dirt, but the smile did not look strange. She raised one finger to her lips before she left. The body went with her.

Darkfall was completely upon them before the troopers returned. Junla and Marma left Jeffenza. Ilissa remained to keep Jeffenza out of the way. Jeffenza made no motion. She had no desire to call attention to herself. Truthfully she couldn't have moved if she wanted to, her muscles were too cramped for motion. Her mind was also too cramped to order her muscles into action. She was busy wrestling with the idea that these women were real troopers who fought and killed like all other soldiers.

Hands hauling her out of her hiding place roused Jeffenza from her trance. She quivered as her muscles were freed from their position. She could not stand. The ropes on the ground were next to her flaccid body. She was lifted onto the horse. Her face was pressed to its side. She closed her eyes. She could sleep like this.

They were gone. The servants stood in a straight line. They held very still. Renfrew knew he could not kill them. There was no need for violence but he wanted to smash something. No one could tell him anything. The four women had vanished into thin air.

"When I went to rouse them the ladies were gone." The whispered words annoyed Renfrew.

"How recently had they left?"

"I never check on my Lady once she dismisses me. Her bed had been slept in. They all had. Their horses are still in the stables."

"The four ladies were spirited out of the castle unnoticed?"

"As a child Lady Jeffenza was always slipping away from her rooms. Even now she escapes without notice. They are the Ladies of the castle. With Lord Jeffeaux and Lady Zona gone, the Ladies are answerable to no one."

The maid was right. It was a large castle and mostly empty now the guests had all departed. He left the group. He climbed until he reached the battlements. He looked into Sarna. He imagined the army marching off to the east. He saw banners flying and the soldiers' voices raised in song. He was wrong. He had watched the training. They would move silent. No signals blazoned across the sky. Grim, studied soldiers would have stepped off into Sarna under the command of the Llweganians.

He knew where they had gone. They had gone into that desert. He would have to go into that desert to find them. They didn't need rescuing. They needed following. They would lead him right to the enemy.

They had ridden up into a great house. Male servants came to tend the horses. Only the lead rider dismounted. She spoke shortly to the servant tending her horse. He nodded as he led the way to the watering troughs.

A female came towards them. She moved slowly, regally. Her dress was rich with color and texture. Jeffenza watched the heavy fall of cloth move with its owner. She felt the clear eyes note her bounds and gag. The woman spoke quietly to the troop leader. The leader turned to glance at Jeffenza. She returned a comment. The woman smiled.

That smile remained in place as she neared the group.

"Greetings daughters and wards of Lady Zona." The words were strangely accented. Jeffenza had to consider the context before she understood the stilted phrasing. Junla nodded.

"Thank you."

"You will be pleased to learn your mother was very well when last I saw her."

"We will be with her soon."

"As you say. I will not keep you. Tell your mother First of this House sends her greetings."

Junla nodded again. Then the woman returned to the building. The horses snorted in the water. Jeffenza wanted to dismount. She was tired of behaving. She was tired of riding. She was tired of being ignored. Junla would pay. For what, Jeffenza had not quite decided yet. As she rode, Jeffenza concentrated on the how.

The house was two days behind them when Jeffenza saw the first signs of a large number of people. This must be their goal because their captors made no attempt to hide. They rode steadily. Past horses and equipment and soldiers and tents, they rode without looking right or left. Finally they reached a grouping of large tents.

The soldiers dismounted. Lady Junla, Marma, and Ilissa swung off their horses. Jeffenza sat trapped on her horse by her tied hands. A trooper entered the largest tent. There was a moment of waiting. Then Jeffeaux came out.

"What is my sister doing tied like this?"

"She was very difficult, brother. She was uncooperative, childish. She nearly got us killed once. I would have left her in the desert." Junla spoke witheringly. "She had no sense at all."

A trooper moved to cut Jeffenza down. Once her hands were free Jeffenza dragged the gag from her mouth. She swung off the horse in a flurry of indignation. Words were boiling to get out of her lungs. Then she saw the rest of the tent's occupants spill into the light.

Jeffenza rushed blindly to Sablor. Relief and fear lending speed to her feet. She flung her arms around him. She rained kisses on the leather over his chest. Suddenly she was flung violently from him to land in an ignoble heap at her brother's feet. Shock at Sablor's rejection kept Jeffenza on her back.

Jeffeaux stared in amazement for a moment. Then he rolled to the balls of his feet. He started to form words to demand retribution but the Harbinger of Death was towering over Jeffenza.

Despite the impending birth of her child, Harbinger was grim as death. Her gravid body seemed capable of all kinds of mayhem.

"In my country a woman may have as many husbands as she can support and satisfy." All eyes stared at the quietly furious woman. "If a woman fails to provide for her husband or to satisfy him he may dissolve the union." Somehow Harbinger swelled to fill the space before and above Jeffenza. "Since we are so lenient in this matter a woman has the right of execution for any and all unfaithful husbands."

Jeffenza stared in shock at Harbinger.

"How many husbands do you have?" Jeffenza's whisper was hoarse and tearful.

Harbinger looked at Petron. She considered her answer carefully. In this grim moment a hint of mischief lit the corners of her eyes.

"Twelve." Petron shook his head at her in resignation.

Jeffeaux blinked at the answer. Lady Zona laughed silently. Marjas and Rodznig groaned. Jorin nodded approval.

"Sablor come here." Even tones echoed in the air.

Sablor looked at his wife. She was filled with the power of their success. Her glory surrounded her. He was part of that glory. If he could bury himself in her he could absorb that power and glory. And she would bless him with the wonder of their shared pleasure. She had set herself an impossible task and was succeeding at it. Her body huge with child was an appropriate symbol. He was married to her. For all his life, no other wife would measure up to her.

"Wife." He knelt before her in submission to her rank over him.

"Do you wish to leave me?" Her words were cold, clipped, a mercy if he did, an agony if he didn't.

"Never for as long as I live."

Tenderness crept into her heart. The young were so intense in their devotions.

"You need only answer for today." A gentle finger touched his face.

"Never for as long as I live." Solemnly with as much the feel of a vow as on their wedding day, Sablor repeated his promise. All her present husbands knelt, their fists clasped to their shoulders. She loved them all so much it flowed from her heart to her face. It transformed her usually strict features into beauty.

"You should never truly love until you are married. It is unwise child." Jeffenza heard the advice in a daze.

Harbinger pressed a hand to her waist. "Come my husbands, Rodznig's heir has finally decided to make an appearance."

Jeffeaux frowned in confusion.

"How does she know the child is Rodznig's?"

"This is her eighth child. Rodznig is the seventh husband." Lady Zona spoke softly.   "It is good to have you safe, ladies."

"Where are we to sleep? I am exhausted." Ilissa dusted the dirt of their journey from her clothes she spoke. One of the troopers led the horses away. Junla hugged her brother and mother. Marma helped Jeffenza out of the dirt. Jeffeaux could only think one thought. His sister had formed an unwise passion for Harbinger's husband. He had seen the woman in battle, huge with child, killing the enemy.

"She is too old for him." Jeffeaux heard the statement. He turned to look at Jeffenza. As his head moved he saw his mother's three guards. The guards that shadowed her every move as the Harbinger's guard did their wife.

"He has had her. He will never want another."

"She isn't even pretty."

"No, she is not pretty."

"I don't understand."

"You wouldn't."

Jeffeaux listened to the interaction between his mother and Jeffenza. Still he could not speak. He stared at the three impassive men that guarded his mother. Men who, he knew, shared her bed. His mother had married those three boys? His mother and them? Married?

"She stands as high as a king in her society. She is not just anybody."

"Those are your husbands, Mother?!?" Every head in hearing range turned to look at Jeffeaux. He blinked as he realized how loudly he had spoken.

"Yes, I married them. So remember that when you deal with them. They have made me promises that they are willing to fulfill with their lives."

Junla stepped back. "Mother, this will take some getting used to. I think we had better get Jeffenza out of the sun. She has had a hard few days."

"I'm sure she made them hard on herself."

"True, but still they were hard."

Lady Zona looked into the bewildered face of her younger daughter. She saw the features that came from her and from her husband. She had loved her first husband. She had secretly despaired of his softness of character but she had loved him nonetheless. In her youngest child and her only son she saw two variations of that softness. Jeffeaux had surprised her. Maybe Jeffenza would show some strength or sense.

"Everything in life does not come down to your own pleasure. You are here and you will remain here because that is what is best for Masfin and our family. This is no game. There is no playing at anything now. Lives depend on actions and inaction." Lady Zona held Jeffenza in a firm grip. Long strides ate space. Jeffenza looked at her stern parent.

Lady Zona did not see the odd expressions on her daughters' faces. She did not hear the whispered conversations of her wards. Her thoughts whirled in her head. She understood the necessity for bringing her daughters to the camp. She worried at the trouble Jeffenza could cause. She turned to Stea.

"Place a guard on this one. She is a potential danger."

Jeffenza felt tears gather in her eyes. Hearing her mother speak so coldly of her broke Jeffenza's heart. Nothing, she had thought, could touch her heart. Indignation swept into her mind but her heart felt the blow still.

"Did you suggest we be brought here?"

"I agreed with your brother when he pointed out your danger. Harbinger would have ignored you. You would not have weighed in any of her decisions. To pacify Jeffeaux and to guard against potential problems with the Masfin troops, she agreed."

Jeffenza watched her mother's retreating back. She had never been close to her mother. They had lived as all Masfin nobles. Nurses raised children and parents visited like fairy godparents. Jeffenza felt the chasm of her culture yawn at her feet. She had nothing to protect her except a brother she despised and her feminine wiles. She smiled at the beardless youth her mother claimed as a husband. His impassive face met her gaze.

Devouring Dragon sat contemplative at the table. Jeffeaux moved hesitantly to his place.

"Where are your guard?" Jeffeaux could still not get the word husbands out of his mouth.

"They sleep the sleep of the innocent." She smiled indulgently. Her face was flushed, her eyes bright but otherwise there was no evidence that she had spent the better part of the previous day striving to bring forth a child.

"Twelve husbands."

Harbinger nodded thoughtfully. "That's about right. I had meant to take only ten. I hadn't accepted a new husband in five years." She bit into a morning cake with gusto. "When Sablor presented his proposal I hesitated. His logic, however, was impeccable. My husbands supported his suit." She sipped her tea. "My last husband was a choice of expediency. He probably regrets this marriage."

"I can't believe you count your Sarnese stooge as one of your husbands. You went to great lengths to make sure he couldn't claim a valid Llweganian marriage."

"The Sarnese ceremony is very explicit. It requires no names only participants. He claimed me as a wife and I shall honor his claim, when the time is right." She lowered her cup carefully to the table. "I would like to give all of my husbands an heir but I am not sure it will be possible. It's not necessary but I would like to do that for them."

Jeffeaux placed his view of sex as a pursuit against hers but could not look at the difference.

"Is sex not important?"

Her laugh, so rarely heard rang out deep and sweet. "I enjoy it immensely. I have to with so many husbands and one of them a stripling lad. It is not an end in itself. It is a dimension of my married life. My husbands married me for my position, wealth and prestige. I married them for political reasons or military ones. Sex is an enjoyable biological function but my intellectual powers are used for other pursuits."

"With twelve husbands you don't have to focus any energy on pursuing a partner."

Harbinger sighed in resignation.

"Perhaps you are right; but, if you had twelve wives what would you do?"

"Court a thirteenth."

"See: if sex is your only focus, a hundred wives or husbands would not be enough. The safety of my people: that is my focus, my passion."

Harbinger served herself a slice of fried meat. Juice ran down the knife as she replaced it on the platter. She licked a stray drip from her fingers. "Tomorrow we leave."

"Leave? You just delivered a child. You can't travel yet."

"I could leave today. My poor husbands are too exhausted to travel, however. Tomorrow we will all be well enough to go."

Jeffeaux took several bites of his breakfast. He regarded his companion between mouthfuls. She had maps spread at her elbow. Soldiers came and went depositing stones on the maps as they came. He was reminded of birds building nests. As he thought of those birds and their nests he realized that he hadn't asked an important question.

"Did you have a boy or a girl?"

"A girl, my family breeds true. Rodznig has sent for his head nurse. He sent for her before the battle began. We expect her today."

"So another dependent joins the train."

"Oh no, she comes with a wet nurse and escort. Rodznig's heir will be safely ensconced in his estate. I wouldn't dream of dragging a child on a campaign if the child were my heir, never mind one of my husbands' heirs."

"You are a strange creature. Don't you love your children?"

"How often did you see your parents when you were growing up?"

Jeffeaux opened his mouth to speak. His words died unspoken. Absently he reached for one of the stones by her hand. Her fingers, hard and strong, swept the stones out of his reach. She turned one in her hand.

"Visit with your sisters today. Ease their fears. Reconcile them to their lot. Lady Zona will be spending time with them also and with her wards. I like your mother. There are few people I would say that about. Be nicer to her."

Jeffeaux frowned at Harbinger. He dared a great deal. He had a sense of security with her. She would not harm him. He never even doubted that. Perhaps he was foolish. But he never thought of her as a danger to himself.

"I can't explain it to you. You would never understand. This is my mother not just some woman. She's my mother. If the roles were different and we were discussing my father I would not be happy. There are certain behaviors that people of her age should follow."

"She's not dead. It's not as if she is likely to produce anymore siblings for you at this point. I was going to release those three priests into the mob to delay action against us and to prevent stories of priest murder at my hands. The mob would have torn them apart. Your mother took pity on them. She provided them with the only protection she could give them against my expediencies. She married them out of kindness. Most good deeds don't go unpunished. You should be glad things have turned out well so far."

"Can you see me returning to Masfin with a mother who had three husbands? They shall say that the Llweganian influence on women is too dangerous. They will embrace the Sarn as the lesser of two evils."

"I have considered this. We might never reach that bridge. There is plenty to destroy us before we get there. When we have to deal with that issue we will. Your problem at this moment is not your mother."

"I know: Jeffenza. She has never taken direction well. I do not think she will be an easy guest."

Harbinger pushed her empty plate away. She gathered her stones into a pouch that hung at her waist; a waist that was already much smaller than the day before, not totally slim but on its way.

"If she can't be an easy guest she will be an easy prisoner. Prisoners are the first hindrances that I dispose of when the time comes. Convince her well. You are reported to have incredible powers of persuasion. Use them now."

Jeffeaux watched the stones disappear into their pouch. He remembered the scene of the day before. He felt again the breath of death that had hung over the players. Then he thought of Harbinger's words.

"I was wondering Harbinger; you speak of love with such a pragmatic vocabulary. Don't truly love until you are married. Have you never seen someone, and irrationally, with no reason, against reason, wanted them, desired them, loved them without thought, almost as a reflex to their being?"

"Is that not lust? How can you love without knowledge of the person you desire?"

"You know them at a single glance."

"Can you ever? Come we have spent enough time on this subject today."

Renfrew squatted in the dust. He fingered the soil. Around him bodies lay in heaps. They had been stripped and animals had gnawed on them. The sun and heat had swollen the bodies and turned the skin odd colors. He could not tell whose troops they were. They had passed several such sites. He did not know if he still followed the trail of his quarry or some marauding band of murderers. All he knew was he followed a trail of destruction.

Why had they never allowed the envoy to present his plans? If they had heard them at least now there would be some clue as to the enemy's whereabouts. All he had to go on was this trail. He hated being reactive. He wanted a plan of action that he controlled. On top of it all he didn't know this country. He would have to turn north. He needed to stay close to Masfin's border. He had to have some reference points. He did not wish to stumble blindly through a strange country.

His troops were not hardened soldiers. They had seen more death on this march than in their entire military careers. They looked at the bodies and wondered. All the bodies were male. He hoped these were Sarnese and Llweganian losses and not Masfin soldiers who refused to fight for Llweganian leaders. If his fear were true there was some hope that he could persuade the Masfin troops still with the Llwegan army to follow him.

Three days after their last grisly discovery, Renfrew decided he hated Sarna. It was brutal country. The days were hot and the nights were freezing. Water was more valuable than food. Small creatures to be eaten could be found with skill but water was so scarce that he thought to turn back every day, twice a day. He sent scouts back into Masfin for water every day since they had started. They were dribbling back now.

He had sent two groups before the last group that returned. He worried that the two missing groups were casualties of the expedition. He could not afford to lose many men. He would need every trooper when he attempted the retrieval of the women. The sun was setting. They needed to establish a camp soon. There would be no moon tonight. Deep in hostile country he did not dare to light a fire, so, everything had to be done by natural light.

Renfrew huddled in his cloak. He took his turn at watch seriously. He had not done this since his younger days. The night air crept persistently down his collar. Cold, insistent fingers pried at his lungs. In the night and this open landscape sound traveled eerily. He thought he heard something right next to him all his watch long. The sound was a normal sound but not here and not at this time. He could not place the sound. He just knew that he recognized it from his past. He was happy when his watch was over and relieved when the morning came.

That day he heard the sound on and off all day. He thought he was the only one that heard the sound. He thought the long days in the empty land had begun to affect his hearing and perception. At nooning he noticed this troop was looking restlessly around the horizon. If they heard the sound then he had decisions to make and madness to fear.

Late in the afternoon one of the water parties returned.

"We were delayed because we overshot the main group. On our turn back we moved slowly because we ran into hordes of Sarnese soldiers. We laid low for a day to let them pass by us."

Renfrew heard the report. His mind raced. That sound was the muted roar of an army. As Renfrew felt the knowledge settle in his mind the watch let loose the alert. As the troopers turned to find their bearings the Sarn soldiers surrounded them. They spoke words that Renfrew could not recognize but understood clearly. He let his hand drop from his weapon.

Stiefis stared at the Masfin general. He understood every word the man spoke. His father had forced him to learn Masfin. He just didn't believe the words.

"You want me to believe that your army is acting without your knowledge or sanction?"

"The Llweganian soldiers were training our army. Their negotiator had been pushing for a joint invasion. One of his apparent superiors came one day. They both left the next day. Then the army was gone."

"All you ever dealt with was men. I find that hard to believe. All the top officers in the Llweganian army are women. You are either lying or…. you are lying."

"There was a woman with them but you can't discuss battle plans with women."

Stiefis laughed bitterly at the Masfin general. "You're not lying: you're an idiot. What's your story about some woman?"

Renfrew did not want to reveal everything. He wanted to keep some secret from this hostile captor but he weighed the situation.

Sometimes the enemy of your enemy can be your friend. He had to take a chance.

"A Masfin nobleman who is related to the King is with the Llweganians. He adds an air of legitimacy to this action. I planned to take his sisters and his mother's wards hostage to force him to return to Masfin; to leave the Masfin army with no doubt as to the criminal nature of their actions."

"And just who is this would be King?"

"You wouldn't know him."

"He doesn't exist."

"No, no he does. His name is Lord Jeffeaux."

Stiefis sat up straight. He turned to share a look with his father.

"He is the nephew of Lady Jessina?"

"No, he has no aunt."

"There are two Lord Jeffeaux's perhaps?"

"No, there is only the one. He is cousin to the King through his mother the Lady Zona."

"Lady Zona." Stiefis stood. He frowned mightily at Renfrew. He paced around the room furiously.

"I have met Lord Jeffeaux and Lady Zona but they had a woman with them whom they claimed to be Lady Jessina."

"The only other close family members of the house of Jeffeaux are the younger sisters Ladies Junla and Jeffenza. Lady Zona has two young wards Ladies Marma and Ilissa."

"She wasn't young. She was older; but not as old as Lady Zona. She spoke Masfin and Sarnese well."

"No one speaks Sarnese in Masfin."

Weirhass looked at his hands. He remembered the calm of Lady Jessina. He remembered her water in the desert. He remembered her ease at ordering people; her ease at riding and her servants' ease at hard riding.

"Who was the female Llweganian?"

"Devouring Harbinger, Dragon of Death some ridiculous name like that."

Weirhass closed his eyes in pain.

"Devouring Dragon, Harbinger of Death: these are not ridiculous names. She earned them in battle. I had the greatest warrior Llwegan ever produced in my hand."

"She's only a woman."

"That is how she stole your army. I believe you. I believe she stole your army. You dealt with her husbands. They have standing and influence in the army but she controls everything."

"Husbands?"

"Yes, husbands; we have many wives, they have many husbands. Husbands and wives," Weirhass stared hard at Stiefis, " you should have tried to get a son of her."

Stiefis smashed his hand onto the table. He gripped its edge to overturn the table roughly. He had had her right there but had let her slip away. She had burned Deskersai. She was coming for them now. Stiefis looked at Renfrew with renewed interest.

"Did she take all your army?" Stiefis asked.

"I am not at liberty to say."

"Come, come now man. This is no time to be coy. Her name when she is in action is Harbinger of Death. When she is at rest she is called Devouring Dragon. When she is finished bringing death to Sarna she will devour Masfin."

Renfrew understood the concept. The Llweganians had been saying the same thing but Masfin had not thought they needed an ally at the time. Now Llweganian action had shown Masfin's error in logic.

"I cannot make promises for my country, but I can present your case to my King and the other generals." Renfrew offered what he could.

"We don't have much time." Stiefis spoke the obvious truth.

"I know. Come with me." Renfrew turned back towards Masfin.

"Do you want to find the women first?" Stiefis stood his ground.

"No, there is no time. I can't do both. If you find them hold them. They can still be used as hostages to turn the army back; if this alliance doesn't hold or it doesn't convince the army to turn back."

Stiefis smiled to himself. He had outwitted the Dragon. It soothed his frayed ego. A small voice whispered in his mind. The war was not yet lost.

As he rode with the Masfin troops back to their king he felt the weight of the war on his heart. The bodies that littered the path of the invasion cut deeply into his mind's eye.

"The reserves that you mentioned; were they trained by the Llweganians?"

"No."

"Are the trained Masfin troops all in Sarna?"

"Yes, once they hear that the Masfin and Sarna are allies they will turn against their Llweganian captors."

Stiefis thought of his household. He remembered the panicked messages from First. He saw his wives laboring in the hot sun. His spirits sank.

Jeffeaux read the missive. He turned the vellum over in his hands thoughtfully. Here was the brake on Harbinger's plans. He would refuse to speak for her to the Masfin soldiers. He passed the vellum to Harbinger's waiting hand. She perused the document. No expression of surprise or consternation crossed her features. Almost it was as if she read a letter from a half forgotten lover.

"You'll have to turn back now. I will not speak to the troops. They wouldn't follow me even if I did."

"True, but I never planned to have you speak to them."

"You think you can convince them to take arms against their own countrymen?"

"I would not ask it of them. Gentlemen," the Masfin commanders lifted their heads to look at her. "I will be coming around to speak to your soldiers tomorrow. I will start at daybreak. I will visit each corps in numerical order. Sleep well."

Jeffeaux paced the space. He watched the commanders leave with impatience. He turned back to Harbinger.

"What are you going to do then?"

"You will have to wait to find out."

"I won't accompany you."

"Then you will have to wait all the longer."

He did not hold to his threat. She said nothing when he met her at the edge of her tent. She shrugged her cloak around her to ward off the chill of the lingering Darkfall. In one hand she held the vellum. In the early light it looked golden.

The first group of soldiers was bleary-eyed and anxious.

"Good day. I have received news from Masfin. King Ranald has entered into an alliance with Sarna: an alliance against Llwegan. You must go home. You have been good comrades. I am very proud to have fought with you.

"I will come against you with all that I have and know. But that is not what you should fear. I will not be able to defeat your combined forces. When I have done all the damage I can do, I will return to guard my borders against Sarna and Masfin.

"Sarna will turn on you. They will know your country and your numbers. They will have positions, fortifications inside your borders. You will experience the slow bleed of constant war that I have known all my life, that all my ancestors knew and that now all my descendants will know. You will become as well acquainted with loss, suffering, and conflict as I am. I would not wish this on anyone but it seems the peace I had thought to steal is gone forever.

"I am sorry I failed you. We will divide up the provisions and the water while your commanders ready you for departure. Good luck."

Jeffeaux trailed behind Harbinger. He tried to find the catch in her speech. He tried to guess her purpose, her betrayal. He found none. She would let them go.

"You will really let them go?"

"Whoever wants to leave, may."

"What does that mean?"

"Just what I said. We shall see what happens in the next few days."

"You expect them to choose to stay?"

"It could happen. The bond of battle is strong. This alliance is a political move. How deep is their trust of the political process? Do they believe the King is wise? Has he been taken in by the Sarnese? Will they be saving the King from himself if they stay? Will they be saving Masfin from the King who has been foolish? There are many possibilities. We will have to wait to see."

"What will you do if they go?"

"Just what I said. I expect they will go. I would. I hope your generals handle them well."

"I had better tell my family to get ready."

"I never said I would let you go."

Jeffeaux stared in astonishment at Harbinger. "How will you keep me?"

"I have your mother and your sisters. You won't leave. If that fails I will hold you forcibly. Just make up your mind: you are staying with me."

"If the Masfin army leaves I will be of no use to you."

Harbinger came to stand very close to Jeffeaux. She drew a line down his face. Then she walked away. Jeffeaux watched her leave. He sighed in relief. She had taken the choice from him.

"Don't worry, I will find a use for you." Her words floated back to him.

Renfrew watched the troops file into the camp. They moved silently, shouting no greetings. He watched for the banners as they passed. His horse shifted under him. He leaned back to stretch the muscles in his back. He was tired of sitting; he could sympathize with the animal. He did not like the serious faces of the troops. He did not like the answers the returning commanders had given to his questions.

Why had she let them go? Why had she practically forced them to leave? What was her plan? He turned to speak with Stiefis.

"Why? Why would she send them home?"

"I am the wrong person to ask." Stiefis wondered if Renfrew had learned that Harbinger was one of Steifis' wives.

"You have more experience fighting the Llweganians. You're the only one I can ask."

"But, they fought with her. They know the answer. One of them must know the answer."

"I hope you are right. There," Renfrew saw his brother's division. He took off down the slope towards the lead group. Stiefis followed having no desire to remain alone on the hill in the middle of these grim looking soldiers.

"Marlin, Marlin are you well?" Renfrew grasped his brother by the shoulder. He smiled at the face that reflected his own features back to him through a murky mirror.

"I am fine, general." The tone was guarded. The eyes were guarded. Renfrew let his hand slip away.

"Welcome home, Marlin."

"We are here. As you wanted. I see you have your Sarn with you. Does he go everywhere with you?"

Renfrew drew back. He blinked at the barely concealed hostility in Marlin's voice.

"You are tired brother. I will see you later."

"Yes, general."

Marlin watched his brother leave with relief. He could not bear the feeling of doom the Sarn had engendered in his soul. He could still hear Harbinger's words of warning. Even now it had begun. His brother had a new appendage. Sarna was looking for a new appendage. Marlin knew he would watch. He knew the whole army would watch. They would wait. Patience was the most important weapon in battle.

Renfrew hurried through his duties. He spent the day assigning duties and responsibilities. He wanted two minutes alone with his brother. That was all he asked. He had to wait three days for his wish. When Renfrew finally saw a clear moment he grabbed it. Stiefis watched Renfrew go, knowing where he went. Knowing he could not follow to ensure the shaky alliance held even on such a minute level.

Marlin was training with his troops. Renfrew watched until Marlin noticed his presence. There was a moment of hesitation then Marlin dismissed his troops. Renfrew would have been happy to wait. He was interested in seeing the Llweganian training methods. Marlin walked up to his brother rubbing a towel around his neck.

"Been busy?"

"Very. You're keeping busy I see."

"It's my duty."

Renfrew frowned at the stilted conversation. He had expected Marlin to ask questions, share experiences. Well he would start.

"You must be relived to be home."

"I am a soldier. I was not reluctant or displeased to fight."

Renfrew heard the implied criticism of the Masfin generals in Marlin's statement.

"One should never fight if there is a peaceful alternative."

"You speak the truth, general."

Renfrew grunted in frustration.

"When you learned of the situation here you must have been eager to tell that marauder goodbye."

Marlin looked off into the distance. He clenched his teeth for a breath then released the breath.

"My country has chosen to side with her enemies against Harbinger. She is now my adversary. That does not mean I have one degree less of respect for Harbinger than I did the morning she came to tell us of the King's decision. She stood there telling us how she was going to provide for us on our march home, then wish us well. Harbinger has two names, when speaking with troops who fought with her, use one of them."

"She stole you from your country to do her dirty work."

"I have drunk water Harbinger dug from the desert. These eyes have seen Harbinger, great with child, fight fiercely in battle. I have heard her compassion as Harbinger sent me home to my country. Harbinger does her own dirty work."

Renfrew swung around in disgust.

"I am surprised you have come back then."

"Just be grateful we did. We have never felt as proud as when we served under those generals."

Marlin turned away completely. He returned to his waiting troops. They closed ranks around him as if defy Renfrew.

Stiefis had discretely followed Renfrew. He had heard every word. He had to duck quickly to avoid Renfrew as the general stormed back to his tent. She has them was all Stiefis could think. She has them. He had to find a way to keep the Masfin army from the Dragon. Or destroy them. The latter would achieve the former. It was in Sarna's best interest in every way to use the Masfin troops at every opportunity before deploying Sarnese troops.

Jeffenza was not unhappy to be held by the Llweganian army. She had more chances to see Sablor if she were with the Llweganians than if she had stayed in Masfin. Now her honor was at stake. She had to woo that man successfully. She could not lose to an old, ugly, graceless, manly female.

Jeffenza did not like being housed on the Sarnese estate of the Harbinger. There were mostly women here. They followed the daily rituals of a nunnery. There were no parties. There was nothing to do but work. She had tried to leave twice; she had been returned twice, delivered to the female First like a bundle of wood. First had placed her under tight security.

Jeffenza now sported the golden chains of a recalcitrant wife. She wore a chastity belt, golden shackles, and bells so her every move even in her sleep was announced.

Every time Jeffenza asked why a Sarnese would aid a Llweganian general First would smile slightly. She would answer calmly.

"Harbinger is my sister/wife."

"But you aren't married to any of the Harbinger's guard."

"No, I am not."

Jeffenza disliked cryptic answers. She waited for the Harbinger's household to return. Surely her mother and brother would help her. Junla and Marma and Ilissa were useless. They spent their time training with the soldiers left to guard the estate; learning to speak, read, and write Sarnese and Llweganian. Generally those three spent their time becoming useless as allies for any of Jeffenza's plots.

Jeffenza sorted her silks. She bent her head over the seat cover in her lap. She frowned in concentration. The pattern was not familiar. She had only the side panel to work. The other panels were being worked by First and Third. This was a seat cover worthy of a king. It would cover the entire chair easily. The silks and colors were brilliant. Jeffenza had no common cultural references to help her guess what the pattern formed.

First looked over Jeffenza's shoulder.

"Good work. A messenger arrived this morning. By tomorrow's Darkfall we are expecting guests. Water will be available this Darkfall for bathing."

Jeffenza did not realize what a luxury a bath had been here. She had no idea the pleasure it gave First to discuss bathing so casually. All she thought was how odd First was to think bathing needed planning.

First was very excited. Third had agreed. Now all First needed to do was to ask Lady Zona if she would allow the plan. Harbinger would not disapprove. First understood Harbinger very well. She would allow this if Lady Zona agreed. First could hardly contain her hopes. Everything depended on this.

The servants began to prepare food for the expected arrival. Every room was aired. Late into Darkfall sheets were prepared for

being aired the next day. First handled the fine cotton sheets for
Harbinger herself. Jeffenza sunk into her bath jingling and
clanking all the way. She frowned at the sight of her flesh
concealed by metal.

All of the household were assembled in the great room, waiting.
Everyone was busy but each ear was cocked for the servant's call.
First could not tell what her hands did. Her eyes assured her brain
that her hands followed the pattern but her mouth could not have
told anyone what her hands did.

When the call finally came First almost cried in relief. At least
her waiting was done for this part. There was a flurry of activity as
everyone put away their busywork. Everyone except Jeffenza, she
would not give anyone the satisfaction of controlling her on this
level. When she was ready to be done she would be. Jeffenza rose
slowly. Her guard had waited until she was ready.

The impassive face told her nothing. She would have been sure
of her impact with the Sarnese women. They fairly danced to greet
the invaders. The Llweganian guards were different. They stood
with her. They paid her no attention other than that. She moved so
her bells rang constantly. The sound grated on her nerves. She
hoped the sound annoyed the guards half as much as it did her.

First hurried to the doors. She did not care if everyone saw her
interest. The door swung open by the servants' hands. Air blew
into the foyer. The staid, quiet building burst into life. Voices
echoed. The sound bodies made as they moved with purpose filled
the air. First smiled at the commotion. They were here. Lady
Zona was standing with Harbinger. The two were speaking as they
entered the building. Then Harbinger caught sight of the waiting
household.

"First, how are you?"

"Welcome home Harbinger. Lady Zona, are you well?"

"Yes, First. What is this?" Lady Zona saw her daughters.
Jeffenza smiled smugly. Revenge was at hand. Her vindication
was looming over First.

Junla gave her mother a light kiss on the cheek. Jeffeaux blinked
at the sight of Jeffenza mincing with her skirts lifted to show her
shackles. First shook her head slowly.

"Lady Jeffenza was unable to follow the rules of the Household.
Since she had been given into my care I placed her under the bonds

of a Hostile Wife. It has been effective. She has made no further escape attempts."

Harbinger eyed the chains. She drew a deep sigh. Somehow she preferred cages to chains; but, whatever worked was fine with her right now.

Lady Zona let loose a deep laugh. She could hardly catch her breath to squeak out her words.

"Her father would have paid his last crop to discover a way to control this headstrong daughter."

Jeffeaux stared at the calm face of First. He noted the way her cheek dimpled as she repressed an answering smile.

Harbinger saw Jeffeaux's interest and First's oblivion. She was intrigued by the restrained excitement in First. Something was about to happen.

"I am hungry. The ride was long and tiring."

"Come, come. There is food for eating and water for bathing."

"Would you mind very much if we eat first? I fear if I bathe I will sleep before I leave the water."

First led the way. She calmed herself by breathing deeply. Tomorrow, she would be able to wait until tomorrow. Though, she had worked up the nerve to ask tonight and did not think she could wait much longer. The food lay spread on the tables. Everyone ate heartily. Wine flowed and talk spewed from every mouth. First turned her bread over and over in her hands. Jeffeaux took the bread from her fingers. He ripped off a piece. Casually he popped that piece into her mouth. First ate unthinkingly. She chewed slowly.

Harbinger had left with her guard. First could not imagine so large a number of people could vanish without notice. Only when Lady Zona and her guard moved to leave did First notice Harbinger was gone. A servant moved to First's side.

"Harbinger has asked for your presence in her chambers."

Jeffeaux rose to escort First. He walked next to her trying to engage her in conversation but First answered so absently that Jeffeaux fell silent. Their steps echoed in the passages.

"First, thank you for coming. Thank you for the bath. You know, in Llwegan each house has a communal bath. The room is spacious and the bath accommodates several persons. Now that you have access to water we should add such a room here." As she spoke Harbinger lowered herself into the bath behind the screen. Petron frowned at Jeffeaux. Jeffeaux himself did not like being in the room. The thought of a naked Harbinger just beyond his line of sight was uncomfortable. His breath rattled in his chest.

"A fine thought Harbinger. I am sure it will happen by and by."

"First do you have something to say to me? That was a very fine meal that you left untouched."

First looked at Lady Zona. She looked at the three priests at Lady Zona's shoulder. She took a deep breath.

"We the first six wives of Stiefis would like to begin proceedings for the Repudiation of our marriages."

Harbinger blinked. She lathered soap across her shoulders. Sablor took the wash cloth from her. He began to scrub her back.

"Explain please." Harbinger bit out the words.

"When a husband is unable to impregnate his wives he may bring them to a priest of Kersai for a Blessing that usually results in a child. Or the wife may go on her own for a Testing which may also result in a child. If there is a child from a Testing the wives may repudiate the husband as infertile and not worthy of husbanding. You have three priests in your Household. Third has agreed to the Testing. There is an altar of Kersai on the estate. We request the Testing."

Jeffeaux laid a restraining hand on First's arm.

"Lady, if you repudiate your husband what will happen to you? Consider what you do."

"Third is the daughter of Weirhass' brother. In Sarnese tradition an unmarried female who is with child has the rights of a son in her family. She may live on any estate the family holds and have any household she desires. We will stay right here. Stiefis will have no claim to this estate with water."

Harbinger smiled thoughtfully.

"The decision is yours, Lady Zona. They are your priests."

Lady Zona looked at her three young men. She did not want to share them with anyone but there was something here: something that would not impact her marriage. Jeffeaux's shocked expression drove her.

"I will discuss this matter this night. We will give you an answer in the morning. I have a question. What claim does the child have on the priest involved?"

"None," Stea answered shortly. "I have never done a Testing before but I did several Blessings. It is a function of my calling. It is nothing like," Stea stumbled on his words. "There is no claim. The child is a gift from Kersai to the family. That is all."

Lady Zona held her face still. A grin was aching to escape. But she would not let it.

"Actually, First, Jeffeaux, could you excuse us? I would like to discuss this with Harbinger."

Jeffeaux felt the insistent tugging on his arm. First dragged him from the room in her anxiety to be sure nothing adversely effected the discussion. She has taken the plunge. They had not refused. She had not expected an instantaneous reply. Well, she had hoped but not expected.

Third stood inside First's rooms. Jeffeaux wanted to enter but First closed the door firmly in his face.

"What did she say?"

All the other first six wives were hovering around First.

"They will tell us in the morning. They did not seem opposed to the idea."

"What do you think, Harbinger?"

"They are your husbands, Lady Zona. I cannot tell you what to decide."

"Could it be to our advantage?"

"Everything can be somehow. If you allow the Testing there will be repercussions we cannot foresee. If we do not succeed the wives will be in a difficult position no matter what First says. If we succeed, no, I will not try to influence you. I will say that I do not plan to repudiate Stiefis."

Lady Zona remembered the precautions Harbinger had taken to keep her husbands from the ceremony at the beginning of their adventure. "I was under the impression that you were not anxious to have any hint of that ceremony being valid. Before we entered Sarna you had many discussions with me about keeping the ceremony false. You chose a name that could not possibly be confused with yours. I thought you sent your husbands away to make sure the rite would not be valid."

"I will honor the marriage because I choose to at my convenience not because I must. If having Stiefis as a husband benefits me, I will claim him; if not, to the desert sand with him."

"I suspected as much. I don't know. I don't like the idea of sharing my husbands."

"I wouldn't like it either. However, they are not asking for a sharing, only his end product. They are used to sharing a husband. They probably look at this differently than we do."

"Zona, there is no pleasure in the act. It is a physical state we achieve through prayer and meditation. I cannot recall any of my actions during this state." Brir spoke quietly.

"Let us not discuss this here."

"May I ask one last question?" Harbinger spoke slowly.

Lady Zona nodded tightly.

"How often is a Testing done?"

"Never in my memory. The husband has to abstain from all his wives for a long enough period that there is no possibility that he conceived the child. Husbands don't usually cooperate in a Testing."

"Ah, thank you."

Chapter 8

Third waited nervously at the altar of Kersai. For an entire month she had abstained from all drink except the holy wine and clear water. Harbinger had decreed and the priests had agreed that the clear water from their lake was the only thing she needed. She had not even looked at her marriage herbs. The priests had said that the herbs were not right for a Testing since they were for the wife of Stiefis. She had counted her days. This week was the most likely time for her to conceive. She waited for the priest. She did not know which one had agreed. All she knew was that the consequences of the sisters/wives' decision was upon them. She was frightened. Not of the act, but of having made a choice. She could do this. Three robed figures entered the altar.

"Welcome daughter. We have come to grant the Testing. So there is never any question all three of us will participate." Third drew in her breath. She watched as the candles on the altar wavered into life. One week, that was all she had to prove the Repudiation.

First sat with Lady Zona. She worked on her needle work. Lady Zona was unable to lose herself in the growth of the pattern. First did not understand the anxiety of her companion but she tried to respect Lady Zona's feelings. First was relieved when Harbinger entered the room. She relinquished her seat gladly to Harbinger. First then joined her sister/wives around the fireplace.

They were silent. Harbinger allowed Lady Zona the space to form her own words.

"What is happening?"

"The Masfin armies are massing on the border. They will make a push in a while. I would do it tomorrow but they will wait. The Sarnese must be gnashing at the bit. I am building a bath. It should be done soon; before the Masfin generals agree to any plan of the Sarn."

"Why build a bath?" Jeffeaux intruded on the women. He drew up a seat. Jorin rose from his seat. Harbinger waved him back. Jeffeaux noted the interaction. Almost he got up, then, he sat with more force than grace.

"I want one here. The ladies will enjoy it. Work is good for the soul." Harbinger spoke absently. She poured a goblet of wine for Lady Zona. Jeffeaux watched the dark liquid flow from its container.

"Will it be finished before we move?"

"I can't say. Lady Zona, was your son always this attentive?"

"No, there must be no other options for entertainment."

"You know there are not, Mother. Besides I am interested in how Harbinger plans to unfold my fate."

"Fate is ever a surprise to me. Tomorrow we all work."

First nodded from across the room. Lady Zona sighed. Darkfall had yet to end. She had grown used to company in her bed. She sympathized with Harbinger's plight all those long lonely months.

"How hard it must have been for you." Lady Zona spoke her thoughts aloud.

"It was not easy. Especially then, but everything passes."

Marlin watched the troops. They executed the maneuver with proficiency. The Sarnese troops finished a hair's breadth ahead of the Masfin soldiers. The Masfin troops were ready. The reports from the border were confused. The Llwegan army appeared. The Llweganian army disappeared at a moment's notice. Stiefis assured them this was to be expected. Marlin said nothing. Renfrew was convinced his brother knew much more than he ever said.

It was hot here. The weather never changed. Dust settled in every crevice of Renfrew's body. Sweat found minute cuts to torture. Still Sarn troops and the Llweganian trained troops did not complain. It was time.

In the hot sun the tents shone brightly. The generals and the King had gathered to meet to discuss the decision to attack. In their field uniforms the Masfin generals looked strange to Renfrew. He himself must look strange.

He felt strange even after months of training in his gear. The Masfin troops wore heavy armor. They spent an hour each day getting ready for battle. The Sarn protection was lighter but still had the mail shirt and plates on the legs. Only the Llweganian trained Masfin troops disdained armor of any kind. They wore silk underclothes with leather outer coverings. On their heads they wore strange hardened leather hats that shaded the eyes and covered the back of the skull completely. They fared much better in the long hours of training but Renfrew feared for them once battle was engaged. The lack of true armor seemed like a real weakness in battle. Still they refused to change their habits. They insisted they had a better chance of survival in their borrowed plumage.

"The Llweganian troops were spotted yesterday, here. As you know water spouts have been reported here and here. So they have water sources in each of these three areas. Historically they carry with them a thirty day water supply. They don't need to do this now but I guess Harbinger does it still."

"They have to return for water sometime. Scout the three lakes."

"We have tried. They are jealously guarded by the area residents. They are known as the Wells of Harbinger."

"Tell them who you are. Tell them why we need to stake out the area."

Renfrew heard the directive. He saw Stiefis' grim expression.

"You don't understand about the value of water in the desert. She has given them water in return for its protection. They can use as much of the water as they need as long as it's there for her when Harbinger returns. That tie is very strong."

The wind finally worked free the tie of the tent. As Stiefis finished speaking the tent flap flew outward. The bright sun flooded the tent. Hot air swept into the tent carrying with it dust. Every eye in the tent watched the dry earth swirl in before a hand grabbed the flap back into place.

Renfrew blinked. This was not Masfin.

"Still send scouts. Some will make it. We will still get some information. Raise up the population against invaders. Agitate."

Stiefis sighed. He did not want to answer with the truth. The Sarn would not waste lives in a low survival situation. Information was not more important than the cost. They were willing to fight in raids. They could fight in battle but rarely did the Sarn confront any enemy head on unless they had no choice. Even now they did not plan to be in the forefront of any battle. The Masfin troops were the safest choice for scouting duty but Stiefis did not trust those who had served beside Harbinger to spy on her. The other

Masfin soldiers did not know the country, did not speak the language.

He looked at the group of commanders dressed in leather. He stared into each man's eyes. They were bland, calm, and almost blank. He could not read them at all. He could not trust them. That was very clear to him. They did not accept the Sarnese judgment of the situation. The Llweganian trained troops were with the Masfin army because their oaths required their presence; that was all. Would it be enough to hold them?

Wind Rider nodded in agreement. Petron held his hand over the nearest lake. He lifted his hand to see the entire plan more clearly.

"Do not forget: this is very important; do not ever cross into Masfin. Stay this side of the border at all times. Our enemy is Sarna. Concentrate on Sarnese soldiers. Don't allow yourselves to be vulnerable to Masfin troops. Defend yourselves against them but attack always the Sarn."

Jeffeaux watched the commanders leave. He waited until the only people left were Harbinger's guard.

"There is no need to limit yourselves on my account." The tone was fretful, sarcastic.

"I do not. Everything I do has a purpose. You are under no obligation to me."

"That I know. I also believe you will not tell me why you have given this order."

"That belief is a true belief. Now I do have some work for you."

It was cold. The dry air burned her skin. On the horizon the thin line of light announced dawning. Jeffeaux shifted beside her. He stayed without urging. At times he thought to protest but those moments rarely lasted. Harbinger reached to lean lightly on his arm. Automatically he took her weight.

"I know you will find this odd but I need you to go to my home away from home. Discover if First is ready to proceed with the rest of the proceeding."

"I'll leave you as soon as you wish."

"Good. You may bring Junla, Marma and Ilissa back with you. Jeffenza will have to remain in First's care. I do not have time to be bothered with her now."

"I'd as soon leave all my family with First."

"I think Junla would enjoy being here. You could use the company as you aren't speaking to your mother right now."

Jeffeaux was tempted to turn his back on Harbinger. Years of manners restrained him. He glared off to one side.

"I'll ask Junla if she wants to come."

"Do that. Your mother gave you life, don't forget that. You owe her some consideration."

Silence answered her. She tightened her grip on Jeffeaux's arm until he could not ignore her. He turned a blank stare towards her.

"I feel somewhat responsible for this state of affairs."

"As well you should. I believe it is the sole influence of your example that has my mother acting in this unseemly manner."

"I have more husbands than your mother but you speak to me."

"You are not **my** mother. I don't agree with your living situation. I can't hold you responsible because you never had any other example. My mother grew up with different values."

"Do you mean to tell me that sex with many partners outside of commitment is appropriate but not inside a commitment?"

"No."

"You and your sister Jeffenza both have had many partners but never made a commitment."

"I am being hypocritical and have double standards but what I do or what my sister does cannot be compared with the behavior expected from my mother."

"Ah, as long as you understand that about yourself I can be content. I need commitments that are ironclad. Your mother has bound those men to her in a commitment I can trust. Your mother has bound them to her beyond betrayal. I am relieved that she has found some compensation for her compassion."

Jeffeaux clenched his teeth. He did not want to forgive his mother or to be reconciled with her. He wanted to hold on to his resentment. He could not envision her as a sexual person. He felt Harbinger's hand slip away from his arm. He turned his head in time to watch her stride away from him. He watched for a moment as the rest of the camp readied for battle. Then he turned towards his tent. He had a job to do.

Harbinger drew a deep breath. The dry air stung the inside of her nose. She smiled. She liked to have an edge to her battlefield.

She looked around her tent. Bernath and Serjanus waited for her. She kissed each lightly on the mouth. Outside the tent Mandul and Wittlar waited with the horses. They would stay by her throughout the fighting. She had missed this companionship during her long sojourn in Sarna. The scouts had reported the Sarn and Masfin positions as of the fall of Darkfall. She looked at the terrain trying to envision the picture of the enemy as it had been reported. Bernath rode to her right. He turned to accept a message from a runner.

"The Masfin lord has left the camp."

"Good."

"I hope he will return." Harbinger smiled at Mandul. He rode on her left hand. He was one of her three left-handed husbands. Harbinger chuckled. Jeffeaux would have been scandalized to know that right or left-handedness had been a consideration for choosing a husband.

"He will. It would be too much effort to have to defend himself if he went back to Masfin. Anyway, he is curious. He will need to know the outcome of this venture."

Harbinger reined in her horse to the left. She rode in silence until they topped a rise. In the morning light she saw the armies spread before her. Her troops were held back. They waited just behind her. On both ends of the ridge her archers waited. She raised her hand. The great bows rose in unison. The steel tips of the arrows gleamed in the rising sun. She dropped her hand. There was a loud twang as the bows loosed. She watched the arrows glide through the air.

Below her the armies raised their shields over their heads. As they lifted their shields Llweganian archers, hidden in the hillside rose from the gathered brush. They fired into the exposed targets. She regretted the loss of the front row of Masfin soldiers, but they were not badly damaged by the attack. A few were weeded out and the generals were shaken by the surprise but no real damage had been inflicted. There was a scrambling as the Masfin commanders flinched at the surprise. The Sarn held their ground. The Llweganian trained Masfin held theirs as well.

"Ho-O." Harbinger called to her trumpeter. She responded immediately. The sound of the horn echoed through the air. Now the arrows were lit. The archers did not aim at the soldiers. They

aimed at the ground near the Sarnese soldiers and the regular
Masfin troops. Some fell uselessly to the ground. Others hit their
targets. They burned a moment then thin lines flashed. To put out
the fires the troops would have to break ranks. None did. Those
pale lines glowed for a heartbeat then the casks buried under
ground caught fire. Huge explosions rocked the battlefield.
Harbinger called again.

There was a rush of sound. The terrain was filled with
Llweganian soldiers. Harbinger urged her horse down the slope.
Her sword swung free of its scabbard. Wind rushed in her face.
She saw nothing except her goal. She would fight half the day.
Then she would withdraw to assess the battle. The troops she
wished to avoid killing were easy to spot. They sported their
borrowed uniforms still. She felt her mouth curl into a half smile
as she thrust down into the infantry around her horse. She swung
her booted foot into a face. Her blade slashed through an exposed
throat. Serjanus passed through her line of vision. He pushed the
crowd back from her. She pushed left.

Always she moved left. The quarry moved little. She could see
the sun flashing on the Sarnese helmets. The Masfin regular
soldiers glowed in their metal casings. Harbinger tried to see how
deep the Sarnese lines were. Then she noted the sun's position:
time to leave. She hated leaving the battle in mid-swing but she
had to see how the fighting was progressing. She reined her horse
around. Her escort turned with her. They fought back through the
lines. Then they were in a zone of quiet just beyond the fighting.
She urged her mount up the steep slope. At the crest Harbinger
turned. Her senses had been right. She had ridden farther to get
back. Her troops had pushed the attackers back towards Masfin.

Time to break off the attack; her targets had moved beyond her
reach. She signaled the withdrawal. Her army began its orderly
retreat. The opposition took advantage of the weakening in her
attack. They pushed slightly forward. Then they met the
Llweganian line again. Her forces fought until the allied armies
withdrew. Again she drew back. It took three tries on the allied
armies' part before they realized they could not follow the
Llweganian army. They could hold what they had but they could
come no closer to Harbinger. By dawn Harbinger and her army
were gone.

Stiefis surveyed the empty field. He listened to the Masfin generals crow over the withdrawal of Harbinger. He knew better. She had not been chased from the field. She had left willingly. For some reason Harbinger had decided to break off the engagement, some reason of her own.

"She is not so fearsome. Not even a day's fighting and she runs away."

"She did not run away: she left."

"It's the same thing."

Stiefis turned to face his conversational partner.

"No, it isn't. Her forces had moved ours back easily. She could have pushed us forever. She chose to leave for some reason. She never does anything without a reason."

"The reason was she could not handle us."

"She was handling us with ease. We need to know the reason."

"Women never have reasons for half the things they do."

Stiefis looked into the relatively smooth face of the Masfin general. Fool, he thought. He is probably easily deceived by his wife. Without saying another word Stiefis walked away. He strode angrily toward his father's tent. No wonder Harbinger had stolen the Masfin army: those fools did not deserve to head an army. No wonder that army stayed tied to her in some way. She had been the best leader they had ever served under. Why, why had she turned back?

Weirhass' tent was filled with silence. Stiefis eased in the opening. He glanced at the sole occupant. His father's head was bent. Food sat at his elbow. Stiefis grabbed a leg of fowl. He chewed slowly as he thought.

Renfrew stuck his head through the opening. Stiefis waved him into the tent. Renfrew entered dragging his brother with him. Weirhass finally lifted his head. He surveyed Marlin and Renfrew.

"We should send out cavalry to watch her. We cannot wait for her to choose the battlefield." Weirhass tone was of a wearied elder best by over anxious youngsters.

"We should send mixed units so our soldiers can learn the terrain." Marlin added a reasonable suggestion raising him in Weirhass' eyes from stubborn insubordinate to trainable insubordinate.

Weirhass looked directly at Renfrew.

"Yes, I'll speak with my fellow commanders to recommend such an action. We must be careful of her, we must be very careful of her." Renfrew answered the direct stare from Weirhass.

Renfrew shook his head. He did not understand the Sarnese fear of this woman. She was a capable leader, he had to admit but their combined armies would easily defeat her.

"Do **you** think she is running away?" Renfrew watched his brother's face as Stiefis posed the question. Renfrew had brought Marlin just for this question but, he did not want Marlin drawn into any treasonous behavior. He felt disaster lay ahead where Marlin was involved.

"No she is simply leaving. Whatever her objective was today she achieved it. She'll be back." Marlin did not even look away from Stiefis. Marlin continued to watch the Sarn's face. Stiefis finally looked away first. Marlin remained silent. Renfrew gritted his teeth. He watched the faces around him. He wanted to be sure no one showed any sign of suspicion. Renfrew knew his fear of unwarranted suspicions was unhealthy; but he couldn't shake the feeling of doom.

Marlin sighed. He imagined the scene beyond the hills. Before there had been shades of grey but the shades were dark enough to know where right and wrong were. Now all he saw was one grey. More and more Marlin's tie to his brother kept him from going home. Only that tie kept him here. Home had become over that hill. That tie might as well be useful.

Marlin signaled his wish to join the scouting parties. A frowned gathered on Renfrew's face. He ignored the signs. Better to be scouting than sitting with the generals. Can't lead from the rear.

Harbinger pushed her hair from her face. The wind pulled at the tendrils. She should cut it again. She had let it grow since she had entered Masfin. Her helmet would fit better if her hair were cut. She pushed it back again. The problem was that the longer she left it the more attached she became to it. She shoved it away again. Wittlar brought a tie. His fingers moved through her locks braiding them. She lifted a hand to pat his busy fingers.

Harbinger focused on the maps. All her opponents' maneuverings had tried to pull her into Masfin. She would not go. They wanted Sarna. Some of them did. So the allied armies would have to come to her eventually. Meanwhile she dug trenches and built fortifications. She controlled water sources and the production of crops. Her grip on Sarna strengthened as they tried to entice her out of the country. She was not happy. Lady Zona touched her hand. Harbinger turned her head.

"A message has been sent from First. The testing has been successful. The articles of Repudiation are being drawn up. First wishes to wait until the child is born before delivering the articles."

"Good for them. How are the Articles delivered?"

"A priest of Kersai delivers them to the husband."

Harbinger smiled thoughtfully. She cast a sideways glance at Lady Zona.

"We will be showing your husbands more adventure then they had ever thought of when they became priest."

Lady Zona nodded. She stood quietly. Her hands rested in her sleeves.

"How does your daughter fare?"

"The same, she has not learned compliance."

"I had not looked for miracles. Jeffeaux did well in his mission. He returned in good time."

Lady Zona smiled shortly. She returned to her letter. She snorted inelegantly. Harbinger frowned in question. Lady Zona did not even look up from her correspondence. Harbinger touched her elbow lightly.

"First does not question your judgment in having Jeffeaux remove my wards as well as Junla. She welcomes your trust and belief in her abilities, however, Jeffenza might have benefited from a familiar face being left behind."

Harbinger laughed. "I'll take her suggestion under consideration. After all First is an honored member of our Household; we should take her advice seriously."

"Not immediately, we should let Jeffenza stew awhile. When First reaches the absolute limit of her patience and skill then we can decide."

"I will trust your judgment completely Lady Zona."

"Send Ilissa. Junla will keep Jeffeaux in line. He will not abandon her. Marma, she is good company of Junla."

"When the time comes, it will be as you have said. That will give First a break."

"We won't be able to call her 'First' for much longer."

"Too true. See how they are moving?"

Lady Zona was lost. Then she noticed the path Harbinger was drawing on the map. The long finger was steady and calloused.

"They are massing for an attack. Do they expect you shall walk right into them?"

"No, that is why I am planning to do it. But I will only seek out that path that bulges over the border; if it is the Sarn army doing the bulging. I doubt the Sarnese will allow themselves to be so exposed."

"Using the Masfin as shields are they?"

"I would if I were Sarn. The Sarn have fewer men. They can burn up the Masfin soldiers cutting down my numbers without reducing their own. I have no interest in affecting the size of the Masfin army so I will concentrate all my efforts on the Sarnese. This avoids loss for me on efforts that gain me nothing."

"Your plan requires more planning than simply attacking whoever attacks you."

"Spending time planning is better than spending time training new soldiers."

The household was very busy. Jeffenza had watched the comings and goings with an eye for an opportunity. She had become quite adept at moving with her shackles. She had spent hours practicing her gait. She did not think she could manage to remove them. Her signs of slavery were well constructed but if she moved very carefully she could gain some freedom. Her goal was to be able to walk over the mountains.

She had some freedom now as the household prepared for the birth of the child. The birth of the child: the way everyone spoke of this pregnancy was ridiculous. They spoke in hushed, revering tones of this godling being born. Lucky for her, their preoccupation might give Jeffenza the opportunity she needed. Jeffenza sniffed.

Ilissa stood in the doorway. Her dark eyes studied Jeffenza. Her hair hung in a simple braid down her back.

"How the mighty have fallen," Jeffenza whispered the words.

"Funny, I was thinking the same thing."

"I cannot change my allegiances so easily."

"Come, come now, I have seen you go from one bed to another in the same night."

"This is a matter of loyalty to my country."

Ilissa bent her body until her face was close to Jeffenza's. Her bland expression was newly learned. Jeffenza almost admired the control Ilissa was exerting on her features.

"Somehow I doubt that. If I did let you go, where would you go? What would you do with your freedom?"

"I would go home. I would tell the King everything I know."

"Which isn't much. Your only value to Masfin is how the threat of violence on your person would influence the Harbinger's decisions. Your value rests solely on your value to Lady Zona and Jeffeaux. The further you separate yourself from them the less your value becomes."

Jeffenza shifted on her seat. The damp of the stone seeped into her flesh. She did not like the gleam in Ilissa's eye. She had to get to Masfin. She could only defeat the enemy from Masfin. Rotting here got her nowhere.

There is nothing so easy as manipulating a stubborn fool. Ilissa smiled at a spot over Jeffenza's head. After a week of lending Jeffenza company, Ilissa had begun to formulate a plan. She left Jeffenza. She needed to consider her choice longer.

Third waddled into Ilissa's line of sight. The smiling women nodded to each other. Ilissa wondered if she should wait until after the Articles of Repudiation were delivered. Jeffenza would not think to mention Third's pregnancy to anyone. Months in Sarna and Jeffenza still had no concept of Sarnese traditions and values. Ilissa grinned. Finally there was something she did better than Jeffenza.

Since childhood Jeffenza had sung better, danced more gracefully, conquered more men than Ilissa. Now, here Ilissa had excelled. Ilissa was in the position of privilege while Jeffenza sat in disgrace. She wanted Jeffenza to remain in Sarna so Ilissa could rub Jeffenza's nose in her triumph; but, Jeffenza would be more use in Masfin.

The Masfin would never harm Jeffenza. Lady Zona knew this. The Sarnese might try but they would risk the alliance with Masfin once they threatened a Masfin woman. Only Jeffeaux might lose his head enough to believe any threats against Jeffenza. That was the variable: could Jeffeaux be controlled? Harbinger had controlled him well so far. Ilissa would trust in Harbinger's talents and strength.

First came to stand by Ilissa.

"First."

First nodded towards Ilissa. "How do you find my charge?"

"As she has ever been. Jeffenza is a good example of why discipline is a proper tool in the formation of character."

"You came from that same Household."

"Ah, but I had loss to mold **my** character: loss of position, loss of opportunity, and loss of family shape you into a different person. You have to be flexible to survive. I do loss well by now. A door doesn't close but a window opens. I am always looking for that window. Jeffenza is obsessing on the door."

"She won't open it on my watch."

"Don't be so quick to promise that. Letting the door close behind her might open up several windows."

First frowned at the statement. Then she saw the statement. She smiled wryly.

Jeffenza did not like being the focus of so much attention. She watched First and Ilissa speaking. She could not hear them but they could mean her no good. She bent her head. She did not want them to think of her at all. If she could become a nonentity, then she would have more freedom. A drift of sound reached her. The words became clear.

"If she were to escape, she would die in the wastelands. Jeffenza is not stupid, only ignorant and helpless. She won't try to leave." Ilissa turned towards the house. First turned with her. Jeffenza watched them leave. Ignorant was she? Helpless was she? She had been brought across that wasteland to get here. She knew her way back.

Once she was back in Masfin she would laugh the last laugh. She would leave too, once she got out of these shackles. She **was** weak. Everything in her life depended on this or that happening first. If she were truly strong she would just go shackles and all. She would need water. She could carry it. Tomorrow, tomorrow she would go. At first light she would go into the wasteland.

Jeffenza struggled with the water skin. She had to cut the straps then retie them so they would hang over her shoulders despite her bound hands. She never knew how heavy water was. She had slit her boots to fit around her shackles. In the dark of dawn she slipped out into the wilds.

"You can't let her die in the desert."

Ilissa considered the shadow at the edge of the compound. She turned to the taciturn Llweganian soldier waiting in the doorway.

"Watch her. Don't let her die. Report back when she is safe."

First settled against the window frame.

"This will add stress to the situation."

"Yes, the Masfin will never allow harm to come to her. The Sarnese will be pushing for threats to her to move Jeffeaux. This could be a good thing."

"Jeffeaux can be controlled?"

"I wouldn't tell him. I would say they are lying, that their threats are a trick; or to downplay her value to reduce her danger. Harbinger will find the right way. She has controlled him pretty well so far. Whatever, Jeffenza is a liability here requiring resources and energy. Let her go."

First shook her head. "I still can't see Jeffeaux being controlled on this issue."

"There is always Junla. Somehow, though, I don't see him going against Harbinger."

"And you have just avenged yourself for thousands of petty slights and malicious hurts."

"You think? Whatever my motivation the action is sensible."

She had forgotten how hot the desert was. The dust and wind caused her great difficulties. She had drunk her water too fast so now thirst stalked her as well as the wild animals. If only she had not been hanging down for most of the ride, she would have remembered the route taken. Her only guide was the sun. Even the stars could not help her. So Jeffenza walked in the heat of the day and suffered through the cold of the night when she should have been moving.

"You were sent to keep her company; not to let her loose in the desert." Jeffeaux paced as he yelled. Ilissa sat quietly on the pillows piled on the rug. She sipped complacently from her wine goblet. Jeffeaux wanted to smash something. He knew the Dragon would not turn aside for consideration of his sister. He knew he was helpless to protect Jeffenza from anything now.

"No Masfin general will allow any harm to come to Jeffenza. The Sarnese will push for her use as a weapon. Of course she is only useful as a weapon if she lives and you believe she lives. So all in all she is more useful as a tool to drive between the Masfin camp and the Sarnese leaders. And she will be happier in Masfin than she was with us." Ilissa placed her empty goblet carefully on the rug under her body.

"My only concern is that she might mention the preparation of the Articles of Repudiation." Lady Zona spoke from behind Ilissa. Light danced on Ilissa's hair as she moved to face the new speaker.

"My pardon Lady Zona but I don't think Jeffenza paid any attention to the Household activities. A pregnancy would hold no interest for her. If no one asks she won't think to mention it."

"You have gambled on that assessment. I hope you are right."

Lady Zona did not want her lending of her husbands to go for naught. She had not thought the act of sharing her three husbands would bother her so. She tried to be as relaxed about the gift as her husbands were about sharing her with each other but she had developed such a sense of ownership it surprised her. She had not felt this way with her first husband; though he most likely had felt that way about her. Her feelings of being married were so different this time around.

"Just the trek through the desert could kill her."

"I sent guards. She will be safe through her journey."

Harbinger touched Jeffeaux's shoulder. "If a threat is made against Jeffenza I myself will go for her. I promise."

"Why should you? She has no value to you."

"She is your family. I will go for her. I promise. Do you accept my word?"

Jeffeaux sighed. He remained still under Harbinger's hand. If she promised him, she would do it. "This is your fault. I told you I wanted her here."

"Yes, you did. I accept responsibility for this turn of events. Masfin is probably a good place for Jeffenza right now. It might become dangerous. It might remain safe. I cannot tell."

"With you she would be safe."

"Yes, but that is not what we have now. She would not be happy here. Will she be happy in Masfin?"

Jeffeaux sighed.

"Yes. You are right. If she can be in Masfin she will be happy. Being under your protection would keep her safe but miserable."

"So let her remain in Masfin for as long as she is relatively safe. Say the word and I will retrieve her. I promise."

Jeffeaux nodded. Ilissa felt her heart smile. Harbinger had been so deft and sincere in her words. The plan had been a success.

Jeffenza woke to confusion. She remembered falling down the ravine. She remembered waking at the bottom of the ravine then being unable to move. Where was she? She must have taken a blow to the head. She was no longer in the ravine. How had she gotten out? Why couldn't she remember? It must have been a blow to the head.

She stared at the edge of the shadow. The sun was creeping by, she had to go. She could not move after Darkfall. Darkfall, she hated it. It brought cold and danger. Things moved and rustled. She could not see the things that moved and rustled. Unlike her captors she could not move after Darkfall. This time she had to cross the waste under the full glare of the sun at all times.

Jeffenza rose to her knees. Under her hand the dirt was sharp. Carefully she heaved up her body. Air left her lungs in a deep sigh. The world tilted, wavered then held still. Gingerly she moved into the sunlight. Quickly she stepped back into the shade. She picked her way through the rocks running her hand against the outcropping as she went. The support and the shadow of the rocks were heavenly but not lasting. Soon she was out in the glare of the sun tramping over the uneven ground of the waste.

Her mouth became coated and sour. The horizon faded then held still. She continued to have difficulty focusing her eyes. She had to pause often to recall where she was going. She kept forgetting which direction she wanted and where it was. She began to repeat directions to herself. Follow the sun until it hits the top. Follow the sun until it hits the top. Wait out the top. Wait out the top. Keep the sun over the right shoulder. Keep the sun over the right shoulder.

Renfrew watched the moon rise with a jaundiced eye. He waited for his brother to pass by him. Marlin was slated to lead a scouting party in the morning. Renfrew wanted to ride with the patrol. Renfrew had been dropping hints for weeks about joining Marlin on maneuvers but Marlin had refused to take a hint. This time Renfrew would leave no room for interpretation. He would inform Marlin that he would come.

The more Renfrew felt excluded the greater he had to push to be included. He also had many questions that could only be answered by going. His greatest question would remain unanswered until someone told him. Why did Marlin and his fellow officers keep so separate from the rest of the Masfin contingent?

Renfrew heard no step. He felt no air but suddenly he knew he was not alone. Marlin stood quietly before him.

"You needed to speak with me, sir?" Renfrew winced at the formality. When they had first joined the service Renfrew had spent useless hours ordering Marlin to address him as sir. Now the small word represented all Renfrew's unease and uncertainty.

"I will be riding with your unit tomorrow."

"We are leaving now, sir."

Renfrew nodded. "I thought as much. I am ready."

"Very well, sir."

The sound of metal echoed in the night as Renfrew's horse was led forward. Marlin winced at the noise. He considered the animal. Then he shrugged. Renfrew looked at his mount. He saw nothing out of place. It was not until he had ridden some miles that he noticed he was the only rider making noise. The sound grew in his ears. He began to envision his demise while the rest of the company moved along, leaving his body by the side of the trail.

As the sky began to lighten Marlin slowed the pace. He drew the unit to a halt. Renfrew shifted in his seat. His impulse was to question why they stayed so still; but, for the first time that Darkfall he was as quiet as the rest of the riders and he did not wish to break the silence. The sun was fully up before Renfrew saw the riders. They wended their way to the group. Each paused by Marlin, handing him something Renfrew could not see. Then they fell into line in the rear.

Marlin rubbed his thumb across whatever was in his hand. Then he tucked the whatevers into his belt pocket. Without a word Marlin began to move. Renfrew followed. The troop moved slowly through the rocks. They came to a large grouping of rocks. Over the increasingly loud din of his horse's harness Renfrew heard the sound of water. His nose twitched at the smell.

Everyone dismounted. Quiet shifting was the only sound. Finally Renfrew noticed that he was the only rider to use tack and saddle. Everyone else rode with only a blanket. Renfrew considered the terrain they had traversed. The ability to stay on a horse without saddle was an admirable skill. Was this a Llweganian taught skill? Renfrew thought he remembered the Llweganians using saddles in battle. He opened his mouth to pose the question then thought better of it. He dared not break the fragile peace with his brother.

Out here, with his unit, Marlin lost the closed off air he had in camp. Here when he said nothing Marlin oozed information. Every member of the patrol worked quickly and efficiently while Marlin studied the rocks of the surrounding area. Even Renfrew knew Marlin was deciding the next day's actions. Watches were posted, plans set and no word was spoken. In the shade of the rocks Renfrew curled into a ball. He drew his blanket over his head. The heat of the sun did not yet reach the shadows.

Renfrew drifted into sleep on the thought that he had not been assigned a watch. Did Marlin not trust him? Were they intending to leave him here in the shadows? Renfrew almost jerked awake at that thought but his tired body overrode his worries.

Marlin reached to shake Renfrew awake. A deep sigh left him as he looked at his brother. The he touched Renfrew gently. Eyes as green as his, opened. Marlin jerked his head once towards Renfrew's saddle horse. He pushed a cup of water and strip of field rations into Renfrew's hands. When Renfrew used the water to rinse his teeth Marlin frowned at the mouth ready to spit out the water. Renfrew's eyes caught with Marlin's; then Renfrew swallowed the fluid. Marlin turned away from his brother to survey the troop.

Renfrew mounted his horse groggily. He had never woken easily. He swallowed the rest of his water. He had to remember that they were in a dry place. Water was not wasted.

All he heard during the night was the sound of his saddle. The creak of the leather as he shifted grew until an entire band seemed to be playing. But Renfrew couldn't abandon the tack. He would be leaving a clue for the enemy. He couldn't ride through this terrain without it anyway.

Marlin watched his brother settle into his seat. The creak of the leather was music to Marlin's ears. Any Llweganian patrol would hear the patrol a mile away out here. Marlin did not want to meet any Llweganians. He did not want to be in the position of having to report on his former allies. He missed belonging with them.

Ten days they would be out here wandering in the wastes. At least the second day was almost over, or Darkfall. Marlin raised his hand. There was breathing that was not his patrol. He turned his head slowly.

The slow steady breathing of a sleeping creature had caught Marlin's attention. Few creatures slept after dark in this waste. An injured or ill animal could be dangerous. Marlin motioned his troop back. He gestured the rear guard in the direction of the sound.

There was a snuffle as the breathing was interrupted. For a moment the night was filled with the sound of motion. Then the guard reappeared. They came carrying a human animal. In the lightening air Marlin could see that the person was smallish. Long hair flung everywhere as the captive tried to break the bruising hold of the soldiers. Bright eyes landed on Renfrew. The struggle stopped. Marlin considered the dark eyes. He sighed deeply. He could guess who she was. No Sarn female would wander this far into the waste. No Llweganian would be so attired. Neither Sarn nor Llweganian would have slept during the night. Only a Masfin female would be here under these circumstances. The Masfin females Marlin knew were in Sarna belonged to Lord Jeffeaux. Here was one of those women. Cut loose. The only reason she would have been cut loose was she was too much trouble to be of any value to the Dragon. So she must be more useful away from the Dragon.

"Do you think she is a Sarnese woman?" Renfrew was staring as the woman.

"No."

"Llweganian then?"

"No."

"What other women are out here?"

"None, only this one, let her free." Marlin spoke to the soldiers.

The captive ran straight to Renfrew. She tried to clutch his stirrup. Renfrew drew his sword. Marlin stopped the downward swing with a strong hand.

"I am the Lady Jeffenza. I am cousin to the King. Take me to him."

Renfrew raised his startled eyes from the begrimed face to his brother. Then he pushed the woman away so forcefully that she landed in a heap.

"Impertinent fool."

Marlin patted his horse's neck.

"I suspect she is telling the truth brother."

Jeffenza looked from the traditionally garbed Masfin who did not believe her to the Llweganian seeming man who did.

"It is true. I have escaped from the clutches of Harbinger and crossed the waste alone."

"That I do not believe."

"You don't see anyone else do you?"

Marlin did not answer. He watched the shadow fade into the landscape. He glanced at his lieutenant. The knowing air in their exchange was one of the many barriers Marlin knew existed to his return to the Masfin army. He had been Llweganian too long now.

"Wellin, take the Lady Jeffenza up behind you."

Jeffenza gripped the waist of the soldier. She tried to snuggle against the back that protected her from the wind of the waste. The spine was perfectly erect. The muscle was rock hard. There was no give in that back. All Jeffenza could do was hang onto the few inches of material that hung at the solid waist.

Jeffenza glanced at the rising sun. They had turned towards Masfin. She would be home soon. A deep sigh left her. She was saved: saved by these strange men, this strange troop.

Renfrew stared at his brother. He waited for the sign to stop. None came. They did not ride back the way they had come. They did not stop to eat or to drink. Through the heat of the day they rode. Renfrew felt the drain such an activity took from him. He felt the heat grow inside his attire. None of his discomfort was mirrored by the troop. Even the female seemed better dressed for this activity than he.

Jeffenza wanted to complain about the pace. She wanted to say: stop, I am tired. But she wanted to get home more. She wanted to bathe, to sleep in a bed, to be away from her captivity. So she hung on for dear life to that hardened soldier. Finally they stopped to rest the horses.

"Where are we going?"

"Back to camp. I am sure Lady Jeffenza has some things of interest to relate." Marlin was glad to have an excuse to return to camp. Every time he went out on patrol he was careful not to find the Llweganians. He did not want to bring any information that would harm the Llweganians back to the Masfin generals or Sarnese leaders. Marlin was positive that Lady Jeffenza would have nothing to say that could betray Harbinger or the lady would be dead.

"This isn't the way we came."

"No."

Renfrew stared at the stars above the rim of the rock outcropping. He had never imagined he would feel that he knew his brother less after this time together. He had thought his brother exactly as he had ever been but with an attitude. Now, Renfrew did not know this closed off person. What had happened with the Llweganians?

Jeffenza drank deeply for the first time in days. She guzzled the water until she thought the water sloshed in her stomach. When she thought the water was going to come back up the way it had gone she stopped. She watched the soldiers prepare camp. They said nothing. Even the Masfin said nothing. She didn't care. She had bested that woman. She was going home.

A blanket was offered to her. Jeffenza looked at the material blankly. They were about to experience the heat of the day. Why would anyone offer her a blanket now? She saw most of the soldiers roll up in their blankets at the base of the stones. She copied their actions. As the sun rose on the world she drifted off to sleep.

They returned to camp in the dark. Sentries called out to them. Renfrew answered the calls. Stiefis came out to meet them.

"Did you find something?"

"Yes," Marlin's tone was abrupt. He could never quite disguise his dislike of the Sarn.

"What did you discover?"

"Nothing."

Stiefis clenched his teeth. Then he saw the double riders. He stared at the slight figure.

"Who is she?"

"The Lady Jeffenza."

"Marlin," Renfrew spoke sharply. He did not yet believe the female.

"Brother I promise you she is who she says she is."

Jeffenza looked at the Sarn. She glanced at the brothers. Why was the only one who believed her dressed as her enemy? Then her attention was caught by the group that was approaching; finally a normal sight.

"Your Majesty." Jeffenza executed a deep curtsey. Her head bowed until she almost touched the dirt.

"Lady Jeffenza." Despite her distressing condition she would be recognizable anywhere. Dulled by dust her white blond hair stood out. The dark arches of her brows bracketed her dark green eyes. The oval of her face was marred by bruises but the shape was still there. "You looked tired, cousin."

"I have spent many days returning home Your Majesty. My experience with the enemy was beyond words."

Ranald stared at the chains on Jeffenza's hands and feet. "We hope you will be able to discuss your adventures later. First you must be rested and have those things removed."

"Thank you, Your Majesty." Jeffenza managed this conversation without ever raising her head above the King's knees. Still she could look up at him and yet remain crouched. Stiefis admired the skill it took to maintain that position while manacled and shackled. Renfrew swallowed his surprise. Marlin watched the show with a calculating eye.

"Perhaps she will have some information for us."

Marlin looked at the Sarn with pity. He could not resist stating the obvious. "If she did she would be dead. She would have been killed the first day."

Stiefis frowned. He did not like the implication of the statement. He wanted to ask what Marlin meant. He pictured his wife. He tried to envision her reasoning process. He had never bothered to spend any time with his last wife. This morose underling probably knew his traitorous spouse better than Stiefis did. Stiefis should have seen through her deception. He was an excellent general. He should have anticipated such a move on the part of the Dragon.

Jeffenza heard the short comment. She bridled at the implication that she had not foiled her nemesis.

"That woman wasn't even there when I escaped. Ilissa was there. She had just returned when I seized my chance." Jeffenza stared defiantly at the faces of her audience. Her words had no impact. Marlin raised his eyebrows then nodded at Stiefis as if to say: what was I saying?

"Why would that woman go through the trouble of capturing me only to let me go?"

"How much trouble were you to keep?"

Jeffenza felt her face flush with rage. "She did nothing to keep me. She handed me over to First. First is the one who chained me like this. She's the one who kept me."

Stiefis watched as the sun caught on the glint of her chains as Jeffenza swung them in the air. He had never seen a set of these chains but he knew of them. He knew the working of them.

"Whose ever First the female is, she knows her lore well. The length and strength are correct." Stiefis turned away from the sight of Jeffenza in those chains. Rage flooded his mind. What Sarn female had dared share the ancient traditions with the enemy? Who was giving comfort and aid to the enemy?

"Will no one listen to me?" Anger, despair echoed in Jeffenza's words.

"Come cousin, We will listen to you. Come away from here." Jeffenza turned towards the kind tone of the King. She looked into his calm face. She was home. She relaxed until she lay face down in the dirt before the King. He grasped her elbow firmly. She stumbled as she rose. That steady hand held her safely. She did not look back at her rescuers.

Marlin watched Jeffenza leave. He had wanted to ask her a thousand questions about the Llweganian army. He had wanted to touch base with his ex-comrades-in-arms. He wondered if his former companions were well or dead. Here, among strangers, he couldn't reveal his deepest wishes, especially to that Sarn. He turned away from the group before Renfrew stopped him.

First watched the guard return. She had a rider ready to ride with the message as soon as the message arrived. Third stood by her. The great swell of her stomach brought a smile to First's heart. She raised a hand to smooth the material over the swell of Third's womb. Then she returned to her watch.
"She is in the care of the Masfin. They have turned towards Masfin."
First nodded to the waiting rider. A weight rolled from her. A weight she had not known she carried until the words lifted it from her. First placed a hand on Third's shoulder.
"Now we can concentrate on a healthy child."
"Harbinger will be happy."
"The Masfin who retrieved Lady Jeffenza were Llweganian trained; except one: they were together yet separate."
First paused as the guard spoke quietly. She nodded that she had heard but made no return comment.

Harbinger read the message. She turned the paper over in her hands. Jeffeaux had relaxed once his sister was safe. This letter from First gave her hope. She did not need the Masfin army back. If she could split the Masfin army from the Sarnese army she would have a clear shot at victory.
A warm mouth grazed her neck. The breath was scented with dry air and water.
"Will they kill her to separate Jeffeaux and Lady Zona from us?"
"The Sarn may wish to threaten Jeffenza harm but she is a womb so they might not urge her death. The Masfin powers will not consent. I will enjoy watching this play out."

Petron stared intently into his wife's eyes. "You do not mean to go there?"

"No, no, I am too busy here. I might go for the Presentation of the Articles of Repudiation. I might return with my lost husband."

Petron hesitated. He wanted to argue a moment longer against any action that took Harbinger into the territory of their enemies. He sighed deeply. If she meant to bring Stiefis back he would have to prepare a plan to deal with a reluctant member of the Household.

Stiefis wondered why there was any discussion. True, she was female. Any female had intrinsic value. Even a Sarn could see that Jeffenza's value would increase if she were dead. Her death served as a warning, a lever, a wedge. But, no, these weaklings looked at him as if he had suggested the massacre of children.

"Dead she is more valuable." Even Renfrew looked at him askance. "All right, threaten to kill her."

"Even if Jeffeaux believed Us, Our soldiers would never follow Us if We threatened the life of Lady Jeffenza. She risked her life to return to Us. She has come to Us seeking protection, offering her aid in Our effort. We cannot treat her so cavalierly."

The King spoke in condescending tones. Stiefis opened his mouth. A hard hand knocked him on the back. Stiefis turned to find himself glaring at his father. The ferocious frown on Weirhass' face drew Stiefis' attention. Stiefis stormed out of the tent. The bright sun slapped him in the face. Their weak-willed allies turned stubborn at the most inconvenient times. Anyone could see the advantage of dealing harshly with this female. Even the Llweganians would see the use of eliminating this female. Of course they would. Stiefis turned to face the tent.

Why had they let her go? What use was her presence in Masfin to the Llweganian cause? Was she truly seeking shelter? How had she weathered the desert unaided? Stiefis noted that he had an observer. The Llweganian-trained brother of Renfrew stood watching him.

"Would you say she is a spy?"

"I would never say such a thing."

"Do you ever speak plainly?" Stiefis' irritation and frustration spilled over onto the ready target.

"I thought my diction quite clear."

"Is there any Masfin left in you?"

"I came when my King called; therefore, I am Masfin."

"I don't think you want us to succeed."

"I do want Masfin to be safe."

Stiefis chuffed in impatience. Never an answer to the question, this one was devious.

"Someday you will learn to trust me. Your life will depend on that trust."

"My life already depends on my trusting you."

"Why do I have the feeling that is not a compliment?"

"Because you choose to feel that way?"

"I believe you will take up arms against your own people, your own brother."

"As you have against your own wife?"

Stiefis blinked at the directness of the statement. It revealed a breadth of knowledge Marlin was not wont to display. Then the nature of that knowledge sunk in. Stiefis had not wanted his relationship to the enemy known.

"One could wonder at your presence here as much as at the Lady Jeffenza's return." Marlin spoke in bland tones.

Stiefis felt his skin redden in rage. "What are you implying?"

"Nothing, I imply nothing. I only wonder aloud."

"Always, she is there, everywhere, always."

"Yes, always," Marlin sighed the words under his breath. He would have said them aloud except he knew his tone would have conveyed more than he wished. He should leave his soldiers. He should return to where his inclinations led him. But, he could not leave his soldiers. The training he had received prohibited him from abandoning his responsibilities. He could not lead his soldiers away from their oaths. So here he stayed praying every day that he would not draw Llweganian blood. Almost he had begun to hope he could die in battle. An honorable death would be preferable to this constant state of inner battle.

Renfrew approached them. They turned to watch him. Stiefis tried to display as much sangfroid as Marlin. It was not easy. All of his hopes rode on the success of this venture. Stiefis squinted at Marlin. Didn't Marlin realize that all **his** hopes should be riding on the venture also?

"So, brother, what say you? What is your opinion on the danger of Lady Jeffenza?"

"I believe we can learn a lot from her return." Marlin spoke quietly.

"You think we should interrogate her?"

"No, her return in and of itself says a lot. She is come home; back to her people, her protectors. Why is there any question of her welcome? Is not our oath to protect those unable to protect themselves? She was stolen away from her bed in the middle of Darkfall. She returned to us at great personal risk. We were discussing killing her? Are you comfortable with the places our allies are leading us? A Masfin who would sanction such a choice, is that the country we are fighting to defend?" Marlin glanced at the shadows. "Excuse me, I have duties to fulfill."

Renfrew watched his brother leave. Marlin's words echoed in Renfrew's mind. He pushed the implications away.

"We should at least debrief Lady Jeffenza. She might have some incidental information for us."

Stiefis perked up at the suggestion. He wanted to begin right now but held his peace. He didn't want too much time to pass before he spoke with the female. She could forget an important detail.

Renfrew drew a deep breath. He approached the King calmly.

"Your Majesty, I beg an indulgence."

Renfrew watched his king turn regally to face him. Renfrew wished he had waited a moment before he spoke. He needed very badly to phrase his request properly. But Stiefis was right; memory spoiled.

"We have so little opportunity to observe the enemy. Lady Jeffenza spent months observing the enemy. Even from a distance I am sure she gained some insight that could help us. She is obviously resourceful and very intelligent. She saw things others would not have noticed. I would appreciate some of her time to help us."

Stiefis watched the expressions cross Lady Jeffenza's face. Most likely she had noticed nothing. She did not seem the kind to remember troop sizes or army strengths. She seemed a pampered, spoiled child; yet somewhere hidden in that head there just might be a stray memory that could help him.

"I would enjoy sharing my experiences with your generals, Your Majesty. If I can in any way aid the destruction of that female I would be very satisfied."

Marlin watched his brother escort Lady Jeffenza to her quarters. He felt a presence at his elbow. His lieutenant stood passively watching the formal farewell between Renfrew and Lady Jeffenza.
"We could get lucky and not return from patrol."
Marlin heard the words. He registered the sentiment.
"Maybe it won't be luck or fate."
"We swore an oath to our king."
"We swore nothing to her."
"And yet."
"And yet." Marlin agreed. He fished in his belt pouch. His fingers smoothed the collection there. They slid through his fingers to jostle against each other.
"We are scheduled out at Darkfall."
"At Darkfall then." It was done. Marlin felt the weight of having made the decision slip from him. The stones had been sent out. He had only to wait for them to come back.

Stiefis had heard the list of complaints Jeffenza made. He tried to picture a collection of wives in Sarna that would so betray their country. He couldn't get over the foolishness of the Masfin female. She could not tell him the name of the estate where she had been for several months.
"They were building a bath house when I left."
"A bath house?"
"A building for a communal bath."
"Communal bath?"
Renfrew understood the difference of cultures colliding before him.
"So there was plenty of water."
"Of course, there's a huge lake on the estate."
That cut down the possibilities. Renfrew looked at Stiefis with excitement.
"That woman wanted the bath house so First made sure it got built."

"Why would First do that?" Stiefis was still puzzled by this Sarnese wife.

"They are great friends those two. They knew each other before."

Stiefis stared in true confusion at Lady Jeffenza. The only friends a Sarnese wife had were her sister/wives. Sister/wives, huge lake; Stiefis knew. He **knew** whose wives were aiding and abetting the enemy.

"Before when?" Renfrew voiced his thoughts aloud.

"Before this whole thing. All the women on the estate know that woman. They quote her. When she comes they spend time with her. They know my mother very well. I think they are more comfortable with my mother. My mother likes them more than she likes me. She's so fond of the Sarnese she has taken three of them to husband. Can you believe that? They masquerade as a guard; guards my foot. They trail behind her everywhere. Just like that woman's husbands trail behind her. When my mother rides around with that woman, the ladies where I was stay put. They keep that house ready for her arrival at all times. You never know when she's coming. No one sends advance notice of their arrival. Everyone just arrives and the house is ready for them.

"First would never turn anyone away. Not if they come from that woman. And my brother, Lord Jeffeaux, follows First around like a damned pet. I half expect to see him sweeping the stones from her path lest they bruise her feet."

"Lord Jeffeaux has seduced this woman?" Stiefis could not believe his ears.

"No, no, First doesn't even see him. The experience must be very humbling for Jeffeaux. Everything is that woman for First. All First does is wait for her."

Renfrew shook his head. "I don't understand."

"Neither do I. What do they see in her? It is always her, her, her or that daughter of hers."

"The Dragon has a daughter?"

Jeffenza smiled for the first time since she had sat down. "All she has produced are daughters: eight of them."

"Eight daughters?"

Jeffenza misunderstood Stiefis' meaning. She nodded gleefully. She thought he could not believe the ill-luck of a woman bearing eight female children. Stiefis could not believe that one woman had born eight living children.

"Does she keep them with her?"

"Only the oldest girl is with them. She is in charge of part of the army. Actually I believe she is a general. I don't understand all of the rankings but I believe part of the army belongs to the daughter and part to the mother. I could be wrong. I wasn't allowed to remain with the army for very long."

"Why not?" Renfrew tried to control his disappointment at the knowledge of her limitation.

Jeffenza frowned as she remembered her welcome at the camp.

"I was betrayed by the Liaison Officer. I believed he cared for me. I still believe it." Jeffenza resolutely thrust her memories away. "When that woman found out about our attraction she had me banished to the estate then placed in chains."

Stiefis tried to envision Seven jealous. He couldn't somehow. Especially of this pampered woman. If the story were true, Jeffenza would be dead. Stiefis had no illusions of the enemy. Harbinger viewed Jeffenza as a harmless irritant. Somewhere in the statement was a fact but it was heavily disguised.

Jeffenza was tired. She had answered every question at least twenty times. She wanted to harm Harbinger but she had no patience for endless recounting of what seemed so degrading to her. She raised her hand for silence; then she turned from her questioners. She left her seat without a word.

Chapter 9

Marlin stood in the opening to the outside. He was looking at Renfrew. His guarded eyes watched the scene. Between his thumb and forefinger he rolled a stone. The stone seemed to catch the light oddly. His steps were muffled as he crossed the space to Renfrew. The stone stopped moving. It disappeared into his fist. That fist rose until it was in the air opposite Renfrew's chest. It paused then opened. Renfrew reached swiftly to catch the falling rock. In the action of the catch everyone's eye went to Renfrew. Marlin whirled, then, was gone.

Instinctively Renfrew looked to Stiefis. Then they both rushed outside. There was nothing. Staring at the empty Darkfall Renfrew realized his fist was still clenched. He opened his hand to look at the stone.

"He's gone back."

"We'll say he was lost on patrol. No need to give anyone else ideas. I wonder if any of his men went with him."

Renfrew heard the emotionless words. He stuffed the rock into his uniform pants pocket. The woman Jeffenza described and the one that drew his brother to break with Masfin could not be reconciled in Renfrew's mind.

Marlin met his lieutenant well away from the camp. He took the reins that were handed to him. Marlin nodded a greeting to Wedell, but his eyes did not leave the troop around him. They all stretched their hands for a stone. None held back. None were missing. They were all serious and pale but there. Marlin did not think of the stone he had left behind. He only thought of the one he now doled out. The responsibility he felt increased with every palm he filled. His certainty increased with every hand that closed over a stone.

Marlin had thought himself almost mad to wish to leave his army. He had worried that he had lost his reason because he could no longer keep his promise to his country. He would not excuse his choice with trivialities over the King or generals. He no longer belonged with this army. He could not go back home if he stayed with this army, so he had to go. He would not be returning alone.

Marlin stared at his now empty hand. Then he grasped the reins tightly in preparation of his swing into the saddle. As he swung free of the earth all his questions faded into history. As he settled on the saddle he thought only of the best route to his destination. He knew where he was going. He knew what he would say when he got there.

"Lady, there are riders at the border. They are not ours."
First rose from her seat. She placed a comforting hand on Third's shoulder. Fifth came to take her place. First motioned the sentry out of the room. They walked in silence to the main hall.
"What type of riders?"
"Scouts; one patrol; they are not Sarn."
"Masfin then."
"They are dressed in Llweganian clothes but they are not ours."
"You are sure."
"They are all male."
First thought of her options. The rider would have already left for the main body of the army to report the incursion. Third was close to her time. She could not be endangered now. Their goal was so close.
"Order everyone to the cellars. I want them to think we have left. Have the animals taken to the far pasture. For once I regret that I am such a good housekeeper. Empty most of the food stores. Leave some broken sacks as if we left in a hurry. All the lights must go to the cellars with me. Scatter some dirt on the floors. Move quickly now."
Sweat dripped down First's neck as she moved up and down the stairs trying to create her illusion. Third had gone down first. Fifth stayed with her through the activity. Everyone else was already in the cellars. She had finished her last inspection when First knew disaster had struck. A dark figure stood in the doorway watching her.
He was not old. He stood quietly but not at rest. She folded her hands across her stomach. She waited patiently for him to speak. In the silence she could hear the breath of the horses outside.
He moved slowly as if not to startle her into flight. His hand moved to his waist in a motion that was familiar to her. When he was quite close to her he bowed. On his way back to standing up

straight he reached out to grasp her hands. He smoothed one open
with his gloved fingers. He slipped a stone into her hand.

"Lady," he spoke in clear Llweganian. "We will wait at the
western shore of the lake for your decision. I am sorry we
disturbed you." His eyes looked into hers with only resolve in
their depths. She knew that feeling. He had reached the door
before she realized he had left her.

"We have sent for Harbinger for help. Someone will be here
soon."

"Good."

"We will be moving about gathering up our scattered animals.
Do not be alarmed."

"Understood."

"If you are come to betray her I will ask to be the first to draw
blood."

Marlin turned at the words and the tone. He looked at the woman
closely for the first time. She was not the type he would have
expected to have such deep devotion to a warrior queen. In many
ways she was not unlike the women of his culture: protected,
dependent. Yet she stood before the unknown calmly and
assuredly. She sought to protect her home and household to the
best of her abilities. He would not have bothered to explain to his
brother why he had chosen to come. He might have articulated to
Harbinger why he had come but perhaps this woman would
understand without explanation.

"It would be an honor."

First lowered her head to study the stone in her hand. She knew
the color and size of that stone. She placed the stone in her
waistband. Her fingers brushed her own stone. It was the same
color but larger. She walked to where the soldier seemed to wait
for her decision. She held her larger rock out to him.

"She will come herself."

"I know. This is her Household. I have met your husband."

"Ah." First could not think of anything to say. She had thought
of Stiefis as an adversary for so long now she could say nothing
about him as a husband; or even to ask a question concerning him.

"And I have met the Lady Jeffenza."

"Well, then, you will have a story to tell."

Marlin smiled. A genuine, truly felt smile creased his face for the first time in more than a season. It crinkled his eyes and lightened his mien.

"She had little to say but said it often."

First wanted to cry in relief. Her greatest fear had been that the element of surprise would be lost. She wanted Stiefis to be ignorant of her plans until the moment of her choosing.

"She might have disclosed something of seeming innocence that held greatest importance."

"You mean besides her hate of Harbinger? That is what she spoke of most. Her only other topic was the endless list of grievances she suffered."

First blinked in surprise. "She was well treated. I never had her beaten. She was even guarded in her escape."

"I know; but she does not." Marlin leaned closer to First. He lowered his voice to a conspiratorial whisper. "She found her way without skill, water or help and has no idea how extraordinary an accomplishment that would have been; a walk in the courtyard with some inconveniences."

First raised a hand to hide her smile. She backed away gracefully but without insult.

"She is a fool. She was safe. She would have been honored as her mother's daughter. She could not see. I do not think her brother does either but he is less foolhardy."

"Lady Jeffenza believes her brother has an eye for you."

First was surprised into laughter.

"As if I would want such a one; he would bring me nothing I need. He has neither a strong back nor talent that would help me with my responsibilities. He has no idea about the work involved with privilege."

"Some women find him charming and pretty to look at."

"That's a lot of use at harvest time. I already have a husband who has no sense of duty towards his wives. Why should I take a lover who has a similar bent of attitude? Where was my husband when his enemies invaded this estate? What protection did he send? When one of his wives went missing what did he do? My dependents are safe because I made a choice. I am safe because I understood the need and acted.

"The one who protects me is devious, ruthless, and strange to my way of thinking. She has left protection for me. She will send more protection to me. She will destroy my country yet keep me safe. Where is he? Hiding in Masfin that is where he is. He has not tried once to see how we fare. He has abandoned us."

Marlin stood still. That was exactly it. He knew with a certainty what she would do for her troops. He knew she would tell him straight. If she could do something she would. If she couldn't she wouldn't promise it. It was not an idea or a set of beliefs or a tradition or shared history; it was the leader herself that drew him. Her actions would validate his choice. Her actions in connection with him personally would cement his devotion.

Harbinger watched the troops settle for the night. She was ready to sleep herself. She could hear her bed calling her. War was so tiring. War was for the young she decided as she stretched.

Harbinger had turned into her tent when she heard the hoof beats. They clamored through the camp. Harbinger hesitated. She hoped the sound meant nothing but her senses felt the urgency of the rider. She had no doubts. Her bed would have to wait.

Sweat streamed from the horse's heaving sides. Puffs of air punctuated the night around her. Harbinger reached to receive the stone. The weight rested uneasily in her hand. She stood as her horse was brought up. Petron stamped on his boots behind her. Bernath wrestled into his jacket. Wittlar pulled on his gloves as he went to hold her horse.

Lady Zona appeared in her tent flap. She looked at the group. She wanted to go with them but knew she would be more use with the main army and Jeffeaux. Enough of Jeffeaux, Lady Zona signaled for her horses. Harbinger watched. She made no signal either way. Lady Zona knew trouble was on the estate. She had ties there. She would go to defend those ties.

"You may get bloodied on this one." Lady Zona heard the flat tone.

"I will make sure the blood belongs to the enemy."

Harbinger smiled. Rather, she revealed her teeth in a ferocious expression. Her face did not lift or stretch: it simply glared. Harbinger was pale with emotion or fatigue. Lady Zona did not know which to blame.

"If we are all ready," Harbinger swung into her saddle. Without pause her troop followed her into the night. They rode without guile or stealth. The dust from the horses' hooves created a cloud in the night air. Across the emptiness of the waste the thunder of the hooves echoed and re-echoed. Harbinger's personal guard was augmented by her horse guard. They were all handpicked for their fighting skills. Harbinger did not look to see how Lady Zona was faring on the wild ride; she had ridden out of Deskersai, she could follow on this ride.

Only when Harbinger saw the fires by the lake did she ease up her pace. She stared at the glow of the fire. She called her troop to a halt. She considered the position of the fires along the lake. Harbinger signaled her troop to disperse in a search pattern. She began to circle towards the fires.

Marlin heard the abrupt halt of the horses. He waited at the main fire. She would come. He would wait. He poured himself another steaming cup of drink. The warm moist steam eased his nostrils in the cool dry air of the night. He watched the edge of the lake. The light of the fires danced on the surface of the water. The lake needed fish. He found it strange to have such a body of water and no insects. His shoulder blades itched. It was hard to wait when you waited for a predator.

"First judged you true?"

Marlin turned from the water. In the flickering light of the fire she looked barbaric. Her helmet was decorated with garish designs that caught the light. Her dark attire blended the rest of her into the night so she seemed to be a head floating above the ground.

"She understood."

"What did you explain?"

"Nothing."

"I see."

"I will cross into the Masfin to chase our prey."

"Yes, so will I."

Harbinger swung down from her horse. She grasped Marlin by the shoulder. The strength of her arm pushed him to his knees.

"I will protect you. I will provide for you. I will bear the consequences of your actions."

Marlin frowned. He did not know the proper responses for a Llweganian oathing. He felt the future rush at him.

"I will fight for you. I will die for you. I will follow where you lead."

"Good then. These are your men. We will stay the Darkfall at the house. At first light we will return to the camp."

Lady Zona sat watching the group. Harbinger looked thoughtfully at Lady Zona.

"How are you called?"

"Marlin."

"Marlin, I attach you to the House of Lady Zona. She is of my House. Her word is mine. When she speaks it is as if her words came from my own mouth."

"Lady Zona," Marlin bowed to his new commander. Lady Zona stared at her new responsibility.

"Once we are at the house, I will discuss with you your broad instructions and your narrow requirements."

Lady Zona rode close to Harbinger. She was uneasy about the situation. She did not like to think soldiers, even soldiers dressed as Llweganians had crossed the border so easily. There were many soldiers on the other side who were similarly disguised. As Lady Zona worried over this a shadow immerged from the darkness. Harbinger turned her head towards the new rider.

"I am not pleased that my civilian dependents sent me news of this incursion."

"I did not judge them to be threatening."

"He spoke to First directly. That is too close an encounter. She was concerned enough to send for me. That is too close an encounter."

There was silence for several moments. No excuses were given. Lady Zona realized that there never would be an explanation given. Harbinger had just given a directive.

"Have there been more crossings that you did not feel I needed to know about?"

"Nothing beyond routine scouting parties. We report those." Harbinger sighed.

"What made you think this group was not a threat to my Household? Remember my household, which is in the middle of a very delicate piece of business, political and personal is your responsibility. This is not a prisoner watch."

The silence became strained. "They were not scouting. They made no effort to hide their passing. They did not engage in military actions. My instinct told me they were here on their own business."

"What if that business had resulted in violence on members of my household?"

"The household never was in any danger. The Masfin soldiers have been dead since their crossing. You just gave them their lives back."

Harbinger sighed deeply.

"The First of this House may send for me whenever she wishes, but, I don't want her to ever feel the need to send for me. They must never feel threatened."

"It was my mistake. I made assumptions that were wrong. I must work on my relationship with First so she will trust in me to make the right decision. I forgot that trust and respect are earned."

"I am glad we are clear on this." Harbinger watched the figure melt into the night.

At least tonight Harbinger would sleep in a bed. Third must be near her time. How long before the patrol was missed? The saddle creaked slightly as Harbinger shifted. Ahead the lights shone in welcome. The gates swung wide at their advance. Harbinger smiled at First standing in the doorway.

"You have met our guests."

"I took him on your advice."

First lowered her head to one side. She glanced at the standing troop.

"I knew you would find them useful. You have a way of turning every situation into good use."

"You can never have too many good, loyal soldiers."

First accepted the compliment with a graceful bow of her head. "And he is cute."

Harbinger laughed. "I have one too many husbands as it is. You are about to get rid of a husband. Perhaps you could find some use for a cute man. He is attached to the House of Lady Zona."

Harbinger swung off her mount with equal parts of relief and grace. "I am sorry that you had to suffer this intrusion. I have already spoken to your troop commander about this close call."

"I only did what I thought would be most helpful. Getting my dependents out the line of fire seemed the most sensible thing to do."

"The confrontation could not have been comfortable."

"I did worry for a moment that the troops were all dead. Then I realized that I might have overreacted."

"If a stranger is in your House uninvited, if a stranger is on your land uninvited you are not overreacting to send for me. I have made this clear to the commander."

"That sounds fair to me." First smiled. "I will have to get used to being taken care of this well. I have to learn to trust again after having to become independent."

Marlin could only hear bits and pieces of the conversation. He did not understand the drift but he could catch the good humor. He relaxed. First was not in trouble for having sheltered his troop. In the shadowed light he did not see the blush that crept up First's neck and cheeks and then subside.

"As to your other proposal: the husband we are shedding was a cute man. We don't need another."

"He seems to have other qualities that could recommend him."

"That is true."

Petron had finished directing the disposition of the horse guard. Harbinger followed First into the domicile.

"How is Third?"

"She is in labor. The pains began shortly after we sent to you."

"Wonderful. Third has remained active?"

"Yes."

"Then things should go well. My mother always said the best way to prepare for labor is to labor constantly."

First could hardly contain her excitement. Only her years of training kept her demeanor calm. She could not envision sleeping this Darkfall. She had not wanted to have the added burden of the strangers at the lake. She had not wanted any distraction, but now she was happy that the Masfins had come. Their arrival had brought Harbinger and Lady Zona. First had never witnessed a birth nor had any training in the delivering of babies. A servant from the Temple would attend a birth. Now two women who had borne children were here to help her.

"Where is Third?"

"She is lying down."

"Well, she should be up. Walking is the best thing."

Lady Zona put a comforting arm around First's shoulders. Harbinger drew off her gloves. She tucked them into her belt. Bernath reached to take them from her. She noted the touch absently. He was right. She would not need them now. In fact she should change from her riding dress. Somewhere here there had to be a clean robe. The impulse passed away. She did not have the inclination to attach an action to the thought.

Sweat dripped into Third's eyes. Her face was flushed with her efforts. The rest of the sister/wives were clustered around her. At Harbinger's entrance every head turned to see who had come. Relief eased each face.

"We will need warm water for cleaning Third and the baby. We also need cloths for the same purpose. We will get you out of these clothes, sponge you down, take a walk. Are there any old clean sheets for the bed?" Finally having something to do the women moved with lighter hearts. Harbinger helped Third undress. The warm water created puddles on the floor as the sweat and dirt were gently removed. The pains came steadily. Lady Zona held Third tightly during their crests.

"Don't forget to breathe, Third. Deep breaths are good. Here's my hand." Third held onto a hand from Harbinger and one from Lady Zona. Their free arms crossed behind Third's back. The support was heavenly. She had not thought she could walk. Walking had become so difficult since the baby had dropped. Her breathing had eased with the drop but motion had become a trial. Upright and walking the contractions did not seem so at odds with her body. Around them activity flowed. They were the eye in the middle of that storm of motion.

Harbinger told stories of her deliveries. She told of battles and comical husbands. Lady Zona described the naming ceremonies of her children. Third heard everything but said nothing. She wanted something. She looked around trying to find what she wanted. Harbinger wiped her face with a damp cloth. The moisture trickled into her mouth. She licked the water from her face. That's what she wanted. More water dripped onto her face. She licked it off.

She wanted to push. She didn't want to walk anymore. She had to push. Her hands tightened desperately on the hands that held her. She could not get the words to leave her mouth. Suddenly the bed was before her. She squatted down. She grasped the edge of the bed. Her body seemed to tighten beyond bearing. Then with her head resting against the edge of the bed she felt a huge thing rush from her body into the waiting hands of Harbinger. She listened for the sound of her child. An eternity passed while she waited. Then a cry, not a thin wail, a loud upset cry filled her ears.

"You must push again. There is the baby's cushion to deliver. Then we will clean you up so you can rest." Lady Zona's sensible voice sounded in Third's ears.

"Are the priests here?"

"Yes," First answered. "They have witnessed the birth."

Third pushed with all her might. She felt a soft thing leave her. Then she gave herself over to the care of Lady Zona. Once she was safely in the bed her newborn was placed in her eager arms. She counted fingers and toes. She held the body for a sweet moment before sliding into sleep.

First received the child from Harbinger. She had watched the calloused hands wash the tiny body. She had waited while the new being was swaddled. Her arms felt weak as she cradled the baby. A child, they had a child. First rubbed her cheek against the bald head. She inhaled deeply the scent of brand new person.

"What name have you chosen for the child?"

First heard the question. She recognized the voice of the speaker. They needed the name to complete the Articles of Repudiation. The discussions over the name had taken up most of the pregnancy. Finally the moment had come. No name from the Sarn tradition would grace this child. Male or female they had chosen the same name. This was a child of war, a child of opportunity, the child of Lady Zona's graciousness.

"Ladizona, this is the name we will call our child."

Lady Zona heard the sound. The accent was different. The stress was different but Lady Zona heard her name.

"I am honored."

Harbinger had finished washing her hands. She looked across the room at Lady Zona.

"I have a mission for your troop. How many witnesses are needed for the presentation?"

"The husband, the head of his Household, and since Third is planning to claim estate rights her father and the head of his Household are needed also."

"Weirhass counts twice so that is three particular witnesses. Well enough discussion. The patrol rides to the edge of the camp. No, a scout returns to the camp with a message that those particular Sarnese are needed at a secluded but not threatening spot to debrief some Sarnese refugees."

Marlin listened to his instructions from Lady Zona's calm face.

"No one is to be harmed. Your objective is to deliver the Articles of Repudiation and to return the three priests unharmed to me. Once the Articles are delivered you are to return. Timing is everything. We will begin an action away from your point of insertion as close to the end of the delivery as possible. You will use this disturbance to cover your withdrawal.

"There are some basic parameters you must remember. Avoid combat on Masfin territory. Your targets are always the Sarn troops. If you have to fight Masfin soldiers use the hilt of your sword whenever possible. Disable disarm, avoid Masfin soldiers. The Sarn are always our primary objective."

"Understood. Are these limits special to us from you?"

"No, they are the standing orders of the army. They may change. When they do, so will your orders. If you have no other option of course you must use deadly force. Your safety is our duty. Can you obey these orders?"

"Yes."

"The priests must be returned. The Articles must be delivered and the priests must be returned."

"Understood."

"Good, I wish you well in your journey. Be ready at first light."

Marlin stepped out into the night air. He had not expected to return so quickly to Masfin. He had just settled his leaving with himself and now he was returning. Don't look at it that way. He had been given a mission. Where that mission led was irrelevant. He caught the scent of flowers in the night air.

"Harbinger is sending you and your troop?"

He turned to face First. Shadows surrounded her. He could not read her mood.

"As you have heard."

"We have worked very long and hard for this."

"We shall not fail. This is our first chance to prove our worth and skill."

"This is very important to us and to Harbinger. We will be free. She will be establishing a right, an exclusive right of control."

Marlin tried to puzzle out what these 'Articles' symbolized.

"When it happens you will understand. Remember everything. I will ask you to tell me what you witness."

Marlin knew she had left. He stood in the night trying to develop a plan to get his quarry to meet with him. Renfrew would have known he meant to join the Harbinger's army. His reappearance would cause some close questioning on Renfrew's part. Did Renfrew know all his troops well? Somewhere there had to be a Masfin outfit. Surely there were some pieces that could be assembled to pass muster before they arrived at the camp.

Dassien felt the weight of his duty. It lay as heavily on him as the newly reassumed mail. He had to be sure to do this right. They would not get another chance. He went over and over his message as he rode.

He reached the tent. Sun beat down on him as he waited his turn. Messengers hurried back and forth between the lines and the tent. Dassien peeked through the flap each time it opened. The Sarnese Stiefis was still inside the tent. Finally Dassien's turn came.

"Dassien reporting." Renfrew looked at the scout. He vaguely noted the corps markings.

"My patrol encountered a small band of Sarnese military still fighting in Sarna protecting a group of refugees. They have come to their border closest to the camp. They are requesting a meeting with Weirhass, Hasshaur, and Stiefis. I promised to come to ask."

Renfrew froze. He was not sure he wanted Stiefis to have contact with any independent Sarnese soldiers. He instinctively opened his mouth to deny the request. Stiefis stood. He leaned over the table.

"Who asks for me?"

"They would not give their names. I am not sure even how long they will remain there."

Stiefis rushed from the tent. Sarnese from Sarna asking for him. Finally his people were rising up against the invader. He had begun to despair. What a day, what a day.

His legs could not eat up the ground fast enough. He did not explain to his father and uncle what was happening. He grabbed them to drag them bodily with him.

"Where are you taking us boy?" Stiefis heard the hard words of his uncle but ignored them. He shoved his father and uncle towards the saddled horses. Stiefis frowned when he saw the Renfrew meant to accompany them. But there was no time to argue with the Masfin.

Dassien considered Renfrew with as little enthusiasm as Stiefis had but he too said nothing. He couldn't see how to dump Renfrew right now. A swift blow to the head would solve any problems down the road.

Marlin watched the three priests prepare the site. The earth was swept smooth. A wooden table was unfolded. The legs were planted in the center of the cleared area. Candles were placed on both ends of the table. A cloth of red and blue was centered between the candles. On the cloth a large single paper was unrolled. A dagger weighted the paper at one end; a bottle, the other.

In the distance Marlin could hear hooves pounding the earth. The sentry signaled the arrival of their guests. Marlin directed his troops to take their positions around the clearing. They all stood with swords drawn when the four riders entered the scene. Dassien quickly separated himself from his companions. He rode until he was behind his patrol.

The shortest priest stood over the table. His hands rested on the edge of the table.

"Are you Weirhass father of Stiefis brother of Hasshaur?"

Weirhass was startled into speech.

"I am."

"Dismount and stand by the red candle."

Weirhass found himself standing where he had been directed. His horse was being held by one of the troop.

"Who is Hasshaur?"

"Here"

"You stand by the blue candle."

The stern eyes of the priest landed on Stiefis.

"You Stiefis stand before the bottle."

Renfrew alone sat his horse. He had not taken his eyes from the strange scene. He had not looked at the troops nor had he noticed where they were.

"I am the Will of Kersai. By his Laws am I bound."

Stiefis stared at the hooded head. He waited for the next move in this strange play. Young hands reached to lower the hood from the priest's head. In the bright sun the shaved skull gleamed. The intricate tattoos terrified Stiefis. This was no simple priest. This was no household priest. This was a priest of the highest order of Kersai. The blood rushed from Stiefis' head as the other two priests revealed their heads. This was a grave matter indeed if three such priests should be here.

"The Third wife, the only child of Hasshaur has sought a Testing from the Will of Kersai. Kersai in His wisdom has granted her petition. She has conceived of the Temple of Kersai a child and borne that child living into the world. The birth has been witnessed. These are the Articles of Repudiation requested by the First, Second, Third, Fourth, Fifth, and Sixth wives of Stiefis, son of Weirhass." Stiefis watched the priest raise the dagger into the air. The dagger slashed the priest's palm. Blood dropped onto the bottom of the paper. The bottle of water was raised next. Its contents were poured into the dry dust of the earth.

"The water of your wives has been emptied uselessly as has the water of this bottle." The priest smashed the bottle on the table.

"Your marriages have been shown to be as useful as this broken bottle. I am the Will of Kersai. His Law is my word. You are repudiated." Stiefis felt the air leave his lungs. Pain deep in his chest radiated through his body.

"Hasshaur, your daughter has given birth to a child. She has the rights of a mother of a child of your house. Weirhass, a woman of your house has given birth to a child. She has the rights of a

- 210 -

mother of your house. She has chosen the home she knew as the wife of the repudiated Stiefis. This is within her rights."

Renfrew understood that this was not a good thing that had happened. The ritual, the meek acceptance of the Sarnese generals bothered Renfrew deeply.

"Who are you that come out of Sarna to declare these things? What jurisdiction do you have over these men?"

Stiefis turned to him in a daze. Weirhass frowned at him. Renfrew feared for his life under Hasshaur's glare. This was very important then. Still he wanted answers. He tried to push his way into the circle. Strong hands restrained him. None of the priests bothered to look at him.

"Wasn't the Temple of Kersai destroyed?"

One shaved, decorated head turned to him. One set of forceful, serious eyes looked at him.

"Yes, but not the priests. Just because the Temple is gone does not mean our duties are finished. We have to work twice as hard to help our people now." Stea thought of the long hours he spent with his wife; learning a new language, two new languages, the life of a soldier, all this and keeping the festival cycle for the household on the estates. Brir had to bite his lower lip to keep from smiling. He did not find his new duties onerous at all.

Stiefis wanted to ask why only his first six wives Repudiated him. Then he turned his head sharply. What would his enemy be doing following the customs of his people? She misrepresented herself so she probably didn't consider herself married to him. This never would have happened but for this war. He had one more grudge against his enemy, his wife, his adversary, his deceiver.

Hasshaur did not hear anything except the statement concerning his daughter. He had felt cheated that his only child had been female. True she had brought security to him and his wives when she married Stiefis but she had not established another household with his name. Now she had. His brother had been blessed with two sons and still there were no grandchildren. His daughter had succeeded. Now she had her own household with his name attached to it.

"The child is called Ladizona. She is greatly cherished."

Another girl, Hasshaur did not repine the sex. Kersai had sent the child. There was a reason he had sent a female.

Ladizona, Renfrew felt there was something familiar in the sounds. He watched as the table was cleared, then packed away. He saw Stiefis stand in the shadows clutching his papers. In the distance Renfrew heard the swell of sound that denoted military activity. He urged Weirhass to hurry away from the clearing towards that sound. Behind him the riders faded into the wasteland. The priests and their guards slipped away from Masfin and the remnants of the Sarnese army. Still Renfrew was distracted as he tried to figure the puzzle of the name. He tried altering the pattern of the accents: La Dizona? No that wasn't it; Ladiz Ona, no again. Lad…

They were at the source of the sound. The Llweganians had crossed into Masfin territory. The camp was in a panic. Horses raced every which way. Tents lay trampled on the ground. How had the enemy passed undetected over the border? Then as soon as he arrived in the camp the enemy began to withdraw. Renfrew sat in shock. He watched the frenetic activity. The orderly retreat of the Llweganian forces contrasted sharply with the manic activity of the camp. Like a sudden shower the invaders were gone leaving confusion in their wake.

Hours later Renfrew had time to wonder at the exercise. The camp had been packed up. Everyone was on the road moving to a secure, hopefully secure, position. The dead had been buried. The wounded were in wagons. Renfrew rode in the rear of the army. He wore a rag across his face to filter the dust raised by the hooves of the army in front of him.

The sentries had become complacent. They had not looked for the incursion because one had not happened. They had thought the Llweganians too scared to cross into Masfin. They had done it and with ease. So why had they not crossed before toady? Why had they crossed today? What was happening?

What had happened? Renfrew recalled the scene in the clearing. He spoke limited Sarnese. His vocabulary was limited to military terms and expressions. He had some basic day to day words but nothing extensive enough to guess at what had transpired with the three tattooed men.

Whatever had happened was not good. Renfrew was dying to ask Stiefis what had been said, but he dared not broach the subject.

Stiefis rode in fearsome silence, deliberately separated from Renfrew for the first time since they had allied. That separation worried Renfrew as much as the scene in the clearing and the raid. This had not been a good day. Renfrew nodded in his saddle. At the edge of sleep a stray thought tickled something he could not quite catch. Then the rhythm of his mount's pace lulled him to sleep.

First stood at the doorway. She leaned into the opening as if she were a magnet trying to draw her heart's desire to her. Darkfall came. She could not see beyond the torches in the courtyard yet still she watched. She began to feel that if she abandoned her post they would not come. She did not see them. It was the rumble of the horses she felt under her feet. The pounding echoed the beat of her heart as she anticipated the arrival. Could she live long enough for them to get here? Without a doubt but she thought her heart would burst before they could reach her. Second came to stand with her. They stood arm in arm waiting. Fifth stood on her other side. First turned her head to flash a nervous smile to Fifth. Fifth stroked her face once in affection.

"They will have succeeded. Harbinger would not have sent one who could not complete the task."

"I know."

Harbinger was the first to enter the courtyard. Dust and blood covered her face so that she looked like part of the night. Her movements as she dismounted suggested the blood was not hers. She flashed a victory sign. First still felt twitches in her stomach. She wanted the priests themselves to give her the copy of the Repudiation.

Lady Zona swung down from her mount with care. Three robed figures joined her. They waited until Lady Zona was composed. Then they left her to approach the waiting women. Third, holding the child, Fourth and Sixth had joined First also. They stood on the top step in the night air. Harbinger came to greet the child. She kept her head bent while the priests arranged themselves.

"The Articles of Repudiation were delivered. They were witnessed by the Head of the House of the Husband and of the father of the mother, by the father of the mother, by the husband of the wives. The marriages of the first six wives of Stiefis of

Weirhass are Repudiated. The rights of the mother of Ladizona are established."

First reached her hand out towards the priests. Her fingers trembled. They strengthened as they touched the paper offered to her. She ran her fingers over the words. Third waited patiently. She handed Ladizona to First as the paper was passed from woman to woman. Ladizona slept contentedly against First's shoulder. The baby's breath stirred the wisps of hair by First's ear.

"So you kept with your decision."

"Yes, there might by some use yet from this marriage. Marriages are dissolved a little differently in Llwegania. I can't let him go because he is infertile. He can leave me if he chooses or I can kill him."

"Very direct."

Marlin heard the words. He looked at the group of men filling the courtyard. He focused on the three that stood with their shaved heads gleaming in the light of the yard. Was that the kind of marriage the priests had with Lady Zona? Would Harbinger have insisted? Would the men have agreed? Would he have to follow that tradition?

"But our traditions are not for everyone. I will hold him to this marriage when it suits me. I will let him go when I have no further use for him. He is my husband by his traditions but he is not of my House as my other husbands are, as Lady Zona is, as you are. I would not trust him at my back." A small chuckle accompanied this statement. Marlin felt the small doubt that had formed in his mind dissipate. "Come, let us relax, renew ourselves, then you can explain to me the structure of this new Household you have achieved this day." Harbinger ushered First into the residence.

Chapter 10

Stiefis sat on his horse. He did not know what he was to do. He could not think to dismount. He did not know where to guide his horse. He could think of nothing. Nothing could find a stage in his mind to launch a thought. All of them had turned on him, all of them.

He did not look at the way they had defeated him. He could not bear the idea of the method of his loss. He had never thought children mattered to him. Procreating was a duty, a burden until this moment in time. Now wives that had never been anything but work and restriction had produced something to be rid of his burden and he was jealous that his wives had succeeded where he had failed.

Weirhass looked at his son. He tried to see where this move would lead the Dragon. Why had she not Repudiated Stiefis? Why had his usefulness dried up? Weirhass assumed Harbinger was behind the Repudiation. Where had she found priests willing to grant her petition? How had she convinced the other wives to go along with her plan? How had she known which wife to fulfill the role so perfectly? The country was occupied. Why bother going through the legal posturing to obtain the property? What was happening?

Weirhass kept his eyes on Stiefis. The wifeless man sat in stupefaction. He had no idea what had hit him. Weirhass had no idea how to comfort his son. As a Repudiated husband Stiefis had no hope of ever acquiring new wives. He had not only lost his wives he had lost any hope of ever having wives again. No priest would countenance a marriage between Stiefis and any woman be she willing or unwilling. Weirhass kept returning to one question: where had she gotten those priests?

Stiefis felt his father's eyes on him. He looked for his uncle. He did not want to be near the man. Soon the story of his Repudiation would be all over the Sarnese ranks. His uncle, ever in competition with Weirhass, would spread the news of his grandchild like wildfire. How could Hasshaur resist telling the whole story of the child? Why would he resist? He could demonstrate how fertile his daughter was while shouting how infertile Weirhass' son was. Stiefis groaned. He rode farther from everyone. He wanted to be as alone physically as he felt emotionally.

"What we need to find you is a woman." Stiefis blinked at Renfrew.

"I hardly think I need any more women in my life ever again."

"Not a permanent woman, you need a whore."

"A what?"

"A whore, a woman for whose services you pay money. The relationship doesn't last longer than the transaction. She gives you pleasure, you give her money."

"Aren't all the women claimed?"

"No. I know just the one. She'll cure what ails you."

Stiefis followed Renfrew unsure what was happening. He didn't grasp the concept Renfrew presented but obviously Renfrew was not going to leave him alone until Stiefis followed. They rode past the straggling troops. Stiefis saw the decimation of the Sarnese corps.

"She has never crossed the border before, why did she today?" Renfrew posited his burning question.

"To cover the retreat of the priests and their guards. In the confusion we lost our guests. I would assume that was the purpose of the confusion."

"What were those priests to her? Are you sure they were real?"

Stiefis paused. He tried to recreate the scene without emotion. He studied the priests. He sighed.

"Yes, their markings and speech were correct."

"So she has subverted three priests."

"Do you hear what you are saying?" Stiefis sat straight in his saddle for the first time since the Repudiation. "Priests in Sarna are not like the clergy here. The priests have all the power. They are everything. If Sarna falls their power is gone. The Llweganians have no gods, no priests. There is no sense in priests joining with Harbinger."

"You speak familiarly of her."

"I have fought her since I took up a sword. Most of our borders with Llwegania march along her lands. She is strong. Her control has grown. She did not always control so much but her neighbors were weak. She has extended her border until we have little room to," Stiefis remembered to whom he spoke. He quickly closed his mouth. "Where are we going?"

"We are here."

Here turned out to be a small building. The windows were covered with pale cloths. The door stood ajar. Stiefis could not imagine what lay beyond the door. The solitary placing of the building, the strange adornments of the windows, the mysterious door all suggested forbidden things. Renfrew dismounted without a second thought. Stiefis followed more slowly. He held tightly to his reins as Renfrew disappeared inside the building.

Once he had begun to see outside himself again Stiefis noted the day. The air was clear and dry. It had a hint of warmth in it. Not warmth lingering from the sun but true warmth that came from Masfin. Stiefis recalled the warm air of Sarna with a feeling of regret. Then he was being called by Renfrew. Still holding the reins of his mount, Stiefis walked towards Renfrew.

Renfrew gently removed the reins from Stiefis' hand.

"Everything is set. You have her until tomorrow sunrise then your time is up. While you have her she will please you anyway you want."

Stiefis entered the mysterious portal. He turned quickly when the door closed behind him. His eyes slowly adjusted to the shadowy interior.

"Welcome."

Stiefis searched the room to find the source of the husky voice. He found her. She was a pale shimmer in the room.

Renfrew rode back to the camp in a thoughtful mood. He went directly to Weirhass. He searched among the wounded Sarnese until he found the older man discussing the status of the wounded with a surgeon. At his approach Weirhass looked up sharply.

"Where is my son?" Worry sharpened Weirhass' tone beyond polite.

"He is safe. He is being distracted."

Weirhass puzzled over the answer.

"We need to discuss today's events." Weirhass returned his attention to the Masfin general. How much did this young pup understand?

"Let us go somewhere else." Weirhass excused himself from the doctor. He strode quickly next to Renfrew. Renfrew tried to capture the feeling of the morning. There was a memory half solid that kept slipping from him.

"This morning," Renfrew spoke the words quietly.

"Where is my son?" Weirhass did not wish to discuss the morning past with an outsider.

"He is fine, or soon will be. He is relaxing with a friend. This morning, why did things happen the way they did? Was the ceremony a cover for the action or was the action a cover for the ceremony? I believe the latter case is the truth, but why? What made three Sarnese priests so important that the Llweganian army would attack for them?" Weirhass sighed. He did not have to relive the moment of his son's humiliation. After the relief, curiosity blossomed. The Masfin was right: how were the situations related?

"Could Harbinger have known that the priests would arrive this morning?"

Weirhass did not answer. He did not wish to reveal his ties to Harbinger. For some reason it was important to him to keep his son's marriage a secret from both the Masfins and his fellow Sarn.

"I believe that the Llweganians attacked to cover the priests' retreat. I have told Stiefis this. But why? How are they connected? I'm missing something."

"There has never been a Repudiation in living memory. The female who was the vessel of the testing was the only wife of my son who could bear a child that would give claim to that particular estate. The estate has water. There are few estates that have that much water. All water is controlled by the priests of Kersai; all water that is except the water found by Harbinger. That female, that former wife of my son, that daughter of my brother, has claim to water not controlled by priests. That control was given her through actions of priests. When we defeat the Llweganians I will be returning to my former place except for that estate. I would have had that water by right of having fought for my home. That female has that water through the grace of the priests.

"I can see why the priests would have braved the enemy to grant this favor to the female."

"So you think this is all coincidental?"

"Yes, perhaps the priests were allowed through Sarna to divert us. Harbinger saw an opportunity. She is cagey."

Renfrew nodded. The scenario fit but only just. It answered more questions than his theory.

"Water, children, women, I have to stop thinking like a Masfin all the time. I need to think like a Llweganian most of the time. She was here, right here. I took no opportunity to study her. In my arrogance and ignorance I let her slip through my fingers."

Weirhass said nothing. He could not be too hard on the boy. He too had let a golden opportunity pass him by. Of course neither he nor Renfrew had really had a chance to know Harbinger better. She had been very careful.

"She is not easily known. None of them are. What is done is done. We have become lazy. She crossed the border very easily. We assumed she could not attack us here. Obviously we were wrong. We will have to guard against her every moment. We have learned from this something she did not want us to know. We can take that lesson to heart."

Renfrew shook off his melancholy. Weirhass was right; strange that this incursion should happen right after Marlin left on patrol. Stiefis knew that Marlin had gone to her. There was no use keeping this secret.

"We have to move. Marlin had not returned from his patrol. All his men went with him. I do not expect them back, ever. This position is compromised."

Weirhass became very grim. "Do you expect any more such losses?"

"I cannot say. It is possible."

"We should take no obvious actions. No need to push anyone away. Still there have to be some precautions to take."

"I agree."

Weirhass shifted in his saddle. He stretched his lower back.

"The female who returned, did she have anything of import to report?"

"She's probably their best secret weapon. She could be an incredibly devious spy."

"That useful?"

"If it happened to her, she will tell you about it without end. Otherwise there is nothing. She was banished from Harbinger's presence; I wish I had that luxury."

"That banishment was useful for the Llweganians."

Renfrew reined his stead around.

"She is, however, a patriot and a heroine. Her opinion is solicited at every turn. Be careful what you say of her and to her, she might yet end up queen."

"Is she a good judge of winners?"

Renfrew chuckled over the question.

Stiefis watched the motes of dust dance in the light. He was relaxed. His body was satisfied. His troubles seemed not so heavy. He owed no responsibility to this female yet she had pleasured him. When he walked out that door he did not need to worry about her. For the right inducement she would pleasure him again. There were some things these Masfins had to teach.

He slid from the bed. His hand was steady as he gathered his clothes. With each article of clothing he donned he felt stronger. The lack of wives or children did not define him. He was more than his ability to husband. He was a very good soldier. He was a good general. He was a soldier and a general with a war going on around him. His abilities were needed by his country now more than ever. He left without looking back.

Renfrew waited outside. Stiefis looked around to see if Weirhass or any other Sarnese soldiers were in sight. He and Renfrew were as alone as they could be in the middle of an army.

"We are moving." Renfrew looked at the activity around them as he spoke.

"Right, where?" Stiefis asked off-handedly trying to speak of anything except his personal life at this point.

Renfrew was silent. He had spent most of the day before in discussions on just that question. It had been hard to come up with a site that none of the Llweganian trained troops had ever visited that was also defensible and accessible to the border. Using the heavy losses of the attack as an excuse the Masfin generals had planned a massive restructuring of the army. The divisions were now a mix of the Llweganian trained troops and the Masfin reserves. Renfrew could not stand one more discussion on the matter.

Stiefis wondered at the continued silence. He stared at the collapsing camp. He felt some of his contentment slipping away.

"We are going to Jalico. It is a small fortress south and east of here. We will have regular border patrols. The engineers will begin to build breastworks all along the border from Jalico."

"Jalico? What are its strong points?"

"It is very obscure. Few have ever seen it or spent any time in the terrain around it." Renfrew spoke the truth without trying to disguise it. Stiefis heard the entire conversation the answer held.

"A wise choice then. The generals have finally seen that they will be unable to defeat Harbinger in a season."

"It was a hard lesson. She might have done us a favor last morning."

"I doubt she would be pleased at that knowledge." Stiefis spoke the words softly. Renfrew hardly caught them. It took a moment for Renfrew to sort the sounds out into meaningful words. Then he understood them. A wry smile tugged at his mouth.

"We will defeat her. I believe that. We have each other. She is alone in enemy territory."

"I doubt the situation makes her uncomfortable."

"Surely it must. Anyone would have to feel the stress of being surrounded by hostile people all the time."

Harbinger bent to place the sleeping child back in her crib. Petron stood at a window reading a missive from the Llweganian Council. Rodznig sat at a table studying reports from the field.

"The Masfin forces are leaving their positions."

Harbinger sucked on her teeth. She passed her tongue along the back of her teeth. The messenger from the Council stood in the middle of the room.

"The Council is concerned that you have left your section of the border open."

"I have my border well manned."

"Pardon, Harbinger, but your border is wide open. Your Rights of Way are unattended. Your Heir's borders and Rights of way are also neglected. The Council is very concerned at this state of affairs."

"My borders have moved an entire country away from their former position. The Sarnese army is in Masfin. The Masfin army is in Masfin. My army is on this side of the border. Have there been any raids in Llwegania?"

"No Harbinger, you know there have not."

"That is right. Even if this move fails and I have to retreat to my former position; the Sarnese and Masfin armies will be so decimated that they will pose no threat to Llwegania for at least two generations. Tell the Council I am minding my borders. They should note them too. There is a very good chance I will succeed in this."

The messenger sighed. This was a comfortable place. Her ride from Llwegania had been uneventful. The residents of the country had allowed her to pass unmolested. She went almost unnoticed. She had stayed clear of the Temple and Altars. She had slept in the wilderness rather than trust the towns and estates but no one had tried to stop her. In fact there had been acceptance in their eyes as they watched her pass.

"It is strange there is no revolt at your back as well as opposition at your front lines."

"Nothing strange there. I am using Masfin skills to bring forth water in the waste. I do not require anything for that water aside from peace. The Temples demand soul, work, fruits of the field. I let the water flow in return for a quiet home front. No mystery there, just sensible husbandry. With water there are crops. With crops there is food and trade. Domestic plenty equals political quiet.

"I do not openly oppose the temples. I do not deny the Priests their ceremonies. I have only co-opted their source of power."

Harbinger sat at the table. She looked at the charts Jorin placed on the polished surface. Even in the warmth of the room the stone of the table felt cool under her hand.

"Anyway, those that might oppose me at home are all in Masfin. The little people here don't care who is in power as long as they are safe. And under me they are safe."

"Do you plan to invade Masfin?"

Harbinger shot an amused glanced at the messenger.

"The Council gave up its right to question me when they refused to join me on this venture. There have been no raids across the borders for which I am responsible. I am upholding my oath. Therefore the Council has no right to question me. Tell the Council how you found your journey. Tell them how peaceful the countryside is. If they are waiting for me to fail they will have to wait a little longer."

The messenger turned her head to one side.

"The question was idle curiosity, Harbinger. Forgive me."

"Ah, well, I am only wedded to men not plans. I will do what must be done. Come you must eat, rest, refresh yourself for your journey home. The cook here is quite talented."

Marlin stood by the door. He moved to allow the woman to pass. She eyed him with interest. He ignored the gleam in her eye. He waited a moment before the feeling of discomfort passed.

"Forgive her. She is of a different tradition. Messengers have no ties, no sense of connection beyond the channeling of information. They have no House loyalties. That is a necessary requirement to insure the objectiveness of their work but it also means they see all people as only transitory episodes."

"But you have messengers who answer to you."

"Yes but they are assigned by lot. They change when it suits their administrators. They are never **my** messengers, they are only my messengers."

Marlin smiled at her use of intonation. Her hands moved through the air when she spoke. They returned to her side. She was ever careful of those she touched. Those she touched, she touched frequently. Her guard, the women of this house, Lady Zona, they all felt the touch of her hand when she spoke with them. Everyone else she maintained a buffer zone. Not a threatening space, not an offensive space, just a comfortable space that said she trusted you, valued you, but you were separate from her in some indefinable way.

"Do we follow?"

"I should advance the border. If I don't they will fortify it. Damn them." Harbinger slammed her fist on the table. She shook her head once in fury. First laid a calming hand on her arm. Sablor crowded her free side. "I would have made a very fine ally. We could have been good neighbors."

"That may still happen. There is the chance that close association with the Sarnese troops will reveal that the tie that binds the Masfin and Sarnese generals is not very strong."

"No, we are too strange. The ways the Masfin and Sarnese cultures are alike are comforting when set against the backdrop of the Llweganian traditions.

"We should quietly follow the retreat. Someone should see where the armies go."

Petron nodded. He reached into his belt pouch. The soldier waiting at the door received the order. Then Petron turned to Marlin.

"Choose two soldiers to pair with the two who are coming. We will send the two teams in to follow the new deployment in Masfin."

Marlin studied the assorted colors in his pouch. He considered each trooper. Then he chose. The stones clicked together as he passed them to his lieutenant. The sounds of hurrying feet echoed in the halls of the building. He listened until a hand touched his sleeve. Marlin brought his attention back to the room. He was looking into the calm face of First.

"Do you think of home often?"

"This army is my home. Since I was a beardless youth the army has been my home. I hadn't realized that this particular army was my true home until I had to leave it."

"What is Masfin like?"

"Green, moist, gentle. There are towns, fairs, cities that hold people and things."

"Is it enjoyable?"

Marlin tried to think of an answer to her question.

"It is boring. In my grandfather's day the lords rose up against the king. There were great battles. The lords lost. There has been no trouble since. The king kept his army in case his power was ever again threatened. We don't even train anymore. It is an honorable station but we had become complacent." Marlin looked at the serious face before him. He had never seen women as ornamental. They had not been powerful or instrumental to any part of his adult life. His mother had been important in his life. He valued her but he could not envision her in Lady Zona's role or First's or Harbinger's.

Once away from Masfin's culture Lady Zona had been able to demonstrate her strength. When crisis had come First had stepped into the role of leader and protector with determination if not ease. He had never thought of the type of women he would respect until he met these three women.

"I have to go." Marlin watched the sun march across the floor. "I have duties that have import, value."

"I know the feeling. For so long nothing I did mattered. There was always someone else there, I was only here. Now every decision I make has impact even though I have thrown away the original source of my position."

"Exactly." Marlin felt a rare smile cross his face. He bowed before he left.

Jeffeaux saw Marlin leave the room. He watched the soldier walk down the hall. There was a swing, a cadence to the soldier's walk that bespoke confidence, training, purpose. A shudder passed through Jeffeaux's frame. His mother was beginning to have that same walk. He turned into the room.

He surveyed the occupants. There was his objective. He moved to intercept her before she became involved in an activity he could not easily interrupt.

"Madame First." He used his most formal tones. His face remained still. He curved his body towards her but not so close as to offend her personal space.

"Lord Jeffeaux, I had not realized you were up and about yet."

"The day starts early with this crew. The day is very fine. I was hoping to accompany you on your ride to check the wellheads."

"I would enjoy the company. Thank you. I was just about to change into my uniform. The troop is assembled already."
Jeffeaux bowed as she left the room. He turned to Harbinger. He thought for a moment.

"Do you have need of me in the next couple days?"

"No, Jeffeaux. I think we will be able to muddle through without you for the next few days. I will be sure to send for you if I invade Masfin."

Jeffeaux still hesitated. He could not get a handle on this woman. He could not tell if she were angry with him, annoyed, or simply laughing at him. He could never feel totally safe in his dealings with Harbinger. Her smile now was so bland that he couldn't see any of her beauty. She looked almost ferocious. But he knew this expression didn't mean danger.

"I had not thought when I offered my support to First."

Harbinger chuckled in real amusement.

"I'm sure you thought, but not of any military or practical matters. It does not matter. It is good that you lend First your company. You'll be able to view Sarna through a native's eyes. It should be a revelation to you."

Jeffeaux retreated from the room while he still felt he was ahead. She wasn't changeable but Harbinger could remember something totally different from the topic of the moment at any second. He didn't want his permission withdrawn. He had never feared a woman until he met Harbinger. Women were always easy for him to use or to ignore. This one was immovable by his charms. She held too much power over his life to be ignored. She could as likely get him killed as make him a king. Neither fate was one of his liking.

He threw his clothes on the floor as he thought. He grabbed his riding gear. He never donned any semblance of a uniform. He tried to deny any attachment to an army even now. His leathers and silks and velvets swung around him. His only acknowledgement of a change in situation was the lack of his bigger pieces of jewelry. It really would not be wise to wear too many shiny objects.

As he entered the courtyard he was an eye catching apparition among the other drab occupants. He swung his saddle bags onto his mount. There was no hum of conversation in the air. The silence bothered him. He wondered if there was true life in the bodies of the Llweganian troops. Even First said nothing. She watched him mount then she turned to lead the troop out of the enclosed area.

Jeffeaux watched as First bent to say a last farewell to Third and the baby. Harbinger raised a hand. Jeffeaux heard the click of stones as rocks were passed from one hand to the other. He would never forget that sound. In his old age when he would hear that sound he would think of this time in his life.

Jeffeaux waited until the estate was a small dot on the horizon.

"So where are we going?"

First laughed. "Do you always rush into the waste without looking?"

"It depends on what there is to see. The where and the why did not matter. Simply going was the only motivation."

First shook her head. She knew why Harbinger had allowed Jeffeaux's presence. This trip was about power. This trip was to keep the knowledge fresh in the minds of the Sarnese people who gave them water. Coming in Harbinger's name would spread a mantle of power over First. That same mantle would drape across Jeffeaux in the eyes and minds of Sarnese watchers. Harbinger was building Jeffeaux into something, something useful. And Harbinger would use any means she had to bolster Jeffeaux's position.

"You should be more careful. The landscape is full of dangers and unexpected pitfalls."

"Ah, but the ride is worth the price of admission. I am away from my main jailer and I will be with the most beautiful woman in Sarna. What man could ask for more?"

"I admire your jailer very much. As for my beauty, I have many attributes other than beauty that are worthwhile."

"That is true. But I can admire all of you."

"Lord Jeffeaux, you are interesting. This is work. I will not be undermined in my duties by anyone. I will not be belittled when we are at the wellheads or in towns or farms or estates. I will order you returned to your jailer faster than you can say wellhead. This journey is very important to me. Do not ruin it for me."

"If you have so many doubts about me, why did you agree to my company?" Jeffeaux spoke with suppressed laughter. He was sure of himself with women. Well, most women at any rate, most of the time except lately so he did not doubt that he had been allowed along to satisfy some desire of First for his company.

"Why? To please Harbinger of course. If she didn't want you here I would have other company."

Jeffeaux reined his mount closer to First. He wanted to look in her eyes for the truth of her statement. There was no flirtatious gleam in her eye.

"What company would you have preferred?"

"That is only the other company's business. Since you are here you may amuse me to pass the time but don't interfere with my duties."

Jeffeaux tried to imagine who would have caught First's attention.

"It's not wise to long after Harbinger's personal guard. She is married to them all."

"They are fine husbands. She is very happy with them. Remember I have shared a husband with Harbinger once already. I am not interested in her guard, fine as I am sure they are."

Jeffeaux tried to follow all the ideas presented in the sentences.

"You didn't like sharing a husband with her?"

"That is not what I said. I cannot imagine she shares husbands she has as her own very well. Nor would I wish to trespass on her areas. She has things that she will share willingly that interest me far more than any of her husbands. If ever I were to take another husband, I would want one like hers."

Jeffeaux rode in silence for a while. "But all her husbands are very different. No two are alike."

"Then I have quite a range to pick from."

Jeffeaux suspected First was laughing at him. She was paying only minimal attention to him. She was not focusing on the horizon as the guards were. She was somewhere else.

"If you married again what would happen to the remainder of your household?"

"Nothing, we would go on as before except this time, hopefully we would have a better husband."

"We?"

"We, whoever I chose for a husband will be husband to all my sisters. We Repudiated a husband, not each other. None of us wish to go to some other First's household. This is our Household. This is our estate."

"Don't you want a husband of your own?"

"A husband is not something you own."

"That is not what I meant and you know it."

First smiled slightly. Jeffeaux knew that this time she was laughing at him. He felt at a distinct disadvantage. He could not argue his point very well because he lacked the experience of marriage. He had only his traditions and observations to fall back on. She had first-hand experience, experience totally different from his traditions and observations.

"Jeffeaux, you aren't even interested in marriage. You live for the thrill of the chase. I don't believe you enjoy the victory as much as the pursuit."

"The victory is very enjoyable, I assure you, for both parties, if that is what you are worried about." Jeffeaux's voice became heavy with suggestion.

This time First laughed outright. "You are incorrigible. And determined. You always came back to your main theme. Even when I take another husband you will persist in your pursuit."

First cocked her head to one side. "Is there any other subject you are able to discuss?"

"You have your next husband already picked out?" Jeffeaux felt a strange tightness in his chest.

"I guess not. Talk to your heart's content. Too bad you couldn't sing your words then I would have some background music for the ride."

"Do I know your future husband? How did you meet? When did he ask you?"

"My Lord Jeffeaux, please pick another subject, now."

Marlin held his finger steady on the map. He turned his head to look at Harbinger. She sat with her elbow on the table. The fingers of one hand were curled over her mouth. The fingers moved to rub one eye and eyebrow. Then they returned to her mouth. Her fingers moved again. Now her head rested on their backs and her eyes were looking at Marlin instead of the map.

"You want me to push our front into Masfin."

"Yes, to the edge of the changes. Just here. No one lives here in these wastes. Very few people inhabit the area just beyond this line. Our front will then be along an open stretch with all the cover behind our lines. No one can move against us without being seen."

"Defensively," Harbinger paused, "ah. I want to draw them to me. I don't want to waste energy and supplies chasing them all over their own countryside."

"Then this is perfect. They will have to dislodge us. They will have to come to us across this huge open plain."

"I will be entrenched in Masfin."

"Sort of."

"There is no 'sort of'."

"This area is new. No one in Masfin feels quite attached to it. It looks too different, too alien. We could almost claim this is Sarna."

"I have no desire to enlarge Sarna, but I hear your position." Harbinger reached to touch the stones the scouts had deposited on the map. The smooth surfaces were cool to her touch. Her other hand reached into her pouch.

Marlin watched the shiny black stones appear along the line he had suggested. The bold line grew steadily. The line was done. It shone bright and dark against the cream of the map. Still her hand hung over the map. Her fingers wriggled once then they returned to her pouch. There was a moment as she sorted her stones. Blue/green stones replaced the milky ones of the scouts.

"I want scouts to know this area as if they had been born there. I am as interested in the terrain as in the troop movements."

Marlin faded to the back of the group. He moved until he stood with Lady Zona. She shifted until he was safely behind her shoulder. Marlin preferred to stay behind a buffer. He felt as if he stepped close to the sun each time he dealt with Harbinger. He would follow anywhere she led. He would dare suggest options for her lead. But being too close to her made him nervous. He wanted to be in the room, but at the edge was his preferred spot.

Marlin watched as Petron gathered up the stones. He wondered who gave Harbinger stones; if anyone gave her stones. He glanced out the window. They would not leave until Jeffeaux returned. Plans would be laid, positions reconnoitered, but no one would move until Jeffeaux returned. She wouldn't cross into Masfin without him. Yet he held no stone of hers. Marlin reached into his own pocket to smooth his fingers over the surface of his stone.

First looked up from the stone in her hand. The veined surface was as familiar to her as her own face. She cherished the weight in her hand. She watched as Jeffeaux walked toward her from the horses. His stride was still confident after four days of riding in rough terrain. They were approaching the first wellhead. All the wellheads were along the Masfin border. Not close enough to represent danger to the travelers but close enough to impact on the balance of power on the front.

The waste was starting to blossom. Shadows of green were appearing. First could smell the change in the air. Jeffeaux blocked her view of the surroundings. Then he sat with a deep sigh.

"And tomorrow?"

"We will reach the first stop. There will be a ceremony. There will be an Act of Reconciliation or Contrition."

"An Act of Reconciliation, you make it sound like a religious rite."

"It will be. The water used to be distributed by the Temple of Kersai. It still is to some degree. In ancient times there was a battle for control of water. The side of Kersai won. In our tradition Harbinger is equivalent to the losing side in that battle. It is fitting that the Battle Maid should destroy the Temple in retribution. That she gives her control of the water to the people is an act of forgiveness and generosity. Depending on how her actions are viewed the communities will choose the type of rite. Whichever Act they choose, we will be her agents, representatives. It is a religious ceremony; remember that, a very important religious ceremony."

"How did religion enter into this? Harbinger does not believe in gods or God that I have witnessed."

First shrugged. "The Llweganians are a very private society. They do not share information readily. How long did you know her before you knew her guard were her husbands?"

"I have met no religious men..."

"Maybe that's your problem. You have no idea what you are looking for so you can't see it. She certainly understood about religion, the politics of religion, the role religion plays in a society, or she couldn't use it so well."

Jeffeaux accepted a dinner plate. The spicy aroma hit him like a hot wind. He hoped there was plenty of bread to cut the spice. Jeffeaux chewed on his bread gratefully.

"But there are no rites, no lead figures."

First shook her head. "You can't argue religion. Belief has no rationale or reasoning. You either have faith or you don't. You have to believe without seeing or your faith is not worthy. When you believe without seeing you take a leap into the unknown, from the not understood into the well-known and completely understood. I believe as I believe, and you believe as you believe. I respect that you believe, and you must accept that I believe."

"Believe what?'

"That Harbinger has faith in something."

"You couldn't be a simple woman."

"No, I thought I was complicated once. I was simple then. Now I am even simpler. I know what I want. I know where I am going. I know how I will get there."

Jeffeaux grunted. "I know none of that. I guess I am complicated by your standards."

"Well I know where you are going and how you will get there."

Jeffeaux looked at her with almost hate in his eyes.

"Where do you think I am going?"

"Over that hill, in the morning, on the back of that horse. So get some rest. You will have quite a show to enjoy at dawn."

Jeffeaux had to bite back his ire. He knew she had meant some journey directed by the managing hand of Harbinger. Or had she? Jeffeaux could not tell with First just what shade of meaning her words held or if she spoke only what she meant to say. Was he wrong to hear double meanings in every phrase? Or was he wise?

First adjusted her robes. In the early morning light her robes glowed. The cool air flushed her skin with a pale pink. Her many braids had been pinned onto the top of her head creating a crown. Her only ornament was a huge water stone that glowed in the grip of a dragon against the fabric of her bodice. She covered the stone with her hand for a heartbeat. The smoothness of its surface gave her courage. She took a deep breath. She did not want to fail in her duty. She comprehended the honor of this duty as well as the political aims of it.

Jeffeaux blinked at the finery of First. She was always well appointed but this morning she was robed almost as a queen. The fine materials, the intricate hairdo, the huge jewel all denoted a person of high position and formidable power. He was not used to thinking of First in any terms but a vulnerable female.

"Good morning, my Lord."

"First, you are taking this very seriously."

"You are right. Are you ready?"

Jeffeaux swung into his saddle. He viewed their escort. They too had donned very formal and formidable attire. Metal gleamed, leather reflected the nascent morning light. He brushed at the material of his tunic.

"We don't have time for you to change. Here put this on."

A water stone chain appeared in the air. It settled around his neck. Jeffeaux watched the links settle on his chest.

"You'll do. Your tendency towards finery has come in handy today."

Jeffeaux fingered the chain as he rode. He comprehended her words several feet after he heard them.

"Women like a well-dressed man."

"That is true. Women like orderliness. A slovenly dressed man does not make a good impression. It is the man who is obsessed with his appearance that has to worry as much as the slob."

"I am not obsessed with my clothing."

"Sit up straight. Chin up. Don't say a word or I will have you silenced. Just sit there and look well-dressed."

Two troopers rode into the village ahead of First. First rode directly beside Jeffeaux. The rest of the troop followed. First surveyed the villagers gathered in the town square over the shoulders of the troopers. The front of the group consisted of three men. One was clearly a priest of Kersai. First studied the tattoos on the priest's head. She noted the cut of the robes and their material. This was no itinerant priest from the Temple. First drew a deep breath.

First moved her horse to the front of the group. She refused to dismount. She used the intimidating height of her mount to bolster her courage.

"I am come in the name of Harbinger of Death, Devouring Dragon."

"Woman, who are you to speak? Why have you come with Sarna's enemies?"

"Who is Headman of this village?"

There was a shuffling of feet as generations of obedience warred with honor.

"I ask again. Who is Headman of this village? I am come in the name of Harbinger of Death, Devouring Dragon, Provider of Water in the Deserts. I am come not to demand payment or obedience. I am come to remind you who gave you this water and of your agreement with her.

"I ask a final time. Who is Headman of this village?"

"I am Headman of this village. I give you this, person who dares to claim the water of Harbinger of Death."

"This is not her water. This is your water as long as you keep faith with Harbinger of Death, Devouring Dragon. This water is used to nourish crops, to chase away the thirst of all who live on its shores in peace with Harbinger of Death, Devouring Dragon, and for those of the Houses of Devouring Dragon, Wind Rider, and Lady Zona."

"I am Headman of this village. I present to you, representative of Harbinger of Death, this priest of Kersai."

"I accept this man as the surety of your bond. Do not forget in our new plenty our past hardships. Harbinger demanded nothing from you and has given you life. This man has given you nothing but demands everything. This is the representative of Kersai. I will present him to Harbinger as the representative of you casting off old lies and ties." First reached into her pouch. She brought her fist out into the light. "I give to you, Headman of this village, the symbol of your agreement with Harbinger of Death, Devouring Dragon. If you have need, send the stone to her. Help will come."

Jeffeaux watched the Headman step to First. He did not need to look to see the color of the stone that passed form First to the cautious man. "This is the symbol of your status within Harbinger of Death's responsibilities. It commands great power. Do not lose it."

The priest tried to reach for the stone. A trooper kicked him away with a booted heel. Hands grabbed the priest away from the Headman. None of the villagers moved from their positions behind the Headman. Jeffeaux watched the group of peasants. They were not that different from the peons in Masfin. Their dress was different. Their coloring was different but the blank expression they wore was the same. So easily they gave up their old order to the invader. There was no tie strong enough to resist the force of- Jeffeaux looked out over the shining water of the new lake- bribery, was that the word he wanted? It was close enough. Their loyalty was not cheaply bought but it was bought just the same. What price was attached to the loyalty of the Masfin herds?

Jeffeaux looked back at the group of peasants. They all touched the stone in the Headman's hand. The look on their faces startled Jeffeaux. It bothered him that he could not immediately place the look. It was important though for his wonderings to translate that look. There was a factor he had not considered.

"Do not allow the waters to be polluted. Only ever take out of the waters. Never return anything to them, not used water, not waste of the body, not waste of the land. These waters must be held clean."

"We hear and obey."

Jeffeaux winced at the phrase. He had not thought to hear such terms on this ride. He was searching the faces of the peasants when he noticed how they looked at him. The expressions were still veiled but they were veiled partly because Jeffeaux was not used to having such a look directed his way. They thought him part of this process. They associated him with Harbinger and First. He would not mind an association with First but not this kind. He opened his mouth to deny that look but First had begun to move away from the group. His horse followed the lead of First's turn. Jeffeaux looked down at his steed in consternation. Even his horse betrayed him, took him farther down a road he had no desire to tread.

The sounds of movement invaded Jeffeaux's awareness. The slight clink of the metal, the muffled protests of the priest, the echo of the horses' hooves on the hard earth, the absolute silence of the rest of the troop, were imprinted on Jeffeaux's memory. He tried to recall days of doing nothing. Hours of pursuit of pleasure seemed unreal to him. He could visualize flashes of color, hear the faint echoes voices raised in merrymaking. He felt the memory slip from him. His horse sidled as it moved through the crowd on the road. Jeffeaux stared at the hands trying to touch him, his horse. He jerked his head looking for the troop. They too were swamped. Panic blinded Jeffeaux for a second.

Then he noticed that the troopers were not defensive nor were they trying to repulse the crowd. They were passing out small items. Not more stones, he thought in disgust. No, they looked like shards of wood. Splinters, pebbles, he watched the way each memento was cradled in the hands of the recipients. What was the use, the intrinsic value of such rubble?

At a sign from First the crowd fell away.

"Remember this day, remember these times. Never forget the desert. Never forget the day Harbinger of Death struck down her sword to make the sands give up their water. The water comes from the heart of the earth. No priest summoned it for you. Devouring Dragon gives you this water. Never forget who set you free from the desert that came from the priests' hands. They took all the water to keep for themselves. Do not forget that. As you drink your first cup of water of the day remember all these things. As you hold the pieces of the Temple of Kersai, remember all these things." First swung her mount's head sharply away from the village. The troop moved as one with her. Jeffeaux twisted sharply to keep pace with them. The priest thumped across his seat like a sack of grain. They had ridden for several moments before Jeffeaux recovered his equilibrium.

"Are you trying out for position of High Priestess?"

First blinked. Her expression of confusion made Jeffeaux regret his sharp words. Then she smiled. He saw a glimpse of someone he did not know.

"I like that. No, I spoke the words the moment gave me. You should marry, you know. It is time for you to secure your line of succession."

Jeffeaux felt a huge fist grip his heart.

"Once we get back I will sit down with your mother." Jeffeaux felt the fist tighten until he could not breathe. "There must be a suitable bride in Masfin who will bolster your position, someone from a strong House. Is there a rival House of your King?"

Jeffeaux felt the fist release with a whoosh. Then he felt a slight shaft of disappointment fill the void left by the fist.

"You have been around Harbinger too much. Marriage is not about power and position."

First shot him a look of ridicule.

"Women have a strange position in Sarna. We are considered as less than a man because our civilization came from the defeat of a woman by a man. We bear children. When a daughter is born there is the cultural disappointment since males are considered better than females, but females mean income to the family. Men pay a high price for their wives. There are as many men as women but every man needs many wives to ensure his line of descent. I am First wife. My husband's family paid the highest bride price for me of all my sister/wives. I held the highest position in my husband's Household under my husband. In Household matters my word was law." First paused. A frown gathered briefly on her face then smoothed itself away.

"Marriages in Masfin are not so different. Your mother has spoken about the many alliances cemented by marriage in Masfin."

Jeffeaux did not want to discuss marriage with First. Something about the subject affected him too much in her presence. Yet he could not step back from the edge this time.

"I like women…"

"No you don't. You don't like or respect them. You like the activity you can pursue with them."

Jeffeaux felt an automatic denial rise to his lips. Then he bit back the words to examine her statement.

"Is that really how you see me?"

"I bet you have friends from childhood who are male; you like and respect them. You desire women, but you don't really like us. Or at least you never consider whether we are likeable as persons. Though I suspect you do like Harbinger. Somehow, in some way you really like her. Even though you are here with me to get away from her, you wouldn't really leave her."

"Me? *Like* that woman? Do you see how she has corrupted my mother? My proper mother now has three, count them, three husbands because of that woman's influence."

"Right, so counting your father that is four times your mother has made the commitment you haven't made once. So your mother is four times the person you are."

"My mother's marriage to my father is in no way similar to the arrangement she now embraces."

"You are so right. Your father provided for your mother. She is now the provider and protector. You are right. Her commitment to her present husbands is the greater commitment."

Jeffeaux snorted his disagreement. "You are deliberately misconstruing my meaning."

"No, I am telling you what I perceive. You don't want to understand. When this is over I want Sarna to be different than it was before. I don't want to be dependent on anyone for anything, not the priests for water, not a husband for my identity. If I have to give them a new icon, I will do it. If I have to give them a new set of prayers, if I have to give them a new female face to associate with their blessings, I will do it."

"Then why are you still called First?"

"Because I am the First. I am the First Sarnese follower of the new order."

"You just can't bear to give up your title. And don't tell me there are no titles in Sarna."

"We didn't need titles. Everyone knew who had power and who didn't. First was a designation. Now it is a name. My name, Harbinger is a name. First describes to everyone what and who I am. In this community and social order, First is my name. What does Jeffeaux mean? It means something more than a designation, doesn't it?"

"It is the name of the seat from which my highest title is derived. I am Lord of Jeffeaux. I am lord of other places but Lord of Jeffeaux is the highest rank I hold."

"Sounds complicated to me."

"Well…"

"Don't explain it to me. I am not interested in the details, just that you have a grasp of the difference between being Jeffeaux and being First. My sisters and I are the First wives to successfully Repudiate a husband. I am First, the first of a Household to have an independent Household. I am the first non-priest to have custody of water. I am so many firsts you cannot comprehend how important they are. I am become First. Before, I was one of many: that many had no meaning for me. Now my sisters are one with me and I am First."

"What is it about this land that breeds such hard women?"

"Llwegania is not harsh. Llwegania is lush and bountiful. They do not need wells that draw water from under the rock. I have only ever heard tales of the glory of Llwegania but I long to see such a place. They say there is a body of water so vast you cannot see land on its far side. It is never cold in some parts of it. Even the night is warm. It is not the land, it is the circumstances that make us."

"Ah, but the land can add to the circumstance."

"True, Jeffeaux, true, I stand corrected. But aren't soft women boring? They have nothing to talk about. They require endless care. They have no thought but for their own comfort. I find soft men boring. They take up too much time and energy."

Jeffeaux opened his mouth to repudiate her harsh judgment on the women of his preference when he comprehended her ending statement. His mouth closed with a snap. Was that really how he seemed in this company?

Chapter 11

Junla turned from the opening of the tent. She rubbed a weary hand across her forehead. She felt the faint scratch of fine sand against her skin. She reached behind her for a damp rag to ease her skin. The scent of water was soothing.

Across the encampment she watched her mother's guard group protectively around her mother. They nodded shortly to soldiers they passed. Her mother was in deep discussion with her colonel. Junla could not guess what they said from this distance but she knew the subject they discussed. Everyone discussed this subject all the time.

Jeffenza had been stupid. This was the place to be. There were more options here. If Harbinger prevailed Junla would become the loyal sister of the new king. If this venture failed, Junla would either be part of the ruling elite of Sarna, a respected guest in exile in Llwegania, or at the worst an innocent pawn who could return to her former life in Masfin. No matter what happened this was the most advantageous place to be. Junla let the flap fall into place. She turned to look at Marma as she finished folding away the last of their sparse belongings.

"Do you think the King and his Council even now are ignorant of what is coming their way?"

Marma kept her attention focused on her task. She watched her hand fold the material along precise invisible lines. She drew a deep breath to answer Junla's query.

"They have the counsel of the Sarnese generals. They have the tales of Jeffenza. They have seen the realities of this war. They have Masfin troops that have trained here. That you ask me that question shows me that you too believe as Lady Zona believes: they have no understanding of what they are facing. They will say the Sarnese are a weak people, easily overrun. They will say of Jeffenza, if she has anything of value to share, is a foolish, weak woman. They will look in distrust at all the Masfin troops who came into Sarna, thinking their troops mean to mislead them."

"You are right."

Marma continued her work. Junla felt the space fill with an unspoken thought that Marma believed but would not speak.

Where was Ilissa? Jeffeaux had been sighted. The camp would be breaking up soon. Where was that female?

Ilissa could be anywhere. She probably had gone on some reconnaissance mission with one of the troops. Ilissa had truly embraced the Llweganian ways. She trained with the soldiers. She ate with them. She went out with them whenever possible. She probably was quite able but Junla did not like the feeling of having someone her mother was responsible for wandering around a war zone. It bothered Junla's sense of propriety. Not that Lady Zona was bothered. No, Lady Zona encouraged Ilissa. Lady Zona herself joined in the training exercises. Junla washed her face again. She let the cool water soothe her nerves.

He woke with a start. He had dozed. As he dozed, dreams of cool water had flowed through his mind. The cool benediction of Prayer Waters flooded his memory. Then he realized where he was.

He couldn't believe the indignity of his position. Hanging upside down across the rear of a horse was so humiliating. His head banged against the horse's side with every step. The smell of the horse was pushed into his nostrils. He had not traveled much by horse. Mostly he had walked or ridden in a cart. Riding on a horse was a warrior skill.

All this focus on discomfort kept him from looking at the two events that caused him the greatest discomfort. How could they hand him over so easily? Did they not honor their heritage? Did they not fear their God? How did one abandon God so completely? Not just one person, an entire village had abandoned Kersai. Was loyalty and reverence so cheaply bought? A glass of water determined the fate of a culture, a society, a system of beliefs?

Those cursed female warriors had him now. They would eat him for dinner. They would burn his body and set his soul adrift in this world. He heard the sound of a discussion. The lone male made weak sounding patterns. The Sarn female- that a Sarn female should be part of this was deeply offensive to him- spoke in clipped, decisive tones. The Llweganian females answered respectfully and shortly. The discussion lasted hardly any time. Then they were turning. No, that was not true; part of the group was turning. His horse and two other horses turned down a different trail. As he rode away, he heard the male whine something. The Sarn female answered firmly.

He began to cough with the heat and dust. He saw his spit gleam on the horse's hide. He watched the moisture wobble with each step of his mount. He was briefly dragged into an upright position. Water was poured into his mouth. His surprise cost him several precious drops of the liquid. Then he was abruptly dumped back on his stomach. The motion almost brought the water back up his throat. He did not want to ask anything of his captors. He refused to try to communicate with them. They would have to stop sometime. When they stopped he would deal with his needs. His whole being began to focus on his bladder. He tried to push his problem away by thinking of the sequence of the morning rites of the Temple, but, each jostle of the horse's stride brought his desperate need to his attention.

Even women of war had to stop eventually. They were human after all, or at least they were animal. Animals had to empty bladders and bowels. His position did not make breathing easy either. Did they intend to kill him with neglect? Females were impossible. He prayed to Kersai to deliver him from the ignominy of his lot.

He felt his horse sidle as his bladder finally won over his will-power. The female guiding his horse looked back at the animal's motion. She spoke sharply to her companion. All motion stopped. Rough hands pulled him from his place.

"Why did you not say you had need? Stupid, prideful action. How are we supposed to know you have need if you do not speak?" The clear Sarnese words surprised him. He blinked at the speaker. "Look at you. All fouled and soon you will stink. Now we have to waste water and time on washing you. We are in the middle of a desert, man. Did you not think?"

The tirade continued as his clothes were roughly cut from him. They were tossed into a small pile. The pile was sorted and folded. Then they were buried under the sand. He watched his robes of priesthood disappear under the sands of the desert.

"The winds will undo your work."

"Stand." Unkind hands drew him into a standing position. Luke warm water sluiced down his legs. There was the sound of

rummaging, and then a shirt was shoved over his head. A strap was placed over the top of his head. On his right the trooper held the strap tightly, pulling his head back in an awkward angle. Both troopers placed their feet
behind his, making him feel as if he were about to fall. Then they placed their left hands down the sleeves of the shirt. The trooper on his right untied his hands. Before he could react the shirt was on him and his hands were secured. Then he was on his back. One of the females was seated heavily across his chest. As quickly as they had put the shirt on him the pants went on faster. His feet that had ever worn only slippers of Kersai since he had reached adulthood were now shod in boots, military boots.

When once more he was hanging upside down, the taller trooper spoke for the first time. She twisted his head towards her.

"You foul these clothes, priest, you go naked." Her voice was husky with dust and effort. He stared into her cold, cold eyes and thought she was the true form of a demon. He did not repeat the mistake. He did not wish to be carried into the enemy's camp naked. He regretted his robes bitterly as he pondered the coming confrontation.

He heard the camp long before he could see it. Over the empty desert the echoes of horses and tack and cooking pots sounded. Soon they would be there. He had never imagined what his hell would look like. He saw patches of tent flaps. They were the color of desert sands. Figures clad in dusty leather walked through his line of sight. He saw legs and feet. He tried to ease the pressure on his neck. He turned his head the other way. All he saw was more of the same. Coming and going all he saw were glimpses of his new world.

He waited while the horses stood still. Both his captors dismounted. His steed stood still. One of the troopers spoke briefly before leaving them. He turned his head again. He caught the last impression of her entering a tent. After a moment a stream of people came out of the tent. He began to count how many. Then the trooper returned. The head strap was hanging from her fingers. He turned his head sharply. He received a cuff for his efforts. The strap bit into his skin. Then his head was lifted up and out.

He stared into curious eyes. A gloved finger traced the markings of his office. They traced the path from the top of his skull down his forehead, across his nose, around his eyes, to the middle of his cheeks. The finger stopped there.

"It's not likely you will finish your climb through the ranks of your priesthood now."

"Female." He managed to inject all his loathing into the one word.

"How observant of you. What was the giveaway?" She let his head drop. "Clean him up. Get him out of my uniform. When he is appropriately gowned bring him to me."

The world swung crazily as he was swung off the horse. Standing, he could appreciate the size of the camp. The spreading expanse of tents overwhelmed him. Strong, steady hands guided him into one of those tents. He stood easily as he was stripped. He stared blankly at the fall of cloth in the hand that reached out to him. He looked from the material to the soldier.

"How..?" His voice trailed off. He felt the cloth swish through the air to land on his shoulders. Swift, deft hands arranged the folds. He rubbed the material between his fingers. Another set of hands appeared. He knew these hands. They had fed him for days. Now they reached out to offer him his clasp of office back. He had thought it lost under the sands of the desert. In his confusion he could not reach the intricate metal device. The hand reached until it touched his shoulder. Quickly the clasp was attached to his robes.

All he could do was marvel at the robe. How did they know which color was correct? How did they have the right color? These were surely demons.

"He'll do." He did not need to understand the language to know what was said. He understood the nod of the head and the final pat to the folds. He was ready to go somewhere. He met some standard. What did he care? There was no one here to whose standard he aspired. He ran a hand over his robes. His other hand was forced to follow. He stepped into the soft slippers. They did not fit. He felt the heel slip as he walked.

The shuffle required by the chains and the slip of the slippers nearly tripped him. He felt a firm hand grasp the skin above his elbow. The leather of the glove was smooth. Under the leather there was no give. He did not look right or left. He suffered the hand to remain. His pride dictated that he not fall into the dusty sand of the desert prior to facing his greatest enemy.

The tent had light from the opening and several lanterns. Still he blinked in the transition from the glare of the outside. As the shadows resolved themselves he was able to study the occupants of the space. He could not place his enemy. He had been unable to see her properly before when she was manhandling him. He could not pick her out from the women who surrounded him. Men were present as well. They stood in uniforms exactly like the female troopers who had brought him here.

"So here is our discerning guest." He followed the sound of her voice. She stood with a group of men. "So this is one of the high priests of Kersai."

He did not know what to say. Words beat against his mind trying to get out but none came. He felt as if he were choking on those words.

"You are very quiet priest. I am wondering what to do with you. Do you have any ideas?"

"Female."

"Yes, that is right. I believe you said that before. You were right then also."

"My enemy."

"Very good, you do have a grasp of the situation." She shifted her weight from her center to her right. The motion was unthinking and threatening. "You are sent as a token of commitment. I really can't toss you aside. But you have no use so I have a hard time justifying wasting water on you."

"I would be proud to be killed for my god."

"I don't doubt it. However, that would serve me no purpose." She sighed. She turned her head to search out someone in the crowd. An older woman moved forward. "I should have a tumbrel built to carry him about the countryside. What pulled the cart of the Battle Maid?"

"I believe the legend has it that she chained lizards to her use."

"Lizards. It would take some time to break them to harness."

"Blasphemy."

"He is so concise, and to the point. You don't like women do you?"

"Women are much cherished in Sarna."

"The implication is that he doesn't like me. That's all right. He doesn't have to like me."

"I despise you, and all your kind."

"There are no others like me. You have met quite a phenomenon. This doesn't help me decide how to dispose of you. I can't keep you chained to my wrist. I don't wish to impose you on any of my Households."

"You could let me go. You have no right to keep me."

"I have you. How I dispose of you is my responsibility."

He paused. "You could kill me."

"True, there are advantages to that course. I will have to weigh the value of your martyrdom to the Sarn cause against the convenience of not dealing with you."

He knew she would kill a priest. She had no soul. Women did not have souls. This one in particular had no soul.

There was quiet in the room. He looked around the group. In that moment he felt his mortality. The judgment he demanded was being made. He had told himself that he knew she would kill a priest, but he had not believed she would kill him. In the reality of the quiet he knew she would kill him. And if it suited her to kill him it would not be to his advantage or to the greater good of his Temple. He could not bend. He had to face his death proudly.

"I'll decide next day."

Junla looked at the priest. She weighed her options.

"I will guard him for you, Harbinger."

At the sound of the clipped words, Harbinger looked at Junla. She stared closely at Junla before returning her attention to the priest.

"I'll only increase your water ration by half."

He did not understand the words. He knew his fate was in the balance. Who was this other one? She looked vaguely familiar.

Junla smiled. "You are not stingy, Harbinger. My own water rations are sufficient for several guests. A half increase will require I increase my baggage capacity. I do not aspire to become a warrior so I have little to do all day. I think I can watch over one arrogant, foolish, helpless male."

Harbinger turned away from the issue. "If he becomes troublesome ask First for advice, she has ways to control difficult guests."

"Thank you for granting me this boon."

A deep sigh issued from the general direction of Harbinger. She turned only her head to look back at Junla and the priest.

"I am sure no matter what happens it will be a boon for you." Then abruptly without taking a breath, Harbinger broke into Sarnese.

"It has been decided for the present that you will be under this woman's direction. Your life is hers to do with as she sees fit. Be careful how you choose."

"How I choose what?" He muttered to himself as he trailed behind the insistent hand. He tried to control the pace by dragging his feet. He only served to make himself fall. Then he was dragged along in the dirt. That frail arm did not look as if it had the strength to haul him along, but it did. There was no pause in her forward motion. This was not the image he wished to project to his enemies: being dragged through the camp. He tried to call out to make her stop. She paid him no heed. They went on until she reached a tent. Then she dropped his lead rope in the dust. Sharp words crowded the air. They were spoken to him. He blinked up at her. She kicked him in the ribs. He tried to grab her foot. A thin whip was brought down on his reaching hand. Clutching his hand to his chest he drew one foot under his body. He kept a wary eye on her. She stood quietly as he rose. Evidently this choice was more in line with her wishes.

"I don't understand what you are saying." He gasped the words. She did not turn to look at him. He shuffled into the tent. Another female sat in the tent. At their entrance she looked up from sewing what she held in her lap.

"What is that?"

"A hedge."

Marma stared at Junla.

"A hedge?"

"He is a Sarnese priest."

"Is rolling in the dust one of their rites?"

"No, I had to drag him here."

"Drag him, that's an interesting way to gather men."

"He owes me his life to a certain extent. I shall remind him of that if ever I need to."

"Ah, a hedge, but, isn't it better to treat hedges with some kindness?"

"I am treating him kindly. He will have to learn his place in order to survive." Junla grasped his chin in a strong grip. She turned his face towards her. "There is no softness here. He will have to learn to be tough and obedient. Or I will be unable to help him at all."

She gave the priest's cheek one pat. "He will have to learn to speak Llweganian. Always speak to him in Llweganian. Never pay heed to anything he says unless it is in Llweganian." She pushed her face into his.

"Speak Llweganian priest."

He heard the words. He did not understand any of them. The tone was implacable. The expression was fierce. He spoke two languages. He spoke High Sarnese and vulgar Sarnese.

He had no intention of cooperating with his captors. As soon as he could, he would escape this situation. He needed to get back to his fellow priests. They needed to know what was happening in the countryside. They needed to develop a plan to counter the peasants turning from Kersai to this group of females.

Junla studied her pet project. She felt the hate that glared at her from his eyes. He tried to stand. She frowned at him. He stood to his full height. She slapped him back down. He stayed down.

He turned his head carefully. This was allowed. He could see the other female who occupied the area. She was still sewing. Her hands moved gracefully, quickly. He felt the rhythm of her work begin to lull him to sleep. His eyes drooped.

He woke with a start as he landed hard on his side. His face was pressed into the dirt at the edge of the carpet of the tent. He spied his captors, asleep, not that far from him. He could escape now while no one watched him. He tried to move from his spot. He rolled to his back. He felt hardness at his back. He ignored the discomfort it caused. He pushed himself up with his arms. He gathered his feet under himself. With a mighty push he sto…ah. Down he went. He cried out as he bruised himself on that hardness at his back.

There was a shifting in the tent. He heard a question shot his way. He cut off his moans. He remained very still. He did not want to draw attention to himself. The question came more sharply. He had to reply. What to answer? He grunted as if still half asleep. There was a pause while his response was judged. Then there was rustling. He heard the soft sounds of someone walking barefoot across the carpet.

He could not see in the darkness. She could. She came unerringly toward him. He smelled her. She smelled of female and sleep. The warm musty smell was unmistakable. A soft hand ran behind him. It tugged at something. It felt the hardness. It pulled him until he sat upright again. Then she left him. Finally he began to breathe again.

He slept in small pieces. Each time he fell over he woke. By the end of Darkfall he was exhausted. His stomach rumbled. He stared out of bleary eyes at the scene beyond the tent flap. He caught wafts of some food. The scent tantalized him. He lay on his side wondering when he would be fed. He needed to take care of some basic human needs as well.

She was back. She spoke to him. He did not know what she said but she asked a question. If she was offering food or something else he did not know but he agreed. She did not understand him. She waited for him to respond. Again he said yes. She turned her head to one side. She called behind her. There was a reply. A glass of water appeared. He reached greedily for the glass. She placed the water out of his reach. She pointed to the water while saying a word. He heard the word in the next group of words she used. Then she said a short sound. The water disappeared. She repeated the long set of words. This time she said another sound. The water reappeared. In those words were the words for water and yes and no. Or here and gone. But she would need him to know yes and no, so those would be the words. He would not speak their language.

She sat a moment longer with him. She waited quite a while. She repeated the lesson three more times. When he refused, she left him, taking the water with her.

Junla ordered another bucket of water. She watched as the servant trudged along with the burden. Someone had pulled that water up long ago anticipating her request. Four days she had repeated the lesson to the priest. Four days he had answered her only in Sarnese. He must be very thirsty be now. Marma had begun to complain about the smell. Junla had refused the priest everything. He was still chained to the same spot in the same clothes. He had not moved. She would not allow it until he used the lesson. So, he lay in his own filth, thirsty, hungry. How long did priests usually fast? How used was he to this deprivation?

She took the bucket from the callused hand. The servant said nothing. He looked at her with an air of respect and suspicion. How far would she go? Junla could not answer that question. She did not know herself. She had never been in this position. She had never had anyone so completely dependent on her for survival. But he had to learn or he would be dead. He would be left for the elements and the scavengers to eat. Harbinger would find a way to have his death lack all meaning for Sarna. Even Jeffenza had had some value alive but this one had no value, only cost.

She was coming. Maybe this time he could steal a drop. The water would fall on his skin. If he turned quickly enough he could get some of it. No, no it was gone, gone. His lower half was damp but all the water was gone. The bucket was far from his reach.

He did not know how long it had been since his capture. He was becoming fuzzy about facts and memories. He spent his time lying on the ground. He no longer had the strength to sit up. This time next day he would be dead. He had never gone this long without food or water. Was it ten Darkfalls? Twelve? He could not tell. The air was hard to breathe.

She was coming. He could smell her. He could smell the water. Water, he was thinking in Llweganian. He would not say water, no the word was, what was the word? It wasn't water it was.

"Water." She heard the faint word. The inflection correct, the intonation was correct. She repeated the lesson she had taught for ten days, five times a day.

"Water, do you want water? Yes. No."

"Water, do you want water? Yes."

She smiled for the first time at him. She lifted him until he rested on her shoulder. She lifted the cup to his mouth herself. Carefully she dribbled the liquid between his cracked lips. His eyes closed in ecstasy. He savored the feel of the liquid flowing down his throat. He rested against the soft support of her body. Her smell surrounded him. His body had won. He lacked the willpower needed for true martyrdom. Water, water, water, yes.

Junla washed her charge gently. She creamed his skin with healing herbs mixed with animal fat. Both the herbs and the fat would help the blisters and sores heal without scarring. She made his bed herself. It was not a bed such as she slept on but on equal to any the troops used.

Her scent permeated his world. All his comfort and well-being depended on that smell. That smell accompanied him when he went to relieve himself. As he ate the aroma of his broth was blended with the aroma of her. Her scent, her touch became his only reality, and the sound of her voice relentlessly teaching him his new language. He spoke only when spoken to. He answered only her voice and her touch and her scent. All he did all day long was obey her direction.

Marma entered the tent. She stood quietly as Junla finished twitching the priest's robes into place. She had shaved his head that morning. The light from the lamps in the tent gleamed on his pate. The dark lines of his tattoos shone darkly against the pale skin of his head.

"Do you think he is ready for this?" Marma spoke in dry tones. She stood with her hands folded in front of her. She had no expression on her face. He paid her little attention. She existed only as a backdrop to Junla.

"I think he will do well enough. You will be polite at all times, correct priest?" He looked into Junla's face. Her expression was stern. There was nothing to suggest he had any room for error.

"I am to speak only when spoken to. I will restrict my answers to yes or no unless otherwise permitted. I must show respect to everyone present."

"Good. Do I look all right?"

He was frightened. He had not been trained in this type of interaction. He fell back on his lesson.

"Yes."

"See how under the most difficult stress your lessons support you?"

He sighed. He had not failed. He was safe. She was pleased. He waited, standing in the middle of the space. Marma stood next to him. She smoothed a hand over her hair. When she was satisfied she removed the scarf from her neck. Her long fingers flipped the filmy material over her head. He felt the fall of the material against his cheek. He caught a gentle waft of her scent. Then his attention was caught by the return of Junla to his line of vision. Marma had distracted him while Junla had changed her attire. Junla was gowned in formal colors. Not the drab shades of everyday work for this event. No, now she wore the deep rich colors of presentation.

He knew this habit was Masfin not Llweganian. No, that was wrong. Color had great importance in Llwegan. He became flustered. He had confused an important fact. No, remember his rules. He repeated his rules. His lips moved as he built a wall to protect him from mistakes. He was brought from his trance by a snap of fingers.

"Come, priest."

He walked sedately behind the two women. He remained to the right of Junla's right shoulder. He stayed an even three paces behind her, varying his speed with hers at all times. He had practiced as he had learned his new language. They had marched around the tent in just this configuration as she taught him words and grammar. With his eyes blindfolded he could do this. In the quiet of the tent he had thought the outside sounds of the camp would interfere with his hearing of her movement. If he narrowed his focus even now he could hear the whisper of her step, the rustle of her gown. If he focused all his attention on Junla alone he would be safe in this environment.

They had reached their destination. Tent flaps were moved for them. He knew where he was.

"Priest, you are brought back to me. Do you know why?"

"No." He spoke in low, retiring tones. He looked at the speaker with carefully controlled features. He would not give offense even by a facial flinch.

"Junla feels that you deserve to know your fate. Today I am passing judgment on several issues. Your continued existence is being judged today. Do you understand what I just said?"

"Yes."

"Do you realize the importance of this event?"

"Yes."

"In your own words tell me what I just said."

"You will decide whether or not to kill me today."

"You understand that if I decide to let you live today, your future behavior could change that decision?"

"Yes."

"Do you have anything to add? Any statement to make at this point?"

"No."

"No? You don't care which way I decide?"

"No."

Harbinger leaned back in her seat. He could see that her stomach had grown since he had last been in her presence. She was growing fat off this land. Then he noticed that her face and arms had not changed at all. He saw that her hand rested protectively over the swell. He lowered his head.

"For now I will leave you in Lady Junla's care. She is doing well by you." Harbinger stood. She stretched her muscles. She adjusted her jacket over the swell of her womb. He found himself staring into her face. He was surprised to find that she was shorter than he.

"Lady Junla is doing you a great service. Be sure you reward her with kindness and respect. I would hate to find that you ever forgot the favor she has done you."

"Yes."

"I think we understand each other."

"Yes."

Junla let her breath go. She nodded to Harbinger. Her mind raced at the implied status Harbinger's last statement gave her.

"I will have to find you husbands, Lady Junla. You are too long unmarried."

Junla's eyes flew to Harbinger's face. Then they flew to her mother's band of guards. Color flushed her delicate features. She did not want husbands from Harbinger. She did not want too strong a link with Harbinger. Unless she could plead helplessness later on, that she had not really wanted the husbands but feared to refuse them.

"An interesting proposition, Harbinger. I am a traditionalist. I would prefer to choose a husband for old-fashioned reasons: advancement, security, position. I am sure you understand."

"I certainly do, Lady Junla. If ever you change your mind I will be happy to assist you in securing husbands with other values."

Looking into Harbinger's bright, shining eyes, Junla knew that the other woman understood her well, very well, too well.

"I will keep your offer in mind."

"I am sure your mother will give me a good reference as a matchmaker." Harbinger smiled jovially. Lady Zona coughed discretely behind her hand. All faces turned towards Lady Zona's guard.

Junla sighed with good humor. "I could only ever hope to aspire to my mother's good fortune."

"And stamina." Only Junla heard the aside. She was surprised into a short laugh.

"Harbinger, I wish to be clear on my goals. Am I headed in the right direction?"

"I am not sure where you are headed, Lady Junla. The road you are on is appropriate for the journey I am taking at this time. I will let you know if a bend in my road comes up that will affect your path."

"Thank you."

"Take your project home. Thank you for coming today. I admire your efforts."

He could not keep his gaze from the three guards around Lady Zona. His last time in this company he had been unable to notice the surrounding crowd. Now he could look at faces. Those three were familiar. In his foggy memory they belonged together. Why they belonged together or why he knew them escaped him at the moment. He could not examine the puzzle. His mind hurt if he stared too closely at the three. Instead he stared at the fall of the material of Junla's gown as she walked.

Seeing that swell on Harbinger put his mind on a track that it had not followed since before he had been chosen by the Temple. He watched the glide of cloth over the curve of Junla's bottom. He could catch a glimpse of the curve of her breast as she swung her arms. Her veil fluttered in the breeze teasing him as it streamed back at him. He slept not ten feet from this woman. Every night he listened to the rustle of her settling in her bed. He listened to be sure she slept before he slid into sleep. Her noises meant an end to his having to learn and to guard against mistakes.

Now as he lay trying to sleep, the sounds of her shifting brought to mind the way her sheets curved around her body. He wondered if the material dipped between her legs. He wondered if the sound of flesh shifting was her arms or her legs moving.

By the time the next morning dawned he had hardly slept. He stood trying to ward off his exhaustion.

"Did you not rest well, priest?"

"No."

"You have less to worry about now than you had before. Today let us begin with the constellations."

He was not happy with the constellations lesson. The groupings were different from his experience. He had no training in reading charts of the earth, never mind maps of the sky. He had to concentrate very closely during these lessons to remember everything. The pronunciation, the words, the names, the positions, the seasons, the time of night all required every bit of his mind.

There was a commotion outside the tent. Noise filtered through the heavy material. There was a loud thump. Then the flap whirled open. A tall lanky woman stood in the glare of the sun. He could tell she was female because she stood in profile. That was the only feature about her he could distinguish. Then the flap fell closed behind her.

"Ilissa, I hardly recognized you."

"Good, what have we here?"

Marma repressed a smile. She bent her head back to her work. She cast a sidelong glance at Junla. He watched the interplay between the three women. He had never questioned the relationship between Junla and Marma; they seemed as sister/wives to him. He considered Junla as the First wife and Marma as the Second. They acted as his mother and her sister/wives had acted. The question from this new woman changed the complexion of their relationship.

This woman was clearly Llweganian. Her dress and her stance were Llweganian. While Marma rarely spoke, always deferred to Junla, this one questioned, demanded an answer.

"This is a good works of Junla's."

"Good works? Junla's? You must be kidding."

"No, she is attempting to preserve his life by training him to be very still whenever danger nears."

Junla was ignoring both speakers. She gripped his shoulder forcing him to return his attention to his lesson.

"This must be the priest I've been hearing about. What do you call him?"

"Priest. It's short, simple, and easy for him to remember."

Ilissa tossed her hardened cap on the table. She shook the dust out of her eyes.

"Ilissa, please leave your dust outside where it belongs. We are quite near the baths. Don't come back until you are swept clean."

"Certainly, your highness." Ilissa swept a credible bow in Junla's direction. Grabbing a handful of clean clothing she left the tent.

He dared a glance at Junla. She was smiling slightly. He relaxed. She was in a good mood. He managed to complete three early spring nights without error. He was rewarded with a gentle squeeze on his shoulder. He was caught unaware for the streak of reaction that sped through his body at her casual touch.

He followed her movement away from him with his head. She lifted the tent flap. He could see nothing beyond her but he knew Ilissa returned. He watched Junla's controlled motions as she stepped aside to allow Ilissa into the tent. He saw the contrasts between Junla's controlled posture and Ilissa's loose-limbed sprawl in her chair. Even in the lamplight of the tent he could see the calluses on Ilissa's fingers. She held her wine goblet with absent strength and grace.

"Have you ranged far?"

Ilissa stared at him as she thought about Junla's question.

"Farther than our journey here."

"It must be nice to be back in familiar surroundings."

"My comrades are familiar."

"Oh."

"But not all of them."

"Ah, ah."

He did not understand the exchange. He did not know why Junla should find any of the statements interesting or informative but clearly she did. She was staring at a distant spot inside of herself. Marma had put down her sewing.

"Harbinger has offered to find Junla a husband or two."

"She has good taste."

"I hinted that I would rather marry Masfin."

"Still aiming for King Ranald?"

"I would bet he is already taken by now."

"Right you may be there. I myself am considering taking a husband."

"You could provide adequately for one?"

"Yes, I won my helm on this last venture. I can provide for three husbands now."

"I guess a helm is better than a dowry."

"It depends. I had an excellent dowry and an excellent sponsor. My sponsor is still excellent. Choosing a husband feels more interesting when one is in possession of a helm instead of a dowry."

Junla tilted her head to one side. She watched the priest as he listened to the tone of their stilted conversation trying to guess its content from the tone of the voices. She smiled to herself her probably was trying to gauge her mood from the sound of her voice. His comfort depended on her mood.

"I always found choosing a husband very interesting."

"It can be more interesting when one has several different criteria to fill the choice."

"What criteria do you have?"

"That I will ponder on this leave. Oh, I have more news. I have a name."

"A name?" Marma scrunched her face at Ilissa.

"Yes, a name earned in battle."

"Oh, right, a name, of course, what is your name?"

"Desert Snake."

"Desert Snake." Marma spoke with reservation.

"For my tenacity, patience, adaptability and strength."

"Congratulations, Desert Snake."

"I must be off. With my helm I got a tent of my own as well as a soldier in training. I can't spend my time indulging in good works."

He watched as Ilissa gathered her few belongings. She bundled them quite expertly. Then she left.

After Ilissa's visit he began to watch men in the camp. He tried to guess what attributes they had that a woman would deem appropriate for a husband. He learned to work the grinding stones. He sat in front of the tent while he worked, grinding grain, watching the troops move through the camp thinking on what made a good husband.

Then everything changed again. He was sitting in the sun, grinding grain, reciting long lists of participles when word passed through the camp.

"Fold tents." The clear, precise words could not be mistaken. He bagged his grain and flour separately but quickly. He disassembled the wheel efficiently. Then he waited for his keeper to call him. "Priest." He turned into the tent. She was transformed, they both were. They stood in complete Llweganian uniforms. She was like a needle of night in the now empty tent. Marma held a drab thing. She carried in a robe draped over her arm. He recognized the color immediately. It was her handiwork but it seemed larger somehow held as she held it now.

"Over here, priest." He stepped close to Junla. She reached towards him. Her gloved hands removed his clasp of office and robes. He stood naked in the shadowy tent. It was dark in the space since all the lamps were gone and the flap was closed. Her pale face seemed to float above the collar of her uniform. It was erotic. She stood so close to him. He was naked and she was dressed in her leathers. Her gloved hands had brushed his skin coolly as she undressed him. She turned back to him. Cool silk covered his upper body past his genitals. A leather jacket covered the silk.

Marma squatted.

"Step." He stepped into silk leggings. He grabbed the material from Marma before she could reach his secret. She waited until he had pulled up the first layer before handing him the next layer. He pulled on the leather breeches careful to adjust himself with some privacy. They had turned from him. Marma was lifting the tent flap. He hurried to get to his place.

In the sunlight he could see the tents falling in large groups. So quickly the camp was gone. Gone too was something else. Females should have no dominion over him. Only after long meditation and the correct herbs and wines should he react in the manner necessary to reproduce. All it had taken today was her touch and her scent. She had managed to destroy him. Not with wiles or seduction, not with any design had Junla wooed him from his calling to Kersai. He was damned. And lost.

Harbinger closed her fingers around the stone the messenger offered. She gave the order the camp had been awaiting for many Darkfalls. Jeffeaux would complain. He would want to rest before moving anywhere but she was tired of resting. Let him complain. First might need to rest. No, First would be anxious to return home. She would welcome the excuse to leave on her final leg of the journey.

The stress of the waiting must have shown on her face. A callused hand smoothed the skin of her forehead. She closed her eyes to savor the pleasure of the gesture. After a deep sigh she opened her eyes. Across the expanse of the field table she saw the tent flap open. The space before her tent was filled with hurrying figures. She could see tents deflating as they were readied for packing. Time to go.

Jeffeaux scanned the horizon. He had been looking for signs of the camp since early in the day. There should be some sign by now. The guard did not seem worried. They were not looking anywhere but straight ahead. Jeffeaux tried to relax. If something were wrong he would know already. He thought, he hoped.

Of course, why would he need to know anything? No one expected that he would do anything so why tell him anything. Why say anything to him at all? The guard in fact did not speak to him often, hardly at all. He had never been so lonely as on this trip. First would speak to him but not of anything he wanted to discuss. First was becoming more like the guards with every passing dawn. She did her work. She discussed politics and power. She waged war in a manner quite fierce and determinedly if nonviolently. She was becoming asexual to him.

Jeffeaux scanned the horizon again. He did not bother to look at the serene face of his companion. Her faith in Harbinger was absolute. Harbinger, she was becoming the only person with whom Jeffeaux felt comfortable. At least she wasn't asexual. A small smile broke the grim features of Jeffeaux's face. Harbinger could never be considered anything but a woman.

The small cavalcade broke over the ridge. Jeffeaux frowned anew. The army was assembling into columns. He urged his mount to a faster pace.

"Lord Jeffeaux, well met."

Sablor spoke cheerfully. He moved his steed until he was abreast of Jeffeaux.

"Is there trouble?"

"No, now that you are returned we are moving. Madame First." Sablor greeted the silent woman beside Jeffeaux.

"Sablor, I return Lord Jeffeaux to your keeping. Please inform Harbinger that I will look forward to her next homecoming."

"Madame First, we thank you for your kind offices. We will send a guard to the estate. They will be at your disposal for the fulfillment of your duties."

"I will do my best to meet those duties."

They exchanged very formal bows that should have looked ridiculous on top of horses but did not. Jeffeaux did not realize the import of the exchange until he sat alone with Sablor.

"Where are we hurrying to now?"

"A better place to press our advantage. Everyone is well. Did you enjoy your tour of the countryside?"

Jeffeaux released his tension. He was used to this type of polite exchange. His court persona reasserted itself on the short ride to the column. He began to wonder that First had not returned with him to personally report to Harbinger; or to receive her direction from Harbinger. He felt exposed riding down the hillside. He felt as if each eye were upon him: a strange uncomfortable feeling that he attributed to his moving across open space with only one companion before an audience of thousands. They rode quickly along long lines of troops.

"It seems as if we arrived just in time. Half a day more and we would have missed you."

"No, you would have arrived in time. We were waiting for you."

"Of course," Jeffeaux spoke barely above a whisper. He looked more closely at the watching troops. They were staring at him. They were waiting for him to take his place before they began their march. Sweat began to form under his collar.

"We are pleased you are back safely."

"Our guards were ever vigilant. First performed her duties exceedingly well."

"How did you find the countryside?"

Jeffeaux grimaced. "Dusty, dry, gray."

Sablor smiled.

"I wonder how the population found you."

"Much as Harbinger meant the people to find me, I suppose."

Sablor was quiet. They had reached the head of the line. Jeffeaux noticed his family members crowded around Harbinger. Her guard parted to allow him the spot of honor next to Harbinger. He bowed to his mother and her entourage. He nodded to his sister and Ilissa and Marma. As he turned to Harbinger he noted his sister had an escort dressed not in Llweganian black.

"Did you find the distraction you sought, Lord Jeffeaux?"

"I had a relaxing ride in the country, Harbinger."

"Good, you must be well rested by now." She turned in her saddle to look out over the line of troops around her. She sat straighter in her saddle. She raised her arm into the air above her head.

"Hoooo Ay." Her arm dropped quickly until she rested her hand on her reins. Then with a sigh the line moved forward.

"I take it we have not turned for Llwegan."

"Very true observation, my lord. Llwegan is not this way. We are moving our lines closer to the enemy."

"You are invading Masfin?" Jeffeaux felt his voice break.

"No, not exactly. I have been assured that our new position is land created in the shaking so no one really has claim to it."

"You will establish territory for Llwegan between Sarna and Masfin?"

"No, we plan to claim the land for Sarna."

"For Sarna?!?"

"I know, I know, but it will serve my purposes better that way. As I control Sarna I am really laying claim to the land for my uses and Llwegania's best interests."

Jeffeaux was quiet for a long time. Then he looked straight ahead at the horizon.

"You are a remarkable woman, Harbinger."

"I can't tell if you mean that as a compliment."

"I'm not sure myself."

"Well either way, thank you for noticing."

Jeffeaux disliked riding so close to Harbinger. Each step they took together placed him closer to the front of events. Why weren't her guards herding him back as they used to do? Jeffeaux studied the faces around them to find an answer. That man with Junla was familiar.

"Who is riding with my sister?"

"That priest you sent back to me. She has taken him on as a prisoner. She has done wonders with his behavior."

"Another priest, have the women of my family become obsessed with religion all of a sudden?"

Harbinger laughed aloud.

"Lord Jeffeaux, I have missed you. You certainly brighten my day."

He heard the words. He understood the meaning. He could not grasp the import. Priests, there were more priests? He wanted to scan the group, the troops, and the army for those other prisoners. Why had he not been placed with those other priests? Where were they? Then he went over every word of the conversation. The priests had to be connected to Junla or one of her family. Who was this man? How was he connected to Harbinger? Who else here was in his family?

His Llweganian was strangely accented. He used words in the wrong order. He was not from Sarna. So he could be Masfin. Was he married to Harbinger of Death? Would she marry one such as him? For political ends perhaps? Where were these priests?

He couldn't think like this. He would be without food and water and comfort again. He wanted to curse. He didn't know any curses. He used to know some, many, but they slipped from him.

He hated riding. He could not become comfortable. His back ached; his legs ached. Junla turned to look at him. His shifting had caught her attention. This might not be good. He immediately relaxed his posture into the position of those around him. He looked straight back at Junla with no expression. She turned away from him. Remember his lessons. Draw no attention. Speak only when spoken to. Answer yes and no whenever possible. Don't think.

Part Two: and Kings

Chapter 12

Jeffenza woke slowly. She savored the feel of the sheets against her skin. The soft slide of silk caressed her as she turned. She opened her eyes. She looked at the room over the curve of her arm. In many ways this room was like her rooms at Malso. The drab colors and stone walls were not different. Here as she woke she could hear the sounds of soldiers and armies and generals. This place has not handsome foreigners or mysterious comings and goings.

She was different from the Jeffenza who had been at Malso though there were cosmetic similarities. She had a real enemy now. She had someone to pour on whom all her hate and aggression. Her good mood evaporated the moment she thought of Harbinger. There could be no peace in her heart until that woman was broken, defeated. Even death would not be good enough for her enemy.

The door to her chamber opened. A servant crept in to deposit a warm cup of sweet liquid. In the morning light Jeffenza could see the steam waft over the cup's rim. Still she did not move. The servant pulled stones from the edge of the banked fire. The hot stones were handled with gloved hands. Quietly the servant rolled the stones over the carpet on the floor next to the bed. Once the chill had been taken from the floor, the stones were returned to the fireplace to ring the pit before the morning fire was lit. Only after the servant laid out underclothes and a morning robe to warm by the fire did Jeffenza stir. She sat against the pillows. The servant brought a warmed shawl to cover Jeffenza's shoulders as she sat sipping her breakfast.

Jeffenza watched absently as warmed water was poured into a bowl. Scented soap was shaved carefully into the water. With a sigh Jeffenza walked across the warmed floor to the fire. She stood still as a cloth damp with the scented water was run over her body under her night gown. She felt the soap being wiped off her skin. Then as she watched the flames, she shifted from foot to foot to allow her stockings to be drawn on her legs. She savored the pampering of being a titled lady in Masfin. She had missed this during her captivity.

When her final choice had been made and her final ribbon tied Jeffenza viewed the completed toilette in the mirror. She looked regal today. Good. She knew everyone thought her an empty-headed girl. Today she would begin to change their minds. Her plans did not include girlish dreams anymore. Girlish dreams had brought her chains and servitude.

She had been fascinated by the equivalent of a foreign prince. Now she had no time for princes, foreign or otherwise. She was stalking bigger game. The thing she envied Harbinger most was her power. In Masfin there was only one source of power for a woman, her husband. The most powerful man to take for husband in Masfin was the King. Jeffenza had made up her mind. She could indulge in pretty men all she wanted later. Now she had only one goal. Was that veil too sheer? No, she looked right, time to go.

Renfrew watched Jeffenza enter the hall. She spoke briefly to everyone. She was approaching him. She would speak shortly to him. She would pretend he had never seen her dirty and sunburned. He would be beneath her notice beyond the superficial greeting. She would condescend to interact with this representative of the ally despite his part in her rescue..no, escape.

Renfrew was not happy. Troops were going missing. Not whole companies as with Marlin, but noticeable numbers. True some would have slipped home. The letters from families begging aid with harvesting or fear for safety of families while armies crisscrossed the countryside were strong magnets. Renfrew feared the soldiers were not slipping back into Masfin. He envisioned troops wandering away into the desert looking for the enemy.

The enemy would have knowledge about every move they had made trying to obscure their position. He should send those soldiers home whose loyalty he doubted except he feared to let them out of his control. He wanted to kill all those he could not trust. He wanted to declare all those who were different the enemy, but he couldn't. He would
become a monster.

Here she was.

"Good day, General Renfrew." She smiled vaguely, slightly.

"Stiefis, was the sunrise beautiful today?"

Stiefis smiled at their running joke. "That is a matter of opinion."

"Someday I promise I will give you my opinion on a sunrise."

"It will be your gain."

"It would be unhealthy for me to be awake at that hour of the day."

Then she had passed them. Stiefis watched her even as she passed onto another group. He admired her manners and acceptance of her position. She liked being a woman. He liked that about her.

"How long do you plan to stay right now?" Stiefis looked at Renfrew.

"What?"

"Are you going to be here awhile? I have things to do." Renfrew sounded impatient.

"Fine, I plan to eat something right now."

Renfrew nodded once. Then he turned from the crowd. He made his way out of the room. He hurried through the building. He had set up his tent on the edge of the courtyard. He wanted to be out of doors, close to the action of the troops.

Stiefis did not watch Renfrew leave. He moved towards his seat. He spoke only with his partners on his left and right. He used his utensils with ease of practice. He smiled politely when required and remained solemn the rest of the time. He was contented. In this moment he did not miss Sarna. He no longer found it strange to sit with women who were married to other men or even unmarried. The food he ate was tasty and the wine he drank was sweet.

In fact his strongest tie to Sarna was Renfrew. Since his Repudiation Stiefis had avoided his fellow Sarnese. He could not stand the pity of his father, the smirking of his brother, the gloating of his uncle. Everything he once had valued had failed him. Even his religion had cast him out. Why should he want to return to Sarna? What was there for him? Arid bleak landscapes? Sand in every bite of food? Begging water from the Temple?

He shied away from the last question. Water had a new source. He placed his wine goblet on the table gently. The food in his mouth lost its flavor. He had a duty to Sarna. His father had brought the disease into Sarna, but he, Stiefis, had trained her in the knowledge that had defeated Sarna. He had caused her to learn all the secrets of the Temple, the rites of his people. She ruled Sarna partly through his actions and inactions.

He sat here enjoying life while his country bent under the yoke of an invader.

He deserved his Repudiation. He deserved the pity and scorn. Renfrew was right to spend every moment planning for battle. The entertainment was about to begin. Everyone was leaving their seats to enter the hall.

Chairs were arranged in rows. Stiefis chose a seat near the exit. He would stay for the opening. He watched the guests arrange themselves. The crowd around the King settled last. She was on the edge of that crowd. She belonged with that crowd. Her well-dressed body and careful posture were exactly what that crowd required, maybe just a little more. She shone a little more brightly than the crowd.

She had a crowd of her own around her. They rivaled the King's in size and glitter. He wondered if she expected the King to notice her with admiration or respect or fear.

He was allowing the petty wars of the court to interest him. He had greater issues to consider. How would he save his people, his country, his culture, his heritage? What did one girl's machinations matter next to his entire world?

He rose from his seat in disgust. He left the whirl of color without a single backward glance. The night air held refreshment and sense. First he needed to put off his useless clothes. Then he would take his duty prescribed position.

Renfrew looked up as Stiefis entered the tent. It had been a long time since his Sarnese ally had put off court dress of an evening. Now was the time.

"They are moving."

"Show me."

Renfrew turned back to the map table. His hand moved to reveal the stretch of land barely inscribed.

"An entire army cannot move without some signs; even an army such as this one. But they are not in the desert anymore. There are no more clouds of dust to give us direction."

"They are headed our way I take it."

"Any way they turned they were. The question is which way did they turn?"

Stiefis studied the map. He tried to trace the path of each position to its logical end.

"We would know if they had gone straight?"

"That we would know. If they passed into Masfin we would know. If they had settled we might know. So I assume they are still moving."

"How many scouts do you have out?"

Renfrew stared at the map.

"Have you dispatched any cavalry?"

Renfrew stood straight. He dared not look at his officers. He walked out of the tent. Stiefis followed closely behind.

"The only men who have knowledge of the terrain I do not dare to send."

Stiefis heard the words. He looked into the dark in the direction he thought she might lurk.

"We have a legend of a monstrous woman who eats men for dinner. She is ugly and manly. She has fearsome teeth and breath. We use it to frighten children into obedience."

"I will tell you something that only my father knows. She came into Sarna as a frail female. She came with presents and bribes. I married her. I took her into my household. I had her trained to the Sarnese ways. I married her." Stiefis drew a deep breath. He stared into the depths of her memories. "What you do not know, what my father does not know is that I found her beautiful, strong, wise, crafty, desirable, frightening. I have seen her draped in cloth of gold and wrapped in the cloak of battle. I have beheld her with bejeweled fingers and goblets in her hands. I have seen those same hands begrimed and holding a sword.

"She has lived in my house, walked with my wives. I had her in my hand but her beauty and power frightened me. I set her on my country. I put her there. I will drive her out or die trying." Stiefis sighed deeply. "Don't judge your troops too harshly. She is like the battle maids we threw out of my culture and I still find her intriguing. Don't you have goddesses whom she rivals?"

Renfrew turned silently. He listened to the sounds of the camp.

"Where will she go? Where is the best place for her to go?"

"Somewhere we will be unable to resist her. Somewhere we will be compelled to push at her. Where would your brother send her?"

"Do you think he has that much influence?"

"She does not fear competence. She uses it. Where would he suggest?"

"I will think on that one. We were never close."

"So I guessed. Brothers can be like that."

Renfrew chuckled. Stiefis spoke from experience.

The stone was cold under his rear end. The wall was damp on his back. The air was dry to his lungs. None of his physical discomfort distracted him from his thoughts. He had puzzled at the question for many days. The land had changed from flat and dry to rocky and dry to mountainous and damp. He sat in their room trying to guess the answer to his query.

He was alone with his mistress. She was deep asleep. Marma was down the hall sleeping in her own room. His lady slept in her bed high off the floor away from stray drafts and rodents. His bedroll was under her bed. He had only to roll under to find his rest. The position of the bed itself was out of most drafts. All he need do was pull his blanket over his head to sleep. But he would spend all Darkfall hearing her rustle above him.

"Priest, what is wrong? Go to sleep."

He could not tell her what his real problem was. He dared not utter his real issue. So the words erupted from him in defense of his innermost thoughts.

"What other priests?"

Junla blinked awake. She turned toward his voice. She tried to imagine where the question came from. She reviewed all her responsibilities' contacts from the beginning. There was only one instance where she could remember this topic arising.

"That has occupied your mind for this entire journey? I am impressed at your restraint and endurance. My mother's husbands are three priests she brought out of the Temple of Kersai at Deskersai. Those are the priests you have been wondering about."

He felt the breath leave his body. He clutched his hands into surprised fists.

"Priests? Your mother is married to priests?"

"Yes, they all seem happy with the arrangement."

Something in him snapped. He surged up in the darkness. He followed her scent unerringly. He reached the bed. His hand found her shape in the sheets. She made a startled sound. He stripped the sheet from her. He fumbled for the end of her sleepwear. He followed the source of her scent. He found her skin. His nose found the heart of her bouquet. His mouth moved to suck at her until he could taste her scent in his mouth.

Junla held still. She swallowed loudly. She had not expected her project to react so violently to her answer. For a heartbeat she had thought he meant her violence. She had drawn her breath in to scream; but once his hand reached for her thighs and not her throat she had relaxed. Her knees fell open to allow him access to her. His tongue was buried as far as it could go into her. Now he was licking upwards. His mouth was tasting every inch of her soft folds. Her hips lifted insistently.

"A little higher, just a little higher," she whispered the words. She shifted again. He heard her. There he found her sweet spot. He licked her, not enough. The caress was sweet torture. His teeth pressed against her. She wriggled. The pressure built. She felt her face tighten in effort. She pushed against him. His teeth opened. He sucked hard. Her stomach muscle clenched. She pushed up, his head pushed her down. He sucked harder. His tongue worried at her. She dug her heels into the bed. A shrill high sound bounced off the walls. The stone sent it back to her. Her head flung side to side as he drank her heavy sweet scent.

She wanted more. She wanted everything. Her feet urged him up. His arms tensed.

"Come here, priest." He could not resist his training. He followed the sound of her voice. As his body moved up the valley of hers she readied herself. She felt his chest drag over her pelvis. It scraped against her stomach and over the rise of her breasts. She lifted her hips; she raised her heels over his legs. Then as he approached her face she felt the object of her desire. Using her heels to urge him forwards while pushing her hand between their bodies she guided him home. He was completely still. She took him as far as she could. She rubbed her body against him. When he lay still she urged him to roll over. As he lay on the bed she raised herself almost off him before plunging back. Her hands dug into his shoulders as she rode his staff seeking her pleasure.

He lay there in shock. He had wanted to find the elusive source of her aroma. He had reveled in the scent and taste of her. His excitement had blossomed as he drank. As with the wine of the Blessing ceremony the wine of her body had urged him on; but, unlike the Blessing wine, her wine did not induce a blanking fog. He knew everything that was happening to him. He felt every blood vessel bursting in his body. He felt the agony of pleasure she was building in his body. He understood where she was taking him but he didn't know where she was taking him. But he was going there, he was going there, he was going there, but he needed to do something. He needed to turn over. He needed to hold. He felt the pain of her bite push him into infinity. His soul seemed to rush from his body into hers. He collapsed as his body deflated. He had no coherent thoughts.

She remembered to pull the bed covers over them. She wriggled to settle him into the cradle of her body. She reveled in the feel of him still deep in her. Then sleep washed over her.

He woke from a dream of warm pleasure to the reality of her holding him with one leg over his hip. She was languidly taking her pleasure. He tensed as he left sleep for the new day. Her hand soothed down his back. The pale light of morning lit her dreamy face. He wanted, he wanted to taste her. His mouth descended until he found her lips. She sighed her permission into his mouth. He shuddered as her tongue caressed his.

He savored the feel of her bare skin against him. Her breasts soft with hard centers rubbed his chest. Her hands traced the shape of his back. And all the while her warm wet tunnel slid along his aching shaft. He rolled onto his back taking her with him. He urged her up and down with worshipping hands. Her hands rested on his shoulders. He watched her body curve up as she took her pleasure. Her breasts bounced in her rhythm. Their pink areolae fascinated him. He watched them quiver and dance. His mouth became dry watching them. Her heavy braid slithered until it brushed his chest. The feel of the fine silk against his skin added to his tension. His hands tightened against the cheeks of her bottom. His fingers splayed wide to cup her.

Her rhythm increased. The force of her thrusts strengthened. He

pushed his heels into the mattress. His eyes closed in anticipation of his release. She collapsed before he was done. He lay shaking in frustration. He waited as she rubbed her face against his chest. He lay still gathering his composure even as he throbbed in frustration. He dared not move. He dared not distract her. She shifted her bottom seating herself more securely. He gritted his teeth. He could not finish and he could not retreat. Each twitch of her body ensured he remained in his wanting state. Her head turned on his chest. She lay quiet for a moment. Then she moved her head. He did not know what to do. Her head moved more, until he felt her tongue lick at his nipple. The pleasure from that spot shot out to his groin; again with the tongue. He couldn't help it. He shifted slightly. Her thighs tightened against his hips. He held still. Her mouth latched
onto him. She suckled first one nipple then the other. Thank the skies she was not through with him.

Oh, he was wrong. She was leaving him. What did she want? She nestled against him. She rolled onto her knees, her tight grip on his arm pulling him over her. This way? Oh, yes this way. He had nothing to hold onto. His hands brushed against her hanging breasts as he tried to find a grip. One hand landed on the sheets, grasping a handful of material. The other savored the shape and feel and resilience of her breast. She butted against him. Like that? Yes, he rushed trying to find his release before she changed her mind.

Harbinger sipped her wine. Over the rim of her goblet she watched her court filter into the tent. She liked this tent. She liked the color of the walls. She liked the carpets. She liked the chairs and cushions. Masfin had some very fine ideas about pampering the body.

Of course one could take this pursuit of comfort to the extreme. She couldn't say anything about Jeffeaux. He was holding up quite well under the strain of campaign life. He was not someone she would trust at her back or side but he did not complain or fall off the pace. He needed to be married. He needed an heir, a son according to Masfin tradition. If he would devote half as much energy to pursuing his duty as he had his pleasure he would be exceptional.

The thought of Masfin traditions turned her thoughts down another path.

"Marlin."

There was a shifting of bodies as the requested person moved from his spot behind Lady Zona.

"Harbinger."

"Sit next to me for a minute."

Marlin lowered himself cautiously. He had never sat in the presence of the Dragon except far down the table.

"Do you have a wife, Marlin?"

"No, Harbinger."

"Good. In Llweganian laws a man can only have one wife; in that one way Llwegan and Masfin are similar."

"Only one wife at a time, Harbinger."

"Ah, yes of course. Our law does not prohibit a widower from remarrying but our traditions frown on it."

"That is different from Masfin traditions." Marlin became pale with fear.

"In Sarna the rules are different."

"That is true. Llweganian and Masfin rules are very different also except for that one similarity."

"You are right, you are right. All three societies are very different from each other."

"That is true."

"But you seem comfortable with Llweganian ways."

Marlin felt his breath leave his body. He was not comfortable right now.

"I am sure you could become used to Sarnese traditions as easily."

Marlin stared in complete bafflement at Harbinger. Her statement had absolutely nothing to do with the conversation he was having.

"The Sarnese have many wives. Take First: she is one of six sister/wives. She would never take a husband who would not take all her sister/wives as well."

"I understand that."

"Do you think you could adapt to that situation?"

"Any man would be blest to have First and her household as his family."

"You are a man of discernment and sense."

Harbinger was quiet as she studied the tent's occupants. Marlin felt his heart return to his body. He realized he had not been having the conversation he had thought but he was unsure what he had been discussing.

"I was one of First's sister/wives until she and her household Repudiated our husband. In Llwegan when a man wishes to court a wife he sends an elaborate written document that presents his wishes, his assets, his strengths, his logic for a marriage to his chosen's mother. First doesn't have a mother anymore. I am her closest approximation for that position. Any of my husbands could help you compose such a presentation. It is an art that they all were very successful in, I think."

She was proposing a match between him and First? Six wives? She was verily ordering him to marry First and her sister/wives.

"What could I possibly offer her?"

"A steady hand, a constant heart, a wise head, a daring nature, you like her. You appreciate her strengths. You admire her character. You don't know how valuable those things are. She needs a strong partner. She has great responsibilities. She needs someone as strong as she is. You will make her a good husband. I know a good husband when I see one."

"You have good husbands."

"All the ones I have chosen are good. I have one out there on the other side who was not a good husband. But he is proving to be a wise general."

Marlin remained silent. No one ever spoke of her connection across the lines. Everyone knew that she kept a tie to one of her enemy counterparts. She was not embarrassed or discomfited by the connection. She almost reveled in it. As if it were a secret weapon.

"Perhaps you will gift your wives with the greatest gift of all; perhaps you will give them children."

Marlin wished desperately for a drink.

"You will like being married. Everyone needs family. Family can have many boundaries but everyone needs some group of people with whom they share a history, bond, affection. Marriage is a good foundation for a family."

"You are right Harbinger, in everything. I have been so focused on the war effort I had not thought of marriage. Are there any

Sarnese rites I should respect in this matter?"

"I told you, you are a wise man. Consult with Lady Zona. She is an expert in Sarnese traditions."

Harbinger smiled at Marlin as he rose. She was well satisfied with her effort. She still had the problem of Jeffeaux and now the developing situation of Junla but solutions would present themselves to her soon enough.

She would need some fine cloth to gift First's household. Masfin tradition also had a place in this ceremony.

"Sablor, find a small group to send into Masfin for materials for First. There is going to be a wedding. The brides will need appropriate Masfin attire. Arrange it for me."

Petron leaned close to Harbinger. "Wife, you are beautiful when you are happy."

"I have always thought happiness was the truest source of lasting beauty."

"How are our numbers?"

"Growing steadily."

Harbinger rubbed the high curve of her belly.

"I have to leave soon for Assize Court. Wind Rider needs to do her Walks. I should do a Walk."

"The demands are great."

"Lady Zona and First will do well here until our return. I want First married before we leave. I will have to solve this new problem with Junla before we leave. It will be good to be home. We will return refreshed."

"I would not want to be gone long."

"We won't be. You know how I hate unfinished business hanging over my head."

"Between the Walk and the travel and the court we will be gone half a year."

"It will lull our enemy into complacency. Our new position will be some time mapping and scouting before we can take full advantage of its potential, and I could use a rest from being pregnant."

Petron chuckled at her final statement.

"You are never so fertile as when we are on campaign."

"I am happy to give my husbands heirs; but, I can't remember a time I was not pregnant right now."

Petron leaned to speak into Harbinger's ear. Jeffeaux watched the conversation from across the tent. He watched Harbinger's skin flush with pleasure at the words whispered in her ear. The tilt of her head reminded Jeffeaux of a young girl flirting with her first beau. Her pleased expression and glowing eyes did not seem at odds with the fierce woman he knew her to be. She would be leaving soon. She had to return to her country to fulfill her duties as the head of several estates. He would miss her.

His mother was set to lead the army. His mother with her generals and her priests and her wards and her children, the idea amazed him. The army would follow his mother? Had she not ridden into the heart of the enemy at Harbinger's side? Had she not ridden out of the Temple of Kersai, fought through the enemy at Harbinger's back? His mother had quite the reputation in this army. After all, his mother was as royal as the King by this army's rules. At least no one expected him to lead any army, especially this army. No one suggested he make any decisions. He went where he was told to go. He was humored and cosseted until he wished someone would expect he do something. He who never thought to raise a hand in effort resented that no one here thought to ask him to make an effort.

Everyone here did something towards the campaign. Everyone here had responsibilities and duties. His sister had duties. In Masfin, where half the privileged slept their lives away, avoiding effort was a victory. Here everyone acted as if he were incapable of anything at all. Nothing was expected of him, not because he successfully avoided effort but because no one thought him capable of effort. He suspected no one would trust him to fetch water never mind an important task. Fetching water was very important here; he could hear Harbinger's amused voice answering his thoughts. He was unimportant here. They treated him the way they would have treated a favored pet mouse.

And yet, he had the most use. The culmination of all this effort would be placing him on a throne. All this was going to end up being in the history books as being for him.

"Maybe I should go with you."

Harbinger looked at Jeffeaux. Her face was blank.

"When you go on your, whatever it is you are going to do, maybe I should go with you."

When Harbinger remained silent, he rushed into speech.

"I could see how to act in an official capacity. Learn the tricks of the trade."

"You expect to use these skills sometime?"

Jeffeaux stared past Harbinger's shoulder. He sighed deeply.

"If I remain behind," he did not wish to say the words. He sighed deeply. "My position will not be strengthened, if I remain. My value to your plans will dissipate if I stay in Sarna. If I go with you, my value will grow."

"That is true. I am glad you brought this up. I had planned to bring you with me. Once we are in Llwegan you will need to be careful. My peers don't like me."

Jeffeaux laughed. "I can imagine."

"I am very circumspect in my dealings with my peers."

"I'm sure, but, you are not a person who is *liked*. I can't imagine you ever inspiring such a pallid response in any person."

"I like you Jeffeaux: you are not afraid of me."

"No, just of what you might do."

"That is part of my peers' problem at home. They fear what I might do, so they try to control me. I won't be controlled."

"I have seen that. You can be persuaded."

"No one's right all the time. I can be convinced by logic or even true belief."

"At least eleven of your peers respected you; they sent you their sons."

"Some thought to control me through my husbands."

"Foolish people."

"I love my husbands; they are the core of my life."

"That is easily seen. Even for love you won't be controlled."

"No. That's not always a good trait."

"You do have a good heart and that does control you." Harbinger smiled at Jorin as he spoke the words in her ear. For a brief second she pressed her forehead against his weathered cheek.

"First on the agenda is the wedding. Then I have to find a husband for your sister Junla."

"Why does she need a husband?"

"If she continues as she is she will get pregnant by her priest. In Sarnese culture that would not be a problem. In Masfin that would result in a spot of embarrassment and some censure. In

Llweganian law she would be in dire trouble I want your position to be strengthened by everything that touches you. If I find her the right husband, that child will cement your position. Then you will have a legitimate heir for your house. I need someone in the right level of society from Masfin."

"You're saying my sister and the priest…What is it about the women in my family and priests?"

"Maybe your female relatives are simply very religious?"

"I can't believe you said that with a straight face."

Harbinger laughed. She threw her head back to let the sound out of her body. She was still chuckling as she rose from her seat. She left so the tent could be dismantled. She had a lot to accomplish before she had to leave for Llwegan.

"Your Majesty, forgive me for waking you."

Ranald turned over in his bed. His coverlet slipped from his shoulder letting a draft of cold air touch his skin. A hand quickly drew the blanket back into place.

"Your Majesty, it is of the utmost importance that you speak with the messenger."

Resigned to yet another sleepless night Ranald got out of bed. He drew a heavy robe on over his night shirt. He stepped into the leather slippers his servant brought from the hearth. He stretched his neck as he rose from the bed. He placed a plain gold circlet on his brow before he left his sleeping chamber.

His anteroom was filled with men in uniform. One man, a boy really, stood in the center of the crowd. The young figure was covered in dust and grime. Fatigue lined his face.

"Your Majesty, they are over the border." Ranald glared at the speaker. He was tired of bad news. He was tired of waging war. He was tired of speaking with soldiers all day long. He was tired of reacting to the movements of a woman.

"Where are they over the border?"

There was a silence as the messenger handed a packet to a lieutenant on the boy's right. The papers rustled slightly as they were passed from hand to hand until they reached the highest aide-de-camp present.

"Obviously someone knows where they have crossed or you wouldn't have disturbed my sleep."

"They have crossed the mountains at Tampello, Your Majesty."

"There are no mountains at Tampello."

"They grew with the Shaking, Your Majesty. There used to be a harbor there. During the Shaking the sea disappeared into the earth and mountains grew, a plain was formed. She has claimed the mountains and the plains for Sarna."

"Someone spoke with her? Without Our knowledge? Without Our permission?"

"Your Majesty, there were some adventurers there, curiosity seekers really; she sent them on their way with this message for us: 'Stay out of Sarna, it belongs not to Masfin.' She will defend the Sarnese border from Masfin incursions with all determination."

"That unnatural woman is trying to claim that We have invaded Sarna?"

"She says those foolish people were army scouts, Your Majesty. This is really Masfin territory anyway, it was our harbor. We did not know Sarna lay on the other side of the water."

"Were they army scouts?"

"It doesn't matter who they were, Your Majesty"

Ranald listened to the argument raging around him. He did not care beyond the fact that the enemy now had a semi-legitimate foothold on his frontier.

"Tampello is two weeks ride from here, is it not?"

"Yes, Your Majesty."

"What is your advice gentlemen?"

"We could cross into Sarna here, Your Majesty."

"The border is undefended?"

"No, Your Majesty, it is well fortified with trenches and traps and troops. She has spent her time building a complex system of defenses."

"We could pass through them?"

"Not before she could move her main force to attack us, Your Majesty."

"Why not? She is a long ride away."

"By the time we assemble the army, move from here to the border, she would have traveled half the distance to us. Then the defenses and the border guards she has in place would delay us for the rest of the time she would need to reach us, Your Majesty."

"Surely the Sarnese people would rise up once they knew their army was returning with us."

No one spoke. Each man looked to his neighbor to break the news of the relative uselessness of the Sarnese alliance in that area.

"No one thinks the Sarnese people will rise up against their Llweganian conquerors?"

"Actually, I think they quite like Harbinger." The young messenger spoke hesitantly, "Your Majesty."

"They like that woman?"

"She provides very well for them. They are living better under her than they did under the old system, Your Majesty."

"She invaded them."

"Your Majesty, everyone who benefitted from the old order is with you except the priests, and the people will not rise up for them. It was a harsh land with a harsh culture. She gave them water, Your Majesty. She gave them life and some control of that life. Why would they rise up against her?"

"Because she is an outlander."

"Everybody there knows of her, Your Majesty. They lived with the knowledge of her all their lives. All their country borders on her country. She was feared because she was a strong defender of her country. She was respected because she was a strong defender of her country. Now she is becoming their defender. She is not strange to them, Your Majesty, the way we are. The Sarnese might not know her daily routine or religious traditions but they know the names of her ancestors and of her children. They can recite her entire lineage. They can tell you the names of her husbands and when she married each one. Everything she did was always important to them. What little gossip or insight they could garner was important. Now they are become part of her story, her myth. They own her in a way, because her life is part of them.

"She is claiming this land for Sarna not Llwegan, Your Majesty. Don't you see? She is holding them so lightly that they have to cling to her to make sure she doesn't let go."

Ranald watched the young face shine through the dirt and fatigue. The boy had been too long in the field to understand so much. War did that. It aged boys into men overnight.

"The question is: how far will she go to defend her country?"

"All the way to the sea, my King, all the way to your throne."

Everyone turned to look at the speaker. Jeffenza shone like a star in the room filled with dark uniforms.

"But she won't sit on that throne, she will place Jeffeaux there. I had wondered why she kept such a soft man such as my brother by her. She needs him to finish her plans. But, my King, my claim is as good as his since it is through the female line. Our child would have the strongest claim of all since all lines would meet in him or her. Harbinger could not refute the superior claim a child of our union would have over that of Jeffeaux."

Ranald stared at the small female daring him to act. If he married her he would not be conferring an honor on her at all. She would be bringing him invaluable help. She would stand as his equal, as his defense against her brother, his rival. He did not want to share his position or power with anyone, especially not a wife or child, but to keep that power he had to do something. He would do anything.

"So be it, my Lady: I will make you my Queen."

Jeffenza advanced into the room until she was close to Ranald. She pitched her voice so only he could hear her.

"And I will keep you King."

Truflo backed out of the room. He stood on the threshold. He watched the generals and advisors surge around the king. He saw the woman place a proprietary hand on the king's arm. He reviewed the conversation he had heard. He fixed the sequence of words in his memory. As he turned to leave he felt a body bump into his. He spoke a hasty apology. He tried to move away from the body, to leave the chamber. The body followed him.

"You know a lot about the Sarnese people."

Truflo squinted up at the face blocking his path.

"That is my job, sir. I am the eyes and ears of the king in the field."

"I had not realized our scouts spent so much time over the border."

Truflo considered his next words carefully.

"I spent long weeks in Sarna."

"You are almost a child now."

"I was an arms runner. That is a job of children."

"When did arms runners get promoted to scouts?"

Truflo knew the prejudice against arms runners in the regular army. He had fought hard against it to gain his present assignment.

"I worked very hard, sir. My commanding officer rewarded merit and potential with advancement."

Renfrew frowned. The time Masfin soldiers spent in the Llweganian camp continued to corrode Masfin values and structure. Since the life expectancy of arms runners was very low only the most expendable of boys and men served as arms runners. They could on occasion rise to the position of a foot soldier but never to a position of importance such as a scout.

"General, I am needed back with my troop. My horse is ready now. May I have permission to leave?" Renfrew waved the youth away from him. Truflo breathed a sigh of relief. This step was done. His list was shrinking. It had started with the leg to enter Masfin. Then ferret out the daily password. Then get into the army headquarters. Then deliver the message. Next make sure the message was believed. Then get out of the headquarters. Lastly return safely to Sarna. He had only one leg left to complete.

Renfrew stared at the retreating figure. Stiefis came up to him.

"You seem to be very interested in the boy."

"There is something in what he said."

"What did he say?"

Renfrew wanted to resist answering the question. Somehow having the words repeated to his Sarnese ally seemed cruel.

"What did he say?"

Renfrew latched onto another part of the conversation. "Who was his commanding officer? That was the question I wanted to ask. He must have known I wanted to ask that question. But he made me let him go before I could ask that important question."

Stiefis shook his head. "He had the password of the day. You see shadows everywhere. Let's congratulate Lady Jeffenza on snaring her king."

"Go congratulate Lady Jeffenza on snaring her king. I have to find this arms runner/scout. I have some more questions for him."

Renfrew rushed to the stables. In the dark air he could see nothing. He could hear the clip clop of horses' hooves as he stood in the night.

"Here, you, did a scout get here yet?"

"He has come and gone sir."

"He can't have been gone long. The night is pitch black. Where does he think he is going? Saddle me a mount."

"Yes, sir."

Renfrew did not consider his state beyond sending for his riding cloak. He grabbed a water bag from a passing groom. The night pressed against him.

"Which way did he ride out?"

"Back the way he came sir."

Tampello then, so be it, he would follow the runt back to his senders.

Two dawns later Renfrew cursed his impulsive decision. How did he expect to follow a scout? He was riding blindly towards Tampello. He knew he would find the youth in the arms of the enemy. He should ride back to Jalico to warn them of his suspicions. They would laugh at his fancies. He needed facts to convince them that the youth had been a wily spy sent to report on the King's positions and movements. Movements the messenger had deftly maneuvered. That unlined face would not be perceived as such a devious deceiver.

Renfrew stopped by a stream to fill his water pouch. He watched the bubbles rise as the air was replaced by water in the bag. He shook his head. He would have to stop for food soon. There had to be a settlement eventually. He had money for victuals. What he needed right now was a weapon for hunting. This entire adventure was a waste of time and ill-considered.

A faint scent of cooking meat reached him. The aroma sat on the breeze. He was riveted to the smell. He stood slowly. The water bag, half filled, hung from his fingers. Absently he gathered the reins behind him. He walked along the bank of the stream following the scent of food. His horse plodded behind him.

He could smell the smoke from the fire. It was very faint under the strong aroma of food. He did not try to disguise his approach. He came straight from the edge of the stream into the camp. He felt his heart stop as he noticed that the camp was empty. That was his only warning.

His horse reared as they rushed him from the woods. He held onto the reins trying to use the potential danger of the animal as a defense against the attackers. A sharp sword severed the reins from behind his back. The blade bit into his water bag. Under him the footing became slippery, dangerous. He titled sideways. He was allowed to fall as his horse was pushed away. He heard the loud protests of his mount to the sudden action. He tried to right himself. A strong hand pushed him the rest of the way down. He saw the fist coming towards him.

Renfrew's first coherent thought was that he could still smell the food. His head ached. His body ached. His pride throbbed. He opened his eyes. The youth sat there, right across from him, calmly sipping water. A plate of steaming stew sat on the youth's bent knee.

"Thought of some more questions for me did you?"

"I mean you no harm. If you let me go now you won't be in any trouble."

"I seriously doubt both statements. Of course I am not in any trouble now. I'm with my companions. We are on our way home."

Renfrew noticed the other occupants of the camp for the first time. Three soldiers sat around the scout. They were hard to distinguish in the early Darkfall.

"I was right to doubt you."

"What tipped you off?"

"You like her too much. You know too much."

"Her names are Harbinger of Death and Devouring Dragon. You may call her Harbinger or Dragon for short. Use one of her names. I do like Harbinger. I have value with her. My commanding officer is familiar to you. He is your brother, General Marlin. I think I will bring you to him as a wedding present."

"General?"

"General, he is of the house of Lady Zona, who is of the House of Harbinger. He is a general and I am a scout. And these are my team members."

"And we are going to Tampello."

"No, I lied. We are over the border, but not there. The armies will pass before us as you go to Tampello; then again as you go back when you find us not there. Of course, I don't mean you personally, since you will be with us by then."

"Then why tell the lie?"

"Because those were my orders."

Renfrew flinched when one of the soldiers came to him. He was chagrined when the woman began to feed him. But he could not refuse the meal. His stomach was too empty to deny it food. After he had eaten his face was washed. A cold cloth was pressed to the bruise on his jaw. There was silence the entire time. Each soldier, scout knew what was supposed to happen next.

His entire journey went like that. He was the only one who initiated conversation. The Masfin youth was the only one who answered him. He did not waste effort on discussion after the third attempt. He waited for his opportunity. It would come. There always were chances if you could recognize them.

"Can you trust the Sarnese, boy?"

Truflo glanced at the soldier Renfrew was watching.

"Yes."

"How can you be so sure? We trusted you and you are one of us."

"I am not one of you. I can trust that woman. She is my wife."

Renfrew saw the smile that passed among the group. He watched the friendly nods the couple made to each other.

"How did that happen?" The question was surprised out of Renfrew.

"She lived in the village near our last encampment. I saw her every day when she went for water. We began to talk. Before I knew it her father came to me offering me her hand. General Masfin agreed. We were married. I am able to support a wife on my position.

"My wife saw how the women were treated and how they acted in camp. She began to train with the soldiers. Now she is a member of my team. We do very well together."

"You are very young to be married."

"In Masfin I would never have married. Who would marry an arms runner? No one would."

"That's no argument."

"No, that is an explanation."

"Perhaps her father sent her as a spy."

"Her father hoped to better her position and to get a child on her. Both his goals were achieved."

Renfrew closed his mouth. He stared at the lanky girl. She had no signs of womanhood, yet, she was a mother. There was a discrepancy in the tale. Unless. That could be. Pregnant women went into battle in Llwegan. His head hurt from all the stresses of his situation. Renfrew closed his eyes to shut out the realities he could not face.

First stared at the group in her courtyard. She watched her servants unloading her gift from Harbinger. She was calm about her upcoming marriage. Her sisters had been happy with the choice. Marlin would be a good husband.

"Harbinger insists that Masfin traditions be included. She was adamant about the dresses. We brought a seamstress with us. She was Lady Zona's own servant." Truflo stood quietly as First accepted the finality of the moment. He understood her reluctance to accept such frivolous attire. She was no pampered lady from Masfin.

"I have a favor to ask of you, Lady. I have sent word about my prisoner here. But I have an assignment that cannot wait on the reply. The sequence of events is very important. I would like to leave my prisoner in your care until Dragon has made a decision about his disposition."

"What kind of prisoner is he?"

"He is the brother of your future husband, Lady."

"General Renfrew."

"Yes, Lady."

"I am very good at keeping prisoners."

"I know, Lady. And at letting them go when it best serves the purpose."

"I am sure our leader will have use for him."

"Thank you, Lady. We will be gone then."

First stared at the old woman who sat on the steps waiting for direction.

"I am called First. Welcome to our house."

"Thank you, Lady. I am an old woman to come so far, but that young man is very persuasive."

"It would seem so. The servants will show you to your room. You have traveled far; rest this day. Tomorrow you will have much to do."

"Thank you, Lady."

First turned to the blindfolded man kneeling in the dirt before her. She could see the similarity to Marlin in the line of his jaw and the color of his hair.

"Clean this one up, fit him with chains, and feed him. I will see him after dinner."

Renfrew felt hands lift him to his feet. Hot sun beat on his head. He could smell water very close. His hands hurt from his bonds. His feet slipped on the ground as he tried to walk after the long hours in the saddle.

He was in a huge stable. Stone walls created deep shadows. He could see only because the place was so dark. After the blindfold of the last few days any light would have blinded him. The glow from the fire did hurt his eyes. He smelled the hot metal. He heard the clink of links. Burly bodies crowded him. His arms were extended. He tried to resist.

"This is very dangerous work. I could easily burn something important right off you. Be still."

Four cuffs, four chains later he was bound. He could raise his hands enough to reach his mouth if he bent over. He could shuffle across the landscape. He could stand, he could walk, but not for long. The weight of the chains would tire him. He couldn't swing the chains. The chains that went from ankle to ankle and wrist to wrist were connected by the short chain that kept his arms just below his chest. That chain was secured to his body by the chain that circled his waist. There were no locks. They were all welded shut. All he had extra was a ring that he knew would be attached to a chain that was attached to a wall. He was a prisoner.

Eating was difficult. He couldn't drink easily. Someone had to hold the cup for him. No one seemed to think it strange. He recognized the pattern of the chains from the ones he had found on Lady Jeffenza, soon-to-be Queen Jeffenza. This was Sarnese in origin not Llweganian. He waited. He wondered what more was to come.

Renfrew walked through halls that echoed with the sound of his breathing. He wondered when the floor would end. They stopped before a huge portal. The wood swung open on well-oiled hinges. He stepped into the room. It was filled with women. They stood in grey dress. They ranged in age by only a few years.

"Stand right there." The words were spoken in perfect Masfin. The accent was faint. His attention was caught by that voice and that language in this place.

"In this Household every member has dominion over you. When you are inside the walls of this house you will be allowed the freedom of your chains until such time as you break the rules. Outside the building you will be tethered. If you become troublesome you will be tethered in the house as well. Our future husband trusts my judgment. He will abide by any decision I make about you. So, I feel free to kill you if the need arises. My word is law in this house. I am First. We are all one in this house. We speak with one voice."

"Is my brother marrying all of you?"

"Yes, that is our way. That is the command of our leader. That is his choice. Why do you ask this?"

"I was wondering how far gone he was."

"How far gone, what an interesting phrase. You did not believe this to be the truth when you asked this question?"

"No."

"You don't believe that he will forsake you for me if I have to kill you?"

"No, blood is thicker than water."

"Water is less plentiful than blood in Sarna. If I am wrong you will still be dead."

That was true. Renfrew stared at the faces of the women in the room. There was a stoicism that frightened him.

"What happens now?"

"You will see. Everything is coming together. You have no responsibilities to concern you now."

"It is the responsibility of every prisoner to escape."

"Escape to where?"

"Lady Jeffenza escaped. She made it through the dessert unaided. I can do so."

First laughed. The entire room laughed. Even the servants laughed.

"If you believe that you are very stupid. Lady Jeffenza couldn't walk to the end of my garden without help. A more useless person I have never met."

Renfrew frowned in thought. Marlin had known the girl had had help. What kind of help?

"Is she a plant?"

"She certainly was a thorn in my side."

"She claims she had no help."

"Lady Jeffenza only ever saw what she pleased to see. She was never the brightest of women."

"She was bright enough to snag the King for a husband."

"A king who made an enemy of the Harbinger of Death? She may marry every king that ever was; she still will not be under the protection of the only power that matters. She turned away from Harbinger."

"She tried to do more than that." First turned to look at Fourth.

"You are right. She had a just defense in ignorance. Harbinger had forgiven her the misstep."

"You're right. It was hard to see that she was Lady Zona's daughter."

"You have a point there."

Renfrew couldn't follow the pattern of speakers. They moved as they spoke so that only First was in the same spot as when the discussion began.

"So is she a spy or not?"

First looked back at Renfrew.

"You really don't expect an answer do you? You can't expect me to give you any information ever that you might use. Relax, follow the rules. Enjoy the peace of our home. You will receive any answers you may expect soon enough."

"I can't understand. Why would you be my jailer?"

"That question should keep you occupied for a while."

Marlin stood next to Harbinger. He read the message again. He understood the words and believed the content. He just couldn't comprehend the truth.

"My brother is a prisoner? First has him."

"What to do? What is your brother's position?"

"He is a general."

"Not his rank, his position."

"Right, our holdings are not as old as Lord Jeffeaux's. They are as extensive. We are not related by blood to the royal house but we remained loyal during the uprising so we have a certain standing in court."

"Good, good. As a wedding present to you I will have him returned to Masfin."

"There is no need for any such gesture, Harbinger."

"There will be a price."

Marlin held very still.

"I'm sure he will be willing to pay. If not he can remain in your care."

Marlin didn't ask the price. He didn't question the decision again. He eased away from Harbinger gingerly.

"Sablor, Marjas, Lady Zona, with me."

The group filed out of the tent. They walked at a leisurely pace through the camp. Lady Zona walked next to Harbinger. She studied the camp as the passed through it.

"Lady Zona, I hear Lady Jeffenza is to wed to Ranald."

"She had ambition always."

"A marriage is very important. Your son continues to disappoint me."

"I can't envision the woman that might match my son."

Harbinger was silent. She could not deny that statement. She could not find the answer to that difficulty.

"Here we are." Lady Zona recognized her daughter's tent. Sablor raised the tent flap without asking permission to enter. In the light from the torch Lady Zona could see her daughter astride the priest. Their skin gleamed with sweat and moisture in the flickering light. Harbinger turned calmly to her husbands.

"Light the lamp."

Lady Zona watched as her daughter gathered a sheet around her. There was a sucking noise as the two bodies separated and disconnected. Harbinger sat calmly to wait for her presence to be acknowledged.

"Harbinger, Mother." Junla was cautious in her greeting.

"Lady Junla, we have a problem."

"Should I dress?" The tone was neutral.

"Not for us. We won't be long. Basically, in Masfin and Llweganian tradition it is not done to have children outside of marriage. In fact the laws against such occurrences are quite harsh in Llwegania.

"I have plans for your brother. His not being married, not having an heir' does not help those plans along. If you have a child outside of marriage my plans would be adversely affected.

"However if you were married and had a child, it would help my plans greatly. It would solve the problem of your brother's lack of an heir."

"You want me to marry my priest?" There was no intonation in her voice as Junla posed the question.

"No, that would be of little use to me in Masfin. You need a husband from Masfin. And, I have found you one."

"Really?"

"Yes. We are on the way to Marlin's wedding. While we are there you will marry his brother, General Lord Renfrew. His rank is acceptable for my uses and his position in Masfin will coincide with any plans you may have. He meets your requirements and my needs. What do you think of my solution?"

Junla sat in the curve of her priest's body. She felt the tension in his muscles. Her mind raced through all the options offered by the plan.

"Will you give me help to guard him?"

"This is the best part: I am going to send him back to Masfin. We will get what we want from him, then we will ship him out. Whatever he does there won't matter. I've imported a Masfin cleric to perform the ceremonies. So you will be truly married. If he denies you it will be a lie. We have him. He probably won't say anything once he is back in Masfin. That won't matter. We don't need him to say anything until we get there. You will have to consummate the marriage. Will that be a problem?"

"No, but I can't guarantee that I will be pregnant from one night."

"That can't happen. You are already pregnant. We have the child, I need you married that's all."

Junla sat in shock. She leaned forward. "How can you know this?"

"I have born nine living children and two dead. I know when a woman is pregnant, and you are pregnant. Now that is decided, you can resume your former seat. We are leaving."

Junla obeyed instinctively. She only realized that she had remounted her Priest in the presence of four people, one of them her mother, when the flap swished closed behind them.

Lady Zona pulled her tunic into a straight line. She ran a finger along the hem of the garment.

"The perfume of love is a wonderful aphrodisiac. Don't you think?"

"I find that often I do not think when I am around you, Harbinger. I simply react or obey. Many of us simply obey you."

"My plan is brilliant. Your daughter has one more option covered. I have given up on your son. This will provide him with a much needed heir. It's the perfect solution."

"You could not have arranged a better ambience for proposing your plan."

Harbinger laughed. "That is true. There was a nice symmetry to the situation. Now all I need to do is devise a way to ensure Renfrew's cooperation."

"I would have thought an interview between you and Renfrew would be the most interesting show, but my daughter must rank as the most of anything and she certainly does in this category."

Harbinger took a deep breath. She savored the smell of the air. There was an edge still. She supposed years would pass before the dryness truly eased. Well she had done all she could. She studied the surrounding landscape.

"You wouldn't want to completely destroy the waste. You like this place."

"As always you read me too well, Lady Zona. We have reached our present goal. One of my problems has been solved, almost. All that is left is the packing."

"I will miss you."

"And I, you. But, I need you here. First and Marlin will handle all the logistics but I need you to keep a steady hand on everything. I need your wisdom to temper their logic."

"You won't be gone that long."

"I won't believe that when I am sitting in judgment. It is my duty, but sitting still looking important for so long a time is not my favorite activity."

"I am sure your communities look to this time as a reaffirmation of your bond with them."

"Most likely they are passing along the hard choices. Well, I never flinched from a hard choice."

"So how will you convince Renfrew?"

"I shall take your daughter along with me. From what I have seen, she should be pretty convincing."

Chapter 13

Stiefis scoured the camp. He tried every place he could think to look. He did not want to blow any cover Renfrew might be using. He did not raise an alarm that might ruin any plan Renfrew was implementing but he searched constantly. Did he believe Renfrew would leave without at least some notice to him? Was he counting himself more important to Renfrew than was true? No one else seemed to be concerned. The army was moving. Everyone had responsibilities that superseded every other consideration. Even Stiefis had duties he had to fulfill and which meant he had not noticed Renfrew's absence for several Darkfalls.

In the midst of all this activity a royal wedding and a coronation had been held. Stiefis watched the couple make promises and assume roles with a jaundiced eye. The elaborate rites and the pompous words bothered him. The Sarnese ceremony was more appropriate. Yet he refused to finish the thought. Both parties were entering this arrangement for the sole purpose of cementing power and position. All goals were fulfilled by the end of the day. They hoped to produce a child but the mere possibility of a child would be as powerful as a child itself for a while. She would never leave the king because she had no child. Being married to the king was her goal and she had achieved it.

Stiefis distracted himself from the lure of self-pity by focusing on the problem of his missing ally. He stared at the horizon as if the line of rock and soil would give up the answer he sought.

"Well son, at least we are hunting again."

"Then why do I feel like the prey? She won't be there. Why would she? Winter is coming. We haven't had that many winter experiences but I know enough about them to know that we will get to this Tampello in time to be trapped by the winter snows. Then she will have all winter to fortify her true position. In the spring we will traipse back here hindered by the roads. She will worry us and raid us until she even picks the spot where we will attack."

Weirhass shifted in his saddle. He rolled his head on his neck to relieve the tension in his body.

"Isn't it time for the Assizes Courts in Llwegania?"

"Only you would remember that, Father. She's not even with her army. They are all settled, resting, growing fat off the new crops in Sarna. But our bodyguard has chosen to go to Tampello. So it's off to Tampello for all those sorry-assed Sarnese soldiers who didn't have enough sense to bed their new wife. If I had slept in her bed one night and she had spoken Llweganian in her sleep all this could have been avoided."

Weirhass snorted. He turned his mount to follow the line of bodies headed out of camp. "She would have spoken Sarnese. Even in her sleep she would remember where she was."

Stiefis turned his head to look at his father. Enough time had passed that Stiefis felt comfortable with a subject that had once been a very sore point.

"Do you ever feel betrayed because you liked her so much?"

Weirhass smiled. "No, I still like her. You have to admire her. I would have happily accepted all this if only we had a son of her body."

"She has daughters father; many daughters."

"I know. I can still dream. But you are right, I really liked her. I envied you from the moment she first spoke. I envied my son a woman." Weirhass shook his head at that thought.

Marlin dismounted. He stood in the courtyard of his new home. He watched the servants come out of the house. They bowed very formally to him. He stood still as his horse was led away. He had come early to be sure, no, he knew everything was in place. He had come early to be here to greet his guests.

He had left his personal troops at the Altar with the cleric who was to prepare the space for the wedding. He drew a deep breath. He had not seen his intended brides since they had accepted his formal proposal. He was nervous. He had never thought to marry. He had never thought to have someone as part of his life in such an intimate way. His wives would have claim on him as no one else in the world had ever had or ever would. The responsibility frightened him. He swallowed the air in his mouth. He used it to push his fears away. They were no use.

Light spilled into the courtyard. Voices filled his ears. On the shallow steps First appeared in the beam of light.

"Welcome, Marlin."

"Hello First. Our guests are one day behind me."

"They will be early."

"There is a final detail Harbinger wants to settle."

"I had thought everything was set." Mild concern colored First's voice as she walked towards Marlin. He extended a hand in greeting. She wrapped her fingers around his gloved hand. He felt the warmth of her through the cured skin.

"We are set; of course. It is Renfrew. Harbinger wants him to marry Lady Junla. That wedding will take a little contriving to pull off."

"He has not enjoyed being a prisoner."

"I can imagine. However, he will not bend easily. He. We will see."

First loosened her grip to smooth her hand along Marlin's forearm.

"We are happy you are here."

Marlin swallowed again.

"I am happy to be here. I just want to be sure. If this is not really what you want, I will stand up to Harbinger for you."

"Don't worry. We are very pleased. This is our choice. You are our choice. We are happy to be marrying you. And we are happy to be helping Harbinger. You will make us a good husband. Our marriage will be good for everyone and everything."

Marlin sighed.

"I know. I've never had a wife before. I want to do everything correctly for you. Even give you the chance to say no."

"Come, my sisters are waiting for us. They have been waiting for a long time."

"How is Ladizona? She must be growing apace."

First smiled fondly. She rested her cheek briefly against Marlin's bicep. Her strides matched Marlin's as they climbed the steps into the house. Women's voices filled Marlin's head. He enjoyed the pampering and barrage of questions. He played with Ladizona until she fell asleep nestled against his chest.

After dinner he fell silent. His bevy of women watched his face fall into serious lines. First nodded to Fifth. The small woman rose from her seat. She shook the keys around her waist until she found the one she wanted.

"Do you wish to go now?" Her deep voice sounded odd from such a small body. Marlin passed the sleeping child to Sixth. He stood slowly. With a nod to the room in general Marlin followed Fifth from the space. He stretched his stride until he pulled even with Fifth. He extended his arm to her in the courtly fashioned of Masfin. She gingerly reached her small fingers onto his sleeve. He placed his other hand over the pale fingers. Gathering strength from the contact Marlin walked towards the cellar door.

On the narrow stairs into the cellar Marlin walked behind Fifth. He placed one hand on her shoulder and used the other to hold a lamp high in the gloom of the stairwell. Their footsteps sounded softly in the darkness beyond the light. Marlin watched the shape of the shadows change as they moved along the contours of the space. There was no sound beyond their steps and breathing. There was no dripping of damp or rustle of vermin. He felt pride in the well-kept household. He would soon be part of this household. He already was. The promise given and accepted was as binding as the ceremonies to come. His thumb moved in an absent caress against the slender neck that was exposed above the line of collar and below the fall of hair. Fifth's step remained steady. They were almost there.

The narrow door looked plain. The sturdy wood and heavy iron hinges reflected no light. The key turned easily in the well-oiled lock.

In the flare of the lamp Marlin saw Renfrew. He saw the startled jerk at the sudden intrusion of light. He saw the chains and the instinctive crouch.

Renfrew saw nothing. The light from the lamp blinded him for several heartbeats. He could smell the woman. He could smell a second person. The odor was heavy with soap and food and something else. Renfrew felt his nose twitch at the scent. Then his eyes became used to the light. He saw his brother standing behind one of his keepers.

"I never thought to see you hide behind a woman."

"I am demonstrating my confidence in my future wives' abilities and my trust in them. If I stand in front of her I am implying that she is less capable than I am or that I do not trust she has you well secured. Fifth has been your keeper because she is considered the best trained fighter of my brides. I would be questioning her abilities and First's decision to place her in charge of you to try to protect her from you."

Renfrew stood quickly. He jerked impatiently at the chain securing him to the wall. He sat back down in a huff.

"This is all for show. I was being treated much better. I did not attempt anything. I don't know why I have been banished to this cell."

"Security reasons: we are having many guests arrive for the wedding over the next few days."

Renfrew raised his chained hands into the flare of the light.

"I could hardly threaten anyone trussed up like this."

"True, but you could see from which direction they came and garner some information."

Renfrew sat straighter. He was completely intrigued by the idea that such a small detail had been thought of by a woman. He would have noted such a thing. His muscles relaxed.

Marlin smiled. He bent to speak into Fifth's ear. She moved to allow Marlin access to the room. Marlin crouched until he was at eye level with Renfrew. He held the lamp close enough to see Renfrew clearly. There were faded bruises from the capture.

"Aside from this cell, have you been treated well?"

Renfrew grimaced. "Like a prince." He nodded at the chains on his wrist.

Marlin reached one finger to a link then he hung his clasped hands between his knees.   "Father always said you had very good instincts."

Renfrew laughed without humor. "He also said following my instincts too closely would get me into trouble."

"You're not in that much trouble. Harbinger could be convinced to let you go."

"For love of you, I suppose."

"No, I wouldn't ask her anyway. There are worse things that could happen to you than being kept here. You would be safe here. When the war ends no matter who won you would be free to return to Masfin."

Renfrew understood the logic of Marlin's statement. He did not like the chains or the control but he was not mistreated nor was he in danger.

"I would rather be with my soldiers."

"So would I. You haven't congratulated me, brother. I am to be married."

"So I have been told. Six beautiful wives, I almost envy you."

"They are good wives. I am very happy. I was a little surprised when Harbinger proposed the match. I did not think I had anything to bring to a marriage that could convince such women to marry me. After all they are all so skilled and competent and have such status that they could choose anyone for husband."

Fifth laid a reassuring hand on Marlin's shoulder. She smiled down at him with pride.

"Well, you are quite handsome, and you sit well on a horse."

Marlin blinked at the compliment.

"I thought it was my steadfast heart that won you."

"That and your position in the House of Lady Zona, and the will of Harbinger. If you were not worthy of us, Harbinger would never have made the suggestion." Fifth kept her smile easily.

Marlin nodded once. Renfrew leaned against the wall.

"She seems to have quite the knack of matchmaking."

"That is true. You will see for yourself soon enough."

Marlin rose on that cryptic statement. Renfrew watched the pair stand in the doorway. Marlin placed a proprietary hand on Fifth's waist. She swung the door closed with a solid push.

Renfrew sat in the dark. He felt for his pallet. He drew his blanket over his shoulder. All he could do was sleep. He could not think or plan. He would have the day back soon. Once it was safe to let him out of the cell. He regretted the rivalry that had always existed between him and his brother. He had no long line of years of interaction to fall back on to bind Marlin to him. He could not tug on a tie that would take Marlin from his present course. Marlin would head down this road to disaster and nothing Renfrew could say would change Marlin's mind.

Renfrew had watched the women interact. He had seen the unconscious actions that demonstrated their affection and respect for each other. He had seen the complete trust they had for each other. He saw how they made decisions together and relied on their leader for guidance in the rare moment they could not decide as a unit. He had watched petty squabbles rise and flee, forgotten, even laughed at afterwards. He had never experienced that with his brother. He wished for that now when it was too late.

Renfrew opened his eyes at the sound of the door opening. A leash was slipped over his head. As he was held still at the far end of his chain Fifth moved past him to disconnect him from the wall. As the chain fell to the floor her strong hand shoved him out of the cell. The relentless pull on his leash propelled Renfrew up the stairs. Once he stood in the kitchen his leash was removed. He was held still by the bombardment of aromas that invaded his senses. They were preparing the wedding feast.

"Take him to be cleaned. Be sure to use the clothes laid out for him."

Renfrew walked through a courtyard filled with soldiers, horses, people of all shapes, sizes, colors. Animals filled the air with their life noises. Renfrew twisted his head every which way trying to absorb all the sights and sounds. He didn't notice his bath. His clothes regained his attention. He ran a hand over the fine materials. Well, he was the brother of the groom. He stood very still as first the shirt then the pants were sewn on him to accommodate his chains.

He followed the servant back to the house. He walked through corridors he had never seen until this day. Finally they reached a set of extremely ornate doors. The servant knocked once. There was a long pause. Renfrew would have knocked again. He was itching to knock himself. Still the servant stood very still. Renfrew tried to resist. He felt the urge to shift position. But his chains would have rattled. He did not want to appear impatient before this servant.

Finally the door swung open. No room he had seen in this house was as richly appointed as this one. Heavy furniture and materials graced the space. Rich metals and jewels gleamed as plates, goblets, bowls, and pitchers. He could have walked into the King's apartments in Masfin.

A lone woman dressed as a Llweganian soldier stood in the room. She was heavy with child. The curve of her body drew his eye immediately.

"General Lord Renfrew."

"General Renfrew or Renfrew is sufficient."

"You have been spending a great deal of time with your Sarnese allies."

"I never was comfortable being called Lord. My father came into the title very unexpectedly and late in his life. I did not ever expect to be so titled when I was growing up."

"Interesting. Do you know who I am?"

"No."

"Do you know how I know who you are?"

"You were informed by my brother or the members of this household."

"No, we met. I remember you. There were many new faces for me to meet and to remember, and I do. You had relatively few faces to remember. I would have thought you would recall me immediately."

Renfrew felt the room become very warm. "Devouring Harbinger."

"Close enough. My names are my titles and I am very proud of them. I worked hard to earn them. But I understand your need to belittle me so I will overlook your rudeness, for now. Will you sit down?"

Renfrew watched her hand. She did not indicate any particular seat. He would choose without any implication. She left him no chance to insult her by his choice. He could still be difficult. He sank to the floor.

"I guess you won't catch a chill though the carpet. My advice is to never give your enemies an easy victory. Expiring from an illness you incur because you are trying to be difficult is no kind of victory; except for your enemy; unless your death would have meaning. Your death would have little meaning right now."

Renfrew regretted his actions before she spoke. He was not sure he could get up again without help. The cell floor had been solid and uneven. The footing had offered him some traction. His new boots were slippery and the carpet offered no grip. He would have to crawl to a table to get up again.

"I will put this chair near you. If you change your mind about sitting on the floor, I will have nothing but admiration for you. You really don't want to be down there while I am up here."

Renfrew sat a moment longer. He eyed the heavy chair with resignation. Then, with a loud rattling from his chains, Renfrew heaved himself off the floor into the seat.

"Good, we can both be comfortable. I wasn't sure I could help you up safely." Harbinger lowered herself gratefully into a like chair. She poured water into a goblet at her elbow. She filled a second goblet and offered it to him across the space. He had to lean to accept it. His chains swung crazily as he moved. They banged against him and the chair. He settled back more slowly.

"You present quite a problem to me."

Renfrew bent his head to lap the water in the cup. He had become quite adept at the maneuver.

"The longer you stay here, the more likely you will learn something I don't want you to know and then I will have to kill you. It would bother me to have to kill the brother of one of my generals."

"My captor thought you would have a use for me."

"I would have to torture you to get any information from you. I don't think you could be persuaded to join me."

"True."

"You wouldn't trade me information for your freedom."

"No."

Harbinger took a long drink from her goblet. She stared at the fire for a long moment.

"I won't just let you go."

"Why not?"

Harbinger looked him full in the face. "That wouldn't be in my nature. I need to have something from you."

"We have agreed that I have nothing to offer you."

"I wouldn't say that." There was a knock on the door. Harbinger raised her head. She waited for a servant concealed in the shadows of the room to move to the portal. As the door opened, a smile of welcome creased Harbinger's face.

"Lady Junla, this is General Lord Renfrew."

Renfrew watched a high ranking Masfin lady curtsey to him. She came to stand behind Harbinger's shoulder. She looked at him calmly. He could see from her body language that this woman did not admire this Harbinger the way everyone else here did. Neither did she hold the Dragon in dislike as Lady Jeffenza did. Rather Lady Junla respected the power Harbinger had and wielded. She understood the dynamics of power in a way Lady Jeffenza did not.

"I can tell that you recognize Lady Junla. She has been a very kind guest in my Household. I think she is somewhat uneasy. I will not let her return to Masfin. She is dear to Lord Jeffeaux and her well-being is important to me. I feel she is best kept safe in my care."

Renfrew tried to read all the meanings in the carefully worded statement. The tone gave nothing away. Lady Junla's stance did not imply an unwillingness to be with Harbinger. Renfrew did not believe that Jeffeaux had ever aspired to the throne but he did think Jeffeaux would take the throne if it were given to him by Harbinger's hand.

"If things don't work out for me as I believe they will, Lady Junla's position will not be very positive." Renfrew tried to be truthful in his answer.

"She will be the sister of the King's wife." Harbinger shot back.

"You can understand if Lady Junla does not consider her sibling to be the best hedge against disaster."

Renfrew bit off his reply.

"I see you understand; however, a well-placed husband would be useful."

"Husband?"

"Yes, if she were married to you and you provided her with corroboration for her story, she would be quite protected."

"Her story?"

"That she was my guarantee of her brother's cooperation so I kept her as a prisoner."

"How would we explain away getting married at your command?"

"Oh, something like you were always in love with each other but never thought to marry. When Lady Junla found out you were a prisoner she begged to marry you. In my desire to keep her happy I agreed. Lady Junla had a master plan. She used the cover of your wedding night to engineer your escape. In fact she becomes a heroine. She will have dared my wrath to free you. I was moved by her loyalty to you and still concerned for her brother, so I will forbear to harm her. You hope." Harbinger sat back in her seat. She placed her hands across the top of the swell of her stomach. A pleased grin spread across her face.

"Pretty good, don't you think? Romantic, heroic, plausible, quite a good story."

"Why should I go along with such a scheme?"

"It gets you your freedom without compromising any of your principles. You do help me out of a spot. Nothing major, yet you are doing Lady Junla a great favor. Since you can't be sure how much of my story is the truth and how much is made up you could be doing a loyal Masfin subject a great service, or a weak woman a favor. Either way, you get back to your army without hurting it or yourself."

"No one would honor the marriage without a Masfin cleric."

"I have one of those. Who do you think is marrying your brother?"

"No Masfin cleric would marry one man to six wives."

"That is true. He is only marrying First and Marlin. A Sarnese priest will perform the rest of the rite."

Harbinger sat up straight. "I will even have you married first, before your brother."

"And then I would be set free?"

"After you consummate the marriage of course. In the morning you would be taken to a place close to the Masfin border then allowed to go free. What say you? Have we a deal?"

Lady Junla left her spot behind Harbinger's chair. She walked until she was close to Renfrew. She knelt before him. She tilted her head until he could see the curve of her neck and the swell of her bosom. Her expression was calm with a hint of fire.

"You will gain your freedom and I will get security. I was stolen from my bed in the dead of night. I stay where I am safe. I am not a decision maker nor am I a power broker. I am a victim of these circumstances. I am trying to make the best of a bad situation. All I need is a safety net for when this path crumbles from my mother's feet."

Renfrew was tired. He was tired of being a prisoner. He was tired of having people pull him about. Even now these women were trying to pull and push him where he didn't want to go. If he went one more time he could never have to experience such an indignity again. What did he care? One ceremony, one night seemed a cheap price to pay for control of his life back.

"My wedding will be first." Renfrew wanted to be clear on this.

Harbinger leaned back again. She released the breath she had been holding.

"I assure you. Do you consent?"

"Yes, let us do this. The sooner this is over the sooner I am out of here."

"Good."

Marlin sat at the table. He looked down the long rows of celebrants. He paid no attention to his brother's dark looks. He cared for nothing beyond the happiness he felt at this moment. He could do anything with his family by his side. With these wives he could guard the entire country until his leader returned. He looked to Harbinger. She smiled at him. She raised her goblet in a salute to him.

"We need music." Marlin heard the words. He turned to look at First. She motioned a trio of servants into position. The sweet strains of a song usually at Masfin weddings filled the air. There were no words to the song, but the voices used no words. They gave the notes in pure clear cadence. First rose. She extended her hand to him. He hesitated. Dancing was not his best skill. It was obvious his wives had gone to a great deal of trouble to arrange this event. Marlin rose. He executed his steps with competence if not grace. First moved through the intricate steps with confidence and a joy of movement Marlin could only admire if he could take his concentration from his own steps.

Jeffeaux bowed to his mother. She joined him on the floor. Junla looked at her new husband. He was staring straight out the window.

"Soon enough you will be gone. Have some manners. Ask me to dance." Junla spoke with the firm tones of someone used to being obeyed. Renfrew reacted from instinct. He lifted her hand onto the back of his. He had completed two figures before he realized he had obeyed an order from his wife: his wife, this woman whom he could not respect or like because of all her associations.

"Don't be so harsh. This is a celebration. Marriage is good. The husband and the brides deserve a celebration for taking this leap of faith. It doesn't matter who they are or who we are. They are newlyweds. Be polite, be happy. The food was good. There was plenty to talk about. You'll be going home tomorrow. There's plenty to be happy about."

Junla moved away to dance with her copartner. Renfrew bowed to the merry face at his corner.

"I like to be in control."

"We all do. Sometimes you have to give up the pursuit of control to regain it."

Renfrew passed Junla under his arm. She reached her hand out in a graceful reach as the dance ended.

"And your priest? The one who shadows our every move? Is he your guard?"

"Do you understand the connotation of guard in this company?"

"Your concubine."

"No, a woman's personal guard consists of husbands only. Husbands like you. Men sworn to a woman on a holy altar. A woman sworn to men on a holy altar. Priest is my prisoner not my guard. He is my responsibility. If I fail in my responsibility he will end up dead.

"Now my mother has three guards. I think my sister was jealous of my mother. As well she should have been."

"And will you have guards?"

"Oh no, I married my husband in a Masfin rite. Marlin used both Masfin and Sarnese rites for his wedding, but I only had Masfin rules. What do you care? Once you are gone what kind of husband will you be anyway?"

"Are you asking me to stay?"

"No. I am reminding you that you do not expect to fulfill your duties that you have just promised me, so don't criticize others for how they arrange their marriages since you agreed to this wedding for your own purposes."

"For my life."

"No for your freedom, your control, your pride. That is different from your life. Some people will only make agreements for their life and even that is instinctual. My priest tried to die rather than to compromise. All you suffered was one day in the dark and a few days of chains."

"I have to get home. It is important."

"Are you so important that Masfin can't wage war without you? Or is it they cannot win without you?"

Renfrew refused to speak with his tormentor anymore. He dragged her from the room. If he had to consummate this marriage in order to escape this situation, then he would do it. Now, before Darkfall got much older.

Harbinger watched Renfrew disappear from view. She sighed in relief. Marlin was happily married. Junla was safely married.

"I don't know how you convinced that man to take my sister."

"Jeffeaux be kind. Your sister has taken the pressure off you totally. She is wed and pregnant. She is providing you with an heir. You need not fear my machinations around your unmarried state anymore."

"Does he know she is pregnant?"

"I didn't tell him. I wasn't present during the wedding night so I can't say if Junla did. But, somehow, I doubt it. Did you say anything?"

"No, I lacked the courage to thwart you."

"Now that I don't believe. You know I have been trying to find some woman fit to marry you for a long time. You resist my every effort. I had almost thought to suggest First at one point. You thwart me every moment of every day on this issue." Harbinger shifted around in her saddle. "And you still are not reconciled with your mother. You are not a parent. You should let me guide you in this instance. Nothing hurts more than when your children are against you. Life happens, things come along, issues, situations develop. Most people don't intend to be a bad parent. In fact what you are defining as a bad parent has nothing to do with you. You disagree with a choice that has nothing to do with you. It's not as if she has chosen to marry you."

Jeffeaux closed his eyes in despair. She could be so uncouth at times. Only Harbinger would have said that.

"Your mother is a person, a woman, not a stick of wood. What's she supposed to do the rest of her life? Live vicariously through you? Your children you haven't had? She's not dead. Even if you had children, why should she not have her own life, joys, and trials? Be fair. Especially be fair to your mother of all people. She gave you life. Let her have her own life."

"Harbinger, we have this argument every day."

"And I will continue to discuss with you your failings. We have a long journey ahead."

"Will I like Llwegania?"

"It is more like Masfin than Sarna in its climate."

"I have forgotten what Masfin looks like."

"Liar, you never forget the land of your birth. You can even remember the way the air tastes. Whether you like remembering or not is another discussion."

Jeffeaux watched the group arrange itself for the journey. He tried to place each face. As he studied the group he noticed a familiar face.

"I did not know Lady Marma was accompanying us."

"You needed a chaperone."

"A chaperone? For what?"

"If you ride with me into Llwegania many assumptions will be made. In fact it would be unacceptable for you to ride into Llwegania without Lady Marma in this group unless you were married to me."

"I rode through most of Sarna with First without any problems."

"Sarnese customs are different and more influenced by my will than those in Llwegania. No woman of standing may have unattached males constantly in her company except during battle. Only my male troopers can be with me and unattached."

"I don't see it."

"That's all right. You don't need to understand everything just accept my statement. Lady Marma has to come. She was happy to come. I think she enjoys seeing new places."

Renfrew tried to remember every turning and rise but he lost track in the first day. His eyes were covered and his ears were blocked. On the third day he gave up. He concentrated on keeping his seat. The ground had become uneven and uncertain. In his blinded state he felt totally dependent on the mount between his knees. He had to trust a beast and a set of hands. They cared for him, transported him, but he was terrified. He wondered if he would feel better if he knew who cared for him. If he had some level of trust before this experience, would he be comfortable depending on anyone to this extent? Renfrew wasn't sure.

He hated most that his mind was free to wander. He had nothing to do all day except to think. Think about what had happened to him. He tried to forget, but the more he pushed himself not to think about one particular thing the more determined his thoughts were to return to his wedding night. More specifically, he could not forget his wife. He could not forget the taste of her skin or the feel of her hands on his flesh. He could recall every detail of the consummation of his marriage with clarity and at times physical discomfort.

The priest, the priest burned in his mind's eye. Renfrew could see the blank faced man. The shadow had followed Lady Junla everywhere; he had stood outside their bedroom. As Renfrew left with his guards he had seen a flash of expression on that face. The only expression the priest had ever shown him. Renfrew recognized the warning, the intensity of feeling the priest was projecting at him. Whatever kind of prisoner Lady Junla thought her priest was, he was a willing one. Renfrew shifted in his saddle. The man was probably her sexual prisoner. Renfrew could easily picture a man becoming addicted to the lady's favors. The lady, his wife, whose favors he would never experience again and whom he - no, he didn't want to see her again.

He should be happy. He was on his way home. He had given nothing of value and had received his freedom. In fact he had received a great deal of pleasure for his troubles. No, he was not going down that road again. He was going to push the thoughts from him. He would try again to guess the routes his guides were taking.

Renfrew turned on his side. He burrowed deeper into his bed. He was cold. He had been noticing the change in the weather for the past couple of days but this morning the cold had seeped into his bones. He could become ill. What were his guides thinking to allow him to become chilled like this? He raised his hand to signal a need.

In his frustration Renfrew failed to notice for a moment the freedom of his motions. He stopped his wave abruptly. Cautiously he opened his eyes. They opened freely, fully, blindingly. The bright light of morning flooded his senses. He sat up quickly. His hand ran joyfully up and down his arms. He was free. He stood quickly.

He was alone. A light snow had fallen. There were no tracks in sight. He had been alone for a while. The snow had cooled the embers and him. Renfrew turned his head quickly. There was his horse, patiently waiting under the protection of a rock out-cropping. Renfrew breathed deep the crisp air. A smile broke free on his face. Everything had been worth the price to be standing free.

Renfrew broke camp as if he were in a race. He was still chewing field rations as he swung onto his steed. He took his bearing from the sun. He never looked back at the clearing or Sarna.

Renfrew knew where he was. He rode along quite happy to be near his destination. It was not until he was almost there that Renfrew realized something was wrong. He noticed the silence and the clean air smell with pleasure until he started to look for the sights of an encamped army. Then Renfrew realized that there were sounds and smells that went with those sights, none of which were present. The landscape was empty. Around him was used space. The abandoned area held only the barest traces of occupation. What the armies had not taken scavengers had salvaged.

In his excitement at his return Renfrew had forgotten the messenger: the messenger who had started him on this path. That messenger who had lured him into the clutches of the enemy and of his wife, had lured the army away from a good position. Renfrew became upset. He should not have forgotten such an important piece of information. Where had the army been drawn? Timbeau? No, he had been under too much stress. Tampello that was the place. He had ridden for several days. He had been taken up hills and down hills, across rocks and through sand. He had known that the journey out had been longer than the trip in so Renfrew had been led a roundabout route to confuse him. The plan had been successful but he knew he had not come from Tampello. The Harbinger could still lead her army there but she wouldn't.

Why would she? She had no need to go to Tampello. Tampello would be cut off for the winter. She would move her army at will through the desert of Sarna while the Masfin and Sarnese armies froze and starved in Tampello. Disease would eat at the numbers.

When spring came Harbinger's army would be well rested and healthy.

Renfrew's mount had stopped. Renfrew looked at the deserted towers of Jalico. The dark stone reflected his dark mood. After all he had gone through to get to it, he would not let the distance nor weather keep him from his army. The clop of his horse's hooves echoed forlornly in the empty courtyard.

Stiefis looked at the white curtain outside his quarters. He could not see the rough wooden shelters of the camp. He could see nothing. He could hear only the rage of the storm. The howl whined constantly. He knew why she had chosen Tampello. This weather was a powerful weapon. Stiefis slammed the shutter closed. The heavy drapes fell into place cutting down the draft. The fire on the hearth belched smoke bursts into the room. The acrid air bothered his throat. He had nothing to occupy his time. Boredom would soon drive him to suicide or murder. He could drink himself into a stupor. That would waste at least part of the day. He could stretch it out to a week maybe.

He watched the dark fluid fall from its container into the cup. He watched the liquid swirl as it filled the bowl of the goblet. But at the end of the binge he would still be bored and frustrated; and worried. No one knew where Renfrew was. Some whispered he had followed Marlin to the other side. Stiefis dismissed that rumor. Renfrew would never side with his brother. Not when his brother had chosen differently than he had and had gone over first. Stiefis understood the dynamics of pride very well, especially in conjunction with siblings.

Stiefis slammed the wine down on the table with enough force to send liquid sloshing onto the table. He strode around the room again. What he needed was a diversion, something to release his tension. The door opened slowly. A helmeted head poked in the doorway.

"Is everything all right, sir?"

"Yes." Stiefis turned away from the twitching face. As the door began to close Stiefis turned back. "No. Are there any women here?"

"Yes sir."

"Bring me one; something young and lovely."

"Certainly, sir."

Just like that he could order up a night's entertainment. Maybe this winter wouldn't be that bad after all. This diversion at least would leave him with a pounding headache no matter how much he pounded with his body all night or day for that matter. Stiefis chuckled at his small witticism. He returned to the table. This time he raised the goblet to his lips with anticipation. He savored the rich wine as he waited for his young and lovely something to appear.

Queen Jeffenza was bored. Her new husband cared more for battle plans and court intrigues than his new wife. He visited her regularly for the sake of implanting his seed in her womb. The entire process took less time than she spent picking out an outfit.

She had power. She had influence. She had the crown. What she needed right now was a good…ness what was this?

"Hold there, soldier."

The young soldier stood still. His hand remained tight around the arm of the young girl. The girl eyed her with fear and suspicion.

"Since when did we start allowing females of this type in the Royal Palace?"

"One of the Sarnese generals requested her presence, Your Highness."

"How does she know any Sarnese generals?"

"Not this female in particular ,Your Highness. His exact words were something young and lovely, Your Highness."

Jeffenza studied the cringing youth and stoic girl. She noted the flushed cheeks and curved body. The girl certainly qualified.

"Which general?"

"Stiefis, Your Highness."

"Stiefis, Stiefis." Jeffenza pretended an ignorance she did not feel.

"The one whose wives divorced him for infertility, Your Highness."

Now that was information about which she did not have to feign ignorance.

"He told you this?"

"Oh, no, Your Highness, everyone in the ranks knows. He is why we had to move to Jalico. When the Sarnese priests came to divorce him we knew our security had been breached. It was quite a scandal in the Sarnese ranks. No one had ever been divorced before in Sarna. And that is the only way a woman can get a divorce, Your Highness." His head bowed again after he had raised it in his excitement to relate his story.

Unable to sire children, that poor man, that poor lonely man looking for comfort on this cold night. A young lovely something, well a queen was a something and she was young and lovely.

"You know the King does not approve of such behavior."

"Yes, Your Highness." It was obvious that the young man was in a difficult spot. He had to obey and did not wish to face Stiefis without a female.

"Take this young lady back to her place. I will explain to General Stiefis myself about the rules of the Royal Palace."

"Yes, Your Highness, thank you, Your Highness."

Stiefis sat at the table. The wine in his cup had been reduced to a small puddle at the bottom. He swirled the red liquid languidly waiting with reined in pleasure for his request to be fulfilled. His head rose quickly at the sound of a knock at his door. He leaned back in his seat. His head turned to face the door.

"Enter." Surprise made him slow to rise. His cup fell heavily on the wooden table. He scrambled to right it before any drops splattered the wooden surface. She was beautiful. Her eyes caught the glow of the fire. Her head sat on her neck with a grace he knew was inborn. Even in the dust of the desert she had been graceful.

A deep sigh filled the room. She did not look at him. One finger tested the surfaces of the room as she strolled around his space. Surprise and the mellow wine held his tongue prisoner.

"I met a young soldier in the hall. He was leading a female of questionable morals through our palace. I can't fault him for obeying a direct order. But he should have explained the rules of this household to you. Women of her profession are not permitted in royal habitations. I promised to make this clear to you."

Stiefis did not dare to breathe. She had come to stand in front of him.

"Your Highness." Women were the devil. They thwarted him at every turn. She stood so close he could smell her scent below her perfumes and the smells of the room.

"I can see that you had a, need, for her services. So I will excuse you this time."

He closed his eyes against the humor he was sure to see in her eyes. From the bend of her head he had seen the direction of her gaze. Those bright eyes had been fastened on the evidence of his desire.

Stiefis nearly jumped out of his skin when Jeffenza's hand landed on him. Her fingers curled to keep him still. Her cool fingers slid inside his pants' opening. They measured his length and readiness. They wandered down to find his twin guards before returning to the center of his problem.

"Of course you are an important ally. We wouldn't want your needs to go completely unanswered." Her hand pushed at his chest until he sat back in his chair.

She wanted to be pleasured, but first she wanted her appetite to be satisfied. She wanted to see and to touch that part of a man she had been required to accept into her body. She studied its shape and taste with her tongue and mouth. She measured its length and hardness. She tasted the hair that made up its nest. She blew across it until milky fluid started to flow. Still it stayed round hard. She would have to suck it dry before she could see what happened when it was not aroused. Well, she was weeping herself. She could feel the wetness between her legs. His hands gripped her shoulders. They raised her until he could impale her. A low keen burst from her. This was what she had wanted.

Stiefis sat still where his visitor had left him. He left his pants open to savor the air of the room. He had thought her skirts would hinder them. He had thought he would explode before he could get her seated on him. He had thought this would be a dull winter. His only problems now were what was the enemy doing and where was Renfrew.

Renfrew looked at the wide expanse of snow. He was not sure how far he had left to go. He had only been to Tampello once, a long time ago. He was still in familiar surroundings. Once he didn't know the land anymore he would either be close to his goal or lost. His water was frozen in its skin. He had to eat snow and to feed snow to his horse. He should let the skin go; he had no need for it with all the snow around him, but habits die hard, and it was a good weapon hard as it was, with a handle even. Food was more difficult. He was almost out of field rations. His poor horse had to work as hard to find food as he did to carry Renfrew. They had to get there soon. Renfrew didn't think he could survive another blizzard. The snow seemed not as deep here. Renfrew dismounted. He began to walk, holding onto the cheek strap of his horse.

The breath from the animal warmed Renfrew as they walked. His feet were getting cold. His legs were tired. A scent caught his attention. Renfrew raised his head. He stepped away from his horse. He pulled the horse along by the lead rein. He lost the scent three times. Then he saw the smoke. A small house puffed smoke out into the clean air. Renfrew climbed on his horse. He sat straight in his saddle. The house looked worn and ragged. The roof seemed to hug the house as if afraid it might fall at any moment. It looked like a palace to Renfrew.

"Hello the house."

The door opened slowly to his greeting. A white haired head appeared.

"Greetings, am I far from Tampello?"

"No, it is two hills that way."

"Will I get there by Darkfall?"

"I don't read the future young man. If your horse is healthy, if you don't stop, if nothing stops you, you will get there sooner. The snow will slow you to the crest of this hill. The army had packed it down from there."

The army, what wonderful two words! Renfrew felt like laughing. He did. He rode away as the old man muttered about youth and fools and snow madness. Renfrew didn't care.

The packed snow was there as promised. Renfrew smiled as he rode down the road. He nodded to the few people he passed. He focused on the horizon. He watched the distant hill grow big. He resisted the urge to ask his mount to race up the rise. The poor beast had carried him faithfully; Renfrew should consider its safety.

The camp spread like a cloak upon the earth. Snow had been moved, stained, piled, and packed. Wooden structures huddles together. Soldiers, animals moved. Their movements seemed aimless to Renfrew. He knew there was a reason for each movement but he did not care. Today the movement seemed like a dance to him. He smiled broadly as he entered the camp.

"Halt."

Good, sentries, they should have been posted on the next hill. He made a note of the problem.

"General Lord Renfrew, soldier."

"What's the password?"

"I couldn't tell you. Bring on the guards. Take me to your superior officer."

The soldier looked at the foolishly grinning man on the sorriest horse he had ever seen.

"I intend to. Trooper Wensew get the captain of the watch."

A young boy disappeared into the camp. Renfrew stayed on his horse. He watched the procedure with pleasure.

"You claim to be General Lord Renfrew, sir?"

"Yes, Captain."

"But you don't know the password, sir."

"Not today's."

"I have sent for someone who can verify your claim."

"Very good, Captain."

"Thank you, sir."

There was silence. Renfrew studied the ease with which his soldiers waited. They did not try to engage him in conversation. They did not shift or fiddle. They waited ready for the next move. Well-trained soldiers, except they should have been posted on the far hill.

"General Renfrew." The surprise, relief that filled the words would have warmed Renfrew at any time. This day everything pleased him twice as much. The sentry melted to one side.

"You are safe."

"Now, I have ridden long and hard. Point me toward a hot bath, a hardy meal, and a soft bed."

"This way, General."

As Renfrew dismounted he looked at the expression on the face of the groom. Renfrew patted his mount's neck affectionately.

"Rub him down well. He has earned a good feed and a rest. He carried me many an arduous mile."

"Yes, General, he doesn't look like much does he?"

"No, but he has great heart."

"Yes, General, that is what matters."

Renfrew watched his companion walk away. No other horse could have brought him home. Renfrew turned thoughtfully into a building. He dropped his outer clothes as he walked towards the table filled with food. His worn, frozen clothes were swept up into practiced arms. His mouth watered at the smell of the meal spread before him.

Each bite was heaven. He had to force himself to take small, long bites. He concentrated on the feel of the food sliding down his throat into his stomach. He sipped his wine slowly. He didn't want to fill his stomach with wine.

A servant waited for him. The quiet presence bothered him. It reminded him of another time not so long past. The poor fellow was only doing his job. The body waited to be his hands and feet, his direction to bath and bed. The servant was there for his orders, not to order him, yet, he could not shake the feeling he was being guarded. He lost his interest in eating, he had become full. Renfrew rose from his seat.

The silent figure led the way. Renfrew followed warily. The sight of the steam from the bath went a long way towards relaxing Renfrew, returning him to his euphoric mood. He could close his eyes, ignore his ever present servant.

The bed was the best. He was alone in the room. He could slide into sleep away from all his memories and realities. He gathered his covers around his neck, turned on his side, and then sleep.

Chapter 14

Stiefis looked around the long table. He watched the diners nibble food and sip wine.

He noted the proper, polite interactions. He kept his eyes away from the head of the table. He did not look once at the King and his Queen. She never looked his way, not once. He only knew this because for all his refusal to turn his head in her direction, his eyes snuck looks. She was relaxed, gracious, contented. As well she should be. He had been buried deep in her not half an hour before they sat to eat. He had had her against a wall in a curtained alcove on the way to dinner. She had her power and her pleasure now.

"Excuse me, sir. A message arrived from the sentries. General Renfrew has returned."

Stiefis excused himself to his father. He left the great hall without one backward look.

"Where is he now?"

"He was taken to quarters, sir."

"Who would know for certain?"

"The sentries perhaps, sir."

Stiefis strode away. He spent several frustrating hours riding around the camp trying to locate Renfrew. Finally he stood inside the door to a room that held a sleeping man.

Stiefis thanked the trooper who had led him here. He drew up a seat. Leaning back in the chair he closed his eyes.

Renfrew opened his eyes. He turned onto his back. There was a funny feeling. He tried to trace the feeling to its source. What did it mean this niggling at his senses? He wasn't alone. He turned his head quickly. There was the source of his feeling. He was not alone. Stiefis sat sleeping in a very uncomfortable chair.

Renfrew studied his sleeping friend. In this moment he realized Stiefis was his friend.

No one else was left to greet him, no family, no brother. Just this ally with his elegant

eveningwear wrinkled and twisted as he slept in that incredibly hard seat.

Just the same, Renfrew was not happy to see Stiefis. He had not decided what he was going to say about his experiences. He couldn't say half of what had happened without feeling like a total idiot. Captured by a boy and his wife, he had been held prisoner by women. His brother had become Sarnese or Llweganian, one of them, but certainly not Masfin. Yet, here was Stiefis watching over him. He owed his friend as much of the truth as possible.

"Couldn't believe I really had returned?"

Stiefis woke with a start. He grimaced as his cramped muscles protested the quick motion. He rubbed his neck as he looked at Renfrew.

Warm water arrived as they stared at each other. Renfrew lathered his face carefully in preparation for shaving. The white soap glistened on his scraggly beard. Stiefis stretched carefully.

"I didn't look for you at first, afraid to disrupt any plan you had. Once you had been gone for a while without contacting me, I began to think you were in trouble."

"Think well of yourself don't you? So sure that I would let you know my every move."

"No just if you were planning to disappear off the face of the world that you might mention it in passing."

"Next time don't wait so long. It was a long cold ride to Tampello."

"Got lost did you?"

"Got took. Got chained up. Got rescued by a woman from a woman."

Renfrew stared at his face in the mirror. He watched his skin emerge from the hair and soap. He rinsed the razor often. As his beard disappeared his hair became more obviously too long. He turned his head from side to side. He really had to see a barer this day.

"So who rescued you from whom?"

"The Lady Junla got me free. You never told me that Harbinger was so strange." Renfrew spoke the word with surprise.

"When I knew her she was doing a very good impression of a Masfin lady. I have had ample time to study the ladies of the Masfin Court and can say with some surety that her impersonation was quite good. Her accent was only fair but I had no example to go by then."

"Well she had the Lady Zona with her to coach her. There were very few ladies more highly placed in the Masfin court then Lady Zona was."

"The ladies of that house are a very interesting lot."

Renfrew agreed silently. He thought of the strong hand in the night and the hot mouth of his 'wife'. He pulled his shirt on with too much force on that last thought.

"So we have a new queen."

"Yes." Stiefis was not happy with this new subject. He brushed the wrinkles in his fine clothes.

"Did you find out anything interesting or useful during your sojourn in Sarna?"

"That the army is not in Tampello. She wouldn't expose her troops to such brutal conditions. That she conjures up Masfin clerics and seamstresses with no problem."

"Masfin clerics? Why would she need a Masfin cleric?"

"My brother is married. I was at his wedding. He's married to your former wives, all six of them. The Masfin cleric was to marry him to First. A Sarnese priest married him to the other five."
Renfrew was not looking at Stiefis as he gave this incredible news. Stiefis could not control the deep pain he felt at the reality of the true loss of his former life: an irretrievable loss that stabbed at his stomach.

Renfrew was held in the grip of his story. He could not keep the words back. He had never meant to mention the next fact. He had thought to forget everything about his experience but he couldn't resist telling. He had to share with someone something more. He couldn't tell of his hours chained in the dark, nor the indignity of his treatment at the hands of women and children. He could blurt out one stone weighing on his soul.

"I got married. I married Lady Junla. After the marriage, during the wedding night, during the festivities I was able to leave."
There it was said.

Stiefis heard the words as if from far away. He was still wrapped up in his own world. As the words hung in the air Stiefis heard them. He looked at them from every angle.

"You married the Queen's sister?"

Renfrew continued to fasten his clothes. He studied the sleeve of his shirt.

"Yes, I did."

"I never met the lady. Is she much like the Queen?"

Renfrew considered the slight, plain woman he had married. Her coloring and style were very dull compared to Lady Jeffenza, the Queen. Yet there was that iron will; that cold calculation of decision juxtaposed with a voracious lustiness which overshadowed her quiet appearance.

"No, they are nothing like each other."

"Ah, then it was pity and not passion that moved you."

"I wouldn't quite call it that."

"Expediency then?"

"Yes, certainly there was a bit of that involved, but, she is intriguing. Yes intriguing that is the word for her."

Stiefis pulled his mouth down in thought. Intriguing, if that was what it took.

"She must have cried when you left. No bride likes to be abandoned on her wedding night."

Renfrew could not keep the memory from intruding. He remembered the trail of her mouth after they had finished. He recalled as her hot breath and quick tongue had travelled down his chest to low on his stomach. There her mouth had marked him with a force and endurance that had roused his exhausted body to readiness once more. Then, seeing his reaction she had laughed huskily. She pressed a quick kiss to his mouth before she left. The words 'don't forget me' echoed in his memory. Then he pushed them away in an attempt to do just that.

"Let us seek out your father. He might have some questions for me as well."

Stiefis held the door open. Renfrew walked through the halls grilling Stiefis on the status of the army. As he heard the questions Stiefis realized he knew few of the answers. He felt guilty. He had been wallowing in pleasure when there were responsibilities and duties to fulfill. Renfrew spoke briskly. Stiefis listened intently.

"It's disease that is killing us."

"Of course, all these bodies crammed in small spaces, poor food, weather, and housing, nothing breeds death like that. We'll probably lose more than if we battled."

"There was little choice in the matter."

"We must teach our colleagues about refusing the line."

"Or at least to get verification before jumping?"

"How was Sarna?"

Renfrew stopped at the door Stiefis was indicating. He waited for permission to enter. He stole a look at Stiefis' expectant face.

"Enter."

Renfrew was saved for the time it took to greet Weirhass. Then he couldn't delay his answer any further.

"I traveled through the country blindfolded. Leaving, well it looked the same as it always did in some parts." Renfrew remembered the smell of water. "Others have water and plants," he recalled the feel of vegetation under his feet as he dismounted. "I was fed foods different from the field rations you brought when I met you. I ate very well considering I was a prisoner. Fresh vegetables, fresh fruit, meat, my keepers had access to an abundance." Renfrew pictured the wedding feast. Of course even in the poorest of villages the headmen and invaders would live well. He tried to compare the spread to an evening meal at court. The wedding had been wasteful. Renfrew closed his eyes. Everyone had eaten. Even the servants had been fed from the feast.

"I had no trouble passing into Masfin. In fact I have to mention this. Why were the sentries so close to Tampello? They should be out on the next hill."

"Do you really think the Dragon is going to march an army here? She sent us here to let the travel and the weather winnow our numbers. The sentries are to prevent spies from coming into the camp."

Renfrew sat with a sigh. "You're right."

"We only increase the likelihood that one of the sentries would die returning from watch or in the blizzards way out there. I wonder where she will order us to march after the thaw."

"We can't even reconnoiter while we wait. I wonder what she is doing."

Weirhass smiled grimly. "She is holding Assize Court. It's that time. Then she will parade around her holdings and her husbands' holdings. Then she will return to the army."

"You know her pretty well."

"Not really, I know what has been observed. Llweganian culture is no more open than Sarnese culture. We have been taking Llweganian women to wife for generations yet I could not tell you much about how their religion works or how their Council is chosen. There are quite a few secrets left to uncover. Harbinger of Death is a very famous Llweganian. We know her better than we know most others. Her lands all border on Sarna. Of what lies in Llwegania beyond her borders I have little knowledge."

"So now that she is out of the country, can we raise the Sarnese against her?"

"We do not know where the Llweganian army is. They know exactly where we are. I am sure that you were allowed to return only because it serves her need or her perverse sense of humor. She knows where we are. She will have units watching our every move. Even if we could leave here safely, we can't without alerting her army and giving her the chance to decide."

"But she is gone."

"She left someone very worthy in charge of her armies."

"If she is so invincible why do we bother?"

"Do you want to hand over your way of life to her? We can only beat her by destroying her army. If we keep whittling away at her army we might have a chance. Part of her army comes from her husbands. Maybe killing a couple husbands will reduce her army substantially."

"Maybe? I need a more substantial plan than maybe."

"I told you we have very little real knowledge of Llweganian political structure. I don't know how the army is attached to Harbinger of Death just how she gained part of it. The only sure way I know of reducing it is to kill it. Perhaps eliminating her husbands could reduce her military strength."

Renfrew thought of how close he had been to her husbands. If he had known how important they were to the military effort….he had had them under his protection for all those weeks before this all began.

"But killing them would be very hard, and any who have heirs of her body well I assume her children would remain loyal and their armies would stay with her."

Renfrew felt a little better.

"So we are back to what can we do to defeat her."

Stiefis sat with a thud. He dragged his hand through his hair.

"Masfin is our hope. She will be unable to hold Masfin as easily as she does Sarna. With our army worrying her border she is back to where she was before she went into Sarna. She has a long border on a hostile country. She has to resolve her position with Masfin. As long as Masfin remains hostile and we can keep her in a constant state of war we have a kind of victory."

Renfrew traced an invisible design on the top of the table. He followed the line his finger made with fierce concentration.

"I'm not sure Masfin can support such a plan. This is a drain on the resources, food, men, that my country is not used to experiencing. Harbinger is used to generations of war as is the country she now occupies. We aren't. Our culture looks to the King to keep the peace. To provide the peace even that is the role of the King. If he can't achieve peace sooner than later his claim to the throne will lessen."

Stiefis paced quickly. He understood what Renfrew was saying. He knew that Harbinger also knew.

"Hopefully the Queen will provide a son to bolster the King's position."

"That would help. Defeating Harbinger is the real goal and without the hope of peace even twenty sons will not secure his position, or a hundred wives of better lineage. If we cannot win a peace, the King will have to seek to negotiate one. And I doubt he will get Sarna back for you. So you must base all your plans on the need to win. That is your only hope."

Stiefis swallowed his words. Renfrew was right. There was no other option. All the troops would have to fight. He could not hold back the Sarnese soldiers from danger. The price of regaining Sarna would be the loss of many lives: Sarnese as well as Masfin. At what price was victory? The Masfin King would exact a price for this war. He would were he king. Sarna would never return to its former state. No matter how hard he fought, or how well he planned SHE had changed Sarna forever.

He would worry about the price later. There might never be a later. He could not allow himself to think like that. He had to believe they would win. He would concentrate on winning. He had to make sure the winning was the result of Sarn plans and efforts. That would offset any claims the Masfin King might make on Sarna after the victory.

Stiefis frowned. "Surely Harbinger's advisors are telling her the same thing. If she pushes war on Masfin long enough the King will have to deal. So, why is she trying so hard to establish Jeffeaux as a legitimate claimant to the throne?"

"A back up plan, a bargaining chip, she cannot be sure exactly which way the Masfin King will go. She does not know him well enough to predict his actions. He might be the kind of person who will never weaken his crown by negotiating a peace. That he would only resist every pressure until the Masfin people make a push to replace him."

Jeffeaux could not believe his eyes. At the border of Sarna there was a dramatic change. Llwegania spread flat, broad, open. Sentry posts dotted the plains. Jeffeaux couldn't imagine trying to defend such a space against invaders. There was no river to mark neither the division nor a mountain range. The desert ended and Llwegania began. Invaders could easily be spotted during daylight but once Darkfall came what kept them away?

Hard fighting, excellent guards, well-trained soldiers, devoted defenders of the country were what stood between Llwegan and Sarna. Jeffeaux understood Harbinger's - no she was Dragon now he had to remember to think of her as Dragon - obsession with defeating the Sarn completely. She must view the border with Masfin as a blessing. Mountainous regions were very strong defenses against invaders.

Watching the countryside blossom into plenty, Jeffeaux could well imagine the need to defend against invaders. Even Masfin could not boast of such fertile and extensive lands; and well-populated. The roads were lined with people as Dragon's cavalcade rode. The crowds gathered in silence. They bared their heads as Dragon passed. They reached to touch her horse and leg when able. Jeffeaux feared to bring attention to himself in the close wall of people. His horse was better used to this situation. He let his mount move on its own; its inclination was to follow Dragon's horse. Jeffeaux had no quarrel with this line of action.

The world seemed frighteningly large. All he could see was earth and sky. At the edges of the world the sky bowed down as if attached to the waves of grass. In the distance at every arc the world blurred from green to blue. Even the desert of Sarna was not as huge as this. He had no sense of distance. He did not know how far he could see. There was a building growing in his vision. It had begun by sitting on the very edge of the world. As they traveled it moved to the center of his circle of perception. Once they reached it they were at the center of the world again; still he couldn't describe accurately what he felt or saw.

Dragon swung off her mount, thankful to be done for the day. She braced her back against a tight fist. The great swell of her child pushed out. When she waged war, her body waged life. Maybe her body would quiet down for a while and once this child was born she could be not pregnant for a space. She was glad to be home. She looked forward to her bath and a bed. Tomorrow she would don her robes of office, tonight her robes of sleep.

Marma watched Jeffeaux pour over the mountain of books in the library at Dragon's largest estate. She could not reconcile this man with the laconic noble she had known all her life. Masfin had as complicated a set of laws but she would bet her best dress Jeffeaux could not even say where to find a list of them never mind what they were. But here in this great house he studied the laws each night then studied their working each day.

Outside, the plains around the house were filled with people. Each day some left and more came. They stayed in tents. Side by side they lived with strangers and neighbors until they left to return to their villages. For those waiting there was the anxiety of waiting but also the excitement of a fair, market day, and holiday rolled into one. Stalls filled with color, the air filled with sound and scent, Marma enjoyed the contrast between the reveling outside and the deadly serious business inside the walls of the great house.

In the middle of the session there had been a one day recess. The household had ventured into the camp to enjoy the revels. Marma had enjoyed the revels. She had savored the break. It had eased her inactivity. It had also given her a marker for how long this process lasted.

Marma shook her head. Why should she question Jeffeaux's sudden aspirations to knowledge? Hadn't she become virtuous since entering the world of Llweganian influence? Staid, proper Ilissa was out waging war, winning booty, thinking of taking husbands. Lady Junla had married, was pregnant, and if rumor was true Jeffenza was now a queen. The world turned on end. Why would Jeffeaux be unaffected by the winds of change?

He was terrified. Sometime between crossing the Llweganian border and the first day of judgments, he had realized that he might end up sitting on the throne of Masfin. No matter how he protested, no matter how much of a fight the Masfin and Sarnese armies put up, Dragon had a chance of winning. If she won he would end up ruling Masfin.

Ruling Masfin did not scare him. He could sit prettily. He could spend money, enjoy privileges with style. The thought that if he were to become king it would be at the hand of Dragon terrified him. Dragon would expect that he rule Masfin wisely so that it never became a threat to her under her rule in Sarna. That thought kept him up late at night. It drove him to study things he had always thought trivial, foolish, the purview of unimportant minions. He closed a book with a deep sigh. He had learned the laws of Llwegania enough to understand the application of a legal system to a social structure. It did not help him with his possible responsibilities in Masfin.

"May I help you, Lord Jeffeaux?"

Jeffeaux was never sure how to address Dragon's husbands. For the longest while he had felt comfortable with Sablor. Any connection he had felt with the youth had been an illusion, a total misconception on his part. The other husbands were really better for him to face. Sablor associated him with Jeffenza. Sablor had ingrained habits that lead him to appear friendlier than his fellow husbands but those habits were not indicative of his real nature. Sablor had little use for Jeffeaux.

Jeffeaux could not know that Sablor saw him as a muddled reflection of what the young man might have become had he not married a warrior household. Jeffeaux did not know that Sablor feared to be categorized with Jeffeaux as a non-fighting man.

"I don't think so. What I really need is a copy of the legal codes and statutes of Masfin."

"I know we have some of that information here. I brought all my work with us. Dragon had some plans of their study. I could ask her if it would be all right for you to study them if she is not using them."

"Thank you. That would be good." Jeffeaux almost regretted his words. Now he had saddled himself with more work. Of course she would have such information. When did Dragon ever leave any possibility unaddressed?

"There's more to taking care of domestic issues than studying laws." Jeffeaux looked up at the new speaker. It was Jorin. Jeffeaux respected this man.

"There's always more to everything. I know that no matter how much I study these, there will always be experts that know better but to be able to put any advice from experts to any use I have to understand what the experts are talking about."

Jorin sat across from Jeffeaux. He drew one of the open books to him. Quickly he surveyed the revealed pages.

"I believe you understand many things very well."

"Yes, one of the things I understand very well is myself. I like my comforts. I enjoy my pleasures. I do not regret my former life. I miss it, greatly, but, I embrace reality. That habit keeps one alive in the face of great odds."

"In your judgment we will attain our goals." Jorin spoke thoughtfully.

"I am known for backing the right horse. I do not know the Sarn leadership at all. They are the variable I cannot judge. I know King Ranald. I know Dragon. I am basing my choice on that knowledge."

Jorin looked out the window at the expanse of Llwegan. "We have had to expend much energy guarding the wide open border. If not for this incredible space we could have solved our problems long ago. The border with Masfin is such a beautiful thing. We truly wished for good relations with Masfin."

Jeffeaux had become used to the seeming non sequiturs of the Dragon's household's conversation. Sometime later he would be expected to remember this conversation, both pieces of it, the long and the short, as if it had never been halted. He was juggling several such conversations. There was his long running discourse with Dragon about his relationship with his mother. Then the one about his duty to marry, at the oddest times, would come up.

Bernath was fascinated with his refusal to learn combat techniques, strategies, anything to do with fighting.

With a sigh of frustration, Jeffeaux pushed the books and papers away. He pushed his chair away from the table. Enough was enough. He needed some distraction. He knew the soldiers assigned to him would follow. He wanted to be away from everything Llweganian. No, that wasn't it. He wanted to be away from the pressures of being under the protection of Devouring Dragon/Harbinger of Death. It was dark night; riding wasn't an option. He couldn't escape the closed in feeling by traversing the very landscape Dragon inhabited.

Marma heard the knock on her door. She pulled a robe over her sleepwear. The material fell heavily against her legs. She opened the door. Jeffeaux was standing in the hallway.

Jeffeaux was quiet. Marma stood patiently, waiting for him to speak. He seemed to look right through her. Then when she tightened her hand to shut the door, he shook his head as if waking.

"Lady Marma, would you walk with me for a little?"

Marma listened to the words. She took a moment to realize he spoke in Masfin. He did not comment on her garb or apologize for the late hour. He simply stood there waiting for her answer. She stepped out into the hallway. The door closed with a solid thud. Jeffeaux did not offer his arm. Marma folded her hands over her stomach. Her hair, loose from its braid hung down her back. Occasionally she lifted a hand to tuck her locks behind an ear.

They were quiet for a while. Jeffeaux seemed intent on some inner conversation. Marma walked steadily.

"I am thinking of starting a cycle robe." Marma felt compelled to speak. "I have been designing the pattern for the past few Darkfalls. As I lie down to sleep I try to envision the sequence of events. Where the cycle should begin? I decided to start with your grandfather's death. At first I thought the most obvious was the shaking, but the more I considered the pattern the more important became your grandfather's death."

Jeffeaux listened to Marma describe the bed covering she planned to sew. He heard her description of the scenes she would piece, the colors she would use. She spoke in Masfin. She spoke of a traditional Masfin activity. Cycle robes were an important piece of family heritage. His own house had a famous collection, going back several generations.

"It is so strange."

"You think so? I thought the gradual transition from pastels of similar colors to bright hues of different colors quite appropriate."

"In that you might be right. Though the implication is that the influence of Dragon was defining and illuminating; I am not sure that is what you mean to say with the robe. No, what is strange is that Ranald is sitting in Tampello fearing that Dragon will invade for the purpose of putting me on the throne. I never thought of my life in any terms, never mind these. I am sure Ranald never imagined a threat to his crown."

"Ranald, not King Ranald: whatever you did not imagine before you certainly are thinking along the lines Dragon is drawing now."

"No one in court will take me seriously."

"Yes, they will. At least they will take your patron seriously. You understand the rhythms of intrigue already. You will know everyone who is around you. It's a ways off anyway. Ranald might still deal."

"Then how comfortable will my life be? He will have to have me killed. In that case I will have to remain with Dragon. Either way I can never return to my carefree days."

"But, wouldn't life be dull? Weren't you bored before we went to Malso?"

Jeffeaux turned in the hallway. He offered his arm to Marma.

"Some days, my dear, I long for boring. Dull is at times a goal I aspire to with all my soul. Constant excitement can become dull and boring in its regularity.

"I really think the part of the cycle in Sarna needs subtle coloring."

"You may be right. I feel that things came into sharp focus in Sarna so I want edges in the robe design. I could use subtle colors that reflect Sarna's pallet but use soft fabrics for Masfin then rougher textures once I get to Sarna." Marma fell silent. She considered the texture and the variety of the materials she would use. In the back of her mind she kept returning to the robe she had worn on her journey from Masfin to Sarna. She was convinced that she should use a piece from that robe. She was unsure how to incorporate it into the work.

Jeffeaux simply enjoyed the act of walking. For several feet at a time he could ignore the questions that snuck up on him when he was least expecting them. Why was he allowing this to happen? Why did he comply with Dragon's most outrageous machinations? This was way out of character for him. He never pursued anything except his own pleasure, his own safety. He could rationalize that his interests lay in obeying Dragon but he was actively participating. He couldn't deny that despite his show of resisting Dragon's plans, he followed right behind her.

"Do you miss Masfin, Lady Marma?"

Marma stared into the shadows created by the fires that ringed the house.

"It is like a well-loved story. I enjoy remembering parts of it. But I know it's not real. It is gone. It will never happen again. If I ever return I could walk the same halls, sleep in the same bed, but nothing would be the same. I feel nostalgic at times. I remember my first ball, my first love, my family, but I would be nostalgic for those people anyway."

"But do you miss it?"

Marma chuckled. Then she looked into Jeffeaux's face. He was serious. The thought was strange: Jeffeaux serious about anything, imagine.

"No. I am happy here. Aren't you? I'm never bored. We live well. Someone else always made the decisions about my life. Nothing has changed here. I certainly am well-traveled. The world is more than Masfin. It is filled with sights and sounds and smells and tastes and people that I had never dreamed of before the shaking and might never have dreamed of until I knew them so well I can dream of them.

"I never heard of a wasteland until I went to Sarna. Now I can dream of it in intimate detail. Would you have believed anyone who told you of a place as flat as this? I wouldn't have, but now I know what flat is. We never went to the ocean in Masfin. Now I want to see it." Marma stopped walking. She stood before a window. He could not see her clearly. She was a dark silhouette with edges that glowed.

"But, you have more to gain and more to lose than I in this venture. So, I can look at this as an adventure while you see it differently."

"I knew how every day of my life would go until I died. Not the minute details, but the general events were clear and I approved. I envisioned some court intrigues; they never can be completely avoided. I knew I might have to make some effort to see my sisters safely married. Eventually I would have to choose a wife to secure the line. Basically I thought my life would be the same from one day to the next." Jeffeaux joined Marma at the window. He actually looked at the groups of people that inhabited the night. He saw the dancers, the talkers, the standing and the sitting people. He saw them still as a group and many as individuals. "A scenario such as this never entered my imagination."

Marma stood still. She was comfortable being this close to Jeffeaux. They had spent many hours much closer physically. In this light she could see none of his new wrinkles from the sun and worry. In this light he looked much as he had in Masfin; except, constant riding and activity had hardened him.

"You don't find the very unexpectedness of this situation a little exciting? When was the last time you wondered how you would entertain yourself?"

Jeffeaux gave a stunted laugh. He shook his head at Marma. He turned away from the window. He extended his arm to Marma. She placed her hand lightly on his wrist. He enjoyed the feel of another's warmth on his skin. He bowed his most elegantly as he left her at her door. Marma stood in the doorway. Light from the fire in her room fell beyond her into the shadows in the hall. She watched Jeffeaux walk away from her. His body was bowed with his inner conflict. Perhaps indecision was the better term. He wanted to follow the safest course. He was having difficulty judging which course was the safest. Would he transform himself into an entirely different person to keep safe? Could he? Could anyone?

Marma stepped back into her room. She swung the door shut. The heavy wood swung easily on its well-oiled hinges. The resounding thunk as it fitted into its jamb was comforting. Marma could not fault Jeffeaux for liking his safety. She did. She liked the sound her door made when it closed. She liked knowing that she could sleep deeply while others watched over her well-being.

Every corridor had light. The shadows did not threaten. They clung stubbornly to the very edges of the halls. In the emptiness

Jeffeaux was surprised not to hear his steps. He has been too long with Dragon to leave such an obvious clue as a footstep. He walked as silently as any warrior. His gait was still his own, at least partly.

She wanted him to deny any desire to be king. That was easy. He knew he would end up dead or king so he had to prepare to be king. How he planned to deny while he prepared was a quandary. He worried too much. He always worried too much these days. He might not live to have to deny planning to usurp the King. He could die under any number of circumstances. He shook his head. She did not want him dead. It was unlikely he would end up dead under her aegis; not if Dragon wanted him alive.

The door to his quarters was ajar. Jeffeaux stood in the open portal. He did not plan to enter a room when he did not know how the door had been opened. He stood irresolutely in the corridor. To leave he would present his back to a doorway. In this moment every doorway was suspect. Then he steadied his nerves. He had been too long at war. Here in this place he could trust the security. There would be nothing physically dangerous in his room. He straightened his jacket. With a deep sigh he entered his suite.

"Lord Jeffeaux, you were a long time in the corridor." Marjas stood across the room. Jeffeaux let his breath leave him in a whoosh.

"Caution, I was practicing caution."

"As you say, I wonder what you expected to find in your rooms."

"After the initial hesitation I realized there would be nothing to find here that would justify my caution."

"You are learning, Lord Jeffeaux. I have come to go over our next few moves. Assizes Court ends in two Darkfalls. Then we will be proceeding to a Walk. The Walk will be half as long as we have spent on the Assizes Court. Once that is done we will appear before the Council. Then we will proceed to the Front. Basically we have spent half our time here."

"Thank you for this update. What will my duties be and boundaries be during the Walk?"

"Good, you are learning. You may never ride next to Dragon. Not even among the guard. If you did you would be considered, under Llweganian law, a husband. The most appropriate place for you will be with the Lady Marma."

Jeffeaux was quiet as he considered the statements. There was a point he had to nail down. "If I ride with the Lady Marma, will we be considered married?"

Marjas kept his eyes on Jeffeaux. He did not turn away. Jeffeaux admired the man's strength of character.

"Perhaps. You come from a different tradition. That tradition should protect you. You are bound by our criminal laws but I don't believe you are bound by our civil laws when dealing with your own people in our country."

"Wouldn't it be best if I stayed by a male trooper?"

"No, that would not be sufficient hedge against accidental proximity to Dragon. You must ride with Lady Marma. We will hope for the best."

"Hope for the best. That will be written on my grave. He hoped for the best at every turn. One has to be impressed at the number of turns I have hoped at." Jeffeaux stood over the table. He pushed a number of papers from one side of the polished surface to the other. He watched his hand as it moved. In the light his rings glittered. He was down to three rings. He needed a new one. Something simpler, bolder was needed to represent him now. He turned to the issue at hand.

"I will not leave Lady Marma's side. I promise. It will kill me not knowing what future Dragon is planning for me. I would appreciate a trooper, a male trooper, assigned to me to answer questions, relay information, generally keep me from wondering what is going on, what is about to happen to me."

"That sounds reasonable."

"Thank you. Have we any word from my - the front?"

"Not since two Darkfalls ago."

"Is that all?"

"Have a good sleep, Lord Jeffeaux."

Jeffeaux nodded acknowledgement to the good night. He was already looking over a book. He sat slowly as Marjas left the room. He could not read anything on the page. He had wanted an excuse to end the eye contact with Marjas. Still he sat looking at the book. Marjas closed the door softly. Jeffeaux knew he was alone. Yet, he could not get up from the table.

He wondered if his mother were all right. He worried that she was facing the combined armies without Harbinger. He hoped she was well. He would not ask about her. He pushed the book away with more force than necessary. He would not become upset. He reached across the table to close the book gently.

Turning from the table, Jeffeaux began to undress. He folded his clothes as he went. He did so without thought. When the pile was done it neatly sat on a chest. His boots stood guard at the end of his bed.

At last she was finished. The Ride would be a good change. She thought the length of the Assizes Court was exactly correct. Just as she was ready to be done hearing cases it was over. The time had been well spent otherwise as well. Dragon watched Jeffeaux gather his notes. Even she had never studied this hard prior to her ascension to power. She had practiced her combat skills. She had studied tactical lessons and enemy outlines, but she had not reviewed laws and regulations. That was not true. She had spent her life absorbing information. She knew two languages before she was married.

Still she had never had to completely change herself. Jeffeaux had earned her respect. The question was, did he see it? Did he respect himself? Did he place any value on respect? Was he simply still trying to learn what he thought he needed to stay alive? She just wished he would take a wife. She had a hard time trusting a man who had no wife. She had hoped that Lady Marma would suit him. He certainly had the opportunity to see the Lady Marma as a good partner. He did need a Masfin wife.

She was having difficulty locating a suitable bride. Lady Zona had not been helpful on that front. She denied knowing any Masfin ladies that would suit her son. There had to be some woman in that country with the appropriate position who would make Jeffeaux a good wife. Lady Marma herself might have a few candidates if she could not bring Jeffeaux to the altar.

Dragon looked out the window of her suite. She did not stand close to the opening. From where she stood all she could see was sky. The rooms were high enough that even the best archer could not shoot into her rooms. Still there was no need to tempt fate. She stayed well away from the openings.

Sarna's deserts afforded a worthy defense. Only the best supplied invaders could storm the country. She thought of the long low houses that caught every breeze of the hot days and hoarded heat for the cold nights. Sarna's desert let her people design houses solely within the restraints of the environment.

Masfin had fortresses and castles. They were used to protect against internal threats but they could bend somewhat to the environment. The mountains gave some protection. Internal troubles could be watched more easily than external forces. They could be held so tightly that they could move without altering the holder.

Poor Llwegan, her rich land gave up food to resident and invader alike. Water poured on all who stood in her. Internal peace did not allow for any freedom in design of living places. Only buildings as tall as this had windows. Tunnels abounded, secret passages turned at every corner, every building from the simplest hut to the grandest estate was built along lines dictated by war. Luckily Sarna had never had the population to support a large scale invasion. But an army could march out of Masfin across Sarna into Llwegan easily. And there could be no real defense against such a force in this flat, open country.

Masfin had to be made weak, dependent, friendly. No building design could defend against a determined army. The winter at Tampello should have reduced the size of the army. Other Masfin troops might have joined her army. With Marlin and Lady Zona in charge they would have the feeling of belonging to a Masfin force. She could not limit herself to the Sarnese forces. She had to reduce the entire army drastically.

A hand brought her from her thoughts. She turned to face her husband. It was time.

"What were you thinking?"

"How vulnerable a country is where the only safe places are in the sky."

Rodznig glanced at the clouds drifting by the opening. He squeezed her forearm once.

"But the sky is the playground of very dangerous dragons."

"Did you ever think that perhaps dragon is just the way the ancients explained a shooting star or a comet?"

"Wife, do you perceive a fault in our training? Do you doubt our logistics? Have you lost faith in our planning?"

"No, I think our fellow Llweganians have become complacent in their security and do not see the danger."

"**You** see the dangers. You are willing and able to secure our borders. That is why you were born. That is why we married you. Sablor's mother had a dream that there was danger and that you, only you would protect Llwegan. Remember, Wife?"

Dragon leaned against the solid wall of Rodznig's chest. She enjoyed the feel of another being in her stance against the rest of the world. She needed this connection to exist. She was the greatest warrior that Llwegan had even produced, and she needed this tie. That was why she could not trust Jeffeaux, because she doubted his judgment and his character as long as he stayed unmarried.

"We need to find Jeffeaux a wife. No one can do what we are doing without another person." She felt Rodznig laugh. She savored the feel of his affection and amusement. He dropped a quick kiss on her forehead. She turned to press a hard kiss on his lips. Then she stepped away from him.

At the door she stopped, then, turning spoke.

"You really married me to secure the borders?"

"I married you because you were the most sensual woman, powerful force, best fighter, lavish provider I could find. I wanted it all. And I got it all, even an heir of the greatest woman I have ever known."

"Those reasons I accept. A woman likes to think she is more than destiny."

"I would never accuse you of being humble."

"I do know my limits. I try to surround myself with people who balance my limitations with their experience, character, skills."

"That is one of your most appealing attributes."

Dragon extended her hand to every household member she passed. Each touch was accompanied with a nod or a smile. These were not her servants as First had. These were related to her. Everyone had a right to call her estate home. They ran the estate, the estate provided for them. There were a few paid retainers who answered to Dragon. They were estateless wanderers Dragon had accepted as her responsibility. They were crowded at the door as Dragon left. She thanked them each for their service. Then she was out in the air of the day.

Jeffeaux was far in the back of the horsed crowd. The only sound was the snorting of the horses. Dragon swung up with relief to finally be on the next leg of her duties. Once she turned her mount out of the courtyard everyone began to move out. When they were gone, silence hung in the house. The going had not diminished the household by a third, still, it seemed silent and empty. Already the house took on an air of waiting. The spring went out of everyone's step. The sense of purpose vanished with the settling of the dust on the stones of the yard.

Jeffeaux rode next to Lady Marma. He checked to make sure the trooper assigned to him was there. Both his troopers were behind him. Once was carrying his books. The books had arrived from Masfin recently. Jeffeaux hoped to spend time with them on the journey. The smaller books he could read while he rode as long as the group did not ride too fast and the troopers guided his mount. He suspected he would want to study the rites and duties of a Walk as well. Marma's project hung at her knee. The large leather sack looked undignified next to Marma's quiet elegance. Still she would not be bored or feel useless while working on her project.

Since he had ridden out of Malso Jeffeaux had not felt either bored or useless. He had felt helpless, frightened, annoyed, and disgusted. His life in Masfin was fading from his memory. None of it seemed real anymore.

"Lady Marma," the young trooper assigned to Jeffeaux spoke hesitantly. "Dragon would appreciate it if you would think of some likely candidates as a wife for Lord Jeffeaux."

Jeffeaux glared at the speaker. When he had asked for a go-between to Dragon he had not wanted one that nagged him as she did.

"Has Dragon applied to Lady Zona for advice?"

"Yes, she had none to give."

"I will think on the matter."

"Why is it so important that I be married?"

Marma looked at Jeffeaux as if he were crazy.

"Of course it matters. Of course Dragon places value on marriage. We are not poor, powerless people. We have great privilege but we also have great responsibility. When a farmer dies unmarried and childless there are legal problems that affect some people. When those who have more leave no direct heirs more lives are complicated. Sometimes entire countries can suffer the throes of difficult legacies. And there is always the question of character."

"The question of character?" Jeffeaux did not try to disguise his confused disgust.

"If you are unwilling to make the commitment of marriage, how can any of your other commitments be respected?"

"What of commitments to ideals, institutions, quests?"

"You haven't made any of those either. You have to commit to something beyond yourself or the avoidance of commitment."

"But I don't want to be King."

"I think the range of your options in that matter has become very narrow."

"What happened to that mindless woman I used to know."

"I was never mindless and you never really knew me."

"I think I knew you rather well."

"There's the Jeffeaux I had thought lost somewhere on the road from Masfin to Sarna."

Jeffeaux paid no attention to Lady Marma's sarcasm. He studied the shadow of her expression. He watched her ease as she sat on her mount. There was no trace of a pampered woman in her posture. This was a hard riding person.

"Maybe it's only that I knew you often."

Marma turned her head to cast a scathing eye on her companion. She did not meet a hurtful expression. Rather, the longish face was thoughtful assessing. He was telling the truth. She had spent many hours in his arms. She could not fault him for that.

"Knew is such a deceiving, misleading term. It disguises a multitude of sins."

"Or activities. It is one of those all-encompassing words that end up meaning nothing instead of the everything it strives for. For someone who used to pride himself being in control this is an outrageous position."

"I think you craved the outrageous. This isn't about control or even winning for Dragon; at least not in conjunction with you. You are a tool, or a girder, for her. She's not trying to make you do something; she is trying to mold you into something. Whatever you do, she is going to use you for her purposes."

"There are some things over which I do have control; one of those things is whether or not I marry."

"Fine but she will continue to shape you into the best possible shape for her uses. The distinction is very subtle."

"I used to spend three hours getting ready to face the day. I used to watch the sun rise at the end of the day. The most important decision I used to make was which function to attend."

Marma laughed. She appreciated the humor in the answer.

"I do miss lying in bed until my body is too tired to lie down any longer."

Jeffeaux watched as one of his troopers hurried to the front of the column. Absently he pulled a book from his saddle pocket. He had so little time to prepare. He really couldn't waste any of it. He was not going to be a king. He hoped but it never was too wise to plan your future on a hope. He hated having to worry about tomorrow. He missed the certainty he had taken for granted, even despised.

Marma studied the bent head. She noted the leading rein attached to the trooper. She sighed. For a second she allowed herself a twinge of nostalgia. Jeffeaux studying a book signaled the end of the world as she knew it. More than the first raiders, or the swarm of black clad female soldiers, Jeffeaux acting in any way responsibly was the end of the world. The new world that was coming was not necessarily a terrible thing, but still she noted the passing of the old order.

Chapter 15

King Ranald watched his door. He could not shake his feeling of dread. He woke every day with the same feeling. It slept in his bed with him each night. It woke before him each day to sit waiting on his chest. With each breath he took he felt the weight of that dread pin him to his bed. What terrible thing did this day bring? What devastating news would be delivered to him this dawning? Each rap at the door signaled a new problem as it had since that long ago day.

He should not wait for a new day. He should rise before the light peeked over the edge of the world. He should be chasing demons before they found their way to his bed. He would call for his servant. One should be waiting right outside the door even now to do his bidding. Ranald stretched his hand towards the bellpull. He felt the texture of the pull between his fingers. Then he drew back. He folded his hands across his chest. His fingers laced closed.

He relied on everyone. His reliance had landed him here in this cold, benighted place. He could not even get out of bed unless he called for someone. Well, he had to change if he meant to keep his crown. His previous actions had landed him in no steady spot.

Gingerly Ranald swung his feet out of bed. As his feet touched the cold floor he winced. He had never been so discomforted in his life. What was wrong with this floor? What had happened overnight to create such a problem?

Ranald stared at his feet as if they were being attacked by the Dragon's armies. They glowed at him in the dark. That wasn't right. There was something missing; oh, right, his slippers. They were resting on the hearth ready to be warmed once the fire was restarted.

The floor stretched forbidding and wide between the bed and Ranald's slippers. Here and there carpets and rugs interrupted the stretch of bare floor. They had to be better than the cold floor. Carefully Ranald stepped away from the bed. He walked to his slippers across the floor's coverings. Once the slippers were on his feet, Ranald realized he could not start the fire. He had slept through every start of a fire in his room. He knew that wood burned but he had no idea how to begin the process.

And, where were his clothes? He could not see them or where they might be kept. He was helpless. Who had made him so helpless? No wonder his entire army had been stolen and was now melting away from him.

Ranald ran back to his bed. He pulled the bellpull with fury at himself and the world. He waited impatiently for the rap that would announce the presence of a servant. Ranald shivered in the cold of the room. He watched the head poke into the room. A sleepy, crumpled face stared at him. Slowly a body followed the face past the door into the room.

Ranald felt his anger and frustration boil through him. He opened his mouth to order his life. The first words that sprang from his lips were roared. They symbolized his fears and desire to be different.

"Where are Our clothes?"

Eyes blinked in confusion. They darted through the room. They stared at his feet.

"Forgive me, Your Majesty. Let me see where they might be."

"We need to know this very instant where Our clothes are."

"Immediately Your Majesty, I will go look right now."

"You will show Us. We will go with you right now."

The servant bowed several times. He began to shake. If the King's clothes had been stolen, the servant would pay with his head, most likely. He couldn't imagine who would want to steal the King's clothes. He walked quickly. He felt the King breathing down his neck as they walked to the dressing room; through the room was the servant's work space where the clothes were repaired and freshened. Then a door opened into a huge space filled with shelves and racks and drawers. The servant lit a lamp just inside the door. The light gleamed on silks and satins. Highly polished buckles of every shape caught the light.

Ranald walked into the room. He stared at the clothes as if he had never seen them before that very moment. He walked until he touched a cloak hanging against a wall.

"Is this everything?"

The servant turned his head in a wide arc.

"I will inventory everything Your Majesty; right now, to make sure it is all there."

Ranald looked at the servant as if the domestic were crazy.

"Don't be stupid. No one would dare steal Our clothes. Everything should be here unless you lost something."

"No, Your Majesty, of course not, Your Majesty."

Ranald waved the servant into the room. The lamp's light jumped as the frightened man followed the King through the room. Ranald stopped to feel a piece of clothing here and there. Finally he made a choice. He pulled items from their shelves. Companion things littered the floor. The servant stood stunned, looking at the things littered across the space. The King had already left the room. Quickly the servant replaced the fallen clothes. He hurried after King Ranald.

Ranald stood in the dressing room. He had shed his night wear. He was struggling to dress in his underclothes. The servant placed the lamp on the table before going to help his ruler. An imperious hand waved him away. The servant unclenched his hands as he watched the various false starts in the process. Finally Ranald had himself fully clothed.

"What are you still doing here? You may leave Us."

Ranald watched the servant scuttle away. He turned to survey himself in the mirror. He savored the feeling of having accomplished this task by himself. The sun was just beginning to light the world. Ranald threw on his cloak. He walked quietly through the corridors.

Ranald stepped out into the cold morning. He watched the light gild the snow. He studied the troopers stir into activity. He wandered through the entire camp. He wondered at the differences of rituals and the similarities. These were Masfin. Those were Sarn. Only a handful of Llweganian trained troops remained. They hovered at the edge of the camp. As the spring melt was reducing the snow, so too was it thinning the size of his army. He could see places where troops had lain down the night before only to be gone now.

He was studying one empty group of tents. An officer from the Masfin troops walked up to him. The man came to stand next to him. The grizzled head shook.

"Another group gone, General Renfrew will not be pleased."

"No." Ranald kept his answer short. He did not look the officer full in the face. He waited for the next line.

"We set guards over them. We split them among the rest of the army. Still they slip from us each day. One or two here, a handful there, gone, every day.

Ranald did not ask to where they went.

"Perhaps they should wear bells."

The officer slapped Ranald on the shoulder. A laugh boomed out into the early morning quiet.

"That's a good one. Though, when they desert despite the bells, the myth and power of them and their training and the army they surge to would become even more intimidating."

Ranald began to understand the import of who had left. He began to understand the drain on his forces was more than disease and homesickness.

"Disease can be countered, deserters can be captured, but traitors can only be executed."

"If we should be so lucky; it is more likely these traitors will kill us first."

Ranald barely restrained himself from stepping back into his role as king. He wanted to know what his advisors kept from him. He wanted to beat the demons to the punch. So, he bit his lip. He watched scouts investigate the empty camp site. He studied the method of searching. He tried to discover the importance in the questions as well in the answers. Finally he could not stop the question.

"What exactly are you looking for?"

The officer looked at the horizon. He pushed the snow from one side to the other with his foot.

"We know to whom they are going. Once we know what they took for the journey we can surmise how long they thought to take to get to their destination. We don't know if they know exactly where they are going or if they were in contact with someone before they left. Does someone come in to persuade them to leave? Does one of the group go ahead then return with the information? Do they decide to leave without clear direction? How do we prevent them from leaving? Our preemptive efforts seem useless. Are they? How do we change what we do to keep this from happening? How can we predict who is going to go and when?"

"You think to find those answers in the pattern of their fires?"

"Perhaps we will find an answer to a question we don't know to ask."

"Were you a cleric before you were a soldier?"

Once again Ranald earned a booming laugh and a forceful pounding on the back.

"Very good, very good, you must come drinking with me one night, when I am not chasing shadows."

Ranald faded from the camp. He wandered back to his place. He had hoped to ease his fears by walking the camp. He had hoped to prove the baseless nature of his fears. Instead he learned of troubles his staff kept from him. At least he could name some of his fears, demons, and perhaps fight them so they did not sit so heavily on his chest.

He cursed his training roundly. He had been trained in legal intricacies and court intrigue. He knew the finer points of physical sport and mental games. Nothing had trained him to keep men loyal to him. That was the battle he was losing. She was destroying his army thoroughly without firing a shot. He had to send out the order to remain loyal. He would compose a royal decree about loyalty and the price of failing in it. He would ferret out all disloyal citizens; have them destroyed as one cut away rotting flesh to preserve life. The procedure was dangerous and painful but in the end the life of his army and his country would be saved. He would not remain King much longer if the war stretched into too many more winters.

Ranald flung his outer clothes on the floor of his apartment. He stepped into his inner chamber. A servant waited to shave him, to dress him for his day of meaningless babble. Ranald submitted to the shave. He did not trust his untried hand with the blade on his face. The clothes, he chose himself and he donned himself. He remained deep in thought as he paced his main chamber.

He swirled in impatience as his military advisors walked into the room. He barely restrained himself as they recited reports and spread papers on the table.

"Useless, you are all useless, this is all useless, this information is useless. Do you know why you are useless and your information is useless? We'll tell you why: because you are all deceivers. You are disobedient and wrongheaded." Ranald paused to gather more air to continue his diatribe. Mouths opened to refute his statements. He raised his hand. One mouth remained open. "Disobedient! We sent you to confer with a visiting dignitary. If you had obeyed Our directive, We would at least have some information about Our enemy. But, no, you ignored her and you have led Us to this place of ignorance. By disobeying Us you abused Our trust in you. Now We discover you have been lying to Us. We ask: why does Our army shrink? You say the soldiers are dying of cold, Your Majesty. You say the soldiers are cowardly, they are running away home, Your Majesty. There is a lie of omission here. No one says the soldiers are changing sides, Your Majesty. Weather We have no control over. Disease is an enemy that creeps unseen and is hard to fight. Cowardice - we have no use for cowards in battle. But loyalty is an issue that can be impacted.

"If soldiers will not fight for us: that is a problem. If they are leaving Us to fight against Us there is only one solution to that problem. We will end up killing them on a field of battle or being killed by them. Therefore, those whom We catch will be executed."

There was silence. No one dared to speak. They waited for the King to give them a sign that they could open their mouths. This morning Ranald looked wild. Color stained his cheeks. Fire burned in his eyes. One brash youngster looked at the frozen tableau. He dared to open his mouth. The words spilled were pitched high and held more air than sound.

"These soldiers are uncatchable. They slip away under the eyes of guards."

"That is a problem We just recently discovered." Ranald frowned his displeasure over this fact at the room in general and the youngster in particular. "We will have to make the choice of leaving very unattractive. How do We know the guards aren't letting them go? Perhaps they are bribing the guards. Perhaps the guards are being derelict in their duty. We do not believe that these men are becoming invisible then slipping away from Us. There is a way to counter this threat. We will pursue every course needed to prevent Our numbers from swelling the ranks of our enemy."

Ranald waved his hand to empty the room. He stared at the papers littering his table. He stared at the papers for a long time.

The lines wavered then flowed until he could not see the words. He searched the room until he found the servant hiding in the shadows.

"Call the captain of Our guard."

As he waited, Ranald gathered the papers. He sorted through them. He built piles, neat orderly piles. When the door opened Ranald turned to face the stoic subordinate standing just inside the door.

"How long have you served Us?"

"Since your father's time, Your Majesty."

"A long time then, captain. We have a special duty for you. You, yourself will be answerable for its execution. Use as many men as you like. Recruit as many new men as you need from any place you want. Just be very sure of the loyalty of those men to Us. You will be answerable with your life for their actions."

"Yes, Your Majesty."

"We want a list of all soldiers who served under the enemy. We want a list of all the soldiers in Our army who have a connection to those soldiers who have turned traitor. We are concerned about the loyalty of the soldiers in Our army. It seems lacking. We need to know who is loyal and who is a traitor. Is that clear captain?"

"Yes, Your Majesty. What do we do with those suspected of such crimes?"

"You imprison them at Our discretion. We will review their cases. We will heal this bleeding wound in Our army. We will be as a surgeon; steady, calm, direct, thorough. This is not an assignment for the squeamish. If you are afraid of spilling blood speak now."

"I am at your disposal always, Your Majesty."

"Good, leave Us."

Ranald felt better. He felt the peace of having made a decision of taking action fill his chest. His army was his defense against losing his throne. He must keep that army strong, healthy, *clear* of infection.

Renfrew watched the comings and goings in the barracks. Soldiers filed in and out at a dizzying rate. They did not smile or exchange greetings. None of them stopped to speak to anyone. They did not pass comments in passing with each other. It was strange to see palace guards so active. Usually palace guards passed this life in a measured tread that went to the end of a corridor and back. No one could question them anyway, they were answerable only to the Captain of the palace guard and that man was answerable only to the King himself.

With a sigh Renfrew heaved himself up from his seat. He looked outside the window. The snow was melting. Soon they would be leaving this benighted place. He would never forget the cold or the frustration of his time here. Other memories threatened to surface. He pushed them ruthlessly away from him. He was here. He had no intention of touching that sore subject.

They had to choose a place to which to relocate. The enemy would be watching for their move. They couldn't stay here. All of Masfin lay undefended from the raids of the enemy. Renfrew suspected that their enemy would wait until they had begun their move.

So the army should begin its removal now. It would be slow and hazardous but it gave them the best chance of reaching some place of security and safety. Renfrew pulled out the maps of his country. He looked at it from a purely military point of view. He tried to remember all the soldiers who had disappeared. He pulled his list from his wallet. He drew out the mustering lists. He checked the names against the mustering lists. There wouldn't be a place in the country some defector did not call home, but perhaps he could find a place that even a defector would hesitate to expose.

There was a knock on his door. Renfrew called an absent sounding enter. There was a sharp boot heel on the floor. Renfrew looked up at the grim looking palace guard.

"You are ordered to the King, General Renfrew."

Renfrew stood without hesitation. He left his papers where they lay. The guard looked at the white sheets that glowed against the dark wood. He waited until Renfrew had left with another guard. Quickly the gloved hands gathered up the sheets of paper.

Renfrew waited in the audience room. Two guards manned the door. Renfrew wondered where the other military advisors were. He regretted not changing his clothes but his training had led his feet immediately out the door in answer to the order. He wished for his papers suddenly. He thought to ask one of the soldiers to bring the maps and the list to him but hesitated to send any guard belonging to the King on an errand.

Renfrew had fallen into a light doze. The sound of heels clicking and the feel of air against his skin broke Renfrew's light grasp on sleep. Renfrew rose clumsily to his feet as his king entered the room. Quickly Renfrew cleared his head. Papers slid from one of the accompanying guard's hands onto the huge desk of the King. Renfrew bowed low. He remained bent until the King greeted him by name.

"General Renfrew."

"Your Majesty, I am honored."

Renfrew remained standing, even as the King sat. Renfrew could see some of the papers. It was very significant to Renfrew that the very same maps that he had been studying were on the desk. Their minds must be running on the same lines. Where were the other advisors? This could be an extremely important meeting. Renfrew smiled.

"You are amused, General?"

"A little, Your Majesty, I was just studying such maps when you summoned me."

"What were you looking for?"

"A secure and strategic staging site for the army Your Majesty."

"Really?"

"Yes, it has been harder than I expected. Even the timing of such a move has become difficult to choose, Your Highness."

"What are the parameters you are using?"

"Well, I hesitate to say, Your Majesty."

"There is something you feel We are unable to comprehend?"

"No, not at all, Your Majesty. I don't wish to appear fanatical."

"Fanatical?"

"Yes, Your Majesty. I am using as one of my parameters a list of all the, I don't know how to say this without sounding inappropriate, the defectors. I was hoping to find some sector of Masfin that has not been compromised. But there is not one home mustering site from which no one has defected. I was becoming very frustrated."

"You were?"

"Yes, but today I had an inspiration: perhaps we can find a site which even the meanest, lowest traitor would not betray Your Majesty."

"An interesting proposition; you are rather fervent on this issue."

"Your pardon, please, Your Majesty, but you have never met the enemy. You have never had your family destroyed by the enemy. You have not been kept in their dungeon. You have not suffered at their hands as I have. I want them wiped, completely wiped, from the face of the earth. I cannot stand the thought that while our army dies here slowly, they are living in luxury and peace."

Or that for one brief moment, he had lost sight of all loyalties and oaths in the honeyed body of one of them. That at night in the loneliness of sleep he dreamed he was back in that dungeon with the moment still to come when his body would erupt in pleasure from the hand of one who rode with the enemy.

Ranald sat back in his chair. This passionate general would never know how close he had come to death. Such single-minded devotion would be a useful tool. It would behoove Ranald to keep this man on his path.

"So when do you suggest We move?"

"First, we must jettison those most likely to defect. There will be no security if we have men running from us to the enemy with reports of our every move, Your Majesty. I know this will be hard for you to hear and to accept about your subjects but she is a witch who has bespelled our men. I have met Dragon, face to face. She is very dangerous. It is difficult for me to say this. I have spent many sleepless nights over this suggestion. I do not offer it lightly. We will have to imprison the remaining soldiers who served with her. I know you will have deep reservations about this move. There probably are many loyal Masfin who will be unjustly punished. After the war they can be freed to return to their homes but for the greater good they must all be confined."

"That is a harsh treatment of the problem."

"Forgive me, Your Majesty, but I believe it is the only way. Then we must move before spring. Our enemies will never expect us to march in this cold. Already the days are getting longer. The sun is melting the snow now. Any new snow that falls will not last. It is best that we go now."

"Go where?"

"I'm still working on that suggestion, Your Majesty. Perhaps someone else, another of your officers will have an opinion on that."

Ranald smiled to himself. His choices had been vindicated by the best source. He has an out for those who sought to criticize his choice. His military advisor had recommended just such a course of action. This day was looking beautiful. Tonight would be the night to visit his queen. On this day of all days she would conceive a son for him.

Jeffenza settled herself. She moved her hips seeking just the right spot. Strong hands held her in place. She felt the skin of his waist against her inner thighs.

She truly enjoyed this part of her life. She took pleasure in the different textures of their bodies. She savored the feel of his hard muscles under her fingers. The scent of his pleasure multiplied her enjoyment. Her pace increased. She could feel the pressure and inner shiver begin.

She was not allowed to bask in the afterglow. Sounds crept into her ears from her outer chamber. Her servants knew better than to disturb her. Her mood turned petulant as she was unable to push those sounds from her mind. The only reason the servants would be allowed to disturb her once she went to bed was if the King were coming.

Jeffenza sat straight up at the last thought. She shoved her body away from her human couch.

"Where are you going? We are not done yet."

"Oh yes we are. My husband the King comes. I can hear the voice of his servant speaking in the room beyond. Hurry, hurry, get up, get out. You have to leave."

"I can't leave. I will walk right by the servant and most likely your husband."

Jeffenza was not listening. She was busy sniffing the air. The scent of sex was heavy in the room. She rushed to the window. She would have to brave the cold. Strong air blew into the room. She scattered scented water on the chair. Her hand, shaking with haste, lit scented candles. Was that enough? Stiefis was almost dressed. She shoved him into her dressing room.

"Go out through the King's chambers."

"That's from the stall floor into the manure pile."

"Well at least you will only be thought a snoop, not my lover."

Stiefis slipped from the room. Jeffenza drew on her robe. She sat in front of her mirror. The room was becoming chill. Through the thin cover of her robe her nipples peaked. Their pebbly outline could be seen clearly in the light cast by the candles on her vanity. She began applying powder to cover the slight redness from the differences of texture she had been so recently enjoying. Next she began to draw a brush through her hair. The soothing action calmed her nerves as she waited for the door to open.

Her royal husband stood on the threshold. He looked odd. Jeffenza wondered wildly what was out of place. What did he see to bring such an intent look to his face? Had Stiefis left some damning evidence?

That look was focused solely on her. The clothes seemed to melt from her royal spouse's body. When had her husband ever undressed in front of her? He did not speak. He did not ask if it would be convenient for him to stay. He said nothing. He simply looked at her steadily. The body that was revealed had minimal muscle and was white with blue veins tracing the skin. Those arms were strong enough to lift her from her seat. He did not place her on the bed. He stood her by the side. Then he bent her forward across the sheets with her face turned to one side. He stretched her arms forward. Then he pulled her hips up towards him. He pushed her legs apart. She wondered what had gotten into her husband when suddenly he rammed home. He pushed in so hard her teeth rattled. He rammed hard and fast pushing down on her shoulders as he worked. Her fingers clawed at the sheets. The quick pounding had nothing of duty. She was nothing more than a vessel for his seed. This time there was an intensity and purpose to the marriage act that had been lacking in their bed.

Jeffenza relaxed. She was not discovered. There was no hew and cry from the rooms beyond. Her husband spoke no words. In her relaxation she stole some pleasure from the moment. She sighed when Ranald was done.

"Mark this well; We have made a son this day."

Jeffenza lay in the bed where her husband left her. She turned her head to watch him dress. She repeated the words carefully. She was not sure she was quite ready to become a mother. What did he know? How could he know anything at all at this point?

Something in the way the words echoed in her head convinced her he was right. She sighed in confusion. Her foremost feeling was relief that Stiefis was sterile so there could be no question of parentage. Still it would be best to break her relationship off with the Sarn. She did not want any questions of paternity. On the other hand no one had found out yet. She had so few pleasures in this place. She was not about to be controlled by anyone if she could get away with it. She could continue until she was obviously pregnant. She couldn't decide now. It would have to wait until later. Right now she had to close that window then douse the light.

Renfrew studied the reports of the last defection. The new measures of the King had been announced to the corps commanders. Each man had drawn a surprised breath. Each man had opened his mouth to protest. There was no precedent in Masfin history for such an action. Then the forceful presence of the palace guard had been noted. Renfrew had spoken up to reassure his colleagues of the necessity of the action. He assured them that there would be no punishment, only detention until the war was over and their actions could not compromise the safety of Masfin. Everyone's goal was to protect their country. Some served by offering their lives. Some would serve through imprisonment. Renfrew did not believe that anyone could really deny the practical solution's merits. He had stood staring at his fellow officers. He had not seen the set expression of the King. He had not seen the raised swords of the palace guards. He had been facing his target audience. He had seen the bodies that had been pushing out of their seats shift back down. He had seen expressions of outrage and disbelief settle into lines of restraint and acceptance.

In his anxiety to choose the right location and timetable Renfrew began to pace. He felt confined by the walls of his room. He enlarged his circuit until he was walking through the halls. He negotiated with himself sometimes heatedly and aloud. No one bothered him. A sound distracted him. A sound that was not appropriate to the location. He was too busy considering his point of view to immediately recognize the sound. If he had recognized the sound he might not have followed it to its source. He might have turned away discreetly. But, he did follow the sound. He puzzled at it absently but never truly listened until he turned the corner into a secluded alcove. He was in shadow. His mouth snapped shut. He held still. There against the wall in the glow of one flickering candle the queen was being taken by a man obviously not her husband. Renfrew backed away carefully. He hesitated only once; when he heard the man speak. Then he continued away from the spot. He shook his head to clear away the cobwebs of surprise and overwork. Had he really seen such a thing? What must he do? Loyalty to the King demanded some action. Loyalty to a friend, comrade-in-arms, demanded another. The greater good demanded silence. Such a scandal would impact the alliance. What was Stiefis thinking? He could not even consider the queen. Did she not fear to compromise her position and that of her children? He would have to keep this knowledge to himself. That was the greater good. For now at least until another good became dominant.

Jeffenza relaxed against the wall. She felt the strength of her lover as he held her. She could not give up this pleasure. Why should she? She had gained nothing pleasurable from her marriage. She had no freedom. She was trapped in this forsaken landscape with nothing to do and no way to amuse herself except these illicit encounters. The King had his intrigues and military matters to occupy him. She should have something fun as well.

Marlin looked at the travel weary soldiers. The group of ten huddled together. Their clothes were tattered and strangely cobbled together as if quickly donned and frequently adjusted for changes in weather. It was not their appearance or their exhausted air that bothered him. They had traveled far to get to him. It was their story that bothered Marlin beyond measure.

He did not insult them by asking them to repeat their tale. The facts they had presented were sparse, clear, and concrete. They were waiting for his reaction. They were looking at him with such an air of expectancy he could not bear their eyes on him.

"I had not foreseen this turn of events."

"No one could have General."

"It is the easy way out."

"But it is not simple."

"No, it complicates things beyond measure."

"We had been leaving in small groups that could travel unnoticed through the countryside. But with this news we stepped up the action. Your own brother is in charge."

"I guess I never knew him very well. I would never have thought he would agree to such an action, never mind advocate it. Imprisoning our own people for a crime they have yet to commit."

Marlin sighed deeply. He felt sadness for the fall of his former home into actions that disgraced his memories of the country. For a moment he thought of his brother when last they spoke. He thought of the lack of distress he felt at their final parting. He had worried that he had harbored envy for his brother's first birth and higher rank, but now he knew that his lack of feelings for his brother were that he had never really known Renfrew.

"This is sad news. It is sad that my - our choice is validated in such a way. I did not leave Masfin so much as join Harbinger, but now Masfin has left me and there can be no reconciliation."

"Exactly. Perhaps we should mourn for a while at the passing of a great state."

"I will discuss your idea with Lady Zona. We are readying for the return of Harbinger to the army. You will be very busy for the next while. As will I. I will however make time to speak with you closely on this matter."

Marlin looked to where Fifth stood by the door. She waited until the group had left. Then she came to him. Her strong hands covered his.

"What are they doing? Ranald thinks to decimate the army to keep it together? Loyalty is not easily lost or won but he could work on earning it. Prisons don't promote loyalty, they promote fear."

Fifth smiled slightly. She pressed their joint hands against her swollen womb. "So this has diminished the Masfin army without one loss from our ranks. This is good. Harbinger will rescue your fellow soldiers from prison. When she rescues Masfin from the clutches of the Sarnese army and the misguided Ranald, she will liberate all those you are grieving for. Her blessings are many and fruitful."

Marlin felt his child move under his hand. She was right. Once this war was over this new madness would be cured. Third entered the room. She waddled along. From her hand Ladizona toddled. The tiny girl child's face lit up when she saw her father. She tried to move ahead of her mother's hand. In her excitement she began to waver. Before she could lose her balance completely Marlin had caught her up. She giggled as she rode through the air in Marlin's strong grip.

"The scout has ridden in. Harbinger is sighted."

"Finally, First was becoming anxious."

"As we all are. It is good to have our sister home."

"Have you told First yet?"

"No, we thought you or Lady Zona might like to give her the good news."

"What news?" Lady Zona met the group at the door to First's rooms.

"That Harbinger will be here shortly. She has been sighted."

"Good. First is determined to wait until Harbinger is here to give birth."

"I thought babies came on their own schedule." Marlin spoke in a quiet voice. He was in awe of the process going on beyond the door. He stood patiently as Lady Zona left him for a moment to answer a question.

"They do in my experience, but First has an iron will. This child seems to be learning at a young age who is boss. Come tell your wife the good news."

"Are you sure she will want me in there? She barred me from her presence yesterday."

"For this she will want you."

Marlin trod lightly into the world of womanly mysteries. He tried to steel himself to the fear of loss and pain this world held. Joy stood in the room but that joy could not be expressed or felt until all chance of loss was gone.

Marlin tested the air. He tasted blood and sweat and effort. Second, Fourth and Sixth all were tending First. There was a servant girl also, since none of his wives could lift much or bend far. He had five more times to go through this agony in the coming weeks. He would rather face an army than stand in this room. Marlin advanced on the bed as if a deadly enemy waited there for him. A figure crouched against the side of the bed. But that body was straining to produce life not threatening to end it.

"First?"

"What do you want? Can't you see I'm busy?"

"Harbinger has been sighted. She will be here shortly."

"About time." First turned to look at the concerned, frightened face of her husband. "Are you sure?"

"Yes, she will be here soon."

"Good. Now get out of here. I don't want you here."

Marlin fled the room. He stood panting on the other side of the door. There were some mysteries that should belong to each sex. One of these in his opinion was childbirth. He didn't see how the Harbinger's husbands could stand to tend her during her travail. Then they must have more courage than he. To get Harbinger with child seemed dangerous enough an endeavor. Witnessing her giving birth would be nothing after that.

"She is well cared for, husband."

"I know. I do not worry for her care. It is how I will be received once this is done that concerns me."

"Some things pass quickly. If she weren't focused on waiting, she would be done and happy, but soon this will be done."

And I will have to suffer through this waiting and this disruption to my household several times more. Marlin smiled. Six children born to him in his first year of marriage; no one in Masfin could boast such a feat. A surge of purely male pride swelled his chest.

"Lady Zona do you have time now?"

"For?"

"I have received an important report from Tampello."

"I will come. Third please take my place."

Lady Zona listened to the tale. She could not stop shaking her head. "And your brother is in charge of this."

"That is what I understand."

"Wouldn't it cause him some difficulty to have Ranald learn just who is married to the mother of the heir of the House of Jeffeaux?"

Marlin snorted in amusement. "Being my brother isn't enough but that might put him beyond the pale."

"This experience had taught me about myself. I have abilities and capabilities that I never expected. I can now say the same about

Ranald. I guess I can say the same about you. And you can say the same of your brother."

There was a commotion in the yard. Riders and horse filled the space. Harbinger swirled into the house. People milled around her. Lady Zona hurried to her.

"First is in labor."

"Good. Let me wash quickly and change. I don't want to bring all my dirt into the room. Well Marlin, I see you are well set on increasing our numbers."

Marlin flushed at the amused tone. He kept his gaze tightly on Harbinger's face. He would not bow his head in embarrassment.

"Come tell me the news."

"This is the biggest news. There is an interesting development in Masfin. They are imprisoning all the soldiers who trained with our army."

Harbinger was quiet for a moment.

"Logical. They are planning to move soon and don't wish to take any potential informers with them. They don't want to kill them. They don't want to leave any behind to swell our numbers. They lack the resolve to kill them and the patience to win them over to their side. Quick and dirty solution that straddles the fence."

Marlin listened to the analysis with a pounding heart. She was extracting data from one move.

"We will have to watch carefully for the move. Once the Masfin/Sarnese army leaves we will retrieve the prisoners. They are our responsibility. See to it Marlin. I want a plan in three Darkfalls."

It was solved as far as Harbinger was concerned. She paid no attention to the larger political implications of the move. She looked for strategic information and things that needed doing.

"This move has politically important fallout that will play to our advantage as concerns Jeffeaux's claim to the throne."

"I am sure. When I need to use them I will, but I hate politics. Jorin deals with all those issues. He and Marjas thrive on them. I'm a doer."

Then Marlin was standing alone in the hall. Harbinger disappeared in the shadows of the corridor. When Harbinger returned she was wearing loose trousers and a billowing shirt. Soft house boots pooled around her calves and ankles. Her damp hair was once again short. Petron followed her closely, as did Bernath. They came to stand with Marlin.

"The first one is the hardest to wait through. You have no idea what to expect." Harbinger spoke softly to Marlin before she entered into the room. Marlin watched the door's opening. He caught a brief glimpse of the activity beyond. He could guess nothing from the few seconds allowed his eyes.

Petron snorted. "As if she ever had to wait."

Marlin gnawed his lip.

"It is best to be busy at this time. The Llwegan way is good. Everyone works. Granted no one works as hard as the wife but there are many things to do. Someone catches the babe. Someone eases the wife's back. Someone runs for water."

"Not in Sarna, not in Masfin, the wives take care of everything. She has thrown me out of the room."

Petron laughed. "She would. Once it is over all will be well. My mother was like that. Her husbands were roundly cursed the entire travail. Then once the babe was born: sunshine and flowers. Five more times to go, poor general, you'll be glad to get back on the campaign trail."

Marlin smiled wanly. There was much truth in that statement. To distract his mind from his worry, Marlin began to consider the plan Harbinger had requested. He kept returning to the political implications. He looked around in his thought.

"Did you lose something?"

"Is Jorin or Marjas here?"

"You need something?"

"All the Llwegan trained Masfin soldiers are being imprisoned. I have to develop a liberation plan. The political implications of this policy are disturbing me. I would like to present my ideas to them so they can consider the leverage this situation gives us."

"You should talk to Sablor and Jeffeaux; they could give you the legal ramifications."

"Jeffeaux? I understand his position in this but somehow I can't see him as a legal expert."

"You do him a disservice. He has studied constantly since we left for Assizes Court. He is quite conversant in Masfin and Llweganian laws and legal precedents. He probably would be more use to you than Sablor. He can discuss the political aspect quite credibly."

Marlin blinked. He started to speak when a loud cry came from the next room. Marlin felt his body slump against the wall. Petron and Bernath caught his arms before his knees collapsed. They propped him between them. The door opened. Harbinger stood in the doorway. She smiled at Marlin.

"Congratulations Marlin, you are a father. First is well. Come thank your wife. Meet your child."

Marlin leaned against Petron as the man led him into the room. Once inside the door Marlin straightened. Petron remained on the threshold. Marlin saw that all his wives stood around the bed except for First who lay holding a small bundle. His daughter sat on the end of the bed barely restrained by Lady Zona's hand from scrambling across the bed to investigate the new baby.

Marlin sat on the edge of the bed close to First. Her hair was wild. Sweat drenched her face and shoulders. The strain of her efforts showed in her face. But that face glowed with such happiness that Marlin had to swallow. That look made up for being thrown out of the room, for spending three days wondering if his wife and child would make it safely through this passage.

"Husband, Marlin, I present you with your son." Marlin felt tears gather at the corners of his eyes. He did not stop them from falling. In a moment such as this a man could show his joy and relief. He stared at the small wrinkled face First bared to his gaze. He touched that face with trembling fingers. He pressed a kiss to the thatch of black curls. He saluted First's cheek with a gentle kiss.

"I am glad to see you are well. Thank you for our child. Ladizona, come meet your brother." Finally the little girl was freed. She carefully moved along the bed until she sat in her father's lap. Gingerly she leaned over until she too could peek into the nest of the blanket. She leaned back into the circle of Marlin's arm.

"Rest First. I'll come back when you are more refreshed." Fourth slipped the child from First's arms. Fifth brought fresh nightclothes. Harbinger herself began to wash First's face. Marlin passed Ladizona to Lady Zona.

Harbinger washed First gently. Head to toe she washed away sweat and blood and discomfort. First drifted between sleeping and waking. She smiled occasionally as she thought of the long held desire finally fulfilled. Harbinger had been right to suggest the marriage. Marlin was a good partner. He was kind and constant. And now the house had a child of a husband. Ladizona was a judgment from Heaven. She was doubly precious because she delivered her mothers from a fruitless union and had brought her household this estate. Even a barren womb could carry fruit from heaven. This child, the children even now coming were children from the seed of the earth. There was vindication in these children.

Poor sweet Marlin, so frightened and helpless before her moods. So valiantly constant in his loyalty, no matter how she had japed at him, he had remained. She had been glad to know he was in the house. She was comforted to know he had stood in the hall just out of sight but not out of hearing. She could hear her sister/wives moving about the room. They were speaking in low gentle tones. How had she ever managed without their support?

Harbinger was speaking to her. She was so glad Harbinger had come in time. Nothing would be so good if Harbinger had not been there. There was a trust First could not deny.

"Come, First, it is time to feed your son his first meal. I am going to raise you up."

First came to complete awareness. She reached her arms out automatically at Harbinger's command. The small shape fit her arms perfectly. The tiny face rooted against her breast trying to find her nipple. Harbinger smiled at the sight.

"Each child is different. I have only nursed one child beyond the first three days but some like to be held under your arm like this. Some like to be held across your chest. Some children do best when you are both lying down. Don't expect that it will work right away. Be patient."

"Patience is something I have learned."

"I know. How are you doing?"

First nearly jumped out of her skin. Her son clamped down on her nipple so hard it hurt. Then there was the sweetest sensation as his mouth worked her breast.

"I think you both have it figured out." Harbinger stood. She stretched her body in fatigue from the long ride and the excitement at the end. "I'll leave you now. I'll have a meal brought to you. Then, you can rest."

Jeffeaux met Harbinger at the door in front of her rooms. He was very quiet. Harbinger waited for him to speak. He followed her into her sitting room. She poured herself a goblet of wine. She raised the bottle to Jeffeaux in question. At his nod she poured him a drink as well. Wittlar was sitting at the table. Serjanus and Rodznig were seated by the fireplace. They were cleaning their swords. The shrip, shrip of the wet stones against the blades was familiar and soothing to Jeffeaux.

Jeffeaux nodded his thanks to Harbinger. Sablor entered the room. He placed two books on the table by Jeffeaux's elbow. Jeffeaux looked at the books.

"This is very unexpected."

"Not really, they are married." Harbinger threw out a misdirection. Jeffeaux frowned at her levity.

"I have known Ranald all my life. We were boys together."

"His power is threatened."

"His authority to rule is based on his ability to keep the peace and to ensure the prosperity of Masfin. Only good actions may proceed from the throne. Am I saying this right? The King has absolute power only as long as he embodies absolute good. His good is demonstrated by plentiful harvests, abundant game, that kind of thing. He must keep the roads safe, the public buildings well maintained. Imprisoning people for something they haven't done but because they might do it even though they have never done anything like it before does not fall into the tradition of the throne."

"Your system of rule has never been threatened by an outside force."

"No, but we had internal strife during my grandfather's lifetime. There was a civil war between the king and the barons."

"Who won?"

"The King. The barons were forced to submit to the throne as the sole source of power and they were summoned to court where the King could keep them under control."

"So the King can do as he pleases, if he is the only power in Masfin."

"Yes, but there is a brake on his power in that the King has a contract with the population of Masfin. If he does not use his power for the benefit of the country he cannot retain it. In fact the people can take the power back from him."

"In theory, you mean. The people have never done this have they?"

"No, but they rose up for the King against the barons on the basis that he had used the power for their good and they wished to keep him on the throne."

"All right, I can see that. But representatives from the population couldn't walk into the throne room, confront the King, say look we all got together for a vote. It is unanimous; the people of Masfin feel that you no longer use the throne's power for the good of Masfin. You are deposed."

"You are right. Ranald would never step aside like that. Still he must present the illusion that he would. He must act as if that were possible."

"Do you see why I hate politics? It is too murky for me." Harbinger spoke in a soft tone to Jorin.

"So what are we to do? Is it worth looking at the implications of this?"

"I will look. I have visions of arguing my way into a throne I have no wish to hold."

"What you need is a nice comfortable wife to bring you some peace at the end of the day. Look at how happy Marlin is. Look how happy my husbands are."

"I don't think Ranald finds any peace at the end of his day."

The room broke into laughter. Jeffeaux frowned at them. Then he smiled. "Nor does Renfrew."

"You shouldn't speak meanly of Renfrew. He got you and your sister out of a tight spot. At least you have an appropriate heir."

"And he is a boy at that. After all your maneuvering it would have been almost apropos if Junla had borne a girl child."

"But she had a beautiful, healthy son, who adores you and on whom you quite dote."

"He is a nice baby."

"He is a nice baby. This from the man who crawls on his hands and knees giving horsey rides. You could have your own nice baby if you would take a wife."

"Don't think I haven't noticed your little plot. You would be happy if I married Lady Marma. You force me to ride with her for months on end. She is the only person I am allowed to speak with in conversation."

"Who else is there? Tell me. I will arrange for her to come here. Ilissa is too much Llweganian now, and she has husbands. You are right; you need to marry a Masfin woman. Name anyone, I will have her found."

Jeffeaux sighed.

"Have you read any Masfin poetry?"

Harbinger smiled one of those secret female smiles that enchant and terrify men. Jeffeaux was caught in the magic of her smile.

"I've had it read to me."

Jeffeaux coughed though the sudden lump in his throat. He forgot sometimes that she was a very carnal person. Until a moment would shine and he could not help but recognize her lusty soul.

"Perhaps I am looking for the kind of marriage found in poetry."

"You would do better to look for poetry that is found in marriage."

"Someday I will have the final say in this."

"Ah, but just what will your words be? Never mind. Marlin is preparing a battle plan. Do you ride with him into Masfin?"

Jeffeaux closed his books. He was no soldier. He would be no use in a fight. But he had not seen his homeland in a long time. These times were showing the many sides of people. Somehow the side of Ranald that was being revealed was not attractive. These choices of Ranald's were wrong, unlawful. Poetry, why was he so caught by the thought of poetry? Poetry, of course he could find the answer was in poetry, epic, saga, poetry.

"I will go. I will prepare a Recitation against the King. I must recite it in three towns. I should recite it before the walls of the castle of Delungor. That is where the original throne is kept."

"Is this separate from Marlin's efforts?"

"It should precede the action. We will be taking action against palace guards."

"You believe the prison is going to be in the palace?"

"No, the palace guards are the only soldiers who are answerable only to the King. They are the only guards he could trust to carry out this order. A move against the palace guard is a move against the King. Before we rescue the prisoners I must recite against the King in three towns and before the walls of Delungor to demonstrate my belief that our cause is just. This will put me firmly in position to challenge Ranald's right to the throne and his power. Are you happy now? Will you forgive me the issue around a wife?"

Marlin stood in the open doorway. He heard the stark recital of fact. He understood the gravity of the step Jeffeaux proposed. Prior to this moment Jeffeaux had always been a pawn, a tool. Once Jeffeaux spoke his first words of Recitation there would be no going back for the courtier. He would irrevocably brand himself a rebel with the first reading of the Recitation against Ranald.

"If you will do the Recitation, I will free those prisoners. But Jeffeaux, you know, I would recommend the wife instead of the Recitation. I like being married." Marlin tried to give Jeffeaux a minor piece of advice.

"I would rather do the Recitation, thank you very much. Sablor, could I impose on you for some help in this matter? This has to be exactly right."

Sablor remembered writing his marriage proposal. Everything had seemed to depend on each word, each punctuation mark. The stress of that writing still burned in Sablor's memory.

"I would be honored. Are there any examples of previous recitations?"

Chapter 16

Lady Zona sat with her daughter. On the floor her grandson played with Junla's priest. There was an odd sense of peace as if the eye of a tremendous storm were passing overhead. Junla smiled at the two tussling on the floor.

"So Jeffeaux has finally chosen?'

"Yes, I hardly recognized him upon his return. The water must be magical in Llwegan."

"Has he spoken with you yet?"

"No. You?"

"No. He nods politely when we happen to cross paths. He visits Renjeaux regularly. They like each other well enough. Still, he is suddenly very moralistic."

"I don't see how he can complain. We are clearly devoted to embracing religion."

"Mother, at least we are married. He is still single."

"Obviously, he has decided to become a monk."

"A monk?" The priest repeated the new word. He turned to Junla for clarification.

"A man who forgoes sexual relations as part of his devotion to a religious life. Usually a monk lives in a community composed of monks. Some monks live alone, separate from all human contact."

He returned to his play with the child. He had never spent time around young children. Having been an only child he had spent his childhood amongst adults. Now he learned all the tricks and joys of childhood from an expert. He found this child endlessly fascinating. When the boy had discovered his toes, well, the dexterity of babies and the determination of babies were incredible.

"I would like to see with my own eyes Jeffeaux writing a Recitation. He has a haunted look. He only relaxes with Renjeaux. He will make himself sick if he doesn't slow down."

"I used to despair that he never took anything seriously."

Renjeaux pulled himself upright using his mother's skirts as an anchor. He patted her leg for attention. Junla swung the solid body into her lap. Chubby hands clapped her face. Junla laughed then pulled her face out of reach.

He wanted to weep. He wanted to freeze this moment in time. He wanted this woman to belong to him. But he would never claim any woman and this woman was already claimed. He lay back on the floor.

"I have to go. We are invading Masfin." Lady Zona stood.

"Marma is coming by later. I am helping her finish a cycle robe. It is quite magnificent. It is very male oriented. I should do one from the woman's point of view. You could help me with the sections." Junla tried to return the conversation to one she was used to having with her mother.

"You write the cycle. I'll go over it. But you must choose all the materials and do the piecing. I don't like the piecing." Lady Zona recognized the strategy.

"Good." Junla could not think of one more reason to delay her mother.

Lady Zona pressed a kiss to Renjeaux's fat cheek. Then she was gone. She met Stea in the passageway. He passed a sheaf of papers to her.

"Speak."

"The top sheets are the first draft of the Recitation. Sablor asks that you check the grammar and the syntax. Next are a list of towns that are candidates for the three, how does it go?" Stea quickly checked his notes. "Right, the three inward listening posts. Does it matter when the Recitation is read in Delungor? Must it be first, last, at a certain time of year? There are several reports on troop activities. Marlin's preliminary plans for the liberation are there. Finally Harbinger asks where you think Ranald will move the army."

"Will Wintraub be back by Darkfall?"

"No, he is still reconciling old maps with the new charts."

"He seems to enjoy cartology."

"It is well he does. Someone must do it and I have no talent for it." Stea held the door for Lady Zona. She paused as he closed it quietly. Brir was at a huge desk that dominated the room. Papers littered the flat surface; everywhere in the room stood stacks of papers.

"Very busy."

Brir sent a smile to Lady Zona. He was trying to organize the reams of paper that represented the debriefing reports of the all recent returnees from the Masfin army. He placed a rock on the pile of papers he was working on. He left his seat to walk around the desk to where Lady Zona stood admiring the clutter. He placed a warm kiss on her mouth. She snared his elbow with her free hand. Stea took the file from her hand.

"Is there a progress report for me?"

"Yes, there is no clue about the intended new headquarters though."

"I didn't expect it. We will have to deduce it. We can narrow the choices though if we keep the criteria that were being used. Tough luck. They can't keep the location secret once they are settled. I'm more interested in the prison. The map should be ready in four or five Darkfalls."

"Will Jeffeaux go on the expedition?"

"I do believe so. His time away has changed him."

"He needed some changing."

"We have all changed."

"Some of us more readily."

"Ah, but you had real incentive. Jeffeaux is simply trying to swim with the tide. His incentive to change was minimal."

Stea took the reports Brir offered. Lady Zona looked around the room one more time. She smiled fondly at both her husbands.

"I am glad you chose life over death. I can't imagine not having you part of me."

"Wintraub talked us into it. He came from a very ambitious family politically. He thought you had some standing with Harbinger. He felt that being married to you would advance him a little more quickly than being a priest in a defunct church of a defeated country."

"You're not trying to say that Wintraub is an opportunist? I wouldn't believe that of him." Lady Zona was laughing. She knew the ambitious streak in her husband. He at least had gotten what he wanted from the marriage. "How were you persuaded Stea? You must have enjoyed parts of the priestly life. The structure, the rites, the sense of belonging all must have appealed to you."

"I did not have the constitution for martyrdom. We could have committed suicide, Brir I am sure would have killed me if I had asked, but I wasn't ready to die. It would have been for nothing.

If I had died trying to defend the Temple, I could have done that. But, to die under the circumstances, I couldn't do it. I think that in the back of my mind I thought once we were bedded I would have some control over you." Stea smiled self-deprecatingly. Lady Zona kissed the straight jaw.

Brir left his wife's side. He returned to the desk. He returned to his work. Lady Zona looked at his bent head. She waited patiently. Stea sat as they waited. Finally Brir looked up from his work. He sighed.

"I did not wish to be a priest. It wasn't until I became a priest that I understood why they took me. They wanted to breed my attributes into the population. It was my duty to my people to be a priest. At first I resented the idea of being forced into another role. Then I realized I wasn't doing anything for you. You were doing something for me. The marriage was for my benefit. You were making promises to me of duty and responsibilities you had towards me. You weren't interested in having children by me, you couldn't have children. Anyway I thought you were the most beautiful woman I had ever seen. I still do."

"I love you too Brir. If we had time I would show you how much but we are conquering the world this week. Back to work."

"We have been conquering the world every week since we got married."

"I know, I know, but it's a big world, bigger than any of us ever knew and when you ride a Dragon it's hard to get off."

Brir laughed as he watched Lady Zona and Stea leave the room. He could remember his first sight of her as she swung off her horse. She did not have the hardened air of the other invaders. There was an air of gentleness that could not be trained out of her. The special treatment she received from the chief invader had confirmed his belief that this woman was different. Despite her harsh treatment of him and his fellow prisoners, Brir never revised his opinion of her as being gentle at her core. The steel backbone, the steady hand only emphasized her caring ways and polite habits. At times Harbinger wore her sensuality like a robe. Lady Zona never showed anything but a polite, controlled face to the world. That excited Brir, because he knew that behind closed doors that air vanished and a sweetly giving taking woman appeared, seen only by her husbands ever.

Lady Zona smiled at Stea. He arranged the contents of the file in accordance to the agenda in his head. Lady Zona studied his bent head. She guided his steps drawing him out of the way of oncoming traffic as they walked.

"Did you read the Recitation?"

"Yes."

"Was its meaning clear? Or did the pair shroud the meaning in phrasing?"

"It is pretty clear. I would like an example of a previous Recitation to put with this one. It would make the discussion more productive."

"I really can't recall there ever being another Recitation in historical records. There is one in traditional stories and I believe there are legal parameters but I don't believe there is an historical example."

"I'll work on the traditional and legal examples. That would be enough. How soon do we need this done?"

"Harbinger wants the prisoners freed before the new moon. As the prisoners are being led to safety Jeffeaux is going to go to Delungor. Then he will go to the three inward listening posts. There is nothing as terrifying to me as the idea that everything rests on my son."

"I thought Jeffeaux was going to recite before the prisoners were freed."

"Jeffeaux does not wish to take the army with him on his journey. He is going to recreate the ancient Recitation. If he won't take protection, Harbinger has been firm about her military plans. The raid on the prison and the incursion into Masfin should afford some protection. She still insists on sending a group of troopers to shadow the group who will attend Jeffeaux."

"Will this affect the validity of the Recitation? Jeffeaux seemed adamant about wanting to be King before we returned to Masfin."

"If Ranald is not truly King then his guard are not truly palace guards. Very thin but Harbinger will not relent. Marlin agrees with her about the risk Jeffeaux is taking."

"You think he would fail Harbinger?"

"Not in this. Perhaps I do him a disservice. I can't imagine that his present behavior is a true character change. Fear is a great motivator."

"Not over the long run, love is better."

"Love? My son doesn't love anyone that much."

"My dear wife, your son adores Harbinger. He might fear her, he might not know he loves her, but trust me, Lord Jeffeaux worships the air that she breathes."

Lady Zona stopped short. She stared at Stea's bent head. He raised a calm face to her startled face.

"He would do anything for her. He will even marry eventually because she so wants him wed. He even dines with us regularly to please her. I only know stories of his former self but such change can only come from some epiphany. He has seen some interesting things. He has traveled far from his former home and life but the only major change that has occurred is his relationship with Harbinger. It is sad. He might die never knowing how greatly he has loved her. I am blessed there. I know my truth." Brir stated calmly what he thought was patently obvious.

"You are right. I never saw it before this moment. He will never see that it was the making of him. He will perceive his capitulation to her plans as a weakness not a strength."

"If it is capitulation, it is not strength. It is strength only if he understands the greater good."

Lady Zona sighed. She drew her husband closer to her side. She soaked his warmth up until the chill of the desert evening was pushed back.

"I will have to say a few words of encouragement as the troops leave to liberate Masfin."

"Do we ride with Marlin or Jeffeaux?"

"Neither, Jeffeaux must have an escort of particular families' sons. Marlin will need a diversion so we are attacking separately."

"This is going to be fun. There's still snow on the ground in Masfin."

"My darling husband you have never seen snow. You have no idea how difficult it is to move in snow. I will laugh and laugh at you when you finally encounter this punishment of nature."

"You do not believe your instruction has been sufficient in this area? There are some facts that were lacking in your telling of the parameters of this experience?"

"If anyone had told you what being married was like would you think it sufficient no matter how detailed the telling?"

Harbinger smiled at the couple as they entered the room. Their good natured bickering was infectious.

"How much work will the Recitation need?"

"I don't know. I will have to study the legal parameters and the traditional rendering."

"Jeffeaux did that already with Sablor. It has the exact form used in the Song of King Minniao. It also fulfills all the legal requirements. My question is, upon reading it, is the intent and the meaning clear?"

"Yes, I am impressed by the thoroughness of the authors."

"Neither dared fail me. Sablor did not relish the floor. Jeffeaux is trying to make up for being unmarried." Harbinger shuffled through the papers on her table. She found the Recitation.

"We need to obtain the tanned skin of a, some kind of small animal indigenous to Masfin. The Recitation must be written on this skin using an ink made from very specific ingredients. We are still working on those items."

Lady Zona took the copy of the document from Stea's sheaf. She began to read the words. This was not a game. She had always understood that. But she had not known the extent of the influence this endeavor had on everyone. She had been growing and expanding. She had been experiencing the joy of freedom and the power to explore that freedom. She had always known responsibility. She had fulfilled her responsibilities and duties under the weight of restrictions and rules. Since she had ridden into Sarna, Lady Zona had found that weight gone. Having the responsibilities and duties had not been a burden to Lady Zona because she could fulfill them without the work of following a narrow path.

This time for Jeffeaux had been totally different. He had been placed in a crucible. His weakness, his short-comings had been burned out of him by the experience of riding too close to the fire-breathing dragon.

"He really can be King." Lady Zona did not realize she spoke the words aloud.

"Yes, he can and he will. He will be a very fine king. He will drive his minions to distraction however. He is driving Sablor crazy about the damned ink." Harbinger considered the copy before her. "It is actually quite beautiful. He must have wooed many a fine lady with his words."

"I thought it was your husband who was the poet."

"Sablor does have a very fine way with words. He doesn't have this power. Listen to this:

The heart of Masfin is broken

Its spirit is bleeding from the cracks.

It seems that the shaking that split the mountains was the act of Masfin denying Ranald's right to rule. It is quite a good mix of poetry and legal points. 'Parted her cloak' is a euphemism I take it."

Lady Zona smiled. "It is an archaic phrase found in ancient works. It means exactly what you think it means. Part of the coronation ceremony is the marriage of the Masfin King to his Bride. Masfin means land, as opposed to sea. There was land, sea, sky. Those were the boundaries of our world, so our word for the place where we lived, the land, is the same. We never thought of Masfin as our country, our state, we don't even have words for those concepts. I have to use Llweganian terms. Masfin means dry land. Curious any way dry land is bound to the people through the marriage of our leader to her. Our right to use the land, our right to live on the land, bring forth food from the land comes from this marriage.

"The wording of the Recitation is that the Bride denies the King and takes another lover to signal her Repudiation of the marriage. It is not that she chose a specific lover from Masfin but that she took strangers to her bed, dangerous strangers to show how dangerous Ranald was to her and her children.

"His action when he sees the new lover is not to shut the rival out, no he sends servants to deal with the intruder. A man sends servants to deal with whores and mistresses not a wife. The next intruder he invites to share the marriage bed with him. He is shown as a coward, a fool, a danger to Masfin. This man is not acting as a husband. Masfin requires a husband. She demands that the husband be faithful, just, and wise. Tradition is that the husband comes from a particular House."

"So this meets with your approval?"

"Yes, so far. I will read it all the way through to be sure. Here is the list of qualified men for Jeffeaux's company. And this is the order for the inward listening posts. One represents sky, one the sea, one time, I guess is the closest word. It stands for the past residents of Masfin. Jeffeaux also needs very specific raiment, and a horse, the age and color are important."

Harbinger accepted the various lists. She began to read them.

"Very complete. I can see that having a priest research the details of a ceremony is the best course of action. Even the type of buckles for the boot is included. Very thorough, excellent work."

Harbinger read in silence for another few minutes. Then she handed the papers to Marjas.

He watched her feed the baby. Her rounded breast was streaked with pale blue veins. He could see the small head bob with effort. He had never thought to see a child of his body, never mind watch him eat from his mother's breast. He would still think of the babe as belonging to others and not to him. This was his training and for the best. The child was his uncle's heir. The child belonged in name to Junla's husband. He was distressed that thinking of Junla as married bothered him. He could not think in terms of possession. He was owned. He could not own. He could not own this child, this woman, himself. But he could store up the sight of this child feeding from this woman. Someday when he was no longer owned by her he could remember this moment with bittersweet joy.

The small head fell back in sleep. She moved to place the relaxed form in its cradle. The material of her clothes hung open. He could see her breasts bob with her movements. He sat very still. He had not been in her bed for a very long time. The last months of her pregnancy and the months since the birth had stretched as an eternity. Still he hesitated. Did he know the rules around this issue? What was best for the woman? How long should she abstain? He wished he could ask but he could not. The sight of her naked flesh aroused him painfully. He studied the curve of her bottom as she placed the cradle safely to one side.

She turned to face him. She made no move to close her robe. She moved slowly across the space until he could almost reach his hand out to touch her. He felt sweat bead on his lip and forehead. She slipped the robe from her shoulders. The material pooled at her waist. He rubbed his hands along his thighs. Casually she cupped her still partially full breast. Absently she circled her nipple with one long finger. He watched that finger. Suddenly her fingers tightened. A long spray of milk streamed to him. It hit him square in the chest. He blinked down at the wet spot. He looked back at her. She still held that breast in her hand as if offering him the same sustenance she had given her son.

He slid his hands around her waist and down until they cupped her bottom. He raised her, leaning his face forward to accept the offered feast. His mouth closed around the brown nipple. His tongue traced the pebbly texture before moving out of the way. He pulled delicately. Milk, warm, sweet milk filled his mouth. He felt her hands move on him. Then she sat onto his lap. He slid home into her wet, warm tunnel. She felt different from his memory of her. She should. Her son had passed out of this same tunnel, stretching her, changing her. Her breast slipped from his mouth as he bent his head back against the cradle of her hands. He pushed her up and down. A tear found its way from his eye. She did own him, body and soul, she owned him. He could never return to his former life. She had stolen everything from him. Her mouth descended until she captured his lips. He rolled them until she was on her back tightly under him. Her legs were circling his waist. Her arms were circling his shoulders. Her mouth was circling his lips. Her tunnel was circling his shaft. As his pleasure burst from him she swallowed his cry and his seed.

"Well, priest, you did miss me." Junla felt her arms as they held onto the lean warm man. Truth was she had missed him; which was funny since he had never been out of earshot from her. Yet she had missed this pleasure. His desire for her was flattering.

She had been the plain sister of a beautiful woman. She had been the plain daughter of a beautiful woman. She had been the plain friend of beautiful women all her life. Men never really had seen her sitting with the four beauties. They had befriended her to meet her beautiful companions. She had rarely felt wanted for herself. Those who were not using her to know the others only wanted to be near one so highly placed.

This man, whose very life depended on her, wanted her. He wanted her despite her cruel treatment of him. He wanted her despite being her enemy. He wanted her with a drive that pleasured her even when he finished long before she had reached any physical release. Jeffenza might have married a King. Ilissa had her three guards. And Marma, Marma would be marrying Jeffeaux, Junla had no doubt about that. But Junla had her own man. In fact she had two, no three, though she was not sure how to count her husband. She had one man who lived only for her. She smiled in the darkness as she rubbed his back. She savored the feel of his muscle under his skin. She rubbed her breasts against his chest. She shifted her body to feel every inch of him she could with every part of her body. She pressed her mouth to the side of his head. He shifted so he held her more tightly. She smiled against his forehead.

Jeffeaux was nervous. He stared at the clothes laid on the camp bed. They were his first new clothes in so long he could not recall his last new set. Then he would not have noticed such a mundane thing. Now everything had meaning. These were not ordinary clothes. They were a special design, ancient and particular: particular to this task. His escort was assembled. His train was outfitted. He stood naked as the day he had been born into the world. He was about to be born into a different world.

He picked up an undergarment. He had people waiting on him. People, how had he been convinced to allow Marma to accompany him? Granted she represented a powerful house, an important house, an ancient house, whose ancestor was mentioned on that fabled ride, but her going was one more step to her becoming his wife. He hesitated in his task as he thought the word and the truth.

A whiff of scent reached him. There she was. She brushed his hands aside. Methodically she dressed him. Each article of the attire was precisely placed on his body. She smoothed the material as she worked. He looked at her as she bent to help him with his boots. Just so in the Song of King Minniao did her ancestor attend Minniao. He waited for her to hand him his gloves. He watched as the cloak clasp was affixed. Then he extended his hands to receive the helmet from her. Its weight in his hands stood for all the responsibilities he was accepting as he took this ride.

"You'll do." Marma spoke absently as she brushed away a miniscule fleck of dust.

"Will I? Do you think? This isn't hosting a few friends in the country. I must do this. To save Masfin I must go. Even if

Ranald offers peace she will never trust him enough to leave Masfin alone. It will be too complicated dealing with Sarna if Ranald remains King. The Sarnese must leave Masfin. They must go home."

"How can they?"

"That will be Harbinger's problem not Masfin's. It is a problem she is willing to bear. Masfin cannot. This war, we will be busy trying to recover for years from this war. This is the right decision."

"Is it a decision that makes it right? All your reasons are good. The real reason you are going is because Harbinger desires it. She judges this the best course of action. You trust her judgment. I have no argument for or against. We are going. You are ready. Everyone is waiting. My Lord," Marma opened the tent flap. She held it steady for him. He stared at the thin sunlight that splashed the ground outside the tent.

Lady Zona watched her son emerge from his tent. His helmet was tucked under one arm. The pale light of dawn caught the shining metal. He looked like a hero from old. The attire, the grim set of his face, the stillness of the moment etched itself on her mind's eye. He was beautiful. Lady Zona sent a glance at Harbinger. Her friend was smiling at the scene. It was a smile of approval.

Marma followed from the tent. The flap of material swung closed behind her. The movement of the cloth broke the tableau. Jeffeaux walked to his mother. He looked into her face. Junla was standing next to Lady Zona. She held her son up to Jeffeaux. He touched a gloved finger to the soft, small cheek.

"Goodbye, Renjeaux."

He wanted to hug his family to his heart but that was not done. And he had been cool to his mother for so long he had forgotten how to be kind. He offered his hand to her. She held it between both of hers for a long moment.

"Be careful, my son."

"This will all be for nothing if I don't make it out alive."

Lady Zona smiled weakly at the attempt at humor. "I am very proud of you, Jeffeaux."

"And not a little surprised, well, so am I. Take good care of my heir, mother."

"I will."

Jeffeaux looked to where Harbinger was standing. He had not been away from her since he had followed First on her trip. At that time apart he had not been active in any real sense. He feared to go into danger without her, but she could not lead here. Nor could she follow. He walked to face her.

"You have the Recitation?"

Jeffeaux patted his belt in answer.

"Good. Be careful, you will be the prime target until you return to us."

"I trust you will keep Ranald's forces busy."

"Still, keep your head low."

"Very good advice."

He could think of no other reason to delay his departure. He nodded to Sablor then turned abruptly to head for his horse.

Junla watched long after the clouds of dust had settled. She held her son against her shoulder. His chubby arms were lax in sleep. Had that been her brother? That man had hardly any resemblance to the Jeffeaux she had known. Jeffenza had chosen incorrectly. Jeffeaux had been a dark horse. Junla buried her nose in the small neck nestled near her face. She savored the smell of clean child. She had ever chosen the opposite of Jeffenza. Always she had come out ahead. Some things still remained true.

Josea turned in his sleep. He woke with a start. For a moment he blinked at his strange surroundings. Then he remembered where he was. Imprisoned, entombed really, at Tampello, a guest in a cell at the will of the King – the King!!! - that's where he was. He had not deserved this. He had remained loyal despite his company's march into Sarna. He had been happy to return to Masfin. He had not missed the Llweganian experience. He did not resent the Sarnese presence in Masfin. If King Ranald presented the Sarnese for allies, Josea was happy. He was a good soldier. He went where he was directed and did what he was told. He never disobeyed an order. He never thought of leaving his post.

Most of his company had left to rejoin the Llweganian army. He had stayed. He had adjusted to a new company, new officers. They had seemed satisfied with him. Now he sat on a cold stone floor, staring at an equally cold stone ceiling because of decisions made by former officers and present officers. He was being punished for having obeyed orders. They hadn't been questionable orders at the time. The officers said *March there*, he marched. That was all. But now, no, a lowly soldier did not ask, did those orders come straight from the King? No, who knew, who knew?

How long ago was it now? Once he could walk the entire length of the world. It would take a while but it could be done. You could know everything there was to know and meet everyone there was to meet. Everyone spoke the same, dressed the same, ate the same, and looked the same. Now he knew nothing. No one would know him; it was too dangerous to know him. Nothing was the way it seemed. Nothing had ever been real. What he had once thought was the world was nothing more than a small corner. He knew that. He had tramped through other parts of the world.

He shifted on his hard bed. The cold of the floor was seeping into his bones. He felt as if the chill had taken up permanent residence in his body. The sound of moisture dripping somewhere kept him awake most of the time. He never slept deeply because of the drip. Just as he would drift into the best sleep he would wake, his body demanding to relieve itself of water. If he were ever freed he would never be the same.

He was alone in his cell. His cellmate had expired from cold and hunger and illness, how long ago? He couldn't say. The poor fellow had not been well before they had been placed in this awful hole. It had not taken long for the shivering bundle to shake to death. No other had taken his place. The loneliness was punishment enough. He was not used to this pervasive silence.

At least spring would some soon. The chill would fade. Warmth would alleviate one of his troubles. He shifted again.

He tried not to dwell on the how of his being there. He had blamed the Llweganians for a long time. If they had never come....but what ifs and blame did not keep him warm or in comfort. He might as well claim his own share of guilt; he had after all joined the army willingly. Now nothing was left of the boy who had left the plow in search of adventure and fortune. He shifted again.

Maybe it was spring already. Maybe the warmth of spring could not penetrate the stone of the prison. Perhaps by summer he would be less chilled: once the summer sun had baked the stone into heat.

He shifted again. Had a day passed? He could not tell. There was no division of time for him. There was only the now.

Josea woke with a start. Where was he? Oh, yes, this felt familiar. He shifted to ease the pressure of his weight against the stones. Sleep deprivation, physical discomfort, isolation, every single moment like every other single moment. He could not remember anything except that everything had happened before. This was his life, existence.

Josea woke with a start. He stared at the food as it sat on the floor. He had not touched it. Nothing had. No bug, no vermin bothered with this abysmal place. It was too cold, too dark, too empty to attract vermin. He shifted again. This wasn't life. This was existence. He stretched a hand to the food. He watched the fingers as if they belonged to someone else. They reached instinctively for the food. His mouth accepted the food instinctively. His brain tried to puzzle its confusion. He shifted again.

Josea woke with a start. He knew the future. He was living the future. There was nothing there. In a minute he would shift. Again. Later he would wake with a start. He had no interest in the future that was coming. His fingers wavered as they started to reach for sustenance. His hand fell against his chest.

Josea woke with a start. He was floating. This was different. He had achieved his goal. He had changed his future. He was warm. He had always thought that death was cold. He had thought the cold earth would cradle his cold body. The dead bodies he had touched generally were cold unless they were fresh. So he had always equated death with cold. But, he wasn't cold. Well he was less cold. Now he was wet. And there were sounds. Why had he thought death would be silent? It wasn't, it was filled with sounds.

"Can he be saved?"

"I don't know. He is very thin. I have never seen someone who had starved to death. I can't guess if we were soon enough."

Marlin looked at the frail body. He stood in the heart of the prison. The guards had fought hard. They had been determined not to be captured. Now Marlin knew why. The ancient dungeons had been used for the prison. Despite reports, despite the scouts' maps, Marlin had expected barracks confinements. He had not believed a King of Masfin would imprison subjects so cruelly for a real crime never mind a crime of association. But, he stood in a stone prison surrounded by men ill with sores, disease, despair, isolation.

"Can they be moved? Today?"

The question was spoken aloud. Marlin did not mean to speak. He was voicing his fury at their condition. Heads turned to look at him. The chief medical officer came to him.

"We must move them as soon as possible. The dry, warm air over the border will be better. They need sunshine, good food, and rest. They will be unable to get any of those here. They should be able to survive the journey in small legs."

Marlin looked at the huddled bodies. He would be protecting a huge train. These were not ready to march soldiers. Harbinger would be on her own until he could safely deliver his cargo. Still such a large target would attract attention. He would be pulling troops away from the pursuit of Jeffeaux.

Jeffeaux's mission took on urgency for Marlin. Ranald was not the true King of Masfin. This was proof enough for Marlin. He did not need earthquakes as a sign. Ranald's actions alone demonstrated his false claim to the throne. No True King would do this to his subjects.

Masfin denies Ranald.
The Mountains split,
strife entered,
because Ranald is not
the True King.

Peace dwells in the
reign of the True King.
The heart of Masfin beats
strong, loud, clear ,
filled with spirit
in the reign of the True King.

But, the heart of Masfin is
broken, and the
spirit of Masfin is
bleeding from the cracks.

Because there is
no
True King reigning
in Masfin.

Masfin, our Mother
rejects Ranald.
She has parted her cloak.
Two wolves struggle
in a death battle.

Masfin, our Mother,
has parted her cloak for them.

Masfin, our Mother, has
taken the striving wolves
to her breast.

She has cast them
upon Ranald to
drive him from her.

She has closed her cloak
to Ranald.
She has left him
with the wolves.

We are the children
of Masfin.
The True King protects
the children of Masfin.
Peace, prosperity, health
are his handmaidens.

Ranald's servants are
war, disease, poverty.

Masfin, our Mother, parted

her cloak, inviting
the wolves that we,
her children might see
Ranald standing with
his true servants.

Did he go himself to
face the first wolf?
No, he sent
his servants.

Did he deny the second
wolf?
No he lay down with it.

He is not the True King.
He dared not face the wolf.
He dared not refuse the wolf.
He is losing his strength.
It is slipping from him.
Rather than gathering it back
he is pushing it from him.

The Reign of the True King
is difficult. The Reign of
the True King is hard choices.
The Reign of the True King
is looking into the
spirit and heart of Masfin
for the True Path.
The Cloak of Masfin is
Always open to the
True King.

Ranald is not the True King.
Masfin, our, Mother, knows
that the only way to
save a family when the
foundation of the house

is weak is to level the
house to build a new house.

We have been alone for
all our memory.
Our house stood well
in the sunny days.
Now we are not alone.
Our neighbors are strong.
Our house will not
withstand the winds of change.
We must pull it down.
We must build again.
We cannot stop the winds.
We cannot build a wall
that will keep the winds
from our house.
We must build a house that
will withstand the wind.
I have ridden the wind.
I understand the wind.
I will not be broken by
the wind.
The house I build
will withstand the wind.

These are the failures
against Masfin, our Mother,
by Ranald.
These are the proofs
of Masfin's, our Mother's,
rejection.
I am the True King.
I am the True Husband
of Masfin.
My marriage with Masfin
will return
peace, prosperity, health
to the children of Masfin.

I stand in the Womb of Masfin,
from where my Fathers came.
I return to take Masfin
as my Bride.
Her cloak is parted to me.
I will enter her as the
True King.
From our Union our Children
will flourish.
I, Jeffeaux, swear, promise, avow,
declare this here at Delungor.

Marma rode quietly. Jeffeaux could not believe the effect
Delungor had had on him. Standing in the empty rooms he had felt
surrounded, not by his guard, but by every King of Masfin who
had ever declared kingship. Then he had felt the eyes of the
keepers on Delungor on him. They were mendicants. They could
not work or own possessions. They had to live simply, waiting to
witness the declaration of the True King. Their existence was holy
but they were not. Their duty was royal but they were not. They
were the lowest inhabitants of Masfin but they were not lowly.
Every township in Masfin sent them food and clothes as they
would always be present for the Recitation. They were Masfin's
guard against tyranny though they did not guard.
    Jeffeaux pulled up. He waited until Marma reached him. She
looked at him with a slight frown.
    "You did not like the Recitation?"
    "It was everything a Recitation should be. Your presentation felt
sincere to me. Do you believe you are the True King, Jeffeaux?"
    "Did the Recitation leave room for doubt?"
    "No, not a hair. I never envisioned you as the True King."
    "I have as much right as Ranald. He hasn't done well. Somehow
I will do better."
    "I never thought of the implications of being True King. No one
has questioned a King's right to rule in my memory. Standing in
Delungor, I felt as if, hearing you say Masfin our Mother, I felt you
spoke the truth. As if some ancient King did impregnate

the earth, take his plow to the earth's breast, and the ancient ancestors of all Masfin sprung from the soil. I know that's not true. I know we are the same people as the Sarnese and the Llweganians. But standing in that hall, hearing your words, I felt close to our traditions."

Jeffeaux watched a lone figure leave Delungor. Soon all Masfin would know of the Recitation. The announcement would spread from town square to village green like wildfire. This was his safest moment. His three inward listening posts were yet to be visited. There were options for every post. Until he reached his first post, Ranald would have to spread the search for him over a large area. This was a false peace.

Jeffeaux glanced at Marma's profile. He took in her calm features. She rode with ease and quiet. This was an arduous journey. She had not tried to avoid it. She was the only descendant left from the original rider. She was the only woman. She did not hold them back. She made little show of her efforts.

He was King now. There were battles to fight. There were miles to ride but he had made his Recitation. Harbinger would remove Ranald. No one would, no one could, deny his claim. He was now King. He had duties, responsibilities. He had always been annoyed at that royal We but the concept was true. He could no longer think in terms of his own wishes and desires. Everything had to be for his people. All the people he had just accepted as his.

Harbinger did not bear that burden. She was not sworn to her people. She had room in her life for personal choice. He did not. He had power over and therefore was answerable to the very least of his people. A True King was not a tyrant, not even a benevolent one, the way Harbinger was. She was a tyrant. She knew it. She decided life and death for her enemies and minions based on her own restrictions, rules, boundaries. She had absolute power legally over everyone in her dominion. Even a husband was not safe from her hand should she wish to kill him.

A True King had to follow a complex set of rules rooted in tradition. Jeffeaux returned his gaze to Marma. And a True King had a True Consort. He had one wife, Masfin, but he had a consort to bear him children. The fertility of his relations with his consort mirrored, represented, and increased the fertility of his marriage with Masfin. Harbinger understood the importance of a leader being committed to one particular person.

"We will pass by Reduni."

"On the third leg, yes."

Jeffeaux took a deep breath. He felt the air pass through his nostrils into his lungs. He pulled his horse to a complete stop. The entire company paused, looked at him. He turned his mount until he looked Marma full in the face.

"Lady Marma, will you marry me at Reduni?"

Marma looked at the outstretched hand. She stared at the face she had known in passion, in play, in frustration. The features were still there. When had the boy become a man? How had that boy become this man? She watched her hand stretch to touch his. Her fingers slipped into his clasp.

"Yes."

"Thank you."

As simple as that? Jeffeaux had expected his heart to burst, his head to explode, his spirit to shrivel but when the moment came it had been so simple. The choice was so right.

He had not died. He turned his head slowly. The world did not spin today. He sat up slowly. He was in a large room. There were others with him. He sat looking on the faces of other people. He drank in the sight of features of beings. To his eyes the room was filled with light. He knew it was not. He could see the few small lamps that shed light on the few patients who were receiving care from the healers. Still that light was bright to him. The door stood open. Through the door he could see occasional passers-by and a corridor and the edge of another open doorway.

Josea pushed to his feet. He swayed. A healer stood as if to come to him. Josea motioned the man away. He steadied himself. The healer watched him cross the room but made no move to come to him. Josea reached the door. He stood on the threshold. He felt fear. He looked back into the room. Eyes watched him. Not with control or restraint but with concern. It took Josea a moment to recognize the concern. Josea rested against the door. He looked at the doors on the opposite side of the room. They were open. He could see the porch they opened unto. Beyond the porch was the harsh horizon he had first seen upon awakening. Between the horizon and the porch was a lush garden. He could see several people sitting in that garden.

Josea could not remember being outside. The green plants called to him. He moved slowly, carefully through the room. He sat on the step down to the garden. His strength had failed him right there. He leaned against the porch pillar. Warmth flooded him. He heard footsteps. Someone came carrying a tray of glasses with a pitcher. He watched them approach. He accepted the tall glass of water. He sipped from it carefully so as to not spill a drop of water. He wanted to close his eyes to savor the feeling of wellness. He did not close his eyes, fearing to discover this all a dream.

A woman, she looked to be the same age as his grandmother, came to sit by him. She took his wrist loosely in her fingers. She looked into his face. He didn't say a word. Perhaps sound would break the spell.

"You look better today." The words were slightly accented.

"I feel better."

"A little weak still, are you dizzy? Is the water staying down? Can you feel your arms and legs?"

"Yes, yes, and yes."

"Good. Broth has been staying down. Do you think you are ready for solid food?"

Josea blinked. He considered his stomach. It felt empty as they spoke. It was so empty he felt nauseous. He placed a comforting hand over his suffering area.

"I don't know. I feel queasy now."

"Do you have a headache?"

"Yes, now that you mention it."

"Good, time to eat. Nothing much and very slowly or it will come back up. Can you remember that?"

"Little and slow."

"Right. Nothing heavy either." She smiled at him with kindness. He watched her walk into the garden. Her attire was wrong. It was not the dress of healers or nurses. He stared at the skirt with its stripes and swags. Here was a truth he had to face.

He stood slowly. Using the pillar that was supporting the roof so elegantly to support his weak body somewhat less elegantly he let his legs adjust to his weight. Carefully he walked across the porch.

Once inside he rested against a wall. His bed, his bed - had he lain on that mattress long enough to claim it?- had been made. The crisp sheets called to him. On a low stool next to the bed sat a tray. He stumbled then caught himself. He made a wide circle around the food. The small stool served as his table. He remembered to eat slowly. He remembered to rest between bites. Slowly his stomach calmed down. His headache faded as he drank. His only problem was that he had become very sleepy. The bed at his back was too far away from him. He placed his hand on the floor next to his leg. He thought to push himself up but all he managed was an abortive attempt. He sat in a stupor. His eyes felt heavy, warm. His body had not connection to his brain. His eyes saw his surroundings, but his mind noted nothing.

Josea watched feet and legs advance on him. He knew that hands raised him from the floor. He felt the bed cradle him.

This time when Josea woke he was more alert. He had questions aching to be asked but he feared the answers. This time he could study his fellow patients. They had been prisoners with him. He recognized the faces of three men. The building was odd as were the dresses of the nurses. He did not wish to recognize his surroundings. He wished to pretend that he was still in Masfin but he knew that all of Masfin was more alike than any of Sarna. It was the scene outside the window that convinced him. He was once again in Sarna. He was awake because someone was gently washing him. The cool cloth was soothing. The pressure of the hand was light. He almost snatched his arm back as it was raised but he didn't. His caregiver noticed the tension in his limb.

"So you are awake again, good. Are you hungry?"

"Yes, and thirsty. Where am I? Have I been here long? How did I get here?"

"General Marlin brought you and many others here for care. This is his wife's estate. You have been here for some time. Everyone has been slow to recover. The body is very resilient but you were in very poor condition."

Marlin was a Masfin name. He knew that name. It was the name of the first company commander to lead his troops back to, to where, or to whom? Had Marlin led his troops to anything or simply away from something? Josea sighed. He felt the cloth begin to soothe the skin on his leg. It didn't matter, nothing mattered. He was safe, in a place other than this world, he was safe. In a strange landscape, in an odd house, among alien people, he was safe. He was fed and well and the cloth passed over his skin, cared for.

"Did the King just let us go?"

"General Marlin laid siege to Tampello. He had to kill many that day. The guards were so shamed at their duty they either ran at the first sight of the banner or they fought to the death, none surrendered. The next battle was getting everyone back alive. Snows came. Cold came. In Masfin the people say that the winter was long and hard because Ranald is not the True King. They say that Masfin has closed her cloak to Ranald so the people of Masfin are suffering."

"Who told you that?"

"They did. I went to Masfin with General Marlin to care for the sick. And I came out again. The people in the villages and the farms told me what I have told you."

"And whom do they say is the True King?"

"King Jeffeaux, he has been to Delungor."

"You know the Masfin traditions very well."

"My husband is Masfin."

Josea closed his eyes. His stomach announced its presence. The sheet felt cool on his skin. He wondered if he would have to ask for his clothes back. Somehow he did not wish to ask for anything from this Sarnese woman who knew his history so well. How long had Sarna and Masfin known each other? Wasn't it only yesterday that the earth had shaken?

"Have you children of your husband?"

"Two boys, they are with my mother. She loves to have them under foot. She loves the sounds they make."

Long enough for a man to court a woman and beget two sons with her. Did he know anything of this Jeffeaux from before the Shaking? No, the name only had meaning since Dragon had swept into Masfin. A True King, that was a story old men told at night after many drinks. No one really believed the earth chose a husband/King. Josea let his eyes close against the thought of a change so momentous that thrones trembled.

There had been a shift generations ago from the king as a power based on his relation to the natural power base. The king had been for some time a non-power subject to the whims of disrespectful barons. Then a king had consolidated his power from a military and political base. This present move by Jeffeaux consolidated the ancient meaning of kingship with the present power base.

Josea did not know what he believed. His devotion and loyalty had been rewarded with torture. He could not give his heart to any endeavor. He was suspicious of everyone. If the ancients had it right, then Ranald was not the True King. None of the terrible things that had befallen Masfin would have happened if Jeffeaux had been King at the time of the Shaking. Josea was too pragmatic to believe that. But another man might have made better choices for his people. In that respect Ranald was not a True King. And Jeffeaux's claim could only be validated by future actions. Convenient.

Harbinger read the dispatch. She smiled happily. He had made her proud. Free of any influence he had taken a wife, no a consort, Masfin was his wife. What was Marma's title? Royal Consort, excellent, now there was real hope for everyone.

"You look as if the war is ended." Harbinger looked up to see Lady Zona watching her.

"Better than that, your son has become a real leader. He has taken a wife. He has made a commitment to someone other than himself or an abstraction. This is wonderful."

"The end of the war would be better."

"There will always be discord in this life. We can only hope to tone it down. To see mediocrity swell into greatness, that is a miracle. He could have gone his whole life being less than the sum of his parts. Now he will exceed every hope. Look at First, She was a petulant child, now she rules Sarna. She is high priestess in a religion she is shaping. I was raised to destruction. I can level a city in a few Darkfalls. Winning a war is nothing extraordinary, it is my function. Creating something, that is the joy, the pleasure, the satisfaction in this life for me."

"How goes your war?"

"Very busy. Marlin was very efficient. He was in and out in so quietly that he hardly distracted the Masfin military. I have had to bear the entire burden of keeping the focus off Jeffeaux's business."

"At least the roads are clear."

"And the population seems to be quiescent."

"For the moment, until they decide which man to back. Both come with foreigners."

"Interesting, is there a Masfin word for foreigner yet?"

Lady Zona thought for a long time. She tried different words until she had to admit there were none. Stranger was not specific enough to be a true synonym for foreigner.

"Enough, time to go. There is a small township that Ranald needs for its metal workers. I will have to deny him their services. Those are my plans. What are yours?"

Lady Zona sipped wine as she looked out the open door. The green of the spring was gentle and soft. Some plants were still hazed with the red of leaves in bud. She had not experienced a spring in Masfin for many a year.

"We are for the sea. If you deny him the land routes, Ranald will have to use ships. We will close the harbors near Jeffeaux's last objective. Marlin and I wagered for the sea routes."

"You both like the ocean. I find it disconcerting. It is beautiful but mysterious. And its air eats metal. I much prefer the desert."

"I noticed. You took which front you wanted. Marlin and I had to take your leavings."

"I deserve some compensation for being Harbinger of Death. Marlin will enjoy the middle route. He will have fun splitting Ranald's forces. He will meet up with you on the beach."

Lady Zona smiled. Only Harbinger would so blatantly admit to her choice based on a personal preference. She lied, though. She had the Sarnese as her duty because it was Sarna. Masfin leaders would head the troops who deeply penetrated into Masfin; a political decision which happily was militarily sound.

At that thought Lady Zona became uneasy. This would be her first combat command. She had spent much time in the presence of military action and decision-making but had never directed an operation. She had Ilissa as an advisor. Her one-time ward was a good fighter with a clear head. Her advice would be useful. Her objectives were clear and well thought out. Her field commanders were experienced. Her troops were well-trained. Her supply train was organized. Still, every decision would mean life and death for her charges and she worried.

"Lady Zona never forget, once we deploy troops we expect death, on both sides. You have two objectives: slow down Ranald's advance, be sure you destroy a large percent of their army without sacrificing a large percent of our army. We plan to fight another day. Resigning the field is not wrong. We can lose a few battles and still win the war."

"Isn't territorial acquisition important now?"

"Soon, but not today. Once Jeffeaux has completed his cycle, then we will worry about territorial acquisition. Then we will begin to push Ranald where we want him to go."

"But a territorial goal would be easier."

"Yes and cheaper and more satisfying and easier to maintain momentum around; but it will have to wait. We are bleeding Ranald's forces and building Jeffeaux's backing. Once those goals are accomplished then we will deal with the nitty gritty aspects of acquisition. This is as much rebellion as an invasion. We are trying to make sure that it is perceived solely as a rebellion by the people of Masfin. That is delicate work. The Sarnese people know they have been invaded. That was a pure territorial acquisition. Remember how quickly we accomplished our goal? The political and social structures have been completely redone to my specifications.

"Masfin is more complicated. I can't tell you enough how exact our movements must be for time and objective and execution. Everything depends on presentation and perception."

Lady Zona sat down. She stretched her legs before her. Her wine goblet rested on the hill of her left knee.

"You really want peace."

"No. My people want peace. They are tired of war. They want prosperity and security. I made them a promise. I keep my promises. Peace is their desire. It is my duty to get it for them.

"I have no idea what I will do with this peace once I achieve it. I have chosen to achieve it in such a way as to insure it for a long time. They won't even need me to keep it for them. I will be obsolete the moment Jeffeaux takes the throne. The process I have started in Sarna is unstoppable. I will retire to my hall to drink and make merry and to relive days gone by. You will have to visit me some time."

"And where do you expect me to go? Back to Masfin with my three husbands? My now extremely proper son will not benefit by my presence. Could we remain in Sarna? You will have to find me some place to oversee in your vast domain."

"I will think on that. I am considering sending you back to Deskersai. There are things that need guarding and disseminating in an appropriate manner. I think you and your household would be the perfect ones to take charge of that most important monument to our victory and Sarna's past."

"The Keeper of Deskersai."

"Has a nice ring doesn't it? Maybe Governor of Sarna? We can't reveal Deskersai's secrets now because of the implications for First and her household but some day when the time is right it must be told. There are priests still alive who would be brutalized if the people knew what they had done for generations. We have broken the cycle. That is enough for now."

"Stiefis would never have been allowed to father a child. So the Repudiation is valid. We do not know if he could have." Lady Zona took the conversation away from a discussion of titles she was not sure she wanted.

"Many might not appreciate the subtlety of your argument. I believe the Repudiation is valid. I always have, but from my tradition. He abandoned his wives. In my tradition Stiefis would have been killed by his wives' families for his actions. In your tradition there is never any separation allowed. According to Sarnese tradition the wives' actions were legal. We have built a new order. We have established new rules. Since you and I had knowledge of the real state of affairs regarding Stiefis' ability to not father children there could be a question as to the validity of the Repudiation."

"The truth is always the best defense."

"That I used a Sarnese tradition to my advantage."

"You and I were the only ones who knew. The wives are blameless. Marlin is blameless. They all acted in good faith. The priests who participated in these traditions for generations all knew the truth as well as we did. And it was legal for them."

"So just ride out the storm. We have to tell First and Marlin."

"Yes."

"Deception can be useful in battle."

"But not with those on whom your life depends."

"Sometimes."

"Never yourself."

"I'll concede that point. If we release this information now, the Sarnese in Masfin will deny it as propaganda. They will call us liars. They won't know it's the truth. Even if they do know; they can't say it is the truth. If they say it is the truth to discredit First they are giving us power, legitimacy so they must deny our report. If they deny our report they can't use it against First and Marlin. They will use Third's Repudiation as proof of the false nature of our story."

"So if we tell the truth we are in trouble."

"No, no, no, no, we are saved. We discovered these documents. We cannot attest to their validity. We only present them for inspection. Those who want to believe will. Those who don't, won't. We will bear none of the burden of proof or culpability. It's beautiful."

"And the Repudiation?"

Harbinger swept her arm grandly. "My sisters are spoils of war whom I have awarded to Marlin: ancient tradition."

"So when do we make this grand revelation?"

Harbinger looked at Lady Zona. She smiled a faint curve of the mouth. "I will have to consult with my guard, First, Marlin, and my close ally King Jeffeaux on this matter. Then I will be able to answer that question."

"Life is complicated for the great among us."

"Ha, ha, I have three, no four cultures and three countries whose interests I must consider with every decision. I cannot make these choices lightly."

Lady Zone leaned forward. "The reason I respect you is that you really think that way no matter how flippantly you speak."

"This will be fun. Now we will look to your family. I have no idea what to do with your daughter."

"Jeffenza? I thought you had given her over to Ranald for worry."

"No, Junla, she is pregnant again by her priest. I can't keep kidnapping Renfrew."

Lady Zona stiffened in her seat. Brir nodded. She grimaced back at him. This was a sore subject.

"Can't we deal with one problem a day?"

"Your son was right: the women in your family do have a penchant for religious men. I could have Renfrew delivered to her bed again. A more appropriate resolution to this issue must be found."

"Once the war is ended she can set up her household with her husband and this will no longer be your problem"

"She could be with child again before this war is ended. Winter comes again to Masfin, sooner than I would like."

"What, you haven't found a way to control the weather?"

"I don't live with priests. I don't have an inside track to godlike powers. North Masfin is fairly temperate. We could remain active in that theater of the war throughout the winter months. Still I will have to arrange the matter of Renfrew."

"Why bother."

"Jeffeaux's position is delicate. I want to prevent any threat to his consolidation of power and legitimacy."

"So Renfrew will be kidnapped from the enemy camp."

"No, he goes out into the field. He will fight in a battle."

"You would arrange a battle to cover his kidnapping."

"We would fight a battle anyway. That is the function of a standing army of this size. One battle, one purloined general two objectives fulfilled by one action."

"I wonder if he will cooperate."

"That will be your daughter's responsibility. Maybe we are looking at this all wrong. We could smuggle your daughter into Masfin to visit her husband. We could think of some mission for her. We would have to surround her with protection but that is a more reasonable and believable plan." Harbinger sighed. She placed her goblet squarely on the table under her elbow. "The other would have been more enjoyable. Only a few can participate in an undercover mission."

Chapter 17

Josea moved warily. He walked with tentativeness of the newly recovered. He still hoarded food. He knew that there would be another meal but his instinct was to ferret away any items that would not rot. The wards were emptying. Everyone had to work in the fields if they were able. The feel of the sun on his back and the smell of the earth in his nose were pleasures Josea had never appreciated until now. Gathering the early crops was marvelous. Life did continue after prison and death. There was summer and the feel of the sun on your skin.

Each morning he woke with a start. He was confused. It still took him several moments to realize where he was. Then he would sigh. He felt disloyal but he was relieved to wake up in Sarna every day. Nothing pleased him as much as seeing the brown hills in the distance. Nothing was the same.

He shouldn't have resisted. He should have returned the first chance he got. He thought loyalty would beget loyalty. He had been wrong. He breathed the scent of cut vegetation. He turned his head to glance at the harvester on his right. He smiled at the person. They smiled back. He could not remember how long it had been since he had smiled. As he worked he could forget everything. He could forget his sense of betrayal. He could forget his ambivalence about his present hosts. He could forget that he would have to make a choice. He still could not choose. He could not completely rid himself of the distrust of anyone who was not Masfin.

It was absurd. He had suffered more at the hands of Masfin leaders and jailers than at anyone else's hands. Most of the time he could interact pleasantly with his caretakers; in moments of stress he would blame all his ills on the Llweganians and Sarnese. He would attribute all the cruelty of his Masfin jailers to the circumstances and not to their own nature. Intellectually he knew the capacity to make such decisions and to carry them out with such fervor was an inborn trait and not one created by circumstances, but he could not accept the fact that Masfins had the capacity to be so cruel. Because then he would have to judge himself.

As he finished his row Josea caught the sound of children playing. The laughter was the perfect music for the clear, warm day. He stood up. He saw the group of small people on the far side of the field. They were running. He thought their nurses chased the children. He was wrong, some of those children belonged to those women. He stared at the shape of the women. Here was the glaring difference from his reality. These women were a family unit because they were all married to the same man. The primary relationship in these married women's lives was not to a husband but to a marriage. They had been an entity before they had gotten rid of one husband. They had remained a group without a husband. They had chosen a new husband as a group. It was too strange.

Riders, important riders, approached. Servants were abandoning the fields. The women and children were leaving the field. Llweganian riders, their black attire and rangy beasts were an eyesore on the landscape.

Marlin dismounted. He bowed formally to his wives. They were flocking to him. Each greeted him with a slight dip of the knee. He extended his arm to First.

"I came a day early to be rested when Harbinger arrives. Did she give you any hint about this meeting?"

"No, she was clear that this is not a pleasure visit nor is it a war council. She implied that this is a family matter."

Marlin slapped his leg with his gloves. He looked off to the horizon, and then studied the group before him.

"What I need is a bath with my wives."

The tension eased. Smiles glowed at him. Marlin thought the effort might kill him someday but he wished to please his wives. They surrounded him with caring and gave him such a deep sense of home that he wanted to give them the one thing he could give them that they could not provide for themselves. They wanted children of him. He tried his best to give them their wish. After his bath he would visit his children. He loved them all. In his heart of hearts Ladizona was his favorite. She had given him this life. He owed her a great debt.

First was nervous. Harbinger had returned early in the morning. She had heard the clatter of the horses as they rode in. There had been no boisterous sounds. The silence had bothered First. She had lain considering the nature of the issue that would bring Harbinger home in such a serious mood.

She wanted to rise. She wanted to rush to Harbinger to get the meeting over with. She wanted to remain in her nest of bedding and limbs. She could not rise without waking her companions. She did not want to spread her gloom to them. She wanted them relaxed and happy and sated for a while longer. Third lay snuggled against her side. Marlin was serving as her mattress. Fifth had an arm flung around her waist. From her vantage point she could see the rest of her sister/wives sprawled across the bed.

This was her place. She could not hide from responsibility. She drew a gentle hand down Third's face. Sleepy eyes blinked at her.

"Time to get up; Harbinger is here." Her quiet mood was contagious. Marlin woke as she roused the others. She met his eyes steadily. He saluted her as she left the bed.

First noted the occupants of the room. Everyone was attired in formal dress. Lady Zona's husbands were garbed in their priestly robes. Their heads were shaved clean. Light from the candles on the table and the sun from the window gleamed on the cleanly shaved skin. The tattoos were dark and fearsome. Harbinger was looking out the window. Several great volumes were on the table where the priests sat. Goblets and wine decanters sat next to the books. First fastened her gaze on Harbinger's face.

"The major function of the priests of the temple of Kersai was as guardians of the reproductive process of the inhabitants of Sarna. The holy herbs, marriage powders were the control device. These books catalogue the entire process from the medicines to the breeding lines. We, Lady Zona and I, have known about this since our stay in the temple at Deskersai. We are going to tell the truth now."

First stood staring at Harbinger. Fourth went to the table. She opened one of the great books. Third wandered until she stood next to Lady Zona. Marlin sat at the table.

Second spoke first.

"There is more."

"Yes. Your marriage herbs were contraceptives. Stiefis was not permitted to father children on you. The Repudiation Rite did not conclusively demonstrate his infertility. We expect several reactions when the announcement is made. We feared a bloodbath of the priests once we reveal this discovery. Not that we had any feeling either way on the issue as pertained to the priests but that the variable and violent conditions were too," Harbinger paused. "I was too busy fighting a war to wish for any other commotion at the time. There probably will be some bloody reactions now.

"I expect that the Sarnese leaders will denounce this as a lie so your Repudiation will not be discounted by them and the present marriage will not be assailed. I believe your Repudiation is valid. I always have. Stiefis would never have been allowed to give you children. Your marriage to him was sterile even if he was not which we don't know. It is convoluted. The priests who made the rules around a Repudiation and who controlled the process of marriage knew that they controlled fertility so they would have known the real reason why wives couldn't get pregnant. To cover their actions they had developed this rite so the rite is legitimate in Sarnese tradition even though it is based on a falsehood. It is legally valid in Sarnese tradition.

"Sarna also has the tradition that captured women are no longer the wives of the defeated men but immediately available for marriage to the captor.

"I myself believe that Stiefis lost all claims to the marriage when he failed to protect or make any effort to defend his wives. In Llweganian law his actions are basis for cancelling the marriage or even execution.

"But this is not Llwegania and you are wives of a powerful man in my army. You are in a position of authority in Sarna. The implications of your situation are immense.

"If we keep the secret then later on there could be disastrous consequences but I feel it important that you know what is about to happen."

Marlin stood. He gathered his wives to him.

"These are my wives."

"Yes. And I will defend your marriage to the utmost of my ability. I do not believe that the Sarnese leaders will acknowledge this information as fact. They might even use your marriage as a weapon against the truth. It is the new community emerging in Sarna which could be impacted. A devious enemy could start a whispering campaign against our ethics. I don't think our enemies are quite that sophisticated. I just want you to be prepared."

First left Marlin's side. She joined Harbinger at the window.

"It is best for Sarna and for our efforts if this announcement is made."

"Lady Zona convinced me of this. The truth is always easier to acknowledge than a lie is to defend."

"I will make the announcement. I will present the books to the Great Wellhouse. I will do this with ceremony and solemnity. It will be a funeral for our past. At that moment we will cease to be Sarna. We will be a new place. Anything that came before will be only history and have no impact or influence or control over our future. We will be washed clean of our past deceits and lies. Our people will never forget it. And anything that was of Sarna will be unimportant."

Harbinger smiled. She felt such a deep respect and affection for this slight woman. First had a strong handle on the intricacies of politics and power and events.

"It will work."

"I have to protect my family. I have finally decided on your name in our community."

"Harbinger of Death and Devouring Dragon are not enough?"

"No, here you are Bringer of Water."

"I'm a bucket."

First smiled. "I see you as the builder of new lives but that is too pretentious and might go to your head. I will now see you as the Bringer of Water."

"Harbinger of Death is much more comfortable. Even Devouring Dragon is less a burden. As you will. Just don't be surprised if it takes me a while to get used to answering to the name. There will be hesitation."

"Time for a change then because you are about to become the Mother of a new nation, culture, society; three in fact, because peace will change Llwegania as well and this will alter Masfin into a new state."

"Llwegania will revile me or belittle our accomplishments. My peers are not happy with this new order we are creating. They think me mad. Perhaps I am but even madness can have its greatness."

"When this is over you will still have much to do. Peace will need new structures in Llwegania just as Sarna and Masfin are building."

"The work of changing Llwegania will resemble war. There will be similar strategies and outcomes. Did Sablor tell you his good news?"

"Yes. He is one closer to having an heir of his wife."

"That is considered quite outrageous in Llwegania. I should not have taken more than six husbands. And I certainly should not have provided so many heirs. I am too ambitious."

"I would have thought greedy would be the word used."

"I am sure it is, behind my back. None dare accuse me to my face. I might challenge them."

"A formal type of challenge I assume."

"Of course with forfeits, big forfeits such as estates and council votes and power and armies, the assumption being that I would win, naturally."

"Very old-fashioned."

"Yes. They simply send advisors. They advise me on my duties to my estates. They send me advisors as to the proper etiquette for Heads of Household as a married person. They send me advisors on diplomacy. They never send me advisors on waging war. But I fear they avoid matters of war in all guises lest I insist they accompany me into battle." Harbinger stared out the window. She watched the figures in the field. "Being a villain is easier and more fun. I am very uncomfortable being near a heroic aura. Lady Zona would wear it much better."

"We can't always choose our own image. I will orchestrate this rite very carefully. I will do extensive research into the matter."

"You can't spend too much time on this, First. I want this done already."

"As with everything. I will have many working on this."

"Simpler is better. There is nothing as elegant as a single line or color or action or words."

"When something is to stand alone you have to be very particular about your choice."

"Borrow Sablor. Lady Zona can you lend a scholar?"

"If you had mentioned this earlier we would not be in this difficult position."

"Just turn the blade. Fine, I have another small matter to attend. There is much to do."

"I will present our plans in two Darkfalls."

Harbinger hurried out of the room. She let go a deep breath once she closed the door on the group. What she wouldn't give to just go home to spend time with her husbands.

Josea watched the lone figure walk from the buildings. After tucking his gloves into his belt, Josea hefted his hoe onto his shoulder. He stretched his legs out far as he walked. The figure walked into the garden that surrounded the barracks. From his vantage point Josea could see the figure pass out of the garden into the training grounds. There was a pause as jacket, helmet, gloves were taken off, folded and placed on the steps. Josea returned his implement to its storage shed.

Curious, he entered the training grounds. He heard grunts and thuds. A lone figure was working on a hanging bag. She seemed to be beating the poor thing to death.

"You can't kill it. It's not alive."

There was a pause. Then the woman turned. He saw her for the first time. Her skin glowed with sweat and effort. Her hair was curling wildly around her face. She did not speak to him immediately. She picked up a towel. Her face disappeared into the cloth.

"Name?"

"Josea."

"Masfin. Prisoner?"

"I am not sure, perhaps."

That brought the towel away from her face. Those eyes pinned him to his spot.

"It depends. If you want to leave you are. If you wish to stay you are not."

"Then I am still not sure."

"My best advice is not to go back."

"I tried that already. It didn't go quite as I expected."

"Whose fault is that?"

"I used to think it was yours. But now I am not sure of that either."

"It is my fault, I assure you. Or my responsibility. I would never shirk a responsibility."

"But you are not the sole cause."

"But I am the only one willing to take responsibility."

"Most likely true. So I can't fault you. I want it to be the way it was before the Shaking."

"I am sure. But that can't be. You have to decide how you want it to be with the changes. You can't take the changes away. You have to accept them, then move on with them." Harbinger listened to her words. She smiled ruefully. Josea stood quietly. He heard the sound of feet behind him. He wondered if he had crossed some terrible line by speaking with this woman.

"How would you like to go back to Masfin, Josea?"

"I can't go back now. I would be doubly damned."

"Not to stay but to facilitate a meeting between husband and wife."

"Husband and wife?"

"Yes, Lady Junla is married to General Renfrew. We are trying to arrange a connubial visit."

"General Renfrew put me in prison."

"Lady Junla is with child. It is important that this visit happen."

Josea felt his eyes lose focus. The thought of helping to fool Renfrew was almost delicious. To know what Renfrew did not. To know years from now a secret that Renfrew would always wonder over.

"It is a pretty time of year in Masfin."

"Wonderful weather for riding." Harbinger did not speak for a long time. Petron and Jorin began a series of exercises. Marjas and Sablor sat apart from the group discussing a serious topic. Rodznig and Serjanus and Mandul inspected weapons and tack. Bernath sat next to Harbinger. Wittler and Neirbo had not come to the area. They were collecting and distributing stones. Harbinger let herself relax in the sun.

"Would I have specific duties?"

"Oh, yes. Every mission is designed to fill two or three roles. So there might be more than a sweet reunion to guard. But I like to have one action serve many purposes."

"Do you believe Jeffeaux is the True King?"

"I have a different god. Duty is my god. I believe Ranald has failed his duty. You ask from an emotional need. I can only be pragmatic. I don't believe in True Kings. I don't believe in divine intervention in mundane matters. That doesn't mean it isn't true. I do believe Jeffeaux will be a good king. I believe he will rule justly, fairly, and sensibly. He wants to do well. If that makes him a True King then he is, for me at least." Josea watched her face as she spoke. She would not hide her thoughts. She had too much assurance to need deception to guard her purpose.

"This won't be dull."

"I shouldn't think so. My life has not been dull in a very long time. Since going to Masfin everything has been interesting."

"Interesting, I can see that."

As Josea walked to the house, Bernath watched him. "If you are going to tell every stranger you come across that Lady Junla is pregnant before we go to Masfin why should we bother?"

"Everyone in the army knows the priest sires Junla's children. We can't hide that fact. We can include them in the epic so that they are invested in the events. We do this for Masfin, not our army or Sarna or Llwegania. In Llweganian and Sarn tradition and Masfin law, if Renfrew claims the children they are his. We have to make it easy for him to claim them."

"And the line of inheritance for the throne? Are we to have another war of succession after Jeffeaux dies?"

"The line of descent is clear through Junla. Her child will be legitimate born in the bounds of matrimony. If Jeffeaux is a good, strong king that will take care of itself."

Junla sat in the dark. She was not happy to have been summoned to Harbinger's presence. Her life seemed to be one long wait for Harbinger's wishes. People came and went on a regular basis. Junla did not try to call attention to herself. She knew that Harbinger knew she was here. Harbinger knew where everyone was at all times. Eventually they were the only two people in the room.

Harbinger spent several more minutes poring over some papers. Then she pushed the papers to one side. She lit another lamp. Junla found her shadow pushed behind her.

"I am trying to place your brother securely on a throne. I send soldiers to their deaths regularly to make sure his crown is firmly on his head. He is engaged in a dangerous action to claim this kingship. It would be helpful if his sister would make some effort to guard his back."

"What can I do?" Junla was puzzled. She could not remember being asked to perform any duties.

"Not get with child when your husband could not possibly have done the deed. Does this sound possibly important, like an issue?"

Junla drew back in her chair. How could she know?

"I enjoy sex. Don't get me wrong. There are ways to indulge your appetites without getting pregnant."

Junla wanted to shrink into her chair. She could not get used to Harbinger's direct manner. Years of contact with the woman had not hardened Junla's shell. She thought herself sophisticated. She considered herself practical. She was no shy flower, but discussing sex so matter-of-factly was uncomfortable. She still cringed at the memory of Harbinger and her mother walking in on her that time so long ago.

"I have arranged for you to return to Masfin for a brief visit with your husband. Be sure you get the job done. Hopefully this war will be over before your next pregnancy and you can make your own arrangements for the issue."

"When do we leave?"

"Two Darkfalls. Be ready. You can take your priest if you wish."

"Do you know where my husband is?"

"Most of the time. I know where all my enemies' generals are most of the time. It is very useful information." Harbinger pushed her seat away from the table. She rubbed a stone between her fingers. "Have you considered your priest? As a person? Have you thought what will happen to him when this is over?"

"I have no idea what will happen to me when this is over. I can't begin to consider what will happen to another person when I have no idea what I will be doing."

"Your brother will be King. Your husband will be a defeated general. Your sister will be wife of a dethroned monarch. Your mother will be advisor to a great conqueror. Your brother-by-marriage will be warden of a vast country. Have you decided where you wish to fit in this scheme? Your priest's entire existence is your responsibility. You will have to decide. You can't just let things happen to you for much longer."

Junla closed her eyes. She did not wish to reveal any part of herself to this woman. She felt closed off from all her strengths and supports in this enclosed space. Closing her eyes did not shut out Harbinger.

"I am only trying to survive. I have trained the priest to remain inside a safe boundary of behavior. I know my responsibilities to him. I feel it every day. Every unguarded moment I think that his life depends on something I have done or failed to do. I didn't initiate the other aspects of our relationship, he did."

"Was survival always your goal?"

"Always?"

"Even before you were whisked to Sarna?"

"I guess. Jeffenza is the ambitious one. I wanted to preserve my lifestyle. I thought perhaps a quiet, prosperous husband would be nice sometime in the future."

"It is clear you understand power very well."

"I spent much of my time at court. I could not help but learn the workings of power."

"So, you have no vision of what you want to happen next?"

"No. Once everything settles then I would try to figure out what I should do."

"Please, get your husband into bed. After the birth of this child be more careful until you have made your decision. Make your decision soon. I have many responsibilities and duties. Your brother has a difficult road to travel. You have to be responsible for yourself."

Junla got up after a few more minutes of silence. She drew her cloak tightly around her body. She pushed away the frightening horizon of the future that Harbinger had pressed her face against. She was so focused on the next moment that she could never look at the next day. She didn't want to look. She had always thought that each day would melt into the next with changes coming so slowly and in such small increments that she would not have to decide or impact on the change. She did not embrace this opportunity to control her own destiny. She trembled before it. She clutched her arms tightly across her stomach. Her head sunk until her chin rested on her chest.

There was something wrong. His lady was nervous. She did not take her cloak off. She sat still in her chair, her swathe of material wrapped tightly around her. He did not rise from his crouch. He soothed the slighted child. The small cries for attention stopped. There was no sound in the tent aside from the soft puffs of breathing.

After an indeterminate amount of time her head moved until her eyes fastened on him. She pushed one pale hand out from the nest of material.

"Come here, priest."

He was uncertain. He thought to bring the child then changed his mind. He crept until he was crouched at her knee. Her hand turned his face to her. Her eyes opaque, oblique, piercing in their regard of him frightened him.

"What am I to do with you, priest?"

The question was rhetorical, he hoped. For he had no answer, he had not thought of himself as separate from her in a very long time. He was not sure he could bear to be parted from her even hypothetically.

"I am going to seek my husband."

His breath left his body. Pain spread from his chest to his heart. He held still in the light touch of her fingertips.

"When we return I will consider your fate."

Light faded from his eyes. He thought he would die right then, if her fingers had not been stroking his cheek so tenderly.

"You will like Masfin. It is beautiful this time of year."

His mind froze. His death receded. Why was he going to Masfin?

"Once I have finished my business with General Renfrew, perhaps you and I can steal an afternoon. Would you like that priest?"

He leaned against her hand in relief. He did not understand what this conversation was about but it was not about her leaving him or supplanting him with another man.

"But once this war is over, what am I to do with you? What am I to do with me?" She raised her face away from him. The anguish in her voice cut at him. "It seemed so simple. I don't see any way out of this tangle for you."

"I am for you." He could not express every feeling in his heart. He could not speak freely; his mouth so long unused would not work easily. He did not even know what he wanted to say. He was so conditioned to obey he could not give comfort in any way except physical. So he pressed his face to her lap. Her fingers moved across his scalp.

"I know but when there is peace what do I do? I can't take this household to Masfin. No one would accept us. We can't stay in Sarna. Maybe we could, yet, I have no way to provide for us in Sarna or Llwegania."

"How would you provide for us in Masfin?"

"I have a small dowry estate. We could live from its income but I am a married woman and you are not my husband. We would be considered a scandal in Masfin."

"You were married at Harbinger's order. Let Harbinger provide."

Junla was quiet. She considered the suggestion.

"I still have my husband and my impact on my brother's throne to consider."

"If Harbinger puts Jeffeaux on the throne, who will be able to shake him off? Sit very still, the hawk will pass."

"Harbinger is concerned. She told me so herself."

"Harbinger has reasons within reasons for what she does. Discuss this with her again soon."

Junla smiled at the face pressed to her. He was right. And peace wouldn't be here the next day. Still she could enjoy the comfort he offered.

First stood before the water basin inside the Great Wellhouse. She straightened the material across her shoulders. The robe fell in a straight flow of blue. Her arms were bare except for a bracelet of black leather. She wore a strap of leather around her neck. It held her stone against her chest. There was no hole drilled in that stone. It was held on the thong by intricate weaving and knotting. She could get it out easily enough. Her hair was free of any adornment and her feet were bare.

There were masses of people waiting for her. She had declared the Truth through every Guardian Village by a Water. Her listeners had been angered and appalled. She had told them to come to this place. They had answered her call. She pressed a hand against the swell of her womb. In this robe her condition would not be hidden. All would see proof of her statements.

"All is ready."

First looked at the speaker. The face had the androgynous lines of youth. The pale blue robes hid any body clues.

"Do you understand what we do here today?"

"No."

"You will. If I do it right. If I don't, we will create another mystery. I hope we reveal a truth."

The acolyte turned away. Those thin arms held out the robes of a priest of Kersai. First accepted the cloth into her arms. Then she left the cool, damp, dark of the Wellhouse.

The bright sun startled her eyes. She closed them to ease the pain. Then she opened them slowly. She walked easily to the place prepared by the lakeshore. She felt the water lap at her toes. Around her people stood so close and so many that she had to look at the horizon to see any earth. Had all Sarna come at her request? The importance of this moment pressed against her even as the respectful crowds did not. She stood inside a great curved metal shell. She hoped the shell would send her voice out into the edges of the crowds. She feared it would not though she knew it would bend her voice far. The acolytes would have to repeat her words throughout the sea of people.

"I have told you of the Great Truth that controlled our lives for generations. You have touched the books and read their words." The words seemed to deafen her. She hoped they escaped to the ears of her audience.

"I have come to these waters, gifted us by Harbinger of Death, Devouring Dragon, Bringer of Water to wash away my past. I will let these waters wash away my sorrows, my anger, my defeats. I shall leave in these waters my bitterness, my pain, and my regrets. When I step out of these waters I shall be new. I shall bring to my life only strength. Nothing that came before will have power over me. The day these waters first saw the sky will be the day my life truly began. I will do this for me, and I will do this for everyone who wishes to leave that past behind, to step into a new life."

Very carefully First dipped the robe of Kersai into the waters. She handed it to the waiting acolyte. The young arms raised the soaking robe until all the wet folds shone in the sunlight. The dry powder dye was activated by the water. In the sun the blue color emerged.

"We will become different by embracing this change; as dye changes this material from one thing to another by accepting the power of the water and sun. Will you accept this from me?"

The crowd was caught. There was a swell of sound. The whisper from the back surged to join the cry from the front. Yes, echoed in First's ears. First walked into the water. She held steady. Marlin had taught her how to swim. She could do this. She did not have to go far, only far enough to immerse her body. She took a deep breath.

The water was cold. The cold bit into her skin and muscles, still she did not hesitate. She lowered herself until she felt her hair spread on the surface of the water. She opened her eyes. She imagined she could see all her bitterness and sorrow float away from her. She rose slowly. She used her arms to balance as she walked from the water onto the shore.

"This will be known as the Lake of our Sorrows. All who drink from this lake will know only joy. Today is our most important day. Today must always be kept."

She did not feel the cold anymore. She stood in the bright sun feeling the warmth on her skin and hair. She was standing in the huge well of silence that only a huge crowd can create. She soaked in the peace of the moment. Then she looked again for the acolyte.

Hands reached a plain wooden cup to her. First cherished the container in her fingers. She dipped a cup of water. She passed the brimming vessel to the nearest watcher. The greying head bent over the drink. First moved away from the shore. People parted to let her pass. Behind her First knew the acolyte was laying the transformed robe on the floor of the speaking shell. First would not look back.

Junla sat uneasily on her horse. She was not comfortable sneaking into her country. This journey was scary. She felt vulnerable. She also felt resentful. A deep sense of responsibility was weighing on her mind. Responsibility Harbinger had forced on her. The troops who protected her were at risk to solve an issue that had importance because Harbinger said it was important. This anxiety, this stress, was a burden Junla carried because Harbinger forced her to bear it.

She was not a child. She could not deny responsibility as much as she would like to, and this made her angry as well. Her moods could just as well be blamed on her pregnancy.

She was not happy to be home. It was beautiful but the familiarity had an unreal feel that made Junla think she was in a dream. The landscape was dear. The shapes of the trees, the flow of the terrain all were instantly recognizable to Junla. It was the wreckage of the countryside that caught Junla's awareness. In Sarna and Llwegania she could ignore the impact war had on people and places. In those countries she had only ever experienced war. She had never seen them in any other state than a state of war. She had left this landscape when it was peaceful, calm, and gentle. Now jagged remains of raids and battles littered the landscape. And there were no people.

No one was out tending their yards or wandering open spaces. There were groups of peasants in fields, guarded. There were caravans of traders, again guarded. Her group kept away from people; still there should have been more movement, more evidence of settlement. It grieved Junla to be in Masfin. It burdened her to be here for the purpose of the mission. And her priest was not happy. He felt threatened by this journey; still, he had asked to come.

Junla would not have left him behind. She trusted no one with his life. Who would care for him; watch over him if not she? He might have displeased someone when she was not there to watch over him. Her son remained with Lady Zona. The bright-eyed boy adored his grandmother. Junla let herself indulge in a moment of memory. She thought of her son as he directed her mother in playing a game. He could hardly speak, barely walk, and yet he knew what he wanted and who should do it.

He was treated as a prince. He knew that everyone would answer his call, provide for his needs. Even Jeffeaux's marriage had not diminished the boy's standing. Junla pushed thoughts of her son away. She did not have time for simple pleasures. This was serious business. There had been a close call with a royal patrol last Darkfall. No deaths had occurred. The leader of this troop had not wanted to call attention to their presence by killing a handful of men. The unwary scouts would never know how lucky they had been. They would never know how close death had been for those moments while the seasoned soldier pondered their fate. If Junla's party had been on the return trip the Masfin soldiers would be dead. Perhaps reality was what weighed on her spirits today.

Junla turned her head to study her companions. The group was a mix of Masfin and Llweganian soldiers. They rode easily together. The years of joint effort forged a bond that transcended culture and history. One soldier was assigned to stay with her and her priest at all times. He seemed new to the group but not unwelcome or unwilling.

Her priest was distressed. Only she could know it. He kept his face still and his body relaxed; but she knew every nuance of his expression and she knew he was not himself. Did he think she would run off into the brush, abandoning him? Did he see Masfin as a threat, an even greater threat than her husband? This was home but she no longer belonged here. She couldn't bring her priest with her. She couldn't leave her priest behind. He was part of her very self now. He had conquered her.

Junla never once thought her priest might be unhappy about the purpose of the mission. She never thought he would feel a sense of ownership for her. She never thought he would fear his ability to allow this mission to be completed. She never thought he feared to fail her. She trusted in his training implicitly. He prayed her faith would not be misplaced when the moment came.

Renfrew tossed his gloves across the room. They landed against the far wall then slid to the floor. Renfrew stared at the offending articles with near hate. Now he would have to retrieve them. He would have to walk across the room, bend over, and walk back to the door. How dare they complicate his life like this? Allies were worse than enemies. Stupid husbands used up precious resources. He had to get those gloves so he could leave. He had to leave to prevent a court rival from discovering Stiefis, that most wonderful ally, having sex with Jeffenza that most chaste Queen. Renfrew would be more destroyed than Stiefis if that slimy favor currying little man discovered Stiefis with Jeffenza. Who had brought Stiefis to King Ranald's attention? Renfrew had. Who had the ear of King Ranald in all matters of military policy? Renfrew did. Renfrew did not bother to notify his aides of his leaving. He grabbed the mount that was ready. He did not care whose horse it was or that voices rose in protest. It was not the King's mount so no one would really deny him the animal. He would have enjoyed the sight of his enemy jumping up and down in frustration, if he had bothered to look back.

"Saddle me another animal."

"You have no other mount my lord."

"Saddle me up General Renfrew's horse."

"I am sorry my lord I cannot do that."

"He has my mount."

"General Renfrew is instrumental in the war effort. His horse must be available for him at all times."

"He is riding my animal. He could not possibly need his right now."

"All the General's horses must be available at all times. That is his standing order. One could be shot out from under him in an engagement and he would need a replacement immediately."

"The general did not ride into battle."

"I do not know to where the general rode. It doesn't matter. I have my orders."

Renfrew bent low over the beast's neck. The poor animal was not swift of foot. Renfrew doubted the stamina of the animal. There were no riders ahead. He might pull the coals out of the fire this time. Those idiots had better learn discretion. They had no sense of self-preservation never mind loyalty or devotion to their group.

Renfrew allowed his mind to wander. He became complacent in his success at beating his rival out of the camp. He entered the courtyard without taking any precautions. He flung open the door. Rough hands descended on him. He was bound and gagged before he could discern that he had been attacked in his own home.

He lay on the floor. He felt his sides heaving in effort to still his heartbeat and to drag air into his lungs. Llweganian, he recognized the dress and stance. Those long-legged women dressed in their unrelieved black stared back at him without expression. He noticed that there were men in the group. He realized that he recognized one. He stared at the impassive face. He could never forget that face. He would ever associate it with his wife. One of the men crouched down to talk to him.

"Welcome home, General Renfrew. Quite a nice little place you have here."

Renfrew started at the perfectly accented Masfin. He looked closely at his captor. He was Masfin.

"Do you know what goes on in your own home? Let us educate you. Quietly now. We wouldn't want to spoil the surprise."

Renfrew felt himself being lifted into the air. He watched the walls and ceilings go by at a dizzying angle. He thought to struggle. Dropping him would cause noise. His efforts made no impact on his bearers. They moved without pause up stairs and down corridors. He heard a door being flung open. There were gasps.

"Don't move. Stay right where you are if you wish to live. There is something I wish you to see, General Renfrew."

Renfrew was now dropped with no regard for his comfort. He lay disoriented for a heartbeat. Then his head was pulled up. His eyes were on a level with the edge of the bed. The covers had been flung back. Renfrew could see a tangle of arms and legs. He knew that the faces his eyes were being dragged to would be those of Stiefis and Queen Jeffenza.

"I was loyal. I thought loyalty begot loyalty. I was wrong. Loyalty begot prison. You put me in prison for the crime of following orders given to me by Masfin officers. I followed my officers into battle and I followed my officers back home. Once I was home I never betrayed my oath. I stayed when many of my own officers left. Did I expect any reward? No, I was doing my duty. And I was imprisoned and tortured for that.

"But what was I loyal to? Look, look at what Masfin has become. My Queen is a common slut. Our allies are using us for their own purposes. What ally would do this if he respected our King? And you come rushing to, what? Protect them? Save them? Warn them? I don't think the answer is that you are here to expose them. They are in your home. You are part of this betrayal. You sent me to prison for nothing. What do you deserve?"

Renfrew felt the pressure on his neck decrease. He slumped to the floor. Rough hands dragged him to one side of the room. The speaker rose to his full height.

"Don't move yet. I am not quite done. You are Stiefis. I know you. Who in the Masfin army does not know you? I know something else about you, and now I know something about your lovely daughter, Queen. The priests of Sarna have been exposed. They have been revealed as cruel manipulators of a most basic activity. First has told the people of Sarna of the breeding program the Sarnese priests used to run Sarna. She brought the holy books to light. The ingredients for the marriage herbs were really contraceptives. The lists of families allowed to have children and those not allowed. Your wives could not bear children because the priests would not let them, not because you could not fill their wombs. So that princess of Masfin is most likely half Sarnese."

"You lie. My marriage was duly Repudiated."

"Under the rules of the priests of Kersai. Those rules applied then. All they meant was the priests allowed your wives out of an unproductive situation. The priests would never have allowed you to sire children."

"This is a story Harbinger is spreading to justify her actions."

"I hardly think Harbinger cares about justifying anything."

"How would you know?"

"She sent me personally to do this mission."

Jeffenza tried to sink into the mattress. She burrowed under Stiefis. Undone, she was completely undone.

"I will never believe you. No one will believe such a heinous lie. The Sarnese people know the power of the priests of Kersai."

"Actually this is the truth but belief is not expected outside of Sarna. The Sarnese people in Sarna do believe." Josea had not heard the priest speak three words together. He almost sat down in surprise at the sound of the deep measured tones.

"She has you all brainwashed."

"It does not matter who believes now. All will believe later and they will remember that she told the truth. That is all that matters."

"Next you will say my wives have not Repudiated me."

"That would be a lie. The ceremony that the woman goes through for a Repudiation is between the woman and Kersai. She states her objective. With a blessing she asks for a sign of Kersai's favor as a wife. In a Repudiation she is asking for a sign that she is right to leave her husband. The only sign the Kersai gives to women is fertility. If after the ceremony the woman becomes pregnant she has her sign that Kersai is agreeing to her proposition. There is no issue of sterility or fertility in a Repudiation. The woman asks can I leave my husband. Kersai says yes by giving her a child, he says no by not giving her a child. These are the dynamics of the ceremony between Kersai and women. The ceremony for the Repudiation of the husband is different but that is a separate issue."

Stiefis stared at the coldly formal face. Sun had burned the skin dark so dark that in the limited light of the room Stiefis could barely make out the lines on the man's face. But after careful scrutiny the lines became noticeable. There was a certain power to those lines. Stiefis felt the shame of his position and circumstances. He was vulnerable to his enemy.

"Are you quite done now? Can we get on with our mission?"

Josea blinked at the abrupt change of topic. He stared at the priest's mouth as he tried to place the words. Then he remembered. His anger faded to the background. He was glad he had seen this. His choice suddenly became wonderfully right.

"Of course, take the fine general to his appointment."

Jeffenza tried to push Stiefis from her. She wanted her clothing. She wanted a better angle to manipulate the situation. Stiefis shifted against her forceful hands.

"Control your slut. We are here on serious business."

"Are you implying that women don't engage in serious affairs?"

"Poor choice of words, Queen. You are a lightweight. You have no business being involved in important matters. It has nothing to do with your sex and everything to do with your character."

Jeffenza realized that the timbre of the voice was not male.

"I am not very comfortable."

"And that is of importance to me?"

"He is heavy."

"You shouldn't pick up a burden you can't bear: there might not be an appropriate place to rest it down."

"Does this indignity serve any purpose?"

"Yes."

Josea dragged Renfrew along the hall. He enjoyed every bump and scrape he inflicted. There was deep satisfaction in returning pain for pain.

Renfrew felt himself hurled into a room. A single light shone. He could not tell if he were alone or not. He could hear only his own labored breathing.

"Well husband, you have become notorious since last we met."

Renfrew felt his body tighten in surprise and reaction to the sound of that voice. Unbidden snatches of memory and fantasy danced in his head. Renfrew strained against his bonds.

"What am I to do with you? The Masfin soldiers of Harbinger's army hold you a monster. Do you have any idea of the conditions in the prison at Tampello? You horribly punished the soldiers who stayed. However appropriate a military decision it was, the choice to imprison innocent men because of an association was terrible for Masfin. That single action sent my brother to Delungor. It rededicated all the Masfin soldiers in Sarna to Harbinger's leadership. It persuaded those poor souls who survived Tampello to finally cross over to Harbinger." Junla loosened Renfrew's clothing. She ran her hands along the skin exposed by her fingers. She could feel the growing tension in her captive.

"One could disclaim responsibility by saying you only carried out an order or made a suggestion that Ranald gave the order, supported the decision. That would be true. You could deny any idea of exactly how the plan would be implemented; but that is weak. Ah, there you are. I knew you would not fail me. Imagine, stressed as you are you are willing to service your wife."

Renfrew lay on his back. He mumbled against his gag. He wanted something. She thought it unwise to loosen his bonds but she was his wife. She owed him at least a chance to speak. She worked the knot free. He wanted only to silence her. He shut her mouth with his. He did not ask why she was here or what her purpose was. If that madman in the next room meant to kill him at least he would die happy. He did not bother to ask for his hands to be freed; though he would have loved to have them active. He simply rolled onto the object of his lust and eased his pain. She accepted him easily. Her legs wrapped around his waist.

When he finished he rolled until he sat with his back against the wall. She sat next to him.

"The prisoners were starved. They were kept in the dark, in the cold. There were as many dead as alive when Marlin rescued them. How could you be part of that?"

Renfrew rolled his head against the wall.

"You can't get away with a glib 'I didn't know how it would turn out'. It was your plan. It was a bad plan. You should have followed up, checked on the implementation. If you had done that you would have seen how wrong you were."

"I was trying to save my country."

"For whom? What kind of country? One that condemns men to death for obeying orders? You are so devoted to Ranald that his remaining on the throne is worth murdering men? If Ranald cannot keep his army, then he does not deserve it. If he cannot keep Masfin, then he is not the True King."

Renfrew bowed his head until his chin rested on his chest. He felt a tightness around his heart. The band squeezed until he could keep the pain in no longer. Horrible sobs tore from him. He banged his head against the wall. There was a scurry of feet. Junla called out to reassure her guard of her safety. Then her soft hands drew his head to her breast. She smoothed her fingers against his hair. He wept until he thought his eyes would crack. Then he lay still against her.

"I have a son. I named him Renjeaux. He is my brother's heir for now. Jeffeaux says he will never choose another. But he has taken a Royal Consort. So my poor son will be supplanted. It does not matter. He will still be my son."

Renfrew listened to the words she used to describe her progeny. He let the sounds pour over him. He shifted his head against her. She let him sit straight.

"You will be reviled when my brother sits on the throne. But you are my husband. I will not deny you. If you need a home, come to me."

"Why?"

"For my son's sake and this child's." Her hand rested protectively over her womb. Renfrew slumped against the wall. He would never forget watching her shadow disappear from the rectangle of light in the doorway; his shadow wife in and out of his life.

Josea was tired of the scene. He was finished here. His mind cleared from its miasma of feelings.

"Either finish your business or get up. I am done with you now."

Stiefis quickly withdrew from his lodging. He cringed at the sucking noise he created as he left. The sound echoed in the room. Immediately as he freed her, Jeffenza rolled away from him. She tried to bury herself in the bedding. Stiefis wondered what their captors would do if he reached for his clothing. There was an odd atmosphere in the room. Everyone waited for something.

Strange noises, muffled, regularly interrupted Stiefis' thoughts. He looked at the other occupants of the room. They seemed uneasy. For some reason they cast glances at the priest. Finally some left to investigate. They returned chagrined. The tension in the room increased. Shortly a small woman entered the room.

There was something familiar about the set of her head and the motion of her hands.

"Hello, sister mine. What are you doing here?"

"The same could be asked of you."

"I am visiting my husband. I don't think you can say the same."

Jeffenza said nothing.

"My poor husband is trussed up in a room down the hall. Once we have gone please be so kind as to free him. I recently had a discussion with a very knowledgeable woman. She gave me a piece of advice that applies here. The King's wife must be above reproach. You got what you wanted. Too bad if you don't want what you got. You chose wrong again, Jeffenza, and you continue to make your situation as impossible as you can. Time to go; come along Priest."

Jeffenza watched her cool, impassive sister leave with her entourage of Llweganian troops. Even those who were clearly of Masfin descent were lumped into that category. Once the room was empty she turned to Stiefis. He was already pulling on his pants. She stretched a hand to him. He never saw it. He was sprinting out the door.

Renfrew sat waiting. Junla had closed his clothing before she left him. He was thankful of that as Stiefis burst through the door. He felt exposed enough without that added embarrassment. Stiefis' face showed concern. Neither man spoke for a long minute.

"Are you all right?"

"Yes, and you?"

Stiefis nodded his answer. He did not comment on Renfrew's failure to ask for Jeffenza. He himself did not care too much about the woman. He could not think of her without reliving the whole incident. He might never be able to look at her again.

"They move with impunity."

"Yes, they know far too much about this land and our habits. I am no longer confident of our ability to defeat them."

Stiefis felt his blood stop as he made the statement. His heart froze in his chest at his own words.

Renfrew did not know what to say. It seemed that even if Ranald lost, a Masfin king would sit on the throne. Masfin would return to some semblance of its former self; but, Sarna, Stiefis' Sarna was lost forever. In his relief for Masfin, Renfrew managed to feel sympathy for Stiefis.

"It does look bleak. We have to go. There is a small man trying to destroy us. He is small and insignificant but he might start something very powerful."

"Don't worry. This won't happen again. He will get no further opportunities. I have begun to realize how very dangerous women can be."

"I concur with that statement." Renfrew thought of his wife. He tried to sort out his thoughts and feelings but could only remember her smell and feel.

"If you get the horses I will escort the Queen."

Stiefis nodded. He felt relief at not having to see Jeffenza alone. Even during the ride he could not avoid her. In fact they should return separately. They needed a proper escort for her. He spent his time saddling the horses trying to come up with an answer to his problem.

Jeffenza clutched her scarf to her face as she listened to the footsteps outside the door. There was as short knock. She waited.

"Your Highness, I am here to escort you as soon as you are ready."

Jeffenza felt a stab of disappointment at the sound of the voice who called her.

"Thank you, General. I won't be long."

She knew. Her play was over. Stiefis would duck down back halls and shadowy staircases to avoid her now. It was over. Well, she made a bad enemy. She let go a shaky sigh. She could not blame him. It had been very ignoble. She could not look at him without feeling, she didn't even have a name for the feeling. In time she might be able to forget everything. She felt her bile rise at the notion that her dear sister had been involved in the scenario.

She pulled her clothing into place. She tried to arrange her hair into some semblance of order. Usually she would stuff it into a hat but it would not fit tonight. Renfrew watched her frustrated attempts to create order. He let go an impatient sigh before he brushed her hands out of the way. He managed a passable braid.

"That sly whore, I wonder what treasonous, devious machinations she is plotting."

"Your Majesty?" Renfrew handed Jeffenza her hat. She secured it with two long deadly-looking pins.

"That slut, my sister, she is up to something."

"Please, Your Majesty, the Lady Junla is my wife. She has every right to be in my home. I would prefer not discussing her in such terms."

"Your wife?"

"Yes, remember, she is my wife. She told me that we have a son. That is the proper behavior for a wife, I believe."

He had not meant to defend Junla but he really did not like Jeffenza. He did not want to make this any easier for her. And he knew that his news would add to her displeasure. There was an irony here. He knew Junla's child was not his and here he willingly claimed the boy, sight unseen. In all likelihood Jeffenza's daughter was Ranald's yet the King would be more than happy to disavow the girl if he knew of his wife's activities. Somewhere the gods were laughing.

"A son you say."

"Yes, Renjeaux. I would dearly love to see him but she felt the journey too dangerous for him. When the war is over I will meet my son."

"She came a long way and spent a long time for such a message."

Renfrew held the last of the doors open. He waited until Jeffenza had negotiated the slippery stairs. Then he helped her mount her horse. They began to ride slowly. Renfrew hoped a unit would pass so he could commandeer an escort.

"We are married and it has been a long time since we indulged our married state." Renfrew turned his mount towards the camp. He spared a glance around the area. There was no sign of their visitors. Nor was there any sign of Stiefis. Renfrew felt a frisson of fear. No, Junla would not kill him yet. She needed him alive until this next child was safely born. The fanatic would have killed him already.

"How do you plan to explain our return together?"

"Your escort was ambushed."

"Simple but not enough."

"It will be. There will have been several actions this night."

"My sister told you this?"

"No, but her movements would have been covered by some aids. The party itself may engage in some action before they gain safe territory. There will be plenty of dead Masfin and Sarnese soldiers before night is done. It pains me to say but it is only the truth."

Jeffenza rode in silence for a while. She studied the air between her mount's ears. She cast several glances at her escort's profile.

"Why won't this war end?"

"It will. I hope," Renfrew did know what he hoped. He only felt a swell of concern in his heart. He knew he desired something with a fierce emotion.

Jeffenza left the unfinished sentence unexplored. She did not care what he hoped. She had her own hopes. None of them seemed likely to be fulfilled. She wished she could find a way to banish Stiefis from her memory, sight, and life. She did not relish seeing him at court or in the corridors of her life.

She could not start a campaign against him yet, as much as she would like to. He had been in her favor for too long. She would have to achieve a gradual cooling of her favor. She did not want her enemies to accuse her of anything. Once she had created a safe distance she could strike.

Renfrew would be harder. He had always been aloof from her. Any campaign against him would be ignored as sour grapes or frustrated impulses. His very distance was armor against her. She would find a way to punish him for his association with her humiliation. All those people seeing her spread under Stiefis. They saw her legs wrapped around his waist. They saw her penetrated by him. They had heard her flesh suck to hold on to him. She shifted in her saddle at the thought of her position. She was the Queen of Masfin. Foreigners and fellow Masfins had witnessed this. She wanted to kill them all. Even Junla was a target of her bile.

"My husband will be suspicious of you, General."

"He has been for a long time. My marriage to the sister of the threat to his throne, my family connection the major officer of his military opponent, are strong reasons to doubt my loyalty. But I am loyal to Masfin with every breath in my body and every drop of my blood. My King knows this. My loyalty has cost my soul everything. Tampello is the measure of my loyalty. What is yours?"

"You have no right to question me, soldier."

"I believe I do, sister."

Jeffenza cringed at the familiarity but could not reprove him. Junla had claimed the relationship. How had her sister met this man? How had they married?

"Yes, your fairytale romance was quite the topic of conversation in the court circles. I can't believe my sister knew you before the war and that I never knew of it."

"Obviously you were never that close. You don't seem very close now. You are certainly different from each other. Look at the choices you have made. My wife certainly has no difficulty believing your behavior. I am certain you can understand how she might not share her deepest secrets with you."

"And still, you have told me nothing."

"If your own sister keeps her council from you why would you believe I would share mine with you?"

Renfrew was answering with the thoughts that popped into his head. His mind was not on this conversation. He was busy scanning the few feet he could see. It was very dark now. He was trying to keep them safe from the dangers of the area. If one enemy patrol had infiltrated the defense perimeter, many could. Renfrew was also trying to build a believable story for their return. His wild card hope was that his assumptions based on previous behavior of Harbinger's army were true. He could cover for their lack of return in that case, but where had they been? What was their reason for being out?

He pondered the entire time they rode back. He almost suggested they part before getting too close but he could not allow her to ride through dangerous ground unescorted. He could only keep moving and thinking.

"You are very quiet."

"I am trying to come up with a cover story for our absence."

"Well I was never gone."

"You think no one will note your return?"

"That's right. I am skilled at this."

"Good, I was stumped for an explanation."

"Never explain, never complain, never volunteer."

Renfrew started as he recognized an old army saying. It sounded so incongruous coming from Queen Jeffenza's mouth. Luckily it was too dark for his companion to see his expression. He did not want her to think him soft or admiring, she was a devil of a woman. She might see his momentary lapse as an opening or weakness or even admiration.

Josea felt free for the first time since waking from his illness. The hate and anger that had held him in thrall all these months slipped from him. He had faced his enemies. He had seen the Queen in her true light. He had held his tormentor captive. He felt relief that he was no longer at the mercy of weak leaders and cruel jailers. He felt sorry for his country but change was not easy. He had experienced the crucible of change personally. There was no easy way to make change.

"It is sad that Masfin has to be destroyed." Josea did not realize he spoke aloud until heads turned to look at him.

"Masfin will not be destroyed. Ranald will. The ruling elite, the military leaders, they will go. Masfin will change a little. It will not be destroyed."

"It is nice to believe in something."

"I wouldn't know. I do know that Harbinger has no interest in ruling Masfin. She only wanted to make her lands safe. She needs a peaceful Sarna for that. For Sarna to be peaceful she needs the Sarnese leaders deposed and Masfin neutral. Those are her goals.

"Harbinger is a border guard. Her estate and the estates in her responsibility all border Sarna. When she took her Household Oath she swore to protect those borders at all costs. That is the traditional oath. She will be the first oathtaker to fulfill it. That is what this is about. She has not been seeking self-aggrandizement. She is not greedy. She simply decided that this was the best way to fulfill her promise to her dependents. She saw an opportunity and took it. I have served under her since I was a girl. I know her well."

Josea looked at the hard-bitten soldier. He felt he knew a little about Harbinger. He had found her charming. He had to reconcile this view of her as a driven person with his memory of a pleasant woman.

"She seems approachable enough."

"She is. That is how she gets soldiers to follow her no matter where she leads. I could swear to any house, but I could only follow Harbinger."

The priest followed the flow of conversation. He tried to distract his thoughts from his feeling of unreality. He had this vision of the two lovers on the bed. In his mind they were Junla and her husband. He felt his stomach heave. He clenched his teeth together. He would not disgrace Junla. He would not show his emotions in front of everyone. He would not display any reaction to the goal of this mission. Junla brought him because she needed him. He would remain capable of providing her with whatever she needed.

Junla cradled her womb with her hand. The journey in had not been arduous. The ride out was almost leisurely. They did not expose her to undue risk; still, Junla was anxious to be done. She almost wanted to push the pace but did not want to risk her child. After everything she had done for this child she did not want to lose it.

Her thoughts strayed to Jeffenza. Her sister had looked so degraded. Naked, cringing, caught in a sordid situation, there had been nothing beautiful or erotic in Jeffenza's wilting figure. Was she that much different from Jeffenza? Jeffenza was cheating on her husband with a lover. Junla felt as if she had cheated on her lover with her husband. Junla cast a glance at the stern profile of her priest. What was his name? An old joke about a child's father being a nameless lover echoed in Junla's head. Both her children had been fathered by her nameless lover. Was he really her lover? Was he merely her sex slave? No he was the dominant sexual partner. She ruled every other aspect of his life and their life together. They weren't lovers. The thought made her sad. She had a lover who was not a lover, a husband who was not a husband. At least she had her son and this child.

Junla considered her son. She thought of how he looked to every male that crossed his path. She knew he looked for Jeffeaux. Her brother had spent time every day with the boy. He adored the child and the boy returned the regard totally. Nurses cared for his physical needs. He welcomed her, but Renjeaux was waiting for the only father he had ever known. Perhaps she did not even have a son. Once again her hand crept to her womb. She prayed for a girl. This one being would belong to her.

"Are you well? Do you need to rest?" Her priest had noticed her mood or her protective covering of her child. She shook her head in answer to his question.

"Let us continue. I want to get home. I want to see Renjeaux."

Ranald slammed his hand onto the table before him. He reached to hit the raggedy messenger who stood before him. He stopped his hand in time. It landed once more in violence on the table.

"He has completed his ride."

"The only variation was his stop at Reduni. This is not against him. He took a Consort there. He is proclaimed. His Recitation is legitimate. The Keepers of Delungor recognize him as the True King. The Cleric of Reduni had declared him the True King and his Consort the Royal Consort. The listening posts have heard his Recitation. Masfin has a new Husband. Will you recognize King Jeffeaux as your True King?"

"No, never, I am the King of Masfin."

"Beware the wrath of Masfin. She has Shaken you already. Beware the Burning. Beware the might of her Husband as he comes to Cast you Out."

Ranald listened to half remembered lines of poetry. He noticed the variation. He wanted to cut this beggar in two. He dared not. The scruffy mendicant was only doing his duty. But he was the King. How dare this insignificant worm question him? How dare this fool mouth ancient, useless lines at him in support of that fop? Ranald reached for his sword. He saw a hand attached to his arm swing the sword until it bit deep into the flesh of the dirty idiot.

Blood spurted in a graceful arc. Surprise, dismay, and then peace transformed the wrinkled face.

Ranald wiped his blade on the rags that covered the corpse. "Dispose of this."

The room was still. Ranald looked at the circle of stunned faces.

"I am King. It is treason to suggest otherwise. A group of lazy, superstitious hangers-on will not spread malicious stories to harm the crown. Anyone who says I am not King will suffer the same punishment. In fact it is time Delungor was regulated to its proper place: the past. Clean it out. No one may live there anymore. Those who will not leave willingly; kill them.

"And I want the head of the Cleric at Reduni on a pike in my courtyard. And the Cathedral at Reduni must be burned to the ground."

There was a moment of complete stillness. Then the room emptied in a flurry of slapping gloves and thumping boots. Ranald sighed in relief. He would not argue his position. He would destroy Jeffeaux. There would be no internal openings for Jeffeaux to take the throne. Just as Ranald destroyed all internal threats to his power he would destroy any internal openings for Jeffeaux.

Mundar stood next to his mount. He watched his fellow junior officers mount. They were embarking on this mission as they had the last with straight faces and locked jaws. There was an air of resolve that frightened him. He had regretted the actions at Tampello. That regret turned to despair and fear as he stood in the predawn light readying to participate in an even crueler action. He had sworn to defend Masfin and the King. That oath chafed under the yoke of his current orders. How would destroying Reduni and Delungor defend Masfin? True, it protected the King but Masfin? Mundar did not think so. Perhaps, just maybe, Jeffeaux was the True King and this was the sign.

How could he ignore such a sign? Mundar swung onto his horse. He looked at his comrades. Then he swung his mount out of the courtyard. He crouched low over the beast. He knew that his comrades understood where he rode. He knew that he had killed himself but he could not stay. He felt the arrow bite deep into his flesh. He felt blood begin to pour from him, but he did not slow down. He wrapped the reins tightly around his hands. He concentrated on staying on his horse. That was his only thought.

"Rider."
Strong Daughter looked at the sentry. She stood quickly.
"Ours?"
"No, Masfin, but he is not trying to hide from us. He is coming straight for our position."
"Send a scout."
"Already done."
Strong Daughter left her seat. She walked into the encampment, then to the edge of the site. She adjusted her tunic against the cool evening air. Horses clattered in from the early dark. In the glow of the campfire and camp torches she saw the arrow quivering in the air out of the back of the Masfin soldier.
Efficient hands dragged the bloodied body from its mount. She stared at the pale drawn face. She thought him dead. Then the eyes fluttered open. She knelt in the dirt by the body. She cradled the head close to her head to hear the words from the frantically moving mouth.
"Delungor, Ranald to kill the Keepers. Reduni Cleric, Ranald to kill, to burn. Do you understand?"
"Yes."
"Repeat."
"Delungor, Ranald to kill the Keepers. Reduni Cleric, Ranald to kill, to burn."
Then she felt the life leave him. She watched the eyes stare at her. It hurt to have such courage leave. It was an honor to witness it.
"Wrap him up. He will deliver his message in person."

Marlin looked at the body before him. He recounted the words in his head. They were so horrific he could hardly comprehend them. He watched the body being respectfully rewrapped. The soldiers carried their burden away. The gallant officer would become part of the Llweganian unit's history and pride. His bones would be buried with their dead. Generations from now when the history of the unit was recited during ceremony the soldier would be remembered. He was deserving of such high honor.

"We must defend them." Marlin looked at Lady Zona.

"No, we must take them. We must take all of Masfin. We will start with Delungor and Reduni."

"They are too far apart. We cannot protect both."

Lady Zona knew this. Jeffeaux was too distant to consult. There would not be time.

"Reduni."

"But Delungor is more sacred."

"Reduni endangers more people. The Keepers of Delungor are protectors of the Masfin people. They will accept their sacrifice as an honor."

"I don't quite think so."

"I do. The most ordinary people can be the most heroic. We go to Reduni."

Marlin had to agree with Lady Zona's assessment. There was no option except to make a choice and this choice was the most logical. Ranald had to be stopped.

"Anyway, Reduni is closer to us. We are more likely to get there first. It would be pathetic if we raced to Delungor only to be too late then be unable to reach Reduni in time." Marlin conceded to Lady Zona's choice.

"There you go. Reduni it is. Then we should take the area surrounding Delungor in answer to the slaughter. I will send to Harbinger."

"Good. Is Lady Junla returned? I want to call in all our units."

"Not yet. Start with the troops in the field. I will follow with the remaining units once they return. And I have heard from Harbinger. We should send Jeffeaux more protection. He will be at even greater risk now."

"I am sure Harbinger will want to send her elite troops to extract him. I will not argue her position this time. I don't care for politics now. There can be no politics, only action. The deposing of Ranald is our only issue from this point forward."

"Agreed."

Lady Zona stood looking at the spot where the slain messenger had lain. She remembered the dead eyes and still body. She had seen violent death many times now. Lady Zona could see that this death had affected the Llweganian commander as well. The boy had been as young as her husbands. She wanted badly to touch her husbands to assure herself of their health and vitality. She wanted Harbinger at her side. She felt invincible standing next to Harbinger.

Chapter 18

The countryside was beautiful. Lady Zona realized that she had not been to Masfin in a very long time. She was enjoying the sights as if seeing it for the first time. She felt no deep connection to the landscape. The vibrant colors and plentiful vegetation seemed too much for her now. Sarna was her home. It had taken this return to convince her. She could not look on the landscape as home ever again. She loved too well the stark wastes and subtle colors of her adopted home to live easily in this environment.

"Deep thoughts, Lady Zona?"

"No, just observations of our surroundings."

"King Jeffeaux should know of our situation by now."

"Will he come directly to Reduni?"

"That is the plan."

"Good. When we take Delungor he should establish his Household there."

"You may suggest anything but I have found this new King to be very clear on his positions and very stubborn in maintaining them," Marlin spoke quietly.

"He will do what he will do," Lady Zona agreed.

"Kings are like that, I have learned. You can only follow behind them or leave them."

"I wonder how we will be greeted by the Masfin populace."

"That is a very potent variable."

Weirhass stared at Stiefis. He could not comprehend the words.

"He is desecrating a holy place?"

"Two, though they are different in their uses and positions."

"Has he gone mad?"

"Don't say that, ever. Keep your thoughts to yourself. He is fighting for his throne in any way he can."

Weirhass thought of their opponent. He thought of the Sarnese people who supported their invader. He stared at the worried face of his son.

"Does he not understand the importance of the people? Did he learn nothing from our mistake? Our own people are supporting our enemy because our enemy takes better care of them. If he does this, Ranald will give his people a reason to turn to Jeffeaux and Harbinger. They will welcome her armies as our people did."

"Never say so. He will kill everyone. He will deny the truth."

Weirhass sat down heavily. He was getting too old to be doing this.

"We are lost. We have to begin to plan our surrender to Harbinger. What can we ask for? How can we return?"

"Ranald could still win." Both Stiefis and Weirhass turned to look at Hasshaur.

"No, that possibility is fading fast. There is little left to manipulate, but we cannot leave. Ranald will track us down to kill us. We must wait."

"They will blame us you know."

Weirhass was looking at his hands. "The Masfin people will say that Ranald's association with us turned him into a monster. We will be reviled everywhere."

"We will be in good company."

"How so?"

"The priests of Kersai were controlling the population. The marriage herbs they gave did not help women to have children; they prevented conception. The proof has been shown to the Sarnese people. We can deny this. We can accuse Harbinger of lying but in the end we will not be believed by our people. We will be linked with cruel priests and mad kings forever."

"You lie."

"No, I was told this was true by one of the highest priests from the temple of Kersai. We are doomed. It is best we stay close to the mad king for a while longer. We would be actively hunted down in Sarna at this point."

Weirhass grunted. He rubbed his face with a weary hand.

"That explains one mystery." Stiefis looked at his father in question. "After I found your mother I searched her room for any clues to why she had done what she did. Anyway, I found all her marriage herbs. She was trying so hard not to have children. Her actions defeated her purpose; poor woman."

Stiefis felt his heart contract. Weirhass had not mentioned his wife in Stiefis' hearing ever. The bittersweet pleasure caught Stiefis. He sighed.

Harbinger sat amid her husbands. Food moved freely through the room. Servants moved also but with a quiet efficiency that deflected notice. Junla sat near her mother. In her shadow her priest was still. They would reach Reduni with the next light. Everything was set. Reports announced the slaughter at Delungor. Jeffeaux had entered the camp. He would be here soon with his new Consort and title. This was a fairly serious affair. So Junla was surprised by the jovial tone Harbinger used when she addressed everyone.

"So, Junla, how did you find your husband? We have been so busy with other matters that I failed to inquire into your mission."

"He was well enough. He is a little unprepared for the reality of war."

Harbinger nodded in understanding. She had seen that with many of her Masfin counterparts and allies.

"I hear your sister was there also."

"Yes, she was engaged in a rendezvous with her current lover."

"Interesting."

"One of my escort recognized him. A certain Stiefis, he is Sarnese."

"Stiefis, you say. Are you sure?"

"He answered to that name. He asked after the validity of his Repudiation from my priest based on the announcement Josea made to him concerning the great Issue of Sarna. At least that was what was reported to me. I was not present during this. I was busy with my husband."

Harbinger smiled a cruel smile, an evil smile that turned Junla's delicate stomach. The husbands around her displayed consternation, resignation, and amusement.

"Lady Zona, did you hear that? Jeffenza was caught in bed with Stiefis of Sarna. What do you think of that?"

"That my daughter is very unwise."

"Thank you, Lady Zona. Ah, here is King Jeffeaux and the Royal Consort Marma." Harbinger rose quickly. She crossed the space to greet the newcomers. A wide smile lit her face. Jeffeaux grasped her outstretched hands instinctively. He clung to her strong hands for only a moment. Then he brought his Consort to his side. Harbinger greeted Marma with an equal enthusiasm. "It is so good to see you. I had not realized how long this Ride would take. I hope you are well."

"The original Ride followed all the seasons."

"This won't diminish your claim will it?"

"No, not at all. The news is very disturbing."

"The reports from Delungor," Harbinger stopped speaking. She turned her grim face away from the couple. "Here is your Lady mother and sister. Do you wish to eat first or to meet with General Marlin?"

Jeffeaux looked at the gathering. Marlin stood. He still waited to be acknowledged. Jeffeaux nodded at the soldier. Marlin bowed deeply. Jeffeaux accepted the deep curtsies from his mother and sister.

"My Lady, wait here. Eat, relax. I will meet with Marlin and Harbinger and my mother for a short debriefing."

Marma sat at the table. Each husband for Harbinger came to her to offer their congratulations on her marriage and the successful Ride. She hoped Jeffeaux would not be too long. She was tired. She did not think she would last long before she fell asleep in her soup.

Jeffeaux studied the map on the table. Light flickered over the lines and symbols. Marlin's voice washed over him. The plans were sensible. The numbers were strong. The ground would be excellent.

"We can't be committed to protecting Reduni. Protecting the population of course is our goal. If the city must be abandoned, do so. It is only buildings. We can build again. Get my people out. Damage his army as much as possible. If you have to trap his army in the city and burn it around him to destroy his army: do it." Jeffeaux knew he sounded hard, but he felt hard. "Did you ever meet my cousin Ranald, Marlin?"

"No, Your Highness." Marlin spoke quietly.

"I knew him well. We grew up together. He was such an ordinary man. As ordinary as a king can be, that is. You would never have guessed him capable of such heinous acts watching in his robes and court. You can't really know some people until you see them under extraordinary circumstances. I hope the people of Reduni accept our help."

The non sequitur caught Marlin unawares. He hesitated over his answer as he regained his balance.

"Our forward scouts have not made contact but the general feeling is of fear and panic. They may be happy for any rescue by first light." Marlin reported.

"Very well. One can't claim hunger under these circumstances but I have learned that a good meal is an important defense in battle. Courage cannot be sustained on an empty stomach. You have committed your troops I see, Mother."

"Yes, I will hold the right flank with Wind Rider. Our companies have performed well together." Lady Zona spoke with the deference due a king.

"Good. I hear that Lady Junla was in Masfin territory recently."

"She visited her husband. She saw your sister Jeffenza. She was copulating with my Sarnese husband at the time. Why is your sister so determined to be involved with my husbands?" Harbinger tried to lighten the mood.

"Because she is stupid. I guess I will not be able to stop you this time."

Harbinger laid a comforting hand on Jeffeaux's shoulder. "I never lived with any of my siblings. I never thought of it one way or the other. I see now that it was a blessing. Don't worry, I can't kill her. It's my husband I can dispatch summarily." The warmth of her hand seeped into the part of Jeffeaux that had been cold since he read the message that had brought him here. The awesome responsibility he had taken onto himself at Delungor had frozen out every feeling once he read that short missive. For this one moment he felt warm. Her strength soaked into his flesh through that casual contact.

He turned to face her without breaking that casual contact. She became very serious. He imagined that he had looked as stern when he took his vow at Delungor.

"We will successfully defend Reduni. We will repel the enemy. We will not need to destroy the city. We will go to Delungor. We will pay homage to the dead there. I myself will bring you the dead body of Ranald. I will lay it at your feet before all your enemies. I will not fail in this." Harbinger said her words solidly as if she were making a vow.

Jeffeaux wanted to say that she did not need to do this. He wanted to say that perhaps it would be better if he killed Ranald or Marlin did. But she could not make him the promise he really wanted. The one he had not known until this moment that he even wanted her to make. He would accept any promise this barbarian queen would give to him. He covered her fingers with his hand. He pressed them tightly against his shoulder then released them. She withdrew her hand from his shoulder. Then she was gone from the space taking his mother with her. He stood alone with Marlin. The soldier waited as Jeffeaux collected himself.

"I used to spend all day deciding what to wear for an evening of entertainment. Now, I am King."

Marlin remained quiet. He looked impassively at the thoughtful man.

"I do not want to be King. I want to be a good leader for our people. I want Masfin safe from all enemies, foreign and domestic. I want children to play happily on hillsides again. I saw no children out playing on my Ride, not one. I will be King. I will be a good king. I promise you that."

Marlin looked into the sincere eyes of the former lazy courtier. The lines of strain were clear on the face. The skin held the yellowish tinge of exhaustion.

"I am attached to the House of Lady Zona, Your Highness. Lady Zona is of the Household of Harbinger. I go where my leader sends me. I follow her orders to the death. I have taken that oath. You need make me no promises. For what it's worth, you are a good king. Harbinger believes it."

Jeffeaux returned to the diners. He sat quietly next to Marma. He answered her questions gently. Everything was as it should be. He turned to Junla.

"I know it is late, but could I see Renjeaux before I sleep? Tomorrow will be too busy and I wish to see him before the battle."

Junla signaled a servant. She issued a softly spoken order. The sleepy child soon appeared. He happily babbled at his uncle. He threw out sounds and gestures of excitement and welcome. Jeffeaux hefted the tot into the air. The squeals were joyous in the air.

Weirhass surveyed the dead. The empty building loomed behind them.

"Soldiers did not do this. Murderers did."

"I am sure you killed civilians during raids."

Weirhass looked at the impudent speaker. Renfrew was not being difficult. He was only trying to make sense of a world gone mad.

"Yes, but we never went on a raid for the sole purpose of killing civilians. Our enemy knew we were coming. They defended themselves. Very well, much of the time. We never went hunting civilians for the sole purpose of killing them. And we never did this to our own people. We had an enemy."

"Sophistry."

"The same back to you. You can't tell me that you agree with this. Don't you find this appalling?"

Renfrew closed his eyes to the sight. He tried to close his ears to the questions as well. It didn't work that way.

"No. You are right. You never went into your own temples to kill your priests. These poor people are not the enemy." Renfrew could stand it no longer. He turned his mount away. "There is nothing more to see here. We had best move to Reduni."

And what will we accomplish at Reduni, Stiefis wondered. Is there an even easier victim there? They should surrender to Harbinger. He should ride to her to arrange the surrender. But, that madman would hunt them down before the Sarnese troops could leave. For himself Stiefis no longer cared. He would pay with his life to leave this nightmare but he had an entire army to consider. He could not condemn them to death.

Stiefis waited until Renfrew was out of earshot.

"Father, if the opportunity arises, surrender would be honorable; more honorable than this. It has to be the entire army. Any left behind will be executed."

"Yes, I will not forget."

"To Reduni, after you."

Lady Zona shared her evening meal with Wind Rider. Their husbands filled the tent with activity. They received reports and issued orders with alacrity. Wind Rider chewed her food thoroughly. She glanced over reports and maps when they were presented to her. Lady Zona sighed. She was relieved that the chains were finished. The trees were still being felled. She could not hurry that effort.

Wind Rider paused in her chewing. She pulled a report back from the done pile. She placed the report on the table next to Lady Zona's plate.

"Do you see this?"

Lady Zona bent over the paper. She followed the line Wind Rider was drawing. "Siege machines?"

"Yes. See all this effort we are expending interrupting the plain before the city."

"Yes, and?"

"We are doing this not only to make the going heavy for the enemy's foot soldiers and cavalry but so they can't bring their catapults to bear on us."

"That seems reasonable."

"If we could destroy those machines before they can be brought into play we would be in an even better position."

Lady Zona considered the plans.

"The whole point of this front is to have an exposed area of action. The same conditions which we are using as a defense against Ranald's army would be used against anyone trying to get to Ranald's machines."

Wind Rider conceded the point with a nod. She continued to stare at the map. She returned to her eating. Still she did not give up the map. She listened to other reports. She answered questions; but her hand continued to whirl the paper on the tabletop.

"They couldn't even use the cover of night."

"No, the moon will be full. There will be light from the camps of both armies and from the city. Whatever darkness lasted between sunset and moonrise would have to be used completely on the sabotage."

"You're right. Too bad Ranald won't delay a couple of Darkfalls once he arrives."

"They still couldn't get back in time. There are three separate missions there: the infiltration, the actions, and the retreat. Each mission would need time for good execution."

"We have the time now. If we could only steal some of this time and place it then."

Lady Zona heard the words. She frowned in thought. She reached for the map. She tapped her finger on the paper as it rested on the wood. She looked at Wind Rider. There was a good reason for this.

"What if the team were waiting for the machines? The group went out now dressed as Masfin soldiers, or local citizens. They could be waiting for the machines. They would cross safely now."

Wind Rider sat up quickly. She waved away a hand that offered another report.

"So, they are waiting there. Under the cover of darkness they dismantle the machines. Now to get them back. They can't stay, because as soon as the damage is done all strangers will be suspect."

"At what point during the battle would Ranald order the machines up?"

Wind Rider spoke to the hand. "Get me that information."

"Every soldier crosses every foot of a battlefield under combat conditions. That's what they do. They will return through the cover of battle."

Lady Zona felt excitement bubble in her. Then she felt the air go out of her sails.

"They will be gone for the changing of the codes. They won't be able to pass through our lines."

"We can have a special code just for them. We will assign specific sentries to which to return."

"What if they can't make the sentries or the sentries are killed?"

"They can always surrender to us. Then during their interrogation they can say the code words. All the interrogators can have access to the words."

Lady Zona leaned back in her chair. She smiled in joy. Wind Rider returned the smile.

Ranald was not happy. Even from three days out reports were announcing the presence of strong defenders at Reduni. Harbinger had gotten there first. Jeffeaux had thrown down the gauntlet at Reduni. Ranald would have to face his rival now. He had declared his intentions. There was no way to break off the engagement without losing strength. Facing the enemy would not be wise. The better ground was held by the defenders.

Renfrew had pushed going around, leaving the field before beginning. Ranald refused the advice. He would meet his enemy here, now.

Stiefis sat on the hillside studying the approach to Reduni. The city sat next to a broad river. The river cut across the foot of a mountain. From here Stiefis could see the gleam of weapons on the mountainside. A sister mountain nestled behind the city. The Masfins loved their walled cities; they kept the wild animals out. The defenders were entrenched before the walls. Any enemy had to cross the plain under the weapons of the defenders or float down the water under the weapons of the defenders. Stiefis ground his teeth in frustration. He turned to Renfrew.

"This is suicide. There is no way to attempt this. Their forces are superior to ours. Their position is better. They sit right across our supply lines. If we fight here we will be slaughtered."

"Yes, to everything. The King will not be moved. He wants Reduni. I would rather die trying to take it than be alive after this failed attempt."

"The war will be lost here. We will manage a few more battles, maybe even a couple of harvests' more resistance, but the war itself will be over."

"It is over already. We are only prolonging the inevitable. Remember to watch your left. You have a habit of dipping your shield on the left as you swing. One of these days you will startle your horse into a buck, getting yourself killed."

Stiefis slapped Renfrew hard on the back. "Take care of your own skin. I have yet to get myself killed."

"There is always today."

Harbinger stood on the ramparts. She watched the cloud on the horizon resolve itself into an army settling for the fight.

"How long do we wait?" Jeffeaux asked the question with a mixture of curiosity and regal command that was amusing to Harbinger. She suppressed her smile before she turned to him.

"Not long, I would imagine. Ranald will not delay."

"You will allow Ranald to control our actions?" Jeffeaux puzzled through his perception of Harbinger.

"No, but we have no need to move. We have Reduni. He is the one who made a statement about his actions here. His character will not turn aside from his avowed actions. He will not have enough sense to turn away. I am sure he thinks we will be an easy target."

As one Harbinger and Jeffeaux turned to enter the tower that punctuated the ramparts. They descended the stairs slowly. The turning narrow steps required concentration to navigate. Once they entered the guardroom Harbinger had commandeered for her headquarters, Jeffeaux crossed to the table that held a map of Reduni and the surrounding countryside.

Jeffeaux looked at the map. The deployed troops looked very formidable to him. The stones gleamed in the light.

"Remember all those times we resigned the field even when it was obvious that we had the advantage? Those retreats will serve us well now. Our opponents will not plan for us to maintain the conflict."

"You were paying attention."

"It seems to me that you spent a long time building a reality just for this moment."

"We always gained our objective. All our previous actions were for a specific objective. Now our previous behavior will be used to a tactical advantage."

"Were we building to this moment?"

Harbinger sat patiently. She smoothed the wood of the table. She chose her words carefully.

"We were preparing for major engagements. Any advantage, edge, weapon that you have you should use. This particular weapon can only be used once if Ranald is sensible. It is the surprise of our actions. You don't always let your enemy know all the actions which you are able to implement. But now we have to wait.

"I have no desire to cross that big empty space under the weapons of an enemy army. Let Ranald come to us. He will."

Jeffeaux watched as Harbinger returned to the ramparts. He watched her legs disappear up the curve of the stairs. He should sleep. Once the fighting began rest would be hard to come by. He returned his attention to the map. His mother and Wind Rider commanded the troops that ran to the river and sat across the water guarding the river. He wondered what his mother was doing right this instant.

Lady Zona stretched her back. She was tired from directing the placement of logs in the banks of the river. These logs were the last fortification that needed installing. Their sharpened ends menaced the river approach. Chains stretched across the water. Any attackers on the river would be delayed long enough for the archers across the river to affect a slaughter. Of course escape down the river would not be very easy for the defenders.

"Zona, you should rest."

"Soon, Brir, we are almost done. How are the forward positions doing?"

"Stea sends that everything is in readiness."

Lady Zona rubbed the slit in her pouch that held the stone announcing Ranald's arrival. Even in sight he was still a half day's march away, she had time to sleep. The last log slipped into place with a thunk as wood hit stone. Lady Zona gave into the firm hand on her arm. She nodded to the chief engineer.

"Well done, sir."

"Thank you, Lady Zona."

Marlin looked across the plain in the advancing Darkfall. The shadow of Darkfall seemed to fall from the mountains onto the plain. His orders were simple. Wait for Ranald to move. Once the Masfin forces began their advance the orders would be issued. His order would be either to go or to stay. If Ranald advanced on the center, Marlin would swing left to squeeze the army. If the army came to him, Marlin would stay while the center moved to crush the army against him. If the center swung to crush the army against Wind Rider's position he was to go defend the center. This would only happen if all the Masfin army were committed to the action. If they attacked in waves everyone would stay to defend their zones.

Marlin was nervous. Harbinger was betting that Ranald would not turn aside. Harbinger had stationed reserves on the borders. They could retreat from Reduni with great difficulty upriver. But Harbinger was expecting to meet Ranald. It made Marlin nervous to commit so much of their army to this one place, this one action. Surely Ranald had at least one general urging retreat. The next morning would reveal the future. Marlin knew he would not sleep well this night.

Marma ran a hand over Jeffeaux's worried frown. He knew he should be glad Ranald had not run during the night. He should be relieved there would be no hurried chase or retreat today, but every battle meant many dead Masfin on each side. He would lose many fine subjects this dawning. Jeffeaux hugged Marma to his side trying to ward off the chill in his heart.

"The day has dawned bright and clear."

"Yes, see there? They are starting to advance."

Marma straightened to see the movement.

"Look at the puffs of dirt." Jeffeaux set Marma away from him. He smoothed her hair back from her face. He smiled down at her staring face.

"Here is your guard, my Consort. They will stay with you in the Cathedral. The Cleric is waiting for you."

"Waiting is terrible."

"I know. Junla will be there with her priest and Renjeaux. You like her company."

"Renjeaux will entertain me."

Jeffeaux smiled in real pleasure. "He is a very bright child. I will envy you your company. I have to wait here without any distractions." Jeffeaux gave Marma a gentle salute on her mouth; then watched as she left. He turned to climb to the ramparts. Petron met him there.

"The Horse are coming."

Jeffeaux spied the cavalry pounding across the space as the sun began to glint off the riders' armor.

"They sound like thunder."

"It will be a shame to kill so much good horseflesh, but they will make a good barrier against the infantry."

Bows twanged as the horses came into range. Ranald would not have time to bring his catapults into range. He would have to move them across the same space that was now becoming littered with dead horses and riders. Harbinger had her own catapults arranged in the front of the city. They were hidden now by piles of brush. They were not loaded with heavy rocks; they held smoldering coals. Jeffeaux watched the lazy spirals of smoke rise from the deep bowls.

Ranald should have tried to bring his machines up by now. They should have been right behind the Horse. No one tried to take a walled city without catapults. Jeffeaux looked for the telltale jerk motion of draft horses behind the cavalry.

"Why isn't Ranald bringing his machines to bear? They should be trying to gain position. Are the darters ready?"

"Yes, they are. There has been no report of catapults. Many were burned at Tampello for fuel. They have not all been replaced Your Highness."

"He thought the city would open its gates to him without machines?" Jeffeaux shook his head in wonderment. "Don't we know exactly the number of machines Ranald has at his disposal?"

"Yes, but, Your Highness, remember, we can't predict when Ranald will bring them into play."

"What could he be saving them for?"

"I couldn't say Your Highness. We are ready for them. Most of the ground before the city is entrenched. We established our lines far enough in front of the city so that the machines would have to be moved behind our lines to be in range of the walls."

"Perhaps the generals on the other side see this." Jeffeaux realized that he must sound as if he were routing for Ranald to win. "It is frustrating to think that the welfare of my people, even soldiers ranged against me, is in the care of a man who cannot make an appropriate decision for their care. For our safety I am glad the catapults have not been brought up. I just worry over why."

Petron studied the horizon. Jeffeaux's point was valid. They needed better information about those machines. He fished a stone out of his belt. The young hand of the runner received the weight. Petron did not even turn to see the young man leave.

"I will find out about those catapults for you Your Highness."

"Thank you, Petron."

Renfrew stared at the crippled machines. They listed like drunken animals. Their buckets hung at crazy angles. The wheels lay in broken heaps. There was no way to repair the damage in time to bring them up for use. The company commander in charge of them stood before Renfrew. He was shaking with fear. Renfrew understood the man's trepidation. There was nothing to be done. The man was dead already. Ranald would not let this disaster pass unpunished. He had no option in this matter. His resignation and frustration translated into a bland tone.

"You are a dead man. Prepare yourself. By the next meal your head will be feeding birds."

The surrounding officers did not hear the words as calm acceptance of fate. They heard the monster of Tampello passing judgment on a poor peer. They looked on Renfrew with stern eyes. They could not disagree with the statement. They could not stand up for the shaking officer without sealing their own doom. Their helplessness and guilt over their own cowardice sowed seeds of great hate in their hearts for Renfrew.

Renfrew looked around for a messenger to send to the King. He did not think when he gestured to a young boy.

"Go to the King. Give him this report. The catapults have been sabotaged. They are useless."

There was complete silence. The boy was pale and trembling. He could not refuse the order but his feet would not obey his mind. Renfrew frowned fiercely at the child. Then he comprehended the moment. He frowned more terrifyingly at the quaking child. The boy swallowed. He wondered if he were about to die because he feared to go to die. Then the commander of the catapults spoke.

"I will personally tell the King of my failure." The commander of the siege machine battalion spoke in a hoarse but firm voice.

Renfrew looked at the still face of the man. He locked eyes with Renfrew for a moment before turning to embrace his fate. The boy slumped in relief. The surrounding officers saluted the commander sharply. Renfrew closed his eyes against the scene. His own cowardice glared in the face of this man's bravery.

He didn't have time for this. He would have to find out later what had happened here. Right now there was a battle to fight. Maybe this setback would convince Ranald to turn aside. He would have to wait until Ranald had calmed down. Many more would go to their deaths if Renfrew spoke too soon.

Josea swung with great gusto. He did not look into the faces of his enemy. Each uniform was topped by Ranald's face. Josea wished to see Ranald die a thousand deaths. He was well on the road today. He began to hum as he swung. The snatch of words spat from his mouth as he worked his sword through the heaving mass of bodies.

"Masfin has parted her cloak." Slash and down, turn, thrust, withdraw. "Two wolves struggle in a death battle. Masfin, our Mother, has taken the striving wolves to her breast." Shove. Careful, watch the ground. A shadow to the right. Turn. Swing a fist, the knife hand, blood spurts, duck. "She has cast them upon Ranald to drive him from her. She has closed her cloak to Ranald, leaving him with the wolves." Josea's voice rose to a crescendo. He swung his blade down with tremendous force on a neck left exposed to him as his adversary maneuvered to slice him. Josea shoved the dying body from his.

"Your King has taken his sister's son to heir."

"At least he can be sure who the mother is."

"What do you imply?"

Josea pushed himself away from his questioner. He smashed the head nearest him. As his victim stumbled, Josea severed a leg from its body. The high pitched scream echoed faintly in Josea's mind.

"I imply nothing. I fight for my country. I state the obvious."

Josea waited for the signal. Overhead he could see the trails of smoke as the catapults flung burning coals down on the rear of the advancing army. He had to remember not to go too far into the field. He saw a comrade fall. He began to work his way left. A hand gripped him strongly. With one heave he lifted the woman. She wavered under the quick movement. Then she steadied herself. He parried on his right trying to lend her his left shoulder for support as she regained her bearings. There was a loud bang. There it was again. In the smoke and dust of the battlefield Josea had lost his way a little.

They were closer to the catapults than Josea had thought. He knew that bang. It was the sound of the bowls of the catapults as they were slammed back into their cradles. It would be dark soon.

"Are you ready?" Josea asked the question softly. He felt the squeeze on his arm. Back to back they began their retreat. They slipped behind pikes and into the trenches. Masfin soldiers tried to follow but they did not know the secret of the pikes. As they became hung up on the wooden barriers archers buried arrows deep into their flesh.

Once he had made the trenches Josea sheathed his blades. He lent his battle made friend his arm. They hurried through the maze ducking the less well aimed friendly fire. The route led them to the city gates.

"Friend or foe?"

"Morning light shines brightest during Darkfall."

"Friend."

Josea was glad to be in the safety of the city. He guided his companion to a healing station. Josea paused to see if he recognized any of the healers. Not here, he didn't see any of his friends. He left to quickly rejoin his unit. He was hungry. He needed rest. Tomorrow would bring more fighting; unless Ranald grew common sense or a conscience overnight.

Pelsen was disturbed. He could not forget the words he had heard on the battlefield. The voice hovered in the air. He had not been able to attach that voice to any body. Perhaps the words would have been less powerful if they had come from some mouth. But they had descended on his ears from the air. They settled in his head. The song was a song of war, a song of celebration. The words were words to send a country into civil war. But it was the statement about parentage that had caught Pelsen in this web of doubt and wondering. He couldn't voice his thoughts aloud. In fact he could not examine his thoughts and feelings very closely now, but later, he would remember this day and this issue.

Petron looked at the grimed face. The eyes were bloodshot. Petron stood with his booted foot resting on the frame of the bed. A similarly dressed man lay in the bed unconscious but stable according to the healers. Around the bed the rest of the unit stood.

"You have been waiting on the plain for Ranald's army?"

"Yes sir. Lady Zona sent us before Ranald's army was sighted."

"Your mission was to disable Ranald's siege machines."

"Yes, sir. Wind Rider was explicit. We completely destroyed them during the night before the battle. Then we rode over with the Masfin Horse. We had some difficulty reaching the predetermined sentries but we were finally able to get to them. The Masfin Horse suffered greatly during the battle. "

"That is how we planned it."

"Yes, sir."

"Have you reported back to Lady Zona and Wind Rider?"

"We sent the stone, sir. I have yet to receive one back. I imagine it will be here soon."

"I am sure you are correct. I wonder when a stone will be sent to me."

There was a tense moment. Petron could not deny the positive aspects of the mission.

He would have been overjoyed if he had known of the mission prior to this moment. This was Winder Rider's besetting sin. She was not tidy about details. Lady Zona usually was; however this time she probably thought Wind Rider had mentioned the plan to Petron or Harbinger or Marlin or someone. They had been lucky this time.

There were footsteps in the hallway. Wind Rider herself appeared to congratulate the troopers. She paused when she saw Petron standing in the circle of light. Her attention was focused on Petron even as she spoke with each soldier.

She left the soldiers with a final smile of approval. Once out of their sight and earshot the smile faded. She walked slowly trying to fade from Petron's notice.

"Don't hang back, heir of my wife. Come closer. Share some information with me. Discuss an important mission with me. Let me know about a situation that might impact my troops."

"It is a bad habit I have. I assume if I know something everyone I know must know it instantly. My husbands complain about this constantly. Once I discuss something, it is over, done, completed, everyone who has to know already knows without my ever speaking."

"You must designate someone to disseminate important information. They must be in charge of it for you. They must keep track of who knows what for you at all times. You have many husbands, pick one of them for this." Petron sighed. He could not deny the effectiveness of the action. There had been no negative repercussions, this time. He felt that Wind Rider would act on his advice. "I am happy. It was well done."

"Thank you. I *will* take your advice." Wind Rider nodded to a passing group of troopers. "I wonder which one of my mother's husbands is her information disseminator."

Petron laughed. "Harbinger need anyone to remind her to share important information? That will be the day. She is closed mouthed about some things, but ask her a question, let her get an idea, you will be wishing she was parsimonious with her words. Those she talks to, she talks to endlessly." Petron slapped Wind Rider on the back. "I will go relieve King Jeffeaux's fears. He has been obsessing about those machines."

Ranald paced in frustration. Nothing he tried dislodged the defenders. Fire and arrows rained down on his troops. Wave after wave of assaults made no impact. He could not surround the city either. There would be no siege. Three days and his forces could not break the center nor turn the flanks. This was unexpected. Always Harbinger had retreated after a day two at the most. Why did she not leave now? What was different now? Or here? Was someone new calling the shots? Who? Ranald never considered Jeffeaux. It would have been laughable. He sent for Renfrew. Obviously someone new was running the show. The most likely candidate was Marlin.

"What is your brother doing?"

Renfrew blinked at the question.

"I have no idea, Your Majesty."

"Harbinger always leaves. Did you bring your Sarnese friend?"

"I am here, Your Majesty."

"Why are they still here?"

Stiefis stood next to Renfrew. He wanted to stand in the shadow so he pushed himself into the light. He endured the wild stare of Ranald.

"This is a war of conquest. It was not before, that was a war of attrition, Your Majesty."

"What?"

"For the past hew harvests Harbinger has been bleeding Masfin of men and resources, Your Majesty. She has been weakening Masfin. Now she has diminished our ability to wage war to the low level she wishes. The conquest begins. She will not leave. She will fight until she is done."

Ranald did not like that answer. He rounded on Stiefis with a deep growl.

"Why do We even bother talking to you? She has never fought against you except before that city of yours. You have never fought her as We have. Head to head, harvest after harvest, We have denied her victory. You have no advice for Us." Ranald turned again to Renfrew. "Someone new is directing that army. Marlin is the most likely guess. We ask you, what is he doing?"

"Following orders, Your Majesty. If they withdraw now I would hesitate to follow. It would be a trap. Let us leave this place. It serves no military purpose. The enemy can't leave here without our knowing. When they move we will be able to draw them to ground of our choosing. Fighting here is playing into Harbinger's hands. Making this an important place gives our actions more meaning than is good. This is only a place; a pretty difficult place for a fight at that. Let us find a better fight, Your Majesty."

"We want this place."

Renfrew pushed his head forward. He looked into the implacable eyes of Ranald. Renfrew dropped his upper body in defeat. Now was not the time to win this argument. Renfrew feared that the only way to win the argument was to see the battle well and truly lost.

"Do we know who commands the flanks, Your Majesty?" Renfrew asked the question in a dead voice.

"No. Immediately We will know. What else?"

"We could reconnoiter the river. Perhaps a water assault is possible, Your Majesty."

"We thought of that. We did not travel with boats. There is no time for building them."

"If we have enough soldiers who swim they could get themselves down the river after Darkfall. They could get behinds the lines taking out some of the enemy as they sleep. It could work, Your Majesty."

Ranald nodded. Swimming was not a widely held skill. He doubted they would find many soldiers who could. They wouldn't need many to reduce the other side by enough to make a difference to a concentrated attack on that flank.

"They could go during the dark. We could hit at dawn while the grisly discovery was being made. That has distinct possibilities." Ranald mulled the options allowed.

Renfrew faded back. He let the other advisors take over. He had tried and he had failed, again.

"Won't they be watching the river?" Stiefis asked in an undertone as the discussion of the plan progress with the advisors.

"It is hard to guard water. At night there are many opportunities; if we can find enough soldiers who can swim well. They will have to swim against the current. Only the strongest of swimmers will have any chance of making the destination." Renfrew spoke absently.

"If you feel the drawbacks are so great why did you suggest this?" Stiefis snapped his question.

"It's all I could think of to give us an edge. We don't need many to be successful. A few could severely damage the enemy."

"Do you think to win this battle?" Stiefis began to assess his soldiers' fates.

"I think to stay alive another day. If we don't win here our chances of surviving another Darkfall shrink. I realized something about myself not so very long ago: I want to live. That is all. I will do what I have to, to live. I don't have any higher goal that that."

"Wouldn't you have a better chance of survival across the plain?"

"Not since Tampello. My only hope is to stay with Ranald. Once he falls I am dead."

"He could kill you at any moment." Stiefis stated the obvious in a very low voice.

"Jeffeaux will have to kill me. Ranald may let me live. I can only hope for that."

"Do you swim?"

"No, I never learned that skill. My brother loved the sea. Not me. I prefer dry land."

"I did not hear that Marlin had died."

"He is as dead to me as I am to him."

Lady Zona was not sleepy. Even the attentions of her husbands could not tire her this night. Her nerves were stretched beyond sleep. She dragged Brir and Stea from bed. She looked at Wintraub's sleeping form. She left him in their bed. Stea took point. Brir stayed by her side.

"Wintraub will not look on this as a kindness." Brir pointed out to Lady Zona.

"One of us must be well rested tomorrow. He will know then I did not mean this as a kindness."

"It is a beautiful night for a walk. I could be happier if the moon were out now." Brir murmured into Lady Zona's ear.

"I was busy admiring you in the moonlight. Now I want to walk. We can check the pickets. That will be tiring."

"And boring." Brir huffed.

"At least we will be doing something useful with our time. I did not wish to study one more map or read one more report. I want to feel free of obligations for a few moments."

"And checking the picket lines will do this?" Brir questioned.

"While we are walking to them it will." A rock tapped lightly on Lady Zona's chest. She stopped. Her hand stopped Brir. He fell quiet and still. They waited until Stea approached. He was accompanied by a unit leader. Lady Zona knew the importance of this moment. There was an attempt by water. She could not see the color of the stones at night. The unit leader was tapping her arm in an abrupt code. Lady Zona had to concentrate fiercely to follow the series of taps.

It was a simple message. Swimmers, numbers unknown, some were being taken even now. There was no notion how many had escaped detection. Lady Zona did not think many had. There were not that many swimmers in Masfin. Still one could do damage. She had to spread the alarm without alerting Ranald she knew. So that meant not lighting the alert fires. They would be wet. At least there was that clue. She returned her attention to the waiting leader. She needed to tap a very concise message. She was even worse at tapping than she was at reading tappings.

She turned to Stea. She would send him to Harbinger. He would be fast and wary. She could trust him to get to Harbinger unharmed. Brir would guard her well enough. She had to send him briefly to get Wintraub. She didn't want her husband murdered in his sleep. She would remain with the unit leader until Brir returned. Stea did not hesitate. He ran into the dark of the night with a brief nod.

Stea dodged any contact in the dark. He had no time to spare. He wished his feet would sprout wings. Each moment he spent running he felt the responsibility of others' lives resting on his shoulders. He was very happy when he reached the gates of the city.

"Halt. Friend or foe?"

Stea had to think hard to recall the code phrase.

"Two suns cannot burn in the same sky."

"Friend, pass."

"There are infiltrators from the river. Beware."

"How will we know them?" The question was flung at Stea's disappearing back.

"They will be soaking wet."

Stea ran on. He reached the door of Harbinger's headquarters. Serjanus opened the door to his pounding. The stern face took in Stea's heaving sides and grim face.

"There have been prisoners taken on the riverbanks. We don't know if they were all taken or if any succeeded in getting by the sentries and the pickets."

Harbinger came into the light. She was drawing on her jacket.

"I told the sentry at the city gates. Lady Zona is spreading the word even now."

"Wake Jeffeaux." Harbinger pushed her helmet onto her head. She fastened the strap under her ear. Her husbands were stamping on boots and pulling on jackets. Harbinger became impatient while they waited. She looked at Stea.

"Sit a moment."

"I must return to my wife. She will be out hunting this infestation. It happened on her flank."

"Catch your breath. You will be no use to her exhausted. Brir and Wintraub are capable. Where is Jeffeaux?"

Vental spoke to the runner who had entered the room. He left quickly. Harbinger followed the interchange closely. She began to strap on her weapons. Her remaining husbands followed suit as they waited for their brother to return. Vental did not look happy when he returned.

"Where is Jeffeaux?"

"We can't find him. His cloak is gone as are his boots."

Harbinger glared at no one in particular. She rubbed the fingers of her right hand with her thumb.

"I want him found." Harbinger left the room so quickly that none of her husbands followed her. There was a moment of hesitation. Their instinct was to find her but her orders had been explicit. They had no choice. Stea watched the men fade into the night.

Jeffeaux wrapped his cloak more tightly against his body. He had often walked the camps at night. Now he felt a kinship with these soldiers who were striving so hard for him. Some of them died each day. Tomorrow some of the men and women he passed a word with now would be dead. He felt he owed these fine troopers his time. Tomorrow he would wait while they fought. Tonight he could walk while they waited.

There was a soft rustle to his right. Jeffeaux stopped walking. He tried to identify the sound. He felt a rush of air. Pain shot through his stomach as he was hit by a very solid force. Instinctively he pushed against the weight. He could not get a grip. His hands kept slipping. Whoever it was he was cold and wet. Jeffeaux jammed his arm against his opponent's throat. The move was effective for a moment. Then Jeffeaux saw stars as his ears rang from sharp blows. In the dark he could not see if his opponent had a weapon. He thought there must be a weapon involved. The arm was raising high.

Then the weight was gone. There was a thud as a heavy object fell. Jeffeaux remained still. He listened to his attacker fight for his life. There were grunts and thuds. There was the sickening sound of bones snapping.

"You all right?"

Harbinger's voice cut the night air. Jeffeaux moved towards the voice. He felt a hand brush his face.

"Whatever were you thinking walking around unattended like this?" The tone was hard, but the hands feeling him were gentle. They found his face and neck. Jeffeaux imagined those fingertips could see the welts rising on him

"We are at war. Even in the middle of your army you cannot be too safe. What would we have done if you had been killed? Even I am dispensable. Wind Rider would receive all the weight of my position. My army would follow her. But you, where would we be without King Jeffeaux?"

Harbinger had him standing. She was brushing his cloak off. She then began to straighten his clothes. Jeffeaux remained docile under her ministering.

"Do you think I have so many friends that I could easily afford to lose one?"

"I am sorry, Harbinger. I felt useless while everyone is fighting. At night I like to watch over their sleep."

"You are not useless. You are not useless." Harbinger closed the cloak tightly against the night air. She tucked her hand into Jeffeaux's elbow. "You are King. How could you be useless? Now I have a situation to report. Lady Zona has discovered enemies in the river. We are not sure how many escaped our notice or what their mission is. We do not want to sound the general alarm because we do not wish the enemy to know they are discovered. We will all have to be extra careful until we ascertain the extent of the infiltration."

Jeffeaux held her hand tightly against his waist. He drew air into his lungs with new appreciation. He had almost died. But for Harbinger, he would be dead.

"I will be certain not to go around unescorted."

"Very good idea."

"Do you think they came specifically for me?"

"They could not have known where you would be this night. He probably didn't even know who you were."

"We could ask him."

"If I hadn't killed him, but he fought like a madman. I had no choice, lest he cut me. I freely admit to avoiding metal cuts at all costs."

Jeffeaux understood her position. Since the war had started he had seen many die from sword wounds that turned deadly when they should have healed.

"There were prisoners taken."

"Yes, your mother sends word this is true."

"Then all is not lost."

Harbinger's mind began to work again. She listened to the noise of the camp. Occasionally a voice raised in communication.

"They will move against our right flank."

"If they assume their mission was successful." Jeffeaux swallowed his fear. "How can we be sure to capture them all?"

"As long as they remain wet they can't hide among us. I will admit this is one Darkfall I will be glad to see the end of. Once the sun comes up all the vermin will be revealed. We have no strangers in our ranks. Everyone knows someone else."

"Your buddy system is useful."

"Thank you. Here we are. I will have to send for my husbands. They are searching for you."

"You sent them all out to look for me?"

"You should feel honored."

"And chagrined, thank you for your concern."

"Just take better care of yourself."

"I promise. I will not put myself in such danger again."

"Good."

Jeffeaux saw Harbinger for the first time in the light of the torches outside the city gates. She would sport a bruise next the next day on her cheekbone. Even in the uncertain lighting he could see the swelling. His actions had brought her that injury. She would never hold it against him. He wanted to reach a hand to that spot, but he could not. He had almost lost his life for failing to bring a guard. He was rumpled and would be sore soon but she bore the mark of his disobedience.

"Forgive me for ignoring your good sense."

"Jeffeaux you never completely ignore my good sense. You eventually hear why I am saying what I am saying. I just fear for you that is all. I will admit I was very frightened for you this Darkfall. I'm just trying to keep you safe. I know you think I see danger in every flower that blooms but I don't overreact. Danger is all around us in this venture. Every step is along the edge of the precipice."

Jeffeaux noted that Harbinger had not called him your highness once this Darkfall. Since Delungor he had felt kingly and not thought of his titles in the abstract. It was pleasant to hear his name, the name he had chosen to keep along with his new title because he liked it so well and had worn it so long. He focused on that because he could not savor the feelings she roused as she admitted her fear for his life. He could not rejoice in the attachment she felt.

This was a new feeling. He had not felt it when he had been a ladies' man pursuing a new conquest. He did not feel it for his life's partner though he greatly respected and was deeply attached to his Royal Consort. He could not put a name to it. All he knew was that it was strong and bittersweet and deeply felt.

"If they are attacking again tomorrow I will need all my rest to endure the waiting."

"Sleep well Your Highness." Harbinger watched Jeffeaux return to his quarters. He looked rather dusty and tattered. She had not been a moment too soon.

Harbinger watched as her husbands filed into their rooms. They glanced at her in quiet expectation. Marjas had brought a cold compress for her swelling bruise. She accepted it without a word. Petron sighed. He signaled that he wished to speak. Harbinger looked him full in the face.

"He will not be unattended again."

Harbinger showed no extreme emotion. She sat wearily.

"I hope not. I would not be pleased to lose such an important component of this campaign through carelessness. The surest way to peace for Llwegania is Jeffeaux King in Masfin. An infant king with a regent would leave open too great a possibility of internal strife in Masfin which could lead to a restive border with Sarna which would disrupt peace in Llwegania. We have to set Jeffeaux safely on the throne. We can't lose everything because we failed to keep him alive while we had him in our care."

"You are right. I became complacent. It won't happen again."

"I know it won't. I trust you. I should have been watching more closely but I wasn't. I allowed other issues to distract me. I assumed that you would automatically take care of this for me. Wind Rider does take after me in this way; I do know it is a fault of mine, and I do try to verbalize everything. Jeffeaux is important. He must be guarded. Lady Junla's children are important. They must be guarded. Are we clear?"

"Yes, Harbinger."

"Since this infiltration was against our right flank, we must watch for an attempt there at first light. Send a report of tonight's events to Marlin, Wind Rider, and Lady Zona."

"Yes, Harbinger."

"Now I am going to lie down. I need to rest a moment before we begin again."

Petron felt his heart contract. He had failed his wife, his leader. He had been contemptuous of Jeffeaux. He had been jealous of the friendship Jeffeaux shared with Harbinger. He had placed Harbinger in jeopardy because he had failed a basic function of his position as Head of Harbinger's Personal Guard. The entire war effort could have been lost this Darkfall because he had failed a basic precaution of setting a discrete guard over Jeffeaux. Now he could not give Harbinger the comfort of his presence because his conscience would not let him rest his body until every detail was reviewed and covered.

Harbinger felt a hand shake her from a deep sleep. She opened her eyes immediately.

"They are massing for assault."

"Where?"

"The right flank."

Harbinger nodded. She sat slowly. Her head was pounding. Her face ached. She went to the dressing table. She splashed cold water on her face to clear her mind from the last vestige of sleep.

"I've been wondering since last night. Why did they attempt the right side? The left flank is more accessible. There is some coverage offered by vegetation at the foot of the mountain. We did not get to clear all of it away. They could have come fairly close. Easier than the water approach."

"The water approach held a greater element of surprise."

"True. Any more reports of infiltrators?"

"Twelve were taken on the riverbank. There was the one you killed plus three more were apprehended in the camp. That makes sixteen known infiltrators. We are questioning our prisoners now about more potential enemies in our ranks. "

"Have they said anything?"

"I don't think they have much to say. So far all they tell us is of their orders to kill as many as they could before capture or death."

"Fine. Where's my jacket?"

Rodznig held the article out to her. She thanked him with a swift peck. Then she left the room.

"Do you think they know who commands the flanks?"

"You would." Jeffeaux spoke as he joined Harbinger and Petron on the ramparts. Harbinger cast a quick look over him to assure herself that he was well.

"Are you comparing me to Ranald as a leader?"

"No, Harbinger. I would never do that." Jeffeaux spoke absently. He was busy noting the dark bruise that filled one side of her face. The swelling must be impairing her vision.

"Let them come. Wind Rider and Lady Zona will not be turned. Tell Marlin to be ready. Bring up the reserves on the right. Have Marlin ready to cover the center as well as the left. We will smash our enemies today."

"We can always retreat. We do not need to win today." Jeffeaux was suddenly anxious for everyone's safety.

"We might not. We do not need to retreat. As long as we deny Ranald Reduni, we win. We do not need to chase him away. We can endure any siege. He can't mount one. He will have to retire from the field soon. He should have already. I don't plan to bring you his head today."

"That's a relief." Jeffeaux noticed that Harbinger was not dressed for battle. Her helmet and gloves were nowhere in sight. Her weapons did not hang on her body.

"You do not go out?"

"No, I will be vulnerable on one side. This battle I will have to rely totally on my army. My husbands are very relieved. I love battle you know. I hate inactivity. I have to wait for my orders to be relayed. I have to wait to see how my decisions impact the battle. I can't act. I have to be still. I hate it."

"I thought you loved peace."

"I think I do. I love the idea of it. I have never experienced it."

"Once there is peace there will be no more battles."

"That is the general idea, yes."

"I'll never understand you."

"Sometimes you have to make choices in life. The easy choices are those that are similar. I love battle. I love the adrenalin. I love the rush. I love the camaraderie. I love the maneuvering. I love the planning, the execution, the inspiration, and the unexpected happenings. It is so exciting and so engaging. It takes all my skills and talents and senses and mind to fight a war. Peace is a state of discovery. Its strangeness is appealing. Its possibilities are intriguing."

"You can't have both."

"I know. Someday I will fight my last battle. Like this. There will be other battles but they will be dreary. They will be done in shadows and back halls. They will lack the pageantry and spectacle of this. Look at the spread of soldiers and horses and machinery. See how the arms gleam in the rising sun. You will tell your grandchildren of these times someday. They won't really understand what is happening now. It will seem like a story you made up. You will never be able to express the real breadth of this and they will suspect you of exaggerating." Harbinger turned away from Jeffeaux. She looked across the day at her opponent. "They will never understand how war affects people. They will think you paint Ranald crueler than he really is to justify your actions.

"That is what went wrong when I first came to Masfin. The Masfin people had not known war in a long time. Your generals would not believe me. The people could not understand how completely devastating military strife is. They had not made sacrifices. They tried to translate our experience with their view of reality. You have to experience war to understand what motivates people who are in the middle of it. How can you second guess what the participants should do when you have not faced loss or fear or pain?

"Everyone on all sides now knows what war costs and what they are willing to do when faced with devastation. These lessons will be lost in our grandchildren's time. Hopefully the lessons of peace will be stronger and better."

Jeffeaux stared at her tense back.

"You are very morose today, Harbinger. We could argue about my mother for a while. That should cheer you up."

Harbinger laughed softly. She nodded. "Yes, let us discuss what title you will bestow on her husbands as recognition of their efforts on behalf of Masfin."

"Titles? I don't think so. I am trying to come up with titles that will be acceptable for their role in my mother's life. We can pass on any formal titles."

"I don't know. They deserve something for their efforts. They have kept your mother safe and happy."

Wind Rider held the stone lightly. She looked out across the flat terrain that fronted her lines. The left flank was the more sensible approach. It afforded some cover. But they were coming to her. She could see them coming in their beautiful straight lines.

"Have our reserves ready to come up."

"Are we to wheel?"

"No, not yet, but I want to be ready. Ah, there you are. Well met, commanders. It is a good day to fight. The enemy is coming to us. Harbinger's forces will attack once we fully engage the enemy. If the enemy turns we will follow. The reserves are coming up now to hold this flank. Commanders, the reserve must hold this position to the last. You may not be turned. No matter what, you must hold this ground. If we wheel, when the stone goes out we rejoin the lines in the center. Then we will return to our position. If the enemy does not turn, if the enemy retreats or continues to advance we hold our positions. Is this clear?"

"Yes."

"Good. Lady Zona will command if we wheel. I will command the field. May the gods of fortune shine on us this day."

Lady Zona nodded to Wind Rider. She had read the report with relief that no one had come to real harm. Not no one, the enemy had lost some men. She suspected that once the chain was raised from the river there would be at least one body tangled in the smaller chains that hung down from it. She was roused from her thoughts by a call.

"Here they come."

"Archers and darters to your positions. Don't waste ammunition. Wait for your shots."

Lady Zona listened to the sounds of the battle, the small noises of commands and motions. In the distance she could hear the larger noises of catapults being readied and horses thundering. She left the staging area.

"Bring me my horse." Lady Zona spoke clearly, calmly as if preparing for a ride in the country. She would be nervous later, once everything was done. At night in her bed she would shiver at what she did this day. It always hit her like that. Afterward she would break down. Now she could not think of the death or the danger, all she could see were problems to solve and issues to resolve.

Renfrew waited for word from the front. From his position all he could see were clouds of dust. He had to rely totally on runners from the battlefield for his information. He did not even know if the night raid had been successful or if it had made no impact.

"General, General, we are attacked in the rear."

"What?"

"The rear sends: We are under attack."

"It would take time to turn to face the enemy. They cannot be many. We are already engaged on the front. The rear must take care of itself."

Renfrew felt his head pound. He wanted to wade into the battle. He would rather face an enemy's sword than remain at headquarters making choices that ranged from bad to worse. He looked up as King Ranald entered.

"What is the news?"

"We have engaged the enemy on their right flank. Our rear is under attack, Your Majesty."

"Their left flank has left its position?"

"I do not know. I only know that they have sent forces to engage us, Your Majesty."

"Their left flank must be exposed."

"They could have sent forces from the middle to reinforce that position or they could have enough troops to field the attack while maintaining their positions, Your Majesty."

""That flank must be vulnerable."

"Our Horse does not send that report. They are silent on this issue, Your Majesty."

"They could have already turned the left flank. They could be engaged behind enemy lines right now. Turn the army to engage the attackers at the rear. We will chase them, overrun them, *destroy* them."

"Your Majesty, by the time we turn it could be too late."

"Then we had better do it now."

"Yes, Your Majesty."

Renfrew stared at the stern face. He gestured a runner to him. He could hardly say the words that would spell disaster. Under the glowering eye of his King, Renfrew spit out the order.

Lady Zona watched the troops stream into the field. She shifted in her saddle. They were away. She held her mind steady. She could do this. It was a terrible thing but she could order soldiers to their deaths.

She sat on a small rise. In the bright sun she watched as Ranald's forces realized their dilemma. She saw the entire army hesitate. She could see what Masfin's forces could not. She could see Marlin's soldiers melt into Reduni to join the center forces. She could watch Wind Rider's fighters push the Masfin army to the center. She could see when the Masfin army shifted to face Wind Rider. Then Wind Rider joined the center. Lady Zona was busy issuing orders to brace her troops for the possible renewed attack. She did not see how small the Masfin force had become. She did not see the center pour its rain of arrow and fire on the attackers that milled on the open field before the city. When she was able to give attention to the battlefield she saw the stream of mounted fighters stream from Reduni to wield death with every blow on the hapless Masfin army. Foot soldiers ran in every direction as rabble.

Jeffeaux surveyed the carnage from his position. He hoped that this would hasten an end to the conflict that was consuming his people. He hoped his mother was alive. He hoped they were finished fighting for a time. There had been enough death over the past several days. But if it meant this war would be over all the sooner he would urge the battle continue.

Renfrew gathered his forces. He did not send for the King. He looked at Stiefis.

"We have to leave now. Any delay will mean an end for this endeavor. We must take as much of the army that is left and flee. Then we will regroup."

"Where do we go?"

Renfrew scanned a map. He shoved it aside. He glanced at a couple more before one appealed to him.

"Here, we go here."

Stiefis committed the site to memory. He left in a swish of the tent flap. Renfrew followed close on his heels. Runners scurried to catch fleeing troops.

"Where are you going?"

Renfrew did not spare Ranald a glance. He spoke over his shoulder.

"We need to regroup Your Majesty. I have ordered the army to a safe place to recover from this engagement before attacking again."

Ranald stood in the dust. He watched his defenses fleeing the field. He saw them slow as the runners spread the word. At least they all began to run in the same direction. On the field all that was left were bodies. In the distance he could see the walls of Reduni. It looked untouched. His living soldiers had abandoned the field. He had to abandon the dead soldiers to the field.

"Where is Our horse?"

"Here sire."

It was hard to accept defeat when he had never had to face it before. He had faced loss but not defeat. He had believed that the enemy would never fight to the end. He had been wrong. She had stayed, and in staying she had won. She could have won anytime. She simply had chosen to leave before. What was she after this time? Was the Sarn right? Had she been playing with him for all this time? How had she known to come to Reduni? Who had betrayed him? He couldn't trust anyone. His officers were useless. Maybe they secretly wished Jeffeaux king. He had to make sure his army was led by those loyal only to him. How could he be sure?

Tampello had failed. She had taken those prisoners easily. The only way to be certain was to kill all traitors. He would have them executed at first light each day; an appropriate way to start the day. He would start with the officers who had known about this current mission. The ones who had ridden with the message; they were the weak link. He needed someone to watch them to see who had broken ranks. He would take care of that first thing.

Renfrew watched the night sky. He stared in the direction of Reduni. He wondered if there was a force planning to march. He wondered if his wife was safe. He wondered if the boy was safe.

"What is wrong, Renfrew?" Stiefis spoke from Renfrew's left
"The horizon; there are no stars."

"They are burning their dead." Stiefis answered absently.

"They burn their dead?" Ranald's appalled tones entered the discussion.

Stiefis turned to face Ranald. He had not heard the King ride up to them.

"Yes, Your Majesty." Stiefis bowed as he answered.

"What barbarians," Ranald sniffed.

"They burn the bodies until the flesh is gone. Then they dowse the fires. The bones are taken away."

"Very horrible." Ranald's eyes grew round in distress.

"It is very warm in Llwegania. The flesh turns putrid quickly. When you have to carry the dead a far distance it is healthy to carry just the bones Your Majesty."

"And where do they carry these bones?"

"I don't know, Your Majesty. I only know away."

"Bizarre people," Ranald made his final proclamation on the subject.

Stiefis remained quiet. He watched the horizon in silent respect for the dead. There was nothing to say; nothing to do but wait.

"Where will they go now, I wonder?" Ranald stared at the far horizon as if it would yield him an answer.

"She will go to Delungor, Your Majesty." Stiefis answered absently. He had no doubt about her actions. He came from a deeply religious people. He knew what he would do. He knew Harbinger understood the power and politics of religion very well.

"It would be for nothing."

"She will go, Your Majesty. That is the logical step to take in her campaign."

"There is nothing there worth fighting for now."

Stiefis swallowed. He could not say too much without implying an insult to Ranald. "We could harry their advance."

"It would give Delungor meaning. Meaning which We just stripped from it. She will move again. Then We will strike."

"As you wish, Your Majesty." Renfrew answered shortly. He did not wish Stiefis to become too involved with Ranald even in a casual conversation. There were too many pitfalls for the Queen's ex-lover to fall into while talking with the King.

"We will have some time to rebuild our arms stores and to let the wounded heal. We will have to choose our next battlefield very carefully. The time will not be wasted, Your Majesty."

"We do not need to go to Delungor, Harbinger."

"Yes, we do, King Jeffeaux. It has been desecrated. It needs to be mourned and rededicated. The country will rise up to support you. You deserve their support. Ranald will gain no new recruits. Who would join him now? The regular people are tired of war. They cannot take much more suffering. You have to assure them that a return to their normal lives is close. We go to Delungor. We establish a border. We push that border until we squeeze Ranald into a corner we choose. But first we go to Delungor. You must heal this country if you are to rule. That healing begins at Delungor. You worry about rebuilding Masfin. It begins now. I will worry about fighting the war. Are we clear, Your Highness?"

"You are a managing woman."

"I take that as a compliment. Now you have a meeting with the city council. I have a meeting with the scouts."

"Do I get to have any impact on this campaign?"

"As long as you agree with me." Harbinger spoke with a very straight face. Jeffeaux could see her bruise clearly from this angle. The sight cut short any words of disagreement. "Of course you do, Your Highness. We will meet this very Darkfall to discuss the military plans I make today. You can point out all my shortcomings then. Why don't you want to go to Delungor?"

Jeffeaux smiled without humor. She always went right to the heart of the matter. There was no avoiding an answer. She would haunt him until he replied.

"If they had not supported my claim the residents there would still be alive."

"Guilt is a useless emotion. It produces no real results or positive action. It controls you and gives you weakness."

"It is very real and strong. It creates bonds and debts."

"It is useless. It is rooted in the past. What good is it? How does it build for the future? Everyone makes mistakes, errors in judgment. You learn from them. They are the lessons life gives you. No one can see into the future. If you do something so wrong that it can't be fixed or forgiven there are legal actions that mete out punishment. Once you face up to your punishment, accept responsibility for your actions, it's over. You can't carry your past into the future. Its weight will suffocate the future. You recognize your mistakes. You deal with them. You move on."

"Everything is not that simple. If not for guilt people will continue to do wrong things."

"People should not do wrong things because they choose to not do wrong things because doing wrong things is *wrong*. We weren't talking about that. We were talking about mistakes which lack malice and forethought. Going to Delungor was not a mistake. You did nothing wrong. Ranald killed those people. He **chose** to do that."

"He wouldn't have chosen to kill them if I hadn't gone there."

"You chose to go to Delungor. You were not wrong. They chose to support you. They were not wrong. Ranald chose to kill them. That was wrong. Ranald's choice does not make the choices of others that came before wrong.

"Ranald killed them. He always had the capacity and inclination to make that choice. How could you let him control people's lives? Not going to Delungor would have been the wrong choice. Those poor souls would still be alive, but Ranald would still be King. That would be a worse choice."

"So, they are a justifiable sacrifice?"

"No, if we had known that Ranald would do such a thing we would have made better choices about their protection. We protected Reduni at great cost and for no real strategic reason."

Jeffeaux nodded wordlessly. He could not let go of his guilt completely. It had been his constant companion since he had heard of the slaughter of the mendicants. He sat wearily.

"I will ask the Cleric of Reduni to accompany me to Delungor."

"Good idea. Any other needs you let me know: I will see then filled. Now I need to review scouting reports and establish a front that will push Ranald to a place of containment for the winter."

"You like to punish your enemies with winter."

"I hate being cold and wet and dirty and tired and hungry and sick. I can't imagine my opponents would like that state any better."

"You equate winter with all those things?"

"Winter creates those conditions more easily than any other season and better than many locations. I need to know how large Masfin's navy is."

"Why? You never mentioned this before."

"This is the first time we will fight near the ocean. We have been fighting an inland war. A navy could impact my ability to contain and control Ranald's moves."

"I don't think we can build a navy by spring."

"Of course not. We could secure harbors, destroy docking facilities, things of that nature. We could push Ranald to a place where the navy would continue to be useless."

"This is a very busy river port. I will ask the council here if they have any helpful information or contacts."

"Good. See, you will be involved."

"Another such winter as the one at Tampello will be cruel punishment on the rank and file."

"If Ranald has any sense he won't allow us to push him to another such place."

"We are back to taking responsibility for one's own choices."

"Very good, you impress me."

"I have to make that meeting."

"Very well, Your Highness."

Chapter 19

Stiefis wondered if there was an end to marching. They had marched until he could not remember what it felt like to sleep in a real house in a real bed. He wondered if there could be an end to fighting and marching before his lungs became engrained with dust and grime. He could feel his body aging and his spirit breaking. There would be nothing left of him soon.

Their patron was becoming strange. He did not look like a person anymore to Stiefis. Stiefis wondered if his perception was filtered by his emotional response to the policies Ranald enacted. He could not see Ranald as a person anymore. All he saw was the butcher of Delungor and the merciless tyrant who woke each day to the spectacle of bloodletting.

Delungor was not even a Sarnese holy place but its desecration ranked in importance to Stiefis with the burning of Deskersai; perhaps even higher, if Stiefis were honest with himself. The Temple of Kersai still stood. The priests had not been murdered even though Stiefis now suspected they deserved punishment for their generations of control. Delungor had been an innocent holy place. It was holy in and of itself because so many people had worshipped in it. Such devotion invested holiness in certain places. The innocent blood Stiefis had seen shed there consecrated the place beyond doubts.

He wanted to go home to his wife. Stiefis was startled by the thought. He searched his heart. He was tired. He was tired of making choices between horrible and terrible fates. He was tired of fighting a losing war. He wanted to stand in the quiet of a place that provided peace and comfort. He wanted to surrender to the one person in the swirl of this insanity who had some answers and power. He wanted to go home to his wife.

He couldn't; not yet. He couldn't abandon his troops and family to Ranald's wrath. And Ranald would be wrathful if even one Sarnese soldier crossed over to the other side. The only thing that stayed Ranald's hand from his allies was their unswerving devotion to the cause.

Stiefis would find no peace knowing what punishment he caused his troops and family and friend. Renfrew would be dead the moment Ranald heard of Stiefis' defection. So Stiefis sat on his horse breathing the dust of late summer. Soon they would have to find a den to hole up in for the winter.

Pelsen fell asleep each night to the words he had heard in battle. He muttered them under his breath as he sharpened his sword. The rasp of the metal against the wet stone seemed a good undertone for the words. He knew Ranald was mad. Everyone knew it. Every morning the proof was spilled onto Masfin's breast.

Pelsen had joined the army two years before The Shaking. He had left his family's farm with the plan to find his fortune and place in the world through the army. He had liked army life before The Shaking. He had liked the structure and clarity of the regiment.

Then The Shaking had destroyed his predictable life. The years of war had destroyed all the things Pelsen had valued. His plans, his certainty had gone up in smoke just as his family's farm had burned to the ground leaving him no place to go, nothing to do but soldier on.

He knew the King had to die. He could not do it alone but he did not know whom he could trust. There was no one to trust except himself. He needed an opportunity. That was all. A window of opportunity to strike a single blow. But the King was surrounded by his Palace Guard at all times.

The words he had overheard in battle presented Pelsen with an idea. They implied a line of action that even the speaker could not have meant to imply. They implied the Queen was an unfaithful wife. Pelsen knew he was easy on the eye. Ladies had sought him out since he had first realized that girls were not the enemy. He could use his looks to his advantage, if he could catch the eye of the queen.

If she fell for him then she was no innocent. She would be as deserving of death as Ranald. He would have no compunction killing her. Even the child had to die. If she was Ranald's daughter she could not live to spread his madness to another generation. If she wasn't Ranald's daughter, well that was the price she would pay. She would be an innocent victim but Pelsen could not afford to take a chance. They all had to die, if the queen succumbed to him.

Pelsen planned his approach carefully. He would not be too obvious. He had to develop a rapport with every Palace Guard he met. He had to find good reasons to pass near the Queen's entourage as they traveled. He would manage. Too much rode on his actions for him to fail.

The hard part would be finding an ally. He had to do this without betraying himself to the list makers. That would be more difficult than getting into the Queen's bed. He would establish himself in the bed first. Then he would wait for an opportunity to strike.

Sablor looked at the terrain. It was completely passable now. He had enough experience with mountains and winter to know that in several weeks there would be snow. That snow would fall until the sides of the pass now visible would be under several feet of impassable white blockade material. One side of the peninsula had a natural harbor. Their guides assured him that once the snow began the harbor would be useless. It would freeze completely during the heart of the winter. In his naiveté Sablor suggested the frozen harbor could create a highway for Ranald's army to escape.

Sablor could still hear the echoes of laughter in his mind.

"We would secure the heights, so some of our troops would be exposed to the dangers of this region."

"You will have the advantage of our cooperation. With that there will be little hardship. We live very well here."

Sablor turned his mount to face the general direction of the harbor. He could not see the water from his vantage point but he knew it was there.

"Is the harbor frozen for a long period of time?"

"No, it doesn't freeze completely for long. Blocks of ice are moved by the rough sea for most of the winter. Any ships would be ground by the ice, not blocked."

"So which becomes passable first: the mountains or the sea?"

"It depends on whom you ask. Freighters who make a living hauling overland claim the mountains. Shipping captains claim the sea."

"So we will have to cover two avenues of escape at the same time."

Sablor turned to Marjas. He did not like the position but it did fit the requirements. The climate was harsh. The area was contained: it had only one small stretch of beach that skirted the mountains on one side.

"We will have all winter to deal with the sea escape route. We can solve that issue." Marjas was assessing the walls of the pass. He liked the setup nature had created. "We would not need many archers to secure the mountain passes. We get the ships out of the harbor before Ranald arrives. During the winter we secure ships and captains so they do not make an attempt to rescue Ranald come spring."

"Seafaring people are a strange lot." The chief guide spoke up roughly.

"Not unreasonable we shall hope. Harbinger does not deal well with unreasonable people."

Sablor turned his mount again until he faced the group of guides. He drew on his familiarity with Masfin traditions and lore.

"Who comes with us to offer your services to King Jeffeaux? Who speaks for your people to the King? Who gives the oath that binds as King Jeffeaux is bound to Masfin and her children?"

Marjas watched the faces reluctantly form into expressions of awe. There was magic in words. The tone Sablor used was stern and deep; a studied voice that was different from his normal speaking voice.

"So, Your Highness, we will need that navy after all."

Jeffeaux looked up at Harbinger's entrance. He adjusted his jacket to cover his shirt completely. Since she had killed to save his life, Jeffeaux was uncomfortable around Harbinger unless he was fully dressed. He did not know what exactly he felt the need to armor against; certainly he had no fears about her intentions towards him.

"You are planning a naval action?"

"I am sorry. I have been thinking so much on this that I am starting in the middle of the conversation. There is a possibility Ranald might attempt to escape from our advance over water in the spring. So we need to be able to deny him that venue."

Jeffeaux looked at the map of the most recent campaign. He did not see any large bodies of water near any of the reported movements. Harbinger studied his face then glanced at the table.

"Not now, come spring."

Jeffeaux looked Harbinger in the eye. "You have chosen a direction in which to push Ranald."

"Yes, Marjas and Sablor are on their way back. They are bringing a contingent of mountain people who wish to swear to you and your throne. I am a little concerned about security but Marjas feels they are sincere. We will learn what we can from them in case they become a threat later."

"You do see danger in every flower."

"Some flowers are poisonous to smell, to eat, to touch."

"Most are harmless."

"Anyway, considering the position of Ranald's army at this point, the number of weeks left until winter sets in, the geographical possibilities, Marlin feels the Takinga Peninsula would be a possible objective."

"Everyone in Masfin knows the reputation of that place. Ranald will not be as easily fooled into going there as he was about Tampello."

"True, we don't plan on tricking him this time. We will give him no other option for movement. We will chase him there until he is caught."

"You plan to drive him before you like animals to slaughter."

"It's a better alternative than having him chase us there and being trapped there with him."

"What if he doesn't go there?"

"The war will last that much longer. Let us try to get him there."

"You are right. I will be at Delungor until you have established your winter headquarters."

"It is a fine defensible position."

"I have to establish some normalcy in Masfin. The day to day administration needs to be set up. The courts have to return to their schedules."

"I am not arguing your decision. You are right in everything. Despite what my peers would like to say I have not neglected my domestic duties. I think Delungor is an appropriate choice for your capital city."

Jeffeaux sighed in frustration. He hated feeling that he had to justify every decision and choice to those who knew him best.

"I don't understand your insecurity, Jeffeaux. You have good sense. You have made a choice based on that good sense. What's the issue here?"

"I will always be Jeffeaux."

"No, you are King Jeffeaux. Forgive me for forgetting the courtesies your actions deserve. We lack such a position in my culture so I am remiss in my duties to Your Highness through my lack of experience." Harbinger stepped back a pace from Jeffeaux. She bowed very correctly. "Lady Zona and Marlin will be leading the campaign to liberate the coastal communities. They will negotiate the surrender of the Masfin navy. They will also attempt to win over the Masfin merchant fleet or if all else fails they will commandeer or destroy all ships they can find. I will be leading the forces chasing Ranald's armed forces. We will send reports regularly to Delungor. Does this meet with Your Highness' approval?"

"Yes, Harbinger, I am very confident Lady Zona, Marlin and you will be thorough and determined in your efforts."

"Thank you, Your Highness. I wish you a safe journey."

Jeffenza was bored. She had spent weeks and months riding from one end of Masfin to the other. She spent her time eating, sleeping, riding…horses. There was no court to speak of, there was no gossip, and there was no entertainment. No one dared to upset her husband. Few dared to come close enough for her to pass the time. They feared to come to her husband's notice in any way, even by way of her.

She was completely alone. She had no options but to spend her time with her daughter and her daughter's nurse. She hated that child. It ran free. It was cossetted and pampered. It had toys and games and joys. It did not suffer from boredom because it knew no better. As long as it was fed and had its nurse the girl was happy. Jeffenza did not understand how people could admire the child.

She had to listen to endless compliments on the child's looks and good-nature. She did not understand why everyone assumed she would be gratified by their pleasure in the child. Someone was coming; time to paste a fond expression on her face. It was only an officer attached to the Command. She paid him no attention. He was ranked way below her notice.

"Queen Jeffenza, forgive the intrusion."

Jeffenza sent a cool glance his way.

"It is time to move out."

Jeffenza nodded. She waited for the man to leave. He did not. He appeared to be waiting for something.

"You Majesty, for your own safety, I have been given the honor of personally escorting you to your mount."

Trying to control her were they? They would see. She went only when it pleased her to move. She sat as the nurse packed the child up. They left her alone in the clearing with the officer. Jeffenza sent a regally frigid look at the waiting officer. Her eyes were snared by the intense expression in his. They seemed to devour her. She felt completely undressed and even mounted in that look. She moved away from that look towards where she knew the horses would be waiting.

She encountered that look often. It seemed everywhere she turned those eyes ensnared her. She had been chased by men before and had been caught. She had chased men and had caught them. Being married to a man who executed those of questionable loyalty each morning had reduced her chasing activities to nothing. There was now an added edge of danger to the chase. It pleased her.

She looked for those eyes so she could ignore them. She sought the officer out so she could cut him dead. She conducted her flirtation under the very nose of her dangerous husband.

Pelsen was happy. He had wondered if he would be able to complete his plan. When he had formulated the plan he had not thought. Not until he had stared into those haughty eyes had he realized there might have been a problem. But there was not. Her imperious air begged for taming and his body was eager to do that taming. Each swish of her skirt as she flounced away from him urged his inner devil on. He would have her spread beneath him begging. And when the time was right, he would douse the cruel flame in her eye himself.

Now that he was certain of his entire plan, he needed to establish confederates in his plot to kill the king. He had to prepare the way more gently than he would need to tread to reach the Queen's bed.

All he had to do was start a rumor. The whispers would gain power and he could watch for the ones who reacted best to the idea by watching their responses to the whispers. The current policy of purging would equally hamper and help him. It would engender the feelings he needed to develop the plot but it would strike fear into many hearts. Well, this was not a proposition for the weak of spirit. They would immediately be weeded out of consideration. Only the most determined would remain.

Pelsen watched the movements of the diners. The meal was breaking up. He was done waiting. He would cement his position in the royal household this night. Right now.

Jeffenza felt the hard hand grab her arm. She felt her scream cut off at the mouth as an equally hard hand covered her lips. She opened her mouth to bite but stopped when she was swung around to face her captor. She looked into the face which was as beautiful as hers in the same way. She glared into the cold eyes but did not bite. She wondered where she was. In the light of the single taper all she could see was that face as it floated in the dark.

No words passed between them. She did not care. All she wanted was to feel the exquisite slid of his muscles against her skin. She undressed under his fierce gaze with a growing tension. She felt his eyes follow her movements in the dim light. She stood unselfconscious while he stared at her. He did not reach to touch her. Just his gaze on her tightened her senses until her teeth ached. She clenched her thighs and the core of her passion began to tingle. Her lungs began to draw uneven breaths. Her diaphragm was not sure how to work. Still he stared at her. She had to relieve her growing tension. She shifted. Still he stared at her. Well she could take care of things. She gripped her breasts and pinched her nipples to agony. She pushed against her hip bones until they ached. She raised her leg to rest her foot on the chair that held her clothes. One hand gripped the back of the chair as her other found the slick folds of her sex. She pushed two of her fingers against her marvelously aroused spot. She rubbed and plucked until her body shivered with anticipation. She never lowered her gaze. He was staring into her eyes and yet he never moved. She was so close. She gathered her fingers to finish when he finally moved.

He grabbed her wrists. In one move he had her turned and pressed tightly to him back to front. He was free from his clothes. He shoved her fingers into her. Then he bent her forward. He pushed and pulled her fingers in and out of her body. She felt his member rubbing along the seam of her buttocks. Her juices flowed along her fingers and her seam and him. Then he was pushing, pushing a finger from his free hand into her there. She clenched every muscle in her ass. Still the finger did not stop. Slowly it pulled out. A second joined it in the next inward push. His fingers and her fingers drove her pleasure until she began to mule in pleasure. Then his fingers left and his long, thick, hard tallywacker covered in the juice from her honeyed passage breeched her. Slowly he moved into her. She keened. She shoved back against him. She felt his testicles slap her seam. Her back arched as she reached a glorious wondrous peak. Never had she come so hard. This was what she had been looking for to ease her boredom.

Pelsen stared at the closed door where minutes before Jeffenza had passed. She was no innocent. He rubbed a particularly sore spot on his chest. When the time came he would feel no compunction killing her. She had shown no hesitation, no shyness, she was a bold adventuress who did not deserve any softer considerations.

Jeffenza leaned against the closed door for a sweet moment before walking sedately down the hall. She wanted to laugh aloud. She had looked for her match in other countries and in royal bedrooms. To imagine he had been hiding in the officer corps the entire time. She was pleasantly sore in places she had not known were all the right places until this very day.

Harbinger rubbed her face wearily. None of her Estates bordered on an ocean. She had no idea how to conduct a war with the added ingredient of water threat. She didn't understand the impact or possibilities of naval engagements. The numbers and sizes of ships did not seem impressive to her. But, what did she know about this?

She understood about controlling harbors in that she knew about controlling centers of activity. How did you deny a ship the use of harbors? You couldn't drain them of water or shut the door on them.

Her head was spinning with information from harbormasters and sea captains. Marlin and Lady Zona were no help. Jeffeaux was at Delungor.

"Wittlar."

"I am here."

"Come closer, my love."

"I know that tone of voice, Wife." Wittlar sat next to Harbinger. He felt her hand descend on his arm.

"I have a very special project for you."

"You don't fool me, Wife."

"I'm in a quandary and need rescuing."

"What is your will, Harbinger?"

"I need an expert on the use of ships and water in war."

"Where do you expect to find such a person?"

Harbinger began to stroke Wittlar's arm gently.

"Sweet Wittlar, you have always been an avid student of battle tactics."

"Sablor is the scholar in our marriage."

"You will do this very well. I need battle strategies, defense strategies, everything. Priests can be very useful in researching things. Ask Lady Junla if you can borrow her priest to help you."

Wittlar looked down at the mystery of ships and harbors that had so frustrated Harbinger.

"You found this very boring, Wife, didn't you? That is why you are passing it off to me."

"It is impossible for one person to know everything. I can know where to look for answers. I need someone who will provide me with the answers to the questions I have.
That is your job."

"I am honored, Wife." The tone belied the words. Harbinger grinned. She rose quickly from the table. She fairly danced from the room. Wittlar turned his head from side to side surveying the piles of reports and charts and books.

"I will need my own priest." Wittlar's voice halted Harbinger at the doorway. "I don't want a priest really. I need my own scholar. I need someone who reads Masfin already. I don't have time for any Sarnese priest to be learning to read a new language. There must be scholars in Masfin. I am willing to make an educated guess here: Lady Zona's priests are the exception rather than the rule. I don't have the time that Lady Junla spent training her priest."

Harbinger stared blankly at Wittlar. She had very few dealings with religious people. She did not think of them very often. Now she had an issue. She knew how many people had been in Sarna prior to her invasion. The records from the Temple at Deskersai had been invaluable to her. She had continued to gather census numbers from First. She had been able to extrapolate how many Sarnese soldiers had fled Sarna based on battle dead from the battle before Deskersai. She knew everything about the Sarnese except the priests. The only firm numbers she had were the four who rode with her army.

She was annoyed at herself for overlooking such a detail. She was not happy that no one had brought up the issue to her. Mostly she did not like not knowing the number.

"I wonder where all the priests are."

"I said I didn't want a priest after all. I need a Masfin scholar."

Harbinger looked blankly at Wittlar.

"For the special project you gave me: the study of nautical things, battles, the like."

"Oh yes, you need a local scholar. Or not so local. There was a University at Reduni. Get a scholar from there. One should be glad to come. The priests, the Sarnese priests, from the temples and the estates, I need to know where they are."

"Of course, Wife."

First stood at the window of her rooms. She watched the children race in the yard. They were concentrating on developing coordination and following directions. It was endless joy for First to see all those children swarming. She turned her attention back to the missive in her hand.

Fourth sat on the other side of the space. She was busy sorting requests for First to attend village festival dates. First shook her head thoughtfully.

"Harbinger wants an accounting of the priests of Kersai."

"The four she has aren't enough?"

"She wants to know how many are still in Sarna and how many in Masfin."

"Why would she need that information?"

"I have no idea."

"They are no use to her if they won't work willingly."

"Harbinger wants to know for her own reasons. I could guess that she simply wants to know. A minor detail she noticed and has decided needs investigating. She will now have some use for a priest in particular, or the information in general."

"Perhaps Lady Zona is looking for a new husband."

First laughed lightly. "He will have to be young and strong to follow the campaign trail with her."

First stared into a distant place. A frown gathered on her face.

"I never considered it until this very moment. Where would I look for a priest? The household ones I assume went into Masfin with the soldiers and Wardens, but the temple priests, where did they go?"

Fourth placed her work to one side. She drew a finger along her cheek in thought.

"There were, let me see if I remember correctly. One hundred plus four in the temple at Deskersai. There were six lesser temples which each house fifty plus two. The only priests that I remember are the four who are with Harbinger."

"I will start with the four hundred and twelve temple priests. Then Harbinger must have the number of household priest from before the war. They must all be in Masfin. Priests always rode out on raids, that was the main function of a household priest."

"But where to begin to look?"

"They won't be hard to distinguish. I'll have the search start near the temples. They are closed, but I think some of the priests would have remained nearby their temples. It's a place to start."

"Do you personally go?"

"No. Maybe; I wouldn't want it to seem as if we were hunting them down for punishment. Despite the horrible things the priests did they were an important part of our culture. I wouldn't want to set the people against Harbinger because I was disrespectful to the priests. I will ride with the search parties to reassure the village Headmen of our intentions."

"That sounds fair enough. Better treatment than they deserve, perhaps."

First ordered her private guard ready for march. She slept dreamlessly the night before her venture. With the new day she rode out of the Estate.

She rode with pleasure during the day and the journey. She loved to see the changes that blossomed in Sarna with every journey she took. She was a familiar sight in all of Sarna. Her colors were recognized in every village. She would have marriages and children to honor all along her route.

She became concerned about something, some indefinable thing that nagged at her as she rode. Her greeting was the same as always. Her parting was the same as always. It was that moment when she stated her quest that gave her pause. The very mention of priests created an enclosed moment of otherness that defied explanation.

They never questioned her. She did not feel threatened or that her position was weakened but her asking created a division between her and her hosts for a moment. Then the moment would pass and she was once again one with them.

At the third temple site she was presented with a priest. He was subdued and docile. He went with her without question. She could not tell his age. He did not speak. He was not disrespectful. He simply did not speak. He obeyed orders but never spoke. First sent him back to the Estate while she continued her journey.

Second received the priest into the house with little fanfare. She dressed him in laborers clothing then set him to work in the gardens. She set a watch over him at all times. At night she had him secured in a comfortable but locked room.

"He reminds me of someone."

"I know." Third was doing an inventory with Sixth. They were preparing the storerooms for the new harvest. They were inventorying the goods, bringing forward the old stock at the same time.

"He is almost like the prisoners that came from Tampello."

"He won't answer any questions. He is polite and cooperative, but he is not with you even when he is standing right in front of you."

"Maybe he's just blessed by the Battle Maid."

"They couldn't be priests if they were blessed by the Battle Maid."

"True, Kersai would refuse them. I forgot. It is easy to forget when you don't follow a way for a while."

Third turned a close eye to a barrel of tubers. She picked one out of the barrel. She held it to her nose. She took a small knife out of her sleeve. She cut the root open. She sniffed the exposed flesh. She ran her thumb across the cut surface. She nodded to the waiting worker accepting the barrel as good.

"I know what you mean. Sometimes I remember the holiday feasts and games as if they belong in a story someone told me over dinner."

Sixth smiled at a worker as he passed with the final old barrel. She waited as Third made a final entry, then followed Third out of the root cellar. She stood next to Third for a breath.

"I will suggest that Second give a report to First on the priest's activities and actions. There is something just a little strange going on here."

Harbinger read the report First sent her. She understood the message layered in the report. She knew the signs. She would have to return to Sarna. She would not have this new culture mired in blood. No matter the provocation, the priests were not worthy adversaries. They had no combat skills. They could not defend themselves. She ruled Sarna. Justice was her prerogative in her domain, and Sarna was her domain.

Marjas slipped the message from her.

"So we ride to Sarna." Marjas muttered.

"We need a plan of action. What will we threaten? No, we can, we must be gentle. I will not beg. Indignation, after all I have done, how could they usurp my rights? Justice is mine." Harbinger ran through the variety of responses that appealed to her.

"The offense was against the Sarnese people." Marjas offered his thoughts.

"And ours. We suffered from raids, losses of life, property, and peace due to policies engendered by priests' actions. We have rights here. It is not honorable to kill someone weaker than you. No true warrior would condone this." Harbinger warmed to her subject.

"I grant you these points, Wife. What will we do with them?"

"We will give them to Lady Zona. She likes priests."
Harbinger's eye lit with glee as she gave her plan voice.

"How many husbands will you have her taking?" Marjas tried to bring reality into the discussion.

"I see your point. They will come under her purview. She will need people skilled in keeping records to run Sarna. We will put them all back in the temple at Deskersai."

"The populace won't like that. They will fear a resurgence of the priests' power once the priests regain their temple." Marjas made a very good argument against Harbinger's plan.

"Then we build another edifice in Deskersai for the administration of the country. The military can be centered in the same building to oversee the work of the clerks. They will all be sworn to Lady Zona."

"So you will explain everything to Lady Zona?" Marjas kept the plan rooted in reality.

" She will have to come with us. Lady Junla should come as well. The sight of her docile priest will help ease the concerns of the population." Harbinger thought a moment before she was able finish her plan. "Just what I wanted to do right now; ride through the desert, when I am carrying the largest child ever born. Did some giant slip into our bed one night?"

Marjas smiled at his wife's fancy. He did not let his concern show. He had never seen her swell so large so early with child. She was fretful because she did not like the physical restriction being so hugely pregnant placed on her. He was worried that she would explode before she delivered. They would have to leave soon or she would not be able to ride. He knew his wife. She would never consent to riding in a cart. Harbinger interrupted his thoughts with her next words.

"We need to issue an edict requiring all priests be turned over to First. First will need more troops to issue the edict and to deliver the priests to her. We need a policy that First can disseminate and follow that addresses the viable concerns of the populace about their continued freedoms and past injustices they have suffered. We need a mechanism in place to ensure the cooperation of the priests with our policy. This mechanism must also meet the needs of the population, real and imagined.

"We should consult with those village Headmen who have proved loyal. We cannot insult those who might be loyal given the opportunity. We cannot create enemies by ignoring anyone. All the village Headmen must come to a forum discussion to give me their concerns, advice, ideas, support.

"We can start with the forum. It must be soon. It can be announced with the edict requiring the priests be given to me. The forum can be held at Deskersai. That means shelter, food everything as if Assize Court is being held. We'll start planning. Set up a consultation with Lady Zona. Use as many of your brothers as you need. I am going to lie down. All this thinking has exhausted me."

He would have laughed but she spoke only the truth. She was tired. This pregnancy was so different from any other. He could not keep a look of worry from creasing his brow. Luckily he turned quickly so Harbinger did not see the look. She would have embraced his concern. Anything that was of importance to her husbands became a priority to her. She had enough to bear.

Jorin lent his arm to Harbinger as she made her way to their bed. Serjanus rubbed his stone as he waited for their wife to leave.

"All the Healer says is that the baby is large. How large? She looks two thirds done. She couldn't possibly be more than four months. She never carries like this. Her hips are wide. She carries across. This one is sticking straight out."

"We can only wait. And keep her comfortable. This war has to end soon. This is her fourth child since first we rode into Masfin. What is her body thinking?"

"We have our instructions. If they are not done when she wakes, she will do it herself, and that is not what we want."

Petron stared at the door through which his wife had passed. He followed the discussion of his brothers.

"Sablor should go with Neirbo to Lady Zona. Jorin, you take Serjanus and Wittlar with two companies into Sarna to First. Rodznig and Cregros, and you had better go as well Mandul, go to Deskersai. The city will need much work. You will need a battalion. Marjas will stay with Bernath to help here. We will come when Harbinger is ready."

Harbinger rested her hand on her stomach. She had never felt this tired. The Healer assured her there was a child in her womb.

The Sarnese healer said so as well. The doctor from Masfin assured her she had no abnormal signs; just this huge womb. Perhaps she had counted incorrectly. The doctor had quailed under the fierce look her husbands had turned his way. He could not know she had born a child recently, and so she could not possibly be as far along as he thought. She would have to resolve the issue of the priests. Wind Rider could complete the campaign, but only Harbinger of Death could convince the Sarnese people to forgo their retribution. She had no choice. She had to go to Sarna.

She was so tired. When had she ever been this tired? She stretched a hand. Marjas answered her signal. He helped her to their bed.

"I need to sleep. Have Lady Zona meet me in an hour's time. Ask if she minds coming here. She may bring her husbands. I will not be offended. We will need them. I want to discuss the possible role she will play; how we can attach the priests to her Household. Also she will need to discuss the rebuilding of Deskersai with us for she will hold it for me."

"Yes, Wife, rest now. We will have everything done."

She was already asleep. Marjas watched her breath lightly. He could see the sheen of dew form on her brow. Heat bothered her greatly during pregnancy. That sheen reassured him that this was a pregnancy and not a false swelling that often led to death. He had watched his mother go like that. It had frightened him to see his mother fade from some mysterious bodily failure. He embraced his fear; it would not do to let fear fester. Like any festering wound it would bring him low at an important juncture. He had to know his fear. He had to live with it. He had to keep it from ruling him.

"She could die in battle." Petron joined Marjas at his vigil.

"She has never gone this far then lost the child."

"No, she also has never grown this large with child this early. She has never been this affected. We know this is one battle she must face alone. We cannot do the work that is most important. All we can do is carry all her other burdens."

"I know life is fleeting. I know we are a warrior house. I know we expect a violent and early death. I do not expect to dandle my grandchild on my knee. Still I would like to, if I do become an old man, be able to look across at Harbinger bent with age. I want in my waning years to reminisce with my brothers in marriage."

"Our faith in our wife is weak. She will not succumb this time either. How far has she brought us? How close are we to victory? She will not let us enjoy the fruits of our labor alone. She will live to crow in Council of her genius and their cowardice. How could she resist the chance to show them all up to their faces?"

Marjas laughed quietly.

"How right you are. She certainly wouldn't let us steal all her glory. Maybe she is right and a giant did slip into our number one night. Or perhaps she is having a dragon."

Petron chuckled. She seemed well enough. She ate. She produced bodily waste. They were all good signs.

First tried to speak to the priest. He answered politely but he never ventured any information. He moved when directed. He fulfilled assignments. He stayed where placed. First rubbed her chin in thought. Perhaps she was too gentle. She could not afford any more time. She cleared her throat.

"Sit here."

He sat obediently.

"Tell me everything that happened to you after the temple at Deskersai fell."

He stared at her. He swallowed sharply. His mouth worked producing no sound.

She watched fear blossom in his face. She had to use it. She could not let him fall into thought.

"What other priests banded with you? What plans do you have to overthrow my administration? To drive Harbinger of Death from Sarna? Are you planning to pollute our waters? To control the conception of children? Tell me your plans."

He swayed. His eyes grew large and round. His face lost color. His hands clutched together in silent prayer.

"We have taken you into our home. We have fed you, clothed you, and kept you safe. And this is how you repay our kindness? You defy me? You leave me little choice but to assume you are guilty of some heinous crime against those in my care. As generous as my care is, Harbinger's justice is harsh."

He rocked in his seat.

"Do you understand me?"

"Yes."

"You do speak. Let us start with a simple question: in what temple did you serve?"

"The third, I was in my tenth year. I had been drafted into the priesthood as a youngster. I remember begging not to go. I was from Brenlau's Estate. Our village was known for producing priests. It was considered a point of honor to send many to the temples. Both my parents had brothers serving on Altars of Kersai. I don't remember what I wanted to do but I remember crying for a long time each night once I had entered the temple school." Once he started speaking he could not seem to stop.

"I returned to my village after the fall of Deskersai. I was protected there. Many of us were. Then the water was given. My village would not be given control of any water. Everyone in Sarna remembers the close ties my village had with the priests. We became reviled. Still the villagers provided for us. They shared their meager supplies gladly.

"When the Truths were made known, when you came with the books, when we could not deny what had been done, the villagers turned on us. They stoned us to drive us from them. They were ravaging animals. How could we blame them? Yet, they had so gladly sent me to that system. They had been so proud to produce so many of the country's priests.

"I traveled long. I remember bleeding. Then I don't remember much. The village that finally took me in tried to follow your edicts. They tried to forgive. Still I was suspect. I was never allowed access to water directly. I was not allowed to speak in public. I could not speak unless spoken to first. I could not speak about Kersai, Deskersai, Sarna. I learned my place. It is a just punishment."

"Are there more priests like you still alive?"

"I do not know."

She regarded the shaking man. She watched his throat work. She did not really believe he meant Sarna or Harbinger any harm.

"You may return to the gardens."

"Thank you. May I ask a question?"

"Certainly. I guarantee no answer."

"What is to happen to me?"

"That is up to Harbinger to decide. Justice in Sarna is from her hand and her hand alone. I only implement her will, enforce it."

"Thank you."

First signaled to her scribe. She had him read the interview back to her. She added her personal impressions. The scribe worked busily to capture her words on paper. As soon as the ink was dry, a messenger rode with the packet into Masfin.

Lady Zona read the report with a jaundiced eye. This would not be easy.

"What would you have me do with these priests?"

"They can keep records well. Every governor needs a staff of record keepers." Harbinger munched on her lunch as she spoke.

"You want us all to traipse into Sarna. Who will stay here? Will you recall Wind Rider from Llwegania?"

"If I have to she can come up but Marlin can handle this easily. My favorite general is keeping Ranald and his army pent." Harbinger shrugged.

"Your favorite general?" Lady Zona looked up from the report.

"General Harsh Winter."

"Rebuilding Deskersai will take longer than winter." Lady Zona resumed her review of the information before her.

"Not for a focused battalion. Anyway the stone shells are still there. By the time the Council is convened the city will be habitable."

"You would build a city in a day." Lady Zona sighed in defeat.

"No, but in less than a season it should do well enough for my needs. I am not thinking of courtiers' needs. We will be hosting people used to simple living. A clean, well-kept place to sleep, good food, they will content."

"Of course, we would not want to insult them with less than appropriate conditions." Lady Zona pointed out.

"Assuredly. However, appropriate does not translate to opulent. My Estates are warrior encampments. We will be housed the same as our guests."

"The edict is ready. First has begun her rounds. We should proceed to Deskersai." Lady Zona reconciled herself to the plan.

"Is Lady Junla ready?"

"Yes. I have contacted King Jeffeaux. He is concerned that we will be away from the front for so long." Lady Zona reported.

"I have sent him reassurance about Marlin. I cannot have our rear in disarray. This issue's resolution is as important as our efforts in Masfin."

"Will you be able to make this journey?" Lady Zona's face softened in concern as she asked her question.

"Not if we delay much longer. I will admit I am worried about this birth. I have never carried like this before now. If I didn't know better I would think I had the date wrong. But I couldn't be wrong. I was still carrying my last daughter when I would posit this conception by my size. I know my husbands are worried. I am almost relieved to have this issue for them to help resolve. A long winter of waiting would drive us all crazy."

Lady Zona agreed with that sentiment. "Do all your husbands come with us?"

"Some must remain, cruel as that is. I don't really need them all. They will have to live with the separation. Bernath is steadiest. He will endure the separation best. Cregros will bear his company well. They are a strong pair. Jorin or Marjas, who will come with us, who will stay? They are both very strong, sensible. Marjas will stay, he is the stronger. Three is a good solid number that will give balance to the group. Serjanus should go to the King. He does well alone. That should ease King Jeffeaux's concerns. The rest will come with me. I might need them to keep this meeting polite."

Mandul stared over the burned shell of Deskersai. Even now, years later it was a mess. From the battlefield before it you could see the desolation. Occasional flitters of movement emphasized the basic emptiness of the city.

"When Harbinger destroys a place, she does a thorough job."

Rodznig grunted his agreement. They had a lot of work to do. No use delaying the inevitable. He kicked the sides of his mount gently. The horse started off with a swish of tail. Neirbo and Mandul followed. The battalion swarmed behind them.

Chapter 20

He watched the conquerors return. He had forgotten how fearsome they were. He had managed to shrink them in his memory. He had softened their features. Their weapons had become puny. All he was left with was a mystery as to how his country could have fallen to such weaklings.

Now he had to face their reality. He had to acknowledge their power. They rode efficiently. They moved through the ruins with ease. They worked like beasts of burden. He could see their muscles bunch and stretch in effort. He could see their efforts result in order.

He watched his own people creep from the wreckage to help. He saw them accepted and rewarded by the enemy. He could smell the food and comfort provided by the enemy. Still he watched from the shadows.

Then, one day he was noticed. A strapping woman saw him crouching in the shadow of her workspace. She called to him. He cringed back. She gestured broadly. He turned his head searching for an escape, a diversion. Nothing appeared. He would have to flee to escape. That would result in unwanted attention. He stared into her expectant face. Carefully he advanced. He hoped his slow approach would cause the invader to grow impatient, to leave, and to let him slip away from her. She waited. Patiently she watched him come close. He would not outlast her. He knew it. He saw resolve in her eyes. Their resolve was a terrible thing to experience. No wonder they had won.

Finally he was within her arm's reach. She extended her hand. It held a portion of field rations. Nothing spectacular, a simple hard biscuit poked through her fingers. It was a terrible sight. It bespoke the entire nature of the Llweganian force in Sarna. They beguiled with patience and generosity. He could not refuse. She would not believe he had had enough to eat in this ruin. No one did. He did not look well-fed. He looked hungry, because he was. Hunger was his constant companion. It lay down with him at night. It haunted his dreams. It woke him in the morning. It drew at his mouth throughout the day. Even his fingers could not refuse the offering. They stretched without his will to grab the food.

Water, in a canteen carelessly tossed to him. Water, the treasure in Sarna, was given without ceremony or concern. He needed that water to soften the biscuit enough to swallow it.

His tormentor watched him eat for only a short time. Then the woman returned to her work. He sat sipping the warm water. The sun beat down on his head. She moved with a rhythm. The swing of her motion lulled him into a light doze. He woke with a start. He curled into an instinctive defensive position.

"I need you to move. I will be cleaning this area next. The sun has moved. Best to sleep in the shade over where I just finished clearing. It is safer from falling masonry." Her Sarnese was only lightly accented. Her grammar was equal to a priest.

He moved at her direction. He continued to watch her work. She did not seem to tire. At dusk she stopped. She was joined by others that had worked near her. They greeted each other in Sarnese. Clearly they meant everyone to know they were equally fluent in Llweganian and Sarnese. The focus of his attention corralled him into following her group.

"You can't sleep in the ruins anymore. We have started construction. No one not directly answerable to our leaders may be in the construction areas."

"Afraid of what one small boy might do?"

"Of course. No one is above suspicion. Small boys could be very dangerous."

"Even pet small boys?"

"Especially pet small boys. They are the most dangerous, sneaking up to bite the hand that feeds them at every chance." She tightened her grip on his collar. He only now realized her ploy. She had lulled him into complacency not the other way around as he had planned.

"We can be hard to keep caged."

"Oh, I think not. We are very good at building cages, if that is what you require."

"I will not bend to your will easily."

"My will is to have you well-fed, clothed, rested, and sheltered. If that is so hard for you to accept, give up your place to those that wish it. Get you to Masfin with the rest of your stubborn citizens."

"I do not wish to leave my home."

"Good. Here is the horse trainers' lot. They will bathe you for you are easy to scent at a hundred paces. Not very effective for sneaking around places. Oh someone is watching us, I can smell him."

He frowned mightily at her. She smiled. A deep chuckle rumbled behind the smile. He screwed his face more tightly.

"Careful, you might strain a muscle in that face. If evil looks could kill me, I would be long dead. My sister would have buried me years ago." He was swung easily into the air. The unexpectedness of his flight startled him into a shout. Strong hands plucked him from the air.

"Oh, this one stinks."

"He offends the senses mightily. Scrub him well. He is determined to shadow our every move. It is annoying to catch that whiff."

He hung between two of the largest hands he had ever beheld. The person attached to those hands was equally impressively large. A jolly face topped that mountainous body. They grew their men large in Llwegania. He attempted no futile struggle. He was carried under one arm by the man. Unceremoniously he was dumped into a large vat of warm water. His clothes were stripped as he sat in the water. They disappeared from the vat. He sat quiescent as he was scrubbed and rinsed and scrubbed again. He had never thought to waste water on such a scale. The shock of the pleasure of all that water on his skin kept him still. As the dirt was scrubbed away his skin gave up the tale of his falls and brushes with others over food and shelter. Old scars and new bruises shone in the lamplight. All he could wonder at was the contrast in his skin color from his arms and legs to his belly.

"That is the work of the sun, boy. It is not dirt bonded to your skin. Out you get. You certainly were home to plenty of creatures. Look at that water. All those floating crawlies were on you. I will have to scrub well today to be sure none who jumped to me take up permanent residence." A square of cloth was passed to him. "Here dry yourself. Then put these on." Clothes were put in his other hand. "When you are ready to eat, we are over there. Come as you please or not."

He was left standing in the puddle forming at his feet. Alone in the heart of the enemy's camp he stood starting to shiver just a little from the air on his damp skin. He knew he would eat this night. He would sleep in a clean safe bed just for tonight. Tomorrow he would return to his plotting from the shadows.

It was not much of a village. Houses stood in two lines down a dusty path. The town well that had once made the village a stopping place for caravans of traders and pilgrims and priestly officials stood in the center of the village. An inn stood near the well, as well as a few tired-looking shops.

No one came any more. Wells that relied on chancy rain and groundwater could not compete with the deep wells springing up throughout Sarna. Villages with agriculture now drew artisans and traders. Villages on routes that led to Masfin or Llwegania or the Estate of First drew caravans. This village was now a forgotten place that whispered only in the faintest memories of old time traders.

So the sight of dust rising on the horizon raised only mild speculation, not expectations. No one stopped to watch for someone to approach. So the village was very surprised when that plume turned into riders sitting in the village center asking for the village Headman.

Pindar warily looked at the riders. He knew they were Llweganian. It did not matter that they spoke clear Sarnese. It did not matter that Sarnese dress no longer was so different from Llweganian attire. These were Llweganian riders. He pulled his coat on with trembling hands. No Headman wished to be called before the military power of Llweganian will. It was instinctive to cringe.

Out he went into the harsh sun. He straightened his hat of office with decisive hands. He would fill the position held by five generations of his family with dignity.

"I am the Headman of this village."

"Greetings. We are sent by First under authority of Harbinger of Death. As Headman of your village you are commanded to attend the Great Assize Court to be held in Deskersai on the next new moon. You may bring with you one companion. If you feel the need of an escort tell us now and one will be sent. You will be housed and fed by the grace of Harbinger of Death once you are in

Deskersai. The question before the court of which you will be a participant will be the disposition of the priests of Kersai.

"Any priests you may have in your custody at this time must be turned over to us on command of Harbinger of Death. They are considered prisoners of war and therefore fall under her jurisdiction at this time. Any priests that come under your protection after we leave may be brought with you to the Great Assize Court or you may send to First for their retrieval. They may not be harmed under any circumstances. Any harm that has been done before this edict is not held to be your responsibility. From this time forward any harm done to a priest is considered an act of rebellion against Harbinger of Death. It will be punished accordingly.

"Are these laws clear?"

"Yes."

"Good. Have you anything to say at this time?"

Pindar held his breath as he thought. He had little choice. He could not risk defying anyone. His village's existence was very much in jeopardy. They could hardly maintain a hold on life. Certainly a clash with these grim-faced soldiers was not in his village's best interest. How long did they have anyway? They had no way to create business. They could not grow more than they could eat. All they had were their homes and each other. He could not risk that. He signaled his brother. No voice raised in denial.

There was a shifting of bodies. He did not turn his head. He knew what was coming from the farthest house. He could see the six bedraggled figures shuffle in his memory.   They had been found in the ruins of the local temple. They were not the original members of the temple. Those priests had been long gone when these had been found. The villagers had forced their prisoners to work the community grinding wheel. Yoked together they had spent their days turning the great wheel. The marks of their yoke were red and raw in the bright sun.

There was no great outcry from the Llweganian force at the sight that met their eyes. The priests were efficiently corralled and led away from the village. The main rider returned all attention to Pindar.

"This is your stone. It must be turned over upon your arrival at Deskersai. You must be there or your village will be considered in rebellion. Is this clearly understood?"

"Yes."

The soldier considered the retreating priests and the wheel. "I will send to First; she will send you two oxen for your wheel. Do not eat them. They belong to Harbinger and must be accounted for to First every year."

"Thank you, understood."

"Will you require escort?"

"No, I know the way. The roads are safe enough."

"Our business is concluded. I go in peace. May your water run clear."

"May your cup be ever full."

Pindar sighed in relief and fear. The rider paused. The clear eyes took in the village as a dying creature. "What was your primary source of income?"

"We were a stopping place on trade and pilgrimage routes."

"You need an industry."

"Yes."

"Does the well dry up?"

"Sometimes. It is fed by winter melt-off from the mountains and occasional rain."

"An underground stream?"

"Yes."

"This is not good farmland."

"No."

"Tough to pasture."

"Yes."

"You need to consider something. Consider, discuss, and bring a proposal with you to present to Harbinger of Death. If she finds it reasonable she will allocate resources to you. But do not mistreat any more prisoners. There are no slaves allowed in Sarna."

"I will."

Before Pindar finished his promise the group had turned to leave. The cloud of dust swirled, created the illusion of the party disappearing into thin air for once the dust settled the troop was out of sight.

Pindar clutched the stone tightly in his hand. He opened his fingers to stare at the striped surface. Brown with a golden stripe it winked at him like the eye of a great beast. He gingerly placed the rock in his pocket. He dared not lose it. Pindar felt his mate come up behind him. She placed a hand on his shoulder.

"Do they mean it?"

"Mean what? The threat, the promise? I believe I must go to this court. I will bring my brother. Or should I leave him in case I do not return?'

"I do not know, husband. Sometimes I think the world has gone mad."

"You may be right."

He sat in the shade. He watched as the buildings took shape. At first everything had seemed to go so slowly that he could perceive no progress. Now every dawn brought new wonders. These invaders surely worked long and hard. He even hated their virtues. Still he could not resist sharing the company of his captors.

He missed the companionship of family and friends. He longed for the feeling of safety home brought. Sitting in the shade, watching the work, knowing that at the end of the day he would be fed, clean, and warm for the night's sleep was very seductive. Despise the source of these comforts, he might. Despise himself for needing these comforts, he did. But he could not forgo them. So he squatted in the shade watching the work.

He dozed. A light touch woke him. He heaved himself to feet. A hand steadied him by the shoulder. He did not shrug it away. He let the wide firm grip carry his weight for a moment as he cleared his head.

"You all right, boy?"

"Yes. My feet did not wake as quickly as my head."

"I know that feeling. Were you born in Deskersai?"

"Yes, my family has lived here for generations."

"It must be comforting to belong to a place."

"Even such a place as this?"

"Even so."

"Do you wish to belong here?"

"No, I belong to my troop. When I am long dead there will be voices raised in song that will sing my name. They will know me through my songs of deeds and my husbands' songs of love. The air which I breathe now will echo my name then. The air which I breathe now will fill others' lungs to produce my name in song. I will live forever because I come from a living community."

He was silent. The idea intrigued him. He did not want to feel attached to such an idea, still it drew him.

"I will compose a song for you, little pet. Then you can have part of my experience, since you have shared your city with me."

"For me?"

"Yes," she filled the air with a few notes. They burst from her lungs in a cascade of beauty. "You will like it."

"What deeds will you sing?"

"That you survived alone in this demolished city. That you smelled terrible when I found you. That you are good at being quiet. That you follow direction well. That being still and watching well are your hobbies. That you like sweets."

"You will write a song with all that for me?"

"I said I will, and I will. I will sing it before the night fire. Will you like that?"

He could not believe anyone would do such a thing for him.

"You can do as you please."

"It pleases you very well I see. Do you know what we need? We need a game of Pass Ball."

"Pass Ball?"

There was a shifting of bodies. Heads turned towards them.

"Pass Ball?" The question echoed through the construction. Bodies heaved from work. In the late afternoon light the dark leather pants and dark silk shirts covered in dust gleamed with a mellow beauty. A ball was produced. Before he knew it he was running through crowds of people trying to snag a ball of leather and sand. It was heavy but easily gripped. There were few rules. Fewer strategies than rules belonged to the game. Hold on to the ball and run as hard and as fast as you could. One of her husbands picked him up to carry him and the ball over the goal line. The move was alternately booed and cheered depending on the side. He laughed. He raised the ball high above his head.

He laughed when he ended on the bottom of a pile of bodies trying to contain the ball. He laughed as he ran after a ball carrier. He laughed as he lay face up in the dust staring at the dying light in the sky. He was still laughing as she carried him to the horse trainer for a bath. His arms clung to her neck as they moved.

He fell asleep in the bath. He woke with a smile at first light. He savored the memory of the previous day. Then he realized he had not slept in his hidey hole. Her hand raised him to his feet. She pressed warm rolls into his hand. He would look back on those days as the golden days of his childhood. He climbed through the shrinking piles of rubble. He watched buildings of sturdy, uncomplicated design grow. The resembled nothing of the old Deskersai, still he did not mind them.

Those days ended abruptly. They were clearing the final quarter. They were near the edge of the destruction around Temple Square. The sight would stay crystal clear for him all the rest of his life. Scavengers, as he had been, were trying to wring the last pilfer before the buildings were brought down. She never saw it. The old, loose masonry fell with speed and heartless accuracy. Before his eyes he saw her crushed. He stood frozen. A soundless scream swelled in his chest. It filled his lungs. It squeezed his heart until it ached. He saw the rest of the work crew rush to her. He saw the blood seep from beneath the stone; not much, she was dead. Everyone knew the dead did not bleed. The blood had been forced from her body by the weight of the stone.

The scream must have gained sound because he heard it. He did not realize it came from him but he knew someone was screaming, hollering. His feet finally moved. He ran at the stone. He beat his hands against it. He howled his pain and rage and disbelief. Tears ran down his face into his open-mouthed rage. Somehow the salt of his tears made his cry fill with agony and anguish beyond simple sound. Gentle hands lifted him away. They carried him away from the scene of the accident. Still he could not stop crying.

He had been too young to remember his parents' deaths. He could not remember the destruction of Deskersai very clearly. He had lived on stories and half memories. He had ingested the bitter moaning of fellow survivors. He had not experienced deep loss for something he could hardly remember. He had not known how deeply true loss could be felt. He had not known that his head would ache from crying. He had not known his tongue would lose the ability to taste. He had not known that tears could fall without control. He had not known sleeping could make you tired.

He had not known that a gentle touch from someone else
suffering the same loss could give comfort. He had not known that
a rite of grief and loss could build ties and bonds. He had not
known these things until he stood by her funeral pyre watching the
flames consume her flesh. He listened to her song. He cried and
smiled as the song of her life was offered with the smoke of the
fire. He was glad for the song of her troop that held her name.
And his voice quavered with those of her husbands as the song she
had written for him finished the rite. The final note sank into the
night.

He watched the water rinse the heat and soot away from her
bones. He waited as each member of her troop drew a line of
mourning on their faces from her ashes. He followed her husbands
to the pyre. He drew the single line of sorrow across his brow.
Then with shaking hands he helped gather her bones into her cloak.
The bundle was neatly tied with white cords. He followed the
husbands to their horses. He stood looking longingly at them. He
did not know how to ask. He had not asked for anything from
anyone ever. He had never had to ask for anything from her. She
had given everything. He placed a hand on the foot closest to him.
He tried to force words from his mouth. The body bent above him.
It grabbed a handful of his shirt. Then he was swung onto the back
of a horse.

He did not ask where they were going. He knew. They were
going to Llwegania. He ate what they pressed into his hands. He
drank when they passed him water. He slept when they stopped.
He would lie down next to her bones. He would rest his back
against them. He thought as he slept her scent and her spirit
surrounded him. Then they were at a great house.

People rushed to meet them. A tall woman spoke briefly. Then
she mounted a horse as well. Together they finished the journey to
the burial mound. He passed with them under the great stone
lintel. He did not listen to the words. He took her cloak after they
removed her bones from it. He watched as her bones were
carefully piled with the other bones of her troop. The shadows
from the torches danced over the thousands of gleaming bones. He
paid them no mind. He did not pay any more attention to his
escort. They were still talking as they left. He wrapped the cloak
around his shoulders. Then he lay down on the stone floor next to

her bones. He closed his eyes to wait to die. He would raise his voice in song no more. Fate had finally broken him.

They were half a day's ride from the burial mound when she realized someone was missing. She drew her animal to an abrupt halt.

"That Sarnese brat is missing."

Her reckless sister's two husbands looked at each other in dismay. They hauled their mounts' heads around. Then they raced back the way they had come. These were the vaunted Harbinger of Death's troopers? They rode off with no plan and no discussion?

"Do you know where he has gone? Have you any idea why he came to Llwegania? Is he a spy? How can you be so sure where we should go?"

They did not answer her. They rode as if a gang of Sarnese raiders were on their heels.

She followed with a grim expression drawing her mouth. They reached the mound well after dark. She stared in amazement as they lit torches and pushed open the mound's door. After a moment she followed them

In the wavering light she could see the pathetic heap.

"He came to die."

Dark eyes caught hers. They were filled with sadness.

"You never understood your sister. You never understood Harbinger of Death. Perhaps you could make the effort to understand a boy who had lost his world twice. He loved your sister and your sister loved him. You will never have a chance to make things right with your sister now. You could help him. You could make things right for him. If you wanted to try."

"Why should I want to help him? Why?"

"Because your sister loved him? Because he is a lost child in need? He follows directions well. He needs a reason to live. Give him one."

"He knows you."

"He needs a mother. He needs you. And you need him."

She looked at the heap. One small hand was thrust into her sister's pile of bones. Those long thin fingers looked so sad. Their slack grip on the long arm bone of her sister was difficult to see. She could see the flesh fading until only the bones remained thrust forlornly into more bones. When she looked up again they were alone. Gently she touched the back covered by her sister's cloak.

"I am Steady Heart." Her voice sounded loud in the curved space of the mound. She stared at the empty eye sockets of her sister's skull. She imagined them filled with her sister's laughing eyes. "Laughing Heart was my sister. When she left I missed her joy. I could never see her as a warrior. I wondered if she would be given a new name but she never changed it. I think she liked being a fierce fighter with a sweet name."

There was no answer. Still she sat rubbing that back. The muscles gradually curved to her touch. The head turned to see her. Dark eyes stared at her.

"Laughing Heart brought joy with her. It makes me so sad to think only Steady Heart remains. I don't know how to find joy. She always gave it to me. I thought when I was very young and foolish that joy was irresponsible, superfluous. Later, I thought it was a luxury. Now I know it is a necessity. And she is gone."

She lay down. Her eyes focused on the ceiling. In the flickering light of her torch she could make out the mosaic decorating the ceiling.

"She didn't want to stay in one place. She didn't want to stay with me. We weren't enough. Why did she have to go?" She turned to look into those serious eyes. Her tears glittered in the torch light. Then fingers touched her tears. At the light touch she felt relief.

"Laughing Heart's husbands say she loved you. They say you loved her. Wolfor would not lie to me. Laughing Heart would not want anyone she loved to lay down to die because she had died."

"When the joy is gone, what use is living?"

"Joy is so rare. So few really experience it. Those of us who have must spread it."

"I have no joy."

"Yes, you do. You have Laughing Heart's joy in you in your memories. You know how to be joyous."

"I can't ever again. I was cold and hungry and dirty and tired and alone until she came to find me. She gave me everything that was important. No one cared if I was warm or fed or clean or rested or happy until she came. No one else will ever care again. I know. I went all my life without her before. No one in Deskersai cared. No one in Sarna cared. No one noticed me. No one saw me. No one looked at me until she came. And now she's gone. The city crushed her. Right there. I saw it. I saw the stone fall. It smashed her to pieces right there. Right in front of me. It took her because it couldn't stand that I was happy. I betrayed my city and it killed her to punish me."

She listened to the rush of disjointed thoughts. Her tears fell faster. She did not resist the urge. She gathered the weeping boy to her breast. She smoothed the tangled hair from his brow.

"I will care. And you will be my joy." Still holding the shaking boy she rose to her feet. It was difficult but she would not put down her responsibility; her gift from her sister.

"I don't think I can go any further."

"I will carry you until you can."

"I miss her so much."

"I know. It will be better here. She played here at your age. There are many who can speak of her. She will feel very close. You will feel her breath against your face as you ride. She will surround you. She will fill you. And one day she will surprise you. You will feel her joy surge through you until you laugh for joy at being alive. She is sneaky like that."

"Why are you Steady Heart? Why is Laughing Heart's husband Warpol?"

She thought he had lost his reason, then she thought of the question.

"Men carry family names. They carry the family names of all the families that ever were so none die. Women are given names that reflect who they are."

He tucked his head under her chin. He stared at the night with blank eyes. He felt his despair surging through his chest. He refused to let it show again. He fought the urge to cry. He pressed his face more deeply into the shelter of her neck. His body began to shake with his contained grief.

She sat on her mount clutching the trembling child. She rested her cheek on his head. Three children she had borne. Three small bodies she had held but never had she felt such pain in a child.

"Sh, sh, it is all right. I have you now. We will miss her together. Our burden will lighten because it is shared. Is she not still giving to you? Has she not given to me this very day? Has she not gifted us each other? Do you wonder what she will gift us tomorrow?"

Pindar watched Deskersai grow on the horizon. He had never been there. All the years he could have traveled for pilgrimage he had not gone to Deskersai. Now he went at the invader's order. As he approached he could see the scars from the war. He could see piles of rubble being crushed for roads. The Llweganians liked to cover their roads with crushed stones. It did cut down on dust. He did not know that this habit was Masfin in origin.

He stared at the swell of people that filled the roads. He had never seen so many people, even when his village had been prosperous. All those people made him nervous. The noise bothered him. He tried to ignore his discomfort as he focused on presenting his stone to the soldier at the gate. He was frightened when his stone was taken. Then he was issued a new stone.

This one was green with black stripes. It glowed between his fingers. He listened closely to his directions. His cousin jostled his arm in excitement. A troop of soldiers rode past. They disappeared into the city. He followed the path of their ride. People swirled out of the way easily and readily.

Scents bombarded his nose as they followed their directions. Food, bodies, ware, horses all gave off scents that combined to highlight the difference of this experience in his life. His group navigated their way despite the assault on their eyes and ears and noses.

"Do you think Deskersai has always been like this?"

"I would think city life the same no matter who held it."

"Pindar you do not sound excited."

"I do not know what to feel or to think."

His sober tone dampened his cousin's excitement. The boy was almost old enough to sit Council. Pindar had decided to bring him because every man might be needed to protect the village but Pindar needed to bring a companion who would not be a hindrance. The boy could fight well and listened to orders. His youth had not seemed a drawback until this moment.

"They could have gathered us up to kill us. Think, you. All the Headmen of all the villages are here. They could easily destroy us all. They defeated the priests and the Wardens easily enough. What kind of chance would we have?"

"If you believe that, why did you come?"

"To protect the village. Disobeying the order would not be good for the village."

The youthful face was transformed by a thoughtful expression. Obviously the boy had never considered the responsibilities that went with being Headman. He never considered that a Headman might have to be heroic in a quiet way. Well, neither had Pindar until this summons had been delivered. Frankly he was not too sure just how heroic he could be.

He had three days to contemplate his fate. Three days of exploring the rebuilt Deskersai to pass the time. Three days of meeting other Headmen, Headmen who did not fear this gathering, Headmen who were happy to answer any summons from Harbinger, did not ease his anxiety. Three days he spent trying to sleep nights, to eat food, to answer the question of what lay at the end of the three days.

Then the slow crawl of time sped to the end. He sat in the great chamber listening to the edict of the conqueror. He watched her lower her body into her seat. Her body huge with child, her body swelled with fertility presiding over the meeting.

"I know you are concerned about the return of the priests to power. I realize that you suffered greatly under their administration. I do not dispute that, nor do I dispute your urge for vengeance. How can I? I have only suffered raids and destruction from my birth because they urged the Sarnese people to a course that was futile and unnecessary and wasteful of both Sarnese and Llweganian lives.

"I always understood the drive to procreate that sent Sarnese raiders over my borders in search of fertile women. I fought against it. I did sympathize with the plight of a people to have children. How could I not? To discover that generations of war were nothing but population control, that my ancestors, my mother, died, because priests were involved in this elaborate scheme made me angry, I will admit. Still no matter how I suffered it is dishonorable to slaughter an opponent not trained in war, battle, fighting.

"Yes, every generation these priests should have said there must be a better way. Yes, every one of those priests should have said I will not participate. I do not belittle their complicity in the crime visited upon you. That is why I will never let them return to power. I will never let them roam free in Sarna or Llweganian or Masfin. They will never have access to control over you again. I promise. But I will not let them be slaughtered or enslaved or abused. I will not have it said I allowed the persecution of priests.

"So you must turn them over to me. I will place them under the control of Lady Zona, my chief deputy in Sarna. She will protect you from them. She will set them tasks that will benefit Sarna but not conflict with my parameters. They are prisoners. If they wish to volunteer their skills as scribes and clerks they may. Or they can spend the rest of their lives contemplating their crimes against you. I will not have their blood on my hands or on yours. They are your brothers, your sons, your uncles, your cousins, and even your fathers. You cannot murder and misuse members of your family and remain unchanged for the worse. I will not permit you to do that to yourselves.

"Now you are gathered here to discuss what kind of place Sarna will be. I have told you what it will not be. Assemble suggestions about a court system, road maintenance, and schooling. Are there some areas that need help to establish trade, industry, and farming? I will be here until the birth of this child. That is the boundary of your time."

She looked so pregnant Pindar could not believe they had the day to talk. Three weeks later he believed he had come on a real mission. He listened to advice from Masfin traders and Llweganian craftsmen. He discussed education for all children when he could not read. He felt part of Sarna in a way his birth had not tied him.

Two months later he still wondered about the reasons to protect the priests. Why were they so important? They swelled the city housing. They moved in quiet and shadow as if afraid to attract attention but they could not prevent the attention. All eyes followed their every move.

Even an uneducated peasant from the barren waste would sense the tension in the very presence of those clergy. There was no lingering affection or nostalgic fondness for the former rulers of Sarna from the great gathering of Headmen.

Yet everyday four priests joined the great work. Three answered to the beck and call of Lady Zona. They moved at her direction. They had freedom of the city. They were her husbands, clearly they were her husbands. One stood with the daughter. He did nothing without permission. He never left her side. He never spoke to anyone. He did not interact with the other priests. He waited on Lady Junla's pleasure. Surely those two women could keep the priests in line if anyone could. He just wondered if anyone could.

Those shadow beings did not seem able to rise up against Harbinger. Even Lady Zona's husbands could not lead a palace coup against their wife's overlord. He did not need to know why Harbinger wanted those priests alive. If she did not want them harmed perhaps that was reason enough for him to agree with her policy. Her policies all seemed to benefit Sarna. He would simply have to trust that she did know better in this instance as well.

He never had the heart or gall to kill them anyway. As Harbinger was providing the muscle power they needed, what did he care what happened to a few broken men?

He returned his attention to the discussion at hand; Harbinger explaining her position on the new prison system.

"When you rule everyone is entitled to your protection from arbitrary implementation of your rules or lack of implementation. I must keep our community safe from harm; external and internal. I must do it within the structure of rules by which our community wishes to be treated. Those people who threaten our community externally I will pursue relentlessly but I will not torture them or condone torture. A clean kill is the warrior's way. Prisoners are treated with dignity. They will be our neighbors when the war is over and they return to their homes. Internal threats must be dealt with as well, yes, but if they cannot be persuaded to our point of view they are to be pitied, placed in a situation which does not threaten our community, but not tortured, not abused, not treated in any way that lessens our stature, impacts on our character as a community. A community is not judged by how we treat the best of ourselves or the strongest or the most liked; we are judged by how we treat our weakest, most needy, or least admired members.

It is easy to treat well those who are helpful and likeable and good. It is hard to be kind, forgiving, and generous to those who have treated us poorly. I cannot take the easy road. We cannot take the easy road. Our community must do the hard thing because we have the courage and the strength and the resolve to do it. We are strong and righteous."

There was a catch in her voice at the end of the speech. Pindar watched as her husbands bent to her. Two sets of hands helped her to stand. She breathed deeply.

"We will have to finish this another time. This child is finally making her appearance."

She walked with the sway of pregnancy that gave her beauty in the eye of every Sarnese male present. It did not matter that that sway was a regular occurrence now. It still held the power to stop a man in his tracks as he watched it pass. Hands with no fear reached to touch that swell as it passed. The husbands allowed the familiarity. They understood the respect and concern and affection that motivated the hands. She could not move very quickly anyway.

Lady Zona turned to the waiting messenger.

"Ride to Delungor. Tell Serjanus it is time he came to us."

Serjanus rode in silence. His thoughts were focused on his wife. She was early. Not as early as the Masfin doctor had suggested but early. She had never come to term of a living child early. She had never gone this long without going to full term. This entire pregnancy had been strange. He did not think he could go through this again in the near future.

He glanced at his companions. Lady Zona would be surprised. Her son the King and his Royal Consort were with him. He should have guessed the King would insist on coming. Jeffeaux knew his life depended on Harbinger bringing this war to a successful conclusion. Serjanus shook his head. He was doing the man a disservice. The Masfin King held Harbinger in great respect.

The roads were lined with spectators as they traveled. Serjanus wondered if his husband/brothers had experienced the same homage as they traveled from the winter encampment. The uncovered heads and respectful bows were somber and raised fear. He did not fear they would mob his troupe. He did not fear they would impede his progress. Their reverence was almost of a funereal march passing. He would have welcomed a rousing fight by the time they reached Deskersai.

He swung off his horse by the last fading light of day. Stable hands rushed to collect his mount. Petron greeted him in the hall.

"How goes it?"

Petron looked exhausted.

"We are still in labor?"

"She could not be active these last months. The Wise Woman is not overly concerned. She says everything is going well."

"If our wife is still in labor everything is not going well."

Jeffeaux heard the tail end of the conversation. He saw the strained expressions. His heart contracted in his chest. Marma rested a hand on his shoulder. He let a sigh escape from his chest at her gentle touch.

She had never labored for four days. Each time she had been brought to bed with child she had been up long before her husbands recovered the next day.

Sablor opened the door to Harbinger's quarters. Jeffeaux caught a glimpse of her pale straining face. He saw her body curved in effort. Then her husbands disappeared inside and he was cut off from her.

It was well into Darkfall when Lady Zona appeared. Jeffeaux was pacing in the formal receiving room. He whipped around at the sound of his mother's footsteps.

"Is she well?"

Lady Zona smiled joyously.

"Yes. She has given birth to two daughters. It explains everything."

Jeffeaux thought his heart would burst in his chest. She lived. Tears ran down his face. He moved to his mother. For the first time in years he swept her into his embrace. He swung her around the room in his arms in celebration that his worst fear was unrealized.

Lady Zona was swamped with joy at the embrace of her child. She had missed him so much.

Jeffeaux put his mother down.

"Harbinger knows you are here. She has asked to see you. She is very tired and a little weak. But she is asking for you."

Jeffeaux left the room before his mother could finish. Harbinger wanted to see him. That was all he needed to know. He paused only to congratulate the new fathers. Sablor still held his heir. He had not expected to have a child this time so his family retainers had not been summoned. He would have the joy of holding his new daughter for several days before she was whisked away to the safety and care of his mother. He did not seem upset at the delay. As the eleventh husband he had never expected Harbinger to give him an heir. A twin birth meant this child, Harbinger's twelfth living child, had been created especially for him. Sablor simply stood in the temporary nursery holding his child, savoring his joy.

Jeffeaux entered the room. Petron looked up at him. With a blank face the First of Harbinger's Household left his wife with her ally.

Jeffeaux sat gingerly on the chair by the bed. He slipped Harbinger's lax hand into his hold. She opened her eyes with a smile.

"There you are."

"Twin daughters, the Sarnese will be pleased."

"Pleased?"

"Yes. They look on twins as a sign from Kersai that the mother is blessed by him."

"I have routed Kersai from these borders."

"But perhaps not some of the superstitions. This will cement your rule and your policies. This sign of fertility will be impossible to ignore."

"How wise of me to decide to have twins just at this juncture."

Jeffeaux smiled. He raised her hand to his lips. He pressed a kiss to her knuckles. She returned his smile. She turned her hand until she cupped his cheek. He pressed his face into her touch.

"You never thought I would die and leave you all the glory of your coming victory did you?"

"No, I knew better."

Petron watched the interchange with a bland eye. He felt a presence at his side. He glanced at the Royal Consort Marma. Some of his displeasure must have leaked into his face.

"My husband will have no peer in Masfin. He will have no one to call friend. Everyone will be dependent on him, answerable to him, under his power. He will be the loneliest man in my country. I can give him support and respect, and yes, even my heart's love, but it will never replace friendship from a peer who owes him nothing. She is all he has left and he will be unable to enjoy that friendship. When this war is done he will have to banish her from Masfin. He will have to prove that he can stand alone, that his Kingship flows from Masfin and not Harbinger.

"And she, she sees the man she made. I thank her for him every day in my heart. To give away such a man is a difficult thing."

Petron stared at the calm, steady woman.

"King Jeffeaux was very wise in his choice of Consort. You are a woman of great strength and wisdom."

"Thank you. Come, show me where I can get something to eat."

Harbinger stroked Jeffeaux's face with tired fingers.

"You look terrible."

"Serjanus rode us hard. The messenger took two days to reach us. We spent two days on the return journey."

"You changed horses often."

"And got no sleep."

"He was foolish. If it had been a regular birth I would have been delivered safely days before you got here. There was no need to rush so."

'We did not mind. Getting here was all that mattered."

"It was time for you to leave Delungor anyway. We have an offensive to plan. It is time to end this war."

Jeffeaux lowered his head to the mattress in defeated resignation.

"I know. We have to end it. My country should not endure one more season of this destruction. It is only that I fear for everyone involved."

Harbinger stroked his head. She rubbed away the strain and worry. She watched as he drifted into a light doze. Towards the end she had feared she would die. She had felt her strength ebb as she strove to produce her children. She did not fear death but she feared to leave Jeffeaux unprotected, her campaign unfinished. Only her great determination not to abandon Jeffeaux to the circumstances she had created for him kept her grim hold on life. He was safely here under her protection. She would recover to wage war one more time. All her husbands but one had heirs of her body. That one would never expect an heir from her so her duty was fulfilled. She could sleep.

Pindar stood in the assembly rooms. He raised a glass in celebration. Twin daughters had been born during this Great Council. As much as it went against his inclination he could not ignore such a sign. Her will was just. The persecution of the priests had to end. He looked into the eyes of all around him. They all realized what he already knew. The old ways had to be left behind. The priests had become unimportant, not threatening. To persecute them was in a way tying Sarna to the past. The past was nothing; the priests were nothing. Let them go to the Lady Zona.

Pindar frowned in thought. He considered his village. His village knew how to care for travelers. That was what they did best. No travelers would come their way again. They did not have to learn new trades, develop new industry. They could, but their skills were useful and needed somewhere else. He would move his village, leave their old life behind in old Sarna. This was a new community. Anything was possible, even giving birth to twin daughters.

Steady Heart sighed. She squared her shoulders as she contemplated the building. Her shadow stood behind and beside her. She had become used to the companionship of silence. She smiled down at the serious face.

"They don't respect me." Steady Heart spoke under her breath.

"So?" Her small shadow dismissed her hesitation.

"It can be wearing." Steady Heart defended her displeasure at the coming task.

"If you say so. Do we have to go in?" The boy offered a way out.

"Yes." Steady Heart sighed in resignation.

Silence greeted her answer. She tightened her grip slightly then started into the building. She was acknowledged with frowning nods. She had known that the reaction to her companion would be negative but she would not leave him behind. He would not have stayed behind in any case.

Finally the silent criticism was made verbal by an elder member.

"This is not a place for children."

"Is there such a rule?" Steady Heart asked even though she knew there was no such rule.

"No, but tradition is clear."

"Where Steady Heart goes I go." The small shadow spoke firmly.

The words were Llweganian but the accent was clearly Sarnese. Stunned silence answered the revelation. The elder member stared at the boy then a jovial expression creased the face.

"The enemy, I have often wondered how they would invade our country. I see they are sending children as spies into the seat of power of Llwegania."

Another member turned to the boy.

"We have been discussing an issue this youngster may help us answer. Little man tell me how likely is it Harbinger of Death will maintain control of Sarna? Won't the people rise up against her soon?"

General laughter filled the room. He watched in disgust as they insulted him and Steady Heart and most especially Laughing Heart with their ridicule of Harbinger and of the campaign.

He waited until the room quieted.

"Before Harbinger, the priests of Kersai controlled who had children, water. The Wardens decided who had land, trade rights, travel permits. Harbinger gives us water, land, freedom of movement within our territories. She builds schools and promotes trade and provides seeds for planting and materials for building. She has just given birth to twin daughters. The Sarnese people will see this as a blessing on her rule. They will never rise up against her." He spoke with the authority and assurance of a survivor. "She destroyed my home. She tore it to the ground and built a new one in its place. She is our conqueror, our invader, our provider." He remembered Laughing Heart with a wrench to his heart. He could see her playing with him in the ruins of his home, giving him joy amidst destruction. "You were not there. You will never understand. You can only believe when I say Sarna will rise up to defend Harbinger. They will never accept the priests and Wardens back; not ever."

Steady Heart placed a hand on her protégé's shoulder. She drew him close to her side in a protective move. He did not resist. The room filled with strained silence. Then voices raised in frustration. Steady Heart listened as conversations swirled around her. She did not try to sort who said what. She listened to the words to remember them later but she didn't pay attention to who said what.

"We will need another avenue. Obviously she has secured her borders well."

"If we believe the words of a child."

"Out of the mouth of babes truth falls with ease and power."

"Ancient saying, of no meaning."

"Have the messengers reported anything to disprove this babe?"

"No, they all agree. Sarna is safe."

"She may lose in Masfin yet. Then that border will be her responsibility."

"She will place her choice on the throne. He will be her ally. Her only opposition in all the world will be here."

"Then we will find that other reason."

Steady Heart knew her companion was looking at her. He was waiting for her to make a decision. She glanced around the room. She would go home. There was little she wished to do here. Standing against her dead sister's choices seemed petty and futile. Laughing Heart had not been wrong in her assessment of Harbinger. The warrior was a good leader and a strong defender of Llwegania. It was past time to go home. She picked up her guest. He placed his head on her shoulder in a familiar motion. He smelled of soap and child and the outdoors.

"Let's go home."

"Please, this place is boring and filled with stupid people."

"Out of the mouths of babes."

"I am not a babe."

"No, you are my little man."

"I won't always be little."

"That is why it is not wise to bring baby predators home with you. They grow into large dangerous beasts that inhabit your house."

He laughed. He had not thought to ever laugh again. Childish laughter burst from him in great gasps. It shook his body. He snuggled his face into her neck again. She had a daughter close to his age. He would have to marry that girl to gain possession of his new home. He decided in that moment his course of action.

"I am going to take your daughter to wife so I can always be your son."

Her heart burst. It strangled her throat. It fogged her brain.

"I will give her to you if you want but you do not need to marry her to be my son. I will claim you as my sister's legacy. You will be my son because we both wish it."

His arms tightened until they too strangled her throat. She bore the pain joyfully.

"She gave me everything, now even my own mother."

She heard the whispered words. They filled her with sadness and joy. He could not know that he had chased her last jealousy away. She could love her sister. She could be grateful to her sister. She could remember her sister. She could owe her sister this boy's love without feeling obligation or anger that it truly came from circumstances created by her sister. This person loved her for herself but they only knew each other through the link of her sister. That was a good thing. Their connection kept her sister alive in their hearts. She could give to her sister by receiving from her sister. It made her happy.

Harbinger rode slowly. Crowds lined the streets in celebration. They cheered her progress. The birth of twins had set off a national holiday. Harbinger waved to the crowds. She kissed babies. She slept in village squares. She was gracious if surprised.

"Do we have time for this?"

"It is a long winter on the peninsula. Much longer than Tampello."

"How much longer?"

"They make their living by weaving wool and logging. They weave all winter. During the short spring and summer they log. They export as much as they can during the short summer. They cannot grow food enough to last the winter because the growing season is so short. They fish some. The peninsula is the nesting place for sea creatures and birds so they hunt for meat. The skins of the sea creatures are much sought after for boots and coats because of their water resistant attributes."

"We are two months into winter. How much longer?'

"At least four months. It's winter six months of the year there."

"I had not realized. Surely I would have remembered if someone had told me."

"They are an isolated community. Not many people know much about them besides their leather goods, wood and woolens."

"How does the wood grow if the place won't support crops?"

"Trees are less fragile than grain."

Harbinger smiled. "Is there anything about your kingdom you do not know, King Jeffeaux?"

"I have much to learn."

"Good answer."

Chapter 21

Renfrew was worried. He could see his name being written on a list. By all he had heard of the criteria used he belonged on that list. His brother, his wife, his contact, his excursion into Sarna all qualified him for that list. That list was death. There was an arrest, no prison time. You went from the arresting officer right to trial. How long did a trial take? The length of time it took to say a name, read a list of required offenses, that's how long. Then the accused was marched to the executioner's block. All this was done in a very efficient manner. Any research or evidence was taken care of prior to the arrest. There was nothing to impede the process of execution. And who would complain? If you complained you were an enemy. You had to have something to fear or to hide to complain. There was no need to bother with proof. Questioning the King's decision was proof enough.

Renfrew looked out on the dark courtyard. The leaping torchlights created a nightmare world that echoed his mood. He deserved to be on that list. Not because of his wife or brother or captivity in Sarna or even his clandestine meeting with his wife, no, he deserved to be on that list for Tampello, for everything he did that kept Ranald in power. But Tampello would keep him off that list. His continued wise council would keep him off that list. His importance to the Sarnese army would keep him off that list.

Ranald needed the Sarnese troops. The Masfin soldiers were melting away. Those Ranald did not kill faded into the ever expanding border of Jeffeaux's kingdom. Only the Sarnese army had no place to go. Only those exiles had no choice but to endure the whims of the mad king. And their leaders were attached to Renfrew. He was their link and so he was able to stay alive. But some day his name would appear on that list.

For Ranald had surrounded himself with men as mad as he. Men mad for power, money, position, all the dregs of the court sat next to Ranald now. They whispered in his ear. They suggested names for those lists. They eliminated rivals and enemies through those lists. Someone would envy Renfrew and in a fit of madness Ranald would let his name go. And this waiting would be over.

This guilt would be assuaged. When Ranald had nothing left to lose, Renfrew would die.

He could kill himself and be done. The thought appealed to him often. But he lacked the courage. He would let someone else bear the burden of his death.

He shook his head. He could not think of that right now. He would not let fear for himself or concern for the doomed cloud his mind. He had to protect the remainder of the army. The best way to protect them was to help them be victorious. There was an opportunity here. They could hold off the attack long enough to rebuild their strength and perhaps field an expedition in the spring. If this winter's camp was not harsh or insupportable.

Renfrew raised his head. The sound that had worried at his consciousness had finally become unavoidable. A small slim man stood in the doorway. Renfrew recognized that shape. His nemesis stood there.

"What do you do, General Renfrew?"

"I am planning a great victory."

"A change of pace for you."

Renfrew remained silent. He would not be drawn into an admission. Any phrase or word could be used against him out of context.

"Not very sociable today are we? Or don't Generals use good manners?'

"I am very busy."

"I guess they don't."

The man began to advance into the room. Renfrew carefully covered his work. He did not want prying eyes touching his work.

"Secretive aren't you."

"I am under specific orders from King Ranald himself."

"I am glad you brought King Ranald up. I am the new Commander of Security for the King."

"I had heard something about that."

"In my capacity I have to interview all the King's officers and soldiers."

"You must be very busy." The implication in Renfrew's tone was a question as to why this small man was wasting his time.

"I have one question for you. Do you believe King Ranald is the True King?"

Renfrew placed his hand squarely over his papers as a seemingly innocent hand tried to pull some of the papers towards it owner.

"King Ranald has declared the concept of the True King to be a superstitious fairy tale. King Ranald is king by right of birth, because the previous king declared King Ranald his heir, because he was crowned by the traditions of our people. There is no True King in the sense that Masfin chooses a king."

There was a moment of silence.

"You are very clever."

"I am King Ranald's man. I will give every ounce of my ability to defend his crown. That is what I know."

"Why?"

"I gave my word. I will not break it. I gave my word to King Ranald."

"That is not stopping your fellow officers. It did not stop your own brother."

"I am myself. I do what I do. I made a promise. King Ranald was duly crowned king."

"What do you think of Jeffeaux?"

"He is ruled by a strange woman. He makes his choices based on values and considerations I cannot trust. His mother goes into battle. What kind of man is he?"

There was little to say to those arguments. They were from the heart and they held no room for compromise.

"Yet, you married his sister."

"She is a traditional Masfin woman. I thought to give her some protection once we win. She is the wife of my heart. I could not deny her every hedge against disaster in my power. It is not her fault she is where she is. She followed her mother and brother's directions as a proper young Masfin woman should do. It is not wise to love the sister of my enemy but when is the heart ever wise."

A grunt greeted this answer. "Her sister left."

"They are very different women. My wife is a gentle, retiring soul. She would not venture into the wastes. I would not want her other than she is. When this is over I will keep her safe. Let her rest away from the center of action. This must be a terrible trial to her." Renfrew spoke his thoughts about his ideal woman. He could not in truth say what kind of woman his wife was except that she has eased his body better than any other. She had given him comfort in the haven of her arms he had not found since, for an agony that ate at him even in his dreams. She had not condoned him, nor had she claimed to understand. In fact she had criticized him and still she had eased his despair. She was a harsh woman to ride into dangerous situations for a goal. But he suspected that he loved her more than life. He suspected that he could respect her when he could not respect himself. And when he could not find peace he would remember his few moments with her as a balm to his spirit and he was calmed.

Some of his emotion leaked into his face. The small man could not rebut the look. He could only feel a sneaking sympathy for a man who could be destroyed for loving the wrong woman.

"So what do you think of your sister-in-law?"

"That she is the Queen. I have found family a difficult association. I try not to have too much. You can't control their actions and those actions can impact you in terrible ways. I believe that the Queen is best served by my remaining a general in her husband's army. Any close contact with me might contaminate her with association with the brother of an enemy general. It is in the King's best interest that I remain distant from them in familial ways."

The small man had to credit Renfrew: he had the correct answers. He did not for a moment believe that Renfrew was as innocent as he portrayed but then it was his job to suspect everyone. And if he derived satisfaction from his work what could anyone say?

If Renfrew was truly loyal he could withstand inquiry. He was the brother-in-law of the Queen. Renfrew had no hint of impropriety or questioning the King in any manner. There was no reason to suspect Renfrew except for his unavoidable associations. Not quite unavoidable in the case of the wife, surely.

"It is not wise to allow our hearts to make such important decisions as choosing a spouse. Take me; I married the woman my parents chose."

"You are lucky that your parents chose someone without siblings."

"How did you know that?"

"It is common knowledge. There is a saying or joke that you are ideal in this position, you have no siblings or in-laws to worry about."

The little man had heard the words whispered.

"Where did you hear this?"

"Actually it was carved in the washroom wall. You are very famous. Even I don't have such distinction."

Renfrew gained only momentary satisfaction from seeing the small man turn beet red from anger and embarrassment. Then Renfrew looked beyond his visitor. There was a messenger waiting. Renfrew waved the man into the room. The messenger skirted the small man. He tried to be as inconspicuous as possible.

Renfrew opened the paper. He read the lines twice. Carefully he gathered his work. He secured it in a leather case. Everything fitted into leather cases. The case was placed with its brothers. Renfrew closed the heavy iron door on the cases. The small man watched the actions. He dearly wished to see what was in those cases. Renfrew turned the key in the inner lock. Then he closed the outer lock. Only King Ranald had access to this safe. Everyday Renfrew prepared a report on the contents of the safe. The King reviewed the contents each day. Renfrew kept his eye on the little man.

"I have to leave. I have an important meeting with our allies. I would not wish to insult them by being late. You see Generals do have manners. Excuse me."

The small man was frustrated. Nothing had been left for him to search. Everything was secreted away or carried off. He was not a military officer. He could not demand to know what the note said that sent Renfrew scurrying away nor could he demand to know the contents of the military safe. He was jealous that Renfrew had this separate tie to King Ranald. He wished to control all access to the King. Renfrew had his separate line to the throne, and he had an independent source of influence. Those allies who put such trust in Renfrew meant a great deal to the King.

Renfrew walked briskly to his meeting. He swung his arms vigorously. He tried to work out his frustrations through physical release of his emotional energies. He was grateful to have somewhere to go. He did not think he could have taken one more second of the small man. He hoped he lived long enough to see the little man fall from power.

There were the Sarnese tents. They were well-cared for and neat. They were precisely aligned and square to the Masfin encampment. Renfrew felt relief to be walking into their orderly environs. He felt safe and free in the strange world of the Sarnese soldiers.

Stiefis met him. They smiled in greeting. Stiefis turned to fall into step with Renfrew.

"Sorry to call you out so late."

"It was no bother. I was already interrupted. Your note was a relief."

Stiefis was quiet. They had arrived at his goal. They bent into the tent. Weirhass stood as they entered. Renfrew waved him to sit down again.

"I am an old soldier."

"I value that, sir." Renfrew sat down heavily. He poured himself a glass of wine. Stiefis sat quietly.

"The war is lost."

"Yes."

No one spoke for long minutes. They all stared into their pasts and their futures.

"Do you have some aim?"

"Keeping as many of my soldiers alive as I can until they are captured by Jeffeaux's forces. It is ironic but I can only keep them alive until Jeffeaux can take them by having them score some victories against Jeffeaux."

"Ah." Weirhass looked down into his goblet.

"You must be very careful, sir. You can't fade into the background easily. You have to watch for….well, my best advice is fight hard for the King. Fight with every breath to give him victory on your way to surrender. I must be honest. We have been too long on this path for me to give you less than my best opinion. Sarna is lost. Your only hope is surrender."

"I see. You say nothing I have not thought. Did you know I like Harbinger?"

"Really, sir?"

"Yes. I have always admired her. You must be very careful yourself. You have many enemies."

"I know. Every morning I wake up surprised I survived the night. Even now I think I hear spies crawling in the dark."

"We have occasional infestations. They are dealt with summarily. I have no use for creatures that lurk in the shadows. It is impossible for a Masfin to pass for Sarnese even in the dark." Renfrew grunted. There were so few Sarnese left, relatively speaking. Everyone knew everyone else. No one could pretend to be a Sarnese soldier. There were no new recruits. The physical differences could be disguised in the dark but you could not pretend to be an unknown member of the group for every member was known and accounted for at all times.

Weirhass took a moment to admire Harbinger for her disguise when she rode into Sarna. She had hidden her physical differences under paint and finery and bravado. He had not expected deceit and so had seen none. Now in a second look he would have seen that she could not possibly be Masfin. Then, he had not questioned her reality.

"Does King Ranald not fear mutiny?"

"Of course. That is the whole impetus for his actions in the mornings."

"No, more forcefully, if the entire officer corps stood up to deny him, the King would have no power. Does he think this will not happen? Isn't there a point at which it has to happen? Can this killing go on until Harbinger crushes the army?"

"Or it collapses from within. I have no idea. I can't be involved. I have to use every ounce of my will and reason to keep the rest of the army alive. I am pushing a great ball up a steep hill. It rolls back on me every day but I must continue to push."

Stiefis pushed away from the table. He felt a great weight of guilt push at him. Somewhere in his actions he could have made a better choice. If only he had made that better choice they would not be sitting here now all staring death - not honorable death but ignominious death - in the face.

"The next moon is the Feast of the Battle Maid."

"I wonder if anyone is making Battle cakes or Maid pudding."

"I love Maid pudding, warm from the oven, steam rising from the hard sauce."

"Yes, I can still smell it. There is nothing quite as tasty. We should go on a raid into Sarna for Maid pudding. There should be Battle cakes cooling on every window ledge."

Weirhass smiled into his goblet. Young boys had gotten into trouble many a time for stealing those cooling cakes. Stiefis himself had suffered the whack of a wooden spoon trying to pilfer the sweet mouthfuls.

"Feast of the Battle Maid?"

"Yes. There are several nights of feasting and dancing and reenactments of the Battle Maid's refusal to marry Kersai. Horse races are held to determine who will be Kersai. The races are very difficult. They range over very rough terrain and last for many hours. It is a test of stamina of both horse and rider."

"How do they choose the Battle Maid?"

"There is no Battle Maid. Her armor is brought out of the Temple. The rider circles the armor five times. She refused Kersai five times so her armor is circled five times. Then the battle begins. But the rider does not battle; he retires with his friends to celebrate the holiday."

Renfrew kept quiet. He thought a rite without a Battle Maid hardly could be called the feast of the Battle Maid. One never argued religion.

"There will be no Feast of the Battle Maid. There's probably some water rite now." Stiefis spoke into his cup.

"Women probably dance naked in a lake or something."

"I wouldn't really mind watching that." Renfrew spoke thoughtfully. He rolled his goblet in his hands. "It has distinct possibilities."

Stiefis blinked at the irreverent tone. He stared at Renfrew. The he looked at his father. Weirhass' face was mottled for a moment. Then a huge laugh burst into the air. Through his chortles Weirhass managed to gather enough air to speak.

"You may be right, especially if the water is cold."

"Definitely."

"You are both disrespectful."

"No, my son, I certainly respect the idea, which was yours to begin with."

"I wonder if there are any Llweganian festivals."

"No."

Renfrew stared at Weirhass' definitive answer.

"They do not have holidays. They only ever work. The closest they come is Assizes Court. That is structured around legal and administrative duties. Llweganians do not have special days for relaxation. Their relaxation is fighting, working, they are a grim people."

"They sound it. I can't see Jeffeaux as fitting in with that crowd. He was a courtier. He spent his time and money on clothes and women."

"He had a lot of changing to do to last with Harbinger. I mean it. I had a Llweganian wife once. She never understood the concept of holiday or feast or celebration. Duty was her god. And work. Those two things only. They are not easy neighbors to have."

"We have found that out. Still, you like her."

"My wife?"

"No, Harbinger."

"Well she is not grim. She is capable."

"Capable? I guess."

Stiefis slammed his goblet down on the table.

"Could we talk of something besides enemies and women?"

"I don't know, those seem to be my best subjects. That and intrigue but usually that includes women or enemies or both."

"There has to be some other topic of conversation. I don't want to be depressed anymore." Stiefis left the tent. Renfrew and Weirhass drank in silence for a while. Then Stiefis returned. He sat heavily.

"You must have a guard."

Renfrew lifted his hand to his head.

"I thought of that but the potential for betrayal is too great. It certainly outweighs any measure of protection it affords. Loyalty is so hard to come by when it is regulated by life and death rules. People will die for you freely when they are allowed the choice. When their lives depend on their loyalty they can only think of protecting their lives. Interesting situation isn't it? How to destroy the one thing you wish to promote."

"You could have a Sarnese guard."

"Oh right, that would look well. I already have detractors because of my foreign associations. My association with you might save my life for the moment, but if I seem to be too close, I would become very suspect. It is a thin line I walk." Renfrew slapped the table with his hand. "I am a soldier. I don't expect to die in my bed of old age. I might die in my bed of intrigue but I can't worry about that. Have you no food to go with this wine? I hate to march on an empty stomach."

"Where do we march?"

Renfrew laughed shortly. "I have no idea. Harbinger probably knows better than I. She is pushing us to the shore."

Stiefis sat heavily. He had a great fear of the water. Since the debacle by the river at Reduni, Stiefis had held a healthy respect for the power and danger of water.

"Will we have to fight on the water?"

"There is a royal navy but it is for show only. We have no enemies to contest with over the ocean. There were pirates, thieves who stopped merchant ships to steal cargoes. The royal navy dealt with them. Wrecking became a more profitable way to steal the cargoes. Anyway the ships aren't very big. They couldn't be used for anything more than transportation."

Stiefis tried to imagine what a wrecker was. "All we would need is transportation: a safe way to move."

"Ships need places they can come close to the shore. They need the water to be a certain depth. There aren't that many places that can accommodate the size of ships we would need to move our men and horses and equipment. Most of the shoreline requires little boats to transport man and goods from the shore to the waiting ships. It would be a nightmare."

"Then we have to secure one of those special places."

"True. Here, I need a map."

Stiefis spread a large map on the table. Renfrew turned it until he was satisfied.

"Here are the natural harbors and the man-made ones. This is the front. How many harbors do you see on our side of the line?"

"Three."

"Right. These two will be shortly lost. This one is where we are now. Let me tell you about Takinga peninsula. It is worse than Tampello. If we get trapped here," Renfrew sighed deeply. He pushed the map from him. "If we get trapped here, we might as well cut our throats. It is a cold water port, which means that in the winter even the ocean freezes."

"I know you hated the desert, Renfrew, but I would take the dust and the hot days and the frigid nights over the winter of Masfin. I don't think this old body of mine can endure another such winter as the one we spent at Tampello."

"I used all my powers of persuasion to prevent coming here to Takinga but my military advice is never heeded. The King only listens to his own advice."

Jeffenza stood by the bed. Her royal husband had sent a message that he would visit her tonight. She had almost sent back that she was unwell but in the last moment had refrained. The gleam in the page's eye told her that he expected her refusal. She would not give in to that expectation. She had to bear a son anyway. She might as well get it over with. She had hated being pregnant. She hated the physical changes. She hated the social restrictions. She hated the pain and suffering during and after. Luckily she could hand the child over to nannies and servants. She needed to have a son. She needed to cement her position as the mother of the future king. So she waited.

The door opened. He stood in the doorway. The years had robbed him of his hair but not his air. He was the King. She stretched out her hand.

"Welcome, Sire."

"Queen Jeffenza, let us see if we can get this right this time."

Jeffenza knew that he meant that they should make a son. He did not care if she enjoyed the act. She wondered if he enjoyed it. She lay on the bed with her nightgown raised only high enough to not impede him. His night robe was still on. He pulled her until her legs hung off the side of the bed. He spread her legs. She felt the discomfort of having him enter her while she was not ready. She lay in the dark wondering how soon he would be done. She listened to his sounds of effort, and yes, she heard his pleasure at the end. All she felt was relief he was done.

"I will come every night until you are with child. I suggest that while I am here you concentrate on begetting a son."

Jeffenza did not mention that there might be a couple of nights when it would do him no good to come. If he were so ignorant of women's cycles she would not enlighten him. Let him find out for himself.

Jeffenza rolled onto her side. She curled until her knees were under her chin. Being Queen was nothing like she had imagined. And the price was very high.

Harbinger stood in the clearing. She looked at the four bodies on the ground. A great sadness welled in her throat. Their dress was not that of deserters or criminals. She rolled one of the bodies over gently. They had been here some time. Even criminals received appropriate death rites. What had these done to deserve such cruel treatment even in death?

"Are there any prisoners?"

"Yes."

"Bring me one."

"Officer or enlisted?'

"Enlisted, they know everything and might tell."

Harbinger waited. She turned each body over. She carefully examined them for clues to their identities. She was sure they were Masfin. She looked up as Marjas returned. He brought a Sarnese soldier.

"Interesting choice. I wonder if he knows anything."

"I can bring a Masfin if you like."

"No, that's all right. I didn't realize we even had any Sarnese prisoners. I thought they always killed themselves rather than be captured."

"That is why I chose him."

Harbinger stood. She faced the grim faced man. She dusted her hands off as she walked away from the bodies.

"I am only curious. Don't worry. I don't think I am about to ask you anything strategically important. You probably don't have an answer for me. These men, why would four high-ranking Masfin officers be executed and left for the animals in the forest?"

"Because their king is mad. He is killing all his officers. You will find their bodies everywhere."

"You can say nothing. You don't have to lie."

"I am not lying. He is purging his army of any who might be tempted to defect to you or wish to follow Jeffeaux. He is mad. Everyone fears him. Comrades are turning each other in. There is a corps dedicated solely to ferreting out any potential weakness in loyalty."

Harbinger looked into the face of her ancient enemy. He had come to her. He had been left to tell her this. She looked into his eyes. He might even be all alone in this.

"Mad and stupid. I won't have to wait long to defeat Ranald if he kills off all his officers. Will their army stand for this? Won't someone stand up to him?"

"There is a plot. It circles like a ghost. No one knows who is in it. It might be only a story to give comfort to the fearful."

"Instead it gives impetus to Ranald I bet; or his corps at least. There must be rot in this body; let us keep cutting until we find it."

"Until the patient is dead."

Harbinger went to stand over the bodies. She studied the chewed features and decaying flesh.

"Can you return safely?"

"If I can't, I will die."

"As you will. Tell Weirhass it must be unconditional, but at least I am not mad."

Jeffeaux and Marlin arrived as the Sarnese soldier left the clearing. Jeffeaux joined Harbinger over the bodies. Marlin went to the last spot he had seen the enemy.

"What was that?"

"The Sarnese leaders have asked for terms. I told him there were none but I would accept surrender."

Jeffeaux knelt to lift one hand. He turned a ring to the light.

"What happened here?"

"Ranald is purging his officer corps. The Sarnese think him mad. They see us as a better option."

Jeffeaux let the hand drop into the dust.

"My sister is married to their madman."

"There is rumor of a plot against him. How much danger could she face if there is a palace coup?"

"How do I know?"

"Have there been any coups in the past? Is there a tradition around royal assassinations? What would be acceptable limits of bloodletting?"

Jeffeaux grimaced. "No. We are not like that. The Masfin people are very civilized."

Harbinger looked down at the corpses.

"Very civilized, I can see that."

Jeffeaux felt tears well in his eyes. He could not envision anyone ordering this act. He felt Harbinger squeeze his shoulder.

"We will finish this soon. I promise."

Marlin bent to look more closely at the bodies.

"I do not know what I hope for, Your Highness. If Renfrew survives Ranald we will have to try him for the deaths at Tampello."

"If he is found guilty I will have to order his death."

"Still I am glad he is not here, your Highness."

"Then I am glad for you also. Come, there is an army we must defeat so we can save it."

Marlin looked at the abandoned bodies. He stopped a passing soldier.

"Take what we need to identify these men, then bury them."

"Yes sir, General sir."

Harbinger stretched in thought. Petron waited until she was done. He held a single stone out to her. Harbinger accepted the stone. She rubbed the smooth surface.

"Something wrong, Harbinger?"

"One of those pesky messengers from the Council. I manage to forget about them for great blocks of time now. I guess there are advantages to being a king, Your Highness."

Jeffeaux thought of the excesses that could arise from a monarchy. He thought that a council was a good brake on the less worthy wielders of power. He did not think Harbinger would disagree with his position. Still, he would hesitate to mention his thoughts on the matter to her. She had such an adversarial relationship with her country's council.

"I wonder what they want now."

"To contain me, to threaten me, to find out what I am up to. Any or all of the above."

Waiting for Harbinger was difficult. One had to sit among the milling crowds of troops and allies. Riding through Sarna had been unnerving. He had thought the mission would have some inherent difficulties, but he had met people who spoke Llweganian at every stop. He had been afforded respect and honor by each person, even once he had crossed into Masfin. In fact he received better service once he left Llwegania.

In Llwegania he had the fine treatment his position deserved but that was all. He received no extra service or better treatment. In Sarna and Masfin he was treated as a high ranking official. He received only the best food and lodgings all along the way. He had been upset to have to be the one to travel so far but now he would volunteer every time the Council needed a message sent to Harbinger.

His pouch was strapped to the front of his body. It was very heavy. He did not know its contents. He suspected it would not be a pleasant communication. The expressions of the Council members who had given him his charge had not been pleasant. In fact he had thought he detected fear, reservation, and uncertainty in the faces that stood behind the missives he carried. If they were planning to cross Harbinger, they should well have second thoughts. He had just seen and experienced the extent of her power and it was a force to be reckoned with.

She was coming. He could tell by the shifting of the crowd's movement. They were clearing a way between him and someone. The only someone he had any reason to see was Harbinger. He did not know her by sight. He had only been a boy when she had last attended Council meetings. Now her heir came instead. He knew what Wind Rider looked like, very well. He could see the same eyes and body language in a small woman. Well, not small, but she did not stand very high. She was speaking with a very tall elegantly dressed man. He was not Llweganian. The messenger wondered if this was the King Jeffeaux who was part of Harbinger's legend. He certainly had the air of one who ruled people's lives.

He had no more time for wondering; Harbinger was standing in front of him. He stood quickly. She waited calmly as he unbuckled his pouch. She took the weight from him with no visible effort. She sat behind her table. Maps were neatly placed away. She methodically filed her notes and other official papers. He could not see the notes. The skins and paper they were written on looked different from Llweganian products so he assumed they were all connected with Masfin and Sarnese business. Finally she placed the pouch squarely in front of her. He stood patiently waiting for her. He could not leave until she dismissed him. He relaxed his knees into a waiting stance.

No seat was offered to him. He could not sit while she read the papers inside. There were downsides to being an official messenger of the Council. His life was comfortable. He received the best of everything. He received more onerous duties than a Household messenger. He thought about this Household. He thought of the messengers who had rotated through Harbinger's care. Perhaps they had more onerous duties as well. They certainly had been in more chancy situations than a Council messenger. He shied away from his thoughts. He could not let his mind wander. He had to remain alert for any sign from Harbinger.

She grunted twice while she read the contents of the pouch. She pushed a large pile of papers to one side. Her husbands began to read through the pile at her signal. She shook her head. Then she laughed.

"They are desperate."

"Is everything all right?"

"Everything is fine, Your Highness. They are trying to bluff with me. They forget, I control nineteen votes on the Council. I have given heirs to all my husbands. My daughter has given heirs to seven of her husbands. I have my own vote. I can block any legal move they try to make. They have no legal recourse. I have done my Walks at appropriate intervals. I have Assizes Court at the proscribed times. My Estate is well cared for. My heir attends Council regularly. The border has been quiet for many harvests. They send so much paper to try to fool me. They can't. Still we will read this through completely to see what there is to see." There was a threat in her tone. He could well imagine the list of enemies she would compile.

"Go, messenger. Rest. I will call for you when I am ready to reply. Soon we will be finished here and I will be able to answer this in person. Won't that set them back on their heels."

He wondered where he was supposed to rest. He hesitated long enough to gain someone's attention. He noted the dress of his own guild; there was something wrong. Ah, yes, the Household messenger would have the trappings of the Household as well. That was the wrongness he saw. He raised his hand in greeting.

"Trying to unseat her, are they?" The Household Messenger smiled in real amusement as she asked the question.

He hesitated. Messengers were not supposed to discuss business. They could speak of guild matters or of road conditions; they could not talk about business. And all politics was business; that was their function. They were the communication lines for the political powers of Llwegania.

"Don't be foolish." The Household Messenger did not wait for his answer. "You can pretend to be separate or above most things but not this. Our entire world has changed. Nothing will be the same. Those who held my position before me knew. I will be lucky. I will see the moment the change hardens into our new road. Sarna is no more. There is only a small threat and that is not from Sarna. Once Ranald is defeated there will be no hostile borders. She will be a kingmaker in one country, a liberator, giver of water in another. What do they think she will be at home? A peer whom they can chastise? They should be afraid. If they had joined her they could have shared in all of this and been her peers or at least close to it. They bet on the wrong horse. They bet on Sarna. More fools they."

He looked into the lined face. He tried to see where the guild masters had gone wrong in choosing this woman. She had fallen from her training.

"I know what you are thinking. I thought the same when I spoke to my predecessor. What is he thinking? Has he forgotten all his training? Doesn't he know the first rule of our guild? There is something about watching the world change that is intoxicating and involving. You'll see."

"I won't be here that long."

"It doesn't take long. You'll be here a while anyway. That was quite a missive you brought. It can't be dealt with in a moment. She is in the middle of a war. She will use her entire allotted time."

He kept his reaction to himself. He did not wish to antagonize his comrade. He followed quietly until they reached a tent. Then he relaxed enough to smile his thanks.

"Rest while you can. We will be moving out soon. This will be the last tent to go."

"I have to get back."

"You will. You ride with the army until she is ready." The hand that opened the flap tapped his shoulder. "You relax. I am leaving with a message for the Council now. When I get back we can share a drink and exchange opinions."

He sat on the cot. These were the least comfortable digs he had used since he had begun this journey. He smiled. He had finally reached the headquarters of the most powerful army and the amenities were Spartan. At least the sheets were clean.

Harbinger was tired of listening to the discussion on the message from the Council. She knew everything she needed to know about the message. It was a threat. She shoved all the papers away from her. Silence fell on the room like a sword. She placed a map before her. It was an old, once familiar map. She went to the fire. She drew a twig from the bottom of the flames. The blackened wood darkened her hands. She placed the charred carbon on the map. With a steady hand she drew a dark bold line on the map.

"This is my border. I am answerable to, responsible to the people south and west of this line." She placed another map on the table. She poured stones onto the map. They crowded each other. She carefully removed stones from the pile. She rearranged the remaining rocks. Then she moved them into a distinct pattern. The pattern was impressive. She shook the stones in her hand. Their clicking echoed in the space. She moved her hand until the clicking hovered over the first map. The stones fell in a small shower along the dark line.

Wind Rider left her seat. She studied both maps. Petron looked the new arrangement over carefully. Jorin looked at the dark line and its fortification. He shifted a couple of stones. She paused in her motions. Then she nodded acceptance of the rearrangement. Wind Rider gathered up the stones. She turned a grave face to her mother.

"This is not a new front. Be discrete, be gradual. Be so slow that to an observer it will not happen overnight.

"Have you abandoned all hope then?"

"No, I am cementing our ability to choose. I won't be backed into a corner even by the Council. You are my heir. Do you have an opinion on this?"

Wind Rider studied both maps. She drew them until they formed one great map.

"So you have decided Sarna's fate then."

"Yes."

Wind Rider left. Harbinger rolled the maps. She placed them in Petron's outstretched hand. She felt her decision settle on her shoulders. It was good they were broad.

She needed to have plans for the campaign against Ranald firmed up. She had to know exactly how many troops she could send to fortify her new border. She needed Marlin and Jeffeaux here but did not wish to alarm them. Where was Lady Zona?

Feet scrambled as someone went running for Lady Zona. Harbinger had not realized she spoke aloud.

Jeffeaux watched Wind Rider leave with a large section of the army. He felt a moment of doubt. Then he sighed. Marlin came to stand at his elbow.

"Your Highness."

"I wonder how far away this rear is."

Marlin said nothing. He looked at the rest of the army which was also preparing to move.

"It doesn't matter, Your Highness. We have trapped them on the Takinga peninsula for the winter. To leave they have to pass us. Our archers will be able to pick them off row by row if they try to escape. The harsh weather will cut down their numbers. Come spring we will decimate them."

"They can escape by ship."

"The seas are very rough, Your Highness. No ship dare them in winter. They can try. They will lose as many men to the ocean as to the winter. The harbor fills with ice. There aren't too many places they can get to for a landing. They can only sail until the sea eats them. We hold all the ports."

Jeffeaux thought of the soldiers who were being condemned to a slow death or a watery grave. "It seems extreme."

"You could demand their surrender again, Highness. Our last two messengers never returned. I suspect they did not defect. From the tales coming from the liberated lands Ranald probably cut them down as they spoke."

Jeffeaux closed his eyes in pain. He hated being King in these moments. People died on his choices, so many depended on his judgment. In extending his terms to save the lives of the Masfin soldiers, he risked condemning someone to death. The risk was almost a certainty. How many lives could he spend on a futile effort?

"Attacking now would get us nothing? Cost us everything? Be a waste of time and lives?"

"Attacking now, Your Highness, would chance us being caught in the same conditions we are trying to use to our advantage against our enemy."

Jeffeaux closed his eyes in frustration.

"But they are our people. We can't forget that."

Marlin felt his heart swell with an emotion he had thought long dead.

"You are right, Your Highness, that makes this a very bitter and difficult war. They are not only our people, they are our families. Your Highness feels this way. I feel this way. I hope that some who are on the other side feel as we do, but they are on the other side. They are the enemy. I have to believe that those who feel one with us have already joined us."

Jeffeaux felt a large grey area open at his feet. Those Masfin soldiers who had joined his army had come because they felt one with the Llweganian forces. Those whom Marlin had rescued from Tampello felt a degree of attachment to him. The people of Masfin who had been liberated regarded him, Jeffeaux as King. Now many Masfin soldiers were trapped in Ranald's army? How many truly followed Ranald? He needed to know. He could not, not ever really know. There were many things he could never know about this situation.

"I am just a little concerned, General. Harbinger would not send Wind Rider simply because she had a vague feeling about the rear. There is nothing vague about Harbinger."

"If it were important, Your Highness, Harbinger would have mentioned it. She still might. I suggest you ask her when the Council's messenger is not near."

Jeffeaux felt easier. There was a simple explanation. He had been looking for a plot when the only real issue was that stranger. The messenger had arrived. Harbinger was sending Wind Rider to the rear.

"Where is the rear?'

Harbinger smiled at Jeffeaux. They were alone in a sea of activity.

"Llwegania. I am concerned about my Council. Wind Rider is guarding our Estate borders."

Jeffeaux smiled across the crowd at his mother. She was busy trying to discuss something with Lady Junla.

"What have you done with their messenger?"

"Nothing. I have another moon until I have to send him back with my answer to their charges. It will take him a while to travel back. Then they will send a reply. By then we will be finished. Ranald will be defeated. I will have more leisure to formulate a response to their machinations."

"They have a legal right to chastise you."

"Yes, if I fail to keep my borders secure. My Sarnese borders are very secure. I have to assume that they have concerns about my Llweganian borders. Wind Rider will see to them."

Jeffeaux reviewed his knowledge of Llweganian law. He could not recall if she had any restraints on her powers. There were consequences if she failed her duty but beyond those explicit circumstances he could not remember any restrictions.

"If your borders are secure there are no qualifiers to your powers. Is that not right?"

Harbinger thought about her answer for a long time.

"Not as long as I am Head of my Household. I have complete control over everything in my Estates. It is like our marriages. I have the right to execute my husbands. I must let them go if they ask it of me. All who stay in my area of influence accept my dictates. If you can't accept my dictates, you leave. You can find someone else somewhere else to provide for your safety, keep the peace, provide for the common good, negotiate between the needs of the community and of the individual. I am considered quite good at those things. Most stay; in fact many have come to me from other Estates. Which is something considering that all my Estates march on or rather used to march on hostile territory. Still they came."

"If all the Estates were run by Heads of Household who were not good, then what? Is there any mechanism to protect people?"

"Not really. The Council is made up of only Heads of Household. If they are bad then so is the Council. You have to have faith. There is always one who is good. There are no absolutes. There are never only good or bad of anything. Anyway everything is changing. Wind Rider could be the final Head of Household of my Estates. Who knows what is on the other side of this venture. I have raised her well. She is a fitting heir. She is wise and strong and fair and has a sense of humor and responsibility. She will be a fine leader. Do you doubt my parenting? Are you saying my example has been poor? Are you saying I am not a good leader?"

Jeffeaux looked into Harbinger's eyes. He could not tell if she were upset or only teasing him or maybe both. He lowered his head.

"I am afraid. What is best for my people? How can I make sure there is never another king like Ranald? I know I can lead them well. I had a very good teacher, the best. How do I make sure that in years ahead they are protected from another such as Ranald? Did this war turn him into this monster? Was he always such a monster and this war only brought it out? Would he have turned into a monster eventually? Questions circle inside my head. I am looking for structure that will prevent this catastrophe."

Harbinger sighed. He took his duty very seriously.

"I would imagine that every system is open to abuses and dangers from within as well as without. There is no safeguard against monsters. You can only give your people the skills to watch for the monsters and the confidence to fight them"

Jeffeaux envied Harbinger her self-possession. He knew he had experienced great change. He had seen the changes in Sarna and now Masfin. He wondered if Harbinger had been touched by this experience, this war. She had to have been. Everyone else had.

She watched the tent opening as items in the tent were carted away. She touched Jeffeaux lightly on the elbow. He walked with her as the exited the canvas structure. He watched the tent collapse. In a billow of material and a puff of dust it was gone. He stole a glance at Harbinger. Did she see the poetry and grace of the collapse or did she see one duty finished? He rarely saw this. Usually they rode ahead while the camp was dismantled. Only on a rare occasion did they ride with the camp. He did not know her reactions around this issue. It seemed strange to him that after so many years of close companionship there were still large chunks of her he did not know.

Harbinger moved towards her mount. There was not much time for anything in her life except work. He could not hold her responsible for a lack of appreciation for the small moments in life. He went to where Marma waited.

He smiled into his consort's worried face. She sensed his moods easily. He wondered if she had always had that skill or if it had developed since their Ride. Standing in Delungor he had begun to believe all the traditions that spoke of the mystical qualities of Delungor and Reduni. On the consecrated steps of Reduni he had felt his spirit hover over him and Marma as they had made their vows.

He dared not mention his new beliefs in spirituality or religion in front of Harbinger. He feared to let his own generals know of his changing perception of the world. He wondered if Marma saw it; if she saw his strengthening tie to Masfin. He was not comfortable with the concept of feelings himself. He wished he could share it with someone. He wished someone would be able to talk him out of his new position.

He sighed. He could envision the crown on his head. It was a simple circlet. He did not know where it had come from but Marma had placed it there at Delungor. The Cleric at Reduni had blessed it for him. The weight of it seemed to tighten around his skull sometimes. Perhaps the metal itself was enchanted. The crown was sending these strange thoughts, impulses, feelings into his mind. He would have to ask Marma where she had found the crown.

Renfrew stood on the shore. The huge waves crested and smashed against the rocks. Snow fell around him in great curtains of freezing death. He had decided hell was a cold place. He turned his head to watch the shadow resolve into a person as it neared him. Deep in the cocoon of cloth and fur Renfrew recognized Stiefis' face.

"We cannot last here."

"No."

"We could try the pass."

"If the snows have not closed it, the pass will be fortified beyond escape."

"It is still open enough if slow going."

"Then there is the rain of arrows and boiling oil and fire to worry about."

"I would rather die fighting than spend another winter letting disease defeat me."

Renfrew closed his eyes against the thoughts in his head and the snow billowing from the ocean. He knew that Stiefis did not plan to die. He knew that the Sarnese army was massing for a great surrender. In all these years Renfrew had supported and defended the King but now he had to choose between his mad ruler and his fleeing friend. He had even pushed Stiefis to this action, this betrayal. He had to betray his King to allow this action to go unreported.

"Will you fight with us Renfrew, my old comrade?"

Renfrew turned his back to the sea. He looked Stiefis straight in the eye. He raised a hand to grasp Stiefis' forearm.

"This is one fight I cannot join. The death for me will be as slow in that battle as it will be in this winter. I have left myself one line of action and that is under the dubious coattails of my King. I wish you luck in your battle."

Stiefis waded through the snow to his waiting horse. Weirhass already sat astride his mount. The swirling snow soon ate them from Renfrew's sight. He remained a long while at his post. He waited until his nose was numb and his hands and feet had little feeling. Only when he was very sure that his former allies had enough of a head start did he walk back to his quarters. He decided he would look for the little man who had annoyed him for so long.

He banged on a well shut door. He felt pins and needles attack his flesh as his hand hit the wooden portal. In the middle of his second assault the wood swung open. Light and moisture poured into the space around Renfrew. He stepped into the room. Impatiently he shoved the hood away from his head. He fumbled his mittens from his hands. He flung the offending items on the table. All the while the small man stared at him in surprise and suspicion.

"Fools."

The little man sat on a very large seat.

"Idiots. I argued and argued but they were stubborn and would not listen."

"What are we talking about?"

"The Sarnese leaders, I tried to dissuade them but they went anyway."

"Went where?"

"They are launching an assault on the forces that hold the pass. They said they would rather die in battle than freeze to death here."

"What?!" The little man surged to his feet.

"They are gone. I didn't believe them. They told me they were doing this. I assembled my reasons. I returned to convince them of the error of their ways. They had left. In a very short time, I walked from the shore to their encampment only to find it empty. They must have been ready to go when they broached the subject with me. They will be dead by morning."

"How could you let them leave?"

"I didn't **let** them leave. I was doing my best to keep them here. They might still return once they realize how futile their action is. Or," Renfrew paused. He rubbed his nose with his tingling fingers. "They could succeed. There is that chance."

"They are dead. Why are you here?"

"You are closest to their camp besides my lodgings. You need to send a messenger to the King. He has to know immediately. I thought the cold might kill me before I could sound the alarm." The little man was smiling his most evil smile. Here was his chance. He would tell the King himself. He would use the opportunity to diminish Renfrew to nothing in the telling.

Renfrew watched the little man disappear. A small grin passed over his features. His days were certainly numbered but at least he had exacted this revenge for all his fallen fellow officers. He could see the future right at this point.

It needed witnessing. Renfrew redressed. The mittens stiff with cold still were difficult to put on. Renfrew persevered; he would not miss this.

He almost did. He did not get close enough to hear the exchange. He managed to see Ranald's face as he heard the news. He watched the sword rise. In a very detached mood he watched the little man's head fly across the room. He could very well be next but at least he had outlived that small person. He had lived long enough now.

Stiefis huddled over the saddle of his horse. He tried to reduce the area of his body exposed to the cold and wind. The poor creature plodded valiantly through the snow. Soldiers floundered and flailed through the deepening obstacle. Renfrew had been right. They would die before they could be killed by the Llweganian forces. Still, he would rather die now than later. There was no way to communicate without stopping. Stiefis thought it more important to keep moving than to speak to anyone so he never knew when the forward scouts reached their destination. He was aware of their success only when a black gloved hand grabbed hold of his halter.

His instinct was to resist the unexpected hold. The cold and his still conscious mind beat out instinct. He looked down into an impassive face. The words were difficult to form. He did not know if it was the cold or the words themselves.

"We surrender."

"I know, sir, I will get you out of this weather. It is not far. Once you are rested I have orders to bring you to Harbinger."

Stiefis released his hold on thought and awareness.

It was warm when he woke. His eyes blinked as he returned to the world of consciousness. He turned his head carefully. He started when he saw his father asleep not far from him. As promised he was warm.

Stiefis moved his head to get a better view of his father. In this light, from this angle, Weirhass looked old to Stiefis, old and frail. Stiefis turned his head away from the sight. He did not wish to see an old Weirhass. He was not comfortable with his thoughts. He wished for a distraction. Otherwise all he could do was obsess in his loss and defeat; and his guilt. Renfrew would be killed. He would be killed for failing to restrain the Sarnese from their retreat. He would be killed because his best hedge against death had faded away in the night. Even for Renfrew Stiefis could not condemn what remained of the Sarnese army to certain death. The guilt, however, ate at him, mocked him as he lay warm and comfortable.

"You are awake, good. Do you remember where you are?"

The final ride from the pass into the territory held by Jeffeaux had passed as if a dream. Stiefis could recall nothing of it; except that it had happened.

"No. Yes. Main body of the Llweganian and Masfin forces with Jeffeaux."

"Very good. You have a meeting as soon as you are dressed."

"My father?' Stiefis turned his head to look at Weirhass.

"He is still very weak. Harbinger has ordered him to complete bedrest. If you wish, she will come here."

Stiefis marveled at the gesture.

"She is most gracious." That thready whisper startled Stiefis and his keeper. "Only, prop me up in the bed more. I cannot meet her flat on my back."

Stiefis swayed on his feet as he readied himself. He watched his father's care from the end of his bed. Chairs were brought in. The few surviving Wardens filed into the room. They sat gently on the seats. Stiefis chose to remain standing. He did not know what motivated him. For some reason, he did not wish to be grouped with the other leaders. He leaned against a wall. Its rough texture pushed him into complete focus of his surroundings.

There was the sound of feet in the passageway. He held in his breath without thought. He did not remember to breathe until he felt his head begin to ache. Then he let the air out in a swoosh. Luckily the sound of the door opening covered the noise.

Grim-faced soldiers filed into the room. Suddenly the space was way too small. They lined the walls. Stiefis felt crowded out of his small refuge. He shifted until he sat back on the end of his bed. Then she entered. Her gaze touched every warden. The sternness of her visage made her inhuman.

"There are no terms." Harbinger made her position clear.

"We understood that." Weirhass confirmed.

"You surrender your men, horses, weapons to me unconditionally." Harbinger was determined that there would be no later recantation of the surrender.

"Yes." Weirhass confirmed again.

"Good." It was done. She let the reality seep into her mind.

"May I ask what you plan to do with us?" Weirhass asked deferentially.

"I am waiting for a reply." Harbinger sighed.

"A reply?"

"From Sarna. The last time I asked the Sarnese people indicated they did not wish you back. I have asked for confirmation on that decision." Harbinger clarified her answer.

"They refused us?" Stiefis could remain quiet no longer.

"Yes. I am considering settling you on my estate borders with my Llweganian neighbors. There would be a certain symmetry, a poetic justice in that arrangement."

"We can't go home?" Stiefis could not wrap his mind around this fact.

"No, the people you left behind do not wish to return to any variation of their former society. Since they are now my responsibility I have to bend to their wishes in this. I fought all my life to keep you out of Llwegania. Now I am thinking of bringing you into its heart. That would put me in a very difficult position with the Council. I hope you appreciate the humor in this situation."

Harbinger advanced into the room. She came to stand by Weirhass. She adjusted the blanket across his chest.

"Father Weirhass, I hope you are improving."

"Yes, daughter."

"I am discussing with King Jeffeaux what he thinks would be an acceptable solution. He is willing to absorb some of you. Your armorers, your horse handlers will be welcome to remain in Masfin. He wants all soldiers and priests gone. Frankly I have no idea what to do with the priests. Their lives are in grave danger in Sarna and I have absolutely no use for them in Llwegania. So talk amongst yourselves, give me some suggestions. As King Jeffeaux reminds me daily, by accepting your surrender I have accepted you as my responsibility. I could probably convince the Sarnese people to accept the rank and file back in their civilian lives. But the officers and the Wardens; I will have to do something else with you."

There was a stunned silence. She seemed genuinely concerned about their plight. They filed past her with fear in their step despite her gentle tones. The room emptied of people until only three remained. Stiefis eyes her warily. She drew a chair next to Weirhass. She smoothed his hair back from his face. She held his head for a sip of water.

"Father Weirhass, you have to eat more."

"I am tired."

"I can imagine. It is a long journey to Llwegania and you must regain your strength to make it."

"So you have decided what you will do with us?'

"No, just you." Harbinger answered Stiefis' accusation without taking her eyes from Weirhass. "You, my husband, will go with your father to an isolated part of my estates on the border of Llwegania and Sarna. Once there you will remember that your surrender was unconditional."

Stiefis felt a huge hand squeeze his heart. The claim she staked was startling to him.

"I never renege on my promises. I allowed you to marry me. This requires that I provide for you. In return I have complete power over your life. All aspects. I hear you were unfaithful to me with Jeffenza. In fact I have witnesses to the deed itself. I only stay my hand because we have never been truly husband and wife. I will honor the relationship to this degree: I will keep you safe and I will provide for you. Because," she left her seat. She walked until she was so close to Stiefis that he could smell her body and see the pores of her skin. "Because there is more to being married than time in the marriage bed. Being married is making and keeping commitments. From my observations of you, you have never been married until this moment. Well you are married now and I expect you to keep your end of the bargain. Which means you have responsibilities to me that you will fulfill.

"I have greatly angered my ally by rescuing you. He felt I should have let you die in that pass. You are my spouse, and I could not forget my duty to you. You might have been able to forget your duty to your first six wives but you will never fail in your duty to me. Are we clear?"

Stiefis looked into the blazing eyes of his enemy. He understood the will that had destroyed his culture and his country. He had given his word. Unconditional surrender meant he could not negotiate or demand anything now. Before he could answer or acknowledge her statements and question, she was gone.

"I was not wrong. I know you have long thought our destruction stemmed from my decision to force you to marry her, but I was not wrong. That marriage saved us."

"Saved us for what?"

"For her tender mercies of course. Stop looking so grim. We are warm and fed and someone is worrying over our well-being. How wrong can that be?"

Renfrew hovered at the door. He hesitated to enter. The King had summoned him. He didn't expect to live long. He had thought himself dead for a long time now. He had nothing to fear, there was no surprise waiting for him.

Renfrew gathered his resolve around him like a cloak. He stepped into the circle of light that surrounded the King's desk. Ranald remained busy for a long moment. Renfrew studied the pattern of papers on the desk.

"Speak to Us about Our late allies."

"They feared the winter, Your Majesty. They were impatient; they could not stand waiting for spring. They are warriors, not soldiers. They decided to face death in battle rather than risk death from the hardship of winter. I wasted time arguing with them. I thought to reason with them as soldiers and generals. They were too different. They were gone before I realized they meant to leave right then. What sensible person would leave right then?"

Renfrew had not thought he wished to live so badly. As his words spilled from him he knew he did not want, was not ready, to die right this minute. He wanted as much more life as he could wrangle.

Ranald did not lift his head to look at Renfrew. Renfrew hoped his voice did not carry any desperation. He was not able to judge the speed or tone of his mouth. All he could do was stand in the circle of light and wait for what would come.

"They rode into battle?"

"They said so, Your Majesty. They took their weapons. To carry such weight in this weather for any other reason would be insane. I believe they lost faith. They no longer believed they could defeat the enemy. For them death is better than defeat but death must be in battle. They are dishonored if they die in their beds."

"They believed Our enemy invincible?"

"They believed they could never return to the Sarna of the past, Your Majesty. They believed their country lost beyond all recall. All they had left was a fight to the death. Better to face that now than in the spring."

Ranald was silent for a long time. He wrote furiously. Renfrew began to feel his legs quiver with stress and strain.

"You were seen on the piers for a long time."

"I was trying to think of a way to sail before the ocean freezes Your Majesty. The move would surprise the enemy, it would give us an edge, it would have convinced the Sarnese to fight with us. I could not come up with a viable plan." Renfrew thought of the crushing waves. Ranald paused in his writing to look up at Renfrew.

"To sail?"

"I am sure the enemy does not expect such a move from us so I thought it would be the ideal action. My first problem was we have no ships available. There is no way to get them here, at least not soon enough to avoid the great freeze. I wasted a lot of thought on that problem."

Ranald laid down his writing instrument. He looked into Renfrew's face.

"Do you think all is lost?"

"It does not matter to me at all, Your Majesty. All I can think of is how to keep fighting. As long as we fight, as long as we resist, they cannot win."

Ranald examined this thought. He considered it from every angle. He liked the thought. Suddenly he no longer wanted to kill Renfrew. The man was truly **his** general and no one else's.

"We had thought to kill you, you know."

"If it serves your plans best Your Majesty." Renfrew did not allow himself to hope. He hung onto his composure. There was still danger in every moment.

"Perhaps We will feel so inclined tomorrow."

"As it pleases you, Your Majesty."

"Dismissed."

Renfrew bowed coolly. He backed carefully from the room. It was undignified but Renfrew understood the logic behind the movement. With his body facing the King he would have a hard time surprising the King with a weapon or hostile motion. Bowing kept him off balance for an attack. Also, as he bowed he could watch between his legs for any obstacles between himself and the door. Still, walking backwards with his fanny in the air lacked dignity; generals should not have to do this. Ranald had read of this ancient art in a book during the Tampello bivouac. Ever since then everyone had been required to perform this little ritual upon leaving the royal presence.

There was a stifled snicker. Renfrew looked up sharply once the door was closed. He glared at the straight-faced guard and the waiting officers. They looked back blandly. He said nothing. He imagined in their position he would have snickered at someone of his rank mincing in that position. He said nothing. He might have at one time passed an amused remark. Now, even though no new Commander of Security had been appointed, he did not wish to gain any type of reputation.

He had turned to stare at the closed door as he thought. His hand curled and uncurled the brim of his hat as he thought. In the spring there would be an offensive. The forces under Jeffeaux and Harbinger would attack. He needed to discover the best place to position the army that would protect it and give it some kind of advantage. An advantage that could be used to negotiate some kind of terms for surrender that would minimize the punitive actions Jeffeaux might take against them all.

"General?"

"Good day, Captain."

Renfrew left never having bothered to discover if the man had been saying goodbye or addressing a question to him. The men left in his wake of silence pondered the fate of this erstwhile general. His execution had been ordered and forestalled many times. Each time the man seemed to have no idea how close he had come to death. He moved in a shadow reality that no one quite perceived or understood. They all thought him quite mad. Yet he still had his head, something the former Commander of Security, his chief rival, could not claim.

He did not curry favor. He did not build alliances. He did not indulge in court intrigue. All General Renfrew seemed to do was to generate battle plans and war theories that Ranald regularly ignored. Still, Renfrew remained alive and a general. Surely madmen and fools were specially blessed.

The thought that crept back into each mind was that the Commander of Security was finally dead. The mad King had killed him. Renfrew lived for no apparent reason. Playing by the rules did not ensure your life. Being a zealot did not ensure your life. Being dedicated to your profession did not ensure your life. The King was mad. In the spring the enemy would come and they would have to negotiate, but the mad King would never negotiate. He would kill the entire army before he was done.

Eyes wise in the ways of suffering and learned in the art of war stared into each other as they realized the truth. Ranald had to die or there would be no negotiated peace. The army would be completely decimated. Harbinger would impose her terms on them. All of Masfin beyond this peninsula was under the heel of the Llweganian invader. To have any hope of keeping their identity the Masfin military leaders had to bargain. To bargain they needed the army mostly intact. It was a terrifying thing to contemplate the assassination of a king. They had all winter to think of their plan and to work up the courage to execute it.

Pelsen watched the growing knowledge of the inevitability of the action harden into resolve. Soon he would be in the company of others who shared his intent. Now they were only beginning to come to the point, soon his whispers would bear fruit. He would take Jeffenza's life himself. He would kill the child too. Only with the blood of all Ranald's family would the wound in Masfin's breast be healed.

It was cold enough to wear a coat. Stiefis wondered what the weather on the peninsula was like. He was a half moon's ride away from the mountains and their pass. There was no need to be closer. The Masfin army was trapped in the bitter winter. Here the combined forces of Harbinger and Jeffeaux rested in relative comfort and plenty.

If he looked out any window, Stiefis knew he would see what he had seen every day since his surrender. Soldiers of all description would be engaged in training. It was constant. He did not join in. He was tired of warring. He was almost eager to begin his exile on the isolated estate of Harbinger. His shadow existence of being a closely watched house guest would end.

He had to wait. He had to endure the pitying looks of Harbinger's husbands as they passed him. He had to bear the burden of seeing Llweganian women controlling the lives of Sarnese soldiers. He had to know that Sarnese women were having children for Masfin and Llweganian men. He had to see priests, priests of Kersai, priests that had delivered his Article of Repudiation living under the protection of women. Because, he had to wait here, because he waited too long to leave Ranald's control, because his father was not yet strong enough to survive the travel to their exile, he endured.

Stiefis followed another turn in the corridor. He was back at his rooms. He opened the door slowly so as to not startle his father. He stood very still. His father sat in a shaft of pale winter light. A woman was carefully shaving him. He could hear the rasp of the blade against skin.

"My dilemma is: how will the trained soldier become part of a peaceful society? They have fought for so many years, how can I reintegrate them successfully? Can it even be done? Will they bring too many nightmares and reflexes back with them?"

Stiefis hung in the door jamb. Sitting on the floor were two of Harbinger's husbands. He knew them all by sight if not by name.

"What if I need them still? What if I have created too many enemies at home and have to defend my Estates from Llweganian forces? Then I fail to bring the peace I have been promising my followers. What if the people of my Estates don't wish to welcome back their soldier compatriots? What if the civilians find my soldiers too changed, too different? You think my biggest problems are what to do with your soldiers. I have as many questions about what to do with mine."

"Have you had any resolution on the issue of the Sarnese troops?"

Harbinger worked thoughtfully for several strokes. Then she rinsed Weirhass' face. She gently began to massage cream into the skin.

"The towns have agreed to accept a handful each as long as the returning soldiers understand the rules they will be expected to follow. The farming communities are a little leery, but because I asked it of them they will also take a few for herding duties. None of the lakeside villages are willing. They are very fearful of having their authority usurped. There is a strip of Llweganian/Sarnese border which has been gifted to my Estates that I might use as the basis for a new community. My perverse nature still feels it best to plop your army intact in camps on my inner borders."

"You have given this much thought."

"I take my responsibilities very seriously." Harbinger finished with Weirhass' face. She moved until Stiefis could no longer see her. He heard the slight noise of a small piece of furniture being moved. Then there was the sound of water sloshing. He waited to hear the indrawn breath that Weirhass always made when his feet were attended to. There was a sigh. The sound of cloth rustling followed. Then a clipping noise began. It took Stiefis a moment to realize that Harbinger was cutting his father's toenails. She was silent as she worked. He could understand that. The feet had suffered from frostbite ad were delicate still. Finally Stiefis heard the sound of a jar opening.

"Have you spoken with King Jeffeaux? Perhaps he will change his mind. After you leave Masfin he might have use for an army."

Harbinger was quiet for a long time as she worked the cream into the skin of Weirhass' feet.

"Yes, no. Once Jeffeaux is safely on his throne he will not want any foreigner or foreign army associated with him. He will need to establish himself as a Masfin King. I would think that foreigners would never again be quite welcome in Masfin. I am content with the few he has agreed to take.

"After all we have been all kinds of trouble from one end of the country to the other. We have stamped our mark on their land, language, culture, politics, and history. You and I, Father Weirhass, we are used to looking at different faces. No, I have to take you someplace else. I'll manage. There, you are done. How do you feel today?"

"I feel happy to have a daughter who cares for me so well. Your touch is light and sure."

"Flatterer. Do you wish to sit a while longer? Or would you like to lie down now?"

"I think I should lie down. I am feeling tired. Doing nothing takes all my energy."

"You are not doing nothing. You are healing. You still have your feet. You lost a couple toes but you still have your feet. That has taken a lot of energy. If you use your energy up doing something else you won't have it to heal your feet. All you have to do now is to eat, sleep and get better. I can't send your son away until you are well enough to go with him. I need you to get better so I can send him away. He drags around my house like the shadow of gloom. It is damaging my reputation that one of my husbands is discontented. I get enough grief about having taken so many husbands in the first place without one of them acting the neglected husband."

Weirhass chuckled. The two men who had sat so patiently were lifting Weirhass carefully from the chair onto his bed. Weirhass relaxed trustingly in their grip. Stiefis could see that this ritual was familiar to all the participants. Harbinger arranged the pillows behind Weirhass automatically. She laid an affectionate hand on his shoulder. Stiefis melted from the doorway. He moved only a small way along the corridor before starting back noisily. He paused in the opening to make sure everyone saw him. He watched his audience coolly. They looked at him blankly. He felt the burden of his debt to Harbinger. She was a more gracious victor than he would have been.

Resentment burned in his heart because she had won. She had not started the hostilities; she had escalated them to a point where his country could not support them. She had taken the lowest order of his society to build an impassible rampart against him. Seeing how his country bloomed, seeing how that lowest order flourished, he could not belittle her accomplishments.

His father had chosen her. Weirhass had decided she was fitting wife material. It was fitting she should tend to him so tenderly. He had given her the opportunity she had needed to defeat Sarna. The three Llweganians left under his watchful eye. They made no greeting or any acknowledgement of him as they left. Harbinger did send one last smile to Weirhass. A servant collected the water and used towels. Oils and ointments were placed away. Stiefis sat in a chair by the bed. He watched the cleanup in silence. Once the room was clear of everyone else, he turned to look at Weirhass.

The grey tinge of death was leaving the skin. He was still pale. His flesh looked as if it belonged to a living person. There was warmth in the hand that reached to touch Stiefis.

"Has the day been interesting my son?"

"Well, I have not been waited on hand and foot by our captors."

"They are not our captors. We came to them willingly. I look on them as our rescuers. We were rescued from the clutches of a madman."

Stiefis said nothing. He took deep breaths to calm his thoughts. He could still hear Harbinger referring to him as her husband. It always startled him to realize he still had a wife.

"Did you discuss anything interesting with Harbinger?"

"The fate of our army. She is still considering what will happen to us."

Stiefis stared at his feet. "I can't imagine why she bothers. She could just send us home."

"She just spent years trying to achieve peace on her borders. She won't do anything that would destroy that peace."

"Whose side are you on?"

Weirhass snapped his mouth closed. He had no real answer for that question. He only knew he was tired of fighting and suffering and seeing others suffer.

"We spent generations raiding Llwegania for wives to bear us children. The entire time our priests were conspiring against us to prevent those children, or to select those children, or whatever. We made war on Llwegania to solve an internal problem that was created by internal controllers. Don't deny that you believe the priests of Kersai practiced that control. You believe it. I believe it.

"So there is a lot of grey here. Most of it surrounds Sarna's culture and actions. Llwegania bore a lot of burden as our neighbor. There is justice that they should be deciding our fate."

Stiefis frowned. He should be rejoicing that a cruel and intrusive force had been removed from Sarna. Many more children were being born under Harbinger's rule. No one would be able to convince the people to throw off her control. They would do anything to have children, even bow to a demon.

The memory of Harbinger seated at Weirhass' feet intruded on Stiefis' thoughts. She had not looked like a demon as she cared so tenderly for his father's needs. She had not sounded like a demon as she discussed her options for the care of her enemies.

She was his wife. She took her connection to him as real in a very important way. He slept in her care. He fed at her providing. He was dressed in her colors as were her husbands who not only slept in her care but in her bed. She was not tall or slim or elegant. She was muscled and short and her slightly rounded stomach bore witness to the many times she had been filled and stretched with a child. None of those realities were problems for Stiefis. It was the bed filled with other men that kept him from really being her husband. He could not conceive of sharing a woman with other men in their presence, with them perhaps involved in the activity. He just couldn't get over his disgust of such a situation.

Stiefis turned his attention back to his father. He saw that Weirhass had drifted into a deep sleep. He looked even older with his character not filling his face. Deep lines had been carved on his face by life and weather and illness. Stiefis was glad of this rest for his father. He was fiercely glad that at least Weirhass' suffering was done. Maybe he could be happy like Weirhass, Sarna's suffering was over. He rose quickly. He did owe Harbinger a great debt.

He could at least repay her by seeming to be happy. He drew a deep breath. Wherever she sent him he would go willingly. Now he would join in the exercise and training programs. He would work diligently during the day with Harbinger's real husbands. He had brains and common sense, both could be used to promote the well-being of the soldiers who had been under his command. He owed both those soldiers and Harbinger at least that much.

As he thought, Stiefis' feet had brought him to the edge of the training sand favored by Harbinger's guard. There was a moment while eyes noted his approach. Then he glanced from their garb to his. His eyes flickered around the area. One of the men left the sand to come to him. Stiefis followed.

They returned once Stiefis was appropriately dressed. It was satisfying to experience physical activity that pushed him to his limits. He enjoyed the flow of motion and even the hard thumps as he landed from a throw. It was more satisfying to watch his training partner land. They spoke little. He had to speak Llweganian because his partner would not speak Sarnese. His accent was not very good. He suspected that his partner spoke fine Sarnese but he was one of Harbinger's husbands and they were treating him as such. So he spoke Llweganian.

At the end of the exercise he went with his new group to the bath house. Harbinger was one of them. She went first into the baths. Stiefis felt a hand restraining him. He looked warily at the owner of the hand. Stiefis searched for his name. Petron, the First Husband, head of Harbinger's guard, therefore Stiefis assumed

Petron was the leader of the group of men who were attached to Harbinger.

"Our wife claims you. I do not deny her right to do so. I cannot. I am responsible for her safety. I am watching you."

Stiefis felt a lump clog his throat. He tried to swallow it down in order to force words from his mouth.

"I only want to help my former troops. I have knowledge and training that Harbinger can put to use for their better care. I have a duty to them. It cannot be fulfilled if I am brooding on my fate and the past."

"Just as long as your talents do not lead you to attempt any harm toward my wife."

Stiefis listened to the possessive pronoun. It echoed in his ears. Petron did not use it to exclude his fellow Llweganian husbands; he used it to exclude Stiefis. Stiefis deserved that exclusion. He wanted that exclusion.

"I will go where your wife sends me. I will do whatever your wife bids me. I only wish to offer her whatever I have that she might wish to use in this time of great change and choice. That is how I can best serve my country. I do not know how to be a husband. I have lost all my wives. I had no idea what a wife could be. I have failed everything in my life. My only friend I sentenced to death to protect my men. If I fail them, I will have killed him for nothing. She is my only hope to succeed at anything. She is all I have."

Petron looked at the wall behind Stiefis' shoulder. He seemed to come to a decision. He turned to let Stiefis pass into the bath.

Stiefis' days became filled with training and discussion. He learned to respect the men who lived with Harbinger. Every meal, every bath, he shared with this group. Harbinger washed each husband in turn. She scrubbed their backs. She dried them and rubbed their skin with oils. He accepted her touch grimly. He bowed his head, closed his eyes tightly, and willed his thoughts to review vocabulary he had learned that day when her hands were on him. At night he slept on a pallet on the floor of the married unit's bedroom. He listened to the sounds of a healthy and happy marriage being celebrated each night in the great bed next to him. As he lived with the group as a whole he no longer believed them decadent fools. He began to understand what kind of woman engendered such a level of devotion. He admired his brother/husbands as men and warriors.

Jeffeaux looked down the table. He felt resentment well-up. She continued to bring that Sarn to the table. He sat comfortably with her other husbands. He ate well and looked very healthy. *His* people were on the other side of those mountains dying of cold and disease and hunger while the Sarn slept in the comfort of Harbinger's bed.

"I see your newest husband is improving his Llweganian."

"That he is. He is providing me with a great deal of useful information. Once his father is well enough I am sending him to a very stark, empty place, he should feel right at home there. He is not happy as my husband. If not for the pesky Council Messengers hanging about I would bother to make him act the part." Harbinger spoke casually. She was busy watching the servants at the door. There seemed to be a discussion on a very hot topic. Harbinger wondered what could be disrupting the workflow. The servants were all highly trained. Something had to be very wrong or very important to allow it to distract them from their duties. It probably would be resolved and she would never have her curiosity satisfied. She missed the parade of expressions that crossed Jeffeaux's face.

"It is a real hardship to sleep in your care."

"He is shocked and disgusted by the idea of sharing a wife with other men. I don't know how he manages. Though the reverse is not true as he had six wives before me. It is odd to think I am married to such a hypocrite. I find it very strange. I have much more in common with Stiefis than I do with you. Stiefis and I have shared cultural history. Our people have known each other for generations. Our cultures are similar with only a few different spins. Whereas, you and I, Your Majesty, have little in common and yet we get along much better. I have always felt very much at home in your company. Don't you find that odd?"

Jeffeaux looked into his wine goblet before setting the rim to his lips. He took a deep swallow. He concentrated on the feel of the liquid sliding down his throat. He fell back on his newly acquired attitude. He smiled graciously in reply before allowing her attention to drift to her other dinner partner. He waited until

Marma looked at him. He found his center in the calming depths of her gaze.

He wanted to be a fair and compassionate ruler. He wanted his people to flourish. He wanted his country to prosper. He did not want his people and country to slide into a national personality that exacted revenge and retribution from the enemies. Their vanquished enemies were going to include parts of their own population. He could only have passion for peace, mercy, and justice, in that order. Marma held the promise of that reality in her calm gaze and encouraging smile. He held on to her strength.

His job was going to be difficult. He was going to have years of hard work ahead of him to heal the wounds of this war. He wanted Harbinger to take all the foreign influences away. He needed her to maintain peace on her side of the border. How she did those things was her problem. He had no right to complain about how she did it as long as she did it well.

Chapter 22

Renfrew stood huddled in his greatcoat. The collar was turned up so high he could not easily move his head. His hat covered his forehead. A scarf was wrapped tightly across his face. Only his eyes were visible in his cocoon. The wind was bitter. The snow was deep and cold and wet. Still, he was glum. The snow was not as deep, the wind was not as bitter as it had been. Spring was coming. Renfrew's continuing hope was that the ocean would calm before the snows melted.

It was an irrational hope, for they had no ships. A calm sea might only mean an opportunity for the enemy to land rather than a chance for escape.

Renfrew turned slowly. North led only to cliffs and a dangerous natural rock jetty that would still need large ships to circumvent. South there was a narrow strip of land that was passable at very low tide. They would be unable to carry any heavy baggage train across it. In fact it was only passable for a very short time during unusually low tides. If the army could get across there it could eat off the land and scavenge for equipment. It was better than waiting to die.

Unless that way was already fortified against them. The water was better. No one would expect them to attempt the ocean route. Still he was back to the problem of ships.

"There is no escape, General."

Renfrew almost lost his balance as he turned to find the owner of the voice. He used the heavy snow to keep his balance. He could not identify the speaker even as he looked right at him. Renfrew remained silent.

"In every direction we are stopped by nature, by circumstance, by external threats. There is only one escape."

"I do not view death as an escape."

"That depends on whose death we are discussing."

Renfrew was silenced by surprise. He could only watch the shrouded figure fade into the dark of the weather. He did not know if the cold or the idea presented to him had stolen his breath but it was gone. He had tried to remain separated from intrigue and politics but now he had been shoved right into the middle of the greatest intrigue of any court. Whatever he did or didn't do, he participated.

Perhaps they would not succeed. Every plot hatched had failed. He could do nothing, hoping what? Hoping they would fail or succeed? Did it matter to him? He was dead anyway come spring. Did he really care if Ranald survived him? Did he care if Ranald or Jeffeaux executed him? Did he care if he died in battle or even in the cold? He had cared a few weeks ago. He had cared enough to talk his way out of execution for the Sarnese desertion.

He trudged back to his barracks. He wrapped his arms around his middle. He tucked his hands under his arms. He bent his head into the wind.

Jeffeaux stood next to Harbinger. He stared at the blocks of troops that were moving into place. Wind Rider had not returned. Still, the map did not look sparsely littered with stones. He wondered at the force stationed at the seemingly impassable spit of beach but Harbinger insisted on the fortification. She had a strong feel for weaknesses in a defense. What he could not imagine were the ships she insisted on.

"We can just wait until the snow melts and pass through the mountains."

"No, the sea will calm first. They might try an escape over water. The snowed in passes will serve as a fortification against their escape. If we come from the water they will have to back into the snow."

"Then we too will be fighting in the snow."

"No, we will push them into the snows of the mountain and keep them there. They will try the passes. We will catch them there. It will be done by summer. If they escape us again we will have another winter or two chasing them. This gives us a chance to end the dying now."

Jeffeaux looked at the map.

"Will Wind Rider return?"

"No, she will be busy with the resettlement of the Sarnese soldiers. If we really need her, she will come. She is a deep reserve. We have the soldiers and the supplies. Your captains assure men they can sail. The armies are already halfway to the embarkation point. This is not a risky, desperate move. It is well conceived and planned. The troops are well-trained and in prime condition. They will be able to execute it."

"Anything that involves water is risky. The ocean is a fickle ally. The army could well end up at the bottom of the sea."

"This is not a battle on water. It is only a transport across it. You are right anything could go wrong. The army could also die in a spring avalanche."

"Perhaps Wittlar will not be successful in organizing the navy."

"Your Highness, Jeffeaux."

He sighed. Wittlar had spent months studying naval movements of the past. He and his assistant had personally interviewed merchant captains and naval commanders. The legwork had established relationships that had borne great fruit. A great fleet was poised to strike on Jeffeaux's command. They sat ready to do Jeffeaux's will all because Wittlar had shown persistence and respect and aptitude. And because all of Masfin thought Ranald a madman. Tampello echoed endlessly. It continued to impact Jeffeaux's ability to win supporters.

"I trust the navy is already organized. That everything awaits my perusal and order."

"Correct, Your Highness. The conclusion of this endeavor awaits only your word."

Jeffeaux understood her position. "All that is left is my meeting with the captains of my navy."

"They are waiting now."

"I could have guessed that. Bring them on, we will settle this today."

"Very good, Your Highness."

He listened to the opinions of the captains. They agreed with Harbinger. They did not see the reason for his hesitation. It would be over. Perhaps that was his hesitation. It would be over.

"If you are all agreed, it is a sound plan. The Sarnese army will be gone before we move?"

"Yes. Everyone has been sent on their way. Everyone."

"Then let us end this war with this action."

"Very good, Your Highness."

Stiefis rode quietly next to his father. Birnher trailed behind. They had been riding across Sarna for several Darkfalls. He wondered if he could really call it Sarna anymore. The wastes were the same, but now they were interrupted by vast stretches of green and the scent of water hovered everywhere. They did not pass close to any settlements. Even the rank and file were affected by the major differences in the country they had left.

Their guard rode with familiarity through this changing landscape. Her daughter was leading them to their fate. He tried to guess who her father was by studying the lines of her face. If he asked she would laughingly deny needing to know. It did not matter to her. She was Harbinger's daughter. Harbinger's husbands were all worthy fathers. They had all raised her.

"I can't believe no one has come to see us. We fought long and hard for Sarna. What kind of people are we? Have we no respect, no gratitude for loyalty, sacrifice?" Birnher snapped wearily.

"Perhaps what we fought to defend had no meaning for them. It is still an occupied country. We are surrounded by a strong force. Who would dare to challenge them for us?"

Birnher subsided. He fell back into place. That dusk they were settling for the night when in fact someone did approach the camp.

Stiefis was summoned to Wind Rider's presence. Weirhass already sat in council with a group of Sarnese men and women. They were well dressed and solemn. Stiefis saw one face he thought he knew. He could not place the features with a name but he knew that person.

Stiefis stood awkwardly in front of the group. He tried to understand why they were looking at him so intently.

"This is my son, Stiefis. He is Harbinger's Sarnese husband." Stiefis turned an astonished face to his father.

"It is good that Harbinger has a Sarnese husband. It cements the tie between us. I am not sure I feel this is the best choice." The accents were not from the ruling strata of Sarnese society, but the tone certainly was.

"Harbinger's household is a military one. She would have little use for a farmer or a trader."

"Lady Zona has taken three priests. Lady Junla has a priest in her household. I would not want Harbinger to choose a priest."

"Harbinger could have had a priest at any time. No, I think this is appropriate. This husband represents the army, the former rulers, who are now under Harbinger's control. A priest? I don't want them controlled. I want them swept away."

Stiefis became dizzy trying to look at each speaker in turn. The conversation was so swift and came from so many different lips he could not find one speaker before the next began. He absorbed the words and deciphered their meaning.

"Ladies, gentlemen, my mother has chosen Stiefis as her husband. If you wish to present another candidate there is a very formal rite around marriage which my mother prefers to use. I would like to inquire as to how many of the returning soldiers, not officers or Wardens, each of your villages would be able to support. We would provide each returning man with a draft animal, one year's planting of seed, three tools, clothing and a small amount of coin. Each village will receive as a gift from King Jeffeaux four barrels of new oil. Harbinger would not expect any community to bear the burden of taking on more than could be handled, and if you are unable to take any we will understand. The planting season is coming and some areas might be able to use some extra hands."

Stiefis could not believe these peasants were being allowed to decide the fate of his army.

"We really need surveyors and engineers. We need teachers and merchants. I can take perhaps twenty. During the planting and harvesting we could use more but not constantly."

"Good, take as many as you can now. We will see if any who remain can be trained for your needs. Then we will make our offer again."

Wind Rider pulled some papers toward her. She spent a moment studying the contents. "You should consider that you will need builders soon. I see there have been many births. You will need houses and shops and roads. The old estate building will do for public use. Families need homes to live in and towns need roads to connect them.

"Masfin's position on the repatriation of Sarnese soldiers is not favorable for the former allies of Ranald. King Jeffeaux is not willing to absorb a significant portion of the Sarnese army. On the upside once the war is over the Masfin Sarnese border will be established with customs and fortifications not as enemies but as separate entities. That means there will be a city at the opening of the mountains. So there will be a great need for day laborers."

Stiefis was exhausted by the time the meal was ended. He had to get salve for his poor leg. Every time he had tried to open his mouth to make a comment on any subject his father had forcefully pinched his leg. If he had realized he was to serve as window dressing ...Stiefis paused in his thoughts. He would still have come. He was on display as an example of how the former adversaries could support Harbinger and even advance her wishes. The fate of his soldiers depended on his cooperation.

He had to admit that Wind Rider was trying very hard for the Sarnese troops. She was planting ideas and possibilities that could turn into real opportunities. Certainly building a new society was better than rotting in a refugee camp.

Harbinger accepted the stone thoughtfully. She placed it in her pouch with a sigh.

"Bad news?"

"No, Wind Rider is doing well. Your captains, are they set?"

"Yes, tomorrow is the day."

"With the tide then." They were standing on the end of a stone pier. Cold wind blew around them. Jeffeaux shifted his weight until they were almost touching shoulders.

"I have promised you Ranald's head."

"I will place no limits on your waging war. I have not yet. Though, I would like to spare Jeffenza and the child."

"I have no intentions against your sister. Have you chosen a flagship?"

"Yes. I would rather go with you."

"This will be hand to hand combat Jeffeaux. You have become a fine King but you never did show any abilities when it comes to fighting. I would have to worry about your safety. It is best that you wait to disembark until we have secured a headquarters on land for you. Then you may join us on shore."

"I will feel like a coward hiding on the ship."

Harbinger turned until her face was fully presented to Jeffeaux.

"We have not fought this long and this hard to place you on that throne to get you killed the very day we plan to do it. You are not expected to be a fighting king. Your promise has been to bring peace to Masfin. I am the warrior here. You are using my skills right now. Your skills will be needed later. Stay on your ship until your generals deem it safe for you to land. Then you may do your king stuff and I will leave the field. Trust me in this."

Jeffeaux concentrated on resisting the urge to frame her face with his hands. He stepped back one step to contain himself. He felt lonely for her already. Because he did trust her, and now because of whom he had become and where he was going, there might never be an opportunity to trust anyone again as he had trusted her, even her.

"I will take your advice this one last time."

"So this is the last advice you will take from me. I might have other worthy suggestions. Don't write me off just yet. If you never take my advice again I am glad you will take this now. Here's another piece of advice, don't stay out in this wind too much longer. No need to die of cold the day before you meet your enemy."

Jeffeaux chuckled at her retreating back.

Renfrew watched the men who worked around him. He wondered who plotted against the King. He wondered if they would succeed. He dragged his mind away from its wanderings. He had real business to do. He had been working most of the winter on a workable defense. He simply had to convince the King to move the army closer to the pass. Being there when the enemy began its move would give Ranald's forces a great advantage. If they could achieve the heights before Harbinger brought her troops into place.

There was a tight silence. Renfrew finally could ignore it no longer. He looked into the faces watching him.

"Do you understand? If we move the army…." Renfrew's words trailed off. He took a deep breath.

"You really are quite good at this General Renfrew. It is not your battle plans we do not understand. We are unable to read your character. We cannot assess the lay of your loyalties, not the lines on your maps. So forgive us this violence."

Caught up in the sound of the voice Renfrew never saw the cudgel swing down on the back of his head. His world dissolved into pain and then darkness.

"Place him in the cells. He might be of use later. He is married to Jeffeaux's sister. His brother is one of Harbinger's generals."

Pelsen checked the time. Renfrew must be out of the way. The household was asleep. He could hear Ranald finishing his husbandly duties in the room beyond. The cessation of noise signaled the end of Pelsen's wait. He was poised to enter the room when he heard the footsteps in the hallway. He would have to wait again. There was no use getting half the job done. If he were interrupted now he would be unable to complete his mission.

He would deal with Jeffenza and the child first. Then he would take out Ranald, or his fellow conspirators would get there. There was a backup to his actions. He would have to be very quiet.

Jeffenza showed no alarm at his entrance. She greeted him with a speculative look. He had set the tone of their relationship so that she would not be wary of his violence. She would be expecting it.

Jeffenza was relieved to see her lover. She liked to cleanse the feel of her husband's touch with the strength and violence of her cavalry officer. Any emotion, feeling, sensory interaction was an improvement over intercourse of her husband. That would be over soon. The doctor would confirm her belief of the child in her body. If the old man had more balls or less fear he would have agreed with her assessment two weeks ago. Her husband was so infamous for his temper even the doctor feared to bear false report. She knew he would rather wait until the child was delivered to say definitively that she was pregnant. She however was unwilling to submit to the useless act one more week, never mind months more. It wouldn't be good for the child having sex much longer. The babe might be dislodged. Not that anything her husband did to her could ever be thought active enough to disturb a hair on her head, never mind a muscle near her womb.

This luscious young officer, he was one to stir every muscle in her body with on look of his eyes. He was giving her that look right now. He looked as if he could rip every muscle in her body from their anchors, bend them to his will, and plunge them back into her. That plunging back into her was a very delicious thought.

He was advancing on her. That's right, come to me. Yes put those strong hands on this weak flesh. He never smiled. He did not smile now. His eyes were always so focused. He never lost himself in their play. Once she would like to see those eyes roll in uncontrollable passion.

His thumb stretched her jaw until her throat was a taut line.

"Well, my Queen, has the King had his pleasure of you?"

"Soon for the last time, soon the doctor will confirm the child I carry exists, very soon. Then we need not worry about nightly interruptions."

"A child, do you know whose?"

"I do not care as long as he stops coming. A child is a child."

He hardened his heart. If the child were his then he was making the ultimate sacrifice to save his country. He clutched the knife with resolution. He did not hesitate. Under the ribs in one swift motion, through the lung and into the heart. She never had the breath to scream.

The look of surprise that crossed her face was so fleeting that he almost missed it. He was glad she knew in the last moment that he had killed her. Time would not permit him to draw out the execution but at least she had known that she died at his hand.

He let her body fall. He could hear his co-conspirators moving through the palace. He had to move quickly to finish his self-appointed task. The child had to die next. Ranald had to know he had no surviving children when he died.

The group of officers moved through the predawn light. They crept among the guards. Those that did not follow died in their sleep.

Ranald was sponging himself clean. He always felt soiled after dealing with his wife. A gentle hiss snagged his attention. He frowned at the interruption. A figure stood in the doorway.

"Your Majesty, we are under attack."

"What!?"

"I came in from the privy. I found the guard dead. We are under siege. For your life rise up, we must go."

"My child, get the princess."

"Yes, Your Majesty, and I will notify the Queen."

The servant spoke to a retreating back. He entered the nursery quietly. He scooped the child up gently so as to not wake her. He prayed she would stay asleep. He started down towards the door when he heard stealthy steps in the hall beyond. He pressed an anxious eye to the crack in the door. All he saw was a blood covered tunic coming towards him.

He rushed through the nursery to the stairs that led to the back kitchen. He fled down into the storage cellars. He searched frantically for a hiding place. He stared at the bins. Carefully he placed the child in the dark recesses of the farthest barrel. Then he crouched by the stairs. He held the cover of a barrel tightly against his chest. He could only wait.

Pelsen felt rage grip him. The child was gone. Ranald was gone. Only Jeffenza lay dead. He tore through the nursery. There were no clues as to where the child could be. Then he heard the clash of arms. There was shouting. He looked out a window.

Ranald was pulling on his coat as he raced through the building. He heard a whisper of a sound. He moved into the shadow of the corridor. He waited. He strained to hear the sound again. When there was no repeat of the whisper he began to move again. He moved away from the royal wing of the barracks. He hugged a wall when once he thought he heard muffled footsteps.

As he reached the door that led into the courtyard, he paused. He could hear shouts in the distance. In the pale light he could just make out slumped shapes littering the courtyard. He gave hardly a look to the macabre scene. His whole being was focused on the swell of sound coming from the shore. He ran through the courtyard with no regard for his safety. Ranald swung the gate open.

"Jeffeaux is here. How?"

There was a cry from the barracks. Ranald returned his attention to the courtyard. How had Jeffeaux infiltrated his headquarters? A group of officers appeared in the doorway. Ranald looked across the space at them. At first he was relieved to see his own uniform. Then he noticed the blood on those uniforms. He took in the set of their bodies and the angle of the weapons they held. There was a sound of glass breaking. Ranald looked up in alarm. A body hurtled from the second story at him.

He fled the courtyard. He raced to the stables. There was a huge cry behind him; then the clattering of boots on stone. Ranald ran with a speed born of desperation. He reached the dark buildings. He breathed in the moist warm air. He thought to saddle a horse if only he had ever learned how. It seemed easy enough on the surface but looking at all the bits and pieces that hung from pegs he was not so sure.

In his fear he thought the sound of his pursuers had grown to a roar. He tried to think of his escape. He could try to ride bareback. He just needed to find a horse he could mount without a saddle and reins.

There was an echo of steel against steel. Ranald was held in thrall as he watched the battle rage in the doorway. He stood close to the first stall. Bodies moved in the startlingly beautiful ballet of a death match. Metal arcs and gleams of reflected light mesmerized Ranald. The sound of grunts of effort and the hiss of steel cutting the air twined into a death chant. As one body fell to the will of the other Ranald let his breath go.

Then he felt the breath of death on his neck. He turned to face his rogue officers and looked into the face of death. He could not see features but he knew he looked at a Llweganian soldier. A sword gleamed in the rising light of the sun. He looked at the shining metal as it swung through the air.

"You can't kill me: I am the King."

"Good, your head for King Jeffeaux, as promised." Harbinger held the head by the hair that still clung above its ear. She stepped out into the open air of the courtyard.

"It seems we interrupted some kind of violence."

Troops swarmed into the barracks.

Harbinger looked at the twitching body that lay on the stones at her feet. "Find the Queen and the Princess. I want them alive."

"Dead." The whisper reached Harbinger's ears. She tilted her head to find the source of the sound. "Dead." She followed it to Petron's fallen combatant. "She is dead."

"That's too bad. Which she?"

"The Queen, I killed her myself. They had to be purged just as Ranald had to die. Nothing of his can be left. She carried a child in her body. The blood had to die."

Harbinger looked into the empty, staring eyes.

"Search the buildings. Bring me the bodies, living or dead."

Harbinger looked back at the walls of the encampment. She could hear the fighting beyond this quiet oasis awash in blood. She glanced down at the head hanging from her hand.

"Find his crown. Put it on the head then mount both of them on a pike so everyone can see. Hang the body over the wall next to the head. That should stop some of the fighting."

The servant waited by the stairs. He strained to catch any sounds he could. His efforts were in vain. His hiding place was so good he hid even from the sounds of the world above. He dared not leave his post to investigate. He could only wait and pray the child remained asleep and that his King would emerge victorious. Sweat poured from him even though the cellar was chilly, chilly and heavy with the scent of soil and the fruits of the earth. He closed his eyes tightly for a heartbeat.

Then he heard the faint scrape of boots. There was no stealth in the sound. Boots and weapons sounded. Back and forth they moved on the floor above. Then silence again. More boots echoed but not in the hurried step of fighting. The steady tromp of purposeful walking echoed over his head.

The door swung open. There were voices in a strange language, then accented Masfin. He held the cover determinedly before him. He was prepared to swing. His breath came in loud gasps. They sounded very loud in his ears. The owners of the footsteps must have heard them. There was a hesitation, then again the accented Masfin.

"Surrender. Ranald is dead. There is no reason to fight. King Jeffeaux will be merciful if you surrender."

He pulled the cover back ready to let it fly at the invader. He never got the chance. Faster than his eye could see, a foot kicked the cover out of his hands. Strong hands, not painful hands, held him captive. He struggled wildly. He was easily subdued. Ropes secured him. Troops spread through the cellar. He cursed wildly. Everything had been in vain. Llweganian arms lifted the sleeping princess into the light. He paused when he saw the gentleness of the hold on the child.

"Send word to Harbinger."

A trooper appeared at Harbinger's elbow.

"Report."

"There is a prisoner in the cells and a servant in the cellars. Both are secured. The servant gave some resistance."

"Any other survivors?"

There was silence. All eyes surveyed the carnage that they had not wrought. Then Petron looked into Harbinger's eyes.

"I believe it might be best that there be no other survivors."

"Let us meet this servant."

Harbinger followed the trooper to the cellar. She picked her way through body parts and pools of blood. And descended into the cellar.

The servant watched the conqueror descend. She did not seem like a monster. She was short and round and calm. Nothing dramatic or overtly evil surrounded her or rode her expression. She took off her helmet. In the torchlight her hair reflected light but was dark and very curly. He had never seen such curly hair. She smiled down at the sleeping child. She reached a finger to touch just behind the child's ear.

Harbinger understood Petron's hesitation to announce that this child lived. The child would bear a terrible burden being the heir to Ranald and Jeffenza. Jeffeaux and his heirs would always be threatened by the very existence of this child. Better for all if this child never lived to see another day. Harbinger stared at the wide confused eyes of the tiny girl. Harbinger thought of her promise to Jeffeaux. She had already failed to keep Jeffenza alive. How could she save this child and maintain Jeffeaux's safety, Masfin's peace, Sarna's existence, fulfill her duty to her estates? Ranald's child had to die today. Harbinger smiled as an amusing solution to her dilemma formed in her mind.

"Hello, War's Gift."

"Hello, who are you?" The child asked in a small voice.

"Your mother." Harbinger spoke in a firm voice preempting any disagreement from her husbands. "I have come to rescue you from the evil people who stole you from me and kept you prisoner all these years."

"Was I very hard to find?"

"Very hard."

"Can I go with you now?"

"You have to go to your father who misses you very much. I must take care of the terrible people who stole you from me. Your father will take very good care of you."

"Will he make me watch men get their heads cut off in the mornings?'

"No, your real father would never make you watch that. Your real father will take you to watch the sun rise over your lands every morning. He will teach you to care for our people. He will love you with all his heart and put what is good for you first in all his thoughts."

"I am glad you finally found me, Mama."

"So am I, War's Gift." Harbinger spoke in Llweganian.

"What do you call me?" The child tried to puzzle the strange sounding words.

"Your true name in your true language. You are War's Gift." Harbinger switched back to Masfin.

"I am a gift?" The child giggled at Harbinger.

"Yes, the very best gift, you will be a good strong woman when you are grown. Won't you reward me for searching and for finding you?"

"Yes, and for giving me a good man for a father. I will be whatever you tell me to be."

"Let us seal our reunion with a kiss."

Strong young arms circled her neck. A wet smacking kiss accompanied the hug. "Mama, thank you for coming."

"I always come for my children no matter how far they roam. That is what parents do. You must learn your native tongue. Never speak this other language unless you have no choice. It has not been good for you. You will speak Llweganian and Sarnese from now on."

"How do I say yes, Mama?"

Harbinger told her. War's Gift repeated the phrase with determination and some success. Harbinger rewarded her with a kiss and a hug. The child giggled again.

Harbinger looked around the room. No one spoke. She looked at the soldier who had handed the child to her.

"Can you get through the pass?"

The trooper nodded.

"Good. Inform my twelfth husband that I send him his heir."

Petron waited for Harbinger to complete her thinking. She stared at the head above the palisade as she stood in the morning sun. Troops moved to and fro carrying messages from the battle. With Ranald and most of his officers dead the battle would end soon. Harbinger sighed deeply. Then she nodded her head once.

"It is fitting that the husband who is not of my bed should get an heir who is not of my body. Sablor, my sweet, go to King Jeffeaux. Tell him the day is his."

Sablor picked his way through the bodies. He swung onto his horse. He turned the animal's head around then plunged out of the barracks. He skirted groups of struggling fighters. The Masfin troops were disorganized. Sablor did not try to deal with anything beyond his errand. Once he had to slash at soldiers who tried to unhorse him but he was able to disengage himself quickly between his sword and his foot.

Finally the shore was in sight. Sablor pounded down the sand. He arrived as Jeffeaux walked through the waves from his dory. Sablor dismounted. He bowed briefly.

"Your Highness, Harbinger sends that the day is yours."

Jeffeaux looked beyond Sablor to the mass of fighting bodies.

"She had Ranald's head as promised." Jeffeaux brought his gaze swiftly to Sablor's flushed face. "Ranald is dead. Most of the officer corps has been killed. We discovered the royal barracks in conflict. There seems to have been a coup attempt. They had not yet killed Ranald. Harbinger had the honor of killing him." Sablor paused. He could find no way to say his next words gently. "We were too late for your sister. She is dead. The only survivors in the barracks are a servant and a prisoner. We have not identified them yet."

"Jeffenza is dead? Her child as well?"

Jeffeaux could not believe his ears. There could finally be peace, but at what cost? He stared at the mass of contending bodies on the battlefield. With no officers or king how did Harbinger expect the rank and file to know that all was lost? There was no one left to give the order to surrender.

As Jeffeaux watched, there was a gradual lessening of fighting. There seemed to be a collective decision to end the contest. "We still need to communicate with the soldiers on the field that their king is dead."

"Harbinger has taken care of that. They should be laying down their arms soon."

Harbinger watched the body fall over the top of the stockade. Then she turned to enter the barracks. The prisoner interested her.

He had to be of some use to the conspirators, but they must have doubted his loyalty. She noted the bodies lying in the halls. They were mostly dressed as servants. Sad that none of the officers had sided with Ranald.

Marjas came up on her right side. She sent him a questioning glance.

"Those nearest the barricades have begun to lay down their arms."

"Good, don't let the birds destroy the head beyond recognition. I still have to bring it to Jeffeaux."

"He is not going to be happy about his sister."

"I had no control over a coup. I had not thought her important enough to warrant assassination and Jeffeaux had not thought her death likely."

"I never cease to realize how different Masfin's culture is." Petron spoke in measured tones. Serjanus had managed to open the door to the cells wide enough for all of them to pass abreast. Rodznig and Mandul took defensive positions by the opening.

Wittlar turned the unconscious body over. Harbinger stared down into a familiar face. Bernath let out a humorless laugh.

"Fate has spared Jeffeaux at least one victim."

"I wonder if Jeffeaux will be allowed to be merciful."

Jorin nodded as he passed Rodznig and Wittlar. "Why wouldn't he be?"

Then he saw just who lay on the stone floor. He sighed. "I see. No, the Masfin people will not settle for anything less than death."

Harbinger watched as Vental and Cregros entered with a report from the ramparts. Rodznig and Wittlar gave up their positions to their husband/brothers.

"We must send to Jeffeaux that we have this prisoner. We should also send to Lady Junla that her husband yet lives." Cregros nodded before he left. Harbinger looked on each face that remained with satisfaction. Then she spoke to Petron.

"We are done here. We can go home. Have an agreement about the borders between Masfin and Sarna drawn up. I want to sign it before we leave. Jeffeaux knows that Sarna is mine. I want him to know that we will guard the border. Good borders make good neighbors."

"Have you discussed this with him? Are there things to which you have agreed?"

"To remove all of our troops from Masfin territory, to keep the peace on the borders these things I have promised. We have already removed the Sarnese troops, so stipulate, that we will prevent any Sarnese soldiers from trying to enter Masfin. I have no problem with Masfin citizens entering Sarna or my Estates in Llwegania with proper documentation and permissions. Finally, any Masfin national who wishes to leave with me may do so. Any who wish to follow afterwards may do so."

"What of the army? Will the King agree to his army following you?"

"Many will stay. This is their home. They have freed their home from the grip of the tyrant. Now is the time for them to enjoy the fruits of their labor. They won't wish to follow me into my new war. It is that war we need to address now. I am never to lie down with peace. I always ride that ugly mount War."

Petron studied his wife's profile. He soothed the frown line from her brow.

"You must give a farewell speech to the armies. They deserve your time. You have spoken with them many times throughout this war. They will want to hear from you one last time."

Harbinger looked at each of her husbands. Every man nodded his agreement. They were right. She owed her soldiers some pageantry, a rite of passage. They had been good soldiers. They had followed her orders well. She could never have secured Sarna without them. She owed them an appropriate leave-taking.

"Secure permission from the King for that as well."

Petron nodded to Jorin and Serjanus. They left on their new business. Harbinger drew a deep breath. She left the cell block without another word.

Sablor remained with Jeffeaux until all the fighting was over. He sat quietly beside the fire during the night waiting for the word to come that would release him from his vigil. Jeffeaux listened patiently to the reports from the field. Marlin was lost in the sea of bodies trying to sort out the situation. Surrendering troops had to be disarmed and assigned rations, clothes, the conditions of their parole. Cregros stared into the dark trying to stay awake. Jeffeaux had greeted his words with a grunt. Marlin had sent back a stone signaling his receipt of the message. Only Lady Junla, across the water with the Royal Consort Marma, did not know.

Sablor swirled the wine in his cup. He poured the last dregs onto the trampled mix of snow and sand at his feet. Lady Zona stood at the edge of the firelight. She had taken the news quietly. Sablor had been glad to signal the survival of the child to her. She had immediately understood the importance for keeping that piece of news quiet. There were many who hated Ranald and everything associated with him. That hate could easily lead to the child's death.

Sablor respected Lady Zona's need to grieve. He hoped Harbinger would be able to come soon to bear Lady Zona's company. He was happy when the shadows yielded his family into the circle of light cast by the fire.

Harbinger led the way. From her hand swung the battered head. She swung it up into the air before Jeffeaux.

"King Jeffeaux, I present you with the face of your enemy."

Jeffeaux stood. He spared not one glance for the gruesome sight. He looked straight into Harbinger's face. His feelings were too varied and strong for him to speak. Absently he took the proffered gift. He passed it to a waiting soldier. The man gingerly accepted the burden.

"I thank you for your efforts on my behalf."

"Your Highness, I am very sorry to report to you that your sister, Queen Jeffenza, is dead. We found her body in her chamber. I thought you would wish to provide her with a proper death rite."

Petron and Jorin stepped into the light. They carried a body draped in Harbinger's own cloak. Jeffeaux recognized the stitchwork immediately. He was nonplussed. He had held a spark of anger all day. Now with one gesture Harbinger melted that anger into sorrow. Jeffeaux could find nothing to say. Harbinger did not wait. She bowed to him shortly then stepped by him to his mother. She placed a comforting arm around Lady Zona's shoulders.

"I am so sorry, Lady Zona. It is a very hard thing to lose a child. I know just how hard." In the edge of the shadows Jeffeaux looked on as Harbinger absorbed the burst of grief from his mother. He saw his mother's husbands hover around the pair of women. Only when Lady Zona loosened her grip did Harbinger relinquish her to the three waiting men. There was silence as the night quiet was reestablished. Harbinger returned to the fire. She crouched before the warmth of the flames. She sent Sablor and Cregros a smile.

"So you have the notorious General Renfrew in your control." Jeffeaux walked towards the fire.

"I have sent for my sister, Junla. She will wish to see her husband before his trial."

"And General Marlin?"

"He has sent that he does not wish to see Renfrew now. Maybe later."

"I presume later will not be long for General Renfrew."

"He will have a trial as is every Masfin's right."

"Everyone knows he is guilty, King Jeffeaux. Let us not be coy." Harbinger looked toward the battlefield that was obscured by darkness. "Has there not been enough death? Cannot King Jeffeaux be merciful?"

"I would like to be merciful. In this I can only be just. After all, Renfrew is married to my sister. His crimes are great and heinous. If I pardon him, there will always be those who might question my motives. I must allow the Masfin people to have their justice system handle this."

"I thought as much, Your Highness. Do you want me to wait until everyone has sworn allegiance to you before I withdraw my troops?"

Jeffeaux shrugged. "I think you must leave us to sort this out on our own. I wouldn't want anyone to say they had sworn to me under the yoke of your oppression."

"Very well, we can get through the pass. As soon as we are provisioned we move out."

Marlin entered his tent. He was startled to find someone there before him. She was sitting very neatly in his single chair. He could describe it no other way. Her constant companion stood behind her.

"I do not know why I am here except he is my husband and your brother." Lady Junla spoke slowly.

Marlin placed his sword on the table. He placed his case of maps next to it.

"I have been around Harbinger and my mother too long. I felt this compulsion to honor the commitment somehow. Have you seen him?" Lady Junla continued when Marlin did not speak.

"No." Marlin replied tersely.

"Interesting, he deserves this punishment. He doesn't deserve the comfort of our presence. Yet, the thought of him waiting all alone to die does not sit well with me."

"He left many others to die alone. I cannot believe that he is my brother. I never knew him well as a person. I am surprised that a son of my parents could have done what he did." Marlin spoke to the emotions he wished she had let him ignore.

"There you go. If he shares your blood how can he be completely terrible."

"He is a monster. You saw the survivors of Tampello."

"Yes, I did. He deserves the punishment he will most surely receive. He did not have the power to establish Tampello. Ranald did that. Renfrew did not run Tampello, nor did he remain in control of Tampello once it was set up. It was something gone terribly wrong. When you mix borderline ideas with insanity all kinds of horrors result."

"No, he should have known from the beginning it was wrong. You cannot argue me from that truth. No matter who administered it, no matter who empowered it, Tampello was wrong, evil. Renfrew should have worked to stop it. He should have left Ranald right then. He should have tried to save the men of Masfin who suffered because of his idea. He had resources and power. He did nothing. He should die a thousand deaths."

Junla sighed. "You are right. He is also my husband. Harbinger would ask for mercy. The war is over. Let the killing end. Let us be merciful to those we have defeated. During the war no one could be more implacable, destructive, and ruthless than Harbinger. I find her very strange. Jeffeaux can't be merciful because Renfrew is my husband at Harbinger's request. So Harbinger has asked that I do one final act for my husband. I agree with you. I do. I also know of Renfrew's deep regret for Tampello. He knows he deserves death. He does not deserve mercy or kindness. If I do not offer mercy or kindness do I become that which I despise?"

Marlin turned away from Junla's questions. He could not think right now. He could only move from one moment to the next. He wished very much to return home. He wanted to lie in the comfort of his wives' arms. It was such a simple wish.

"What does your priest think?"

Junla frowned. She cast a glance at her silent companion.

"What does it matter what he thinks? This is not about the priest. This is about my duty to my husband. It's a very short duty. I only plan to share the rest of Renfrew's life, not he the rest of mine."

"Do you have plans for your priest afterwards?'

"After what? He's not my priest. I only did what I had to do to keep him safe. I taught him what he needed to know to survive so close to Harbinger. He was a chief priest of Kersai at the temple at Deskersai. His life expectancy was very short if he did not learn to be very still. I trained him to be totally still. Do you know how many priests are left alive in Sarna? Since the Revelations about the Sacred Writing from the temple?"

Marlin nodded wearily.

"He is my responsibility. Just as your brother is my commitment. There is only one thing left I can give to your brother to honor my commitment. I intend to try to give it to him."

"You still haven't told me what you plan to do with this priest."

Lady Junla stood. She moved past Marlin. Her shadow followed closely. As she passed, Marlin placed a hand on her arm to detain her. Lady Junla ignored the insult. She motioned her priest to relax. Marlin was under a great deal of strain.

"I will give him a choice. He may join his fellow priests or stay with me."

Junla wrapped her arms around herself as she entered the cold night.

"A choice Lady?"

"Yes, you may decide your own fate at last."

"Have I angered you, Lady?"

"No, you deserve a choice. I deserve for you to make a choice. Who wants to be with someone who stays with them because they have no choice to leave?" Junla was trying to decide what her best course of action was. As Renfrew's widow she would be unable to remain in Masfin. She would be a hindrance to Jeffeaux in his bid to establish a new dynasty. She would not be welcome in Masfin by the people either.

She could join her mother's Household. She hoped she would get a child of Renfrew. Her two sons were staying in Masfin. Jeffeaux had claimed them as his heirs and would not relinquish that claim despite their connection to Renfrew. He had simply adopted them and called them his sons. A very Llweganian or Sarnese attitude as far as Junla could see.

Junla was brought out of her reverie by a strong hand around her arm. She was swung around until she faced her priest. He pushed his face into hers.

"Do you think to abandon me so easily?"

Junla was deeply insulted. "I would never abandon you. I want you to choose to be with me or to go. I will not make it easy on you. When have I ever been easy on you? You must choose."

"How can I choose? I am nothing except what you make of me."

"There is something in there besides these trappings of obedience. See how you defy me. Choose, tell me what you want, right now."

His mouth worked soundlessly. He could not seem to remember how to speak. She waited patiently. She did not try to sway him. He stared into her steady gaze.

"I stay with you."

"Good, now you know where I am going. I have arranged for you to stay with my mother's Household until my return."

"I will not always obey you."

"There is no shame in being wrong sometimes."

He shot her an oblique glance and accented it with a grunt.

"Though you can waste time and effort." She continued.

"Nothing is wasted when there is a lesson to be learned."

Junla sighed. "I can see already that I will live to regret my compassionate urge to save you."

Renfrew woke with a splitting headache. He placed a hand to the spot that hurt most. He immediately drew his head back. He looked around. He could not see anything very well. He wondered if it were his injuries affecting his sight or a lack of light. After a few moments he was able to focus his eyes. He looked into the concerned face of his wife.

"Need another child legitimized?"

"No, I am here to bear your company for a while before your trial and execution."

"They are one and the same?"

"The evidence is very strong against you. You cannot claim innocence about Tampello."

Renfrew bent his head. She was right.

"I should simply claim guilt and let it go at that."

"A trial would give you a few more days of life."

"What would I do with those?"

"You could let me offer you comfort. It is the best I can offer."

"You hope to get a child of me?"

"I hope to give a child to you that you will not completely die. You are not completely evil."

"That child would grow up under the stain of my guilt."

Junla laughed. "Everyone will assume that the child belongs to my priest. Anyway, I will not be living in Masfin. I go to Llwegania or Sarna; certainly I will not stay in Masfin."

Wearing his royal robes he sat at his royal desk on his royal chair, he felt as if he were in a coffin. He was alone in that room staring at the final decree of peace which he had signed that very day. His finger ran lightly, hardly touching the skin under his name: Jeffeaux, King of Masfin.

He knew the moment Harbinger entered the room. She stood behind him.

"This is the room where my sister drew her last breath. Ranald's allies have found a new protector, new lives. My sister and her child are dead and your husband is safe in the fortress of your protection." Jeffeaux spoke with tightly leashed anger.

She stared at her ally. She knew his moods very well. She understood his anger and frustration. She had it in her power to defuse his ire, but she would bear it a moment longer. He would be unable to vent his feelings soon. He would have no peers. Without peers he would be unable to gain satisfaction from venting. Spilling anger on weaker and dependent people led to guilt not relief.

"You know I take my responsibilities seriously. I do not shirk them because they are unpleasant or inconvenient. He is my husband. I have an army of seasoned soldiers dependent on me and beholden to me for their lives. I am married to one of their own. I am about to return to a Council both angry with me and terrified of me. It suits my purposes to have that army in my control, on my estates, at my shoulder when I face down the encroaching, waffling, greedy, jealous members of that Council. Yes, our former adversaries now flourish under my protection. They are reviled in their homeland. Their allies are sleeping in Death's cold embrace. I am all that stands between them and oblivion. I rescued them. They understand me. They know me. They respect me. They are my tool, my army now. And I will strike at the heart of my enemies with the sword I have fashioned from my spoils of this war."

Jeffeaux stared in horror. He felt as if he had never known this woman. "I thought you promised the Sarnese to find them homes in Sarna."

"The population will not accept them. I always knew that. The promise was easily given. Wind Rider is trying her best. That army is mine now. I might never have to use it. Just my possessing it might control the Council's actions. I can hardly wait to see their faces the first time the Council watches me bring my Sarnese husband into a Meeting."

"Did I ever know you? Who are you?"

Harbinger advanced on Jeffeaux. She smiled into his face.

"I am the same woman I ever was. I will do anything I must to secure the safety of my hereditary lands. I have sworn to do this."

"Does this army stand as a threat to me as well?"

"Jeffeaux." He heard the hurt in her voice. He was too angry to apologize.

"Jeffeaux, I am sorry. I was wrong. I should have sent someone to protect your sister. I did think she might be in danger of violence if a coup occurred. Sparing her would have been wiser for the conspirators; still she obviously was in danger. She was your sister. You cannot condone the murder of an innocent woman. She had character flaws, but they were not crimes. Ranald's death you could pardon, but Jeffenza's, no. Not because she was your sister but because she had no part in any of Ranald's reign of terror. Sparing her would have been the strategically wise move. I should have done better by her."

"Well, she always was chasing your husbands. Why should you care what happened to her?"

"Because you care. Because Lady Zona cares. I did care. I just misjudged. I never thought they would really kill her."

Jeffeaux let loose the breath he had been holding. "Neither did I. Especially the child. How could they kill the child?"

Harbinger looked out the window at the milling army. "Have you considered my request to address the army before I leave?"

"Trying to steal another army?"

"No. Goodbyes are expected of colorful leaders. I think I qualify for that position."

"Colorful." Jeffeaux released a ghost of a laugh. "I shall send out the order."

"You must get used to the royal we. Now that you are married to Masfin you are in fact a plural being."

"I will not miss you ordering me about."

"You will miss me though."

Jeffeaux almost cringed at her close hit. He heard her take a deep breath. Then he felt the heat of her right behind him.

"I have sent my newest daughter to my twelfth husband as his heir. I believe it was the proper thing to do under the circumstances."

Jeffeaux started. What did this have to do with anything? Then he stopped feeling. Sablor had claimed her last living child born of her body. She had borne none since. What child was she talking about? Why would she be talking about one of her children when they were discussing Jeffenza's child? True she could be angry with Jeffenza for having sex with Stiefis. Jeffeaux heard his thoughts in relation to the conversation. Harbinger had sent a child to Stiefis. Then he understood what she said and why she said it.

"He will cherish her as is fitting. She will live long and well in his house."

Jeffeaux bent his head. He was relieved, yet still jealousy burned in his heart because Stiefis should have claim to her and he did not. He felt a hand on the skin of his neck under the heavy royal wig.

"You once asked me a question that I did not answer. Do you remember? We were discussing love and husbands. I will answer it now. Yes.

"I had ridden well into Darkfall. I was in a strange land. I entered an alien building and saw a group of foreign beings. My eyes beheld a bejeweled, beribboned creature with long curls and high-heeled shoes. I stared into his painted face and irrationally, irrevocably, I loved him. He is long gone. I miss his mincing step and languid hand movements, the way his eyes roamed the world looking for pleasure and amusement. I loved the sound of his voice. Not just the voice, the tones and rhythm of his speech. I would argue with him just to hear his voice. He was such a fey, delicate creature, and I loved him. I will always love him.

"I had to destroy him. For my country, for my people, he could not remain. I had to send him away from me. In his place is a man I respect and even admire. A man who is able to make the same choices for his country and people that I have made for mine. He is a man who, if ever I had a son, I would wish the boy to grow into such a man.

"It is hard to leave such a man with a whole heart. It is hard to leave the only living reminder of a man I love so intensely. You can win the battle, and even the war, and still lose the only thing that was of any value to you personally though you gain the entire world for your people.

"Miss me as much as I will miss both of you; the one I destroyed and the one I made."

Jeffeaux felt his chest begin to burn. His lower jaw tingled and ached. His throat closed against itself.

That hand turned his face until he was looking into her serious gaze. Then she was too close for his eyes to see her. He could smell her. He could feel her heat. Then his universe shrunk to his mouth as she took it in a fierce kiss. The experience was everything he had ever fantasized and was nothing he could have imagined. Her lips and teeth and tongue took his mouth and soul from him. He wanted to rise. He wanted to hold her against his body. Before he could gather his senses to raise his hands she was gone.

He heard a sound. He thought it was a groan from his chest. He knew. It was from his chest. It was the sound of his heart breaking. It was the sound of the shards of his heart falling into his soul.

He clenched his hand tightly as if trying to hold onto the moment of revelation as if trying to stave off that eternity of pain and loneliness. He released his fist to reach for the bellpull. An aide-de-camp answered the summons.

"Send to all regiments: there is to be a general assembly. Once all the soldiers are present, notify Harbinger of Death that her revelry is ready."

"Yes, Your Highness."

Should he send her an outline of unacceptable topics? Should he try to limit her words? How could he? He would trust in her. He would trust in her desire for, her interest in his wellbeing. She would not weaken his position in any way. She needed him strong. She needed his throne sturdy. She loved him. She would not risk him personally. He should send for his mother. He needed to speak with her and with Junla. Even Marlin should be consulted before they all left for Sarna.

Lady Zona looked up from her packing. She had very little to do. Still she enjoyed the act of folding. The scent of freshly laundered cloth made her smile. Years on the campaign trail had taught her to cherish the luxury of clean clothes. A small sound alerted her. Then Junla filled the doorway.

"Daughter."

"The trial has yet to start."

"We must leave. I have to take up my governorship."

Junla stuck out her chin. She had never questioned any order during the war, but now, she was tired of having so little say in her life.

"What if I do not wish to move? What if I wish to stay, at least until the trial is over?"

"It will do Renfrew no good to have you here. It may hinder the King, your brother, to have his sister, the most infamous war criminal's wife present during the trial."

"How will it reflect on me to abandon my husband during his hour of greatest need?"

"How will he feel to have you witness the testimony of his heinous crimes? How will he feel to know he leaves you unprotected in this country?"

"I am the sister of the King."

"And of the former Queen. You put your brother in a delicate position by staying. It is safer for everyone, including you, to leave now. You are my heir. You come with me. You have much to learn. You will swear to Harbinger on my death. Your heir will swear to Harbinger's heir on your death. You have much to learn."

Junla stared at her mother.

"What are you saying, Mother?"

"Who else would be my heir? I am too old to bear children. Daughter you may not sit on the fence any longer. There is only one side left for you. Marlin and First are important leaders of Sarna. They provide security, culture, structure, community. They are of **my** Household. They answer to me. I am sworn to Harbinger of Death of Llwegania. I must build whole new systems of education, trade, public works, justice, everything. I am answerable to a very powerful ruler. I have very able husbands but I need my heir's help. I need my heir to understand all the workings for her tenure."

"I don't want to be your heir."

Lady Zona laughed. She stroked her daughter's face.

"Good, too bad, you are. You are not some peasant able to choose your own road. You are the descendant of Kings. You are the mother of Kings. I know you are flexible. I know you understand power. I know you are strong and smart. I know you have courage and compassion and good sense. I will teach you how to wield power."

Junla took a deep breath. She felt her companion's hand on her shoulder. He must be smiling. She had forced him to change to survive whether he wished it nor not. He now could watch her mother force her to bend to another's will. As long as she could keep this child, what did it matter? She could very well swear to Harbinger. She could govern a country she detested.

Marlin stood before the heavy wooden door of the cell block. There was only one prisoner inside. Harbinger would be leaving soon. He did not have much time. He didn't need that much.

He had left his meeting with King Jeffeaux in a black mood. Lady Zona insisted he come here before they left. The King had agreed. Jeffeaux had sited his own lack of farewell with his late sister Jeffenza. Why was he here? What could he have to say to the stranger on the other side of the door? Duty was a painful spur. He nodded to the waiting guard. The door swung open.

Pale light wavered in the space. Directly opposite the open door was the only occupied cell. Marlin stood in the doorway watching his brother. Renfrew listlessly turned his head. He watched Marlin approach through his bars. His expression was carefully neutral.

Marlin noted the comfortable temperature of the area.

"It is pleasant enough."

"Very pleasant as prisons go."

"We won't go that road."

Renfrew nodded. "Better not. I seem to be in chains when we meet these days."

"We all make choices. I am leaving at first light. I won't be returning to Masfin. My Lady Zona is the Governor of Sarna. I will be her military commander. Once I cross the border I will cease to be Masfin."

"You ceded your right to call yourself Masfin seasons ago."

Marlin tried to see himself in the man who was his brother.

"Why?" Marlin knew he was asking about Tampello. So did Renfrew. Renfrew chose to ignore the knowledge.

"That is my question. Why did you abandon Masfin?" Renfrew stretched as tall as his chains would allow. "How could you? And don't mouth to me some story about a True King. You no more believe in that old story than I do. Did she capture you in her web? Do you love that strange woman?"

Marlin did not try to evade the question. He did not pretend ignorance.

"I do believe King Jeffeaux is the True King of Masfin. He is the first True King Masfin has had in generations. He is the True King because he acts like one. He takes his responsibilities very seriously. As long as he lives he will be the True King. He will be as a husband to Masfin."

Renfrew snorted his distaste, "He is that female's pawn."

"No, once, at the beginning. Now he is a very good king."

"If you like him so well, why leave?"

"I am Harbinger's man. She has given me everything. She cared for all her soldiers. When we were cold, she was cold. When we were hungry, she was hungry. She led us into battle. She did not order us into battle. I am a soldier." Marlin stepped into memory. "You should have seen her ride out of Deskersai. She was large with child. Blood, smoke, soot, and sweat streaked her face. Her sword swung with force, deadly accuracy, agility. She laughed. She rejoiced to be with us.

"We accomplished great things with her. You weren't there. You never stood by her as she fought. You never felt her care of her armies."

"Leader worship is dangerous. Nothing you have said explains your complete change of loyalties."

"What was I in Masfin? What ties did I have?"

"What ties? We are blood."

Marlin laughed. He shook his head.

"How many years had passed between conversations? When had you last seen me before war came? Do you know? I don't. Six Darkfalls never pass between greetings from Harbinger and her soldiers unless she is on her Ride. She remembers names and faces and instances and children and sorrows. She orders soldiers to their deaths. They go willingly because they know she does not waste their lives on futile, useless efforts. How can you not love a leader like that?

"You took me for granted, General. She valued me. I have ties of blood now. Ties that are eternally binding but they are not more binding than those ties of the heart which I chose and which chose me."

"You simply chose the side that opposed me. You could not stand to be second to me in anything."

"That may have urged me to weigh the options. I do not know. The generals were making assumptions and placing no value on people who I knew were capable and competent. Watching their discussions convinced me they were not the best choice for me, not for Masfin. I was not wrong.

"Sarna was a danger. That danger would never have been neutralized by the military decisions being made back then. King Jeffeaux is a better King for Masfin than Ranald ever was or ever would have been.

"The Shaking happened. Once that happened everything changed. We are better because of the choices I made, not the ones you made. My making different choices would not have prevented the changes the Shaking wrought."

"I did what I had to do to preserve the army."

"Why?"

"Why what? Preserve the army? Masfin needed that army. King Ranald would have ravaged the land if the army failed him."

"How? Without the army what power did he have? In the end it turned on him. By letting the army dissipate you would have saved its soldiers, Masfin, and perhaps even Jeffenza and Ranald. You loved that army. You could not give up that army. You destroyed it trying to save it."

Renfrew grunted. He looked away from his brother's clear gaze.

"So you have come to say goodbye."

"Yes, and to let go my anger with you. My wives want me to give up my anger. Your wife wants me to forgive you. Harbinger would grant you mercy. She says that war is a crazy thing. She is a warrior. The Sarnese are warriors. They fight for land, possessions, and women. Harbinger fights to defend her country. This war was not like that. She did not understand how Tampello happened. She could see that trying to establish control led to actions that in retrospect were unwise and useless. She was appalled, shocked, dismayed, at the slaughter at Delungor. She knew then that Ranald would do anything to protect his power. When you follow a power hungry leader you will do things you never thought possible for your own protection. Absolute power corrupts absolutely and your leader can turn on you in the blink of an eye. There are no warriors or soldiers in an army led by such a person, only survivors willing to do anything to please a crazy person. She said I should have pity on you. She said I do not have to forgive you. She said you did terrible things to stay alive. It is instinctual. It is not a question of whether or not you have the courage to give your life to a good cause or not. When dealing with insanity you often cannot see beyond the moment.

"Soldiers expect to lose their lives. Their leaders often take those lives by mistake, incompetence, ignorance, fate. Tampello was leaders taking lives of their soldiers through desperation. Delungor was the sign that courage of a warrior was needed to stop an evil. From that moment, the soldier's duty, the warrior's honor, required that your life be given up in the good cause of destroying Ranald.

You could not stop trying to save your own life at the expense of many others."

"I would have died for nothing."

"At least you would not have taken any more innocents with you. Letting the soldiers leave might have cost you your life, but it would have saved so many others."

"I never even considered that road."

"I know. It is most interesting that we are of the same bone, background, country and yet we made such different choices and led such different lives. The importance of minute differences during war is incredible. Goodbye brother. We shall not meet again. For what it is worth, I no longer despise you. You should have come with me that night."

"I could not, for you had chosen first."

"Such a small detail to hang a war on."

"As you said, it is the small things that count in war. If you see Stiefis, tell him I wish him well."

"He will say you should have left with him."

"That he will. You still had chosen first. I could not bear to have made the wrong choice when you had made the right one."

"I was lucky that the right choice for me was the good choice as well."

"Farewell, brother."

Marlin nodded in reply, for Renfrew would not fare very well at all. He did not look back as he left the cell block. He kept his eyes focused on the horse waiting for him. He could hardly wait to lose himself in the embrace of his family. He very much wanted to be home. First he had to stand by his chosen leader. There she was. The crowd was huge. How could she possibly project her voice over such a distance? There were riders amidst the crowd. She would have given her words to the riders. They would speak as she spoke. Everyone would hear her words and see her as she spoke them, even if they could not hear her voice.

Harbinger sat on her horse. She knew the King stood on the dais behind her. She would speak from her horse. It felt right. She looked out at the crowd. She saw individual faces in the sea of bodies. She heard bodies shift. She watched the battalion flags snap in the wind. She felt the muscles of her mount between her thighs. He shifted his weight. She tightened her knees then she relaxed her seat. They had been a good army. They had followed orders. They had adhered to training. It was a fine day, a good moment to savor their victory.

"This is my fare-thee-well. You have been fine soldiers. We have fought well together. Now you will be even better citizens. You have traveled your entire country. You know it better than any of your forefathers. This country belongs to you as it never did to your forefathers. You fought to protect this country from an outside force. You fought to protect this country from an inside threat. This country belongs to you, and this King belongs to you, because you were willing to pay the ultimate price.

"We know you won the war. Now you must win the peace. You must build a country worthy of the price our comrades paid. You must build a country able to withstand such a terrible price.

"We are comrades, you and I. There will be songs written about our deeds. You will tell your history to citizens who were not yet born when we tramped the length and breadth of Sarna and Masfin. In time there will be more alive who do not know those things than there are veterans of this conflict. They will say: those things could not have happened. Your memory will seem faded. You will say: did we do those things? They will say you exaggerate, it is not as the songs tell it. You will say: do I remember rightly? Was Tampello awful? Was Delungor reprehensible? They will say look how prosperous, how wise, how strong we are: we could never have had such a war. They will say peace is so good it is worth keeping at any price; no threat is worth war.

"They were not here. They did not see the raids that led to war. They will see the Sarna of contentment. They will never know a Sarna where people are subjected to horrible, secret restrictions. They will not know a people desperate to have children as neighbors, because you gave them a prosperous and fertile people as neighbors. You gave Sarna the circumstances to be a good neighbor. They will not have a ruler so desperate to save his power that he would kill all his people, leaving no one left to deny his claim. They will not know what it is like to live though this time, and so they will not believe.

"You and I know how it was. It was a terrible time. You suffered greatly. You have paid a very high price for this peaceful future. We saw the blood at Delungor. We watched the most beautiful and terrible sight of Ranald's army marching across the plain before Reduni. When everything fades, remember this was real. Don't let them convince you of your faulty memory. We lived through these things.

"Because we lived through these things we are always together. Our ties are as strong as blood because they were forged in blood. I honor these ties. Should we never meet again it will always be as if we had just shared a meal last Darkfall."

She sat looking for a last breath then she wheeled her mount. All her Household guard streamed behind her. She galloped until they were out of sight. Then she pulled her horse to a slower pace.

Marlin rode close to Lady Zona. He studied the expressions of the Dragon and her husbands. They were not euphoric, pleased, even contented. He turned his head away from the group. He did not wish to intrude. Lady Zona had no such qualms.

"That last messenger from the Council, he carried bad news?"

"No, just a posturing that can be easily ignored."

"I won't be satisfied with that."

Harbinger sent her a glare.

"I won't be dissuaded either."

"The marriage structure in Llweganian society was developed to ensure that the widest variety of traits was passed on through generations. The limit on the number of husbands a woman may have is her ability to keep them happy in bed. A woman may abuse the system by marrying many men to acquire their lands, armies, votes in Council. To protect against this the Council may demand a demonstration of the reality of a marriage. This is a very old statute. It has not been invoked for generations. Until now, they have not sent me such a request."

"Harbinger, you have produced many children in the time I have known you. How could anyone question that you are married to your guard?'

"Ah Marlin, it is not these husbands' marriages they question. It is my Sarnese husband they doubt I have had."

"Has he sent a petition?"

"No, they claim to have a witness of an invalid marriage."

"Who would witness against you, Harbinger?"

"A Messenger of the Council."

"I thought the Messengers had a code against spying."

"An oath and a system of laws that I may invoke against the Messenger, but that will be a moot point if I am caught in an invalid marriage. So I must get my shy Sarnese husband to bed me before the entire Council. And I will have no time to convince him of this. The Council will meet us at my Sarnese husband's Estate."

Marlin thought for a long moment. He looked to Lady Zona.

"Did you witness this wedding, Lady Zona?"

"Yes, as did the husband's father."

"I was at the Repudiation. Harbinger did not Repudiate her Sarnese husband. By the Sarnese laws they were married and are married until a priest of Kersai sets their marriage aside. Are not marriages by any society other than Llweganian valid?"

"Fine point. This has nothing to do with the validity and everything with power. The easiest way to consolidate my power at this point is to bend to the Council's will, to demonstrate my married state in public."

"Easiest only if you can get your shy husband to agree."

"That is the sticking point. Forgive the phrasing. Do you doubt my ability to arouse my husband beyond his shyness?'

"Never, Harbinger. I would never underestimate your abilities in any arena. May I go home to my wives?"

"Not up for a public display of marital affection General Marlin? Again, phrasing, I know. That's all right, I will allow for your Masfin sensibilities. You don't need to know everything about me. A little mystery is good. I think you need to quarry stone."

"Stone, Harbinger?"

"Yes, I will build a wall: long, high, wide, sturdy enough to keep jealousy at bay."

"I have never seen such a wall. There must be very special stone for such a wall."

"You are right, there. Quarry it for me. I will be needing tons of it."

"Perhaps the world will shake again, build your wall for you."

"I am not that powerful yet." Harbinger let a hearty laugh escape her belly. "You are a sly fellow, General Marlin. Get home to your family. I have a pretty man to bed."

Lady Zona watched her general ride away. She had remained quiet during the discussion.

"Will there be war?"

"It seems War is my True Consort. I think Stiefis will lie with me before the required witnesses. If not, I will defend my marriage with force of arms."

Lady Zona remained silent for a goodly space. Harbinger did not rush her. They rode in companionable silence.

"What if Stiefis asks to have the marriage dissolved under Llweganian law?"

"That is the question. He has sworn that he is my husband. I have never tested his resolve in that matter. I will see if he has grown any honor in the course of our marriage."

"That is a difficult plant. One can never be sure of the soil or seed or fertilizer or weather or passing winds. The seemingly surest seed under the wrong conditions or even perfect conditions will throw up a weed. Then out of nowhere honor will sprout from a nothing seed in the middle of a storm. You can never tell with honor."

"Lady Zona, you are so right, and it is nerve-wracking to trust my life's work on such a chancy thing, but there you have it. When husbands are involved what can a woman do but throw the dice, then hope everything turns out well?"

Harbinger sent a sidelong glance to Petron's profile. His sour expression caused her to grin.

"What say you, husband? You believe there is a man I cannot get into my bed? If I put my mind to it?"

"I would rather fight all of Llwegania than accept that boy as my brother."

"He is older than some of my husbands. If I can avert the shedding of any more blood by accepting this man as my husband I will do it. I am sick of lying down with War. I want to wallow in peace. You have trained him well. He is loyal to his family and friends. Since he came to me, since I rescued him from Masfin, he has honored our marriage. I will have peace if he will bed me."

"Once you put your mind to it you could have bedded Ranald himself."

"I never thought of that solution."

"For that we will be forever grateful."

"Come you to witness this, Lady Zona?"

"Would it help you?"

"No, nor would it hurt. You would be incidental."

"Incidental was never something to which I aspired: I think I should get my Household to Deskersai where I have many momentous and important tasks to perform in the service of the Bringer of Water. I might need to have an army over the border to defend your marriage."

"Good point, get to your Estate. Wait for my orders."

Harbinger watched Lady Zona ride away. Husbands, soldiers, retainers followed the new governor of Sarna. Harbinger glanced at those who remained. A small smile curved her mouth.

"With that our numbers are much as they were when we first rode out of Llwegania to meet our fate."

"We certainly still have the same issues with the Council as then."

"They never questioned one of my marriages before."

"It is an attack on our position. How is that different?"

"You do well to remind me of the heart of the matter. I would not want pride to blind me."

Stiefis stood on the parapet of his castle. The towering height had given him vertigo when he had first taken possession of this Estate. Now it gave him strength. Also, it was a wonderful escape from greedy scheming people who were filling up his space.

His wife's messenger had bade him welcome these grim-faced people with gracious demeanor and watchful eye. They were her rivals and peers. He had heard enough veiled comments to know they had come to contest his marriage. He would not lose another wife. He was done giving away things that were his.

Surely she would not allow this. She had adhered to their vows throughout the war. She had cared for his father as a daughter by marriage would. She provided for him; she sent him an heir. She considered him her husband. She would not give him up because these petty people tried to maneuver her. He had come home. She would not make him leave.

A cloud rose on the horizon. Some of his anxiety stilled. She would be with him soon. He gathered his cloak tightly to his body. She had never mentioned his infidelity. She knew. She had sent him the child.

He had recognized the child immediately. He had not known how badly he wanted a child until the little girl had arrived. Hearing the messenger announce that this little girl was now his heir had affected his breathing, his soul.

He would never forget the moment her eyes met his. She had glowed. She had flown across the yard into his arms. He had taken one look at her adoring eyes and been lost.

"Mama says she had looked for me a long time. She said you were very happy I was found. She promised you would never make me watch heads get cut off. She said you loved me very much. I am so happy to be home."

"I am very glad to have my daughter where she belongs. I am very sad it took so long to find you. I am very sad you had to see all those horrible things. I will show you good things, I promise. I will love you more than any other father ever loved a child to make up for all the years you had to miss a father's love."

"I am so glad Mama found me. I am so happy to be back with my real father."

They had been inseparable since that day. She filled his life with constant joy. He would not give up his daughter. He would do anything to ensure his child stayed with him.

The cloud resolved into a long line of black. The purpose of that line held power and determination. That was not the line of someone coming to bow to the will of others. She was coming to claim her husband. She was coming to demonstrate the validity of her marriage. He was not naïve. Words would not suffice. An old-fashioned public bedding was the only answer to a charge such as this. His anxiety grew again. Would he fail her? Would his nerve allow such a display?

The line began to have a voice. He could hear the rumble of the horses' hooves against the earth. The voice would swell to thunder as she neared. She had aroused more than one man in her life. He would trust in her ability to arouse him. Though none of them had borne such burdens as he. They had neither his background nor his stresses.

The voice swelled to thunder. That thunder filled him until it surged his blood. She was finally here. There was excitement in him at that thought. He rushed to his wife.

He burst into the courtyard as the first rider entered. He recognized his family immediately. He ran lightly down the shallow steps to greet them.

"Husband, your house is bursting at the seams with guests."

"They have been arriving for days. Invasion must be a national pastime."

She laughed at his attempt at humor.

"Voyeurism more like." She had advanced until there was hardly a hand's breadth between them. He bent to share a kiss of peace. She allowed the gentle salute.

"I had begun to guess as much."

"Feeling up to the show?" She placed only the slightest stress on up. All the husbands caught the joke. They smiled hesitantly.

"Indeed I am. Anything to get rid of them. Guests are like cooked food: both begin to smell after three days."

The smiles became grins.

"A Llweganian ceremony then as we have already been blessed by a Sarnese priest."

"Before dinner?"

"Not so fast. We should play with them a little. Let them think they have a chance. Let us feed them a very fine feast, then dash their hopes to the ground. They have caused us some inconvenience and insulted us greatly. Causing them some pain will be good."

Stiefis was quiet. He soaked up the feeling of belonging to a group, a group united in a winning endeavor.

"Is the marriage validity ceremony complicated?"

"Very simple, all your brother/husbands must be there and the Council."

Stiefis nodded gravely. "The entire Council?"

"Every one. They are all here. I had watchers reporting to me as they arrived. I didn't want this to be invalid because they pulled a switch on us."

"My father will have to be there as well. It is only fitting."

"As you wish."

"And your heir, but not mine; she is too young."

"That is within reason. How is our daughter?"

"She is very well. I have not thanked you for my heir. She is the greatest gift."

"I thought as much, hence her name."

"I awake everyday eager to see the world through her eyes."

"I hope her mornings are good."

"I take her riding everyday as you promised I would."

"Good."

Stiefis extended his arm in a very Masfin courtly manner. Harbinger ran her hand along his arm until her fingers rested on his wrist. It was a Masfin woman's trick. Seemingly genteel but slightly outrageous, the pressure of her fingers was a long slow caress. He had not been with a woman in a very long time. The slide of her hand reminded him of that fact. His flesh trembled.

Flechse watched the interplay of wife and husbands with a frown. He had a clear view from the window of his room. Behind him his wife and his two brother/husbands conferred with an ally.

"Tell me again why we have done this?"

All discussion ended at his request. He did not turn from the window.

"We need access to Sarna and Masfin for trade. Devouring Dragon controls the entire border with Sarna. All trade delegations need to establish permissions with Devouring Dragon to reach Sarna and Masfin. We cannot deny her the right to demand control of permissions. We can only eliminate her control of the border by dismantling her marriages. The marriage to the Sarnese is the most vulnerable. So we attack there."

"We have based our charge on the chance comment of a messenger."

"A Messenger of the Council has a certain patina and aura that lend legitimacy to our charge."

Flechse turned from the window. He straightened his cuffs. He pulled his tunic into a perfect line across his hips.

"Once one marriage is dissolved it will be easier to attack another one."

"A fowl shoot really, they will fall without a fight."

"They will be relieved to be out of such an old-fashioned repressive structure. Twelve husbands, what man wishes to be one of twelve husbands? She will be stripped of everything. It will be something to watch. When must she answer the charges?'

"She has until two Darkfalls from now."

He smiled at his wife. Waterwoman was pretty and young. He had been glad when their parents had proposed the match. He was not First but he was Second and she had taken only three husbands. Women took fewer husbands now. No one took more than six. Devouring Dragon had twelve and her heir had seven. Nineteen Estates tied up by two women. One woman controlled the entire Llweganian border with Sarna. She had been too greedy. He would see her fall. She would learn a lesson. He could hardly wait.

"Can the timetable be pushed up?"

"No. We are using an ancient law; we have to follow it to the letter. She has until that particular Darkfall to demonstrate her marriage. Be patient. Tonight, the next or the next, it does not matter, we will succeed."

Flechse sank into a hard seat. He stretched his legs before the fire. It was fitting that an ancient law would be invoked in this antiquated pile of stone. The Sarn would be happy to be freed from a marriage that landed him in this hole. Not a single modern convenience graced this place. Flechse sniffed his disdain at his surroundings. Stupid woman, thinking she could rule the world, restrain his actions. She would fall soon and he would have helped push her.

When Waterwoman had first broached the plot, he had smiled in glee. The Guild Leader's reluctance to back the story had been a sticky moment. The man's old-fashioned ideas of honor and oath-bond had been laughable. He did not understand how power worked now. He did not see the importance of careful manipulation and veiled statements. Flechse liked the deviousness of this plan. He enjoyed the intricate dance of this play. He raised a goblet of wine to his mouth. He sipped the wine. It was very fine wine. It tasted of exotic places and different climes. He had never tasted such fine wine until his stay here. This wine should be available to him whenever he wanted it. He should not have to wait for a visit to Devouring Dragon to have access to such fine wine. The wine highlighted the need to conclude this play successfully.

Evening bells sounded. Flechse dropped his feet to the floor with a loud thud. He finished his wine in a large gulp. He followed his wife from the room. Tens of bodies whirled in the halls. They proceeded with the air of a market day. There were laughter and loud words. Victory hung in the air. The entire Council filed into the Great Hall with smiles and joy. Flechse loved the irony of the vanquished providing the victory feast.

The hosts were already in the hall. At the head of the table the Sarn sat with Devouring Dragon at his right. That was fitting since this was his Estate. Other Sarnese sat as well. All her husbands were there as well as her heir with her husbands. Servants moved along the tables. Flechse sat with a glad heart. He ate heartily. He watched the head table with suppressed animosity. Soon the mighty would be cut off at the knees.

Stiefis watched the crowd of invaders with a jaundiced eye. He saw how they laughed and chatted and toasted one another. He ate with barely contained hostility. They would not take anything from him. Under the table he felt his wife's fingers on his thigh. She caressed his leg with steady strokes. She spoke with Petron in idle tones. Her fingers pressed strongly into his flesh as she flirted with her First. Those fingers wandered higher and higher on his thigh as the meal progressed. Finally she was stroking his most vulnerable and responsive muscle. She sent him a sidelong glance. He returned her look with a tight smile. He certainly was ready to prove his marriage valid.

He could stand the guests no longer. He wanted them gone, out of his home, out his life. He wanted the question of his right to his home, his child, his wife answered to his satisfaction.

Flechse watched the intense exchange of expressions between the husband and wife at the head of the table. He felt a flutter of unease return to his stomach. They had looked married earlier this day. They looked married now.

Then the Sarnese husband raised his goblet.

"A toast to my wife: there is not a luckier man than I. I have worthy brother/husbands. My Estate is productive. I have a wonderful heir given me by my wife. My family and my dependents are well cared for. All this is mine for giving my army to my wife. Drink to my marriage."

The goblets in the room were raised to lips. The Sarn took a deep swig. Then, he slammed the goblet down on the table.

"My marriage is in doubt. I was married by my traditions, and only a priest of Kersai may call that marriage into question. But I am now a Llweganian husband, so I will swear to my wife in the Llweganian manner."

Flechse watched the knife slice the steady hand. He listened to the words with horror. Then the Sarn was sweeping the table clear. He pulled his wife onto the table.

Harbinger looked into the face of her husband. He was grinning. He was going to enjoy defeating an enemy. She pulled on the laces that confined his weapon of choice.

Stiefis gently undid the laces that shielded his wife from the rest of the world. He sighed to find her ready. Obviously she liked the challenge of their situation as much as he did. With one hand he steadied her hip. His other hand grasped the nearest Council Member.

"Watch, since that is your purpose here, watch as I demonstrate the validity of my marriage."

Stiefis pushed into the final corridor of his journey to his new life in Llwegania. He was finally home. He released the gasping Council Member with a shove. He anchored his arching wife to him. She shook her head in frustrated pleasure. He would not relent. He would not rush this consummation. He would make every man wish to be him. He would make every woman wish to be Dragon. He would make everyone wish to be them. He was demonstrating his power. His power to husband this woman, to raise his child, to run his Estate ,would never be threatened again. He would leave no room for doubt.

Without breaking his connection he raised Dragon's torso until she was flush with his chest. Tightly controlling his desire he began to plant gentle kisses on her groaning mouth. She was not a gentle woman. Her hands made strong through war gripped his head. Her mouth devoured him. Her tongue swept his mouth stealing his breath. Her thighs, strong and insistent, flexed around his hips. She began her own demonstration of power. He lowered her back onto the table. He pushed their bodies until they lay full length on the wooden surface. They rolled until she was on top.

"So the Battle Maid has finally defeated Kersai?" She spoke in priestly Sarnese.

Stiefis smiled brightly. She was supernatural. She was strong and female and in charge of his pleasure at this moment. It was not shameful to cede victory to such a conqueror. Defeat at her hands was sweet indeed.

"Yes. It is fitting a new nation rises from our courtship." His Sarnese was no less educated. "The Battle Maid's celebration of victory is not so bland as Kersai's."

"What fun would a celebration be without satisfaction?"

Stiefis pulled her down until their faces met.

"There will be satisfaction, my Wife, I promise."

"I have learned to trust your word. You have become a good husband."

"I will show you how good a husband I have become."

He rolled her. She gripped his hips with her powerful legs. Her back arched off the table. He cushioned her head with one hand as he set a furious pace. All the while they laughed at their victory and power. Then he could no longer resist the pull of her inner muscles as they tried to milk him dry.

He rested only a moment on her. He no longer wanted an audience. He wanted his bedchamber and his brothers around him. He eased them both off the table. He closed her clothing before he adjusted his own. She smiled at him gently.

Then the First of the House of Harbinger of Death spoke.

"We are all ready to demonstrate the validity of our marriage. You have invoked a very ancient statute which has not been invoked for generations. We have answered your charges. We assert that this is an assault on our sovereignty. Therefore our borders are closed. All Harbinger's Estates, all those who answer to an heir of her body, all those of spouses of heirs of her body are closed in accordance with the ancient traditions which you have invoked.

"By next new moon we expect a head. Messengers are not to reveal any intimate details they may witness in a Household during the performance of their sworn duties. If they break this oath, the Household so betrayed may demand the head of the Messenger, the head of the Guild Leader, or the head of the Estate where the guild resides. As the Messenger broke oath to report falsely about a proscribed subject, we expect one of those heads by the next new moon. If you fail to comply, we will consider the Council in default and therefore illegal and non-binding."

There was complete silence as the marriage partners of Harbinger of Death left the room. Flechse stared blankly around the room. He felt his blood rush to his head. He could not control his words.

"He wasn't supposed to defend his marriage. He wasn't supposed to want to be married to Devouring Dragon."

An elderly Sarn rose to his feet. He leaned heavily on a cane. He pushed his head forward to catch everyone's attention.

"My son remained married to Harbinger through a war. That marriage is valid. She commands our army by our choice. Sarna would not rise up for us but they will for her. She is the close ally of the newly crowned King of Masfin. You don't pull this Dragon's tail unless you are ready to lose your head. She is no little country squire. I have found her to be a formidable adversary and an amenable conqueror. King Jeffeaux benefitted from having her as an ally. Choose your position very wisely."

"That request is based on a law none expect kept. No one expects Messengers to refrain from comment. We all count on the law not being kept. There hasn't been a beheading in years." Flechse pushed his tankard of ale away. He pulled it back. He took a deep breath to release it with force.

Wind Rider snorted. "The Council evoked an ancient statute to threaten my mother's marriages. She complied with the ancient tradition. You set the rules. Play by them. That head must be delivered, or the Council's existence is false, corrupt, and invalid. We are not an elegant family. We do not indulge in petty posturing or shady maneuvering. Proof you wanted, proof you got. We waged a war for many years to secure Llwegania's future peace. We return home not to thanks or victory songs, but to demands and betrayals. What a thankless lot you are. Eat the bounty of my mother's efforts. Then consider whose head you will deliver." Wind Rider stared right at Flechse. She raised her knife slightly away from its scabbard. Then the blade slid back down with a click. Flechse raised his hand to cover his throat. Already he felt the bite of cold steel in his flesh.

He could not send the Messenger's head or the head of the Guild leader. It was his head or his mother's. His mother who had vehemently opposed the move, she would stand for him. She would die because of his mistake. She had no other heir and no possibility of conceiving one at her age. He had no heir yet.

Flechse looked into his wife's eyes; he could not blame her. He had participated in the process. He did not want to remain married to the one who had killed his mother. He could not leave her until she gave him an heir. Who would marry him now? Funny he had come to witness the end of a marriage. He had not expected it would be his.

Sablor's sister Soft Step of Westering watched the play. She had resented her son being supplanted by the heir sent by Harbinger. She could not deny the gift. Younger twins were considered special because they were born specifically for the husband. An unexpected gift sent to insure that husband had an heir. The superstition was old and shaded in mystery about just who sent the second twin, but it was ingrained.

That twin, that heir ,gave her power. She administered an Estate that was part of a great force. True, she cast her vote at Council at Harbinger's direction. True, her brother was Head of the Estate. Her favor was curried because she was her brother's sister. Her son was courted because his uncle was married to a powerful woman. She was feared and respected in a way she would not be as Head of Westering. Westering was safe as it had not been in oral memory. Her mother's dream had been true.

First read the letter twice. She put it down. She read it again. A surprised sweet laugh echoed through the house. Her sisters looked up from their work. Their children stopped their play. Marlin turned into the room. Her laugh sounded so rarely. She smiled. She exuded contentment. She rarely laughed. Now she could not seem to stop. Third picked up the letter. Then she too laughed. She covered her mouth with one hand and clutched the letter to her breast with the other. She freely passed the letter when Sixth motioned for it.

Marlin watched as all his wives dissolved into laughter. Even the children laughed, echoing their parents' hilarity for no known reason. He smiled at the sight.

"Oh husband, you should have stayed. You should have witnessed the spectacle. I would have liked to hear you describe it."

"What spectacle?"

"Stiefis bedding Harbinger on the dining table before the entire Council. I would have given anything to be there."

Marlin blushed. He could not keep the blood from creeping into his face. Even the thought of witnessing the public display made him uncomfortable.

First retrieved the letter. She was still chuckling as she smoothed the paper.

"When Harbinger suggested Stiefis bed us as a group, he fairly sent her flying from him. That he should have to perform before all those witnesses," her chuckling erupted into giggles again. "You should have seen his face when I said I would agree to such a thing. And now to think. Silly man. He got what he deserved." She placed the paper on her desk. She advanced laughing and giggling on her husband. Her sisters joined the surge. Marlin watched as his wives advanced on him. He retreated towards their rooms. Stiefis might be up to public exhibitions but Marlin had no intention of demonstrating the facts of life to his children. His wives were happy to chase him into their boudoir.

Lady Zona, the Governor of Sarna, read the letter with a sigh of relief. She let her head rest back onto her shoulders. She felt a great weight leave her. A gentle smile creased her face. Stea looked up from his writing.

"Good news, love?"

"The best. Devouring Dragon, Harbinger of Death, Bringer of Water has demonstrated her marriage to her Sarnese husband to the satisfaction of the Great Council of Llwegania. There will be no open hostilities in Llwegania for now. Finally, we have achieved peace for Sarna."

"The best news truly, love. The bedchamber must have been very crowded."

"How narrow you are. The Great Hall of course. Harbinger would not be hemmed in by so confining a space for such an act. Or rather her twelfth husband would not be so hemmed in. A fine meal, and dinner entertainment as well, were the offerings of that particular host."

"We shall have to review any invitations to Devouring Dragon's Estate with an eye to their wording. We will need to be very clear on what if any entertainment is offered."

Brir entered the room. He looked at the smile on his wife's face. "Peace is secure I take it."

"For today at least. What is your news of the day?"

Wintraub entered close behind his brother.

"We have to review the plans of the new outpost at the pass into Masfin. General Marlin is wondering what type of wall Devouring Dragon is building. He wishes to know what kind of stone he must quarry. Lady Junla feels unwell today. I sent a healer. The priests have been housed but they need occupation. Stop me when you think we have reached enough issues for one morning."

"It is a good thing I have so many hands at my disposal. Be sure to add fulfilling my duties as a wife."

"Should I schedule that before, during, or after dinner?" Stea spoke with a sly undertone.

"We dine in our chambers? I will notify the servants." Wintraub looked askance as Lady Zona and Stea burst out laughing. Then he took the letter his wife handed to him.

Brir received the letter last. He chuckled as well then sobered quickly.

"When I visited Lady Junla she had a request of me. King Jeffeaux has extended a limited visitors' permission for one of her family to witness the execution of her husband. She has asked if one of us could go. She would like a cleric or priest to attend. None of the Masfin clerics will attend him. None that came with us will go. I said I would go."

Lady Zona advanced on her husband. She laid a hand on his face.

"Masfin religion is very complex and tied to rites and rules and great tallies of deeds. Forgiveness and understanding are not always an important aspect of the system of belief. Repentance and redemption are not as important as strict adherence at all times to the Canon of the Church. After all, a lifetime of misdeeds cannot be erased by last-ditch regret."

"I should refuse?"

"Not everyone can be strong and embrace their fears. Everyone stumbles sometimes. Renfrew did terrible things. He helped Ranald maintain his grip on Masfin. He deserves his punishment. He also deserves a chance to repent, to seek redemption, to be comforted. Go with my wholehearted support."

Renfrew stared at his visitor. He blinked in the light. Finally he was able to see the face. What was a Sarn doing here?

"Hello, General."

The man seemed to know him. That was very interesting. For a brief moment Renfrew wondered at what point he had met this man. This Sarn did not look like any of the warriors Renfrew knew. Renfrew stared in thought. There was a detail here. The face was inscribed, this was a priest. He did not know any priests but his wife's.

"A priest, I am sent a priest. Jeffeaux seeks to demean me even now. I want a Cleric, a good Masfin Cleric."

"The King has searched all of Masfin. He can find no Cleric willing to minister to you. It seems the slaughter of the mendicants of Delungor brands the followers of Ranald as heretics, a specific type of heretic that precludes the services of Clerics. King Jeffeaux was not happy, but he could not order a Cleric to your side."

Renfrew drew an unsteady breath. He pressed a hand to his face.

"So he sent to Sarna for a priest."

"He sent a message to your wife that he could not find a Cleric. This was a simple courtesy. The Lady Junla asked me to attend you. Lady Zona agreed that I might come. It is fitting. I am no longer a priest but I can offer the comfort of a family member as you wait."

"A family member?"

"A father by marriage; I am that to you. In Sarna, religion revolved around bloodlines and water rights. The fertility of the people and the land were our province. I have not much practice in offering spiritual comfort or advice. There is an ancient holy text that I often recited when I was lost, afraid, confused."

Renfrew shrugged in indifference. Brir took the gesture as consent.

"I have translated it for you. I am sorry the poetry is lost in translation, but I am not a poet."

This is a story of passion, in its many forms.
In the beginning there were the Sun and the Moon.
Together they traveled through the Sky over the Earth.
In the beginning the Sun saw only the Moon.

As eons passed the Sun saw more.
The Earth blushed rosy from the heat of the Sun.
The Earth caught the Sun's attention.
The heat of the Sun's passion cracked the Earth.
His fingers of warmth crept into her crevasses.
The warmth and light of the Sun mixed with the dark and damp of the Earth.
Man was born.
The betrayed Moon ran in anger until she inhabited the Night Face of the Sky.
Still she loved the Sun.
Sometimes she slid back into the Day Face of the Sky
To catch a glimpse of Her Husband.
The Sun occasionally recalled his Wife.
He would call her to cover him.
But, always he returned to the Earth.
The Moon would try to win her Husband back.
She constantly changer her shape.
Still her Husband loved the Earth best.
Sometimes in the Night Face of Sky
The Moon would hide her face in despair.
Sometimes She would not even grace the Night Face.
The Sky held the Sun and the Moon.
The Sky surrounded the Earth.
He knew their passions and their loves.
And he was lonely.
Then a beautiful daughter of the Sun and the Earth gazed long at the Sky.
She noted his moods and shapes and shades and loved him.
She danced to him of her love.
She danced in the shining of her Father.
She danced in the glowing of her Father's Wife.
She beat the tempo of her love out with her feet on her Mother's breast.
Sky answered.
He caressed her with gentle winds.
He kissed her with soft rains.
She laughed and whirled and raised her arms to him.

He surrounded her with spirals of wind and scents he gathered
from all the Earth.
They were happy.
They loved.
One Darkfall the Moon became angry.
Angry that her rival's child was so loved.
Angry that such love was displayed.
Angry that her light gave lovers joy of each other.
So she crept her pale fingers into the sleep of a man.
She called that man to where Sky's lover danced.
She clothed the woman in irresistible light.
The man fell upon the woman.
The Sky looked on in fear and anger and love.
The Sky sent a lightning bolt to kill the man
To save his lover.
Alas, his aim was true.
He killed the man.
He killed his lover.
The Sky, horrified, devastated poured tears onto the Earth.
The water softened the Earth until she began to melt into Sky.
The Earth felt herself slipping away.
She raised High Mountains to stop her slide into infinity.
The water filled the Bowl of the Earth.
Soon all the Children of the Sun and of the Earth,
All that crept in the Earth were drowning.
The Earth cried to the Sky to stop.
He could not.
The Earth cried to the Moon to stop the Sky.
She would not.
The Earth cried to the Sun,
Save our children.
The Sun pushed the Night Face of Sky until the Day Face showed.
The Sun pleaded with the Sky.
The Sky could not stop his grief.
The Sun heard all his Children crying in agony.
The Sun raised his hands in the Sky.
The Sun and the Sky battled.
Sky convulsed and twisted and shouted.
The Sun prevailed.

The Sun dried the Earth.
Sky never wept again.
Sometimes they battle still.
But the storm is brief and The Sun always prevails.
And everything is
The Sun, the Moon, the Earth, the Sky and Man.

Renfrew shrugged.

"And the meaning for me is?"

"Even the elements of our world are fallible. Even they experience strife. And yet the world still exists." Brir closed the book with reverent hands. "You have cheated death many times. There is no other plan you can make today. Despite all our struggles and your passing the world still exists. Make your peace with the world. What ritual would a Masfin Cleric offer now?"

"None. I have earned this punishment through my crimes. There is nothing left to offer me."

Brir ran his hand on the cover of the book. He frowned in thought.

"There is a Llweganian tradition. An offender may offer apologies. You may seek forgiveness from family that you may draw comfort from their relationship as you face death. You are my son by marriage. Your wife has asked that I attend you that you might benefit from any comfort available. It does not seem wrong. Will you accept my company at least?"

Renfrew wanted to push the offer away. He did not want to accept that this last challenge would be his last. His mouth would not issue the rebuff.

"How fares my wife?'

"She is well. She is preparing to bring her child into the world. There is much rejoicing in Sarna at the birth."

"Really? I had not realized Lady Junla was so popular, or even known."

"She is Lady Zona's daughter. Her child will one day be the Governor of Sarna. The birth will be a great event in Sarna."

"My wife's child will rule Sarna?'

"As a child of hers will one day rule Masfin. She is the mother of Kings."

"Yet, unlike her sister, she never seemed to covet such a role."

"It is true the Lady Junla is contented to hold a healthy child to her breast. She is happy in her Household."

"In striving for nothing she has gained everything. That is ridiculous. What a poor example."

"How little you know your own wife. She well understood the nature and workings of power. She chose wisely. She bent when necessary. She demurred when possible. She listened to wisdom and ignored folly. It is a quieter path but the journey is difficult and laborious."

"I am foolish. I am jealous. She will live to see her child grow to adulthood. I will not live to know if it is a boy or a girl."

"That is perhaps the greatest tragedy of your life."

"No, the greatest tragedy is that I allowed sibling rivalry to guide my choices, and men died for it. I knew Ranald was insane, and I did everything I could to keep him in power rather than admit my brother had been right."

Brir stood up. He had heard the sound of the guard coming to escort Renfrew to his execution.

"Do you wish to make that apology now?"

"What?"

Brir gestured. "The time grows short. Do you wish to list your regrets that I might share your burdens?'

"I am sorry." Renfrew could not seem to articulate any more than that. "I am sorry. I am so sorry. I am so sorry that I placed my pride of accomplishment and intellect before the good of my fellow man. I am so sorry that I could not admit I was wrong. I am so sorry that I had to keep proving I was right even though men died for my proof. I am sorry I so feared Death that I kept throwing other men at him to keep him from me. I am so sorry."

"I hear your regret. I hear your admission of responsibility for the horrors of war. I hear them and I still call you family. I still share this moment with you because we are family." Renfrew closed his eyes. There was no silence. In the quiet between the two men fell the sound of footsteps. Keys jangled. Clothing whispered. Then the key was turning in the lock.

"It is time, Renfrew. I will walk with you if you like."

"Yes. Tell me the story again but this time in Sarnese that I might hear the poetry."

Renfrew walked to the pace set by his jailers. He let the sound of Brir's voice pour over him. It was beautiful poetry. The sound did give him comfort. Too soon they entered the small chamber under the court. He looked at the chopping block. His hands were tied behind his back. The collar of his shirt was tucked under itself, clearing his neck of any impediment to the executioner's blade. The executioner wore a black hood. Renfrew tried to see the eyes in the slits of the mask but could not.

His knees were locked. Renfrew did not think he could bend them. A strong hand forced him down until his neck rested on the block. His mouth was dry. His eyes were painfully dry. He felt the smooth wood against his neck. He thought he would vomit. He saw the shadow of the executioner as the man stepped between the light and him. He saw the shadow of the blade raised in the air.

"I am so sorry."

The blade swung down.

Spring had come. The trees flushed the red of branches about to bud. The scars of war on the land from the war were fading. Early plants had started to cover anything that did not move. Mansa pulled her cloak around her. She did not know why she had traveled back to the place of her birth. Perhaps she came to lay ghosts at last. Perhaps she thought she would find peace hiding in her old house.

The war with its companions, disease and famine, had claimed her husband and children and parents and brother. Still spring had come again.

She found the village with some difficulty. The tumbled houses and unkempt streets were effective disguises. She almost missed the house where she had been born. The collapsed roof and gaping windows were depressing.

Mansa clutched her cloak tightly. She heard a sound in the town square. She advanced warily. Peering through cracks in a wall she watched the lone rider. Years and war had greyed his hair. Nothing could change the line of posture. She watched as he raised the bucket to drink, then she could restrain herself no longer. She raced to him. The bucket swung back into the well. The rope sung as it bore the weight of the bucket's fall. Still clutching the sides of her cloak Mansa spread her arms in joyous welcome. She seemed a bird as he swung her into his embrace. Home at last, she was finally home.

Darkfall was coming. King Jeffeaux leaned against the window frame to watch the oncoming dark. In these moments he could still feel her mouth pressed to his. He could still hear her words echo in his ears. He missed the sight of her, her strength.

A gentle touch broke his reverie. He raised the tapered fingers to his mouth to greet her with a gentle salute. Her head rested against his arm.

"For what do you watch, my King?"

"Monsters. When I was a child I feared monsters came with Darkfall. When I was a man, I cast out that fear."

"And?"

"I do believe the child may have been right. There are monsters. They just don't always live in the dark."

"The man did cast them out."

"I still watch for them."

"We will watch together, my King."

King Jeffeaux gathered his consort to his side to settle them in to watch the dark fall. To remember with amazement, incredulity, regret, and bittersweet joy things he could not believe had happened. How could one miss such times? How could he? Quietly, gently, Darkfall came.

and Lovers

Epilogue

"Momma, tell me the story."

She bent to tuck the blanket more securely around small shoulders.

"I tell it every night. Surely you know it by heart."

"It's my favorite Momma."

"All right then." She never minded telling the tale. It had been her favorite as a child as well. Her grandmother used to recite the story for her.

"And the day came when Dragon sent her Masfin daughter by her Sarnese husband back into Masfin. The Gift rode a strong steed worthy of the daughter of the Dragon. The trusted steed galloped through the empty grasslands of Llwegania. He carried the Gift through the barren waste of Sarna. He even breached the Great Gate of Masfin to carry the Gift into Masfin. Finally the Gift arrived at the palace."

"The Wondrous Palace, Momma." The correction was given in a small determined voice.

"Finally the Gift arrived at the *Wondrous Palace* of the King. She walked into the mighty Great Hall where the King, the keeper of the Crown, Marma, and all the courtiers were meeting. The Gift walked right up to the King. She did not bow. She did not pander. She reached out her hand. In her hand was the Final Stone. It glowed in the light of the Great Hall. The King stared long at the stone. Then the Gift spoke:

"The Old Dragon dies."

"The Old Dragon Dies." The child corrected.

"The Old Dragon Dies, the Gift said only once. The King touched the stone with a trembling hand. He reached for the crown on his head. He bowed low to the keeper of the Crown, Marma, as he placed the crown in her hand. He left the Great Hall. He left the Wondrous Palace at Delungor. As he left Masfin the Great Gate opened never to shut again. As he rode through Sarna the

barren waste blossomed into a garden. As he entered Llwegania the empty grasslands filled with game and fowl.

"At last the King and the Gift reached the House of the Dragon. He swept into the house to find the Dragon lying in her great marriage bed surrounded by her remaining four husbands, her twelve other daughters, their households and heirs. Wind Rider, the mighty heir of the Dragon came forward. She bowed to the King. She turned to the bed. She spoke in a steady voice:

"Mother, the True King Jeffeaux is here."

"The Dragon opened her eyes. Her weak dying body quickened at the sight of his beloved face. Her eyes and mouth lit with a smile that chased the darkness from the room. Her voice was low but strong:

"My beloved you have come."

"Yes I have come to take you on our last Ride. We must see the land we have created one more time."

"I knew you would come. I waited for you."

"I had to come. Where else would I be now but with you for the rest of our eternity?"

"Everyone sighed in the room to see such devotion. The grandson of the keeper of the Crown Marma, who was also the First Husband of the granddaughter of Wind Rider, came to kneel beside the bed. He spoke in respectful tones:

"Oh Great Dragon, I beg of you the honor to carry you to your horse that you might begin your journey with the True King Jeffeaux."

"The Dragon never took her eyes from the True King Jeffeaux. She raised her hand to rest it in the king's grasp.

"I grant you, Jeffeaux, grandson of Jeffeaux, that honor."

"And they rode on the Great War Horse into the shimmering of the horizon. To this day if you stand in the House of the Dragon and look to the horizon in the shimmering of the day, you can see them. When you stand on the steps of the Temple of Kersai in the shimmering of the day and look to the horizon, you can see them. When you walk through the garden of Delungor in the shimmering of the day and look to the horizon you can see them. They ride the plains of Llwegania and the gardens of Sarna and the shores of Masfin guarding the world they gave to us."

"Ah, Momma, I love that story."

"So do I."
"I want to say the last part."
"Then say it, my sweet."

"THE END."

About the author:

Elizabeth Murphy grew up with Greek Mythology, Arabian Nights, and Winnie the Pooh. Her favorite books are **The Count of Monte Cristo** by Alexandre Dumas, **The Zero Stone** by Andre Norton, and **Little Women** by Louisa May Alcott.
She has had several careers including waitress, retail manager, lighting designer and nutrition services supervisor. Her two constants in her life have been her writing and her best beau.
Ms. Murphy enjoys walking through the parks and forests of the great North West, camping, and entertaining for the brave souls willing to share her adventures in cooking.